Pr
c

"Brilliantly
—Ro

"Readers will relish the paths to the final battle . . . a delightful finish. . . . Fans will enjoy the latest entry in the Sinclair mythos." —Genre Go Round Reviews

"A stunning story . . . never-ending action and political intrigue will keep the reader interested until the last page." —Fresh Fiction

Lightborn

"[An] engaging mix of chaos, angst, and manners . . . including genuine surprises." —*Locus*

"This story world is highly complex and certainly unique. . . . Readers should find the plot and players fascinating. . . . What will the imaginative Alison Sinclair come up with next?" —Romance Reviews Today

Darkborn

"Alison Sinclair's *Darkborn* plays like a sweeping historical novel in a teeming preindustrial city whose residents are divided into those who can only tolerate light and those who can only exist in darkness. A sprawling cast of characters argues and schemes and practices magic in secret—until a calamitous chain of events reveals the whole city to be under siege from a mysterious and ruthless enemy. Despite swift action, broad conspiracies, and monumental life-and-death stakes, the heart of the book is a delicately rendered love triangle that tracks the human cost of any grand adventure. I can't wait to read the next book about these complex and engaging characters."

—National bestselling author Sharon Shinn

continued . . .

"Alison Sinclair's unique world of two societies, mortally divided by sunrise and sunset, provides a fascinating backdrop for a fast-paced thriller of politics and intrigue. Delightful!" —National bestselling author Carol Berg

"Fast-paced and crammed with dangers to its main characters, *Darkborn* goes beyond romantic suspense to explore their complex personalities. . . . It's a fine start to what looks like a truly interesting project." —*Locus*

"[A] wonderful read, with an intriguing setting populated by appealing and memorable characters."
—Lane Robins, author of *Kings and Assassins*

"Intriguing paranormal romance." —*Publishers Weekly*

"Sinclair's descriptions are vivid. . . . The magical world building and great characterization make this the kind of book you hate to see end." —*Romantic Times*

"A complex book with many layers. . . . The best part of the book is the characters and their relationships with each other." —The Book Smugglers

Shadowborn

Alison Sinclair

A ROC BOOK

ROC
Published by New American Library, a division of
Penguin Group (USA) Inc., 375 Hudson Street,
New York, New York 10014, USA
Penguin Group (Canada), 90 Eglinton Avenue East, Suite 700, Toronto,
Ontario M4P 2Y3, Canada (a division of Pearson Penguin Canada Inc.)
Penguin Books Ltd., 80 Strand, London WC2R 0RL, England
Penguin Ireland, 25 St. Stephen's Green, Dublin 2,
Ireland (a division of Penguin Books Ltd.)
Penguin Group (Australia), 250 Camberwell Road, Camberwell, Victoria 3124,
Australia (a division of Pearson Australia Group Pty. Ltd.)
Penguin Books India Pvt. Ltd., 11 Community Centre, Panchsheel Park,
New Delhi - 110 017, India
Penguin Group (NZ), 67 Apollo Drive, Rosedale, Auckland 0632,
New Zealand (a division of Pearson New Zealand Ltd.)
Penguin Books (South Africa) (Pty.) Ltd., 24 Sturdee Avenue,
Rosebank, Johannesburg 2196, South Africa

Penguin Books Ltd., Registered Offices:
80 Strand, London WC2R 0RL, England

Published by Roc, an imprint of New American Library, a division of Penguin Group (USA) Inc. Previously published in a Roc trade paperback edition.

First Roc Mass Market Printing, May 2012
10 9 8 7 6 5 4 3 2 1

Printed in the United States of America

Author's Note

Darkborn concluded with Telmaine, Balthasar, and Ishmael beginning separate journeys. *Lightborn* tells the story of Telmaine's return to Minhorne to face further Shadowborn intrigue and the consequences of her own and others' secrets. *Shadowborn* begins with Balthasar and Ishmael on their mission to the Borders to avert a Shadowborn invasion, and continues the story past the end of *Lightborn*, to its conclusion.

One

Ishmael

These riders are good, Ishmael di Studier thought, ruefully. Otherwise he would have heard them before they were almost on him, even on the pleated and twisting old post road. And then he would have been behind the wall on the far side of the field, well out of range of sonn, rather than crouched in a dip behind a boundary marker a mere twenty yards from the road, impersonating a rock. The riders—however many there were—were traveling with muffled hooves and carefully wrapped metalwork, on horses trained to be silent and easy in darkness. They had crept up on him. His inability to tell their numbers—six? eight?—was testament to their quality.

If they were friends, he knew how they would be riding: in two staggered lines, spacing precisely maintained, each one listening and casting sonn to his or her own side. It was an order and discipline he had developed with them. They might well be friends, since the ducal order to raise the Borders for possible invasion should have the entire Stranhorne troop turned out on alert for Shadowborn. Perhaps even with instructions to find him as well.

But they might also be enemies, search parties ordered out on the archduke's warrant for his arrest. Worst of all, they could be soldiers from Minhorne, sent to the Borders on that same warrant. Ish had no doubt that the warrant had included instructions that he was to be brought back unharmed; equally, he had no certainty that those instructions would be followed, not for a fugitive charged with a lady's murder and sorcery.

He sensed diffused sonn, scattered back from the tall grass and tares around him, and thought rocklike thoughts. Midnight damp seeped through his steadying knee and a painful cramp settled in his calf muscles. He dared not shift his weight. The riders would have hearing as acute as his own, and some of the veteran border troopers had intuition that seemed akin to magic. And if his profile broke that of the marker, a bowed spine did not echo like stone.

A horse stamped and blew, and despite himself, he twitched. He could have sworn that he made no sound, but a woman's voice carried clearly through the night. "Ishmael, is that you there?"

He knew the voice; a held breath went out of him in a sigh. "Yes," he said. "I'm here."

Gloved hand on the boundary marker, he pushed himself up. He had hiked and jogged upwards of thirty-five miles in the latter part of the previous night and the earlier part of this one, carrying a pack and weapons, and he was no longer twenty, as his knees were informing him. A little stiffly, he made his way back to the party on the road.

The woman on one of the two lead horses grinned triumphantly down at him. "I *thought* I caught a movement. You're slipping, Ishmael." She was not that much past twenty herself, a leggy young woman, long hair braided and wound around a broad brow, features too marked and mouth too wide and mobile for conventional beauty. She wore a practical jacket and a divided riding skirt, had a rifle slung over her shoulder, a revolver and a knife at her hip, and another knife in a boot sheath. Hers was hardly the typical attire of an heiress, even in the Borders, but she was a delight to sonn, nonetheless. He returned her grin with one of his own. "You're good, Lavender—you're all of you good—and y'well know it."

Smiles widened around him. He did not recognize any of the six men and one woman with her, but they'd all know him by reputation as Ishmael di Studier, Baron Strumheller, hunter of Shadowborn, and mage. For all he was no longer most of these things.

"Nicholas," Lavender di Gautier said, "give him your horse, and mount up with Thalia. The two of you will be easier on a horse than the baron and I." The youngest and lightest of the troop swung down and dutifully handed over the reins. Ishmael took a moment to free his rifle from his pack and strap his pack behind the trooper's provisions. The horse tried to sidle; he cuffed it, growling at it for taking him for a novice.

As he climbed into the saddle, she said over her shoulder, "You want we should head back, or finish the loop round the Pot?"

Back would be to Stranhorne Manor, her family seat, and his destination since he had jumped off the southbound coastal train just before Stranhorne Crosstracks. The Pot was a small, perfectly round lake at the bottom of a steep-sided pit, immediately recognizable on any relief model. Almost certainly it had been made by magic.

"Back," he said, though not without thought. But after spending yesterday in the open, in a day-blind pitched in shadows, he would feel much happier with stout walls around him.

"Come up by me."

His lips quirked with amusement at the confident command in her voice, even toward him. The others smoothly rearranged themselves as he eased his horse forward. They were good; neither the baron, her father, nor her twin sister would have allowed her out with anything else.

"Are you all right?" she said in a low voice.

"Aye," he said. "I am now."

"We heard"—there was a slight tremor in her voice, despite herself—"we heard you were dead."

"Came closer to't than I like, I'll admit," he said. He tried for an easy tone, but that near miss had probably cost him one of the most precious things he had. Two lives—especially those of Lady Telmaine and her daughter—should be a fair exchange for his lost magic, but if someone were to ask him outright, he could not honestly swear that he would not rather have died.

She would never ask him, but she knew him well enough to hear something of it in his voice. "I suppose," she said, "I'll have to wait until Stranhorne to hear all of it. I presume that is where you were bound."

"Aye."

"Well, you're safe now."

"That's more your promise than th'truth," he chided her. "For all it's welcome."

"This warrant for your arrest—"

Had her father told her both of the charges, or just the one? With the city broadsheets being delivered every night by train, she could not have remained ignorant for long. "False, both of them."

"I *know* they're false," she said with spirit. "I know *you*. Surely the archduke—surely Lord Vladimer—"

The less said about the archduke's attitude, the better. "Until Lady Tercelle's true murderer is produced, suspicion will remain on me. And as to th'other"—he weighed what to say, given that he was not supposed to talk about this at all with her—"it's for Lord Vladimer t'do the convincing of my innocence, since he was the one I supposedly ensorcelled. He's a wily man, and it no doubt suits his purposes to have me leading this chase."

She made a disgusted noise but expressed no further opinion. "Then what about this ducal order? All it tells us is that the ducal order of six twenty-nine was suspended, allowing us to mobilize troops beyond our allotment to guard the Borders against threats. Who are we supposed t'be guarding against? We've not seen claw nor hair of Shadowborn all this summer."

She showed her youth there, Ishmael thought, believing that quiet was good. He'd spent the summer in Strumheller as fidgety as a man in burlap britches. The Borders took their name because they abutted the boundary of several thousand square miles of uninhabited land, the Shadowlands. The mages who had laid the Curse that made the Darkborn had lived near the center of what was now the Shadowlands. Some residue of that, or other, terrible magic, had given rise to the Shadowborn, marauding monsters that were the Borders' constant hazard.

Ishmael had passed the better—or worse—part of twenty-five years fighting Shadowborn, first as a trooper for hire, then as a professional Shadowhunter, and ultimately as Baron Strumheller, organizing an integrated system of warning and defense that had about halved the casualties from Shadowborn incursions. In twenty-five years, he had never experienced a summer so ominously quiet.

He had fretted and roamed and listened, but it had been Lord Vladimer Plantageter, the archduke's brother and spymaster, who had raised the possibility that this might be a prelude to Shadowborn activity more organized and extensive than any they'd encountered before.

"Here's the short of it," Ishmael said. "Th'archduke sent the ducal order on th'urging of Lord Vladimer. There's been Shadowborn at work in th'city, Shadowborn with seemingly the wits of men, the gift of taking on the likeness of others, and an appetite for chaos."

He heard her catch her breath, though with admirable discipline, she did not turn her attention from the road ahead.

"I'll tell th'whole of it in Stranhorne, but these Shadowborn were nearly the death of Lord Vladimer—which was the second charge laid against me"—sorcery, the mere suspicion of which had landed him in prison—"and were th'death of upwards of a hundred and fifty Darkborn in the Rivermarch, when they set it alight during the day." He had nearly been one of those, too, having escaped by a combination of experience, knowledge of the history of that old and none-too-salubrious district, and luck. He had been spending his luck prodigiously of late. "It's likely"—indeed, he was certain of it—"that the Shadowborn had the doing of the murder that's been laid at my feet, since Lady Tercelle herself had dealings with them." Intimate dealings, which he would explain to all of them once they reached the manor. "Seems," he said with grim amusement, "that I'm in no great favor with them."

"Ishmael—," she said, and fell silent. He could almost hear the hum of her thought. He had first met Lavender and her sister riding with the Stranhorne border troop in boys' disguises. The disguises had been done quite well, and the rest poorly, so he had torn strips off both their hides for being more of a hazard to themselves and their fellows than the Shadowborn, sent them home under escort, and assumed that was that.

"What about Strumheller?" she said.

Ishmael shrugged slightly. "The order of succession was sent and signed, and the barony has passed to Reynard. My brother has no great love for me, but he's got too much sense t'meddle with the arrangements and men I put in place—not with the Borders on alert. You'll have no weakness on your flank."

"Reynard *can't* hold on to it, not with you still alive."

Having disinherited Ishmael, their father had spent years grooming Reynard to succeed to the barony. His brother had never forgiven Ish for being reinstated, or for the two or three times he had turned up since, alive after long absences. Best to change the subject. "How's your sister? Is she keeping well?"

Unlike Strumheller Manor, which had been reduced to smoldering rubble in the border uprising and civil war of two hundred years ago, and rebuilt as a whole, Stranhorne was a seven-hundred-year-old architectural accretion. There were rumored to be ruins three times its age buried underneath its foundations, but Xavier Stranhorne had dryly observed that even he would not knock down his manor to confirm, historian though he was. Inspired by the fate of Strumheller Manor, the Stranhornes had turned their minds to fortification. South- and west-facing walls were doubled and as sheer an ascent as stonemasonry could make them. The top three stories had sniper windows overlooking an open killing ground strewn with noisemakers, and on the roof were three mounted cannon, a detail that appalled Ishmael, who had fought a shipboard action beside cannon. His ears had rung for hours after. The gardens on the east and the courtyard on the north were protected by a fifteen-foot-high wall with enclosed guard posts. There were two gates, the main one into the courtyard, and a smaller, seldom-used one into the gardens on the east of the manor. The massive courtyard gate was now opened and closed by a steam winch, one of the few concessions to modern technology that Stranhorne allowed.

Even if the features had been added with a mind to repel Darkborn attackers, they should do very well against Shadowborn.

The headquarters for the Borders troop had originally been a ballroom on the northeast side of the manor. It was a late addition, conceived last century as a stage for the high social ambitions of one of the baronelles. But after her triumphs, the tiered balconies, the elevated orchestral platforms, and the lush reliefs and scrollwork had grown shabby with decades of neglect. Tradition held that sometimes the ghost of the baronelle could be heard weeping for its ruin, though from what Ish knew of the lady, weeping with rage was more likely.

The courtyard and ballroom were bustling. The courtyard was full of horses, mules, and carts; the ballroom was full of men and a number of women, milling around the entrance to the armory off in one intimate gallery, the mustering station for departing and returning troops, and the entrance to the kitchen. Troops were generally young and inevitably hungry. A final group was gathered around a huge relief model in an open side gallery. A woman was stretching over it to place a marker, her reach slightly impeded by the swell of her abdomen: Lavender's identical twin, Laurel, married a year, and five months' pregnant.

At her shoulder, to Ishmael's not unmixed relief, was her father. Most Darkborn were relentlessly modern in outlook; Baron Xavier Stranhorne was an exception, having personally taken an ax to the first telegraph pole raised on his land. He was a relatively young man, only a few years older than Ishmael, and well educated, with a degree in history from the university in Minhorne and a lifelong interest in scholarship. His opposition to "progress" had equal parts Borders obduracy and considered decision.

His opposition to magic was equally uncompromising. The first time Ishmael had called on him as Baron Strumheller, Stranhorne had taken him into his private library and delivered an ultimatum: "I have opened my doors to you, sir, as a peer and a neighbor. But should you exercise or even discuss your unnatural practice within my halls, my doors will be closed to you forever. Do you wish to dispute this?"

"These are your halls, sir. I do not." Stranhorne nodded—he had the refreshing trait of not needing to beat down an adversary who'd submitted—and the matter was settled. Ishmael had scrupulously respected Stranhorne's prohibition, and Stranhorne had scrupulously extended to him the courtesies of a peer and host. Were it not for Stranhorne's daughters, their relationship would have remained that of cooperative but distant neighbors. Ishmael would have regretted that.

Lavender hailed her father and sister cheerfully. "Told you we'd find him." Turned her head, sonning the gathered troops. "Pay up!"

He might have known there'd be a pool as to who might retrieve him.

Xavier Stranhorne's face was unreadable, which was not reassuring; the scholarly baron was not particularly demonstrative, but he did not hide what he felt. He said, "Welcome, Strumheller"—which title was no accident, undeserved though it was. "I'm afraid I'm greeting you with awkward tidings. Your sister sent a telegram from Strumheller this evening. Ferdenzil Mycene's been charged with the warrant for your arrest. He's on his way with a dozen mounted men."

Lavender caught her breath, her expression horrified. "Mycene! What was the archduke *thinking*?"

There was no love lost between Stranhorne and the Duke of Mycene and his heir. Mycene's territorial ambitions included the extensive archipelagos off the Stranhorne coast, including the island home of the late Baronelle Stranhorne. And the warrant was for the murder of Ferdenzil's betrothed, Lady Tercelle Amberley. For the sake of his peace of mind, Ishmael was glad he had not known Mycene was hunting him.

"Mycene's also got a prisoner: the physician who was traveling with you."

Ishmael had been afraid of that. When Ishmael had decided to leave the train, his ally, Dr. Balthasar Hearne, had gone on to Strumheller to carry word to Ishmael's brother and sister that he was still alive. Ish hoped the physician had not suffered for his willingness to act as messenger and decoy.

Laurel stepped forward and hugged him firmly. He returned the hug, gladdened to feel her girth. The last time he had passed through, she had been worrisomely thin and sick with early pregnancy. He was not surprised to hear her murmur against his ear, "Library—we'll join you." Laurel had always been the cunning one of the pair.

"We can give you provisions," Lavender said urgently. "Get you away on a fast horse."

"No," said Ishmael and Stranhorne together. Ishmael continued. "I was coming to Stranhorne, whatever befell. You need t'hear my report. You need to know what's behind the ducal order."

"That can't be more important than your freedom, surely," Lavender said.

"I think it is."

"Then let me intercept Mycene," urged Lavender. "Misdirect him." Her father got a pained expression on his face; Lavender was a notoriously poor liar. Laurel just said, "Lavender, *think*."

This was best not discussed in an open hall. With this many men and women around, there were bound to be those who, for the best or worst of reasons, might reveal information to a man carrying the archduke's warrant. Ishmael nodded to Stranhorne and worked his way through the group, returning handclasps and greetings as he went, but not stopping. Alone, he made his way to the baron's study. Which seemed to have had several more shelves added, though he would have sworn there was no room. In a bunker built of books alone, Stranhorne *could* hold off a

Shadowborn army—but that whimsy was rapidly followed by the sobering awareness of possibility.

Stranhorne, Laurel, and his younger son, Boris, arrived promptly enough to prevent Ish from nodding off in a soft armchair. Lavender was downstairs, organizing sweeps, knowing that if her father did not tell her everything, her sister or brother would. Stranhorne served Ishmael brandy from a bottle sequestered behind a particularly forbidding tome, and rang for lemonade for his daughter and son.

"If you hoped," Stranhorne said, sitting down with his own brandy glass, "I'd shield you, I'm likely to disappoint."

Ishmael *had* hoped that; he could not deny it, at least to himself—hoped for shelter, for time, for help. "I know," he said, without rancor. "Would have been one matter to have city agents arriving hours or days behind me, but here's Ferdenzil Mycene hard on my heels. The last you want is t'give him time to take the measure of Stranhorne's full assets when y'think you might come to need them against him, someday that might be soon."

Stranhorne sonned him crisply, but it was no secret that, should the Duke of Mycene and his son act on their ambitions to annex the islands, Stranhorne would support his late wife's people, in arms, if need be. With the men and women that Ishmael himself had helped train to fight Shadowborn. Ishmael added, "His knowing that you know he's taken me is some security that he'll return me to Minhorne for trial, and not just stake me out for th'sunrise."

"I think I can make sure of that."

"I didn't murder Tercelle Amberley," Ishmael said. "Th'appearance was cursed compromising, I'll admit, but I'd been lured to be discovered with the body still warm. I'd hoped to prevent harm to her, if she'd been blameless, and get some answers if she hadn't."

Stranhorne's nod said that he accepted that. "We've been stockpiling munitions," he admitted. "And rotating our reserves in for training. We know that Mycene has been building up a presence in the isles. We weren't sure that this business about the Shadowborn wasn't a distraction. The city has never taken much interest in Shadowborn before now."

"Lord Vladimer has," Ishmael dissented.

There was a silence. "Vladimer," said Stranhorne. "Yes."

His opinions of the archduke's brother and spymaster had to be mixed, Ishmael thought. Vladimer was the best of allies to those whose interests aligned with his brother's policy. And the worst of enemies to those whose interests did not. The former Baron Strumheller well knew where the archduke's policies did not entirely serve the Borders. "In this, at least," Ishmael said, "Vladimer's our ally."

"Ah, and what would 'this' be?"

"You'll have t'know first that this touches on the matter that you asked me never t'discuss within your halls. There's no getting away from it."

"I somehow thought it might. Go on," said Stranhorne, no promise of forgiveness in his tone.

Ishmael waited until the servant had delivered the lemonade. Then he laid out the story: Vladimer's suspicions that the lack of Shadowborn activity indicated that the Shadowborn might be organizing their forces for the first time in history. The apparently unrelated scandal of bastard twins born to Lady Tercelle Amberley, Ferdenzil's betrothed, by a father the lady claimed, impossibly, to have been Lightborn, or at least to have been able to move through the day. Attending physician Balthasar Hearne's suspicion that the twins might be sighted, as no Darkborn had been since the Curse was laid. The murder of Tercelle Amberley, and the attempt to frame Ish for that murder. Lord Vladimer's sudden, uncanny coma, attributed to sorcery. Ishmael's arrest on suspicion of murder and sorcery, his imprisonment and escape. Rescue, rather—he skated lightly over his condition at that escape. The reappearance of Lysander Hearne, Balthasar's long-missing brother, claiming Tercelle Amberley's children as his own. And Ishmael's confrontation with a Shadowborn at Lord Vladimer's bedside, in a ducal summerhouse full of people unconscious under its influence. Alive, the Shadowborn had resembled Lysander Hearne. Dead, it had not.

He did not tell them about Lady Telmaine, Balthasar Hearne's wife and Ishmael's unexpected ally, a lady of courage and spirit and a mage of considerable strength. The lady had hidden her magic all her life, terrified of social ruin. And who was he to condemn her, he whose father had summarily disinherited him? His feelings for Lady Telmaine were nobody's business but his own—and hers, admittedly, since they were both mages. And he did not tell the Stranhornes about the price he had paid to save her life. A mage drew upon his own vitality to power his magic, the efficiency of that drawing determining the strength of the mage. Ishmael had been born as weak as mages came, but he had still succeeded in holding back an inferno around Telmaine and her daughter when her magic failed. In doing so, he had permanently damaged the connection between his vitality and his magic. The least use of magic now risked killing him.

"These Shadowborn have strength," he said to Stranhorne. "To change one's form—it's what underlies magical healing, only we regard it as a perversion of th'use and won't try it—but to fully change one's form argues considerable strength. Th'one we met was able to hold an entire household under ensorcellment—though it may be that it was at its limits, which made it vulnerable t'me." A lie, but he could not tell them that Lady Telmaine had valiantly set her untrained magic against it, distracting it enough to let him in range. "They seem t'like fire as a weapon: the burning of the Rivermarch, the firing of the warehouse where Lady Telmaine found her daughter."

"Mmph," said Stranhorne. Laurel was listening intently, while Boris was sitting very still, obviously thinking rock-like thoughts, to Ishmael's well-hidden amusement. Boris was seventeen and only lately admitted to his elders' councils. "You'll understand," Stranhorne said at length, "how much I'd like to disbelieve you, but Max sent me an account by courier of Lord Vladimer's report to the dukes and barons, and it tallies with what you say. The ducal order has been extended to the dukes—they're allowed to mobilize their own reserves."

Ishmael, mindful of tender young ears, did not swear. The Dukes of Mycene had held the archducal seat until two hundred years ago, and that Sachevar Mycene still coveted the seat was common knowledge. Sejanus Plantageter was secure—after forty years as archduke he ought to be so—but still . . . giving his rival leave to bring forces into the city . . . Vladimer would surely have argued with him vigorously, if he were able.

"Lord Vladimer?" he said. "Was he there? How'd he appear t'Max?"

Max Stranhorne would never have been able to tell if Vladimer were suffering any ill effects of the ensorcellment, aside from the effects of the experience itself—which could not be discounted. Ish himself had sensed nothing, and Lady Telmaine would surely have said . . .

"Lord Vladimer gave the report. Max thinks he may have been hurt—possibly ill, but Max thinks hurt. What prompted the extension of the archducal order," Stranhorne said, distinctly enough that Ishmael knew he was aware of Ishmael's distraction, "was the death of the Lightborn prince."

On the other side of sunrise lived the Lightborn, as utterly dependent on light as the Darkborn were on darkness. Both races had been created together by an eight-hundred-year-old act of magical vengeance. For eight hundred years, Lightborn and Darkborn had shared the land, trading, negotiating through paper walls, but never able to meet face-to-face. For much of the land, Darkborn and Lightborn cities, towns, and villages were separate—the Borders themselves were almost empty of Lightborn, for reasons no one among the Darkborn understood—but Minhorne, the largest city, was held in common, and the seats of Darkborn and Lightborn rule were separated by fewer than five miles.

The death of a Lightborn prince was not in itself an unusual event: Lightborn custom allowed the ruthless culling of faltering, incompetent, or corrupt leaders. But Isidore was a seasoned, steady statesman of no more than Ishmael's age, who had for twenty years survived the machinations of his wife's relations—she was the daughter of one of the potentates of the southwest desert—not to mention the ambitions of his own.

"How?" Ish said.

"Magic," Stranhorne said. "The lights in his rooms failed."

Darkness was as rapidly fatal to Lightborn as sun- or mage light to Darkborn. It left a tacky residue that smelled, distinctively and repugnantly, of old blood.

Even as a student, Stranhorne would never have lived in the areas that Ishmael had; he would never have smelled that odor for himself.

"I understand that the lights are magical talismans enspelled to absorb and reradiate sunlight," Stranhorne said.

He understood correctly, as Ishmael would expect. Though they had never discussed it, he knew from other directions that Stranhorne had as much theoretical knowledge of magic as any man who was not a mage. "The prince is protected—layers deep—by mages," Ishmael said. "Anyone tried t'annul the magic on the lights, they'd know; they'd warn th'prince and they'd stop it."

In the aftermath of the laying of the Curse, the last remaining Lightborn mages had begged protection from the most powerful of the emerging warlords; out of that had come the compact ruling magic on the other side of sunrise. A mage could not use magic against a nonmage except by publicly declared contract with another nonmage. Mages were indemnified against all harm done by law of contract.

"It doesn't make sense," Ishmael said slowly, "that the mages—the Mages' Temple—would have lifted its protection from Isidore."

"Yes, but—" Running footsteps outside, the snap of a floorboard, and Lavender threw open the door. She shut it hard and stood with her back to it, as though pursued. "He's here," she said in breathless anger.

"Mycene?" said her father, calmly.

"Ishmael has to get away now. He can leave by the east gate, through Mother's garden."

"And go where?" said Stranhorne, but to Ishmael, not his daughter.

Ishmael said nothing. Vladimer had sent him south to make sure the Borders were prepared to defend themselves, and then if no invasion materialized, to scout the Shadowlands personally. And *he* had come south to make sure that the Borders—Stranhorne and his own barony of Strumheller—knew what they might be facing. He had done that.

And now . . . Stranhorne had it right. Ishmael could keep running and be nothing but a trouble and a distraction to men and women who needed to keep their minds on the true enemy—and possibly get himself mistakenly shot by one of Stranhorne's own patrols, in this time of high tension. He could demand sanctuary, and divide Stranhorne's family, setting the twins against their father. Or he could surrender, let Mycene take him north, and trust to the law and events proving his innocence. He had no doubt Vladimer had turned his own formidable resources to the task, though Vladimer would have troubles of his own—Sejanus extending that ducal order, for one. *And,* Ish thought ruefully, *Vladimer has perhaps a little too much confidence in my ability to survive.*

At least if Mycene took him back to Minhorne, he would be near Vladimer and Lady Telmaine. He was worried about them both; Vladimer because he had already been ensorcelled once, and Telmaine because he and her husband had left her to guard Lord Vladimer's back. Her strength, coupled with her inexperience, had its hazards.

"Laurel," Stranhorne said, after a moment. "Go downstairs; greet Lord Mycene. Settle him down if he needs settling—tell him ten minutes."

"Ishmael," Lavender appealed to him.

"There's no point t'it," Ishmael said, projecting calm. "I could go pelting about the countryside, but he'd likely find me within two or three days—the man's a good soldier, a good leader, whatever else we may think of him—and I'd be two or three days more weary. This way's safer for me." *And all of you,* he thought. "It's not as though I think I'll get left out of th'fight somehow."

Laurel, passing, rested her hand on her sister's arm and said something to her, too quietly for even Ishmael to hear. Lavender's shoulders slumped. Laurel slipped out and closed the door behind her.

"Did you get it all moved?" Lavender said to her father, her tone flat.

"I think so, but I'd like you and Boris to go down and make sure that it is—and that it's well concealed, or at least well disguised. There's no reason for Mycene or his men to go into the cellars, and we'll keep people on them, but I'd not put it past them to try."

"Nor I," Lavender growled. She opened the door and stalked out, her younger brother trailing her.

They listened for a moment as the footsteps receded. Stranhorne rose, took Ishmael's glass from him, and refilled it. "I wish it didn't have to be this way," he said, passing it into Ishmael's gloved hand. *Hospitality or anesthesia,* Ishmael wondered.

"Y'can't afford to give Mycene reason to demand a search of the manor under th'archduke's warrant," Ishmael said, stoically. "Not with a cellar full of munitions bound for the Isles. I'm grateful you took my report in full. My sense is that whatever's coming is coming soon, now they've broken into th'open in the city."

Stranhorne balanced his glass on his fingers, shoulder against a crammed shelf. "But what's coming? That is the question." He sonned Ishmael. "You know I have material collected from the period of the Curse and after."

"Aye," Ishmael said. "I'd heard that. But asking after it would have been treading too close t'matters you'd asked me not to speak of."

"True," Stranhorne said, soberly. "A dictate I hope not to live to regret."

Surprising himself as well as Stranhorne, Ishmael laughed. "In all truth, it never occurred to me t'ask. Even before m'father sent me on my road, my tutors had to nail my breeches to the chair. Heresy, in this household, but there 'tis." He set down the glass, still half full, and said more seriously, "But I'd be glad of the dunce's version. First of all, who might be in th'Shadowlands?"

"I know nothing for certain," said Stranhorne. "In the second and third century after the Curse, multiple expeditions went into the Shadowlands. Those that returned reported a barren land—previously, magic had been used to alter the weather patterns to bring rain—that was otherwise uninhabited. Those that passed beyond a certain line some two hundred miles in never returned; we do not know why. Shadowborn entered the written record late in the third century, and became an increasing nuisance through the fourth, leading the archduke eventually to withdraw support for campaigns into the Shadowlands." Which led to the establishment of the Borders baronies, and eventually to the Borders uprising and the war of Borders' independence, and the order of six twenty-nine that limited the Borders' standing forces. That history Ishmael had not only had hammered into his thick, juvenile skull, but had personally contended with these past twenty-five years. Stranhorne continued. "But *if* there are men in the Shadowlands—and I remind you I have no support for this—I might speculate that they are descended of the mages who were involved in the laying of the Curse, though why they should have waited eight hundred years to make themselves known, I can't say."

"Known other than by the Shadowborn and th'Call," Ish noted. The Call—the Call to the Shadowlands—was Ishmael's personal curse, a bizarre ensorcellment that was a legacy of his years roaming around the Shadowlands. Nobody knew what made it take hold, but every year, dozens of bordersmen and -women followed the Call, and none was ever heard from again. Stubbornness, distance, trusted guards, and, on occasion, chains had kept Ishmael on the right side of the border. "Lord Vladimer had it in mind for me t'go and find out. He was concerned that there was mischief behind the unnatural quiet of this summer."

"He was right, but that was risky for you," Stranhorne said, which amounted to gushing concern. "You are assuming that the Shadowborn—as we know them—are related to this. Suppose they are not. Suppose they are an entirely separate problem."

"From where I sit, th'separation seems academic."

The corner of Stranhorne's mouth quirked at the slight truculence of tone. "Though *if* there are such mages, their quiescence is still unexpected, given the type of . . . powers attributed to the mages prior to the Curse."

"There's fair magical strength on the Lightborn side," Ishmael noted. "Maybe the Shadowborn hesitated to tangle with the Lightborn, and we've been the beneficiaries."

"Which raises two more questions in my mind: first, how much do the *Lightborn* already know about these occupants of the Shadowlands, assuming they exist?"

Ishmael spread his gloved hands. Minhorne, as well as being the seats of both governments, was also the headquarters of the Mages' Temple, which ruled magic on the other side of sunrise, and, effectively, among the Darkborn as well. There were few Darkborn mages whom the Lightborn recognized as strong, the Lightborn having carefully cultivated strength among their lineages while the Darkborn left mages to arise by chance and scrabble for survival when they did. The Temple was not given to advising Darkborn of their doings, much less allowing them a say.

"You realize," Stranhorne said, "that that might make sense of the prince's death, if the Lightborn have formed an alliance with the Shadowborn. Second," he continued, while Ishmael was still taking that in, "tradition says that the magic that laid the Curse killed all those involved. But am I mistaken that all our experience of present-day magic is that any persistent magical effect—talismanic magic or ensorcellment—depends on the survival of the mage responsible? As the saying goes, magic dies with the mage."

"Aye," growled Ishmael. It was an adage entrenched in law—the legal penalty for sorcery being execution—and the one sure way to free the victim of all influence. Ishmael's growl was less at the reminder of his own jeopardy than at what Stranhorne implied. Magic, rooted as it was in the vitality of the mage who worked it, never outlived the mage—with the one great exception. After all these centuries, nobody gave thought to the possibility that the Curse was *not* the exception, even with the example of the long-lived Lightborn archmages before them. "You're saying that you think one of the mages who laid the Curse *survived*?"

If *they*, whose Curse the Lightborn lineages had for centuries tried to break, were the Shadowborn, then even he must despair.

"It is entirely speculative, you realize," Stranhorne reminded him judiciously. "I think it highly unlikely that those involved in the laying of a malevolent curse eight centuries ago would have waited all this time to make themselves known to us—not when it has been evident for centuries that we would prosper. But it *is* the simplest explanation for the anomaly."

"Curse it, Stranhorne," Ishmael said, with deep feeling, "not even Vladimer had that notion." He had to remember, though, the first time he and Vladimer had spoken about this, Vladimer had no more to go on than the extraordinarily quiet summer in the Borders. And the second time, Vladimer was newly awakened from ensorcellment and very shaken.

"Vladimer's a man of the modern age," Stranhorne said. "I am a historian. . . . There are ruins in the south desert that date back thousands of years, and outside the Sundered Lands I'm told there are other ruins, other deserts, oral traditions of other magical catastrophes. Perhaps this is merely a cycle that repeats itself."

Ishmael drained his brandy glass, wishing it were three times the size.

"When you first called on me," Stranhorne said, "I considered forbidding you my halls. To this day, however, I have not regretted my decision to receive you. Although," he remarked in a lighter tone, "some of my peers—and particularly their wives—were appalled at how you have corrupted my daughters."

"I had th'inborn proclivity to work with," Ishmael said, shakily.

"I'm quite sure it came entirely from their mother." There was a silence of weighing and sorting of words. "My prejudices obscured my recognition that that domination was not the only seduction magic offered. You were born with as much secular power as any man could wish, and yet at the age of sixteen, you rejected that for magic."

"M'father had more t'do with that than me."

"You need not have brought your magic to his, or anyone else's, attention," Stranhorne pointed out.

As Telmaine had, gifted with far greater power—and greater sense, perhaps—than he. Facing back across the years, he considered the stew of conviction and rebellion that had led him to compel his father to recognize the magic in him.

"When your father disowned you, I spoke up in support of it. When he reinstated you, I knew he had been forced to it. When you inherited, I wrote the archduke, urging him to refuse to sign the order of succession."

"I knew that at the time," Ishmael said. "I fully expected y'to run me off your lands that first time."

"I gave it some thought," Stranhorne said. "Even though everything I had heard of you was to the good. It is the virtues of mages, the good they do, that persuades people to discount the evidence of history—and so the cycle repeats. . . . How soon will you be back?"

The unexpected question took him by surprise. "I'll be—" He cleared his throat. "I'll be working t'get loose the moment we clear your gates—you can count on that. If I'm brought to th'city, I'll have Vladimer's backing, and his testimony that I meant him no ill." Though with a charge of sorcery and a suspicion of influence, that might be less an advantage than otherwise. "But if th'situation changes here, you can be sure mine will."

Stranhorne set his glass down and relieved Ishmael of his own. "Our ten minutes are up, I think. I've sent for Jeremiah Coulter from the Crosstracks, to test that warrant. If there's any crack to be found in it, he'll find it."

Ishmael

The Stranhornes had managed to pen Mycene in the ballroom, even if Laurel's smooth delivery was sounding rather strained as they came through the door. Ishmael's pursuer was almost toe-to-toe with the lady, though he was at a disadvantage thereby, being a good six inches shorter than she. His face was distinguished from commonplace by its asymmetry; one cheekbone noticeably higher and narrower than the other, one eye slightly offset relative to the other, nose slightly displaced by an old break. His hair was fine, straight, and pulled back from a high forehead into a braid or a queue, which had been tucked into his collar. He wore a greatcoat split for riding, heavy weight and of highest quality, and well-rubbed breeches. A holster rode on one hip, and the sheath of a long knife on the other.

Half a dozen of his men were lounging or sitting about, seasoned troopers conserving energy. The remainder must have been delegated to tend the horses. Dr. Balthasar Hearne was standing slightly to one side, haggard and road worn and, except for a too-large jacket of Borders style, still dressed as Ish had left him, but alive and apparently uninjured.

"Ishmael di Studier," Mycene challenged him. "I have here a warrant for your arrest for the murder of my betrothed, Lady Tercelle Amberley, and for suspicion of sorcery against Lord Vladimer Plantageter." His head twitched toward a man leaning against the wall with folded arms and a cynical expression on his face. If he'd never met the man, Ish would have taken him for a smuggler. Which he was said to have been in his youth; nothing teaches a clever man the law like the evasion of it. Sensing their sonn, Jeremiah Coulter shook his head slightly; the warrant was sound.

As Stranhorne had said, and Ishmael had expected. The brandy or Stranhorne's conversation, or the combination, had stunned him sufficiently that "I surrender myself to your hands" came out evenly. But he was glad that Lavender was in the cellar. Laurel merely chewed on her lower lip.

Mycene seemed perplexed, as a man is who pushes hard at a supposed obstruction, only to find it yield. "Right," he said. "Hand over your weapons. We're going north."

"There isn't a train until tomorrow," Stranhorne said. "The northbound express will have gone by the time you reach the station."

"Then we'll ride," Mycene said.

With a quiet sigh, Balthasar Hearne swayed and slid to

the floor in a dead faint. There was a slightly embarrassed silence at such unmanly behavior, and then Laurel settled carefully to her knees beside him, feeling his pulse. Before her pregnancy, the Strumheller surgeon had frequently drafted her as his assistant, for her cool head, steady hand, and ready understanding of terse orders.

"This man's exhausted," she reported. "He won't be traveling any farther today, unless it's in a coach."

Mycene shook his head in curt disgust. "Then we'll take a coach."

Stranhorne said, "You have maybe four hours to sunrise, which will put you in the inner Borders. I daresay you will be able to find lodgings from one of the households, but then you have—what?—another ten hours the next night, at best. A coach would slow you down even further. And given the ducal order, I think I would be fully within my rights to refuse you the use of fourteen or fifteen horses from my stables until this crisis is over, despite your warrant."

His lawyer gave a buccaneer's grin.

"I offer you the hospitality of my household until tomorrow night," the baron continued, reasonably. "We will deliver you and your prisoners to the station, where you will be able to catch the train up to the Summerhouse Terminus, and the first day train to Minhorne."

Boris was failing to conceal his dismay—no wonder his sisters always cleaned him out at cards. Ishmael was impressed by Stranhorne's nerve, and alarmed at the risk he was willing to run—on Ishmael's behalf? With a cellar full of munitions and an active plot to support the Isles, Ish would have punted his enemies out the door as fast as possible, never mind decent. Or perhaps Stranhorne hoped to continue that intensely disturbing conversation.

Ish would rather be carried off north in chains.

"I accept your invitation," Mycene conceded, sourly. "But I'm setting a guard on both those men. Di Studier's under arrest for murder and suspicion of sorcery, and Hearne for aiding and abetting. I'll have *you* up for aiding and abetting if they're not both on the train north tomorrow."

"Less risk having him here than rousing his suspicions as to what we had to hide," Stranhorne murmured to Ish a few minutes later, on the stairs. By the fourth flight, they had opened up a little distance between themselves and Mycene's guard, who had had a hard ride in his train. "We'll keep him and his men well fed and wined, and make sure they don't go wandering and meeting locked doors. We know who to keep away from them, too."

"And y'blame Lavender on your wife."

Stranhorne cocked a half smile at him. "Of course. It's Laurel who's all mine. . . . We'll dine just after the sunrise bell."

Balthasar Hearne was sitting up in bed when Ishmael came in, Stranhorne having persuaded Mycene to leave the guards outside the rooms his prisoners were to share. Balthasar was still fully dressed, except for jacket and boots, with a quilt thrown over him. He seemed tired but quite alert. He waited until Ishmael had closed the door, and said, abashed, "It was all I could think of to delay them. I'd already exhausted every other argument."

"It was convincing," Ishmael allowed, relieved and privately amused. *Curse it.* A man yearning after a married woman had no business liking the woman's husband.

"Not bad," Laurel allowed, judiciously. "For a man." To Ishmael she said, "Father managed to stall them? Then I'd better go and find something to occupy Lavender—it's too late to send her out again—and check with the housekeeper about dinner." She swept out.

Ishmael clasped hands with Balthasar. "Good t'find you again," he said, and sat down. "Did you make it to the manor?" Since the age of sixteen, he never had been able to refer to Strumheller Manor as "home," for all his sister's chiding.

"After a delay. Mycene was waiting at the station," Balthasar said, the tightness around his mouth betraying what his stoic face tried to conceal. "They questioned me." No small ordeal for a man beaten nearly to death under questioning less than a week ago. "They affected not to believe me and they took me up to the manor, claiming you might somehow have got past them. It was close to sunrise, anyway." So Reynard and Noellene had had the dubious pleasure of entertaining Mycene and his arresting party over a day. "Your sister was gracious and most relieved to learn that the reports of your death were mistaken. Your brother could not be faulted as a host, but he . . . gave me a message for you. He said that this time he would settle the inheritance in court."

"Ah, well, that's no surprise," Ishmael said. "He's not a bad man, m'brother, just too often disappointed." Even Reynard's marriage, arranged by their father, had been a disappointment. After ten years of childlessness and increasing estrangement, his wife had insisted on a divorce. "I'm like one of those alley cats, always turning up when y'think you've sonned the last of it."

"Your sister expressed her disappointment that you did not send your brother a personal letter."

That made him grin: Noellene had been born when Ishmael was sixteen, and had inherited their city-born mother's beauty and refinement—but she was enough their father's daughter to strip hide with her tongue when truly riled. She was probably right about the letter, but what was done was done. "Y'could explain as well as I could . . . And then you came on tonight. Hard ride, was it?"

"I cannot say I remember the last half," Balthasar admitted. "I just concentrated on staying with the horse."

"No mean feat, in that company. Now, I've some news t'give you, and it's not good. I think Stranhorne and I both need to hear your take on it—given you've served terms on th'Intercalatory Council, and live shoulder to shoulder with a Lightborn."

"Floria, yes."

"This does concern your—" He wasn't sure how he could, or should, characterize Balthasar's relationship with his neighbor. They were as intimate as a man and woman could be who would never meet in the flesh; that he knew. And he knew how Balthasar's wife felt about it. "Mistress Floria," he said, sidestepping awkwardness. "Since she's vigilant to the Lightborn prince. Isidore's dead."

"*Dead?* How?"

"Lights failed in his rooms during the night."

"That's—not possible," Balthasar said. "The prince's lights would be enspelled by multiple mages. They could not fail unless all those mages died at the same time."

"Or unless the magic was released or annulled."

"Not . . . possible," Balthasar insisted.

"Unless the Temple lifted its protection from Prince Isidore."

"In the whole of the history of the compact, the Mages' Temple has only once canceled contracts with a prince, with ample warning, and only after that prince had abused magic and mages egregiously. Isidore had no such history—and no such warning. Floria would have told me if there had been any hint of it." He paused. "Shadowborn?"

"That's my thought," Ishmael said grimly. "Which means strength enough t'overwhelm Lightborn high masters. Or collusion."

He waited, sonn playing over the other man's face as he thought that through.

"That we haven't already met that kind of strength doesn't necessarily mean it's not there," Balthasar said, slowly. "It may simply not have been needed. But as for collusion . . . No, I think that if the Lightborn were involved, even the Lightborn mages, they would make their demands directly. They have survived by the compact between earthborn and mageborn. Lightborn magic," he said, an appeal audible in his voice, "is not *chaotic*."

"I hope you've the right of that, Hearne."

"Have you heard again from Telmaine since she contacted you on the train?"

"No," Ishmael said. He caught his hand's unconscious movement to his chest and laid it casually down, hoping Balthasar had not noticed. "I know th'turn I had frightened her. She didn't understand before what it meant, the damage I had taken."

"You should have made that plain to her and to Vladimer," Balthasar said, levelly. "We made our plans assuming that you and Telmaine would be able to use magic as a line of communication."

"Curse it, Hearne—" He checked his defensive reaction. "You're right. I should've. I'd not let myself think how bad it could be. Now let it be."

Balthasar Hearne let it be. "The prince should not have died by magic. The Lightborn police abuse magic. *They* should have dealt with the Shadowborn we fought, not us. Are you certain that what we are dealing with is Shadowborn, and not factionalism within the upper echelons of the mages, both Darkborn and Lightborn?"

"A mage war," Ishmael said. *Sweet Imogene—Vladimer, Stranhorne, and now Balthasar.* He should have begged the whole bottle from Stranhorne.

"Yes," said the physician, simply, and waited.

"Some Shadowborn—glazen, for instance"—he indicated where the scars ridged the corner of his mouth, since he knew Hearne already knew that story—"use magic in their hunting. They're animal and it's instinctive, but I know the sense of it, and I sensed the same magic in the one at Vladimer's bedside. It's unique—Telmaine sensed it, too—and you doubt the Lightborn would collude."

"I think," Balthasar said, slowly, "knowing what I know of the Mages' Temple, the Lightborn would either dominate or be forced into submission. And if the Lightborn dominated, then it would be a lawful domination, not a chaotic one."

As a bottom-ranked mage, Ish had almost negligible dealings with the Temple, but listening to the Broomes—the leaders of the commune of mages within Minhorne—he, too, had formed an opinion of lawfulness to a fault. "The last possibility Stranhorne put to me was that th'Curse is not an exception to the way of magic after all, that one of Imogene's conclave, or even Imogene herself, survived to hold it."

"That's . . . always been a possibility," Balthasar said, sounding more thoughtful than rightfully terrified. "Although given the attention that the mages have paid to the Shadowlands over the years, if there were that much magical strength anywhere in them, they should have found it."

"I'm told that if a mage has good control or isn't making use of his strength as magic, then it's near impossible to know that a given vitality is his—unless you know that person. And there's nobody on either side of sunrise of an age t'know Imogene."

"Eight hundred years," Balthasar said a little faintly. "If Imogene had the viciousness to do this to us in the first place, then she would not wait eight hundred years to finish it. And if she were experiencing a belated remorse—"

Ishmael snorted. "Like no remorse I've ever met."

Balthasar took a deep breath; Ishmael could hear the waver in his diaphragm. He held it, then steadily released it. "There are a number of these scenarios that you and I simply cannot do anything about. You are a first-rank mage suffering from severe overuse." At least he had been kind enough not to say "disabled." "I have a very rudimentary sense of magic, I'm told, which lets me sense magic on the scale of a weather-working, but nothing else. So"—his voice was strained but firm—"our obligation remains unchanged. Find out what is going on, and get the information to the people who can do something about it."

Ishmael set a hand on his shoulder and stood up. "Which we have done, for the moment. The next thing is dinner and a wash for both of us. The ladies won't thank us for coming in reeking to the rafters of sweat, mud, and horse."

Balthasar

Dinner was served just after the sunrise bell, in an intimate dining room in one of the newer parts of the manor. To Balthasar, the occasion had the unreality of a parlor drama, as though comfort and security were already more novel to him than pain and danger. A few hours ago, he had been pounding along the roads in Ferdenzil's train. Now, in borrowed formal clothing, he was dining on snails imported from the Scallon Isles in the company of Ishmael di Studier, Ferdenzil Mycene, Baron Stranhorne and his son, and the ladies of the house.

"We were sixteen, you understand," Baronette Lavender said, extracting a snail from its shell with an economical twist of her two-tined fork.

"T'be presented the following year," Baronette Laurel said. "That was, if Lady Calliope di Reuther had any say in it. She'd chosen to take an interest in us poor, motherless things." Wisely suspicious of exotic foods, she signaled for another serving of smoked chicken.

"Find out if either of us could be polished up sufficiently for her darling boy," Lavender said, maliciously. "As if we'd be fool enough t'place ourselves within her reach."

Balthasar decided not to mention that said darling boy was married to his wife's close friend, Sylvide. He could not, however, dispute their assessment of Lady Calliope. The twins' father listened with an expression of benign amusement; he, no doubt, had heard it all before.

"And," Laurel said, returning to their joint tale, "we'd been reading all the wrong kind of literature."

"Aye," Ishmael rumbled. "That you had."

"In those stories," Lavender explained cheerfully to Bal, "all a girl needed to pass as a boy was to have boys' clothing and a cap. It was always the cap falling off at some untimely moment that gave them away. *We* made sure that *our* caps were proof against a gale."

"We'd ridden short, local circuits with the Stranhorne troop," Laurel said. "We'd heard *all* about Baron Strumheller, who'd Shadowhunted for more than twenty years, and we were all afire to meet him." She gave Bal a rueful smile. "We'd no idea the female walk was different from the male."

"Well," Lavender said with a sly grin, "that's what he *claimed*. But we'd also no idea what kinds of entertainments there are up in the city that'd teach a man to know a woman in man's garb." Ishmael opened his mouth and, wisely, Bal felt, closed it again. "Have you visited the burlesques, Dr. Hearne?"

Bal remembered one of the early lectures in his training concerning the difference between male and female anatomy. Even then he had recognized the lecturer's considerable achievement in managing to bore sixty young men with the intimate details of the female body. He decided against attempting to reprise the feat, though he tried to emulate the tone. "I'm doubtful that theater would have given you any better source material for your impersonation than your adventure stories. . . . I take it, then, that Ishmael recognized you were young women."

"The moment he met us," Lavender said. "Though he did not take us aside until later, after he'd judged our competence. Then he tore bleeding strips off both our hides and sent us straight home, under escort. We were too shocked even to cry."

"It wasn't that he shouted or insulted us," Laurel explained. "But he told us in explicit terms just how unprepared we were for the style of fighting he expected, and how we were putting at risk our lives and the lives of the men who'd be with us."

"We were in disgrace for *weeks*," Lavender said. "Admittedly, there were compensations. Lady Calliope quite lost interest in us as prospective daughters-in-law. And"—she settled her chin on her sinewy hand and cast a teasing burst of sonn over Ishmael—"once we recovered from the shock, we were in *love*. Sixteen, remember."

Ishmael found diversion in his plate. Ferdenzil Mycene's expression was somewhere between intrigued and appalled. Bal understood it, for all he thought himself progressive in his attitudes. Everything about them was outrageous, from their first-name address to a man so many years their elder, to their ease in discussing things that city society would have found mortifyingly improper, to their readiness to take to the road with the troop. Yet he could not but hope that in fifteen years he would share a meal in such comfort and informality with his own grown daughters.

"We spent the entire winter and spring and half the summer trying to make up the deficiencies Ishmael had so mercilessly pointed out. And then we took the train to Strumheller, all escorted and proper, to prove that we were fit to be troopers."

"He allowed as we'd improved," Laurel said. "And, miracle of miracles, he got Father to agree that we could ride escort on visitors and such on the near Borders."

"I am surprised," Ferdenzil said, though his tone implied something stronger, "that your father permitted it."

There was a brief, disconcerted silence; perhaps the ladies were not used to hearing city prejudice manifest at their own table. Stranhorne merely murmured, "I'm at times surprised, too."

"It's th'glazen," Ishmael said. "One of the most dangerous Shadowborn. About the size of a large dog, most of them, but they can ensorcell a man so he'll let himself be eaten alive. Only men; we do not know why. A woman with a steady hand and nerve can save a dozen lives, if not more."

This silence had a different texture to it. Bal remembered Ishmael's lawyer telling him that the scars on Ishmael's face, scars no mage of any strength should carry, had been made by a glazen. If these young ladies knew him as well as they seemed to, they might know that story.

Ish himself broke the silence. "Though it wasn't as troopers I wanted them."

"Indeed, no," said Lavender with a laugh, and waved a hand, inviting him to elaborate.

"Two baronettes, raised t'be chatelaines of a manor, able to manage a staff of a hundred or more and oversee th'organization for events involving hundreds. They'd won the help of the men of their troop, so I knew they'd the leadership. I'd give them two or three summers' seasoning, then set them on the logistics. Took some doing for their father t'agree, but I think he's judged the merit of it long since."

Stranhorne, his smile dry, raised his glass toward Ishmael.

"And that," Lavender said, "is what we've been doing for the past three years—managing the planning, provisioning, and tracking of the Stranhorne Borders defenses." She smiled sweetly at Ferdenzil. "Shocking, isn't it?"

Ishmael softly cleared his throat. A warning, Bal thought.

"And does your husband approve?" Mycene said to Laurel. She was married, Balthasar understood, to the Stranhornes' envoy to the court of the Dukes of Myerling, in the Isles.

"Not at the moment, of course," she said, demurely. "But I met him riding escort."

"Do many of your women ride with the troop?" Ferdenzil said.

Ishmael's face, alert and unsmiling, turned toward Lavender. That he nudged her foot under the table, Bal could not know for certain, but he suspected it from her twitch. She said, coolly, "Are you one of those who believes where the language says 'men,' that only men need apply, Lord Ferdenzil? Our standing troop numbers are within the ducal order of six twenty-seven, men and women both."

"I fail to see how women can be an asset to a troop, then. Women lack the strength and the will to fight."

"Raw strength, maybe, but a gun in a woman's hand is as deadly as in a man's," Ishmael said, "and they've often the sharper ears and the better judgment as to when t'shoot."

"But none better than you," Lavender said, staunchly. "I was there when he dropped a scavvern at six hundred yards, by ear. He was ahead of us on the road, and the first thing we knew was when he shouted the warning and shot. Could you shoot a Shadowborn at six hundred yards, Lord Ferdenzil?"

"I would not try," Ferdenzil said. "Sonn is sure; anything beyond, and you're a danger to your own people."

"A different kind of warfare," Ishmael said, setting down his spoon and addressing Mycene straight, one man sharing his experience with another. "Once a scavvern's near enough t'sonn, you've got two shots, maybe. Our people know our routes, know t'respond to our challenges, so we can challenge and shoot t'sound, as long as th'fighting formation holds. Once it's gone, then yes, we have t'shoot to sonn, rather than risk harming our own."

Lavender Stranhorne folded her hands before her plate and shifted in her chair, as though she were tucking her feet beneath her. "Then if you don't care to shoot beyond sonn, you cannot care much to sail the Islands, Lord Ferdenzil," she said in a silken tone.

"On the contrary, Baronette," Mycene said, carelessly, "I find the islanders' methods of addressing the problem of navigation most ingenious."

"But, alas, controversial," Bal murmured, drawing the

attention of both parties. He took a well-timed sip of wine. "I have served several terms on the Intercalatory Council that mediates where the common affairs of one race impinge upon the other. The choice of shore sites for the signal bells and message drums can be contentious; after all, the Lightborn *sleep* at night."

"It's always seemed t'me to be a brave thing t'do," Ish remarked. "To sail in these waters, trusting knowledge of the seas, skill in reckoning speed and direction, and the sound of the bells. A man's sometimes glad to be too preoccupied with his belly t'worry about the rocks."

"And what," Lavender said, "would you say of a man who goes Shadowhunting at sea?"

"I am well aware," Ferdenzil Mycene said, coldly, "that di Studier is a folk hero in the Borders. But I am here with a warrant for his arrest for the murder of my betrothed, Lady Tercelle Amberley, so you will forgive me if I do not share your admiration."

"Lord Mycene," Lavender said, "*Baron* Strumheller is more than a folk hero. He's the man who organized the baronies to *stop* this scourge of generations from preying on our towns and villages, when all your fine northern dukes and lords gave us were distrust and suspicion and threats to rule us in rebellion if we raised the force we need."

"Lavender," said Ishmael, "the warrant for my arrest is signed by the archduke, with the law of the land behind it. As is the ducal order enabling the raising of the Borders."

"Yes," said the baronette bitterly, "now the Shadowborn have come to the city." She stood up. "Excuse me, Father, Lord Mycene. If I stay, I will say something I will regret. Though not nearly as much as I should." She left, skirts swinging with her long stride.

On their way back to his shared suite with Balthasar, Ishmael continued the twins' account. He had done his utmost, as he promised their father, to keep them to less-risky duty, escorting noble visitors on the inner Borders roads. Their single encounter with a Shadowborn had occurred on an illicit jaunt into the highlands while Ishmael himself was far down in the interior, helping organize the Odon's Barrow troop and reserve. "Never came quite so close t'fainting on my feet as when I read that letter," he admitted. "I was glad t'leave the hide stripping to their father." Who had, Laurel had assured him, done a superb job of it, one quite worthy of Ishmael. "It was Laurel's shots took it down. Lavender's better on the range, but Laurel's got the cooler head."

Once they were in the suite and the door closed, he said more soberly, "The way the ladies are pleased t'tell it, the troop's an adventure. I didn't know the rest until months after. . . . The year before my father died and I was still Shadowhunting for hire, I'd been hired on by a lady in a little manor on the boundary between Stranhorne and Strumheller. Her son, fifteen years old, the lord of the manor, had vanished off the road. We were nearly four weeks in the Shadowlands but we found no trace. . . . The boy and Lavender had known each other from childhood, and were set on marrying when they came of age."

"And the young ladies didn't tell you."

"No. It was from their father I learned it."

Two

Ishmael

For the second night in a row, Ishmael awakened to the sound of dripping and running water, though this time the sound was coming from high overhead, and not from rain drumming on a day hide stretched above his face. He could not hear birdsong, only the voices of a manor very much awake. He had overslept. He started to sit up and abruptly became aware of another presence. He snatched for a revolver that was not there—Mycene having thoroughly disarmed him—before his sonn resolved the form of the man reading in the chair across the room. "Hearne," he noted, drawing his arm down. "What's th'hour? I'd have thought Mycene would have had us on the road as soon as the sun was down."

"He would have," the physician said, laying his book aside, seemingly oblivious to the meaning of Ishmael's abortive movement. "But there's nearly two feet of snow outside."

If Balthasar had snatched off his warm quilt, it wouldn't have brought him upright as effectively. "Two feet?" He had had no sense of magical weather-working whatsoever. Sweet Imogene, he must have slept like the dead. Balthasar, too.

"It stopped snowing just after sunset, I'm told. Baronette Lavender has sent some parties out on skis and snowshoes, to determine how wide the effect is."

"But none of the regular sweeps," Ishmael said. "Is that

what you're telling me?" He threw back his covers. Balthasar started to lever himself stiffly out of his chair, intending to return to his own room. Ish waved a casual hand at him. "Stay," he ordered. "I've nothing y'haven't sonned a hundred times before. You understand what power's needed t'influence th'weather."

"Yes," Balthasar said. "That kind of working would take several Lightborn high masters, and is probably beyond the reach of living Darkborn mages."

"Stranhorne will understand that," Ishmael said.

"Will he have shared that understanding?" Balthasar said, in sober assessment.

"That is likely, considering. The man's no fool."

Ishmael lifted clothes laundered of the odors and grime of the road, and went into the adjacent dressing room to wash and dress. Clad, he padded past Balthasar to the outer wall and lifted the bar and opened the shutter of the narrow, light-sealed window. It was unglazed, since its purpose was defensive. He propped a foot on the low bench on which a rifleman would kneel, and pushed his head through the gap—it would not pass his chest or shoulders—then inhaled deeply and listened. The doubled walls were wide, but the gap widened to the outside, allowing a sniper a better-than-sixty-degree arc. Snow: there was no mistaking the scent of it, but the air was warming and he could smell the grass and scrub of the Borders rising on the wind. The thaw would not be long in coming. Could he console himself that the mages who had called the storm down on them lacked the strength or commitment to keep the cold? Or had it already achieved its purpose, pinning them down, preventing the Stranhornes' sweeps?

He could hear voices from his left—children, screeching delight at this novelty, and two or three adults—and swung his head to better place them. They would be within the enclosed garden to the east, since there was nowhere else for children to play in time of high alert. It had been the baronelle's garden before she died. He was fully oriented now, and unnerved by more than the snow. He jerked his head back in, closed and tested the shutter automatically, and turned to face his traveling companion. "Hearne," he said, "I need your help."

"Anything," the physician said.

He would rather, he admitted to himself, be facing down a scavvern with a butter knife. "Y'know the reason we were t'meet in the first place."

"Lord Vladimer thought my skills might be useful to you," Balthasar said. "In dealing with the Call." Balthasar Hearne had a growing reputation in the treatment of addictions and other irrationality; his success with one of Vladimer's other irregular agents, Gil di Maurier, had attracted Vladimer's attention.

"Aye. You've an interest in the treatment of compulsions." He passed a hand down his face. "I've th'strongest urge to go straight downstairs, out the door, and start walking southwest as fast and far as my feet will take me."

"That is all?" Balthasar said.

Of course he would miss the significance of the direction, not knowing that for as long as it had ridden Ishmael, the Call had pulled him due south, not southwest. "Yes," Ishmael said, fighting impatience. "That's all th'Call is—an urge t'go into the Shadowlands and not come back, even knowing it would be the death of me."

"Is there any basis to this compulsion—a sense that someone important is waiting for you there, or that you have something to do?"

"No," Ishmael said. "It's just th'urge t'go. Southwest." He almost felt as though he had lurched in that direction, but sonned no reaction in Balthasar's intent face.

Balthasar said, "Sit down, if you would, Baron."

He waited until Ishmael had sat down and then said, "Have you ever lost control to the extent that you started to move in that direction without intending to?"

"Not waking," Ishmael said through a tight jaw. "I'd sleepwalk when it was at its worst. Wanted a guard, sometimes chains."

Balthasar's lips compressed, whether at the implications of someone sleepwalking during daylight or at Ishmael's measures. "And are you close to losing control now?"

"No, but it's strong, and th'direction's changed. All these years, it has pulled south. Now it's pulling southwest."

"Southwest, but still into the Shadowlands." He paused. "How do you interpret that?"

"That whatever or whoever is holding th'Call on me is moving. Likely moving north." *Toward Strumheller.* He sank his fingertips into the arm of the chair.

"And what have you tried to break the compulsion?" the physician said.

"What haven't I tried, Hearne? Magic, of course; overspent myself often enough to drive th'futility through my thick skull. Phoebe Broome tried. She'd have asked her father, but her brother Phineas tried t'send me off the first months I was in their commune, and wound up taking a mild case of it himself. She was afraid her father'd get in too deep and suffer worse. The mage who'd had me as student tried. I downed various potions and medicines, too, though it was as well I'm hard t'poison, or some of your colleagues would have done for me."

"Did you ever approach a Lightborn mage?" Bal said.

"Had some correspondence with one, but we'd never th'intimacy for me to raise the question with him. Darkborn mages tend not to want t'attract their attention that way—they've the greater power and they think to rule magic on both sides of sunrise. I've always wondered if they weren't the more vulnerable to th'Call, though if Lightborn were lost in numbers in the past, we've no record of it."

"Floria never seemed to have any difficulty talking about Shadowborn."

"Mistress Floria's not a mage," Ishmael said flatly.

A thoughtful pause. "What do you know about therapeutic hypnosis?"

Ish shrugged. "Not so much."

"Most important, in this instance, is that it has nothing to do with ensorcellment or subordination of the will. I am not a mage—as you well know—not a fairground magician, and definitely *not* the hypnotist in a sixpenny melodrama." That emphasis suggested past trying experiences. "I could not induce you to do anything that you might not wish to do."

He paused. "If you wish to touch-read me to know the truth of that, you may."

Ishmael did not move. It was a generous offer, given that Ishmael's presence, as well as Telmaine's confession of magic, for which Ishmael was also responsible, had perturbed Balthasar's happy marriage. Ishmael and Telmaine had at no point acted improperly, but there was a warm, mutual attraction between them. "I've got many wishes best not acted on," Ishmael said, truthfully.

"I've never known anyone who didn't. But I'm not talking about impulses, although hypnotism can be very useful in subduing impulses, even quite compelling ones. Will you let me attempt to hypnotize you, Baron? It may be that I can augment your resistance to the Call."

"Aye," Ishmael said. "Have at it."

But now, as years ago, when he was trying to elicit the fullest strength from his magic, Ishmael was hampered by his hyperacute senses and keen, worldly awareness, the consequences of years of vagabondage and Shadowhunting. He knew there was danger outside; he knew danger had to be attended to. Every voice or closing door, familiar or otherwise, snapped him from his trance.

"Hold," he said at last, and leaned forward, rubbing his temples to coax away an incipient headache. Balthasar sat silent, his expression a professional mask.

"Maybe I should have said t'you that I was not that good at th'exercises that mages use. The mage who took me on when I couldn't stick in the Broomes' commune had th'idea t'overwhelm my vigilance. He had me down at the fish market when the barges docked." Balthasar's grimace proved that he, too, had visited the fish market at that time—probably as a cash-strapped young student after cheap, fresh fish. Ishmael grinned. "It seemed t'work, Hearne. So maybe—"

Telmaine's silent scream, the sear of magic across his awareness, caught him completely unguarded. He felt his body spasm with the shock of it, and then he lost all sense of himself as the reverberations shuddered along his nerves. Their passing left him in a state of desperate uncertainty.

He willed a silent voice to speak, longed for a whisper or even a wisp of vitality that would tell him if she prevailed, whether that was a shriek of mortal injury or a battle cry. He could not endure— He must— He must not try to— The crushing pain in his chest nearly caused him to black out, and left him sweating and shaking and afraid he had groaned aloud. His teeth were locked, hard enough for his jaw muscles to spasm, and he felt chilled and nauseated. Balthasar's fingers probed his pulses, felt for his stuttering heart; through his touch, he felt the physician's recognition and concern at this second episode. He lifted his head groggily, finding himself propped half in, half out of the armchair. "Cursed . . . habits," he managed, and, struggling to think, let his head fall back.

He had sensed Shadowborn—he could not mistake them. Sweet Imogene, had another Shadowborn found her? They knew there were at least two in the city. If so, had Vladimer been there? Judging by what she said of her encounter with the first Shadowborn, her best chance—perhaps even her only chance—of survival was to have someone present with a ready hand and a revolver, and Vladimer was as good as Ishmael at close quarters. But there had been Lightborn magic in that sear, too. Had she run afoul of the Lightborn mages, despite his best hopes that his warnings and her own aversion would restrain her from contravening their laws on the use of magic? Or were the *Lightborn* in league with the *Shadowborn*, as Stranhorne had suggested? It would explain the magical taints, and why she fell under attack.

Sweet Imogene, what was happening in the city?

He roused himself at the rattle of small bottles as Balthasar unrolled his medicine pouch. "No need to dose me," he said. "It's just th'effects of overreach again."

Balthasar paused and said, firmly, "You have to stop trying to use your magic."

"Th'head knows; it's just slow t'reach the reflexes." He pushed himself up too soon; he had to lean forward, head in his hands, until his heart rate steadied and the pain in his chest eased.

When he raised his head, Balthasar was waiting for him. "Was it Telmaine?"

The man was no mage, but he had witnessed Ishmael's previous spasm while talking to Telmaine, and she would be foremost in his mind. In a few words, not sparing either of them, Ishmael sketched what he had sensed.

Balthasar's shoulders bowed with guilt. "How could we do this to her?" he whispered. "How could we put her in such danger?"

"Th'job needed done, and she's the best we have." His choice of tense was deliberate.

"I'm her husband, Strumheller," Balthasar said. "I promised when I married her to cherish and protect her, and I sent her into danger."

There was not much Ishmael could say; Balthasar knew what they faced, knew what it had already cost them. And Ishmael knew how he felt—indeed, he envied the other man his right to express it. "We'll be bound north before sunrise," he said, half prayerfully. "If Mycene has his way."

They ate breakfast in near silence, having exhausted speculation as to what might be happening in the city or outside in the snow. Mycene would not release either of them, though they heard Lavender arguing with him in the hall. Nor would Mycene permit the twins to visit them. He was convinced that the young women were plotting Ishmael's escape, whatever their father said. He was quite right, if Ishmael knew his baronettes. And who was to say Lavender had not been right when she had urged him to ride out before Mycene arrived? If he had, he would have been out in the snow—or beyond the snow, with whatever might be out there.

He persuaded Balthasar to dose himself out of his medical bag to relieve the aches of the previous night's ride. The dose, breakfast, and lingering fatigue made him drowsy, sparing Ishmael his too-sharp attention and his too-imaginative worrying about Telmaine and what had happened in Minhorne. Like Vladimer and Stranhorne, Balthasar could imagine disasters that might never have occurred to Ishmael. That left Ishmael to listen to the snowmelt running in the gutters and feel the Call dragging on him.

Stranhorne himself arrived while they were eating lunch. His face told them the news was bad. "Roads have cleared enough that a post rider made it through. I've had a telegram from my elder son in Minhorne. The archduke and several others were injured this morning in a magical attack. The archduke suffered severe burns; he may not live. A regency council will be instituted for the emergency, and the heir will be recalled from their summer estate. At present, the main suspicion falls on the Lightborn."

That was what I felt from Telmaine, Ishmael thought in horror. The Shadowborn's cursed fire raising again. Were Lightborn involved as allies or agents of the Shadowborn? Or had they, too, opposed the Shadowborn attack, finally involving themselves against these rogue mages? It would be a bitter irony if the Lightborn had been trying to protect the archduke and now were blamed—but that was the way the world worked. And Telmaine—was she alive or dead? If the archduke had been attacked, she would have done what she could to stop it; he could not imagine her doing otherwise.... She had abundant power but precious little experience, and what he had sensed suggested her situation had been desperate. All that beauty, refinement, and strength of personality and magic, burned, perhaps dead—because he was not there.... "Vladimer?" Ishmael asked, because he could not ask first about Telmaine—he had no reason to ask about Telmaine—and she should have been close to Vladimer.

"Lord Vladimer appears to have suffered a mental collapse, having shot and killed a lady guest."

"Who?" whispered Balthasar, and then in a near shout, *"Who was she?"* He controlled his voice; it shook with the effort. "My wife ... was a guest at the palace." His thoughts would have followed the same course Ishmael's had, likely more swiftly.

"It was not your wife," said Stranhorne with compassion. "The lady's name was Lady Sylvide di Reuther. My son made no mention of Lady Telmaine."

Ishmael remembered the lady, a sweet-faced featherhead, gossiping with Telmaine at the archducal ball—about Ishmael's reputation, as he recalled. Why Vladimer would have had cause to shoot *her*, he could not imagine. Was this some residual effect of the ensorcellment? Had the Shadowborn ensnared him anew? Balthasar had surmised that Vladimer had not told them everything about his encounter with the Shadowborn, and Ishmael was certain he was correct.

"Did your son say anything about whether . . . Lady Sylvide's form changed in death?" Balthasar said.

"He did not," Stranhorne said, slowly. "Is that possible?"

"Aye," Ishmael said, grimly.

"It has to be Shadowborn," Balthasar said. "If the archduke dies—"

The archduke's heir, being his youngest child, was only twelve, little older than Sejanus Plantageter himself had been when he succeeded his own father. "The regency council'll be Imbré, Rohan, Mycene, and Kalamay," Ish said slowly, thinking aloud. The three other major dukes, and Claudius Rohan, who had sat on the regency council for Sejanus's own long-ago minority and was Sejanus's closest friend; no one would deny him that service for Sejanus's son. Imbré was the only other one of that long-ago council still alive.

Balthasar Hearne understood the political implications as well as either baron, perhaps better, for he had served several terms on the council mediating Lightborn-Darkborn affairs and understood the stress points intimately. Neither Mycene nor Kalamay had any tolerance for Lightborn. Sachevar Mycene—Ferdenzil's father—coveted the land they held, and Xerxes Kalamay found them and their magic to be an offense to the Sole God.

If their neighbors had turned against them, the Darkborn were terribly vulnerable. As they had been a hundred years back, when the genocidal Lightborn Odon, styled Odon the Breaker, set out to rid his lands of Darkborn.

Stranhorne said, "I've commissioned a special train to take Lord Mycene and his men to Strumheller, now the thaw is well advanced. It'll be faster than the coastal express, but you'll likely have an overday stay in Strumheller or some point north—with Lightborn unrest, the railways won't want to risk day trains."

Ishmael agreed. Balthasar's face was grim. Likely recalling the abortive attack on the day train taking Telmaine and him to the coast to save Lord Vladimer. Lightborn, Telmaine had said. "We need to go north as soon as we can now," Bal said.

"Father," Lavender's voice came from outside. "Get *out* of my way, you knucklehead. This is an emergency. *Father!*"

Stranhorne himself crossed over and opened the door. "Let my daughter pass," he told the guard. "If she says it is an emergency, it is."

Lavender half fell through the door, muttering not entirely under her breath about the guard's habits and antecedents. "The inbound post coach just arrived," she said, anticipating her father's reproach at her language. "The post riders from Upper Eastbridge and the Heights didn't make their rendezvous. Several carts of wool were due into Lower Eastbridge from the Heights; they didn't arrive. A midwife who went out in that direction last night to attend a childbed hasn't been heard from, and no one who lives in that direction has made it to work or market. Dyan's mustering and mounting a double squad to take the road to Lower Eastbridge, to scout. Post coach is going on to the Crosstracks—"

"Under escort," Stranhorne said.

"Yes, a squad—Carlann's taking them. Laurel's writing the telegrams to send t'Strumheller and points south along the wires."

"Strumheller Manor and Crosstracks, both," Ishmael said. His brother had to get the word, with no dithering. If Stranhorne weren't so obdurate, they'd be able to send the telegrams from here. Ishmael had had Strumheller Manor wired the month he inherited, although nine years later, his engineers were still working against skeptical villagers, distance, gales, rain, and frost in their efforts to string and maintain a working network along the hill roads. "The railway head office, too: they'll need to decide on th'trains." Which likely meant that he would not be heading north under guard tonight, if the trains were stopped and Stranhorne could not spare fifteen horses. "And Lord Vladimer in Minhorne. Plain text; no cipher." If Vladimer were incapacitated and couldn't read it, others would; it might push them into action.

Though, given the regency council, that action might not be what he wished. Mycene, for one, might take advantage of the archduke's incapacity and the pressure on the Borders to make his move on the island territories. Unless the archdukedom itself proved the greater plum.

The Plantageters would have to look to their own interests. Ishmael had all he could manage in the Borders.

"I need a telegram sent to my wife," Balthasar slipped in. "She was staying at the home of her sister, Lady Erskane. Ask her to wire that she is all right."

Lavender nodded and said to her father, "We're sending a squad south toward Stonebridge and Hartman's Barrow. They'll meet up with the squad quartered in Stonebridge and swing out by the Barrow."

"Double squads," Ishmael said. "Even from here. Same orders as th'ones to Eastbridge. And pass the word to th'post coach to hold their outbound runs."

"Already done," Lavender said. Then she said, "Will you lead the squad to Upper Eastbridge? You're one of the best we have still."

Lavender didn't know about the strengthened Call—didn't know that his risk from it was any graver than at any other time since he'd known her. Balthasar, subject to the constraints of his profession, kept silent, though Ishmael heard the breath he drew.

Stranhorne shook his head. "Mycene would never allow it."

"Or he'd insist on a guard on me," Ishmael said. "And the last thing we need is men in the squad who haven't been trained in the way we fight—or have you forgotten th'hide-stripping I gave you and your sister, all those years ago?"

She said with feeling, "Never."

"I'll be put to good use here, getting the manor ready."

"Do you think," Lavender said, sounding younger than her years, "it might come to fighting here?"

"Aye, I think it might. Those are ominous signs, as y'rightly understood. But we've got solid walls between us and them, and without the walls and the killing grounds, they'll rue the hour they crossed into our lands."

Except, he thought, *they have magic, and magic powerful enough to bring snow in late summer.* Her father knew that. But Lavender—it did not matter whether she knew or not. She could do no more than she was already doing, and would do it less well if she were frightened. "If y'can get me out of this room," he said, "I'll do what I can to take Lord Mycene and his men in hand. They'll be no danger t'anyone but the Shadowborn shooting from snipers' holes in th'upper stories." He gestured. "And they may take t'it."

"And this is good *how*?" Lavender muttered.

Ishmael grinned, despite the weight of his worries and the drag of the Call. "Th'enemy of your enemy, girl. It'll be all to the good, them knowing what we've been up against, all these years. Make them think twice about troubling your kin in th'Islands."

"Who is taking the squad south?" Stranhorne said, neutrally.

She set her lips, an answer in itself, and then said, half blurting, "Laurel and Boris will be here, and one of us—"

"Not necessarily," Stranhorne said. There was a silence. "Be careful."

"As a city lady guards her reputation." She kissed her father's cheek, clasped Ishmael's gloved hand, and made a strategic retreat before either Stranhorne or Ishmael could raise further objections.

"Stranhorne," said Ishmael. "I owe y'an apology. I promised to keep them out of danger." If he'd been born a sixth-rank mage, he'd be able to *lift* Laurel from here to safety in a moment—and he would have, even if her father banished him from his manor and she boxed his ears for it. But he couldn't even argue for sending her to relatives in the inner

Borders if the trains were stopping, and he could not pretend the roads were safe.

"Are you?" the baron said, tartly. "I had no idea you were responsible for the Shadowborn."

"Get me out of this room, please, before I start tearing through th'walls. Hearne, too. Is Linneas here?"

"Yes," Stranhorne said, the hint of weary amusement telling Ishmael a familiar story. Linneas Straus was physician and surgeon to the Stranhorne troop. As regularly as the turn of seasons, his daughter's husband was sacked from his latest job, the growing family descended on Linneas's home in need of shelter, and Linneas took refuge in the manor. "It's that," he'd said to Stranhorne, "or y'sit magistrate on my trial for killing th'wastrel."

Balthasar would no doubt learn all that and more once he met the physician. "Linneas Straus is the physician who takes care of the manor and the troops," he said to Balthasar. To Stranhorne: "Hearne's got city hospital training; be useful should things get busy. He might be able t'help us prepare for numbers of casualties. We've never dealt with a mass attack before." It would also keep the physician distracted from what might be happening in Minhorne. If his need was anything like Ishmael's, he should be grateful.

"And we can only hope we're not dealing with one now," Stranhorne said. To Balthasar: "Linneas doesn't have a city education—he was trained by apprenticeship, as were most of our surgeons—but he's been physician to the manor for thirty-odd years. Attended on all my children's births."

Balthasar took the caution as intended, though for him, at least, it was not needed; he had little city professional arrogance about him. Ishmael added, "And never mind his sense of humor."

"I'll have a word with Mycene," Stranhorne promised, and left them.

Balthasar sat down. "Oh, dear God," he breathed. "Vladimer was right."

"Seems t'have been," Ish said stoically.

"You think they'll need me?" Balthasar said.

"They might. But there's another reason I want us out

and about. If it comes to a siege, and it might, the manor's walls are strong, and its defenders skilled, but if there's an agent inside—if there's a Shadowborn inside—then that'll do them no good whatsoever. Remember what we found in th'archducal summerhouse: th'entire household ensorcelled into sleep. If that's done here, they'll have no chance."

"Have you sensed something in the manor?"

"Maybe. It comes; it goes. I've taken damage, I know, but I *daren't* let this pass."

Balthasar said, slowly, "If I were a Shadowborn shape-shifter, and I wished to sabotage the effort to defend Stranhorne, then I would try to replace you, Baron Stranhorne, or one of his children."

"Aye," Ishmael said. "That'd be my thought, too."

The physician's voice was oddly tense. "Perhaps *I* might sense it, if it is mage enough."

"Y'didn't sense th'one that wore your brother's form."

"I was flat on my back, weak and panicking with the threat to my daughter."

His probing sonn, his braced posture, revealed his purpose. Ishmael grunted. "You've more nerve than sense, thinking t'spook a Shadowborn when you're alone with it and unarmed."

Balthasar said, unsmiling, "You were out of contact for more than twenty-four hours."

"Well, I'm m'self. And this close t'you, I think I can be sure of you, too."

He waited, and was relieved to hear the change in the physician's voice. "A mage or mages strong enough to bring on snow in August would have the strength to breach even these walls."

"We can but hope they've a need t'preserve this manor. I wish I'd a sense of th'way they worked. It seems so erratic—oblique one moment, excessive th'next. Vladimer'd be able to get a sense of it. I can't." He pushed that worry aside; they had to deal with the dangers of the moment. "I want us t'try to smoke out any Shadowborn in the manor *before* their forces reach us."

"The Shadowborn who impersonated my brother, trying

to get me to tell him where Tercelle's twins were, did not attempt to touch-read me. It may be that Shadowborn do not have that ability. If they don't, we can check on each other, ask each other questions that superficial acquaintances would not be expected to know. But if they do—"

"In this flurry, we're likely safe enough. But you'd be best t'take care not t'be alone, or with one or two. That includes Mycene's men."

Balthasar's expression changed again. "What is't?" Ishmael said.

"Something I noticed during last night's ride . . . Something I—" His expression was frustrated. Plainly, Balthasar Hearne was not used to having his memory fail him. "You were about spent," Ish said. "It'll come t'you."

In the hall, an alarm bell clamored. "What—?" said Balthasar, as Ishmael moved.

"Call t'arms," Ishmael said, opening the door, and walking straight into the sonn of Mycene's guards.

Balthasar

To Balthasar's relief, they were all spared finding out whether Ishmael was prepared to stop, or how far Mycene's men were prepared to go in stopping him. Young Baronet Stranhorne arrived at a run. "My father's compliments," he gasped out. "You're all wanted in the ballroom immediately."

A diplomat in larval form, Balthasar thought, since he was sure that Ishmael was the one truly wanted. They arrived in the ballroom at the same time as did Mycene himself, who sonned them with a scowl and gestured, with a taut flick of the hand, for Balthasar and Ishmael to precede them. The ballroom, busy when they passed through it on arrival, was barely controlled mayhem now. Balthasar smelled blood, despite the dense overlay of gun oil, gunpowder, wet wools, leather, and sweat. By the turn of his head and the narrowing of his lips, Mycene smelled it, too. From the far side of the ballroom, a man shrieked through clenched teeth, and sonn resolved a bucking figure on a table, with others holding him down. Balthasar started in that direction, but a hard hand on his shoulder jerked him back. "Stay," the guard said.

"I'm needed—"

"*Stay*," growled Mycene. "I'm not having you take advantage—"

"Sweet Imogene, Mycene," Balthasar said, exasperated, "where would I *go*?"

A group of men and women wearing the uniform and livery of house staff thrust past them in disregard of Mycene's temper and rank. Most carried long-barreled guns, some more than one. Ishmael had explained that the south and west sides of the manor overlooked ground cleared, leveled, and strewn with gravel and the brittle shells of dried nuts, and cross-webbed with trip wires strung with rattles. Nothing could approach unheard. The narrow upstairs windows served as sniper posts. Mycene allowed the reservists to pass with no more than a grunt of sour approval. From within milling bodies and pulsing sonn, Balthasar could hear Laurel's clear voice issuing orders.

A man with one arm directed them to the side gallery, where they found Baronette Lavender, her father, and as grim, weary, and battered a group of men as Balthasar had ever managed after a brawling night in the Rivermarch, where he worked intermittently as a physician. They were gathered around a large relief model, which Balthasar recognized as being of the immediate area.

Mycene thrust forward. "What's happening?"

Stranhorne sonned him, nodded curtly, acknowledging him as a peer, but spoke as much to Ishmael as to Mycene. "Shadowborn, in force. Scavvern, balewolves, some kind of winged Shadowborn—no one's given a clear description. Ensorcelled animals—attacks by dog packs, horses, cattle, and goats, even mobbing by *sheep*. We've got envenomations, reports of beetles of some kind. . . ." He jerked his head toward the door, where the shrieks from the man on the table had diminished to a muffled keen, with an intermittent strangulation that Balthasar read as convulsions.

"Stonebridge"—Stranhorne pointed to a marker—"has

been overrun." The bell tolled, a slow, steady knell beneath his words. "We've got survivors pouring in the gate as we speak. Laurel is marshaling sweeps to bring in all those we can rescue, because we'll have to close the gate before the Shadowborn force reaches us. The squad quartered at Stonebridge was evacuating the town when last heard of. We've no word on Hartman's Barrow or the hill villages beyond. We've sent riders out to the Crosstracks, to raise the alarm, warn the railroad, and send telegrams to Strumheller and the inner Borders. Strumheller's our best hope of quick reinforcement, if we can hold the tracks and stop the wires from being cut. At least it's early in the night—we've got hours before we'll be completely unable to defend ourselves. If you want to take your chances on the road to the station, then we'll mount and supply you. But I'd not refuse a dozen good fighting men." He said that without a smile, without any play on the irony of his recruiting his enemies; the situation was too grim for that.

Mycene's grunt signaled neither assent nor refusal, but he leaned forward slightly, gathering himself for action. He was already committed to this fight, whether he knew it or not.

To Balthasar, Stranhorne said, "Are you up to helping Linneas? We've got casualties." He had noticed Balthasar's stiff movements. Balthasar simply nodded. "Good." To the one-armed man he said, "Erich, take him, introduce him."

In the ballroom, the reek of terrified, wounded, and sick people was even stronger, the noise louder. Somewhere, a woman was screaming wordlessly, a monotonous descant of horror, chopped by regular, wheezing breaths. To Bal's left, a small child's voice said, "Ma, Ma, Ma," with a dreadful persistence; worst of all, it went unanswered. He heard Erich say to someone, "We need t'get them calmed down and cleared somehow."

Erich slung Balthasar toward the narrow corridor into the former ballroom kitchen, now—for the sake of its stoves and drainage—turned surgery. The Stranhorne surgeon was already at work, hands digging into a man's belly. He barely acknowledged Erich's introduction: "Here's th'city man, Linneas, t'help you. Name's Balthasar Hearne." Bal noted that the man on the table still wore his boots, and tallied that with the set to the surgeon's face and the viscous strings trailing from the drapes onto the floor. Without a word, he stripped off his jacket, rolled up his sleeves, and went to the sink to scrub his hands and forearms with harsh carbolic soap. Behind him, he heard an instrument fall, with no sound of a fumble or missed catch, the tiny sound like the last stroke of a distant sunrise bell to a man too far from shelter. The sound of a body being lifted was always different after life was gone.

He let a few heartbeats elapse before he turned. Linneas Straus was a heavyset man in his fifties. He swept his sonn over Balthasar, approving his bared arms with a grunt. "Y'know what t'do?" he said.

"If I don't, I'll ask."

Balthasar lost track of time. Smell, hearing, insight—all narrowed to contain only the utterly necessary. He administered anesthesia. He helped pin down a slight boy while Linneas amputated his ruined arm above the elbow, and cleared vomit from the boy's mouth before he choked on it. He set swift stitches into the lacerated back of a young woman, knowing that for all his care, she would be scarred for life, if she did not take a fatal infection. Worse than the clawed ruin before him was the low, monotonous sobbing that did not change, no matter how deeply the needle pierced. One of the women acting as assistants whispered to him that she was infant mistress in the Stonebridge school, and that the school . . . She left the sentence unfinished. Balthasar completed his suturing, the attendants carried her away, and he let the sound and the information slip out of his mind. He knew to be grateful that it was not him but Straus who must decide who to set aside as beyond all help. Like the man with the crushed skull whose agonal breathing had so often faded to silence and then rattled into life again that when he finally died, nobody noticed at first.

Voices floated in from elsewhere. Lavender or Laurel said, "Father, we may need your word to close the gate soon."

"Oh, Mother of All," the other twin replied, "there hasn't been time for everyone—"

"We ran into what's left of the Stonebridge squad." This time it was Lavender. "The Shadowborn vanguard is three miles back. We've moved the armory into the second-floor gallery, and we've filled the ballroom and the lower floor with refugees, and set anyone whose nerves are up to it to reloading upstairs. Ishmael's handling that.... Curse Mycene, he should have been out on the roads."

"How many have come through the gate?" he heard Stranhorne say.

"Just over a thousand, by my count," Laurel said, her voice a half whisper.

Stranhorne said, perhaps to no one in particular, "At last census there were upwards of seven thousand between Stonebridge and the Barrow, and another three thousand in the hill villages between here and the border with the Shadowlands...."

Balthasar fumbled and dropped his scissors. "Curse it, city man," Linneas barked. "If you need a break, take one. This is likely just th'start."

Someone offered him a mug of tarry tea, sweetened and laced with brandy, and meat jerky and dried fruit, which he soaked in the tea with no regard for gentility. Then a man delirious with pain planted his foot in the center of his stomach, and he nearly lost everything. By the time he was done wheezing and retching, the man had slipped meekly under anesthetic, his last resistance spent. Balthasar braced himself against the table and, still bent over, set to work. Linneas Straus remarked, more cheerfully than before, "No need t'feel ashamed of yourself there; he's th'terror of tavern brawls from the Crosstracks to Stranhorne Port."

Three

Ishmael

Life had taught Ishmael patience, and experience, priorities. So he wasted no spleen on his frustration at being mewed up in the manor and tripping over guards every time he turned around. He had nervous snipers to settle, reloaders to deploy, ammunition runners to direct. With so many of the regulars out on the roads, trying to bring in as many refugees as possible, the majority of the manor's defenders were reserves, trained only as far as would comply with the ducal order: manor servants, wives and sons and daughters of reservists, and young troops in training. And Ferdenzil Mycene and his men, who had listened when Stranhorne had refused to let them out on the roads because of their inexperience in fighting Shadowborn.

I might even start to respect the man, Ishmael thought wryly, *if Mycene keeps being reasonable.*

He wished he had had a chance to have Mycene and his men test shoot some rounds, to give them the feel of the weapons and distance. They weren't as used to handling rifles as they were shorter-range weapons, though several had trained and fought at sea—and Ish, no sailor, had to respect anyone who could master both his weapons and his stomach on a rolling ship. But he had no idea how close the enemy might be and would not risk losing any surprise there was to be had.

"So the idea is we shoot to sound," Mycene said, softly.

He knelt on a sniper's rest in a southern gallery in the fifth and topmost floor of the manor. Ishmael was propped against the wall to his right. Ishmael had half of Mycene's men in this gallery and half in the next, alternating with seasoned Stranhorne reservists. "Have you ever fought these kinds of actions before?"

"There's been th'odd incursion reach the manor before, but not in this force."

"If we'd had time to prepare, I would have suggested volley fire. With the range these have"—he gave a light, possessive caress to the barrel—"we could have started on them as soon as we knew they were within range. You don't appear to need to stint on ammunition."

Was that as innocuous an observation as it seemed? Ish thought, remembering the munitions stored in the locked cellars. In this stir, they hadn't been able to keep the wrong people away from Mycene. But coordinated fire would have been a cursed excellent idea to have had earlier. They were too used to fighting in the open, in small bands, against a haphazard enemy.

He sonned his captor, kneeling relaxed in the sniper's rest, his weapon resting ready on the ledge. Ishmael hadn't needed to correct his posture or settle him down; plainly he was one of those calmed by the approach of battle.

"How large is this force?" Mycene said, voice barely carrying.

"Unknown, except by measuring th'numbers they overwhelmed. Stonebridge was seven thousand people, a fifth of whom were weapons trained—" If Mycene didn't have an idea already of how large a reserve Stranhorne retained, he would before this night was fought out. "And a good squad."

"And what had Stonebridge in the way of defensible positions?"

"Only the terrain: it's built on a hill. Th'only reason the manor is walled and built for defense against force is that Strumheller was burnt to the ground during the civil war." By, as Ishmael recalled, an army led by one of the Mycenes.

Mycene turned his head and sonned him for the first time. "You think we can hold this manor?"

"Depends," said Ishmael, surprised to find himself inclined even toward that much truth.

Mycene returned his attention to the night. "And, of course, there is the question of magic. My father has a fixation with it; I never understood why. Always seemed unmanly to me."

"Nothing unmanly about th'strength needed to bring snow in late summer," Ishmael gritted.

"No. It slowed us detecting their approach very effectively. Have you given any thought to what a retreat from here would be like?"

"Aye," Ishmael said. "Bad."

A humorless smile turned Mycene's lip. "Worse if there's no planning for it, that I can tell you."

Mycene had suffered a dire defeat during his first campaign against an insurrection in his family's holdings on the south coast. He'd been young—twenty-two—and entirely too confident. His father had had to issue pardons and make galling concessions to ransom his son. Mycene had never let himself be caught out again.

Ishmael said, "Aye, nothing like one's own mistakes t'teach one. I'll put it to Stranhorne." He'd be surprised if one of the Stranhornes had not already thought of it. He shrugged off the wall. He wanted another circuit, to steady anyone who needed steadying and to take a last sense of anyone holding or loading a weapon. It might be futile. At this stage, he could not tell whether someone was nervous because of him or because of what might be moving in the night. And although he had intermittently had a transient sense of something that might be Shadowborn presence or magic, it was so faint that he was almost persuaded it was a phantom of his damaged mage sense. But surely—surely if he stood toe-to-toe with a Shadowborn shape-shifter or weather-worker, he must sense that strength.

The question as to what he would do then was one he had no answer for.

He moved away, the guards starting to follow. "Let him go," Mycene said, loudly enough for Ishmael to hear. "There's no hiding for him anywhere this side of sunrise.

Nor for anyone who helps him." Ishmael nodded over his shoulder by way of acknowledgment of the sentiment, if not the fact, and continued down the gallery. Behind him he heard Mycene say, "And where by the Sole God is di Banneret?" A murmur. Mycene snorted. "He was told not to eat the sausage."

Ishmael spared a moment of sympathy for the hapless di Banneret, who would have the insult of his fellows' mockery added to the wretchedness of his guts.

He moved from rest to rest, remembering to make a little sound to warn the taut-nerved snipers that he was coming. Speaking of mistakes teaching, he'd more than once nearly been shot by one of his own people before he'd learned not to pad noiselessly up behind them.

They seemed good, steady. Mycene's men, too, though most were wary of him, and a couple hostile. One of the hostile ones was a bordersman—by the accent, down toward Odon's Barrow—and one of those who handled a rifle with ease. Maybe later he would learn the story.

Boris caught him between rooms. "Father needs you," the youth said, breathlessly. He leaned closer. "The guards?"

"Called off."

"He needs you in the cellar," Boris whispered. "Take the east stair."

"Finish my circuit for me, would you? Make sure everyone has some food or drink with them, and preferably *in* them. You, too," he added, when Boris gulped. "Not a good idea t'start a fight on an empty gut; just makes y'shakier. Your sisters should have told you that."

"Yes. But," he blurted, "I'm not a fighter."

"Nor's your father, but there's a use for thinkers, too." He clapped the young man lightly on his arm, knowing not to press. He'd been too terrified to eat the first few times he had gone up against Shadowborn. And he had been even less a fighter than Boris when he had been cast out into the world. No village or town guard would take him, so it was Shadowhunting or banditry. "Go and check on your people."

"Ishmael," the young man said desperately, "the Shadowborn are less than three miles away. What do I say if someone asks?"

"Tell them the truth. Morale is one thing, trust another. What you do and say affects their trust in your family. So tell th'truth. That goes double if you've heard something about one of their families. Swap in one of the loaders if they're shaky; let them go with no reproaches." He paused. "You'll do well. Y'come of good stock, and you've solid people around you. They know what t'do. Your part is mostly to steady them."

The east stair, Stranhorne had said, which meant hurrying without appearing to hurry the length of the southern corridor, and down five flights into the cellar. It also meant that he encountered only two or three people on the stairs, since most of the movement was up and down the western and central staircases. Only the southeast portion of that wall had sniper cover; the northeast was walled, with a watchtower on that wall guarded by a squad of men. A squad because they had no means of retreat.

One of Stranhorne's men unlocked and opened the door at his knock, and led him through the cellars to where the baron and a knot of men stood around a pyramid of boxes of munitions. Stranhorne stepped quickly away from the pyramid, moving to block Ishmael's sonn—but not before Ishmael had recognized the detonators attached to one of the boxes.

Stranhorne took his arm and turned him toward a wall. "I'll trouble you to tell me," he said in a low voice, "what was the first thing I asked of you?"

Identity check, thought Ishmael: Stranhorne or Laurel, or both, had been thinking ahead. "That I never discuss or engage in my unnatural practice within your halls."

Stranhorne released Ish's arm with obvious relief and waited. Aside from the damp cold of the cellars, Ish sensed nothing foul or chill around him. He shook his head slightly. Interpreting the gesture, Stranhorne said, "We need to think about what happens if they force an entry."

"Y'already are," he noted.

Stranhorne gave a grim smile. "You tell me: how strong

would a mage have to be to survive this many tons of stone dropped on him?"

For a moment Ishmael felt like that queasy and terrified seventeen-year-old facing his first fight. "I don't know," he said. "If taken by surprise—" The Shadowborn that he and Lady Telmaine had faced together had been strong enough to ensorcell an entire household, and more than Telmaine could hold for more than a minute or so—but that minute or so had been long enough for him to put three bullets into it, and it had not been strong enough to survive those.

"That's the aim," said Stranhorne. "My engineers tell me there's a good chance we'll be able to drop the first and second stories into the cellar."

There is a reason, Ishmael thought, *why intellectuals make a plain working man nervous.* "And get out alive?"

"It's not a suicide plan," the baron said, though there was an edge in his voice that said even if it were, he would carry it through.

"The difficulty is," the baron said, "to work best, we need to be sure that if they do force entry, it's through the east gate. I don't know whether they're capable of punching holes in the walls, but if they come in through the north gate, we're going to have to leave to the east, which will put us behind their lines, or break out through that bricked-in entry to the west. I've got a couple of engineers up there preparing t'blow it."

"Y'ever heard Lord Vladimer on th'subject of plans that depend on enemy cooperation?"

"No," Stranhorne said. "But, then, I've not been in the habit of making them."

Except for the danger in which they all stood, Ishmael could have wished Vladimer were there. If anyone knew how to arrange enemy cooperation . . . "Whichever way we leave the manor could be encircled. We might have to fight our way through. Mycene was cautioning me about the difficulty of an unplanned retreat."

Stranhorne tipped his head back, listening and sensing the mass of stone buttressed above their heads. "I've read the histories of the civil war, and of the wars in the four and five hundreds. I knew there'd be some difference between sitting at leisure in my armchair and fighting a war, but this . . ."

This was not the time for Stranhorne to lose confidence in himself. "Every hour we buy gives time for the Crosstracks and th'inner Borders to prepare, and gives time for reinforcements to come."

"Did they tell you that only about a thousand people have made it in so far?"

He could not have told that from passing through the bedlam of the ballroom. "No," Ishmael said. "They didn't."

"I tell myself that if the Shadowborn were moving that fast, they may not have found or caught most of these people. But there is another explanation—that they may simply have slaughtered them."

Numbers or magic, Ishmael thought. *Either will do.* He could not simply exhort Stranhorne not to despair, or try to chide or shame him out of it. Nor could he leave him in this mood.

"If it's the manor they want, we can hold numbers," he said, at his most stolid. "If it's not the manor, if they roll past us, then we can muster and attack to their rear, though no leader of any sense would leave a force numbered and armed as we are"—not to mention vengeful—"at their back. So if they've any sense, they should make sure the manor has fallen first before they move on, and we should hold until reinforcements come from Strumheller." *Assuming by the direction of the Call that Strumheller has not been similarly besieged,* Ishmael thought. They should not count on timely aid from the north, not with Sejanus Plantageter down and the regency council in control.

"If it's magic," Ishmael said slowly, "and we're speaking of mistakes, those of us in the city should have put this before the Lightborn Temple as soon as we began t'wonder at it. If it's magic, and they force an entry, then your plan's as good as any. I'll be less than no help t'you against magic. I . . . held this back, thinking not to risk it reaching Shadowborn ears"—and because of his own cursed cowardice in speaking of it—"but I did something in Minhorne that likely finished me for magic. Bad overreach, means I try to tap my vitality and I drain it to th'dregs. Nearly done so twice already. I've still got th'touch-sense and maybe I'll still sniff out Shadowborn if they're close and strong enough; I've yet t'test it. But the rest—everything else—is gone."

He waited out the other man's silence. Stranhorne would be the last to acknowledge his grief. "In one respect," Stranhorne said, slowly, "I'm glad. It means I don't have to ask you to wait down here with us, in hopes that you might resist an ensorcellment long enough to throw a switch. I can trust that you'll do whatever it takes to get my son and daughters to safety, and as many of my people with them."

"Not something y'need t'ask, Stranhorne."

"Good. I'm not courting death; I've far too many books left to read. Or I will have," he amended wryly, "until we throw these switches."

"Think on it as having an excuse t'go shopping," Ishmael said.

"Now *that* is something your sister might have said."

Over their heads, eerie amongst the muffling, echoing stone, the alarm began to sound. "I need t'get up there," Ishmael said.

Stranhorne held out his hand; Ishmael clasped it.

Then he went up the stairs at a run, spilling onto the top floor to the sound of staccato firing, except for the far gallery, where he could hear crashes of massed fire; Mycene putting his notion of volley fire into effect. It was as good a use as any to make of him and his men. Ishmael ducked into the nearest room, a guest suite adjacent to the one he and Balthasar had occupied. The four slits were manned, all by Stranhorne reservists or retainers, one firing and one reloading, or at one of the slits, two snipers spelling each other. Those he recognized: a teenage brother and sister from the Crosstracks. Nobody reacted to his sonn.

In the next room he found what he wanted, a man he recognized as skilled and seasoned, who was interspersing his steady firing with brief instructions to his less experienced fellows. Ishmael set his back against the wall. "What's happening?"

"Noisemakers started cracking just before we sounded the bell. We shot some to sound, but the racket's too bad. At least they haven't brought th'cursed cannon into play upstairs." He tilted his head. "What're they doing down in th'gallery?"

"Mycene, trying coordinated fire."

A grunt from the bordersman.

"Are y'holding them?"

"Too soon t'tell." A sideways cast of sonn. "Y'shooting, or just idling?"

The corner of Ishmael's mouth tucked in, tugging at the scars. "Have no fear, I'll have m'turn. I—"

The man swore and jammed his shoulder into the slit, bracing himself with an outstretched leg as he strained to angle upward. He shot twice into the sky, grunting as the recoil pinned his shoulder against stone. Ishmael remembered then that Stranhorne had mentioned flying Shadowborn. Before the man spoke, he was running for the eastern stairs, one of four that opened onto the roof. In the stairwell he almost collided with Lavender di Gautier, bounding up the steps by twos and threes. She greeted him with gladness changing to shock. "You're not armed!"

Mycene's men had refused to let him carry even a knife, but it was an unforgivable oversight not to have rearmed as soon as Mycene loosed his jesses. Ruthlessly, she stripped the two troopers with her of their second revolvers—the ones she carried would never have suited his much broader hands—and thrust them and her own knife into his hands, and sent the junior of the two scrambling downstairs to rearm them. "You're not armored, either," she complained. She and her companions wore helmets and armor, hardened leather with metal breastplates and shoulder guards. The sound of shouts and shots from overhead forestalled any argument. She took off like a deer, leaving them scrambling in pursuit.

"Di Gautier," she yelled warning as she launched herself through the door to the roof, Ishmael's lunge for her belt falling short. His sonn caught her as she skidded to one knee in the open, revolver raised. He felt a surge of sickening Shadowborn magic, and then something dropped down at her back, wings spread. Shooting it risked shooting her. Ishmael converted his last stride into a dive, slamming into scaled knees and bringing the Shadowborn crashing down on him. He threw it clear with the strength of terror, fending off a raking foot with his left arm. Two shots sounded simultaneously, and its thrashing became uncoordinated.

Lavender gripped his uninjured arm, adding her hoist to his scramble up. "What *are* these things?"

Sonn confirmed that the creature was moribund, and he took a sense of its shape: winged, deep-keeled breastbone, manlike face, clawed hands and feet—claws that would have stripped her rib cage to bone, had they connected. He was shaking slightly and fighting to subdue his gorge; whatever subtler sense was lost to him, the magic around these Shadowborn was as foully potent as anything he had ever met. His left arm was achingly numb and he could feel the sticky warmth of blood between his fingers. He was glad the contact had been fleeting; he had no desire to touch-read that. "N-nothing I've met before."

"You all right?" she said, sharply.

"Overhead!" a man shouted, and reflexively they all three ducked as guns fired from three directions—Sweet Imogene, some idiot was shooting inboard with a rifle!—and with a screech, a Shadowborn fell splayed on the deck. Ishmael and Lavender bellowed simultaneously, "Sound positions and form up!" Lavender added, "Abandon rests. Form up on the stairwells!"

Ishmael's lips drew back in a seasick grin. *Brilliant girl.* They needed to defend the entrances to the manor now, not the periphery, and positioned around the stairwells they would have clearly defined quadrants to cover and would be less likely to shoot one another. And they also needed only one voice giving commands. "Troop's yours," he barked, and lunged for the stair housing. In the shelter of the eaves, he dropped to one knee with a jar that nearly made him heave, but held his revolver steady, angling above the head height of a crouching man, as figures scrambled across the rooftop toward them. Seven, eight, ten men—one supporting the other, who was stumbling and holding his thigh.

"Some cursed fool *shot* him," the first man accused.

Lavender shifted aside from the door to let him pass into the stairwell. "Everyone sound off!" she called, and was answered by ragged shouts from three directions and scattered yells from elsewhere. The nearest was a woman's voice, and Ishmael sonned her figure just starting to move toward them from one of the sniper's positions. Then sonn caught a plunging shape, and the woman shrieked and fell beneath it. Ishmael and the man next to him shot as one, and the Shadowborn reeled away and toppled from the edge of the roof, and did not rise again in the air. Nor did the woman rise, though she stirred a little, giving a bubbling sob that suggested a torn throat. Ishmael felt the other man start to move and blocked him with a rigid, bloodied arm. "No," he growled. "We need t'stay here."

The man clubbed his arm with the hilt of his revolver. But from his other side, an older man said, "He's right. Here they come."

Ishmael missed the first round, for the blow had awakened the pain in his clawed arm. Sweat running down his face, he balanced the revolver and fired upon anything that dropped from the air. He'd fallen into the easier task, he realized, having ducked for the outer stairwell; Lavender and others on the inside had to clear the area between the stairwells, without inflicting casualties on their own. With his arm screaming pain and the waxing and waning sense of Shadowborn making his head reel, he was less of a hazard here than there. *And, Mother of All, she is good,* he thought, listening to her shouted exchanges with the other groups, coordinating fire.

"How many of these cursed things are there?" muttered the man at his side, reloading. Ishmael's revolver clicked dry, and he jammed it into his waistband and drew the second. As he did so, vileness washed over him. Instinct wheeled him around, clear of the eaves. He sonned the Shadowborn even as it alighted on the stairwell roof above Lavender, folding gracefully on the crouch, claws extended to rake. Someone screamed warning at him, and he felt a gust of downdraft on his sweating neck. Knowing exactly the choice he was making, he braced the revolver with both hands and placed his bullet beneath his target's prominent breastbone. As he did so, he felt a metallic puff past his cheek and a hot burst of liquid on his neck. He smelled blood, sharp and rich, and grinned in crazed gratitude at his savior.

Then the dying Shadowborn toppled against him, the bare skin of its forehead brushing the bare skin of his neck, its thoughts invading touch-sense, the reek of its magic enveloping him. Under its weight, physical and psychic, he pitched forward onto hands and knees, aware of a roil of impressions that either body or mind or both must reject, so that he was either going to be thoroughly sick or simply pass out. Hands caught his jacket, hauling him into shelter by the collar and armpits, the urgent handling and brushed touches by his own a blessed antidote to the intimate sense of Shadowborn. Someone pushed his revolver back into his hand. "Thanks!" he croaked. "We need t'keep aware of the roof over our heads. And I need t'come through. . . ."

He switched his revolver to his injured hand, dropped to a crouch, and scuttled to Lavender's side. "Y'all right?" Lavender said, as he straightened up beside her.

"Been worse." He caught her sleeve, pulled her ear close. What he had to say had an even higher priority than having her undivided attention on the killing field. "I'd a touch-sense of that one. The mind's more man than animal. It wasn't chance that dropped th'other above you."

She gave an indelicate curse. He doubted she understood all the implications of the information, but knew she would understand what she needed to, here and now: these were cunning, mindful foes. "You've it in hand here," he said, with a private prayer to gods real and imagined that this would continue. "I need t'get down to th'north gate."

"Yes," she said. *"Go."*

He went, managing to be a turn of the stairs out of their hearing before the aura of Shadowborn, exertion, and injury overwhelmed him. The bout of vomiting was as short as will and self-control could make it; fortunately for his legend, it went unobserved. He'd owe the house staff a tip for the cleanup. He wiped his mouth on his sleeve and lurched down the stairs at a creditable run, already hearing shouts and shots from the direction of the ballroom. Sweet Imogene, if they forced the entrance, with the ballroom full of the weakest of refugees and the wounded—

He veered off on the third floor and ran for the door to the roof of the ballroom, which in the ballroom's glory days had held a rooftop dance floor. Now it held guard positions, but was usually only lightly manned—and if no one had thought to reinforce the guard, and they had been taken by surprise . . . It had a door to the third story wide enough to admit three in promenade, as well as a servant's side door. He wheeled around the final corner and sonned the door still closed, blessedly intact and barred. His sonn caught the figure of a slight man, hands to the bar, and for a heartbeat he thought it was Balthasar Hearne. "Hoi!" Ishmael bellowed. "Hold there." The figure whirled and plunged down the main stairs, moving far more spryly than he would have expected of the travel-worn physician. He would have pursued, but the servant's door opened and what stepped across the threshold was not Darkborn. He slammed against the wall and fired, two-handed, into the doorway. Curse it—he had neither the time nor the dexterity to reload, which left him with five bullets and a knife. "Stranhornes!" Ishmael roared at the top of his lungs. "To me! Ballroom roof!"

Balthasar

Trouble on the roof, Balthasar had registered someone saying outside some time ago. Straus had cocked his head, listening; he nodded grimly and went back to itemizing the many faults of his son by marriage. He and Balthasar were repairing the muscular back of a young drayman who had used his carriage to ferry the weak and wounded in the retreat from Stonebridge, and shielded his last passengers from attack with his own body. With fixed concentration, the Stonebridge apothecary dripped chloroform onto the mask over the patient's face. He had hardly spoken since he stumbled in the gate with the youngest of his brother's children in his arms. His own oldest daughter was upstairs with the defenders, but none of the rest of his or his brother's families had reached the manor, and no one could tell him whether they were alive or dead.

The drayman was carried from the table alive, though neither physician thought well of his chances. They had washed the wounds extensively and cleaned them of shreds of cloth, but the tissue damage was so extensive that they could not completely debride them, and Shadowborn lacerations infected easily, Straus muttered grimly as they stood side by side, scrubbing the blood off their hands. "Likely be dead in days, even if we're not overrun. . . . Y'any good with a firearm, city man?"

"No," Balthasar said.

"So I take it you've not got one?" Straus, Balthasar realized, was armed: his sonn outlined the shape of a revolver under the other man's surgical apron. Was the surgeon prepared to fight?

"No . . . should I?"

"Not if it makes y'more hazard to th'wounded." Straus sonned him. "But there's some would like t'have a bullet for themselves."

Rather than die under Shadowborn teeth or claws. Bal understood. He knew there were some to whom the manner of death mattered, who believed that some deaths profaned body and soul. He was not one. Most deaths were ugly. He shook his head.

Straus said no more on the subject. "We'll take th'scalp wound next, if there's none worse next door."

Next door had been an intimate dining room for the baronelle and her circle. Bridal and naming-day cakes would have sagged under the weight of the decorative molding and piping. Rows of pallets held men and women waiting for surgery, recovering after surgery, or dying in the greatest possible comfort. Mostly now they were quiet, drugged or weak or resigned to pain, so that he could hear the sobs of the young woman rocking in a chair in the corner. Bal sighed. Her sister had gone into premature labor during the retreat. The child must have died. Perhaps the mother, too.

"Hearne." Stranhorne's one-armed aide wove between pallets to accost him. "The baron—Strumheller—wants a word with you. They've taken him over t'the briefing gallery. Not bad hurt," he added, as he registered Balthasar's reaction. "Baronette Laurel is stitching him. Get her off her feet for a while." Then he said, loudly enough to be heard by patients and helpers alike, "We've fought them off," and, quietly, to Balthasar, "though it was a near-run thing."

In the side gallery, Ishmael di Studier was leaning back in one of the chairs, arm extended along a narrow table. Laurel di Gautier was suturing two oblique lacerations on his forearm. Ishmael's teeth were set in a roll of leather and his sound hand was locked on the arm of the chair, but otherwise he endured without flinching.

She had obviously done this before, by the speed and deftness with which she set the sutures. Possibly even to Ishmael himself, given the ease with which she touched the mage. Balthasar waited as she tied off the last few. "I'm done," she said quietly, and began to clean the skin. Ishmael unclenched his teeth and removed the tooth-marked leather. He snagged a towel from the stack at her elbow and wiped his face and soaked hairline.

Balthasar cleared his throat, attracting their attention. "Hearne," said di Studier, hoarsely, before he could speak. "What did Lord Vladimer say first when he came to?"

"Ordered us not to move, or he would shoot to kill." That he would not forget, for his heart had nearly stopped as Telmaine had moved and Vladimer had shot into the floor just beside her head. He had not thought Vladimer would bluff.

Ishmael's shoulders did not relax. Deliberately, he held out his sound hand. "Touch me," he said. "Above th'glove. I've sound reason for asking," he added.

Balthasar hesitated, but could not persuade himself a Shadowborn would have willingly let Laurel inflict such pain on it as Laurel had just done on Ishmael. He pushed down the cuff of Ishmael's glove, fingers seeking his pulse and finding it, fast with pain and the aftermath of exertion, but full and regular.

The pulse jumped; Ishmael hissed out a breath. "Sorry," murmured Laurel.

Balthasar released Ishmael's wrist and stepped back. "Ask me," Ishmael said.

"I'd not have touched you if I had any doubts," Balthasar said, as the mage must know. "What was it you wanted to talk to me about?"

"First thing is, I just went skin t'skin with one of those Shadowborn." Laurel's head jerked before she caught herself; Ishmael, his head turned toward Balthasar, didn't notice. "Wasn't meant, believe me. The thing was dying, toppled against me." He stopped; Balthasar realized he was fighting nausea. "Foul with Shadowborn magic—"

Laurel paused in her cleaning to pass him a small towel that smelled strongly of mint, even at Balthasar's distance. Ishmael wiped his face, inhaling deeply of the scent. "*Cursed* unpleasant," he said with feeling.

"But informative," Balthasar said.

"You have that way . . . of cutting to th'essence." He paused as Laurel propped up his hand and began to bandage his arm. Her head was cocked, listening. "It was a formed mind that touched mine. Not a sane man's, but no beast's, either. Th'thing had once been Darkborn—I'm sure of it."

"*Ishmael,*" said Laurel in horror. "You . . . could sense that?"

"Aye, m'lady. I shouldn't be speaking of this in front of you—"

She shook her head crisply. "Father's prohibition might have made sense in the past, but it makes none now. We need to know what we're fighting." She split the bandage with a stroke of the scalpel and knotted the ties neatly around his wrist. "So, they're . . . transforming Darkborn into Shadowborn." Her head came up; she sonned him. "Lavender knows?"

Thinking of her twin's lost love? Or her twin exposed on the rooftop?

"She knows. Can't be sure on that," Ishmael said. "Just that they've minds closer t'men than beasts. Though th'implications are ugly, for th'ones lost." He rolled his head on the back of the chair. "Second thing, Hearne, is I don't suppose y'were up on the third floor a little while ago?"

"No," said Balthasar, uneasily.

"Thought you mightn't have been. Trouble is, I sonned someone much like you trying t'open the door to the rooftop dance floor. He bolted just before th'servants' door opened and a whole scourge of Shadowborn tried t'pile through. I got reinforcements just as I shot myself dry."

"They've infiltrated us," Laurel said for him. "Come in with the refugees."

"You . . . didn't sense anything?" Balthasar said, cautiously.

Ishmael grimaced, scar jumping. "I sensed plenty," he said. "Was ready t'heave the whole time I was on the roof and fighting them in the hall. It wasn't false heroism kept me in place," he said to Laurel. "But no, I didn't sense anything from any particular one—but if they'd any sense, they'd have been keeping clear of me."

Stranhorne arrived with his one-armed lieutenant. The scholarly baron now had armor over his shirt and a holstered revolver at his waist. His hair was untidy and matted—with blood, by the smell. He shook his head as his daughter opened her mouth. "Not mine." She passed him a towel, pointed him in the direction of a washing basin and jug set on the side table. "Mother," she said, firmly, family shorthand, maybe, for *Mother would insist* or *Mother would be outraged* or *Mother would have hysterics.* Somehow, knowing the late baronelle's daughters, he couldn't believe it would be the last.

Laurel sketched in their conversation so far as her father scrubbed his arms and blotted the worst of the gore from his hair and leathers. Stranhorne said over his shoulder, "So, you've not lost it after all."

"Aye, it seems not. Though a man with a burned tongue might still taste spices, if they're strong enough."

"All right." Stranhorne turned. "We've fought off the first wave. And we need to take a moment to decide what else of our tactics we need to change—we obviously hadn't thought through the implications of having Shadowborn come in force from the air. We've still got about four hours to sunrise. Strumheller, what's your best guess on whether they're liable to be active after?"

"M'best guess, Stranhorne, depends on past experience, which has shown itself a poor guide in this."

"Take it nonetheless," the baron ordered.

"If they were once Darkborn, then they may be bound by th'Curse as we are." *We have the father of Tercelle's children to falsify that hope,* Balthasar thought, but did not say. "If they come by day, then they don't want us—don't want us to change or t'eat or any of th'other things they could do with our flesh. And if they come by day—it galls me t'say this—we can't fight them. We can only hope to burrow deep t'survive."

Something in Ishmael's face, something in Stranhorne's, disturbed Balthasar. "And how likely is that?" Stranhorne said in a still voice.

Ishmael hesitated. His voice sounded almost studiedly impersonal; unusual for him. "We might be able t'close some of us in your lower cellars, so that it'd be more trouble t'the Shadowborn t'dig them out than they'd care to take. Predators don't waste energy and don't put themselves at risk. They're in our territory, enemy territory. But we've never had them come at us in such force before."

"Should we evacuate now?" Stranhorne asked. "If the message reached the Crosstracks, and the telegraph is running and the tracks are clear, a relief force should be at the Crosstracks by nightfall. They might even be there already."

"We'd likely lose more doing that than waiting for the relief force," Ishmael said. "Unless we can be certain there's some they want more than others, and that they can tell us apart, if most of us went on the road, most of th'Shadowborn would follow."

There was a silence. Then Laurel said, quietly, "There is one other option."

Her father and mentor waited. "You know what it is," she said, "but you won't say it yourselves. Ishmael says they have minds like men, and we've certainly discovered that they will exploit our weaknesses and attack our commanders. If they're intelligent, we might be able to negotiate with them."

"Negotiate our surrender, you mean," her father said, though not harshly. "Nothing we've met suggests it would be otherwise. They need not speak to communicate their intentions most eloquently. If I thought we'd gain anything by it, I'd swallow my gorge and negotiate, but nothing they've done suggests they have aught else in mind but slaughter and domination."

"Father," she said, carefully, "would your answer be the same if they were not using magic?"

He frowned, not at her but at the thoughts her question inspired. "Truthfully, I can't know," he said. "But magical or nonmagical, we can judge them by their deeds. Strumheller, in my place, would you negotiate?"

"Never," Ishmael said, without a pause. "Maybe I'm influenced by the sense of the magic and the touch of the mind—but nothing in their deeds, as you say, suggests they recognize our right t'live in peace. Our best hope is t'bloody them; then they might listen." He rolled his head. "Hearne, what's your say?"

Balthasar, slightly startled at the question being referred to him, weighed it. His spirit rebelled against rejecting outright the possibility of negotiating and perhaps sparing lives on both sides. But years of torment by his brother, years of work amongst the oppressed and dispossessed of the city, and years of listening to and observing his social betters had all taught him that to many, negotiation was weakness, an invitation to further cruelties. He said, "Negotiation would only be productive if we had something they want—aside from our lives." *As food or slaves,* he did not say; it stood implied.

"I know," she said, quietly. "That's my thought, too.

But—" Her hand strayed to her rounded abdomen, and she did not voice what else she thought.

"As long as we can hold the manor, we stay," her father said. "But we should lay the groundwork for a retreat, as Mycene says. I'll get started on that. Laurel, I want you to rest. Hearne, you'd best get back to the surgery. I know we took casualties in the courtyard and on the roof. Strumheller, I've a request of you that will seem decidedly hypocritical, given the opinions I've expressed as late as last night. But we're fighting for our lives, here. I want you to find that infiltrator—or infiltrators. If they're Shadowborn or shape-changed or ensorcelled, you'll be able to tell, if you come close enough."

Close enough to touch, he meant. Close enough to read, unconsenting and perhaps unawares. Ishmael had told Telmaine that that was contrary to the code he lived by. His face stoic, Ishmael got to his feet. "I can do that."

Ishmael

Aside from the leadership and the vulnerable points, the points he would expect a Shadowborn to undermine were the roof, the entrances, the armory, and the munitions. Which had him roaming from rooftop to cellars like an unquiet ghost, three of Stranhorne's troop dogging his heels for his safekeeping. The sense of Shadowborn magic had dwindled since the attack, but not gone entirely, and when he reached the roof, he realized why—the damp night had turned to sleet and wind, making him shiver with more than cold. He found Lavender and Jeremiah Coulter at the southwest corner, supervising the lashing down of one of the three cannon underneath an improvised shelter. Coulter stroked its flank as covetously as a horse thief might a prime mare, his misspent past having included a stint as a pirate's gunner. Ishmael cautioned, "Y'realize that thing'll deafen everyone on the roof and below." That he knew from painful experience. He never wanted to be near cannon fire again.

Coulter grinned. Lavender frowned through the rain dripping from her hat. "We'll use it if we need it."

"Give me a head start at running first," he grumbled. "A word, if y'don't mind."

She let him draw her away. "This weather's not natural," he said, quietly.

"I don't need you t'tell me that," she said. "I know by the queasy expression on your face."

He'd thought he was concealing it better than that. She smirked, reading his mind.

"Boris said you gave him the talk," she said. "Are you about to give me the talk?"

"You don't need that talk. This is another one. If y'hear the retreat, retreat. Y'understand?"

"We'll have to disable the cannon. . . ."

Entirely sensible, with their enemies able to land on the roof and turn those cannon on the stairwell entrances. "If y'hear the retreat, y'won't have much time." Five stories down to the ground, and may the Mother of All Things—including of fiery young women with more courage than sense—guide her choice of a stair. He could imagine nothing worse than being down in the cellar with Stranhorne, knowing they must light the fuses, and knowing she was trapped above them. He still didn't know whether Stranhorne had told her what he planned—it was time he did, for the sake of the people with her—but it was not Ishmael's decision. "*Promise* me you'll get your people down and clear. Spike or throw the cursed cannon off th'edge of the roof if you must, but do it fast. We'll need you on th'ground to help with the breakout, and we don't want you cut off."

"I *promise*. Now you promise me, no more one-man stands."

"Not my choice—"

"No excuse," she said, sternly. "You told me that yourself: y'have to think ahead, leave yourself maneuvering space. Promise."

He promised, and he meant it as sincerely, he supposed, as she did. Time and circumstance would determine whether one or both of them would be forsworn.

She leaned forward as though to kiss his lips, and at the last instant faltered and brushed his cheek instead. He could not kiss her back—it would not have been proper, even if he had been willing to intrude further on her thoughts—but he brought up his gloved hand and cupped her cheek. "Please try to stay out of trouble."

He wanted to pull Coulter or one of the senior troopers aside and order them to make sure she did retreat, but knew she would be rightfully furious with him, instead of merely irritated, as her fleetingly sour expression attested. She wasn't a teenage enthusiast anymore, and she deserved the same respect he would give any fighting man or woman. Maybe it was as well that he'd never had a daughter. . . . He made his circuit of the men and women with her, trying as best he could to sense any additional aura of Shadowborn over the miasma rising with the rain. *Trying too hard,* the fierce pain in his chest warned him. He had no choice but to sit down on the wet gravel and pass off the spell as momentary dizziness from his injured arm. He went down the western stair, deliberately using the busier stair so that he met as many people as possible. Imogene's tits, he could only hope his movements were as unpredictable to any Shadowborn trying to evade him—assuming they'd even bother—as to himself.

Laurel was resting, on her father's orders, in a curtained corner of the ballroom. Neither her father nor she had wanted her to go back to her rooms, he because he wanted to be sure of her whereabouts in a crisis, and she because she had the opportunity here to listen. She whispered her suspicions of two groups who had passed her; he promised to check them.

The baron himself was in the side gallery with several of his troop, stooped over the relief, reviewing the route and deployment for a retreat. Ishmael circled, attentive to any recoil of the men and women he passed or any perturbation of his senses, but nobody shifted more than simply yielding him room. Stranhorne stopped him as he made to withdraw. "Raining again?" he said.

"Aye. Cursed near sleet."

By the tucked-in corner of Stranhorne's mouth, he understood the implication. He moved with Ishmael to the doorway. "Can we expect relief by sunrise?" he said, quietly.

A sensitive question, Ishmael admitted. If they didn't, he would not know whether the enemy had cut them off or Ishmael had failed in his duty to prepare for his own decease and the transition to his brother's rule. He had thought he planned well, but had never imagined the transition happening in the midst of such emergency, where a speck of grit in the mechanism could produce a fatal stall. And his marred relationship with Reynard was more than a speck. Noellene had been right: he had owed Reynard a full account, whether in person or in a letter—even though he might be certain that Reynard would believe not a word of it. But when events taught Reynard otherwise, then he would have that information.

Too late to regret that, either. He said, "Troops have been on th'alert or on the move all summer. Reynard's had the ducal order, and he's had Hearne's account. If the rider reached th'station, and the telegraph wires aren't cut, then they'll be moving as fast as they can. Reynard's no trooper, and he knows t'stay out of the way. And even if he doesn't, Noellene will set her hand to it."

Stranhorne smiled at the mention. "She will, that." He was fond of Ishmael's sister, and she of him, though not fond enough to marry, much to the vexation of Reynard's then wife. She had schemed for Noellene's respectable send-off from Strumheller. After Reynard's divorce, Noellene had settled in once more as chatelaine, and seemed likely to stay there. Notwithstanding her dainty beauty, citified airs, and expensive tastes worthy of Lady Telmaine herself, Noellene understood the Borders defense as well as her brothers. If Reynard needed spurring, she would apply the spurs.

"So, t'answer your question, I'm hopeful of it."

"But we should plan to hold out for the day," Stranhorne finished for him. "If we're not forced to retreat. Any hint of Shadowborn—inside?" he appended.

"Truthfully, be difficult for me t'tell, but I'm on it. Where's Mycene?"

Mycene and his men were in the courtyard, having reinforced the squad guarding the main gate during the worst of the attack. The Shadowborn had again made targets of the leaders, more successfully than on the roof. The defenders' mind-set had been too slow to shift from thinking of Shadowborn as unreasoning beasts capable of savagery but not tactics. Stranhorne probably owed the integrity of its north gate to Mycene and his men. *That is a less uncomfortable notion than hitherto,* Ish thought, slightly amused at how differently they greeted him, having now met Shadowborn for themselves. Mycene was no friendlier, since he still had every reason to suspect—or maintain the appearance of suspecting—Ishmael's involvement in his fiancée's death. However, Ishmael doubted he would ever again liken the profession of Shadowhunter to that of rat catcher, as his father had done more than once in Ishmael's hearing. Ish exchanged nods with Mycene's men and words with Mycene, noted they were down to eight, and accounted for three wounded—one seriously and two of whom they expected back shortly—and the hapless di Banneret, who knew no better than to eat sausage from a street vendor's cart.

Which made him think of the wounded, and wonder how Balthasar Hearne was holding up. He shied from entering the dining room, ward for the most seriously wounded. Arrant cowardice, he knew. He would have found it hard even when Stranhorne's prohibition against using his magic was on him, and now, now that he knew he was no longer able to help, he faltered at the door, at the sounds of murmurs and groans and of someone—a woman? a young boy?—sobbing brokenly.

As he stood there, a woman made to push past him, and he recognized one of Stranhorne's housekeepers, a sharp-tongued, sharp-witted woman who was an exacting manager for her portion of the staff. He could rely on her to know exactly who was doing what and where. He caught her arm. "Dr. Hearne, Dr. Balthasar Hearne—could y'please tell him that I'd like a word with him?"

"But, Baron," the woman said, startled, "he hasn't returned since he left with you."

Balthasar

Balthasar followed the orderlies carrying the stretcher for his last case into the ballroom to assess the next, and found Ishmael standing inside the dining room–turned-ward, hands pushed deep into pockets and shoulders hunched. "I need a quick word," the baron said, curtly.

"Is it your arm—"

"Nothing medical," said the baron, his expression strangely unreadable. "Nothing needing done here. I just need a word."

Balthasar's first thought was of Telmaine—that Ishmael had sensed more from Telmaine. That thought had him untying his apron even as he truthfully protested, "I don't have long. I shouldn't leave at all."

"A moment—that's all I ask."

Balthasar trailed Ishmael's hurrying heels across the ballroom, up the east stairs. Ishmael brusquely deflected attempts to accost him with a "Later" or "Ask the baronettes."

Their room on the fifth floor was in use. Ishmael steered him to one on the second that was now largely cleared of furnishing and carpets, except for a dozen beds bare of mattresses. He recognized the packs propped against the near wall as belonging to members of Mycene's troop—this was where the troop had been billeted. The beds themselves would have been stripped of their mattresses to hold refugees and wounded.

"Have—Is it Telmaine?" Balthasar said as soon as the door closed.

"Telmaine?" said Ishmael, startled. "What about Telmaine?"

Not, then. "Have you found an infiltrator?"

Ishmael smiled. "In a manner of speaking."

Balthasar felt the heart within him chill, as though he had suddenly gained the sense of Shadowborn magic that Telmaine had described. That smile was no expression of the man he knew, for all the cast of face and the scars were the same. Sweet Imogene, he himself had warned Ishmael of just this eventuality. But, tired and caught up by the false

Ishmael's urgency, he had let down his guard, missed the clues of the lapses in accent and Ishmael's failure to show concern for Telmaine—indeed, now he thought of it, Ishmael's expression down in the ward had been wrong, oblivious to the suffering around him. Balthasar had been caught by the very ruse he had warned others against.

He swallowed and said, "This cannot possibly work. Ishmael himself is in the manor." He prayed this was still so, but surely the Shadowborn could not have caught Ishmael off guard.

"I *know* he's about, curse him," the Shadowborn said, hands fisted. "But it already *has* worked."

On him, for whichever reason the Shadowborn wanted him. "I'll be missed," Balthasar said, steadily. If the Shadowborn killed him and took his form, only Ishmael would be able to tell—until or unless the Shadowborn found himself faced with a chloroformed patient on a surgical table. The thought in itself was bleakly cheering; the prospect of how far the Shadowborn might go in his masquerade, sickening.

He kept such thoughts off his face and out of his voice. "You came with Mycene's men, didn't you? You were the young man—di Banneret—who lent me a coat. A coat that was too big for me—and for you." That was the inconsistency that had been nagging him, why a guardsman traveling light would carry a coat that did not fit him. Sweet Imogene, if he'd only remembered in time . . . "What is your name?"

"My *name*?" said the Shadowborn, taken aback at the unexpected civility.

Good; keep him off balance. "Do you not exchange names amongst your people?"

That smile again, a triumphant malice in it. "We *do*. Oh, we *do*, and you'll *like* learning mine. . . ." The Shadowborn abruptly moved with a crack of floorboards quite unlike Ishmael's near-noiseless tread. Balthasar recoiled, his sonn ringing off the bones in the other's skull as he pushed his face up to Balthasar's.

"Where are my sons, Balthasar Hearne?"

I should have shouted out, Bal thought, *while I still had a chance.* A claw balanced his carotid pulse on its tip, and his mind went blank with terror. "I don't know," he whispered. "Truly, I don't know."

"You sent them away," the Shadowborn breathed in his face. "Where to?"

"I thought they'd be safer if I didn't know," Bal whispered in turn. "Can you not read the truth from me?"

It was not a safe question, but an urgent one. He had thought the Shadowborn who had impersonated his brother, Lysander, claiming to be the father of the twins, had tormented him merely for the pleasure of it. But if not, if these Shadowborn could not touch-read, and if he survived to convey the information . . .

The claw tip stroked downward; he clutched at his throat, but his fingers found merely a stinging gash and a trickle, not a gush or even a spurt of blood.

"Truly," he gasped, "I meant them no harm. Or their mother, either."

"What did she tell you about me?"

"She said you had come to her in the daytime, traveling through the day. She was afraid the children would not be fully Darkborn. And they were—*are*—not. But they are also beautiful, healthy little boys, for whose safety I pray."

"But *she* was not safe," the Shadowborn said, in Bal's face. "She's *dead*. So why should *I* care about your stupid prayers?"

"I am deeply sorry about Tercelle," Bal said. "But my prayers are my own. I would not dare to ascribe their value to anyone else. Much less a member of a people about whom I know virtually nothing."

"You think you know nothing about us?" the Shadowborn said, grinning savagely. Then the grin tightened, as at some mental or physical effort, and the bones of it *shifted*. There was something intrinsically revolting about bone moving like muscle beneath the skin, but even if there were not, he had already met the phenomenon, lying pinned on Vladimer's bedroom floor as his brother's semblance warped to that of a stranger's and the nails of his poised hand elongated to shredding talons. Ishmael's face re-formed as a much younger but still familiar one. The young man—boy, no more than sixteen—smiled his older brother's mocking smile.

"Not such a stranger, am I, now? *Uncle* Balthasar."

The smile was there, the lips and narrow nose were there, but the cheekbones were more pronounced and the eyes more wide set. Lysander's features, mingled with another's. Mingled, as Balthasar's were with Telmaine's in their two small daughters.

Balthasar broke for the door. There was no planning in it, simply a raw impulse of flight. The Shadowborn caught him on his first stride, arm around his chest. A calloused palm slammed up underneath his jaw, pinning his mouth closed; fingers closed on his nose, blocking off all air. Bal bucked and thrashed, staggering with the Shadowborn, bringing them both to their knees. As they toppled, the Shadowborn twisted them both, throwing Bal down beneath him. Bal's injured cheek ground into the floor. His head pounded with air deprivation; he convulsed with the urgent need to breathe. His head struck the Shadowborn's jaw, and he frantically jerked it up again. The Shadowborn gasped out, "I am *not* letting you go. You *will* obey me."

And Balthasar *felt* the ensorcellment enwrap him, turn his muscles to meltwater and his will to . . . nothing at all. "Lie still," the Shadowborn said in the boy's voice, and he could not move, stripped of even the most primitive survival reflexes. He was all but unconscious when the Shadowborn released his mouth and nose and let him gasp in air.

"You are my father's brother," whispered the boy against his ear. "You are *family*, and so you should love me. Love me the way you love your own children. And *obey me*. The way you would obey your *God*."

With hopeless fascination, Balthasar observed the fragmentation of a mind from within. The ensorcellment would not extract from him a father's love or a believer's obedience, but it would crudely exact a slave's devotion. Even so, he recognized the plea in the demand, and some part of him responded to it with pity—this monster was little more than a child. A third portion of him weighed the experiences of Vladimer and Tercelle, the knowledge he had through his sister, Olivede, of magic abused, and knew that he was lost. And a fourth knew both reason and resistance, silently enumerating the ways the Stranhornes and Ishmael were equipped to deal with the enemy in the house. *Ishmael* must sense this ensorcellment. He choked on the slave's cry of warning and ground his aching cheek against the floor to stifle it.

"Get up," said the boy, in Ishmael's voice. Reason said, *Test his power*; the slave said, *Obey*. The conflict made him as clumsy as a partly strung puppet, but the slave brought him to his knees. The boy slapped him with sonn, jerking him to his feet. Reason said, *Ishmael's sonn was never so coarse.* "That's the way," the voice said, fully Ishmael's once more. "I want you"—a pause, to ensure the message was understood by Balthasar and the ensorcellment—"to go down to the ground floor, to the eastern gate, and *open it*. And don't try to warn anyone."

"I . . . will not," Balthasar said. Even as he did so, he felt himself take his first step toward the door.

"You will so." He smirked. "*She* didn't want me to learn how to do this, but I learned it all on my own. So go downstairs—don't worry; they won't eat you. They'll know you're mine."

"Guarded," Balthasar said, unable to stop himself.

"It won't be, by the time I'm done with"—the carpet in front of Balthasar burst into an arc of flame; he had barely enough time to register the heat before it was quenched—"my little diversion."

Four

Ishmael

Ishmael turned at the sense of someone beside him. Laurel di Gautier was at his shoulder, blanket trailing from her shoulders. "I heard," she said in a low voice.

He bit his tongue on suggesting she go back to her rest. He needed another mind on this, one not distracted by a clawed arm, the Call, and the miasma of Shadowborn weather-working. "Wc need t'find Hearne and this Shadowborn. Any ideas?"

"You are quite certain," she said, "about Dr. Hearne? He met these Shadowborn earlier than any of us, didn't he? I was less worried about him because I didn't expect Shadowborn to have his skill." The corner of her mouth twitched. "Linneas Straus wouldn't have just anyone working in his surgery."

"Unless th'Shadowborn are subtler by far than I take them for, the man I touched not an hour ago was th'same man I met seven days past." Unless along with the shapes they stole, the Shadowborn were also capable of stealing memory and knowledge; if so, only their actions would reveal them. His heart started to race, making his left arm throb in tempo. His fingers found their way to his holstered revolver.

"I've had a late, unwelcome thought," he said. "Should have had it long since. There was one man of Mycene's I've not met, supposedly laid low by a sausage. We know a Shadowborn was in th'city: maybe he came down in Mycene's train."

She nodded. "I'll have someone—two someones—check," she said. "But what we need to know—"

From the east corridor an alarm began to ring, its rate frantic. Along the halls he heard a shout of "Fire!" His first thought was of the munitions, and the men waiting by them. He said to Laurel, "I'll go." Stranhorne was just emerging from the side gallery, his one-armed aide at his side. Striding by, Ishmael said, "Don't know; going t'find out."

The rhythm of the alarm told him it was on the third floor of the southwest corner of the manor; the Stranhornes had anticipated the difficulty of tracking sound through the ancestral pile. He had an unpleasant feeling he knew which room. Collecting seemed to go with the Stranhorne blood. In recent generations, it had expressed itself in bibliophilia, but several of the past barons had collected hunting trophies, including trophies of Shadowborn. Stranhorne's grandfather had offered the collection to the national history museum in the city. Given that Shadowborn defied orthodox taxonomies, the museum had declined most of those, so they were kept in a long gallery and storeroom off the south hallway.

Which made this arson what? Editorial comment? Revenge? Sick prank? Ish supposed he should be grateful the interloper's sense of humor or strength did not extend to animating them, setting the pack of false-toothed balewolves and mangy-pelted scavvern roaming the halls.

Smoke, harsh with burning straw and fur, and Shadowborn magic brought him to a halt just before he collided with the milling mob of manor staff, reservists, and ambulatory refugees summoned by the alarm. Boris Stranhorne was in the midst of the horde, valiantly trying to impose order and purpose. He didn't have the mass or the voice. Ishmael did. A lungful of air gave him the volume, and smoke in his throat gave him an ominous rasp. "We need th'hose run from the main water tank now!" he bellowed, making those nearest him bend away like wheat under a downdraft. "And a bucket chain from the main scullery."

They probably couldn't reach the former taxidermist's workroom, which was off the gallery, and furthermore he had no idea how long it had been since anyone had worked the taps in there; rust-locked taps or sludge-filled pipes would do them no use. "And all who's not got a clue how to drive a hose or pass a bucket need t'get yourselves out of this corridor. Now!"

Several staff members and reservists, wielding buckets, had already arrived. One reported, "We've gone for the hose, Baron. Where should we—"

Where indeed? It wasn't just his roaring that had cleared the bystanders: the smoke was thick enough to stir, and the heat, when he put his face around the open door, was ominous. The air roiled and twisted as his sonn reflected from the interfaces between ribbons of heated air. It was hideously reminiscent of the day he had been caught in the burning Rivermarch, having gone to ground after an encounter with the Shadowborn in a brothel incongruously called the Rainbow House. As far as he knew, he had been the sole survivor of all the ladies and clients. He closed the door on the blaze, hoping to contain the smoke and starve it of air. "We'll not quench this one without th'hose," he said. "Soak the walls. Soak the floor—and we need to soak the floor upstairs. We need t'make sure it doesn't spread." To Boris he said, "Tell th'ones who're running ammunition to keep their senses about them—we need to know if there are any others kindling—and get any of th'other youngsters who still have their wits about them t'help."

A bucket chain had formed, with buckets passed hand to hand down the line. At least they did not have a carpet to worry about; Stranhorne, like Strumheller, was furnished for the wear of a large household that was a center of government, industry, and defense. Overhead, Ishmael could hear running feet, furniture being dragged, and urgent voices, as the rooms overhead were cleared so that the floors could be soaked. He set his back against the wall, staying out of the way, keeping his chin down to mask his hard pulse. The reaction was a response to the bite of smoke in his throat and the memory of the Rivermarch. At least outside was still dark and not daylight—if a night full of Shadowborn could be said to be less murderous than the sun.

As a crew from the stables came dragging the fire hose—already spurting water over floor, wall, and people alike—the alarm began to peal again, signaling that the Shadowborn had renewed their attack.

Boris clutched at Ishmael's left arm. Ishmael winced, though he kept his voice light. "D'y'get the feeling that this is just not our night?"

He pulled Boris away as the fire-hose crew threw open the door into the gallery and turned the hose full on the interior, and a great belch of smoke and heat rolled over them all. He dropped to a crouch, bracing himself on his throbbing arm, alert to their coughing and ready to move in if any were overcome by smoke. Boris half fell down beside him. Ishmael said hoarsely, "Get down t'your father—tell him what's happening. Then spread word about a fire watch. Soon as they've control here, I'll move on. I need to find who's causing this."

Balthasar

The laminated outer door of the baronelle's study led into a vestibule between inner and outer wall, with an ironbound outer door as stout as the one into Strumheller. Balthasar wept silently as he wrestled down the two heavy bars bracing it, wept for his futile belief that he could evade this ensorcellment, and now for his remorse at what he was about to do. He could not stop himself: could not stop himself lifting the bars, turning the handle, setting his shoulder and then all his weight against the door, falling outward into the rain.

He tried to cling to the lintel, but even so, the ensorcellment was driving him forward. It came to him that this must be something akin to what Ishmael felt as he struggled against the Call. How could he ever have prided himself that his skills would be of any help, any help at all . . . ?

The ensorcellment harried him across a garden, turned wild in the storm. It punished him as he lost himself among the hedges. Beyond the wall he could hear wolves howling. Overhead, stone split and stone chips sprinkled over him; the snipers had tried to range on the sound. He scrambled along the base of the wall, almost on all fours, as bullets ricocheted. High in the air something screeched, drawing the snipers' fire.

And there . . . was the gate. His sonn caught the hard, rough profile of the arch, the smoother finish of the gate. It was a wide gate, but still not wide as a street. Yes, it might pass an army, but not all at once.

Two-handed, he forced the key to turn, felt a mechanism yield and the dead bolts draw in with a ragged thud. He felt the gate shudder as a body threw itself against the other side, and heard claws grind.

"Balthasar Hearne—stop!" cried a woman's voice.

The gate flew inward as something lunged at it from outside. He heard a tearing snarl, heard a shot. A bundle of fur and bristle skidded past his feet; he recoiled from its snapping jaws.

Twenty yards away stood Laurel di Gautier, alone and cxposed, head hared, skirts bound to her legs by the wind, rifle to her shoulder, lips drawn back in a face stony with intent. Ishmael had praised her cool head, and Balthasar understood why as she shot and shot again into a gateway seething with Shadowborn with a calm precision he would not even have expected in his own capable wife. He crouched in the lashing rain, helplessly arguing with the ensorcellment that orders to *open* the gate did not preclude closing the gate, counting the shots, and wondering how long before she needed to reload, how long before the rain penetrated her rifle, how long before she missed, how long before one of those flying Shadowborn . . . Laurel slung the rifle on her shoulder, no time to reload, and in the same motion drew a revolver right-handed, and the next Shadowthing through the gate gained but one bound on her before she put it down. She took a pace forward. She meant, he realized, to clear the gate and close it if she could, before she shot her last. He willed her on, even if he could do nothing to help her.

Something dropped out of the sky to her left. She pivoted and fired, then managed to catch the next wolf with barely a beat. Another Shadowborn landed to her right, between Balthasar and her. He discovered then the limits of *open the gate and warn no one.* He surged out of his crouch with a rock in his hand, and with all his strength—and knowledge behind it—drove the pointed end of the rock through the fragile bone in the Shadowborn's temple.

She gasped, "What—" and shot and shot again into the gate.

There was no explaining, not in these circumstances, even if he could struggle sufficiently free of the ensorcellment to do so. He cast into the air, his sonn dissipating in seething rain and wind, but still catching at its limits something up there. He flung the rock at it. While evading the landings, she had lost all the distance she had gained. "Inside," he begged. *"Please."*

"No," she said.

He threw himself at her, intending to manhandle and drag her if he must—no planning, no timing. She swung her revolver; he did not hear the shot or feel it except as something like a punch in his side. He found himself half turned and down on one knee. More by reflex than by any urgent need, he put a hand to his side and felt the cold rain turn warm. There was strangely little pain. *Traumatic anesthesia,* the clinical part of his mind noted.

Behind him, the archway and wall blew in, as though struck by an immense fist, collapsing in a jumble of falling stones and blocks almost at his heels. The hem of a wet skirt flickered in his sonn, and he heard her take the first few running steps before rain and wind swallowed them. *She shouldn't be running,* he thought absurdly, *not in her condition,* and started to get to his feet. Stones ground behind him. Something huge and bristled set its paws on the dead thing beside him, and he froze, still as a rabbit. The wolf—larger than any wolf he'd ever heard of—sniffed speculatively at the belly of the dead one and then extended its head to nose Balthasar's bleeding side.

His sonn caught a small female shape, a hand reaching

out to cuff the wolf's muzzle. "Mayfly, leave that alone. You can eat it later."

Rubble crunched as a second person moved up beside him. A man's voice said, "Not him, Midora. Sense the ensorcellment."

"So he is here. Little *bastard.* Where's *Jon*? If he were in trouble and Sebastien ran—"

"Enough, Midora; Jonquil's dead," the man said, calmly. "We all felt him die. And without him, without his knowledge, what could Sebastien do alone in Minhorne?"

"Let's get this over with," the woman snarled.

Balthasar started to turn his head, to sonn the speakers, and felt a man's hand resist the motion. He flinched, trying to keep skin from contacting skin, opening him to the touch of what was surely a mage. "Best not draw attention," the man advised. To his companion: "Let me deal with Sebastien. He may be unpredictable, and he has obviously been learning."

"That little half-breed—"

"Ariadne's son," the man said flatly.

"Why bother? You won't keep him alive, after this. Emeya'll have him roasted—and with your blood for a sauce, if you're not careful."

A hand rested lightly on Balthasar's gripping fingers. "You're hurt," the Shadowborn noted, dispassionately. Then, startled, said, "That profile: *Hearne*. No. You must be another relation. The brother, perhaps. Well, well, well. I think we'll just—" Searing agony spread out from his wound, as though the Shadowborn had applied a cautery iron. Balthasar would have bucked or screamed, had he been able to move; instead, and this time in truth, he fainted.

Ishmael

Ishmael came headlong down the stairs, impelled beyond all caution by the nearby sense of Shadowborn magic. He reached the door to the baronelle's private study as Laurel burst through it into the hall, slamming it behind her, and caught woman and rifle as she stumbled, keeping them both upright. She was bareheaded, hair and dress soaked, revolver in hand, shaking as though fevered. She took a drowning sailor's grip on him. "Please be Ishmael," she gasped.

"Aye," he said. "I'm th'one y'told you loved Jeremiah Coulter." It had been a brief, intense, and fortunately one-sided infatuation when she was eighteen; he had never told anyone else what she confided.

She pressed her wet head against his chest and let him support her. "Something just destroyed the wall into Mother's garden," she gasped. "It doesn't make *sense*. Why'd he open the gate if they could destroy it that easily?"

Like her father, always thinking. "Why'd who open the gate?"

She lifted her head, taking her own weight again. "Dr. Hearne—or something in his shape. The corridor was unguarded." *Drawn off by the fire,* Ishmael thought, now understanding that mischief. "I got there too late to stop him. Things were coming through; I shot, trying to clear the window t'get the gate closed. Two of the flyers had a go at me. I killed one, Hearne got the other with a rock, but then he came at me. I shot him—pure reflex, and a wound only, I think—then the wall blew in and I ran. I just left him. I don't know what he was—But I—But why'd he open the gate if they could destroy it that easily?"

If it were Balthasar, then he had been ensorcelled or otherwise coerced, and might already be dead. Even if he were not, it would be death to open that outer door. "We'll get t'him as we can," he said. "But y'did the right thing. They could be through th'outer wall any moment, but at least they've chosen to force th'entrance best for us. Get the word t'your father. He'll want to sound the bell for the muster. Y'need to check the main way's clear." He eased her away and took the revolver from her hand. "I'll buy y'all the time I can."

She bit back appeal and thrust her ammunition pouch at him. Her face was full of the words she had too much sense to speak.

"If they've the minds of men, they've maybe the curiosity of men. I'll make of that what I can. And if not"—he finished reloading and closed the firing chamber—"by then, I'll know which one t'shoot first." Not to delude himself, he reminded himself that he likely had only one shot. He felt magic build on the other side of the door. *"Go,"* he said.

One shot, he thought. The question was whether to take it—and likely bring magical retribution down on himself and anyone within range—or risk not being able to take it at all. Hand on the door, he felt the shudder of the assault on the outer wall, and through the door heard stones grind on one another. Sweet Imogene, how much of the wall were they bringing down?

He threw open the door and set his back against the lintel, exposed as it was, so he could cover both inside and out. His sonn delineated the gape in the wall and the rubble heaped tidily to either side, swept clear of the breech by the magic that had made it. Even the dust seemed to part. Two figures were coming through the wall into the study, the taller stooping slightly, and as near to side-by-side as the breech allowed. He said, consciously deep and forceful, "You can hold where y'are, if you would. I want a few words."

"And who might you be?" The voice was a light tenor, a singer's voice with a careless delivery that suggested easy power or studied manner.

This, Ishmael thought, *is where I ensure myself a conversation or a very quick death.* "Strumheller."

"Strumheller? As in Baron Strumheller?" Magic swirled around him like a polluted river in winter, and he was glad of his empty stomach and the bracing lintel. He concentrated on not letting his aim waver. "You're supposed to be a mage. What have you done to yourself?"

His lips drew back from his teeth; he had just had the welcome thought that the overreach spared him the need to keep a bullet for himself. "Bad overreach, dealing with one of your kind's ugly fire tricks. Your name, sir?"

"Do you expect that to mean anything to you? It's Neill."

He was correct; it did not mean anything. To sonn, Neill was a rangy man in his twenties with a rawboned build that

Ish would have interpreted as late developer or idle skiver, depending on how charitable he felt. Perhaps this was Neill's usual form; perhaps not. He was dressed in a jacket made of irregular pieces of skins and leather, an embroidered shirt, and leather trousers. Even from where he stood, Ishmael could sense his magical strength. And sense, too, it was not entirely under control. Neill felt—allowing for the thoroughly repellant Shadowborn aura—like one of the stronger mages at the Broomes' commune, early in his learning and gaining capability faster than control. The difference was that the young man from the commune was fifth rank and conscientious. This man was far stronger. And Shadowborn.

"And the lady?" Whose shape was surely not her own, not with that aura of strength around her. She stood no more than four-and-a-half feet tall and had the diminutive, inhuman beauty of an expensive doll. Except for the curl of her lip. "Get on with it, Neill."

"We agreed we'd do this my way," Neill told her, without turning. And to Ishmael: "I'd like to talk, if I may, to Baron Stranhorne."

"Talk?" He'd met some smooth rogues in his time, including Rivermarch enforcers, but none of them had blasted in a man's wall before turning on the charm. Though he supposed Jeremiah Coulter might have, before he reformed. "If you'd wanted t'talk, y'could have knocked on the front door with a card. We're not couth by city standards, but that's still th'way it's done."

A sardonic smile. "You have me there. Call it . . . evolving strategy. For one thing, I believe you have something of ours." He raised his voice, and power rushed past Ishmael. "Sebastien," he said.

Ishmael had thought—no, he had hoped—that the Balthasar Hearne that Laurel had slammed the door on had been the Shadowborn. The falseness of that hope was confirmed by a blast of furnace heat at his back. He whirled—no resolution could have prevented him, whatever he put behind him—to face flame. He thudded back against the lintel, but by the time he turned his head again, he was completely ringed by fire. He could feel the skin on his face beginning to sear. His soaked clothing and hair would give him only seconds.

And then the blaze was quenched, gone as though the fire had never been—but for the heavy smell of wood smoke, scorched fabric and leather, and hot metal. He sonned the slight figure standing at the hall corner, swung his revolver, and just as his finger began to tighten, the smell of hot metal impinged itself on his wisdom. Cursed thing wasn't safe to fire. He removed his finger from the trigger, gasping slightly.

The newcomer—the very Shadowborn he had been searching for—was a youth of fourteen or fifteen, sixteen at the most, and surly and scrawny with it. He also had a disconcerting resemblance to Balthasar Hearne, though an incomplete one. He stood with fists clenched, arms almost vibrating with thwarted energy—his magic, though very strong, had not fully emerged.

"Why'd you do that?" he shouted past Ishmael. "That's the Shadowhunter."

"I'm interested in keeping him alive," said Neill, from closer.

Without turning his head, Ishmael passed the overheated revolver to his left hand, drew the other with his right, leveled it to where sound told him the man's chest would be. "I'm not likewise minded," he warned.

The woman said, "Sebastien, get in here."

Ishmael's sonn caught the boy as he started forward, jerking and palpably fighting every step. The woman's magic was the most mature of the three, deft and slick, and he had no doubt she could have crafted an ensorcellment that would have brought the boy running eagerly to her side, not this rough puppetry. Ishmael rolled his shoulder around the lintel as the boy drew near, not wanting to let him within striking distance or take his muzzle off the man's chest. Though there was no denying, with the power around him, that the revolver and even his presence were barely more than a gesture. Much as he wished to listen to the sounds around him, to know how the muster was proceeding, he concentrated on present and place. He did not know how much these three were capable of reading without touch. He trusted the Stranhornes to waste no time evacuating. In turn, he must give them all the time he could.

He wished he could be reassured that Neill seemed in no haste. Was he, as his countryman or kinsman—the one who had seduced Tercelle Amberley—had been, immune to daylight?

The boy, struggling still, lurched up to the woman. Deliberately, she raised a hand, transformed to the sinewy, scarred knuckles of a prizefighter, and hammered his cheek, sending him sprawling across a chaise longue and spilling half-hemmed baby clothes to the carpet. Neill, who had not intervened, said then, "Midora, enough."

"It is *not* enough," she said. "He killed Jonquil."

The boy snapped from dazed to accusing, arm outstretched toward Ishmael, ending in a quivering arrow of a finger. "*He* killed Jonquil! I wasn't even there."

Futile as it likely was for him to try to deflect attention from Telmaine, it was already established habit. "Bullets in heart, gut, and brain," Ishmael confirmed.

A gesture from the man, backed by a gush of his magic deflecting hers, spared Ishmael's life, if not his churning stomach. He'd be cursed if he'd vomit at their feet, but much more of this and he would. "Jonquil must have got careless," Neill said. "You may be good with these things"—a casual gesture toward the revolver—"but you're not up to his weight otherwise."

"Where were you," the woman said to the boy, "when he shot Jonquil?"

"More to the point," said Neill, "why are you here?"

The boy, sitting on the floor, drew his knees up to his chest and hugged them, rocking slightly, holding his bruised face. "I was in Minhorne. Jonquil had gone to the summerhouse. He was going to wake up Vladimer and . . . and then kill him." That hesitation suggested ugly things. "I felt Jonquil die. I went down to the station, waited for Vladimer to come back. That was the order, wasn't it? Kill Vladimer. Kill Vladimer. Kill Isidore. Kill *him*." He gestured to Ishmael, but Ishmael hardly registered his own name for the company it kept. "But Vladimer had a mage with him. She turned my magic back on me—*burned me*."

"In other words," she said scornfully, "she scared you, and you ran away. *She's* going to skin you, boyo."

"I thought it would help if . . . I sent someone to open the door."

"Which we hardly needed, now, did we?" Stones hopped from the two mounds of rubble and began to dance around him on the floor, jumping like vicious mice. He raised his hands to protect his face. "Neill!" he wailed.

Behind him, in the corridor, Ishmael heard a soft whistle. It penetrated his careful inattention as, he thought, it should have penetrated his sleep. His lips twitched in something that was almost amusement. *Fall back and join us, indeed.*

But if they were to execute Stranhorne's plan, they needed the Shadowborn to be committed, in the depths of the manor, before— *Don't think*.

He shot Neill. He did not try a second shot or wait to sonn his fall; he hurled himself away from the door, even as the boy screamed and a furnace blast of flame roared out from the lintels on either side. His wet clothing sizzled. Thank the Mother—or the drunken patron god he had invented for himself—his face had cleared the doorway. He threw himself to one side, rolling, as behind him the ceiling caved in—more than caved; was smashed in, the fragments of plaster and shattered beams hammering down and bouncing up to hammer down again. Someone fell screaming; a young boy, one of the ammunition runners. Ishmael lurched back toward him, even though he knew the boy was already beyond anyone's help—he could hear it in the sounds he was making. He was surprised that he himself was still alive—that Midora could not distinguish his vitality from the boy's. But the Shadowborn could bring down the manor themselves in trying to kill him. He let out a roar, putting into it all the fury and despair and revulsion at the child's hideous death, and then letting its authentic tones turn to a shriek, as though he himself had been caught by the falling roof. The stones' frenzy redoubled. *"Ishmael!"*

screamed Lavender. And, *"Let me go!"* He could not even answer her, else he'd undo his own ruse; he could only pray that they managed to hold her back from fatal recklessness. He backed away as soundlessly as he could on booted feet down the southward hall, while behind him the storm of debris raged. Just before he stepped around the corner, his wits caught up with him and he said in a low voice, "Di Studier—" Bullet impacts burst from the far plaster before a voice barked a cease-fire. He whispered, hoarsely, "Aye, it was a good, bloodcurdling shriek, wasn't it?"

"Come," said the voice—that of Stranhorne's one-armed lieutenant. He sidled around the corner, making himself the leanest possible target, and into the sonn of the group of a handful of men, advance guard on the corridor from a barrier built ten yards up. One of them, a jumpy marksman by the tremor in his hands, said, "But we heard—"

"They brought the roof down, and with it, one of th'ammunition boys. He's dead now."

"Stupid little sod," muttered the lieutenant. "Should have been at the muster already. Must have gone back to pilfer."

He must say that, Ishmael thought. *He must say that and believe it, that the boy deserved that death.* Reaction caught up with him, and he had to brace himself against the wall. "Fall back," he heard the lieutenant say, and two men caught his arms. The men behind the barricade pulled it down enough to let them scramble over, which Ishmael did well enough, and slid to his haunches in its rear, back against the wall. "Sorry," he said to the one-armed man. "Bit much, that."

"Aye, well, it's not over. Baron wants them well committed before—"

Ish lifted a cautioning hand. "Not sure how much they hear . . . There're three. Man, woman, boy. Shot the man; we'll find out if it sticks. He seemed t'be the leader, also th'one willing to talk," which might make the shooting regrettable, but he did not want to find out that the Shadowborn were stalling him to their advantage, even as he tried to stall them to his. "Strong mages," he said, grimly. "Very strong. Boy's a shape-shifter—probably came with us in the guise of one of Mycene's men, th'one supposedly laid up with street-cart belly. Darkborn or Lightborn mage that strong could pluck th'thoughts and plans out of our minds, though these don't seem to be behaving that way. May not be able; may be toying with us."

"Can't do anything about that; no sense worrying," the one-armed man said. "Baron wants you leading th'vanguard. He figures that anything needs to be fought through, you're best t'do it. Mycene will have the rear; nothing for them t'be a danger to there but Shadowborn, and he's a cursed good fighter. Be a good thing for th'Isles if he did get killed."

Ishmael noted the compliment, backhanded as it was; he'd had similar ones paid to himself, not the least by his own father. And Stranhorne's election of him as leader of the van was a high compliment indeed. But where did that put Stranhorne himself?

"People of Stranhorne!" Neill shouted.

Ishmael, to his shame, jumped.

"We are not interested in wholesale slaughter—"

"Could'a fooled us," someone muttered.

"If you lay down your weapons and surrender, you will be treated well."

Nervous snickers and scornful oaths, silenced by the one-armed man's throat-slitting gesture. Ishmael added the signal to mute sonn, which the one-armed man conveyed forcibly.

Ishmael started again as Lavender's clear voice called, "What do you want?"

"Who are you, *woman*?"

Don't tell, don't tell, Ishmael willed, and did not hear her reply as the pain in his chest wrung breath and thought from him—*idiot!* She wasn't even a mage.

The Shadowborn was saying, "We want the manor, and enough staff to keep it livable, and we want the family."

Was that brassy, confident voice the voice of a man whom Ishmael had mortally wounded not minutes ago, or of the stripling impersonator? And then his question was answered by the sound of his own voice. "Y'can tell them everything's all right. Y'can hear I'm fine."

Erich's hand slammed into his shoulder, pinning him against the wall, before he was even aware he had moved. He got the point: if he so much as hiccoughed, the hand would be over his mouth. He tapped the other man's wrist in acknowledgment, and waited, breath held, heart pounding.

"Do you really expect us to believe that?" Lavender said, without a tremor of uncertainty. *"Shadowborn."*

He could hear the quick breathing of the men around him—not the one-armed man, who knew how to make no sound, but one with a distinct wheeze, and two who were snoring, at least to his ears. From farther away, around the corner, he heard stones grumble and slide. Magic swelled sickeningly, and he heard stones grind on wood. "Down! Everyone *down!*" he roared, full voice, and threw himself flat, catching Erich by the belt and hauling him down, and twisting and kicking the feet of the nearest man out from under him just as the first stones ricocheted off the wall at the corner. A woman—*please not Lavender*—screamed from around the corner, and the improvised barricade before him shuddered violently under the barrage of brick, spars, and plaster. There was a thud of plaster on bone, and a man sprawled back from his place at the barrier. Ishmael rolled over and sonned, catching distorted shapes of fragments passing overhead. He heard yells from farther up the hall as the missiles reached the second barricade, but he'd noticed the barrage was thinning, seeming to travel high.

On the far side, he heard a crunch and a scrape, as of claws on wood, and felt the barricade tremble slightly—and his sonn caught the balewolf just as it scrambled onto the edge of a side-turned table. He rolled to his feet with a shout of "Wolves!" His left hand went out and caught the brute's shaggy throat, and with the power of his legs and back behind it, he heaved it backward off the barricade, a feat he would never have ventured, let alone accomplished, in cool blood and sobriety. It landed, leaped, and caught someone's bullet in its jaws. The entire corridor heaved with them. He heard yelling from the far corridor, and running feet approaching behind. Over his shoulder he shouted, "Fall *back*, *back*! We can't hold here." Maybe they could, but the enemy had to commit, had to come as deep as possible into the manor, and as long as they thought that the beasts were overrunning the defenders, maybe they would hold on the magic. Bordersmen could fight monsters, but magic . . . He caught the collar of one man who had not moved, who knelt still, fixedly firing and firing, and all but launched him down the corridor after the others. And then they were running back, two men carrying the one who had been felled by the stones. The one-armed man, covering the rear, went down beneath the claws of one of the brutes, but a second man ducked in with a knife the size of a short sword, impaled its open jaw, and slit its throat, while a third dragged Erich clear.

Above the abandoned barricade, the ceiling fell in, crushing the animals beneath it. He heard Neill's cry, "Midora!" with a choke of pain at the end of it, and the woman's laughter. Then from overhead he heard shooting—someone, two someones, firing through the cavity in the roof. Suicidally brave, with the ceiling coming down in pieces, but that let the defenders pile through the gap opened for them in the barricade, and fall to their haunches and knees for reloading. "Shit—," someone gasped. "Aren't I dead? Aren't we all dead?"

By some miracle, none of them were, though several were bleeding from stone or bite wounds, and the man who'd been felled at the barricade was unconscious with what looked like a grave head injury, and another was likely to bleed to death from his torn groin, despite the best efforts of his fellows to staunch it. It was a wound Ishmael himself could have dealt with once. The one-armed man recalled his attention from bitter regret. "If they've not held th'other side, we'll have some trouble on the retreat."

Truer words were never spoken. If the defenders in the north corridor had to fall back into the vestibule and entrance to the ballroom, then he and the others would be cut off. They would have to retreat into the cellars. He took a deep breath, aware of his own shakiness. How long since he'd eaten or, even more important, had anything to drink? He rasped, "Anyone got water with them?"

Someone passed him a flask; he drank, using the moment to think and to listen to the far side. He had not been able to listen to what was happening elsewhere while he was scrambling to save his own life, but from the sound of firing, he believed they were holding. Had to believe they were holding, and that Lavender was still alive. *So much,* he thought ruefully, *for Stranhorne wanting us in the vanguard.*

How long had it been? Long enough for the muster and breakout to be ready? He corked the flask and handed it back to its owner with a nod, then said to the one-armed man, "What's the signal, then? Ours, that we're breaking contact, or theirs that they're breaking out?"

With a crash, the ceiling collapsed, carrying the two snipers with it. Both were women. Ishmael surged to his feet. The defenders shot frantically, but there was just too little time—one had no chance at all to rise, while the other had no sooner gained her feet than a wolf leaped for her throat and dragged her into the mass. Her blank, terrified face and her wide, crying mouth seared into his memory. The man whom Ish had hauled from his post at the first barricade screamed obscenities and shot and shot and shot again, oblivious to the hammer falling on an empty chamber.

"Ishmael!" It was Lavender, her throat raw. "Break—break now." And then Ishmael heard a sound he would never again be able to mistake, any more than he would the magic that fuelled it—the *whumph* of erupting fire. He moved before he thought. Ten strides took him to the door into the central gallery, through which he plunged in utter disregard of what might be waiting on the other side. Nothing was; he sprinted the width, hit the door, threw it open; met smoke and the roil of heat and flame to his right. He yelled, "Lavender!" and heard her answer, from the far side. He shouted, "Y'have to run—run through. Run t'my voice. I'm clear." How long? He felt magic pour over him, heard a *whumph* behind him, and the gallery ignited. He roared, tasting blood, "Fall back, fall back to the muster!" The men on the other side had to come through the west gallery or hall, or go down to the cellar, and they had to do it now.

Two figures suddenly burst, solid, from the flame: Lavender, leading the young troop who had given up his horse to Ishmael. She almost fell into his arms, as her sister had. He did not greet her with an embrace, but with frantic slaps at the smoldering edges of her clothing. She twisted and shouted, "I'm through. Come! Come! Come! *Come!*" To her urging, raw with need and nothing like command, they came in twos and threes, bursting out of the fire on courses toward her.

Jeremiah Coulter wore his buccaneer's grin. "Reminds me of a ceremony on one of th'far south islands. . . ."

Ishmael heard running and stumbling feet on wood behind them, and turned to sonn the men and women from the barricade. He could weep with relief that they'd found their way. They helped him catch and slap down the men and women emerging from the fire. The one-armed man was not with them. The one on whom the leadership had devolved said, "Erich went down to the baron. He said they'd break out through th'south."

Through the bricked-up entrance they'd need to blow to get free. *Sweet Imogene.* He caught Lavender as she moved, with a harder grip than he'd ever taken of her. "No! Your place is here." He couldn't tell her her father would be fine. "We need t'get clear, and we need t'get clear now."

The last through the fire, a young woman, caught Lavender's arm. "Ronina and the Prescotts—they won't come—"

Ishmael stepped forward, almost up to the fire. "Y'come and y'live, or y'die right here!" he challenged.

In answer, he heard three shots. Lavender, beside him, made a sound like a puppy crushed beneath a wheel. He said, hoarsely, "This is it—sound the breakout."

"The fire . . . ," she whispered. "If it reaches—"

"Erich's gone to warn." He caught her hand. *"Come."* He led them, a ragged, wounded, indomitable band, into the ballroom, but she had to force him to release her so she could sound the bell—Mother bless that Stranhorne had at least been willing to allow mechanical bells. She threw the switch and the final retreat began to peal, thin against the building roar of fire. She turned back to him, crying, but unaware of it. He said, "We'll be back, lass. We'll be back."

She plunged ahead, toward the heaving mass of people pushing out the far doors, and Ishmael followed.

Balthasar

Cold roused Balthasar where he lay, rain, close to sleet, needling his exposed skin. Breathing hurt, every inhalation pulling at his side. Beneath his hand, he could feel icy rainwater pooling on the outstretched wing of a dead Shadowborn. He could hear the spatter of wind-driven rain, and a bell ringing in staccato bursts. And he could smell fire, the rank smoke of wood and fabric.

His hand jerked, twitching his soaked sleeve out of the puddle. He closed his fist, opened it. Not ensorcellment; the stiffness of exertion and cold. Making himself move, making himself lift his head, rise on his elbow, sonn around himself, was one of the most urgent efforts he had ever made in his life. Sonn caught shapes moving, and something growled. He froze. The movements came no closer, though the restless shapes continued to prowl. His sonn, probing the rain, delineated the gaping wall, the neat channel of cleared rubble.

Moving very slowly, he pushed up his shirt, explored the wound with his fingers. It was closed, though puckered and drawn. He remembered the Shadowborn touching him, the pain. Yet it had been a curative pain.

From deep within the manor came a low, rumbling belch. Through the flagstones he felt a vibration, and, with the next, louder—an explosion, he realized—he felt a distinct twitch, as though the earth itself were shrugging. The very walls of the manor wavered with the force of the third explosion, and the ceiling slumped into the gap. Warm air rolled over Balthasar, reeking of a munitions factory. From beyond the wall a bugle blared and a winch whined. Then a yelled command, a volley, another shout, another volley, and he heard wheels and hooves—a great many of both—on pavestones. A woman's voice screamed, hoarse with shouting, "*Drive! Run!* All speed to the Crosstracks. We hold the rear!" The manor shuddered again, though those massive walls remained intact. The woman—Lavender or Laurel—shouted, *"Father! We hold the rear!"*

This made sense of the whispers and exchanges he had overheard while he worked. The Stranhornes had planned for defeat, planned for retreat, planned even for betrayal. He listened with shuddering exaltation. The coaches would be carrying the wounded and those unable to keep the pace on foot. Anyone who could walk and run would do so, carrying those they could, and those who could fight would be on foot and horse in the van- and rear guard. Laurel and Lavender Stranhorne would be riding with them. But he feared now that he understood some of the silences that had fallen around Xavier Stranhorne, and the exaltation went out of him. Someone must have fired the charges placed inside the manor, someone who had chosen to risk being entombed with Shadowborn invaders in the gutted interior of his manor.

With a few more tired coughs, a few more tremors, the manor settled into its warrior's death. The wheels receded into the night. Wind and rain drowned the running footsteps. The bugle cried again in thin defiance, and then all that remained was the dwindling noise of hard-shod hooves. His skin was so numb he could not know either the temperature or the force of the rain. Sunrise would not be long coming.

At that thought, and regardless of what else prowled around those ruins, he staggered to his feet. The first step almost pitched him back into the puddles, but he shuffled toward the manor, though whether to shelter or succor, he did not know. What was not already destroyed in the explosion would be burning. Anyone living in that shell would not long remain so. Balthasar was dizzied by the war between free and ensorcelled emotions, an impotent, murderous rage that he knew was close to insanity, and a helpless pity for them all, including that child monster who held him enthralled. He hoped—how he hoped—that the Stranhornes had not left any of their own alive, but knew that some must have barred the entrance to the ballroom to the last, and some of the wounded would not survive the journey—he remembered Linneas's revolver—if they even began it.

Within the gap, he heard someone cough thickly. He barely caught himself from revealing sonn, and pressed his back against the wall, listening to the crunch and slither of stumbling feet on the untidy rubble.

"Don't—," a man's voice grunted.

"Let me—" Balthasar heard a bubbling groan, and the sound of rain-wet leather slapping and slithering against the wall. A familiar young voice gasped, "Neill—Neill, what do I do? *Help me.*"

The ensorcellment jerked tight on his viscera at that "Help me" and dragged him forward. The boy crouched, his hands bracing Neill's shoulders against the rough wall. Neill's patchwork jacket was gone. Of the once-fine shirt, only its side panels and shoulders remained; the sleeves were in rags, and the front torn open. To the right of his sternum was a cavity in the flesh that frothed at every exhalation. With that wound, he ought to be dead. But he was obviously capable of healing magic, of a sort.

"I need—," Neill gasped, and Balthasar jumped violently as something bristled and muscular thrust against his legs, pushing first him and then the boy aside. The balewolf padded up to Neill and pressed its muzzle under Neill's hand and whined, like a solicitous hound. A second joined it. Silently, first one, then the other, sank to the wet rubble, their bristled flanks moving feebly as though they were exhausted. The cavity in Neill's chest no longer bubbled.

"Why didn't you—?" the boy protested, his tone hurt.

Neill said, roughly, "Don't be a fool. You'll need your vitality." He summoned two more of his surviving wolves to him, and their limp bodies joined the rest. The man stroked the nearest bristled heap gently.

Something moved within the smear of smoke and nascent heat, and from the ruined interior staggered a huge wolf moving on lacerated paws, its fur soaked—the smell was that of blood—and hide burned. Neill pushed himself painfully around to gather it in. "Ah, Mayfly," he said hoarsely, resting his face on the gory fur. The wolf let him lean on it, mild as a sheepdog.

"What—?" the boy began, plaintively.

With a swift strike that belied his injury, Neill caught his chin in one hand. "How, by the . . . Mother could you . . . *not* find out . . . that the cellar . . . was full of explosives?"

"It was not my fault!" the boy cried, struggling free. "How was I supposed to know? No one taught me enough."

The wounded Shadowborn gurgled a laugh. "D'you think . . . you're *alone*?" He fell back against the wall, throwing his hand up to bark knuckles against the stone. "I wanted this manor intact. Its *library* alone—" He swallowed down the confession and let his head drop back. "Midora's dead," he said, flatly. "Beam fell on her; couldn't help. Could barely keep myself alive." He snorted wetly and swept a wrist across his nose. "Speaking of overconfidence."

"I'd rather it was her than you," the boy said.

The man's expression was one common to the elders of antisocial juveniles everywhere. He turned his face toward Balthasar. "You're Hearne's brother. The physician."

"He's mine!" the boy said, sharply.

"I can sense that. You poor sod . . . not the least idea what's going on, by the look of you. Don't know whether to pity or envy you . . ." Behind Balthasar, something grumbled deep in its massive throat. He could now smell blood, ordure, and warm, wet, living fur. An atavistic sense told him he was ringed by Shadowborn. Neill raised his hand as he went to turn. "Don't—," he said, softly, and the ensorcellment reinforced that injunction. "They won't harm you, as long as you just stay as you are. I try not to repeat my mistakes." He rolled his head on its stone pillow toward Sebastien. "What happened in Minhorne?"

"We killed the Lightborn prince!" the boy blurted. "Set up the magic on the munitions—everything was going fine. Jonquil ensorcelled Vladimer, was going to let him slowly die, keep his people disorganized, but then Strumheller became involved. And even though he was accused of the ensorcellment and . . . and murder, he was directing other people toward us, and Jonquil thought he could hurry Vladimer's death as well as trap Strumheller's allies. But Strumheller was working with a mage, a *strong* mage—it wasn't the Broome woman; it wasn't any one of those we knew about—and she managed to resist him, and Strumheller . . . He *shot* Jonquil dead while *she* held him."

Telmaine, Balthasar thought, and desperately tried to stifle the thought.

"I got some of Jonquil's agents and waited at the station for Vladimer, but the mage was there again—I didn't think he was supposed to work with mages, and she turned my fires back at me. I was . . . I was alone. I was," he said in a small voice, "scared."

"I can understand that, Seb, but Emeya won't be in a mood to listen. You need to go back to Minhorne and finish up what you and Jonquil were ordered to do, and you need to do it before Emeya gets here. *Come!*" The boy jerked forward as though a rope had been hooked to his breastbone. "Trust me," Neill said, as he laid the back of his hand against the boy's cheek. "This is going to hurt me more than it hurts you." The boy stiffened and whined through his teeth, and Balthasar's body tensed in ensorcelled protectiveness, remembering the man's searing touch. But, fortunately, before he could otherwise react, the man's hand fell away and he slumped sideways onto his elbow, arm across the oozing hole in his chest. He had tapped his own vitality to work whatever magic he had on the boy, and paid for it.

Sebastien scrambled away, but only until he bumped against one of Neill's wolves, which growled at him. Then he crouched, staring at Neill, mouth opening and closing. Slowly, Neill raised his head. "I've shown you how; now would you *get going*, before *she* calls us back?"

The boy lunged out of his crouch to catch Balthasar's hand, though Bal's sensation of it was no more than of a jar at the end of a stick of wood. And then the boy threw his arms around him, and Balthasar felt an instant's disorientation before they fell.

Ishmael

Someone caught Ishmael—by his left arm, curse it—and hauled him close to shout in his ear, "Baronette wants you! Up front in the grand coach." He pointed, though how, in the shambles that was their retreat, he knew *where* to point, Ishmael did not know. He was supposed to be in the vanguard, but the van was already well up the road and Mycene had it. Stranhorne's plans notwithstanding, if ever a man was temperamentally unsuited to be rear, Mycene was. By the croaking shouts from his right, Lavender was mustering Stranhorne to guard the rear. Sharp woman, but with that throat, she'd be living on hot lemon and honey for the next week. So Lavender was with them, and Laurel. "The baron?" he shouted. "Boris?"

"Don't know about the baron. The baronet took a mauling. He's in the coach."

Holding his throbbing arm against his chest to spare it further insult, Ish struggled forward through the mob. He had not been privy to the planning of the retreat, but he had the essence: troops to the van, rear, and flank, running or riding; wheeled vehicles—everything from the Stranhorne state coach to a coal man's wagon—just behind the van, drawn by horses, mules, oxen, and teams of men harnessed together; and a long train of foot travelers following behind. With the fugitives from the west, the manor staff, and reservists, they had thirteen hundred people to get to the Crosstracks, five miles away. *And only two hours to do it in,* he thought, hand going out to steady a young woman who was lugging a screeching, thrashing child of three or four. In this press, a child that size could unknowingly be trampled.

Feeling the strength in his grip, she appealed over her shoulder, "Take him, please, sir. I can't carry him and keep this pace." He realized she was not a woman, but a girl, twelve or thirteen, tall for her age, but slender. Not a mother, then—a sister or cousin or nursemaid, or simply someone with a pair of empty arms. He accepted the burden. "I've to go forward past th'wagons. I'll find him a place." He hoisted the child over his shoulder, which spared his ears the howls and his wounded arm the little fists, and continued forward as rapidly as he could. The noise did seem to help clear his way.

He handed the winded but still gamely protesting child up onto a covered cart, where he joined a crop of small ones and their harried caretakers. The jouncing had already made several of them sick, and no doubt the rest would follow. He quickly assessed the solidity of the cover over their heads. It would do. It would have to do.

He found Laurel riding shotgun to one of her own coachmen, a rifle across her knee. Four members of the Stranhorne troop were keeping a high watch atop the coach. He swung up on the running board beside her, head level with her waist. She reached down, and they exchanged a lingering arm clasp. She wore a heavy leather jacket, too large for her frame, over her loose dress and stout riding boots, and someone—probably not she—had tucked a plump cushion behind her back. Her hair was caught back in a braid beneath her helmet. Her face was composed, even stern. He could sense her influence in the calm assurance of the people around her. He'd always known she had courage and a cool head, but this was more than he would ever have expected of her or her sister.

From beside and behind her, she produced a holster and a brace of revolvers, a pouch of ammunition, and a staff—all his own, he realized, as he took the holster in hand.

"Lavender's at the rear. Your father?" he said, knowing he could not spare her.

She shook her head once. "The way the manor was burning, the way it went up . . . he and the others may not have had time to get out." Her voice was small and tight. "We can't spare anyone to go back."

"Y'can spare me, I think, though your father'll take my hide, since his orders were t'get you clear. But it's still only a few minutes run t'get down to the southwest corner."

"Assuming," she said, "you meet no trouble."

"Assuming that," he said. "But I doubt I'd make any great difference t'you here."

"Then there's Dr. Hearne," she said.

"Who'd be th'first after me t'tell you you'd done the right thing by leaving him, if his mind was his own. But, yes, I'd try for the baronelle's garden as well."

"You shouldn't go alone."

"I'll move fastest, going alone." He hooked his right arm around the leg of the coachman's bench, and quickly checked both revolvers. Not that he didn't trust her, but he'd worked too hard to instill good habits in her and her sister.

"Ishmael . . . ," she said. "Please take care."

He briefly covered the hand on the rifle stock with his own gloved one. Being in the open air had restored him, and he felt as though he could run for hours. Illusion, but it should carry him where he wanted to go. "Who's the best we've got on th'south side?"

"Dyan." She pointed.

He wove through the crowd until he found the squad leader holding a firm seat on a young thoroughbred that had more spirit than sense; it was Boris's favorite horse. He should have asked after the baronet, but too late now. Trotting at Dyan's stirrup, Ishmael pointed out his course. He would fall out across the field, keeping level with Dyan and his squad until he was out of range of sonn. Anyone he found, he would bring up the rear.

I should do something about my cursed legend, he mused as he scrambled over a stile and angled his path across the new-mown field. *Anyone thinking to attempt this ought to be told he's daft, and tied up and thrown into one of the sick carts for his own good.* Stranhorne would have plenty to say, though a man who'd torch munitions in his own cellar was hardly one to condemn. But Stranhorne's trap had shifted a balance; Ishmael could feel it in the air. The rain had lightened to a drizzle and was almost warm, and he could sense very little of the Shadowborn's former strength.

On the far side of the field, he followed the wall until the corner and the gate, opened the gate, and slid through, onto the manor grounds. He moved as quietly as he was able at that speed. He could still hear the retreat: not even abject terror could keep quiet that many horses, carts and carriages, injured men and women, children and infants. But he could also hear the hiss of the wind through drying stubble, the chirp and flutter of an early rousing bird, the flap of a tarpaulin weighted down under stones—all the ordinary sounds of the area. The wind was in his face, blowing from the manor, so it would not betray his presence. Though with the heavy reek of smoke and munitions, he would be hard-pressed himself to smell anything before he came on it.

He knew the manor grounds, having spent a number of enjoyable nights training with the twins and cadet members of the troop, trying to teach them how to move silently and with the minimum of sonn, and how to place and number others in the dark. In addition, he had a perfect, and unwelcome, lodestone in the form of the Call. All he needed to do was keep driving himself away from it and keep from thinking that its strength made his leaving the retreat doubly foolish. With a momentary lapse in concentration, he might well find himself walking southwest.

He had the choice of following the wall of the manor or coming directly across the warning field. He chose the latter; the wall would be shelter, but would also restrict his direction of retreat. He wondered if he should regret that decision; the dry sticks were soaked, but he still had to navigate over sliding stones, crunching gravel, and deadfalls deep enough to break his leg, if he missed being impaled. The wind was blustering and shifting, pushing and lifting the smoke and stinging ash, and when the smoke shifted away, he could smell violent death and the beginning of rot. He stepped carefully around the crumbling edges of a pit occupied by several wolves. One struggled weakly on the stakes that pinned it, and a second was gnawing on the carcass of one of its dead companions. A few yards in, he came across the first of the Shadowborn brought down by the fire from the manor, more wolves, the first scavvern—a young one, by its growth—and one of the flying Shadowborn, crumpled and broken-backed in death. *Who might that have been before?* . . . Some thoughts were simply best not had. The wind shifted, and he shielded his face against the ash, trying not to cough, until it was done playing with him. Not far now. He moved forward, listening ahead of him, listening through the muffled crackle of the fire, the creak of heated stone, for the sound of voices, even for the sound of moaning. To his right, a wolf howled out its pain, and several more answered. He could no longer hear the retreat, and he was stricken by the sense that should he also throw back his head and howl into the emptiness, none of his own kind would answer.

He did not know when exactly he gave up hope, but it was gone by the time he reached the southwest corner. He could not even have said where the bricked-up entrance had been without going right up to the wall and examining where the stones lined up one atop the other. There was no breach in the wall, no place for Xavier Stranhorne, Erich, and the men and women with them, to have escaped.

He forced himself to move. He had less than two hours before sunrise, and he dared not linger around the manor. Even if there were nothing more dangerous than the dead, the snow and the battle might have scattered or silenced the wildlife he was used to using as a sunrise alarm. And he would not be safe to sleep out now, with the Call gnawing on him. It would be ironic if he were to be caught by the sun, after all these years.

The years of vagabondage and Shadowhunting saved him. Thought might be dulled by exhaustion and loss, but instinct was not. He heard *something*—a breath, a muted growl, the breaking of a wet stick—or smelled *something*, the sweat or breath that, rank though it was, meant something was living. At its very limits, sonn caught the shapes flowing along the south face of the manor, toward him, along the narrow, quiet band between the wall and the first layer of gravel.

Exhaustion was swept away by adrenaline. He shot, four times, to howls, and turned and sprinted along the base of the wall. He had no cover or vantage there, and if they were to come at him in numbers, he needed the gates and the gate towers, for cover, a vantage, a chance to reload. He could not hear movement behind him, for his own pounding effort and tearing breath, and, having committed himself to run, he dared not twist to sonn. And there, the northwest corner, the wall around the courtyard, the turn—

The foul chill of Shadowborn magic rolled over him. Ishmael switched direction on a stride, zigzagging away from the wall, across open grass toward the road. He heard and felt the rasp of a wing close overhead, pivoted, and swung with the staff, fouling its swoop. It grounded gracelessly, and he shot it even as it spread its wings, then plunged back into the dubious shelter of the wall. Back against the wall, he sonned wolves closing in on him from the direction of the road itself.

No chance to reload. He caught the first on the road, switched guns, and shot the second on the embankment and the third on the road. *Four more shots left.* Two wolves in the lead from the side were dealt with, but there was more movement beyond them. *Two rounds in the chamber, and eighty yards to the gate.* He coiled to run, but even as he did so, from the direction of the road came a whimper, the very sound he'd heard a dog make, decades ago, just before a Shadowhunt—only the third he'd ever been on—turned into the bloodiest disaster he'd ever been in, barring this.

"The size of three stallions crossed with your worst nightmare," he had said to Ferdenzil Mycene. This scavvern was only somewhat larger than a cart horse, but that made it all the faster. It rolled forward on the knuckles of its long forearms, and as it reared to strike, his sonn caught the hard echo of its talons and the envenomed spur on its wrist.

He shot it in the center of its mass. It reeled but did not fall; scavvern were cursed difficult to drop with a single shot, whatever his legend said. He dropped the staff and steadied his revolver two-handed, readying his last shot, knowing he'd have to try for a pith. Then it would be staff and knife work for as long as he lasted.

A woman's voice said, "Ishmael di Studier!" He sensed a surge of Shadowborn magic, as potent and vile as any he'd known, and the Call itself, like a steel cable, wound round his spine. The staggering scavvern, the milling wolves, and he were suddenly moving as slowly as if caught in winter honey. Only a small adjustment was necessary in his aim. A man shouted from behind the wolves, "Ariadne, look *out*!"

The woman screamed, "Lysander, no!"

Ishmael fired, and a second shot echoed his. He grunted at the punch in his belly, then agony briefly voided his mind of all capacity to reason and locked his jaws on a howl. His legs buckled, spine split, or as nearly as made no difference. He slithered down the wall and flopped facedown in the mud. The scavvern, toppling, barely missed him, sluicing him with mud from its fall. Half-smothered, mud filling his mouth, he remembered how, drunk, maudlin, and smelling nothing but the reek of the city, he had prayed to be able to mingle his ashes with Borders earth. Mud would do—his father would no doubt deem it fitting. He was bleeding hard, bleeding out, but he could still hear the approaching splashes of the mage and the man who had shot him. He could sense her foul power gathering around him. Well, they were welcome to his sorry carcass, but he'd make doubly sure. He reached into his magic.

<Not. Alive.>

Five

Balthasar

The sense of falling was brief, and ended with a hard landing on tiled floor. Balthasar's knees bore the impact, and the pain left him braced on knees and elbows, dizzied. *Magic,* he thought, *this has to be magic. But to what end?*

"*Yes,*" he heard the boy gasp out, "I *did it.* It's so easy. It's so *easy*!" he half wheezed, half screamed. "You lousy bitch, it's so easy." Then he slumped down on the floor, head on his arms, shuddering with reaction.

Beneath his hands, Balthasar felt dry tiles, not wet flagstone. The air was chill, but no rain fell. He could smell the dust and dried-flower scent of a house long closed up, though that was overlaid by a faint odor of rot, like neglected kitchen refuse. He turned his head away from Sebastien and softly cast, resolving an ornate arch over a doorway. To the left, another arch and stairs . . . the interior of a house.

He knew this house: it was in Minhorne. His brother had brought him here once, bragging of the scam that had ruined a man and laid his property in Lysander's hands. Perhaps it was justice that the house had been Lysander's own ruin. When he grandly gifted it to his inamorata, Tercelle Amberley—though her family owned half a dozen houses much finer—it provoked that last, fatal quarrel with his mistress, a possessive, volatile young actress. Which ended with her dead and Lysander sobbing in Balthasar's room, pleading for the help of his fourteen-year-old brother in smuggling the body out of the city, to leave for sunrise.

Help that Balthasar had, to his everlasting regret, given him.

This would be the house that Tercelle had fled to after she left her twin sons with him—the house Telmaine and Ishmael had traced her to. It was also the house she had died in, murdered, surely, by the Shadowborn.

"Get me something to eat," Sebastien said, faintly, into his arm.

In the kitchen, Balthasar exchanged his soaked jacket and waistcoat for an overlarge but thick servant's vest he found hanging on a peg. He retrieved bread, hard cheese, chutney, and honey from the pantry, not trusting the prepared meats, and made sandwiches sweet and savory. Also in the pantry were bottles of light beer, familiar to him from his student days, though that label was well beyond his budget then. Opening a couple of bottles hardly constituted a debauch, and the beer was probably safer than the water.

The boy had crawled over to the carpeted stairs and was sitting on the lowest step, head in his hands. He cast a wavering sonn over the tray as Balthasar laid it on the step beside him, but promptly seized a sandwich with each hand, eating alternate bites and swallowing almost without chewing. Balthasar had seen street urchins gorge so when set before food.

He had no appetite himself, but he knew he needed food to counteract the shock and hypothermia. He doggedly worked his way through a honey sandwich, each ashy bite washed down with beer. Turning the bottle in his hands, he supposed he should be glad to have no illusions that drink could rid him of his memories, because he understood as never before the desire to crawl into bottled oblivion.

"Why?" he said at last. "Why all this? Why Tercelle? Why Stranhorne?"

Sebastien shook his head. "You're better not to know."

Ignorance had not spared him before this. "Where is my brother?"

"Dead."

There was venom in that tone, enough to mark it as wish more than truth. Balthasar therefore did not answer it with conventional regrets. "And your mother?"

"Dead."

"She must have been a strong mage."

"I don't want to talk about them," the boy said. He lurched back against the stairs, pulling at the waistband of his breeches. "I feel sick. I've never *lifted* beforc."

The magical mode of transport, an instantaneous transfer between places. His sister, Olivede, had described it to him, though it required at least sixth-rank magic to achieve, and Olivede had not the strength. She had said more than once how glad she was to be spared both the burdens and the temptations of high-rank magic and not be other than she was—a skilled physician and reliable third-rank healer.

He turned over in his mind the scene he had witnessed just before they had come there. "Who is the woman you mentioned, who would have called you?"

"You shouldn't ask so many questions," the boy said.

It did not quite mute Balthasar, just thickened his tongue and made speaking laborious. He ate half of a cheese sandwich and finished his beer, feeling the slight detachment that came with beer quickly drunk. The boy sipped distrustfully at his bottle.

Balthasar tried again, "Why are we back in the city?"

Sebastien shrugged. "Orders."

Balthasar set down the bottle. "I'm going to try to light the stove," he said. "I'm soaked through. And—"

Sebastien's stiffening, his astonished gasp, interrupted him. The ground beneath them shook. An immense concussion cleaved the night. Balthasar came to his feet, swinging his head to try to fix the sound. He recognized it as an explosion, a huge one, larger even than the disaster of several years ago at one of the distilleries. But there were no factories in that direction, only more rows of streets, parkland along the river, the river itself, and the estates on the far side. He heard a bizarre screaming whistle from overhead, and then, from his left, another, lesser explosion.

Sebastien jackknifed, leaping to land on his feet beside

Bal. "Yes!" He punched air. "Yes, yes, yes. They've finally *done* it! *That* for your caution, Neill, and *that* for your power, Jonquil."

Oh, sweet Imogene, Balthasar thought. Sebastien had said something about ensorcelling munitions. Was that a ship or ships blowing up on the river? But who should have been bringing munitions into the city? Had the dukes insisted on arming themselves as well, now that the order of six twenty-nine was suspended? He heard another crash, another shriek of passing . . . artillery? Were they at war—Darkborn against Darkborn? Darkborn against Lightborn? He turned his head again, checking his orientation. In *that* direction was the river, the artery of trade and communication, and on its far banks, the great city estates of several of the dukes, including Duke Kalamay, hater of Lightborn and mages. And in *this* direction was the city center, the Lightborn prince's palace, the Mages' Tower.

From outside, he could hear screams. If Lightborn walls had been breached, anyone caught outside would die, swiftly if the light were more than a glimmering, and slowly and in agony otherwise. He could not leave anyone to that, whatever the risk to himself. He lunged past the capering boy, turned the door handle, and found it locked. He groped one-handed for a key that was not there, still twisting futilely. Even in its light-tight frame, the door shuddered from another barrage, and then he felt a wave of unease and dizziness, followed almost immediately by an explosion in the air, and another, even greater one, to his right. Then the reverberations faded away, leaving only a deep bell knelling and no living sounds outside at all.

Magic, he thought. *Magic enough even for me to sense.* He heard a whimper behind him and turned to sonn Sebastien on the floor, arched and shuddering with a convulsion. He dropped by his side, examining him for signs of injury, signs of anything that might have triggered the seizure, then rolled him over on his side, bracing him there with knees behind his back, protecting his head from the tiles. He did not know the boy's medical history; he might be epileptic, but from the coincidence, Bal had to suspect that this was magical. And if he were part of whatever had happened—as his triumph seemed to indicate—then he might be under attack by the Lightborn. Olivede, Balthasar's principal informant in the ways of magic, was merely a third-rank mage, and a determinedly peaceable one at that. He had no idea what might happen should mages turn magic upon one another.

Except that it was certain to be dangerous for the bystanders.

Even if he could run, he had nowhere to go in the light-polluted night.

Sebastien went limp, his head lying heavy in Balthasar's cradling hand. "They can't be . . . can't be . . . ," he whispered, drew in a whining breath, and began to convulse anew. Balthasar braced him, counting out the seconds. When the fit passed and did not immediately resume, he stripped off the servant's vest and wedged it behind Sebastien's shoulders, and bundled his wet shirt beneath the boy's head. Then he ran in search of the household's medicine cabinet.

To his surprise, he also found a full obstetrical kit, complete with forceps, anesthetic equipment, bottles of chloroform, and antiseptic. Initial, but not considered, surprise: Tercelle Amberley would have made alternate preparations for her confinement, had Balthasar turned her away from his door. His hands shook with chill and the intensity of his wish that he had done so, as he gathered bottles into a small pouch. But if the seizures continued, he would be able to anesthetize the boy.

When he reached the hallway again, Sebastien was lying curled up on his side, and for a moment of hideously conflicted relief, Balthasar thought he had died. Then he coughed, and the ensorcellment tightened like barbed wire. Balthasar knelt beside him, hand on his shoulder, sonning his face. "Sebastien?"

"They couldn't—," he whispered. "Couldn't have been able to—"

Balthasar probed his head, eliciting no wince; felt his

chest and belly, finding no tenderness; felt his pulse, finding it fast but strong. "Who couldn't have been able to do what?" he said.

"Shouldn't have been able to annul—"

Annul . . . magic in which the boy had invested his vitality? That might explain the seizure.

"Are you . . . safe?" Balthasar asked, stumbling over the words, the question, the conflict between ensorcellment, compassion, dread, and smoldering anger that made such a question a deeply resented obligation.

"They shouldn't . . . have been able to . . ." He managed to lift his head, and, with Balthasar's help, sit up. "They shouldn't have been able to *do that*," he said plaintively.

"Do what? What were those explosions?" Balthasar asked. He did not think he had ever less wanted to know the answer to a question.

"The Mages' Tower. We blew it up."

A simple statement, bereft of boast. The Mages' Tower was, by Floria's account, the dominant feature of the skyline, a tower occupied by high-rank Lightborn mages, men and women whose healing power granted them life spans four or five times the length of those of ordinary men and women, who could raise storms to their will, transport themselves and others between places . . . as the boy just had then. The dynamite needed—

Sebastien scowled at his skepticism. "We *did it*."

"You'd never have been able to place enough dynamite—" *Not with the vigilance,* he wanted to say, *not with the city watch.* But who knew how many in the city they already held under ensorcellment, to act for the Shadowborn or simply turn their attention away? How many other men and women had been forced into the position he was in?

"Not dynamite. *Guns*. Great big guns."

Great big guns. Despite his exhaustion, despite his resistance, he made the connections. "That was why you were interested in Tercelle." The Amberleys' industrial concerns were munitions and artillery. It was that, not the old love affair between Lysander and Tercelle, that had drawn the Shadowborn to Tercelle Amberley. As Lysander had said—

and Floria, more kindly—he was a sentimental fool. "They were the ones who—"

"No." A grin peeled back the boy's lips. "Duke Mycene and Duke Kalamay—*they* did it. We didn't even need to ensorcell them. They did it all on their very own. *We* just had to ensorcell the munitions." He drew his knees up to his chest and hugged them. "But they shouldn't have been able to . . . ," he whispered.

"Ensorcell the munitions to—"

"Make them extra lethal," the boy said. "This way . . ."

He put his clammy palm on Balthasar's wrist, and Balthasar's breath left him, crushed out of him by the pain in his chest, the overwhelming sense of dread and mortality. He could not even cry out.

Sebastien lifted his hand and released him, leaving him propped on his hands and gasping in shock. "*That* way."

Balthasar could not speak, so profound was his sense of near death and his realization of how much hope he had placed in the Lightborn mages having the will and power to end these atrocities. If even the Lightborn were vulnerable . . . Yet they *had* retaliated—he had sensed that himself. . . . "They *did* annul your magic, didn't they?"

"No," the boy said, his voice breaking high. He forced it down to a growl. "Say that again, and I'll annul *you*. They *can't* annul our magic. They can't *sense* it. I just overreached. It was me and Jonquil ensorcelled the munitions, and Jonquil's dead, so it was just my vitality in there, and *I overreached.*"

"What . . . do you mean that the Lightborn cannot sense your magic?"

"Just what I say—they *can't*. They can't sense us, and they can't sense our magic. Haven't been able to do it for centuries, but you can bet they've kept that a deep, *deep* secret. We didn't even know ourselves until . . . well, until. Lightborn can't sense Shadowborn magic; only Darkborn can. And Darkborn aren't that strong."

If the Lightborn mages could not sense Shadowborn magic, or if they could sense it but could not counter it, it made terrible sense of their indifference to the Darkborn's travails. The Lightborn mages had united to call down a rainstorm on the Rivermarch as it burned, but the target had been the fire, not the magic that set the fire.

"So they were no threat to you, but you still attacked the tower."

"We had to. They couldn't sense our magic, but they could still attack *us*."

"But *why*?" Balthasar said, angry now. "What is it all for?"

"I shouldn't tell you."

"Why shouldn't you tell me? You've ensorcelled me. I can't betray you."

"That's not—" He stopped himself.

Balthasar waited, shaking slightly with anger and exhaustion. *Not* what*? Not the way it works?*

Sebastien buried his face in his knees. "It's been happening a long time," he mumbled. "I don't know what it's all about—it's best not to ask—but there are two of them. Lady Emeya and another one. They fight each other, but they want the lands, the whole lands."

"And they hold you—and others—ensorcelled."

Sebastien lifted a face that held in it the same hopeless exhaustion Balthasar had sonned in child factory workers. "Some want to stay. *I* wanted to stay."

There was a time to ask, *And now?* But it was not now, and not because of the boy's readiness or uneasiness. Balthasar himself was not ready to hear. "But your will is your own," he said.

A silence. "My head really hurts."

"You've had a seizure," Balthasar said. "Had you had them before?"

The boy did not answer, his lower lip set sullenly.

"Let's get you upstairs," Balthasar said. "You'll feel better when you're warm and lying down." He helped Sebastien to his feet and steered him toward and up the stairs. In the first-floor master bedroom, he helped the boy out of his soaked clothes—the trousers soaked with urine as well as rainwater, he realized—and toweled him down, got him into a clean nightshirt, and coaxed a dose of chloral hydrate down him. The seizure, or the uncertainty about his magic, had left the boy dazed. Balthasar spread quilts over him, smelling the fragrant must of old herbal sachets, and started to turn away.

The quilts rustled. "Don't go." A child's voice, a child's plea.

"I need to change out of those wet clothes. I'll become ill otherwise." It was obvious that healing was not amongst the boy's skills.

"Come back quickly."

Balthasar obeyed, rummaging in the spare-room wardrobe for a heavy, smoky-smelling sweater and coarse trousers that were too large for him but would be warm. One of Tercelle's male relations, he presumed; they could not belong to either Lysander or Mycene, both of whom were slight. He stripped, washed the blood off his side, wincing at the tenderness of the closed wound, dried himself, and quickly rinsed and wrung out his clothing as best he could. Then he dressed, drawing the waistband tight to hold it up on his hips.

Sebastien was still awake when he returned, fighting sleep like a child. Balthasar found himself straightening the covers, as he would for one of his daughters. Sebastien's eyes shifted—watching him?

"It's strange," he said. "Having you here. It's like having . . . him."

"My brother?" Wiser to say that than try "your father."

"He was . . . He looked after me. But then . . ." A long silence. "He wanted to take her away. He said he *had* to take her away. And if I wouldn't go, then he'd leave me behind. He said if it was her or me, he would take her."

The words were childish, the anguish was that of a young child's abandonment, and Balthasar could well imagine Lysander saying that to a child. He reminded himself that he could not imagine what Lysander had experienced among the Shadowborn. "Was she in that much danger?"

"Yes. No!" A long pause. "Emeya would have killed her."

"But you didn't know that at the time," Bal said. *Because people seldom do, even when it is there before them.*

"No," he said. He turned on his side, away from Balthasar. "I don't want to talk anymore. Be quiet. Stay."

Balthasar sat listening to the tolling of the warning bell, a sound he had heard only once before in his time in the city, when the collapse of an ill-built tenement had spilled light into the night. But those were poor artisans, with only enough light to last out the night, and though scores of Darkborn had been burned, few had died outright. The breached walls of the Mages' Tower would have blazed out like a beacon, and the Lightborn would have surely laid claim to the last hours of the night in a bid to rescue survivors. He could not escape and live, even if he had not been bound by the ensorcellment.

He heard a snuffling snore; the boy had rolled over to sprawl on his back. In sleep, he might have been one of the waifs Balthasar had treated in Olivede's Rivermarch clinic: half starved, half wild, street bred and street reared, neglected and abused. He could not hate the boy—and was that ensorcellment or pity? *Pity,* he thought, and rejected the thought—and then brought it back to reexamine it. His thoughts limped with exhaustion, but even in his weariness, he had a sense that he was close to something important. *Love me,* the boy demanded. An adult might thwart the wishes of a child out of love; as the father of two lively little girls, he found himself doing that more often than he ever wanted. For him to juxtapose his feelings for his daughters with his feelings toward this boy seemed an obscenity, but . . . if he had an escape, he sensed it lay there.

He would need his wits intact to know his way when it opened before him. Rather than strain against the ensorcellment by trying to leave the room, he found a spare quilt and a pillow, laid down the pillow, wrapped himself in the quilt, and stretched out on the rug in front of the cold grate.

Balthasar

Balthasar woke to the muted crackle of an untidily laid fire in the grate, and his brother kicking at his bare feet. "Up," Lysander said. "I'm having visitors. You get to play butler."

"Sebastien?" Balthasar said tentatively.

"Yes—oh, the shape." He smirked. "You like it?"

He did not like it. His memories of his brother were of taunting and torment shading to outright cruelty, ending in coercion to conceal Lysander's capital crime, but nevertheless he rebelled at the thought of his brother's living likeness being passed back and forth amongst these Shadowborn like an old sock. "No," he said. "I don't like it."

Sebastien scowled down at him. He was wearing a slightly outdated, formal suit that would have suited a lord's heir. It might have been Lysander's, since Lysander liked to dress expensively and above his station. The young mage seemed recovered after last night's collapse, but there was a hectic energy about him that Balthasar had seen in young addicts and young gamecocks intoxicated by their own recklessness. The first, he had treated; the second, he had, generally, outplayed. "I need to be older," Sebastien said. "Or they won't listen." He kicked Balthasar's feet again. "Get up. And dress decently. There's clothes in the wardrobe."

He left. Balthasar crawled out of his bedding. He could not tell what time it was; his watch, soaked once too often, had stopped. There were no familiar sounds to cue him. In his and Telmaine's home, the staff's routines demarcated night and day as crisply as the bells outside. In the old, narrow house he had inherited from his parents, he could tell the hour from the mutterings of the walls and roof as they warmed with the sun, and from the sound of Floria White Hand's movements next door.

His own clothing had barely begun to dry; he could still wring water out of the cuffs. Groping in the wardrobe, he found a shirt, pressed trousers—loose at the waist and slightly long in the leg—and a formal jacket and coat, both decently plain and smelling of tired lavender and long storage. He washed and dressed, wincing as he stretched the scar in his side, found a comb and pulled it through his unwashed hair, and decided not to bother to search for a razor. Despite his sleep, he was draggingly tired, but he knew his tiredness was as much of the spirit as the body, that it was despair that sapped him.

Sebastien was standing in the vestibule as he came down the stairs, toying with a large, ornate door key. "You look awful," he said, as though Balthasar's haggard aspect gave him personal offense.

"I can do what's needed," Balthasar said quietly. Sebastien would not hear the other meaning and the prayer in that.

Sebastien's response was interrupted by the doorbell. Key in hand, he crossed to the door. His smirk back over his shoulder, his expectant pause before he turned the key, jolted Balthasar to full understanding. Protest jammed in his throat at the realization that Sebastien knew precisely what he was doing—as Lysander knew what he was doing—and panic rendered him mute.

He had only enough time for a single step back, as Sebastien turned the handle and threw open the door on daylight.

Six

Floria

Politics made for strange bedmates, Prince Isidore used to say, though Floria White Hand had never foreseen it applying to *her*. She was a vigilant; her prince's allies were her allies, and her prince's enemies her enemies. This she had learned when head-high to her father's belt, as he had learned from his father, and he from his, and so on, back ten generations.

How, then, did she come to be standing—albeit with her back to a solid wall—in a gathering of the very people she had spent eighteen years protecting her prince *from*?

In the center of the room, the dowager consort Helenja glowered at her sister. Helenja was a heavy woman, deceptively so, given how quickly she could move when inclined. She had a southerner's coloring, and the ornate construction of her dull auburn hair was in the southern mode. Her usual dress, southern in its earth-hued simplicity, was decorated with ribbons and a sash in bright red, in scant acknowledgment of her mourning.

In Sharel, Floria could see the young Helenja, despite the slight physical resemblance between them: Sharel was lean, dark, and straight nosed, where Helenja was bulky, auburn, and had a nose that had been broken by a fractious horse. Nevertheless, Sharel's arrogance and swift certainty of judgment evoked the arrogant young consort who had thought to conquer Isidore's court.

"Of course he's a hostage!" Sharel was saying. "You said Fejelis grabbed him just before they all disappeared. Orlanjis would never have gone willingly."

The dowager consort looked past Sharel, toward Floria. She was squinting slightly, as though looking at a bright horizon or suffering from a headache. "Orlanjis," Helenja said, grittily, "couldn't have made his support for Fejelis more plain. Mistress White Hand, come here."

Floria did not want to expose her back in this company, but she and Helenja had established a sketch of an alliance around their desire to find Prince Fejelis and his brother. Moreover, she'd never fight her way out. She obeyed.

"Tell my sister what *you* saw," Helenja said.

Why Sharel should believe Floria's account of the disappearance of Fejelis and Orlanjis, she had no idea. For eighteen years, Floria had been vigilant and food taster to Fejelis's father, Isidore, on account of the magical asset that protected her against poisons—most of which had been plied by the southerners.

Perhaps, she thought bitterly, *I have become credible because of the part I played in Isidore's death.*

Stonily, she reported, "The prince's sister"—to refer to her by either her birth name or the name given her by the mages was equally fraught—"came running up to Prince Fejelis and Captain Rupertis in the vestibule of the palace, to tell them that the high masters had Magister Tammorn, who had been working for the prince, and were planning to burn out his magic—"

"Why?" Sharel interrupted. "He's a mage."

"Magister Tammorn is a sport," Floria said. No need to explain what else the Mages' Temple had to hold against Tam, aside from his birth outside the Temple's carefully cultivated lineages. "Prince Fejelis went to the high masters and attempted to persuade them to release Magister Tam and to join with him in dealing with the Shadowborn."

In defiance of centuries of protocol shielding the archmage from earthborn contact, the young prince had appealed directly to the archmage for an alliance. His appeal had been bold and moving and might have worked, except that Fejelis had made a tactical error. "He let it be known that he believed that lineage mages could not detect Shadowborn magic."

"Was he mad?" said Sharel.

"Look out the window," Helenja said. "And tell me."

Out of the window was the Mages' Tower, that thrusting assertion of the mages' ambition, wealth, and power, which had shadowed the palace and streets beneath it for two hundred years. Its upper dome was gone, its upper stories collapsed in on themselves and fallen in slabs over the streets and buildings below, its middle and lower stories punctuated with jagged holes. The bright dust of its ruin was still settling out of the late-afternoon sunlight. That the destruction had been wreaked by material means—explosive shells from Darkborn emplacements on the far side of the river—everyone knew, but it was already widely rumored that the lethality had been magically augmented. And surely no enemy the mages sensed could have struck against them so preemptively.

"Mad, no," Helenja said, judiciously. "But unwise to have said so outright." She inclined her head toward Floria. "Continue."

Floria believed the silent archmage might have been weighing Fejelis's appeal, but her interpretation was unasked for. "Prasav"—that was Fejelis's oldest cousin on his father's side—"stepped forward to accuse Magister Tam of having been responsible for the prince's—Prince Isidore's—death, under Prince Fejelis's instigation. He suggested that the prince and Magister Tam were lovers."

Sharel snorted at this expression of northern bigotry.

"Fejelis asked the high masters to confirm that he and Tam were innocent of the prince's death. They made no move to do so. Vigilants under Prasav's command"—some of them suborned members of Fejelis's own guard, Rupertis among them, and she owed *him* an accounting at her first opportunity—"took aim at Fejelis. The mages raised no objection, though there was no formal rescinding of contracts."

That made Sharel's eyes widen. the system of contracts by which earthborn secured the services of mages were sacrosanct. "Orlanjis tried to push Fejelis out of the line of fire. Magister Tam deflected the bolts, and then he, the prince, and Orlanjis disappeared."

"The Temple staged a coup," Helenja said, bluntly. "They have set Perrin up as princess—a mage princess, against seven hundred years of compact. Fejelis and Orlanjis were removed by Magister Tammorn. *His* motivations are obscure and his destination even more so. None of *my* mages"—a cold glance in their direction—"claim to be able to locate them."

"And what are you doing here?" Sharel demanded of Floria. "You're Isidore's."

"And, ironically," Helenja said, with a smile that told Floria all their old antagonism was merely suspended, "the instrument of Isidore's destruction." She paused, letting Floria fully appreciate that statement.

"So that rumor about the talisman is true?" Tam believed that, under ensorcellment, Floria had carried to the prince's rooms a talisman enspelled to annul the magic of the lights on which he depended to survive the night.

Floria did not answer. The downward flicker of Sharel's gaze alerted her to her right hand, working on the pommel of her rapier. "Do *you* believe in the Shadowborn?"

For eighteen years she had guarded Isidore, as her father had Isidore's father and uncle before him, and her grandmother, Isidore's grandfather, unmoved by attempts at assassination, threats, seduction, and bribes. Nothing but magic could have made her part of the murder of her prince—yes, she believed in the Shadowborn.

Law might exonerate her of anything done under ensorcellment, yet she had murdered her prince and forfeited her honor, and she would do anything—make any alliance—to make and take recompense for that.

"Yes," she said. "I believe in the Shadowborn."

"And what do they say?" Sharel said, head turning toward the mage.

"The boys are not within the city; of that my mages are certain. Beyond that, they need a direction and distance, or time, to find them."

"If they are caught outside at sunset—"

Helenja glanced toward the window, at the slant of light and depth of shadows. "They won't be," she said.

"How can you possibly know?" Sharel said.

"Fejelis is levelheaded. If he has survived the *lift*, he will ensure they survive the landing."

She could not know. Tam's feat—*lifting* himself, Fejelis, and Orlanjis—should have been beyond a mage of his official rank, even before he had endured the high master's questioning. Misjudgment in such extremity was likely.

"Whatever," said Sharel, "got into Orlanjis?"

"The boy is fourteen, a bundle of emotions," Helenja said. "That mage won't have dropped them at random; it'll be a place he knows. Floria," Helenja said without turning, "you know this mage, I believe. Where would he go?"

Floria drew close the calm she had learned as a courtier in a mage-ridden court. "Magister Tam was born in the foothills of the Gyrheights—the Cloudherds," she explained, giving them their southern name. Tam would never return there, even in mortal danger, but Sharel need not know that. The southerners romanticized their origins. "I know he likes the west coast." It was not precisely a lie; he had visited the west coast once, but talked of it often.

Tam had not gone back, though, after he had met his artisan lady, Beatrice. They had a three-year-old son and a six-month-old daughter, and if Helenja did not already know about Tam's family, then Sharel's inquiries need not progress far before she came across them.

She would deal with Helenja to safeguard Fejelis's rightful position as Isidore's heir. Isidore had made her promise the night Fejelis came of age—the night Isidore died. But she also owed Tam her life; his magic had deflected those quarrels from her own heart, as well as her prince's. She had a blood debt to repay.

"No matter," said Helenja, when Floria said no more. "Start looking; I am expected in an audience with the 'princess.' Floria, with me."

If Helenja and Floria made for strange bedmates, Floria found herself thinking some minutes later, then whatever would Isidore have made of *this* orgy of the peculiar?

She stood at ease, back to a wall, gaze shifting around the room, clashing and glancing off the gazes of the other guards and witnesses ranked around the wall. Across the room, her former friends and colleagues in the prince's vigilance eyed her suspiciously, questioningly, or speculatively, according to their natures.

In the center of the room, beneath a rose skylight, was a round table, its edge and legs carved with ornate geometric scrollwork, decorated with silver, and inlaid with mother-of-pearl and ivory. On the far side sat Perrin, two hours' princess of the Lightborn, and aged a month for every minute of it. Whose idea was it that she sat in that chair, the high, flaring back of which diminished her to a child's proportions? She wore a prince's red-and-blue morning jacket, and her light hair had been hastily caught up in a style suggesting a prince's caul, with deep blue beads threaded through. No one dared re-create the true prince's caul, lost with Fejelis. By her height, her sandy hair, and her light gray eyes, she was Isidore's daughter, but Floria had never seen that hunted expression in Isidore's eyes, or even in Fejelis's.

On either side of Perrin sat the two whose alliance had pitched her into power. On her right was a solid, unremarkable-looking woman in crimson jacket and trousers. The crimson was higher necked and more opaque than any ordinary Lightborn should have been comfortable wearing, which meant its opacity was magical. Her glittering chains of rank showed her to be one of the surviving high masters, the leaders of the Lightborn Mages' Temple, and spokesperson for the archmage—definitely not unremarkable, was Magistra Valetta.

On Perrin's left sat Prasav, dressed as politic in crimson mourning and the green caul that marked his rulership of several northwest provinces. Beside him, sleek and predatory, was his daughter, Ember, in the guise of her father's secretary. She watched Perrin as a well-fed cat might a caged bird, idly considering possibilities for later.

Closest to Floria, Helenja laid her hand down on the table with a soft click of gold filigree rings. "So, Magistra," she said to Valetta. "Are you able to tell me yet where are my sons?"

"Regardless of whether we complete his deposition," Prasav added smoothly, "Fejelis is a disruptive influence."

"Nobody," Perrin said, "is completing Fejelis's deposition. I told you both," she emphasized, with a look at each of her power brokers, "I am not taking the caul stained with Fejelis's blood."

Floria had to appreciate her courage, if not her sense. A princess who refused the caul was no safer than a prince who had lost it.

"We are not interested in contracting to locate the princes, but we *will* find Tammorn, and we expect the princes will be with him."

Her use of "princes" could not be anything but designing. While Fejelis lived, only he was entitled to the address, but it was to the mages' advantage to have their brightnesses at each other's throats, not least because of the lucrative contracts protecting them against each other.

"When you do," Perrin said, firmly, "since my brothers are earthborn, not mageborn, they should be placed in the custody of the vigilance."

Where they will last only as long as it takes the first suborned vigilant to reach them, Floria thought. By chance—for it surely could not be the thought—Perrin's gaze intersected hers. The princess's face tightened, as though she had just tasted something unpleasant. The fading—Floria hoped—ensorcellment that lingered around Floria? Perrin, like Tam, was a sport mage. And sports, Fejelis had asserted, *could* sense Shadowborn magic.

"Well," she heard Prasav say, "shall we talk about the Darkborn? We've two hours before we meet with Sejanus Plantageter."

He and others cast an eye toward the sunlight shining in the west-facing window, low, slanting, and yellowing. Since the Darkborn archduke and his retinue could not travel by day, they would arrive at the meeting place after dark and cede the second hour of the night onward to the Lightborn.

"That assumes," Helenja said, "that he lives to reach the Council Chambers."

The meeting was to take place in the Intercalatory Council Chambers, the only space designed for such encounters, though it was hardly the environment their brightnesses—or the Darkborn aristocracy—were accustomed to. The council was of relatively low status, and its representatives not aristocratic. Floria's neighbor and close friend Balthasar Hearne had been serving intermittent terms on the council since he was of age to do so. He had described the chambers to her, the several rooms of various dimensions, to suit different-sized groups, each one bisected by an opaque paper wall supported and reinforced by heavy mesh. Darkborn and Lightborn could hear one another perfectly through the wall—as she could attest, having spoken to Balthasar through such a wall for most of the days of their lives.

Prasav stared across the table at Helenja, open distaste in his expression. "If you mean anything in particular by that, Helenja, may I suggest you think again, *now*. We want reparations from the Darkborn, not war with them."

Helenja snorted. "Ever the mercenary, Prasav. Do you really think that what they did last night—last *night*—can be paid for in money alone? If you have any doubt, look out there." She stabbed two fingers toward the window.

Magistra Valetta's was the only head that did not turn. Rumors ran through the palace of high masters crushed in their beds or quenched as their lights were buried.

Helenja leaned forward slightly. "Magistra, how are we supposed to decide on our demand for reparations from the Darkborn if we do not know what lives were lost?"

"The value of even one life is incalculable," the mage said without expression.

"Yet we are going into negotiations with the archduke of the Darkborn and the men who were directly responsible for this atrocity," Prasav said. "We will demand justice for your murdered people, but we will also demand reparations. And it will not come cheap."

"The city," Helenja said.

The others looked at her, Prasav frowning, Ember with eyes narrowed in speculation, Perrin with pale, parted lips.

Valetta blinked.

"Tell them we want Minhorne," Helenja repeated.

"I very much doubt they'd agree to that," Prasav said. "No matter what we held over them."

Helenja's fist closed. "The Darkborn live here on our sufferance. They depend on our goodwill. Our light is more deadly to them than their darkness is to us: any light kills them, but only complete darkness does us. Minhorne's the only city of any size where we have to live like this. It's unnatural."

"I refuse to put my name to—," Perrin said.

"Minhorne's the largest, most prosperous city in the Sundered Lands." Ember's voice glided smoothly over the princess's objection. "Arguably, it is this way because Lightborn and Darkborn economic interests have become intertwined to their mutual advantage, at least among the earthborn. Losing their industry and innovation at this time would cost us more than we could afford."

Prasav's daughter, indeed. Where the entire Lightborn realm was impoverished by hundreds of years of contracts with the mages, Prasav's scrupulous—plenty said "ruthless"—economies had let him husband his wealth.

"Then let them live underground," Helenja growled, "the way they used to. There's a whole network of underground streets."

The buried streets linking the older parts of the city were hundreds of years old, and Floria had heard Balthasar's description of their condition—most damp, some collapsed, others more sewer than thoroughfare.

"What about you, Magistra Valetta?" Ember said. "What do the mages want from the Darkborn?" She leaned back into the sunlight to regard the mage, her face grave and concerned. The only death Magistra Valetta would acknowledge was that of Lukfer, a reclusive mage of strong but uncontrolled magic whom the mages accused, with his student Tammorn, of spreading false rumors about the Shadowborn.

"We have yet to measure our injury," the mage said at last. "But we wish to hear what the Darkborn have to say. The streets *will* be safe for them."

Magic kept those lights burning. Magic—particularly high-rank magic—could quench them.

Perrin spoke softly. "We, too, must live to reach the council chambers."

Prasav said, with distinct impatience, "We have it taken care of, Princess."

Perrin turned her silvery eyes on him, and for a moment Floria saw her father in her.

"My daughter," Helenja said, before she could speak, "has a point. Please describe how exactly we are to avoid Isidore's fate."

"When the bell sounds, runners will leave the palace, carrying lights. They will string the route so that it is as brightly lit as the corridors of the palace. We will not travel together, and we will carry lights of our own. If there *were*"—a cut of the eyes sideways toward Magistra Valetta—"such a thing as Shadowborn, I doubt they would be able to swallow the magic in that many lights." He folded his hands and said to Helenja, "*I* am satisfied with the arrangements; whether you are is up to you."

Helenja acquiesced with a tilt of her head.

"Shall I suggest," Ember said, evenly, "that we hear what the archduke has to say—how, for instance, he plans to deal with those responsible—and assess our injuries further before specifying the reparations we seek?"

Prasav said, "I think not. I am in a mood to demand." He smiled coldly across the table. "So let us demand the city, and let them take the proper measure of our outrage."

Ember dipped her head slightly in acknowledgment.

Magistra Valetta said, "Agreed."

Perrin, the princess, licked her pallid lips and said nothing.

Balthasar

I should, Balthasar told himself, *have realized what Sebastien was capable of.* Given what Tercelle Amberley had said, given what Sebastien had said about his parentage. But first there was that moment of sheer, abject terror to pass through, before he realized that he should already have been dead, if he were going to die. Sebastien was half Darkborn, half Shadowborn, and perhaps immune to the Curse—he had at least wondered about that possibility. But *he,* Balthasar, was not immune. . . . Yet here he stood, before a door open on daylight. Sebastien had been mage enough to bring them here; now the boy had proven himself mage enough to shield them both from daylight. Not even the Lightborn high masters had achieved that.

How can we fight these people, Balthasar thought, *Telmaine, Ishmael, Vladimer, and me?* He swayed where he stood.

Sebastien thought it a fine jape and greeted the newcomers with suppressed glee more suited to the boy he was than the man he was pretending to be. "Welcome, Captain, Johannes. Come in; bring your lights. Don't mind my brother; he's a little nervous about the sun."

A gust of heated air swept around the two men standing on the doorstep. Balthasar reached out with a shaky burst of sonn. The younger had the build of a man who labored for a living and the clothing of one who did no more than subsist by it: his vest was sleeveless and his trousers ended in a ragged hem. He wore thick-soled sandals with heavy, close lacing. His only adornment was a knot-work bracelet on one wrist. The older man was lean and supple, and Bal's sonn picked out the indistinct texture of fine, soft lace in his sleeves and leggings. He carried a rapier and a pistol on his belt, and the fluid balance of his movements reminded Bal of one of the Rivermarch enforcers who was also a fencing master; it was how he imagined Floria would move.

"Balthasar," Sebastien said airily, "fetch us some of that excellent beer."

"None for me," said the older man, gravel in his voice.

Lightborn would not accept food and drink from those they distrusted.

"Nor me," said the younger.

"Then come through to the sitting room."

"I'd as soon speak here," the older man said.

With the door open? Balthasar wondered. His mind was beginning to clear of the panic inspired by the threat of sunlight. He took in more details of their stance, their position—close to, within lunging reach of, the door. Their distrust could not have been plainer if they had shouted it.

"Balthasar, these gentlemen represent two of our allies, Captain Rupertis of the Palace Vigilance, and stonemason Johannes of the artisan's progressive movement. Gentlemen, my brother, Balthasar Hearne, Darkborn."

Heads turned toward him for a long moment. Was he so obviously Darkborn to sight? It must be so; Sebastien appeared pleased by their reactions. Then the older man turned his attention back to Sebastien, while the other continued to face Balthasar. The self-styled progressive movement demanded revolution and the formation of a republic, and simultaneously rejected all forms of technological innovation, especially Darkborn. They were marginal, but not as marginal as Balthasar would have preferred. But Rupertis... He knew Rupertis by name, as one of the several watch captains of the Palace Vigilance. A captain of the Prince's Vigilance, suborned or ensorcelled... What did that mean for Floria?

"Now," said Sebastien, with Lysander's smile, "what have you to tell me?"

"Why didn't you tell us that you planned an attack on the tower itself?" Rupertis said.

"Why should we?" Sebastien said, folding his arms. "You didn't need to know."

The man's jaw tightened. "Well, here's something *you* need to know. Isidore's dead. Fejelis has disappeared. And the Lightborn now have a *princess*—Princess Perrin, ruling with the backing of the mages. Your shells *didn't* kill the archmage *or* the head of the Temple Vigilance. And they've taken over. Is that what you wanted?"

Sebastien's smile had faded. "Who's Perrin?"

"Isidore's and Helenja's eldest daughter. She showed at ten as a mage and was taken into the Temple."

Sebastien shrugged. "Not a problem, as we've told you before."

"Are you sure? Perrin's a sport—born outside the Temple lineages. Fejelis claimed that lineage mages can't sense your type of magic, but sports can."

"That's impossible," Sebastien said, voice rising. "Lightborn can't sense our type of magic."

"You'd better hope they can't," Rupertis said, flatly. "Fejelis contracted with a sport mage, name of Tammorn, perpetually on the outs with the Temple, but strong. Fejelis claimed the shells that hit the tower were ensorcelled, and the sports dealt with them."

Sebastien's breathing was quick and shallow. "It didn't happen that way."

There was a grim satisfaction in the set of the man's lips, hearing, as Balthasar heard, the wavering. "Fejelis put this to the archmage and high masters, in front of their brightnesses. They didn't like that, I could tell you. Prasav made a play for Fejelis's deposition, right there and then—had to, I figure, since if Fejelis had made the contract with the mages he was asking for, we'd never have shifted him—and the high masters stood aside when we drew on Fejelis. Cursed shame, I thought, but I had my orders." From his tone, one would never know that he spoke of the murder of a nineteen-year-old man. "That sport mage of Fejelis's swatted the quarrels aside and *lifted* himself, Fejelis, *and* Orlanjis out of there. If the mages know where he took 'em, they're not saying."

He waited for a reaction, and then said, dangerously, to Balthasar's ear, "But it doesn't actually matter to you who is prince, does it?"

Sebastien, too, heard that undertone. "Of course it matters," he said quickly. "That was the agreement: we help deal with Isidore and with Fejelis, and leave the way clear for Prasav. We'll help deal with Perrin and the mages. They're lying; they're hurt."

"Was it Beaudry's own plan to quench himself after he put a crossbow bolt through Fejelis?" Rupertis said. "We found his residue bundled up in a black tarpaulin. He didn't even try to get away."

"I don't . . . ," Sebastien began, and checked himself. "I didn't order him to do that."

"Floria White Hand is still alive," Rupertis said. "Fejelis put a warrant out on her himself, sooner than we expected. We sent a team after her, but the woman's as sharp as her rapier. She cut through the screen into her Darkborn neighbor's house. Got out that way—" His face swung toward Balthasar. "*That's* where I've heard the name. So you're part of this, too."

"*No*," Balthasar said, fiercely; that much the ensorcellment did not forbid. "Never of my own free will."

The captain's face clenched, as if he heard an accusation. "You'd understand better if your rulers had beggared you with taxes to pay mages to protect them against other mages. My family used to have lands and a name—his did, too." He gave another jerk of the head toward Johannes. "We were bled white by taxes from our lord and by our own Temple contracts. We turned vigilant, hired swords, but decades of service, decades of practice . . ." He flexed his sword hand. "We're no more than glorified footmen, hired for a show of wealth, because earthborn are *cheap*, and when the money finally runs out, we'll slip another step down toward begging in the streets."

From his council service, Balthasar knew the price that the Lightborn had ultimately paid, both for the original compact with the mages and for their own murderous customs. By the compact, mages could not use magic against earthborn in their own interests, but could be contracted to do so by earthborn—and thereby indemnified of the consequences. Over time, as the tradition of deposition of heads of houses established itself, anyone at risk must contract with the temple for their protection, against threats both magical and secular. Now, after hundreds of years, much of the wealth of the princedom resided not in the hands of the prince and their brightnesses, but in the hands of the mages, who had much less interest in employing earthborn. And every year the number of starving in the provinces and vagrants in the city increased.

"Isidore tried to fix it, but he's been bled white, too." A grim smile. "They're all fussing about the prince's caul having gone with Fejelis, but the thing's no more than wire and glass. Some of our lineage turned jewelers, and I have their word on it. Prasav is the only one who's been able to hold on to his wealth; he seemed the best bet, the best gamble, for those of us who'd rather not be eating the garbage from the streets."

"I have served several terms on the Intercalatory Council; we know, as much as anyone can know on the far side of sunset, how it is with you. What"—another question for which he did not want to know the answer—"was the warrant for Floria—Mistress White Hand—for?"

"The deposition of Isidore. Fejelis said she'd been ensorcelled to take a talisman to the prince's rooms, a talisman that would annul the lights around it."

"*No*," whispered Balthasar. "She served him all her adult life—"

"Tasted every dish he ate," the captain confirmed. "Closer than a wife, to Helenja's ire."

For a long moment, ensorcellment or no, Balthasar simply hated the Shadowborn. How many people's loyalty, how many people's despair, had they used to craft their way to power? For their design was power, he had no doubt of that. They did not care which Lightborn became prince, because their aim was their own ascendancy. Did Rupertis know what he worked for?

Johannes spoke for the first time, his voice suffused with anger. "We've got the Prince's Vigilance out on the streets. We'll have mages' vigilant investigating, and assets questioning. Tempe Silver Branch is questioning the people arrested in front of the railway station. No one can lie to her."

"That's their problem," Sebastien said. "If they were stupid enough to get caught. You *said* you wanted a revolution. What's that song you sing?" He affected a nasal, though true-pitched tone. *"Streets running with blood and fire."*

"There was a servant with Isidore when the lights went out," Johannes ground out. "Nobody cares about *him*—it's all Isidore, Isidore—but he was my cousin, one of *us*! You're no better than the rest, you callous bastard." His hand went to his knife—and was enveloped in flame as the scabbard and pommel caught fire. Rupertis slashed with his dagger at the ties on the sash, yanked them, let the scabbard fall with a clatter of metal and a scattering of ash. Even in those few seconds, the blaze had almost completely consumed the leather.

Johannes slowly folded to his knees, holding out his burned hand before him.

Balthasar started to go to him, but Rupertis spoke, and the tone of his voice made him pause. "Fejelis said something else. He gave a name to the magic and to the people who practiced it: Shadowborn."

Sebastien was breathing quickly, suppressed glee and horror in his expression. "Shadowborn are a Darkborn myth."

"Moving from dark to light," Rupertis said, half to himself. "Ensorcelling men, burning—" Balthasar took a step forward. Ever after, he would be uncertain whether it was his professional instinct to defuse conflict or an impulse born of the ensorcellment to draw Rupertis's attack on himself. He was too late for anything more. Rupertis's rapier came from its scabbard like a breath driven out by a blow. Sebastien fell backward with a screamed, *"Stop!"* but Rupertis had already started to uncoil in a lunge, as oblivious to command as a falling boulder. Sebastien shrieked a word or a curse, and the captain's body exploded into flame of such intensity that Balthasar threw his arms up to shield his face. He heard the man's last breath roar out in agony. The blazing corpse dropped to the tiles with a meaty crunch that—like the sizzle of meat and fat, like the stench, like the postmortem spasms as muscles cooked—Balthasar knew he would be revisiting in his nightmares. The blade clattered to the tiles and broke.

Too late, far too late, Sebastien cried, "Stop!" and the flames went out.

Johannes staggered to his feet, eyes bulging with horror. He backed away, one step, two, three, stumbled backward and through the door, colliding with the lintel without a cry. Sebastien did not appear to notice his leaving. "He made me do it!" he cried.

Balthasar, repelled though he was by the sentiment, could not entirely disagree. Perhaps death had been Rupertis's intent; perhaps it was simply a risk he had accepted in trying to kill the young mage.

"I've never burned a *man* before," Sebastien blurted, still facing the body of the man he had killed. "I'm not a monster. I'm not. They said I'd be if I stayed. Just like they said."

Balthasar swallowed. "It was a reflex," he said, and before the boy could seize too hard on that as exoneration, he said, softly but sternly, "But if you are going to use your magic to defend yourself, you *must* learn different ways to do it."

Sebastien turned on him. "How am I supposed to learn?"

"Neill seemed willing to teach you."

"*She'd* stop him. *She* doesn't want me taught."

He was tired of pronouns and circumlocutions. "Was your mother the one who warned you about becoming a monster? A powerful mage needs training, or even with the best will, he can do great harm."

"None of *them* want to teach me. Save Neill, and *she's* got him so ensorcelled—"

"Sebastien," Balthasar said, "what do you want? *You*, not Emeya."

"It doesn't matter what I want."

"Your mother and father got away from her."

"They left me behind."

"You *chose* to stay behind, you said. I doubt, with your strength, they could have taken you against your will. But I don't think you know what you chose then. You know better now."

The boy did not answer, his face sullen. *"Smell, Sebastien,"* Balthasar said, almost in a whisper. "Is this what you want to be?"

Sebastien's throat worked on a suppressed gag. "I *hate* you."

Balthasar flinched, but said steadily, "You ensorcelled me to care, and therefore I must care if you court destruction. From what Captain Rupertis said, someone did counteract the ensorcellment on the shells. You felt that last night."

"I *know* it worked. I *felt it*."

Balthasar was courting destruction himself now. The boy need not call fire to burn him, not with the door open to daylight. "If you make the Temple come for you, they will destroy you. If you go to them now, they may spare you. You have a form of magic new to them, and if you can prove that you were acting under the influence of another, then their laws may protect you." He could not convince himself that it was a certainty, even under Lightborn law. Yet he was certain that if the boy continued on this course, it would be to his own end. Under Darkborn law, Sebastien would be condemned to death for sorcery. If nothing else, if he had fathered Tercelle's twins, he was guilty of sorcerous seduction.

"You don't believe that," Sebastien said dully. "You think they're going to kill me."

"You haven't been taught what you need to know," Balthasar said, "about magic and about morality. I would make them understand that."

Sebastien stood a moment longer, head turning from the charred and reeking corpse to Balthasar and back.

"You do not have to do this," Balthasar said.

Sebastien suddenly straight-armed him, hand to the chest, making him stagger. "Be quiet. Go back to your room. You're not turning me against her. You *can't*."

Floria

Floria raced sunset across the bridge. Conspicuous to hurry, and risky to go straight, but what else to do with the time she had? As it was, she would have to return after dark, under the archduke's proclamation granting the Lightborn part of the night, and hope to make it back before anyone thought to look for her—whether with benign or malevolent intent.

Breathlessness forced her to slow from a sprint and then to a jog. Her ribs ached; her throat was raw. She was still feeling the effects of being nearly drowned in the fountain outside Bolingbroke Station. Up on the crowded hill of New Town, sun warmed red walls and white roofs. To her left was Darkborn land, the estate of Duke Kalamay, and the raw, brown wound of the mages' retribution and the explosion of the guns and stored munitions that had carried away half the hill. Nestled in deep shadow, the house itself still stood untouched, but the sky above it was smudged with smoke from outbuildings near the crest of the hill. The last time she had crossed this bridge, there had been smoke in the air, too, the smoke of the burning Rivermarch.

She glanced down at the dock below the estate; it was intact. If the occupants of the estate were wise, they would leave later tonight. Fejelis had today put almost every vigilant at his command on the streets to protect Darkborn, but she would be surprised if Perrin extended the order tomorrow, so she doubted Kalamay's grand house would be standing by tomorrow night. Mycene's estates were in the country, in Darkborn lands, but pity help the city household that had had him as a guest, if the rioters knew.

As she reached the far side of the bridge, on the road approaching, she met a party of two dozen guardsmen and -women. They looked like they'd had a long, hard afternoon, and were dusty, weary, cut, bruised, and carrying three of their number on stretchers. "Mistress?" one called, though it was a hail, not a challenge.

Barely checking stride, she rasped, "Nothing for you, unless one of you's a midwife."

They shifted to let her pass, with weary well-wishes. There was more than one gray or balding head with experienced eyes in it, who might well think to ask a few questions about a fair, running woman with her particular collection of bruises, dressed for court and armed for trouble. It would be too much to hope that her rash stand in front of the railway station would not be one of the stories told in the barracks tonight.

Worry about that later. Up the hill she ran, feeling every stride in the center of her chest. The bundled lights in her backpack bounced on her shoulders. She had her hand on Tam's gate when she thought to wonder what kind of talismans and protections he kept around his house. Would they recognize her as a friend in his absence? What if he had thought to ensorcell them against Shadowborn magic, including the ensorcellment that still lingered about her?

From the house there came an infant's screech: Tam's daughter had a voice proportioned to her will. *Nothing else but to take the risk.* She eased cautiously through the gate. No unseen barrier stopped her, no sudden weakness collapsed her, no roar of thunder met her. She padded across the garden, trying to steady her breathing enough that her voice would sound normal. Beatrice was wary of her at the best of times.

Her pull on the doorbell elicited a sweet carillon and a clamor of, "Mama, mama, mama, atta*door*, *attadoor*." There was a thud, as of a small body striking the door, and Floria winced. For some, "head-on" was not merely a metaphor.

The viewing hatch opened; Beatrice's pale face floated in its frame. "Floria?"

"Issadaddy?" the unseen child demanded.

"Let me in," she said. "Please."

"Tam's not here."

"I know. And I know when and how he left the city. Will you just let me in?"

Beatrice closed the hatch. Floria drew her stiletto—if the woman would not let her in, then she would force an entry—and pushed it quickly back into its sheath as she heard the bolt slide back. The door opened slowly. Beatrice stooped to keep a hand on her son's collar, her posture wary. Disappointment filled his upturned face and eyes at the sight of her. "Isnadaddy."

A crash behind her made Beatrice whirl, releasing the boy. The red-haired baby, propped up in a chair, had hurled a wooden toy onto the tiles, and was glaring at Floria. She could feel the little boy trying to squirm past her legs.

"Is there someone who can take the children while we talk?"

"Have you come to tell me he's dead?" Beatrice said tensely.

Tam would surely not have left her uncertain of his survival after the tower was destroyed. "He's not dead. But he's in trouble. Do you have anyone you can go to for the night—someone you know who would shelter you?"

The baby screeched. Beatrice moved to collect her while her son mounted an assault on the door. "Did he send you?"

"Tam *lifted* out of here with Fejelis and Orlanjis, saving Fejelis from deposition. Helenja has Sharel trying to find where he might have taken them, which means learning more about Tam. It won't take her long to learn about you."

Beatrice's lips pinched. The southerners' reputation in New Town was dismal; they were loud, reckless, destructive in their entertainment, and careless in making reparations. They had disrupted more than one market with their rumpus, and while more lay behind the failure of Beatrice's family business than a single stall full of broken crockery, Beatrice's thoughts about southerners were far from charitable. "It's too late to go anywhere now," she said.

"There's to be a meeting between their brightnesses and the Darkborn court, and an hour after sunset the bells are to be rung to allow their brightnesses to travel to the meeting place. The Darkborn will keep to their houses. You can move then."

"I never—"

"It's not common knowledge. We don't want any mischief done under its cover. We'll not meet anyone in New Town."

And if we do, she resolved, *I will deal with them.*

"I don't think—No." Her fine lips set. "*If* I decide to go, I'll go first thing tomorrow."

"And if the southerners come for you tonight? They're used to the desert, used to traveling by night."

"I'm not taking the children out on your word alone, Mistress Floria," she said, narrowly. "For one thing, I hardly think it will help us to make our way to safety if my son and daughter scream in terror the whole time. I thank you for your concern, and I will act on it if I choose."

This was the woman who had refused Tam for nearly five years, though he was as decent a man and besotted a lover as anyone could ask. And she had a point about the children and the noise they would make. Floria might have been able to concoct a potion, even from household herbs, to sedate the children; if she hadn't had water on the brain as well as in the ears, she would have *brought* a potion.

"All right," she said. "When you go, don't take any talismans with you that Tam made. Nothing, not even protection or toys for the children." Some of Tam's uses of magic were playful and inventive. "Mages would be able to trace you through them." She wondered whether to mention that the Temple might be taking a renewed interest in Tam's lineage, given the strength he had shown. If they were, there was probably very little any earthborn could do, and they, at least, would treat the children well.

She had her hand on the door when she heard the sunset bell begin to ring. The first hour of the night was for the Darkborn. She turned back, ignoring the resentful expression chased off Beatrice's face. "Make yourself at home, Mistress White Hand. I must go and put the children to bed."

That was a ritual that would occupy her for the better part of the next hour, Floria suspected. She made her way through into the social room and sat down on one of the long couches. Her first glance had already measured the room and eliminated all threat in it; now she studied the brightly painted tiles mounted on the walls and in brackets in alcoves, Beatrice's former livelihood. In the corner was a clay sculpture, a tree with coiled and twisted roots and huge, enameled copper leaves. The tree drew her eye and made her uneasy. It suggested turmoil, unhappiness. Though when she had said as much to Tam, he had laughed and said she did not understand artists. Being a mage, he could not avoid knowing what his lover felt, that she liked him well enough, but she did not love him—though he could be consoled that she loved no one else better.

She was hardly one to judge the bargains others made, she who frequented the vigilants' house of companions, when she felt the need. Perhaps it was time to engage a matchmaker, as more than one of her relatives had suggested, and cease to be so choosy. Or accept that the priceless magical asset against poisons she had inherited from her father would pass to one of her cousins or their children.

Old thoughts; useless thoughts. Better to spend her time thinking what else to tell Beatrice that would make the woman move the moment the sun came up.

Balthasar

Sitting in the room, resting as best he could, Balthasar listened to the sunset bell and then to the voices in the vestibule beneath. This time, Sebastien's informants were Darkborn; he was sure of it, though he could not hear the words. The ensorcellment would not permit him to leave the room. Presently, he heard the door beneath close, and feet come quickly up the stairs. The door gusted open, slamming back against the wardrobe behind it. "You!" The carpet around him burst into flame. Balthasar scrambled into a crouch on the cushion of the chair.

"You didn't tell me about your *wife*!" Sebastien shouted, in Lysander's voice.

Balthasar started to stand, and then realized that standing would place him above the full heat of the blaze. "No," he said, more faintly than he would have liked. "I didn't."

"You ought to have. She was a danger to me! She helped murder Jonquil." That last seemed to turn his anger more calculating. "Well, it doesn't matter." It wasn't just the shimmy of the flames that distorted his face, Balthasar realized. His voice completed its shift toward the boy's. "Your wife's *dead*."

The edge of the cushion was catching. "Put out the flames, please," he said, arm shielding his face.

Sebastien quenched the flames with a sweep of the hand, his expression ugly. *"Did you hear what I said?"*

"I did," said Balthasar. He took a precious moment to compose himself, and stepped down and over the scorched carpet. "I have no reason to believe you."

Sebastien's hands closed into fists. "She tried to use *our* magic and lost control. She nearly killed the archduke, and then she came back to heal him, and they captured her and he had her executed. They put her in a room with a skylight and opened the skylight."

That made two of three implausible statements. The only one believable was that if Sejanus Plantageter were hurt, Telmaine would try to help. "As I said, I have no reason to—" And he remembered what Ishmael had sensed from Telmaine while they were in Stranhorne, and what Stranhorne's son had telegraphed to his father. And that the archduke, judicious ruler though he might be, had a profound distrust of magic. That was enough for the ensorcellment. An abyss of belief and despair gaped beneath him.

The boy's hands loosened their clench, and his lips eased into a smirk. That was worse; that was Lysander's smile of considered cruelty. "You *ought* to have told me," he said. "I'd have been able to save her."

"She would never give in to you. And I refuse . . . to believe she is dead."

"Believe it," the boy said.

At the words, the ensorcellment twisted inside him, trying to tear out his hope, tear out his heart, tear out his love. It wrung a sound from him that was midway between a gasp and a groan, the sound of a man who had taken a mortal injury. There was no argument reason could make against the imposed conviction that Telmaine was dead. "I *will not*," he said, strangled. "I will not."

"Tidy yourself up," he heard the boy say, dismissively. "We've a visit to make."

His body moved, somehow. He wondered that a man could endure so much pain and still live. He could barely draw breath for it; he found himself leaning, dizzied, against the side of the wardrobe.

Promise me, Telmaine had said, as they began to reckon the danger they were in, *that if anything does happen to me . . . promise me you will still live for, love, and care for the children.*

Their daughters, who were sheltering with Telmaine's formidable elder sister. Florilinde, who had a fascination with all things mechanical, and little, strong-willed Amerdale, whose sixth birthday was a mere two weeks away, and whose one immovable desire was for a kitten of her own.

Amerdale will not have her birthday in a city ruled by Shadowborn. Whatever had happened to Telmaine; whatever happened to *him.* Balthasar pushed himself away from the wardrobe. His hands sought the pouch of bottles he had taken from the medicine chest and obstetrical kit the night before. He remembered the pleading *Don't leave me* from the night before and set the thought, *Chloroform, for painless surgery* first and foremost in his thoughts as he wrapped the small bottle of chloroform and pushed it into his pocket. *Morphine, for the relief of pain,* and a syringe, in the other pocket. He did not count himself as religious—it had always seemed to him that religion was a product of psychological frailty as well as a triumph of imagination—but now that he stood face-to-face with his own psychological frailty, he whispered a prayer as he rose: that he be given the moment he needed, the opportunity he needed, for he surely could not choose.

He followed the boy, once more in his Lysander form, down the steps, to the tolling of a warning bell. Sebastien had said the night had been ceded to the Lightborn to allow their brightnesses to travel to negotiations. The air that brushed his skin felt like night air, just after sunset, though with Sebastien's ensorcellment on him, he did not suppose it mattered whether it was night or day. Nothing much mattered. Not the tolling bell, not the eerie, huddled quiet of the city beneath it. He heard no voices from the streets, no carriage wheels, no horses, not even any machinery. Only the wind stirred. Sebastien said, disgruntled, "There aren't any coaches. I don't want to waste myself *lifting*."

He is afraid, Balthasar thought, insight penetrating his dullness. He roused himself. "Where . . . are we going?"

"Your council chambers. The Lightborn princess—whoever she is—and her nobility. They're *all* going there to meet the archduke and his council."

Balthasar forced himself to pay attention to the undertones of that gloating. He said, quietly, "You do not have to do this."

The boy in his brother's shape halted and swung on him. "Do *what*?"

"Whatever you are planning to do—" No, that was weak. "Kill the archduke, kill the princess—is that it?"

"You don't think I *can* do it? I'm a strong mage."

"Yes," Balthasar said. "I think you are entirely capable of it."

"Good."

"I also think you do not understand what you are doing. But for me to make you understand—for me to even start to make you understand—between here and the council chambers is quite beyond my capacity."

The admission stirred a vague impulse of alarm. He needed to care—he needed something to use against the ensorcellment. "Tercelle's children—they *are* yours, aren't they? Truthfully?"

"You don't think I'm old enough?" Sebastien challenged.

No, thought Balthasar; he had been nearly ten years Sebastien's elder, and still not old enough, when the midwife set Florilinde in his hands. She had thoroughly disapproved of him, he recalled. Telmaine had told him later that she had been outraged to have a husband underfoot who fancied he knew *something* about childbirth. He stopped with a gasp, remembering her laughter. It felt as though he had just scraped a scalpel across the raw wound of her loss. "Did you feel anything—anything at all—for Tercelle Amberley?"

Sebastien caught him by the arm and swung him around, wrenching aching muscles. "I *loved* her, stupid! She was so beautiful. The way she spoke, the way she held her head, her grace—she wasn't like the women where . . . where I come from. It was just once, for me and her, the first time I ever . . .

I didn't expect . . . I didn't think about . . . I didn't even know she was pregnant. I couldn't even look for her because Jonquil would have known. And it was all for *nothing*. Jonquil had her killed. When I felt him die, *I danced*. And if anything's happened to my sons because of you, you'll die—*horribly*." He spun and started running, slowing to a walk halfway down the block. He might have been sobbing. But if he had been, he was composed again when Balthasar caught up with him.

Balthasar considered and rejected several questions, among them whether the men who had nearly beaten him to death had been sent by Jonquil or Sebastien himself. "What . . . would you like to do after this is over?"

"What do you mean?"

"I mean, once you have done what has been laid upon you to do," Balthasar said, choosing his words carefully. "What will you do then, if you had a choice?"

"Get away," Sebastien said, head down. "Take my sons and . . . live far away from people. I'd set magical talismans all around, so that no one would approach, and if anyone dared, I'd raise storms and lightning. I'd build a house for them, out of stone and earth. We'd eat fruit and berries, and we'd raise oats and barley and potatoes, but not lettuce—I hate lettuce. And meat. We'd collect stones—beautiful stones—and make mosaics. You're laughing at me."

"No," Balthasar said. "No, I'm not."

Perhaps he did not entirely keep the sadness from his voice, for Sebastien halted. "You didn't believe all that, did you? *That's* where I'm really going to live."

Balthasar oriented himself to Sebastien's grand gesture and the direction, and realized he must be pointing at the Lightborn palace. "I've heard it's very beautiful inside," he said, "though much of the beauty is in the colors, and would be wasted on such as myself."

Sebastien stared at him. "Would you *like* to *see*?" he said, unexpectedly. Balthasar tried to conceal his sudden dread that the boy was about to turn his magic on him. "Doesn't the dark . . ." His voice suddenly trailed off, but Balthasar heard, quite clearly, *frighten you?*

"I was born in darkness," Balthasar said, mildly.

"You nearly wet yourself when I opened the door."

"So would you have," Balthasar said, "if you'd known your whole life that sunlight would burn you to ash. . . . I wish I understood magic better, to know how you were keeping me from burning. It's an . . . exceptional thing. Your people must understand the Curse very well."

"Yeah," Sebastien said, "we do."

The Intercalatory Council Chambers were just within the boundaries of one of the newer Darkborn districts, small row houses occupied by the homes and offices of minor civil servants and not-yet-established professionals. Had he married according to his station, he might well have had his first home there. A couple of streets away was the start of an equally modest Lightborn district that for two or three hundred years had been home to Lightborn artisans, artists, and craftsmen. He liked to believe both districts had prospered in unexpected ways from their proximity. The outer walls of the council chamber had been plastered smooth, so that the Lightborn could paste posters, which offered the people's commentary on politics and society. He could rely on Floria to describe those that his colleagues on the council were too politic to translate.

He set a hand on the wall as they approached the steps, and felt damp, lumpy paper. The lumps compressed as he pushed at them: fresh paste, hastily applied. And then his hand brushed something tacky, and he caught the smell of blood. He halted, midstride, the memory of those hours in surgery coming back to him. Sebastien, on the stairs, turned. "What is— Ugh! Leave it! Leave it. Nasty thing."

"What—"

"Leave it! It's vile!"

Balthasar pulled a handkerchief from his pocket and wiped his hands, keeping his mind closed to the stickiness. Sebastien rattled the handle. "They're locked!" He threw his weight against the doors, unavailing. "I'll have to burn through!"

"No!" cried Balthasar, remembering the stench of smoke rolling out from the gaping wall of Stranhorne. "I know where there's a key."

Distrustfully, Sebastien watched as Balthasar hoisted himself up to the lowest rank of gargoyle. Floria had been appalled when she learned about it—why, she demanded, didn't they just leave the door unlocked? His groping hand found the key, spilling it onto the paving stones with a clatter.

Sebastien simply stared at it, while Balthasar slithered down, collecting moss on his borrowed formals. "Tradition," he explained, as he bent stiffly to collect the key.

Sebastien stood at his shoulder as Balthasar plied the key and pushed the door open. Deep in the building, a bell rang, and Sebastien started. "What's that?"

"The council works day and night—it's best someone's warned when the door is opened."

"You didn't tell me." He caught Balthasar's arm. "Do they keep explosives here, too?"

"I don't know any reason for them to."

"You'll die, too," the boy threatened.

"I might count that a mercy," Balthasar said, and cursed himself for the indulgence. He said, more quietly, "We don't have to go in."

"Yes, we do."

He opened the inner door, and found himself caught by the sonn of half a dozen armed men of the archduke's guard. Instead of the pistols that formed part of their usual ceremonial regalia, they held revolvers as modern and, he had no doubt, deadly, as Ishmael's.

Sebastien jarred up against him, catching his arm. "What is it? It's dark." Belatedly, he used sonn, and caught his breath.

Balthasar croaked, "Wait!" What inspiration might have come to him, he would never know. A door flew open at the end of the hall, and a compact, handsome man built like an athlete threw himself out to confront them, followed a step behind by his own sister.

"Lysander!" Olivede cried out.

"No!" the man said. *"Shadowborn."*

Bal recognized Phineas Broome, the fourth-rank mage who was one of the coleaders of the commune that Olivede belonged to. "Kill them!" shouted Phineas.

And Balthasar heard the thunder of revolver fire from behind him as Sebastien *lifted* both of them the length of the hall. Shouts, an explosion. His wild backward cast of sonn caught the guards as they spilled aside, thrown or throwing themselves away from a figure who was simply falling amidst a feathery echo that Balthasar knew as spurting blood. He started back down the hall in trained response, and behind him he heard Phineas Broome groan deep in his throat. The mage stood with arms outspread as though to bar the door, face contorted with extreme effort, the muscles in his neck like ropes. The smell of smoke thickened the air, though Balthasar did not know where from. He gasped, "No, Sebastien. *Remember how it smelled!*"

A backlash of heat seared his face as Sebastien fleetingly wavered and the weaker mage prevailed. And then Phineas cried out and fire flashed up his clothing, from trouser cuff to collar. The door to the main chamber slammed open and a revolver boomed. Sebastien lurched; the flame unwrapped from Phineas like a cloak, and then Balthasar heard a man's mortal scream, felt the heat, and heard and smelled, for the second time, a man being incinerated alive by Shadowborn fires.

In the move he had rehearsed in his mind a dozen times, he pulled cloth and bottle from his pocket; twisted out the plug; dropped it, freeing his hands to sluice the chloroform onto the cloth; and discarded the bottle in turn. He caught Sebastien around the chest, clamped the rag across his mouth and nose, and held him with all his strength in a travesty of an embrace. He could feel, against his wrist, the warmth of the boy's blood. In Sebastien's ear he rasped his half-deranged babble of justification: *"I can't let you do this. I can't let you destroy yourself. You would destroy yourself. It is because I care for you that I am doing this, because you demanded I care. . . ."*

The boy wailed something unintelligible, muffled by the rag. Bone and muscle rippled and swelled beneath his arm; claws dug into his wrist. Heat mounted around him; he could smell the acrid stench of singed wool and hair, and pressed his face to Sebastien's neck, praying that the mage could not turn the fires on them both. With one last uncoordinated rake at his hand, Sebastien slumped against him. Balthasar half collapsed, half guided him down to the floor, and then squirmed urgently out of his smoldering jacket. In unconsciousness, Sebastien had shed his borrowed form, and Balthasar, panicked by the memory of the Shadowborn who had transformed as he died, tore open his collar until he had exposed the bleeding wound at the join of neck and shoulder, and sonned the pulse in his throat. *"Olivede,"* he said, *"help me."*

"Busy," she gasped, from inside the council chamber. *"Sweet Imogene—"*

He heard, then, a pistol hammer being drawn back. He dropped forward onto his hands, shielding the unconscious body. Two men dragged him to his feet, their expressions murderous. Both wore the livery of the Duke of Mycene. "No," he shouted, trying to struggle free, as a third man went down on one knee and laid his revolver behind Sebastien's ear.

And then, blessedly, the archduke's voice cut through it all. "Hold."

The moment teetered; Balthasar sonned the tension in the finger that rested on the trigger. Then one of the men who held him rasped, "Aaron, wait. This is too cursed quick."

Balthasar felt, more than heard, a growl of approval from the gathered men.

Olivede said, breathlessly, "Please, someone give me a hand here—"

Of Phineas Broome, he could sonn only his booted feet. The archduke gave some quiet orders; someone in the rear ranks dragged him clear.

"Balthasar Hearne," the archduke said.

"My lord archduke." The expression on the archduke's face killed his last hope that Sebastien had lied. He could not imagine any other reason why he should sonn shame as well as raw-nerved suspicion on that face.

At his feet, Sebastien moaned. Revolvers leveled. Balthasar crouched and held the chloroform-soaked rag over Sebastien's nose until the boy stopped twitching. He could not even say "I'm sorry," in case regret weakened him fatally. "I'm going to stop the bleeding," he said, asking no one's permission.

"Explain, please," said the archduke, "how you come to be here? Who is this . . . boy?"

"I have heard," Balthasar ground out, "what happened to my wife." He went on before anyone could speak. "Whether I shall ever"—*forgive* would have been the honest word, if not the most politic—"reconcile to it is . . . a question for another day. I am still a servant of the state, still *your* servant. But this boy is my brother's son, and I claim his life."

No one questioned his assertion, but, then, the proof was there in the resemblance. Nor did they respond to his claim. It was enough for the moment that they not interfere. He opened the boy's jacket and shirt to expose the narrow, childish chest, pulled off his own shirt, and tore strips from it to make a compress and bind it down. It was awkward, clumsy work, but he got it done.

"Lysander was living among the Shadowborn," he said as he worked. "He fathered a child by a Shadowborn mage. There are at least two factions of Shadowborn. Lysander and his wife fled from one to the other, but they did not succeed in taking their son. I first met him, though I did not know it, at Strumheller Crosstracks; he arrived in the guise of a member of Mycene's troop. In Stranhorne . . . do you know that Stranhorne was overrun by Shadowborn?" Stark, and not the way to break such news, but he was past delicacy.

"We do. The details are scant and we don't have time; the Lightborn should be here very soon, unless it pleases them to make us wait. Go on."

"With the help of another mage who survived the destruction of the manor, he brought me here."

"As what? His collaborator or his captive?"

"His captive." He paused to wind a strip of bandage around his wrist, and from his pocket fumbled the morphine and syringe. He cleaned his hands as best he could, and with still-tacky fingers he filled the syringe and used his knife to slit Sebastien's sleeve and expose the thin arm.

Sebastien moaned and rolled his head weakly. Balthasar placed the tourniquet, braced his arm, slipped the needle into the vein, and injected the drug. He released the tourniquet and hung over the boy until sure his breathing was steady. He could hear men moving past him, three men carrying another, and Olivede giving steady instructions despite the strain in her voice, to the accompanying drone of a prayer from Duke Kalamay.

"You seem most concerned for someone who has held you captive," the archduke observed.

"The boy is sixteen at most, and has been cruelly used," Balthasar said. "Ill taught—fire and shape-changing seem to be the magic he knows best. The other mage, the one Ishmael di Studier killed at Vladimer's bedside, was the elder and the dominant partner."

"You will have to keep him drugged," the archduke said, "and if that does not kill him, and he does not die of thirst or hunger, we shall—"

For almost the first time ever, he heard Sejanus Plantageter fail to complete a sentence. He was glad of it: his desperate accommodation with the ensorcellment would not survive a threat of execution for sorcery. He shuddered, the ensorcellment racking him. "I know," he gasped, "that this situation cannot pertain indefinitely."

"Indeed," said the archduke, grimly. "The situation will assuredly change, and possibly not for the better. Let me be plain: is your will your own?"

"As long as I believe that I am acting in *his* interest"—a desperate belief, held fast, despite accumulating evidence of harm—"then I believe my acts will be my own. I am quite certain that permitting him to continue on his planned course would only lead to his destruction."

"So ensorcellment is amenable to solipsism."

"He is a *boy*, Your Grace, uneducated, unsophisticated, abandoned, and abused. He has the emotional maturity of a young child. He demanded first of all that I love him as I love my own children—impossible, but it gave me latitude to act for him as a father would. As his father," he said harshly, "*should* have."

Sejanus Plantageter pinched the bridge of his nose. "I am under the impression that the Lightborn could not sense this ensorcellment," he said, slowly. "Thus your acquaintance, Floria White Hand, was able to deliver the ensorcelled talisman to the prince's room."

Balthasar realized a beat too late that the statement had been a test of what he himself knew, and his reaction had betrayed him. "I was not thinking . . . about that, Your Grace. About other things, but not that."

"Mistress Floria was, I understand, quite unaware of her own ensorcellment. That was why I permitted your wife to be condemned to death. I had no other way of being certain that my mind was my own."

Balthasar said, in a voice that shook with repressed feeling, *"You were wrong."*

There was a silence. "I am truly sorry," the archduke said, and his face twisted as he heard his own words. "I said that to your wife—"

"Wait," said Balthasar, forcing himself to reason through numbing grief. "Sebastien said . . . Sebastien said that none of the Lightborn could sense Shadowborn magic—he believed that no one could. But Ishmael di Studier could. Phineas Broome could—sense it and fight it. And when the attack was launched on the tower, Sebastien reacted as though the Lightborn had somehow counteracted or annulled it—"

"They demolished the gun emplacements."

"But there was also an ensorcellment on the munitions, Sebastien said, to make them . . . to increase their harmfulness. The boy's vitality had been used to support the magic—"

"Only that?" said the archduke, very still.

"I don't know," said Balthasar, "but I do know he suffered a seizure immediately after the emplacements were destroyed."

"Sejanus." Claudius Rohan, the archduke's closest counselor and friend, shouldered through the group of guards. "Sejanus, the Lightborn have arrived."

The archduke turned away, paused. "I'll spare the boy's life for the moment," he said, his back to Balthasar. "I will not promise more."

Telmaine

So this is life after the worst has happened, Telmaine Hearne thought, as the Borders-bound train rattled south across an uncertain landscape toward an uncertain end. Across the train compartment from her, an old man sat kindling a taper made of newspaper with the touch of his fingers, a delighted smile on his imp's face. Even with her inexperience, she could sense his magic delicately eliciting a fine rill of flame along the edge of the paper, like a feather stroking sand.

A feather plucked from a very dead bird, she amended. Farquhar Broome was himself Darkborn, but the magic he was toying with had originated with the Shadowborn themselves. And though Shadowborn magic did not actually smell, it left her with the unsettled conviction that she *had* smelled something thoroughly foul.

"Father," protested Phoebe Broome, but resignedly.

Her father quenched the flame with a belch of that nauseating magic, and held out the taper to Phoebe. "Try it, dear girl," he invited. "Just do as I did."

Dutifully, Phoebe took it. She was a tall, switch-thin woman several years older than Telmaine, her dress so plain as to be masculine, and her manner awkward and self-conscious—except when she forgot where she was and who her traveling companions were. Her father, too, was tall, of an indeterminate age, with a wizened-apple face that wrinkled into merriment at the least invitation. His suit and coat had to be at least four decades out of date. Had Telmaine encountered them under other circumstances, she would readily have typed them: difficult father with long-suffering daughter; he charming in his disregard of social convention, and she carrying a double burden of it. But had someone been so indelicate as to mention the name Broome to Lady Telmaine, the duke's daughter, she would have cut the speaker dead. Mages, even the leaders of the largest and best organized commune of mages in Minhorne, were not discussed in polite society.

And yet here she was, sharing a train compartment with Farquhar Broome, said to be the strongest living Darkborn mage, and his daughter. Here she was, a condemned sorceress, spared execution by the archduke's last-minute, secret orders, carried out by Vladimer with imaginative scrupulousness. Would anyone, even the archduke, know that that heap of ash in the execution room was not hers, with her own wedding rings and Balthasar's silver love knot cushioned on it?

She imagined some footman or courtier laying the jewelry in Balthasar's hand. She imagined her husband's face—imagined what she would sense if she touched him—and bit her gloved index finger until it hurt. She had not even dared leave Balthasar a message—save an oblique word to Floria White Hand, of all people, safe on the other side of sunrise and accomplished in keeping secrets—for fear she might compromise the ruse. But when would Floria be able to pass the word on, if she even would? How long would Balthasar think her dead, and what would he do in the meantime?

Phoebe Broome slipped her gloves from her long hands and laid the gloves aside, and then unwound a thin, controlled ribbon of magic, quenching the flame almost as soon as it came into being. Farquhar Broome beamed approval. "Not nearly as unpleasant when you do it yourself, is it, now?"

Phoebe smiled back, reluctantly. "No, Father."

Telmaine sank a little deeper into her seat, determined not to attract their attention. Earlier, she had demonstrated Shadowborn fire setting to them—having learned it, entirely against her will, from the Shadowborn themselves—but even her most tentative and careful coaxing had created a burst of flame that had instantly burned the taper to a strip of ash. She had just managed to quench it, leaving their compartment reeking with smoke.

That was not the worst. Across from her, Lord Vladimer

had jolted upright in his seat, snatching at his revolver. She had gone utterly still, terrified, knowing what he remembered: that catastrophic breakfast, Telmaine's uncontrolled fires blazing up around Vladimer's brother, the archduke. She herself remembered her dear friend Sylvide crying, "Lord Vladimer, no!" and throwing her arms around Telmaine just as Vladimer fired. He had been aiming at Telmaine—aiming to kill her magic with her—but with his right arm wounded and his aim unsteady, he had mortally wounded Sylvide instead.

After a moment, Vladimer deliberately removed his hand from his holster, his bony face a sick mask, pulse beating hard in his temple. He apologized to the Broomes for alarming them, and excused himself—to rest, he said, completely ignoring Phoebe Broome's efforts to ease the atmosphere or mind his comfort. The mage was as gauche as a provincial sixteen-year-old. *But, then,* Telmaine thought, *how should Miss Broome, mage and social outcast, know how to behave around a duke's daughter and the archduke's half brother?*

She heard Farquhar Broome tear another strip from the broadsheet and fold it, and sensed another pulse of Shadowborn magic. "Now, my dear"—Telmaine sonned him holding out the unlit taper to Phoebe—"try to set it off. No, don't take it; I'm not quite sure how vigorous—" The taper burst forth with a jet of flame several inches high; Farquhar Broome promptly dropped it. Magic leaped out from father and daughter and the taper was snuffed, leaving a scorched ring in the broadsheet. Farquhar Broome shook his fingers, then lifted the sheet and explored the hole.

"I wonder that they have not refined it," he said. "It should be possible. It's an intriguing approach to latency. I'm sure it could be applied in other areas."

It already has been, Telmaine thought. The murder of the Lightborn prince had been carried out with a talisman, spelled to annul the magical lights Lightborn needed to survive the night.

She sensed, passing between father and daughter, a ripple of magic, such as she had sensed passing between Phoebe and her brother, Phineas, when she had listened to—spied on—their conversation with Lord Vladimer. Then Phoebe got to her feet, politely excusing herself so she might check on the well-being of the fifteen or so mages who comprised the rest of their party. As though the group was not well able to communicate even through walls. Telmaine repressed a sour little smile. She could recognize an engineered opportunity.

Farquhar Broome turned his face toward her, his smile now only a memory in the lines of his face, though his expression was gentle. He was as circumspect in his use of sonn as Ish, she had noticed; perhaps magic substituted, or perhaps he was simply accustomed to other people taking care of him. "Dear lady," he said, "what a shock this must be to you."

Statements of the obvious were not confined merely to vapid society matrons, apparently. She said tightly, "I have lost my reputation, my place in society, and but for the archduke's clemency"—belated, secret, and ambivalent clemency—"I would have lost my life. I am well aware that with another man"—Duke Mycene, perhaps, or, Mother of All avert it, Duke Kalamay—"I *would* have lost my life. I don't deny what I did. I don't deny my responsibility."

He nodded, as though none of that took him by surprise. "It was a serious thing you did, and a brave thing in coming back. Your sureness in healing is remarkable, for a young woman who has kept down her magic for most of her life. With your strength, my dear, *someone* should have recognized what you are."

"I was always careful to stay away from mages," she said. Until Ishmael, who had guessed within minutes of meeting her. But, then, Ishmael did not allow prejudice to interfere with his perceptions, and *he* could hardly reject outright the notion of a nobly born mage. "My husband is a physician, and I had Ishmael's—Baron Strumheller's—guidance, too," she said, challengingly. Phoebe Broome had come close to expressing the sentiment that Ishmael was not a suitable preceptor for her.

"You do understand, dear girl, that you cannot go on in

this fashion. Your magic—well, it is like a ball gown. Once it is out of its box, then it will not be pushed back in again, not without violence to its fine fabric."

And what could a seventh-rank mage and a man know about ball gowns? But she understood. The magic she had kept tucked well within her skin was restive now. "I know I need to learn how to control it," she said.

He smiled his imp's grin. "And I believe you will do well."

Assuming, she thought, *we survive what we find in the Borders.*

As though one of his threads of ambient magic had snagged the thought, he said, "There is another painful matter I must bring up, dear lady. That nasty thing in your mind will give you no trouble in and of itself now, although had Ishmael been less timely and sure with those firearms of his, you would likely not be sitting here."

"That nasty thing" was a legacy of her battle with the first Shadowborn that had tried to kill Lord Vladimer. She had come away from that encounter with a cyst of Shadowborn presence in her, an infection or parasite of magic forced on her by the Shadowborn. With the Shadowborn's death at Ishmael di Studier's hands, the magic in it was extinguished and it could no longer ensorcell her, except that the Shadowborn had also given her its knowledge. Her experiments with that knowledge had awakened her magic in dangerous ways.

"I will not use it again," she said, a heartfelt wish.

"Dear lady, you must. Or, rather, you may have no choice. Why do you think we have been amusing ourselves with tapers and fire? It is because we must understand this magic before we meet it. We are already under strength—I am quite sure of that. You have not sensed ahead, have you? I thought not."

"Why?"

He shook his head. In the last few sentences, the fey manner had slipped away. "We may have right on our side, but we simply do not have the numbers or might to match the Shadowborn. We are fortunate in Lord Vladimer, who is certain to favor an oblique approach—he is renowned for it. But he will be the first to insist that we need all the information we can get if we are not to blunder into a confrontation we cannot win."

"I will tell you everything I can," she said.

"Though it pains me to say, that may not be nearly enough, because your understanding of magic is a novice's, strong as you are. It would be of immeasurable help to us if you would permit me or my daughter, Phoebe, to examine the Shadowborn's *gift* directly."

For a moment, she resisted understanding that he wished to touch the thing in her mind, magic to mind. Through stiffened lips, she said, "I cannot believe you are making such a suggestion to me, sir."

She hoped—she fervently hoped—that she was convincing in her outrage.

His smile was very sweet. "I am," he said, without apology.

Should she leave the compartment in umbrage? Order *him* out? She had a distinct feeling that he would not oblige. He could sweep the knowledge from her mind with the barest effort, as she had the knowledge of his plans against the tower from Duke Kalamay, and then he would know.... Frantically, she pushed down the thought.

"I know this is far too soon," he said, as though, she thought dizzily, he were an impulsive suitor offering a premature proposal, "but please give it some thought. Neither Phoebe nor I would ever force you, *especially* now that we face a living demonstration of violation of our principles. Compose yourself, dear lady; we do not want to alarm the good people on this train, or disturb young Lord Vladimer's rest."

Then she was alone in the backwash of his magic, for he had not even opened the door to the compartment. She gulped at such a casual display. How could she possibly resist? She thought she smelled smoke and frantically made her mind blank, holding her breath. When she had to breathe, it was only the stale air of the compartment, like old cigar smoke, that she inhaled. Perhaps she had only imagined the smoke.

Sweet Imogene, the thought of Farquhar or Phoebe in her mind appalled her, though not nearly as much as it would have before she had met Ishmael. Ishmael she would, and had, let into her mind without hesitation. Society had not the least notion of all the improprieties possible through magic—*she* had not had the least notion.

If she could only speak to Ishmael, she would have laid her confession before him, even though . . . even though . . . Would he understand how she had come to know about Duke Mycene and Duke Kalamay's plans to launch an attack on the Lightborn Mages' Tower, undeclared and unprovoked—except that to such men, the very existence of the tower, and the mages it housed, was an offense. Would he understand why she had misused her magic so? He would understand why she had taken the knowledge to Vladimer, trusting him to act on it? Ishmael was deferential to Vladimer's greater cunning. And she thought he would understand why Vladimer had chosen to do nothing.

But that was because, after years of service and friendship, he knew Vladimer, and Ishmael's was not a nature given to outrage or bitterness. He would not hesitate to condemn Vladimer's silence, but he would understand it. She could not trust that the Broomes, who barely knew Vladimer, would be forgiving.

Vladimer—and she—could not do this alone. They needed the Broomes and their commune. She could not—

A woman screamed in full-voiced horror. Telmaine lurched to her feet, sweeping aside her skirts, and threw open the door as Phoebe Broome cried out, *"Phineas!"*

The mage was standing in the corridor, bracing herself against the walls, her father at her side. "Phineas! Oh, Mother of All, *Phineas*." She stretched out an arm, back along their track, and Telmaine could feel the magic streaming out of her.

"What is it?" Vladimer said, harshly, from behind Telmaine. He was framed in the door of one of the two state-

rooms, supporting himself against the lintel, coatless, hair disordered, and shirt loosened.

Phoebe gave another cry of "Phineas" and fell to her knees, curled palms held up before her, as though cupping water or life. Behind them, mages crowded the corridor; behind Vladimer, the door to the engine opened and one of the engineers stepped through, revolver drawn.

Phoebe lifted her face to her father. "Why didn't he call on us!"

"It was too quick, dear girl." He put his hands beneath her elbows and lifted her with an implausible ease. Telmaine sensed magic. Phoebe hung, limp as a pennant, on its prop.

She heard Vladimer dismiss the engineer, assuring him that he would take care of it.

"I just felt my brother die," Phoebe told them all, between sobs. "I don't know what happened. Olivede is there, but I can't get her to respond. I could feel her pouring out magic . . . healing. . . ."

"It is not death you felt, dear girl," Farquhar said.

"Then why— Oh, *no*. He feels like Ishmael. He feels just like Ishmael. Phineas— "

"Telmaine," said Vladimer, so close behind her that she could feel his breath.

"I *don't know*," she answered the implied demand for information. Phineas Broome had been lately in the service of the Duke of Mycene, though exactly why he had taken such service, perhaps only he knew. He claimed loyalty to the state, protecting Vladimer and the archduke from a dangerous mage—Telmaine herself. Vladimer inferred he wanted access to the Mycene armory for his revolutionary associates, and using that inference, Vladimer had struck a deal with the mage: silence for silence on Telmaine's escape. Telmaine had been immensely relieved that Phineas had not joined them, that his actions appeared to have estranged him from his family, because Phineas *knew* about Vladimer's silence over the tower.

If Phineas had remained with the Duke of Mycene, and Olivede Hearne had been there, then it was not too far to assume that the archduke was there also. And if by "he feels like Ishmael," Phoebe meant that he felt dangerously overspent, burned out, that meant the *Shadowborn*—

Vladimer said, "In here," in a voice meant to be obeyed.

"My dears," said Farquhar to the rest of his party, "we will tell you as soon as we are able."

He steered the stumbling Phoebe into the compartment, moving as steadily as if he were walking through the halls of the immense, immovable archducal seat. Phoebe subsided limply into her seat, with a murmured, "I'm sorry."

Vladimer sat down. "Magister Broome," he said, in a voice that caused Telmaine's stomach to clench. "Inform me."

Farquhar Broome sighed. "I wish I could, dear boy. . . ." Vladimer's lips thinned dangerously at that, though whether it was the evasion or the solecism, Telmaine didn't know. "I cannot sense either Phineas or Olivede now; there's too much Lightborn magic blocking me. They are quite a bit stronger than I."

"Lightborn?"

"It is customary, particularly when sensitive negotiations are proceeding, to block magical surveillance."

"Magister Broome, I could order this train to turn around, this minute."

"Dear boy, what would that possibly achieve? What is happening in Minhorne would be long over by the time we reached there, and what is happening in the Borders very much needs attention."

Vladimer accepted that with obvious reluctance. "Were the *Lightborn* responsible for the attack on your son?"

"No," Phoebe said, faintly. "It *was* Shadowborn. It felt stronger than Phineas. He was trying to stand against it. . . . There was fire . . . and he . . ." She put gloved hands to her face. "I'm sorry, Lord Vladimer, but he's my *brother*—"

"And was *my* brother there?"

She swallowed. "Yes," she said, more steadily. "Yes, I think he was. I don't know where they were, but I don't believe it was in the archducal palace. There were other people there—you'd know who should have been there better than I. But the first thing I sensed for certain was Phineas's alarm, and panic and pain—agony—as he tried to quench the flames. And then I felt him wring himself out with the effort, and—from Olivede, Dr. Hearne's sister, and not as strong as Phineas—I sensed only healing effort, on a man. Two men. And . . . emotional turmoil, something to do with family. She wouldn't, or couldn't, respond to me. And then I lost all sense of them."

"The Shadowborn have used the guise of Lysander Hearne in the past; perhaps they did so again. That would certainly disturb his sister—it did his brother."

"Yes," said Phoebe. She put out a hand, groping, and after a moment, her father took it.

Vladimer braced himself as the train shook and rattled over uneven tracks. "When we arrive in Strumheller Crosstracks, I will immediately wire north for information. But if you learn more by other means," he said through his teeth, "I need to know."

Balthasar

Duke Mycene was dead, despite Olivede's efforts. Phineas Broome was still alive, but barely so, his heartbeat irregular and his blood pressure very low. They had no stimulants for him. One of the archduke's guards had been gravely injured when his revolver exploded; only his fellows' quick work with tourniquets and pressure bandages had kept him from bleeding to death. The others were all burned, lacerated, and half deafened, but still standing. The archduke had left two with the physicians and casualties in a side hall, and taken the remaining three with him into the main conference room. Balthasar could just hear the voices from there, the words themselves indistinguishable.

"Balthasar," his sister said, lifting a face that seemed to have aged twenty years in minutes, "I am so sorry about Telmaine. I had no idea that she was mageborn. If she had only trusted . . ." Her voice faded.

For Olivede, there had never been any question of not following magic, or any expressed regret at the life and place in society that she gave up to do so. But the open, sensitive girl had become a guarded woman, bruised by the many hurts the world dealt her kind, and Balthasar was not certain that she knew how much she had changed. He did not think she could understand—could have understood—his wife.

Olivede pushed herself to her feet and came along to where Balthasar sat beside Sebastien, whom he had made as comfortable as possible on a long, padded bench. The bleeding had almost stopped; the boy snored slightly in his drugged sleep. There was a suppressed revulsion in Olivede's face as she sonned the boy, though whether it was at his magic, his actions, his resemblance to their elder brother, or all three, he could not know.

She took Bal's bandaged arm—he had strapped it properly with the help of one of the guards—in hers, checked it, and let it go. Wasting magic on so minor an injury was out of the question. "I can't annul the ensorcellment on you," she said in a low voice. "I haven't the strength, even if I had much left after"—a twitch of the head toward where the body of Duke Sachevar Mycene lay in an improvised shroud. Even so, the smell of his death tainted the air. "He so *willed* to live. He gave everything to the struggle. How could I give less?" Her smile twisted in a peculiar mingling of compassion and repugnance. "To him, the only profanity in magic was that he had none himself. He liked power."

"Be careful," Balthasar breathed. "If Kalamay—"

"Between Mycene and Kalamay and the Shadowborn, they murdered dozens of Lightborn mages," Olivede said, as though she had not heard, her head still turned toward the dead duke. "But that death was obscene." She sonned him. "Balthasar, you're in as much danger as I am from Kalamay. You *cannot* protect this boy."

"I *must*," he said, throwing all the weight of meaning he could into the two words and imploring her to understand.

She masked her face with her hand, denying him the chance to sonn her expression. "The Lightborn are preventing me from reaching anyone, but I don't suppose Master Kieldar could come, until the curfew is raised." Even in here, they could hear the warning bell. "Phineas needs more than I can do for him, and Phoebe must be frantic. I didn't respond because I . . . didn't want to explain." She sighed and sat down beside him, her worn skirts folding almost silently—unlike Telmaine's starched, scented rustlings—and slipped her arm around him. "My poor little brother," she said quietly, "you've sustained a dreadful loss. I cannot imagine what you have been through. But you have your daughters to think of. Just remember— "

She brought up her hand as though to draw his head against her shoulder. He sonned the bare skin, thought of the ensorcellment, and ducked out of her embrace. And then realized what she had meant to do: spend the last of her magic in rendering him unconscious. "I am not distraught with grief," Balthasar said angrily. "At least not distraught beyond reasoning."

"Balthasar," she said. "Please let me— "

From the main chambers, they heard a shout: "Will you listen to me!" Balthasar's experience of the archduke was slight, generally gained as part of a large audience to Sejanus's masterful public performances. He had never heard the veteran statesman even raise his voice in anger, much less shout. He took a step toward the door.

"Not with that ensorcellment about you! If any of them can sense it— "

There was real fear in her voice, but, still angry with her, he disregarded it. "I know more about the Shadowborn than anyone here. I'm used to conducting business with Lightborn—six terms on the council, Olivede! And if there *is* someone who can sense it, my ensorcellment would be proof— "

"Of further Darkborn involvement. *Don't*, Balthasar. There's at least one high master in the building—I can sense the strength. It's important—it's vital—that this is dealt with as a matter between earthborn. If the Lightborn mages decide *we* had anything to do with it, they'll crush us like cockroaches. Phineas— "

"If it were to be dealt with earthborn to earthborn, would they have a high master with them?"

"Archduke's orders were that none of you were to leave," one of the guards said civilly from his station beside the door. In deference to his injuries—his face was bound with cloth torn from a pennant—it was a seated station. But if his hand on his revolver was not quite steady, it was purposeful. *Brave men,* Balthasar thought, *knowing what they guard here.*

Olivede wrapped her arms around her ribs. "Phineas went to warn Dukes Kalamay and Mycene about Vladimer's mage, who was your own Telmaine. But because he was involved with them, he might be accused of ensorcelling the munitions that destroyed the tower."

He could not keep his temper; she sounded so frightened and forlorn. He lifted his scorched jacket and put it around her shoulders. She leaned against him with a sigh, and he rested his cheek cautiously on her hair. "I'm sorry," he whispered. "I'm sorry you have to fear your own people as well as the Shadowborn."

She pulled away, wrinkling her nose. "Ugh, Bal, that ensorcellment is revolting."

She had worn exactly that expression at twelve when he had run to her in outrage after Lysander had pushed him into a pigsty. Though the muscles of his face moved like clay, he smiled at the memory.

They heard the door to the main council chambers slam open, and a moment later, Sejanus Plantageter swept into the room, a brace of Mycene's guard scrambling ahead of him. Balthasar found himself up and standing between them and Sebastien before he was aware of having moved.

Dukes Imbré and Rohan followed the archduke together, Rohan lending an arm to the oldest duke. Then came a young man who, by his resemblance to Xavier Stranhorne, was surely Maxim di Gautier. At his shoulder was a stout older man who steered his young baron with the gentlest of touches and cast a challenging sonn over Balthasar and Olivede. In his other hand, he held a staff in a grip that dared anyone to menace his baron. Duke Kalamay followed, fingers kneading an amulet that Balthasar recognized as one distributed to followers of the Sole God as a shield against magic. Behind Kalamay came his heir, whom Balthasar knew as a clever man of malicious wit and considerable theological knowledge, and one who took as much pleasure in demolishing the fallacies of faith as those of skepticism. He stumbled on the threshold, caught himself against one of the benches, and lifted a face sagging with shock. "You said there was nothing to it. Nothing," he said, to his father's back.

Imbré laid a hand like a gnarled root on the archduke's shoulder. "Well, Sejanus, now we know."

"W'can't yield, of course," said a stocky man in a Borders accent, setting his stance before the archduke.

"You shall not treat with mages," Kalamay said.

The archduke ignored him. "Lord di Gruner, while yielding is as repugnant to me as it is to you, I cannot ignore the fact that, should they choose, they could trap us in our homes, day and night both, with their lights. I doubt most households have more than two weeks' sustenance to hand, and the poorest will have less. Not to mention the havoc it would cause for business and trade."

"Are they," Maxim di Gautier spoke up, hesitantly, "a legitimate government? Is this princess a legitimate ruler, or does authority still properly vest with Fejelis?"

"Of whose whereabouts we have no idea," said Rohan.

"I got the impression," the archduke said, "that neither did they." He started to pace. "I should not have let myself be thrown by the fact that they brought forward a woman. I think even Vladimer stopped keeping a dossier on Perrin when she dropped out of the succession. I thought if Fejelis went down, it would be Orlanjis. And his mother, likely—Odon's granddaughter, indeed. I wonder if this order of expulsion was her idea."

"Our people won't stand for it."

"Indeed they won't—and I wonder if theirs will, too. Oh, there's feeling against the Darkborn—the riots and the vandalism tells us that—but there are sectors of the economy and parts of the city that owe their prosperity to trade with us." He paused, his expression one of concentrated thought. "We are vulnerable to the light, but we have other, subtler means to hand. But I think I do not want to discuss *any* of our options until we are well out of this building."

Balthasar got stiffly to his feet. "Your Grace," he said, "am I to understand that the Lightborn still insist this is a matter between Lightborn and Darkborn—that they do not accept the part played by Shadowborn?"

Sejanus hesitated briefly—whether because of Balthasar's insignificant status or his involvement—and then said, "You understand correctly, Dr. Hearne. As far as the Lightborn are concerned, the attack on the tower was entirely Darkborn. As to what happened just before their arrival—they didn't even acknowledge that."

But even lineage mages should have been able to sense Phineas and Olivede's efforts, and the injury and deaths of Darkborn on this side. So how much of the denial was authentic and how much politic? First and foremost, the Mages' Temple served its own interests, and those interests would not include admission of so profound a vulnerability. Mages contracted to the various members of the Lightborn nobility would obey the letter of their contract—no more. But what of the princess herself? She was born outside the lineages, to a family with no known magical members. Was her magic of the sport form?

He said, slowly, "My ensorcellment makes me immune to daylight. As long as that ensorcellment lasts"—as long as Sebastien was allowed to live stood implied, he hoped—"I would be able to go into the courts of the Lightborn and act both as envoy and as living proof of the existence of the Shadowborn. To my best knowledge, even the high masters would not be able to reproduce the feat of allowing a Darkborn to survive in light, or a Lightborn in darkness. If they cannot sense my ensorcellment, yet there I am, alive, they must ask themselves why."

"Bal—," Olivede began, and fell silent at a gesture from the archduke.

"If they do not simply kill you to restore congruence to their worldview," Plantagetor pointed out.

"I believe that I will be sufficiently intriguing and offer sufficient possibilities that they will keep me for study."

"Why should you take the risk?"

Because I hope the Lightborn will spare the boy, he told the ensorcellment. "Your Grace," Balthasar said, "I have served several terms on the Intercalatory Council, as my father did before me. I know about and care about the relationship between Lightborn and Darkborn. I have a family connection to the Shadowborn. I have been their victim—it was only by my wife's and Ishmael di Studier's doing that I did not die twice over. I have lost my wife to a series of events that *they* initiated. Regardless of what happens to me, I do not want my daughters—or even my brother's twisted child—to live under Shadowborn rule. By their acts, I know them. I can do this. I am *uniquely* qualified to do this."

"How much of this is your own will, and how much . . . his?"

"He has never intimated that I should cross the sunrise, but as long as I believe that I am acting in *his* interest, then I believe my acts will be my own. As I have demonstrated, I believe."

"And how is your crossing over in his interest?"

Balthasar swallowed; he had not wanted to be asked that question, much less answer it truthfully. "Because I believe that Lightborn law will be more lenient to his crimes than Darkborn, and that the Temple mages have the strength to train and discipline him properly, which we do not."

There was a pause. He could not tell, from the archduke's face, what he was thinking. "We have received what amounts to a demand for complete submission to Lightborn rule and a surrender of the city itself. The Lightborn deny that Shadowborn exist, and blame Prince Isidore's death on us, though they cannot say how we might have achieved it. Mycene's and Kalamay's guilt in the destruction of the tower and the deaths of mages is inarguable. One more offense, and I do not think they will refrain from tearing down our walls. How am I to know you will not be the agent of that offense?"

"It is my belief," Balthasar said, "that Floria's ensorcellment was the work of the other Shadowborn mage, who was also the one responsible for ensorcelling Vladimer." A muscle ticked in the corner of the archduke's mouth at the mention of his brother's name—Bal wished he knew more about Vladimer's condition. But what was said was said. "That Shadowborn could keep Floria unaware of what had been done to her. The boy does not have that ability. I have been aware of my actions all along."

"While unable to control them," the archduke said. Balthasar turned in appeal to Olivede, but the archduke said, "Miss Olivede is your sister, and I am barely acquainted with her. Her efforts to try to save Mycene's life and ease his passing speak well of her—but I cannot take her word regarding you."

"Your Grace," Balthasar said intensely, "*am* I the man you would send on an assassination? My marksmanship is risible. I am no mage. I may know drugs, poisons, and anatomy—but I would be entering a Lightborn court where assassination is a mechanism of succession and their brightnesses surround themselves with layers of secular and magical protection. The fact that Floria had to carry a talisman to the prince suggests that such magic cannot be centered in a living body, and therefore I argue that I cannot be carrying such an ensorcellment. If you are concerned about anything else I might be carrying with me, then have me stripped and searched before I go.

"You *need* the Lightborn to accept the existence of Shadowborn, Your Grace. I am the best proof you have."

Seven

Fejelis

A hand on his shoulder woke Fejelis, a hand that snatched itself back as he snapped upright. His head connected with a chin; she thudded back on her rump on the floor. "Ouch!" Watering, honey-gold eyes squinted at him.

Wit finally overtook reflex, and Fejelis recognized his hostess and surroundings: Jovance, mage turned railway woman, in the hut in the Darkborn Borders that she shared with three others—her brother, Jade, and a young couple, Midha and Sorrel. Rather too few hours ago, by the way he felt, he had stretched out and gone to sleep on a pallet on her floorboards. He had simply trusted to Tam's judgment, and his own assessment of her—which was admittedly not unbiased, another unexpected aspect of the situation. He tried to untie his tongue for an apology.

"Sorry to startle you, your brightness," Jovance said. "But we've been asked to mount a guard outside for some Darkborn trains coming through. How are you with a rifle?"

". . . Isn't it still . . . ?" He just avoided asking the obvious question; of course it was still night, and of course she knew that. ". . . Depends on the size and speed of the target. Overall, fair to middling." Against a target, anyway; he had never had a taste for hunting live game. "Jis—Orlanjis—is better than I am."

"Sooner have a crossbow," his younger brother said. He was nervously finger-combing his long red-gold hair, trying to worry loose a snarled residue of his ornate coiffure. His face was pale beneath his desert tan. But Orlanjis had spent seasons in the desert with their southern kin; he had hunted and bled his kill, dressed, cooked, and eaten it.

"If we need one of you, we'll need both," Jovance said, rising smoothly on strong legs and reaching down a hand in a worn leather glove to draw Fejelis up. He tried to convince himself that the shirt he had slept in was long enough to preserve decency, groping drafts notwithstanding. Her eyes glinted with mischief, noting his knees-together, slightly hunched posture.

The need to distract her, as much as the need for information, prompted him. "Trains, you said?"

"Yes. It's an hour after sunset—again, I'm sorry I had to wake you so soon, after you walked all that distance, carrying Tam." *Which my body doesn't need to be reminded about—thank you, Jovance.* He felt nineteen going on ninety. "The Darkborn manor of Stranhorne reports being overrun by what they describe as an army of Shadowborn, which seems to have swept through some of the outlying territories. They managed a retreat to Stranhorne Crosstracks just before sunrise last night—they're ferocious fighters and well organized, which means anything that could overrun them is thoroughly bad news. Now they're trying to evacuate wounded and noncombatants by train. They'll have armed guards, but they want us to mount a watch in between trains. It's good we're six." She did not count Tam, who had been incapacitated by his exertions getting the three of them there, and was lying unconscious in the small bedroom. Her lips compressed. "Not quite what Tam was hoping for, bringing you down here to supposed safety."

Another, less stupid, question occurred to him, about how they could shoot, looking out into darkness from light, but he decided he would let that, too, answer itself. As well as the one after that: if she were able and willing to use magic offensively, they need only wait to find that out, too. He suspected she was strong, but did not know how strong.

Jade lobbed Fejelis underwear and a pair of trousers that were short in the shank but otherwise a passable fit. His own clothes were impregnated with the dust of the fallen tower. Fejelis pulled the clothes on, tucked in his shirt, ran his hands over his unkempt hair, and accepted a rifle offered him. He confirmed it was unloaded, noting that it was of Darkborn manufacture. *The blind Darkborn are certainly accomplished at killing at a distance,* he thought grimly. The rifle had an interesting attachment, a long tube set parallel to the barrel with a lens mounted inside. Peering down it, he could see the glint of curved glass, the wink of focused light at its center. "One of Tam's artisans thought that one up," said Jovance, "attaching a telescope to a rifle."

He knew Tam's artisans, or some of them. He considered them *his* artisans, too, since, in a guise other than heir, he had been an irregular visitor to their cafés and workshops. Jovance said, "Tam described the design to my"—a small flinch—"grandfather." The grandfather who had died in the destruction of the tower. "Lukfer arranged for some samples to be made up and sent them down for us to try out. He worried about us. If you can tolerate having your eye right up to the end of the cylinder, it gives remarkably good magnification, and cuts out ambient light."

Fejelis sighted the grain of the scarred wooden floor, the knobby edge of the carpet. The prickling around his shaded eye grew into an ache like severe eyestrain. ". . . I think I can do this," he said. ". . . But the fog . . ." When Tam had set them down, the fog had been too dense for them to do more than find and follow the railway track itself.

"Still there. The telegraph says Stranhorne's had snow, wind, violent rainstorms; a mage in their party said it was mage weather. The first train left Stranhorne an hour and a half ago, so it has roughly another hour before it reaches here, and another half to reach the Crosstracks. It's carrying a couple of the Stranhorne family themselves. There's another about half an hour behind it. So we've time to go out and drill getting the lights and ourselves into and out of place fast. We'll get a signal as it passes each station, so we'll know when to close up."

She glanced at Midha, who did not speak, and went on. "Everyone get four lights and sling them to either side, and then take up ready positions." Midha opened the door on darkness. Fejelis's mouth went dry, remembering the hallucinatory chiaroscuro of the night before as they hunted for survivors in the rubble of the fallen Mages' Tower, but Orlanjis all but threw himself down the black maw, and Fejelis had to follow. The hut stood on a platform, fifteen feet in the air, with a covered deck all around, so that—in light, without fog—they should have had a fair vantage. Now they could barely discern the line of the railroad tracks.

"Too slow," said Midha to Jovance. Fejelis guessed that he would ordinarily have been in charge, but he, like the other two, would rather Jovance deal with their unnerving guests. She had once been a Temple mage. Thus prompted, she had them try their deployment in pairs, with two riflemen covering the diagonals while the others slung lights; that went better. While Sorrel went back into the hut to monitor the telegraph and put on the kettle for what promised to be a long night, Jovance had both Fejelis and Orlanjis shoot several rounds at a marker, the nearest of those they used for target practice, and the only one they could make out in the fog. They established that though Orlanjis was the better shot, he could not use the closed sight. Jovance exchanged Orlanjis's closed sight for an open one, warning Orlanjis of the difficulty he might have seeing.

"I've night hunted," Orlanjis began . . . and in the middle of the sentence brought up his gun, squinted through the sight, and fired, lurching a little at the recoil. In the mist across the tracks, something howled its outrage. Orlanjis fired again, steadier now, and the howl ended.

Jovance said to Midha, "Let's ask Sorrel to telegraph the Crosstracks, get details of what we're up against." To Orlanjis: "What was it?"

"Don't know. Large . . . animal." On the last word, his teeth chattered and he clenched his jaw.

She clapped his shoulder. "Bigger target, then. There's too much light for Darkborn out there, and too much darkness for Lightborn, so feel free to drop anything that's not us."

She has a vigilant's gallows humor, Fejelis thought, exchanging glances with Orlanjis along the length of the platform. Bright though they were, the lights were chill and dim compared to sunlight, and Orlanjis's face was wan and damp with the lack of sunlight, settling mist, and fear. With his vivid imagination, the night must be full of horrors. For Fejelis, the greatest horror was the possibility that he might have brought Orlanjis here to die. After years of having had his brother held up to him as the southern faction's favorite and his nearest rival, the last thing he had expected was that a single, impulsive act on his part would have won Orlanjis's loyalty.

Then he saw Orlanjis swing his rifle toward him and thought for a brief and terrible moment that he had won nothing. Orlanjis fired, and just behind Fejelis something scraped against the railings. Fejelis threw himself flat, rolling, and stared up at the man-sized but not man-formed creature clinging by one hooked talon to the rail. Its chest was deep, with a prominent breastbone and hollow belly, and its pectoral muscles worked as its wings fluttered. The jaw and lower face were a man's, but the eyes were barely visible. A fine pelt covered the head and torso. Orlanjis and Jovance fired together, each from their corners. Skin split, blood gushed, and the Shadowborn thudded down to straddle the railing and slither like a half-filled bag of sand off the railing to the ground below. "For the Mother's sake, *watch*," Jovance yelled at him. "The fog conceals them!"

In the doorway, Midha said, "Stranhorne Crosstracks says that some of them can fly—"

Panting, Jovance said, "We *noticed*. You want to take this corner? I'll cover the front, get us ammunition. Your brightness—"

". . . Yes, fine," Fejelis said, before she or Orlanjis turned to look. He climbed to his feet, picked up his rifle—thanking the Mother of All Things Born it had not discharged—drew a deep breath, and stepped up to the rail. The mist roiled, its motions disorientating; he fired twice at phantoms before he saw his first creature and spooked it into Jovance's line with his misses. He heard several shots from Orlanjis's direction, followed by an unnerving pause. From between them, Jovance rasped, "When you're reloading, say, 'Cover me,' so we can."

Fejelis shot at ripples of mist, at dark, solid, moving shapes on the ground. Twice he left a wounded Shadowborn that Orlanjis or Midha dispatched. "Reloading," he croaked, and had just realized he had nothing to reload with when she pushed a pouch into his hands. "Your little brother remembered *his* ammo," she chided him, before Jade's *"Cover me,"* summoned her around to the far side.

The mist seethed, though his adrenaline-sharpened vision and even the uncomfortable sight found nothing solid. Orlanjis yelled alarm and shot wildly. Fejelis broke discipline to throw one swift glance over his shoulder—

—To see one flying Shadowborn tear two of Orlanjis's lights from their hangings, even as another dropped on him from the roof. Orlanjis pitched forward, without a sound, beneath its weight. From the far side of the hut, Jovance shouted, "Hold your posts!" Fejelis remained mesmerized as the falling Shadowborn seemed to rebound, thrust skyward against gravity, and then both Shadowborn simply burst as though an immense fist had crushed them. Meat, bone, and gore spattered the platform, the roof, the ground, Orlanjis. The unstrung lights whirled above Orlanjis's head.

"Fejelis—*outward*!" Jovance shouted, dropping to her knees beside Orlanjis. "I have him." He whirled, eyes raking the mist, his finger twitching on the trigger. He had no idea how many hours later it was that Jade said, quietly, from his side, "They're gone." He pried the rifle from Fejelis's grip and turned him to face Jovance, who was supporting a trembling, blood-spattered Orlanjis. Jovance released Orlanjis to his embrace; under his hands, he could feel rent fabric part over whole skin. "Thank you," he breathed over his brother's shoulder. "Thank you."

"I, for one," Jade said, "might have wished she'd done that sooner. That was a bit close."

"Easy for you to say," said Tam's tired voice from the door. "It wasn't your magic."

"I didn't want to find out they could sense me when I

couldn't sense them," Jovance said to Jade. "But, yes, I nearly held back too long." To Tam she said, "What're you doing up?"

"Well . . . ," said the mage, burying his hands in the pockets of a ragged dressing gown. "I might have slept through the shooting, but when one of those things landed on the roof above my head—you have no idea how vile that magic is—and you let rip . . ." Fejelis hoped his face wasn't as green as he felt at the reminder. Yet he grinned with relief at seeing Tam awake and upright, if as heavy-eyed and ashen as a man recovering from a three-day bender. The mage smiled back with a rueful shrug of the shoulders as he glanced around them, apologizing for the failings of their haven.

The bell, loud, insistent, made them all jump. Jade said, in horror, "Mother's milk, the train—" The Darkborn train, which they'd all forgotten, with Darkborn guards riding outside. "*Inside*, now." He and Jovance dove right and left, harvesting lights, while Fejelis half carried Orlanjis into the hut, lowering him carefully into the chair nearest the fire. He'd apologize for the stains later. Orlanjis's eyes were dilated, black pupils in dark irises. He looked as he had looked when he learned of their father's death in darkness.

Tam said, "Get warm water with honey or sugar down him; it will take the edge off the shock."

By the time Fejelis came back into the little living room, Jovance was spilling an armful of lights onto the floor inside the door as Midha dropped the bar on the door. They looked at each other with the stunned expressions of survivors, expressions Fejelis had grown far too used to seeing around him.

"Have they gone?" Midha said to Jovance. "Is the train in danger? Is there anything on the track?"

The mage's golden eyes became hooded. She stood quite still, except for the flexing of her left hand, in the center of the close little room. Tam's brow tightened as though in discomfort. "Now it's clear," she said, and took a step toward the chairs. Finding them occupied, she sat down on Fejelis's pallet, beside the stove, knees drawn up to her chest, face hidden.

"Hot water and honey for her as well," Tam said, mildly. "Maybe something stronger for the rest of us."

"Don't you dare," said Jovance, lifting her face. "Coming over all fatherly doesn't mean you're not overspent. So stay out of this."

Tam silently parsed that sentence, his lips moving. Jovance made a gesture that Fejelis knew from the streets and the vigilance, caught his eye, and looked sheepish. He managed to grin at her.

The "something stronger" was bedeeth tea, an infusion of a desert root with stimulant properties, with a jolt of what he supposed was brandy before it ate its way through the cask. He wondered how Floria White Hand's magical asset would have reacted to it. Tam docilely sipped hot water and honey. Fejelis crouched at Orlanjis's side, steadying his cup and ignoring the tackiness on his hands and the tears trickling down his brother's face. They fell silent, listening to the growing clatter of the approaching train, riding its tracks under control of a Darkborn driver, in the faith that the combined efforts of Darkborn and Lightborn kept the tracks clear. The noise was joined by a fine vibration Fejelis felt through the soles of his feet. Then the vibration coarsened to a shake, and to the accompaniment of chattering crockery in the kitchen, the train passed beneath them and receded into the night. Only the reek of engine smoke remained.

He was not the only one who let out the breath he had been holding.

"Eight carriages," Jade said, "maybe nine." He looked at Sorrel, who nodded. "The Crosstracks said nine."

"Engine'll need some maintenance after."

Jovance opened and closed her left fist, staring at the wall in the direction of the departed train. "I don't sense anything ahead of them," she said, sounding strained. Then she dropped her face onto her knees with a poorly muffled obscenity. "That's a trainload of pain and grief," she said, face hidden. Jade eased himself down on the pallet and put his arm around her shoulders.

Sorrel got up hastily. "I need to check if the other huts are all right."

"Mother's milk," said Jade, grimly. "If any of the others— No, save your strength," he said to Jovance. "We'll wait for the telegraph. There's nothing much we could do anyway."

They waited in silence, listening to the tap and clatter of the telegraph. Sorrel returned, mug in hand; by that and by the ease of her movements, Fejelis could tell that the news was good. "Several skirmishes just outside Stranhorne Crosstracks. No one seriously hurt."

"Nat and Les?"

"Checked in fine."

Jade said to Tam, "Les—Celeste—was the first Lightborn ever taken on by the Darkborn railways, forty years ago. She didn't tell them she was a woman and six months' pregnant at the time. She's worked most of the track from Stranhorne to the Southern Ocean, and what she hasn't, Nat—that's her eldest son—has. They've got family at every branch office who've been after her to give up the huts and move into town—and been agitating even more since she broke her hip a few weeks back. *She* says she plans to end her days as grease on the track."

A gruesome image, Fejelis thought, who had recently seen far too many residues of quenched Lightborn, but at least Orlanjis was no longer staring or crying. He seemed distracted by the character sketch, and hopefully missed the allusion.

Tam stirred. "Do you know whether the train had to fight off Shadowborn?"

"I can't say, Magister Tam," Sorrel said, diffidently. "The train has not stopped, so we haven't had any reports from it, but it is within five minutes of schedule . . . which means it hasn't had to slow down."

"And none of the other huts came under as strenuous an attack."

By Midha's expression, he, like Fejelis and Jovance, knew where Tam was going, and did not like it.

The question had to be asked. ". . . Is it us—me?" Fejelis said, correcting himself.

"Or me," Tam said. "Or me and Jo. It can't be Jo alone,"

he said to Jovance. "They attacked before you started using power." He hesitated. "Jo—"

Her head snapped around. "Don't be stupid." Tam put a hand to his head, his freckles even more prominent. He had, Fejelis realized, just attempted to speak silently to her. She glared at Tam, then Fejelis. "Your brightness, he'd like me to take you out of here. I could, but I won't abandon my brother and my friends."

He did not like the idea, did not like it in the least, but he owed it consideration. *You'll never have the luxury of doing something simply to impress a girl,* he remembered his father saying, dryly. If he were the danger, if their attackers were still working according to some plan that sought the decapitation of both governments, and they knew he had fetched up here, then they would all be safer with him gone. But where to?

Tam, watching him, sighed. "Forget I asked," he said. "Curse it, Fejelis, I'm—"

"We're *all* still alive," Fejelis said, firmly.

Jovance put her hands down on the pallet on either side of her and stretched out her legs. "At least we've ammunition and a defensible position here. I just have to hope that my chucking magic around hasn't *attracted* attention." Her eyes flicked sideways, and met Fejelis's briefly. She was not talking only about the Shadowborn.

Midha said, "We'll just have to deal with what happens when it happens. Jo, can you keep a sense of what's moving outside, say for half a mile around, until we get organized?" She nodded. "Then let's all have something to eat and work out watch schedules. Master Orlanjis"—Fejelis was relieved at how quickly Orlanjis lifted his head—"you're first up for a shower and change of clothes. Don't stint on the hot water; we've plenty. I'd like two of us outside, except when there's a train passing, and one on the telegraph, but the others have to get some rest—"

"Should we go down and check the line?" said Jade.

"We'll not be able to cover enough line to justify the risk. We can barely see two hundred yards with the fog."

"Is clearing the fog a higher priority than sensing for

Shadowborn?" Jovance said. Tam opened his mouth; closed it. Mages seldom tried weather manipulation solo, even on a very limited scale. Even Tam, with his aptitude for handling inert matter, found it exhausting.

Watching Midha's expression, Fejelis thought that although Jovance's magic was no secret among them, her companions had never seen it so decisively demonstrated. Perhaps they did not understand her limits. ". . . Since it's dark," Fejelis tendered, "and our vision and ability to move would be restricted anyway, I feel it would be a waste of strength."

She gave him a grateful glance. "So we hold out here for the night. There aren't many Shadowborn come out by day, usually, even though the Curse doesn't seem to affect them—or so the Darkborn say."

"There is one other possibility to consider," Tam said, slowly. He looked down at his hands. "You, or even I, contact the high masters—"

"No," said Jovance, and then looked sideways at Fejelis, conflict in her face.

This wasn't the time to think his argument through before he spoke, he sensed, though he would have appreciated the chance to consider. His impulse, which, as ever, he distrusted, was to refuse. "If another attack comes, we should surely have some sense that our situation is becoming desperate. *Then* we could call for help."

"And if the high masters cannot make up their minds as quickly as you can?"

"Don't . . . refuse just to protect me," Tam said.

Fejelis cleared his throat. ". . . And who were those three crossbow bolts aimed at? Besides . . . my mother's family has an ugly history with the Darkborn. I would like a chance to rehabilitate it. The Borders seem to have become a front for this war, and though we Lightborn are not many, we have three assets that the Darkborn do not: the ability to see, to move by day, and strong magic."

"Two mages, one of whom is gravely overspent," Jovance pointed out. "And we're just here to do a job."

". . . I know this is not fair. I know it. Yet all four of you were prepared to stand guard in the night, at risk of your lives."

"That's our job: safety on the railroads. Not the whole Mother-blessed Borders."

"Jo," Tam said, "stop arguing for the sake of argument."

She rounded on him. "Someone has to. Oh yes, you read me right: I've never had any sense of self-preservation. But what about them?" Her snapping hand indicated her friends. "He's his brightness Prince Fejelis Grey Rapids. Are any of you going to argue with him?"

"I'd like to think I would," Midha said, though he did not look at Fejelis as he said it. "If it were to keep us all safe. But we've got too many friends on the other side of sunset—" Now he looked at Fejelis. "The routine can get cursed dull at times, so we write a lot of letters, and the owners don't mind if we use the wires when there's no official traffic. We've come to know and like a number of Darkborn rather well, in Stranhorne Crosstracks and along the lines. We're in."

Floria

Beatrice spun out the exercise of putting her children to sleep, but returned before the hour was over. Floria laid before her the other information she had: that Tam had successfully escaped the Temple's binding, that the Temple might therefore be interested in the lineage they had before this disdained. As the bells changed their rhythm from warning of darkness to warning of light, she left the woman sitting on the couch, staring into space. She had done what she could. In the foyer, she unpacked and strung lights around her waist and across her back, leaving both hands free. Below ground level in the palace was an unlit room that vigilants used for practice in moving and fighting, with only the lights they carried. Nothing and no one should hold the power of terror over a vigilant.

Or so her father had said, the first time he pushed her through the door into the darkness.

At first, she saw nothing but the near walls, the dim forms

in the garden at the edge of the spray, and beyond that, nothingness. She closed her eyes and listened for any movement out there, besides the wind that came up around dusk. She and Balthasar had used to play listening games, ear to ear on either side of the paper wall. She could not match his hearing, but listening with him, she had learned how to use her own better. Hearing no threat, she opened her eyes and moved away from the door. Now, across the river, she could see a faint linear glow that marked the route to the council chambers. There appeared to be no other lights in the dark streets: *good.* She moved quietly to the gate and leaned against it. She could afford to wait a while, to ensure that no one would use the curfew to come for Beatrice.

She waited until she saw that the lit route traced out by the princess's party had begun to shorten; their brightnesses must be on their way back. Once they had reached the palace, once the lit way had been dismantled, the night would be returned to the Darkborn. If the mages remained adamant about that, they had the means to enforce it. She did not intend to outstay her welcome. She retraced the route as quickly as she could and more easily, since it was now downhill. The moon was just coming into view over the slopes to the east, giving an eerie glitter to the water on the river. A false promise, since should her lights fail now, the moon would merely illuminate her death. The thought raised a cold sweat, chilling the shadowed skin of her scalp, and despite her training, fear forced her on until she was almost running.

She had almost reached the palace, almost reached the wide street—now dark—that had been used as their brightnesses' corridor, when she heard scuffling, and then an angry, familiar voice. "... What you are doing is criminal."

The reflections on the walls lurched as she halted. It could not be—no Darkborn could be alive, not with this much ambient light.

She drew her revolver. If it were not Balthasar, then there was only one other person it could be.

She heard the voice gasp in pain. She remembered that gasp: she had heard it from the other side of the wall as two men manhandled Balthasar on a search through his house. He spoke again. "The curfew was laid for one purpose and one only: to permit your princess to travel to a meeting with the archduke—"

She stepped around the corner. Three men and a woman—southerners, by their dress—encircled a fifth person. Seven servants, personal light bearers, ringed them. She recognized two of the four as members of Sharel's retinue. One of them held an ax at half ready. Another, a pry bar. The third was restraining *him*. She had an impression of a lean frame; dark hair; pale skin; mottled, stiff clothing; a back arched in an attempt to ease his pinned arms. The southerners were too close for her to take a clear shot without the risk of one of them fouling it, and if they held what she thought they held, they were dead or enslaved already. They just did not know it.

"—not," he finished, "to terrorize Darkborn with gratuitous *breakings*."

He sounded so like Balthasar in his quiet fury at the greed, stupidity, and indifference that crippled factory workers or kept the old underground streets a disease-breeding sewer. How *dare* the Shadowborn mock her by so perfect an impersonation?

"What are you, cripple?" the woman mocked. "Some kind of Darkborn-lover? Some kind of darkness freak?"

Cripple? Floria remained still. Should she call out, hoping they would give her a clear line as they turned?

The man who held the pry bar lowered it, saying uneasily, "Marle, there's something off here. Where are his lights?"

"I don't need lights," the creature who was not Balthasar said. "It's complicated to explain, but I must speak to your princess or to your archmage as soon as possible."

"I don't think so," said the man holding him. His movement took Floria by surprise—took them all by surprise. He pulled his captive backward, pivoting. Floria glimpsed a white profile, whiter than any Lightborn she knew. She tracked with the revolver, her wonder intensifying. Why was the mage letting himself be manhandled? She heard the woman say, "But we can't—"

"Got to," the man said with a grunt. "Don't want him telling anyone." He heaved; Floria glimpsed a shape hurtling into the shadows. She heard a body land and another of those sounds of pain terribly familiar from the far side of the wall.

The revolver cracked before she knew she meant to fire. One of the hanging lights shattered, raining glowing fragments down on the head of the servant who carried the stand.

One of the southerners went for the rifle slung over his shoulder. She shot him in the leg. He fell, shrieking. Then she shot out another of the lights. She didn't have nearly enough bullets to threaten them all, but the psychological effect should be enough. She said, making sure her voice carried, "Leave one set of lights and go."

"Mistress White Hand—"

"Go!"

The woman was crouched by the wounded man, trying to get him to release the hands gripping his thigh. "He needs a mage," she said, urgently.

The man glared out of the circle of lights, his longing to fight palpable even across the distance. But the most belligerent of his companions was wounded, the woman had abandoned all fight, and the other man was standing paralyzed. He seized one of the stands of lights from a servant and threw it down, and then gestured the other man to help the woman. Floria watched them go, unmoving, guard up, revolver trained. Yes, he turned once, his eyes promising vengeance. She had made an enemy there.

And she'd have him up before the judiciar for this night's work. Even if the judiciary were indifferent to the Darkborn, they'd care that he had intended murder by darkness—never mind that what he intended to murder well deserved it.

On light, deadly feet, she ran forward, revolver raised.

He was still sitting on the ground with the fallen lights beside him. He was holding his left wrist, which must have taken the impact of his fall, in his bandaged right hand. She realized immediately why the southerner had called him "cripple." She had seldom seen a blind person, and never one whose eyes were not visibly marred by the process that had destroyed his sight. Yet his dark eyes were flawless, with a brown, healthy iris and glossy cornea, except that his pupils were constricted and his wandering gaze did not fix on her.

As quietly as she approached, he was still aware of her. "*Floria?* Was that you speaking?"

She sighted the revolver on the center of his forehead.

"Please," he whispered. "Of all people, not you."

Her lights spilled over his face, lighting the pallor of an invalid who seldom saw the sun. A narrow, intense face, a scholar's—or a fanatic's. Blinded Lightborn, knowing themselves destined to look on darkness for the rest of their days, frequently committed suicide or lost their minds. On one side of his face she could see the red, shiny marks of newly healed wounds—like knife marks—from his ear to his jaw. His clothing was too thick, too opaque, to be wearable, particularly in this light, and with that uneven, natural dye reminiscent of the little box that Balthasar had given her—and that the Shadowborn had used to craft the talisman that had killed her prince. On his index fingers were matching silver rings. She had seen a pair of rings identical to those when Balthasar had slipped them into the *passe-muraille* to show her. Sitting against the paper wall, he had talked until he was hoarse about his wedding and the marvel that was his wife.

He said, almost in a whisper, "I wrote you a letter when I was thirteen. It was the first love letter I ever wrote. I imagined a meeting between us. This isn't . . . what I imagined."

She still had the letter, read once and unopened all those years since. She had been eighteen, Prince Benedict had just been deposed, and childish imaginings had seemed very distant. "No," she said. "Because you are not Balthasar."

He took a shallow breath. "I told you what Tercelle Amberley said: that her lover had come to her through the day. I now know who the man—men—were who used her so, how they moved through the day and what they wanted from the Amberleys. I know why the children were born sighted."

"A Darkborn can no more live in light than a Lightborn can live in darkness."

"I am living proof to the contrary. Which is why I *must* speak to your princess and the mages of the Temple."

"I can't allow that."

"Floria," he said, so familiar. "It *is* your voice. Were you with the party that spoke to the archduke?"

"No, I had a separate errand."

"How much do you know?"

"I know," she said, "that their brightnesses do not believe in such things as Shadowborn. I know that I do."

A beat; pain crossed his face. "Prince Isidore," he said, compassionately.

She did not answer. She would not let him feed on her pain, whatever he was.

She heard the bells change their rhythm, signaling warning to the Lightborn that their part of the night was at an end. If she let him up, if she risked leaving him alive, dared she bring him to the palace for questioning and punishment?

Whom did she serve? Isidore, who was dead, but who had commissioned her to watch out for his son, and Fejelis, whose steadiness in the midst of chaos and disaster had won her respect.

Would it help either of her princes if she took a Shadowborn into the palace?

It would be proof of her innocence, and of Fejelis's. And a . . . curse on their enemies.

Her voice rasped. "Stand up."

He did, clumsily, holding his wrist close to his body. She ignored that; injuries could be faked to put an opponent off guard. But his clothing jarred her. Mages could ensorcell clothing to appear opaque, but the cloth usually retained the texture of the sheer cloth most wore.

And he carried no lights, nor did he ask to pick up the fallen stand.

"Turn around," she said, testing him. "Walk. Back to me—look round, and I'll shoot."

He turned without hesitation to face the darkness, and began to walk in the direction of the palace. "Floria," he said, "I am so very sorry about Isidore, about the tower. If we'd realized faster what it was we faced—"

"Don't talk," she said. For all she knew, he had woven an ensorcellment into the words.

He continued a half block in silence, then spoke again. "Telmaine . . . is dead. Part of me simply does not care if you do shoot me. Except that I would rather it not be you. And I have undertaken to do what I can to persuade their brightnesses that another force has been working to destroy the peace between us."

"Your dukes had more than a little part in it themselves."

"Yes," he said. "Duke Mycene is dead—he faced down a Shadowborn. Duke Kalamay—I think the archduke will deal with him as soon as he can, but his power is compromised. Telmaine—I don't know how much you heard, how much they told you, but my wife was a mage."

"A *mage*?" Prejudiced, proper, jealous Telmaine . . . She reminded herself, forcibly, that this *could not be* Balthasar, but why should any impersonator think she would care about Telmaine, with whom she had no more than a speaking acquaintance?

And who could not be dead, whatever he said, because she had freed Floria from her prison before her lights ran out.

He was speaking again to the night before him in as bleak a voice as she had ever heard. "She had had no training, and she went up against—fought—a Shadowborn. I don't know what he did to her, but something went wrong with her magic. I can't believe she would willingly have harmed the archduke, much less nearly kill him." He halted without warning, and she nearly jammed the revolver into his back. "Keep moving," she said.

"She healed him, but they took her prisoner. Took her prisoner and put her in a room and opened it to the light—they executed my beloved wife for sorcery, and I was not there to protect her," he finished in a gasp, suffocated by pain.

She remembered Telmaine—or the voice that sounded like Telmaine—saying, "Tell Balthasar we spoke. It is very important."

If this were a Shadowborn, it might think to disarm her with Balthasar's grief, not knowing that she would know it lied. Or be soliciting information, if Telmaine were, implausibly, a mage. "Keep moving," she ordered.

After that, he did not speak again until they reached the walls of the palace and passed through into the gardens. And then she saw him falter before her, heard him faintly breathe, "Sweet Imogene. I never imagined . . ." She did not have time to walk him around to the rear, bring him close to the terrible ruin of the tower, which was just as well—if he were Shadowborn, she would not give him the chance to gloat, and if he were not, if he were, impossibly, Balthasar, then she could not inflict such pain on him.

When, she wondered, *did I begin to doubt?*

Since she was not in attendance on their brightnesses, she had not come to the door of greater privilege, but one of the doors of lesser privilege favored by the vigilance, because it gave them quick access to most of the places vigilants needed to be, including their own internal barracks. At the top of the steps four vigilants stood within a shelter of light, watching them. She recognized Captain Lapaxo, the most senior surviving of the captains. Parhelion had died at his post with Prince Isidore. Beaudry had apparently committed suicide or been murdered after making an attempt on Fejelis's life. Although, given that Rupertis had apparently transferred his allegiance to Prasav, perhaps *he* was in charge of the vigilance and Lapaxo exiled to guard duty. The captain's eyes, tired and suspicious, moved from Balthasar to Floria and back again, seeing exactly the same anomalies she had. "Mistress White Hand," he said, neutrally.

"I need a mage to question this man, urgently."

Her prisoner said, "A lineage mage won't be able to—"

"Would you kindly *be quiet,*" she said, tense with doubt and the potential for disaster.

Lapaxo said, "Go through; wait inside." She heard him

ordering one of the other three, the last two to take down the lights and close up, to follow. He joined them, flanking Floria and watching her prisoner. It was easier to think of the prisoner as such now, to believe that whatever he was, it was not what he appeared to be. Out in the night . . .

Inside was a short, wide vestibule with another vigilant post at the end. To those guarding it, Lapaxo signaled, *Bring a mage.* A woman disappeared through the door beyond the post.

"I would quite like to sit down," her prisoner said diffidently.

"It won't be long," she said.

It wasn't. The vigilant returned not only with a mage wearing the badge of the palace judiciary, but with Tempe Silver Branch of the judiciary—not mageborn, but magically endowed to detect lies, as Floria was magically endowed to detect poisons. The mage was less than Floria had hoped for, merely third rank, born of the lineages, and quite likely as young as her oval face. She was dressed entirely in mourning red—tunic, trousers, headband, and gloves. Her wheat-colored hair was meticulously braided into multiple neat loops, attesting to vanity, poise, and an understanding of the need to maintain appearances. Despite that understanding, she had something of the harrowed, heavy-eyed look common to many of the younger mages in the aftermath of the tower's destruction. Though where most of them looked merely stunned, her eyes smoldered with rage.

Floria said, "Magistra, could you please tell me what this man is? I warn you, he may be dangerous."

"How so?" said Lapaxo, and she realized that her prisoner was not the only one under suspicion.

"He claims to be Darkborn. Indeed, he claims to be a close friend of mine. That is, as we all well know, impossible."

"Even so, you don't quite believe that," Tempe said, quietly.

Floria laughed bitterly. "My notion of what is and is not impossible has been somewhat tried of late."

"Where did you go tonight?" Tempe said.

"To warn someone that the southerners might be about to take an unwelcome interest in them. I would prefer not to say who." Especially not in the company of a mage. "I will say—listen to me, Tempe—that the party I went to warn constitutes no danger whatsoever to any of their brightnesses, the vigilance, or the Temple."

"Truth," said Tempe, somewhat reluctantly. She turned her attention to Balthasar. "Who are you?"

Floria had been vainly hoping that she would not start with that question.

"My name," said her prisoner, "is Balthasar Hearne."

Both Lapaxo and Tempe looked at her; they recognized the name. The mage did not. She had not moved, had not shown any indication of initiative. Absorbed by her own anger, she would do nothing without a direct order.

". . . And, yes, I am Darkborn."

The mage's lip curled. "Do you want me to examine . . . him?"

There was a silence. Tempe said, as uncertain as Floria had ever heard her, "He is speaking the truth—as he believes it. Lapaxo—"

Lapaxo returned the mage's glare with his own, one of a captain of vigilants. She was the one who dropped her eyes. "Please, Magistra."

She jerked off her red glove and tucked it into her belt. "Fine," she said. "Hold him."

"There's no need," their prisoner said.

"I'll determine the need," the mage said, shortly. "Hold him."

Floria took one arm, Lapaxo the other. The mage said to Balthasar, "I'm going to touch your face."

"I know," he said. "My sister is a third-rank mage."

The touch was almost a slap, though it quickly softened as she took hold of herself, her hand molding to his cheek. Floria watched her face as her magic penetrated his thoughts, watched her expression shift from anger to confusion and then, abruptly, to deep pity. Floria could not see his, though he shivered a little in their grip.

The mage dropped her hand and stepped back. "He

needs a healer, not me," she said, staring at their prisoner in undisguised pity and dismay. "He's—he's quite mad. He is convinced he *is* Darkborn. He believes he was held prisoner by these Shadowborn, ensorcelled by them, made able to walk in daylight. He believes he is on a mission to prove that the Shadowborn exist and are responsible for everything that has happened. He believes he is blind, believes it so strongly that I cannot see through his eyes, yet he behaves as though he is able to see. Something terrible must have happened to him. . . . If you were to make inquiries among the people who lived around the tower, you might well find someone who knows him."

Their prisoner made a sound that might have been the ghost of a laugh or the ghost of a sob.

Tempe said, "Does he intend anyone harm?"

"No," she said, with certainty. "He wants to save us—Darkborn and Lightborn both. Even the Shadowborn. He cares. He cares passionately. And he grieves." To their prisoner, she said, awkwardly, "I'm so sorry."

Floria said, "Do you sense any ensorcellment about him?"

"No!" The mage bristled at that question, taking it as accusation.

As a pure-lineage mage, she would not.

"Thank you, Magistra," Lapaxo said. "That answers some of my questions."

She dipped her head, turned away, and left at a walk just shy of a run, fleeing the presence of a man driven mad by tragedy.

Their prisoner sounded shaken. "She's wrong. I'm not mad."

Lapaxo said, tiredly, "We'll hold him here, under guard. Find his family in the morning." If they had survived. And even if they had survived, what was the likelihood of their being able to pay for a healer to restore a mind so broken?

Yet that voice. That manner. Every word he had spoken, every action he had taken, *was* Balthasar. Perhaps she was as mad as the mage said he was. She said, choosing her words carefully, "May I look after him? I brought him here."

"And why was that?" Tempe said, promptly.

"I couldn't leave him out there," she said, truthfully. "We were due to hand over the night, and he'd already run into some of Sharel's retinue, who'd been amusing themselves by battering in Darkborn doors."

"They came through half an hour ago," Lapaxo said. "Spitting fire and swearing vengeance against you."

Their prisoner said to Tempe, "Then I wish to lay charges against these four individuals, by the compact of eight sixty-four, dealing with matters of legal transgressions across sunset. The charges will certainly involve property damage and assault." He held up his wrist, the swelling and new bruising prominent on the pale skin. "I was in imminent danger when Mistress Floria stepped in: by their words and behavior, they did not intend me to survive as a witness. There may be further charges, depending on what else they did."

For once, Tempe seemed at a loss, caught between the insistence of her asset that he believed every word he said, and her own certainty that he was severely delusional. She said, weakly, "I'll . . . send a clerk to take a statement."

"Thank you," said their prisoner.

"Permission granted," Lapaxo said. "I'll want a guard on you both."

That was precisely what Floria did not want, but she took what she could get—them past the guard post and into a small holding suite. It was starkly lit and equally starkly furnished, with a modest living and eating area, three beds in separate rooms, and toilet facilities. The prisoner investigated the stretched mesh of the seating with interest before sitting down and leaning back. "Floria," he said, in a strange, wondering tone. Then, purposefully, "Do you think I could get ice and a strapping for this wrist? I don't think it's broken—there's no tenderness at the expected spots—but it's swelling. And then I *have* to speak to a mage who can actually detect this ensorcellment."

She was not going to tell him that the only sport mage in the palace, as far as she knew, was the princess herself. She decided to deal with the practicalities, and spoke to their guard, requesting bandages, ice, food, and drink, and a dose of painkiller from the vigilant's store.

The vigilant returned with the medical supplies and the food and drink. She mixed a dose of the painkiller into juice, sweetened it with honey, and tasted it. She had half expected recent events to have undone her efforts in educating court in the futility of poisoning her. But it was unadulterated.

She offered it to him, not certain whether he would take it. He put their shared thought into words. "I'm trusting you haven't put something in here that will knock me out until morning." He did not mention a simple, lethal dose, though if he did not think about the possibility, he *was* insane.

"I'll call in Tempe, if you want. Let you ask me in front of her. She wouldn't let me poison you."

He considered her thoughtfully for a few heartbeats longer and then drained the glass. "I must get you to teach me how to make medicines palatable," he remarked. "Most of the ones I was taught to prepare taste thoroughly vile."

Despite his seeming calm, she saw his relief as moments passed and he felt no ill effects. "My wrist?" he prompted.

Wary of touching him or letting him touch her, she pulled up a stool. It was her turn to feel relief when she took his arm and nothing happened. His skin was pale and cool, with a slight rash or chapping across the back of his hand, and no calluses of manual work or sword training. She examined the wrist, feeling the tendons and probing the fine bones, ignoring his flinches—provoking them, even. He let her hurt him, enduring. "I don't think it's broken, either," she said at last.

He relaxed as she wound the coarse mesh of the bandage deftly across his palm and around his thumb. "Do you remember," he said, "mixing up a hangover cure for me, after my friends and I celebrated passing our final exams?"

She did; she had been worried about him—about Balthasar—as he had been so miserably ill. She finished strapping the wrist. "Let's have something to eat."

Somewhat to her surprise, Tempe did respond to their request, sending a clerk to record both the prisoner's statement and hers in his impeccable shorthand. The prisoner's account was precise and well observed, including details of appearance and posture. The mage must be right; he *could* see.

Or he was Darkborn, and Balthasar Hearne.

She needed to know for her *own* sanity.

The clerk gathered together his materials and started to rise. The prisoner said, "Wait." And when the clerk looked at him—and away from those disturbing eyes—he said, "I have a request that you take down another statement, under the seal of the judiciary."

"Under the seal of the judiciary" meant that the statement would enter permanent record. The judiciars considered the integrity of their records as sacrosanct as the Temple did their contracts.

The clerk looked at her for confirmation; she nodded slowly. Whoever and whatever their prisoner was—mad or sane—he understood Lightborn law, and under that, he was fully entitled to make such a statement.

"It may take a little time. Would you like something to eat or drink?"

The man shook his head vehemently, and Floria felt the corner of her mouth twitch. Of course not; not in the presence of a notorious vigilant assassin whose asset made her immune to poisons.

In a measured voice, the prisoner began, "My name is Balthasar Hearne, and I am a physician, born Darkborn in the city of Minhorne. I am an adult of sound mind and a citizen in good standing, and I make this statement of my own free will to place on record my knowledge of the troubles that beset Minhorne, specifically the burning of the Rivermarch, the assassination of Prince Isidore, and the destruction of the tower of the Mages' Temple."

She knew part of the story, but not all, and certainly not what had happened in Stranhorne and after. His account of Captain Rupertis's treason and death brought her to her feet, fists clenched. She rang for a guard and demanded that Rupertis come down and see her. The guard told her that Rupertis had not reported in, having left on an errand during the day. After that, she could not sit down again, but paced while, in a still place in the center of the room, the man told his story. The clerk's moving hand faltered several times during the narrative, as did their prisoner's voice, but he told it to the end, listened as it was read back to him, and signed in an uncertain but recognizable script when the last sheet was offered to him. "Put that before your Mistress Tempe, if you would."

He managed to hold his composure until the clerk left, and then he laid his face in his hands.

Her last disbelief had crumbled, listening to a voice she had known for close to thirty years speaking without a mis-chosen word or misplaced inflection. She sat down beside him, resting an arm along his spine and gently kneading his neck as though he were another vigilant. "You need to pull yourself together," she said, quietly. "As soon as Tempe reads that, she'll be along, wanting to hear you confirm it to her asset. You're liable to find yourself up before the Temple or the princess very shortly after that." She closed her hand on the tendons of his neck, pulling gently back. "Balthasar, sit up and listen to me."

He let her draw him up, his head in profile to her. She said softly, "It's a dangerous thing to show weakness in the Lightborn court. Whatever you feel, whatever anger or hurt or grief you're carrying, you *must* conceal it. Otherwise, you won't be believed. Otherwise, you'll be a target." Those were, she recalled, the very words her father had used to her, nearly thirty years ago. They were words she had used to any number of vigilant cadets in the years since.

He turned his head. "You said my name. You believe me."

"I believe you. But if others do . . . you have to know that they may decide this ensorcellment makes you too dangerous to live." First, they would want to extract all the information from it that they could.

He leaned back, his face drained of emotion. "Why do you think I dictated it under a judiciary seal? Even if I die, my testimony has entered the record."

Clever. And no less than she would have expected of Balthasar. She reached for the dish of hot towels that had come with their meal, finding them still somewhat warm. "Let's get you tidied before they come for us."

Telmaine

"We'll be into th'Crosstracks in a matter of minutes, m'lord," the engineer addressed Vladimer, ignoring his companions. "All seems t'be clear."

Vladimer was sitting with his sound shoulder propped against the wall. He roused himself. "You've made better time than I expected. My compliments to you and the rest of the crew."

The engineer paused. "Aye, well," he said, in his Borders accent, "I'd as soon we none of us had t'do this again."

"I would add my wish to yours," Vladimer said, dryly, "if I thought it would be heeded." The engineer touched his cap lightly and started to close the door, but Vladimer spoke again. "Even if it does appear to be clear, I want you and your crew to be on the alert as we come into station. Given what happened the last time I got off a train." When he and Telmaine had been ambushed by a Shadowborn and his agents, leaving Vladimer wounded and an engine and carriages blazing.

"Aye, my lord," said the engineer. "That y'can count on."

"Though I trust," Vladimer said with grim satisfaction, "that should the Shadowborn try an ambush here, they will meet with an unpleasant comeuppance."

The bordersman's expression flickered at the reference to Vladimer's traveling companions, though not with the prejudice Telmaine might have expected; he appeared almost gratified by the prospect. Telmaine wondered if he were from Strumheller. If he were from Ishmael's barony, that might explain it.

"Do you expect there to be trouble at the Crosstracks?" Phoebe said as the door closed.

Vladimer leaned his head back. "Better to expect trouble and have none, than not expect trouble and walk into it. I have no idea of their numbers or how they communicate, although I would deduce that at least in Minhorne, they are relatively few, since they have caused as much mayhem through their agents as directly. It may be we have been able to keep ahead of them—assuming that none of the nonmageborn in your community were serving them without your knowledge." Phoebe did not rise to that lure. "And assuming that Sejanus and his staff have been able to maintain the fiction of my incapacitation."

The drawn cast to his bony features gave the lie to that "fiction," in Telmaine's opinion.

There was a silence; then Phoebe Broome drew in an audible breath. "Lord Vladimer, I would like you to let me hold your revolver until after we arrive."

The extraordinary demand startled Telmaine into sonning her. She found her leaning forward with a determined expression, all trace of the gauche, socially intimidated woman gone.

"If you will not let me or one of my people heal you, then you should let me have the revolver. If Ishmael were here, he would insist."

"Would he, indeed?" said Vladimer, in that brittle tone that intimidated Telmaine every time she heard it.

"He might weigh the risks differently. But, tell me, Lord Vladimer, would *you* leave a man in your condition in charge of a loaded weapon?"

There was a silence—in which Vladimer must remember, as Telmaine did, Sylvide's death—followed by a rasp of clothing, a snap of a holster. Telmaine's sonn caught the passing of the revolver, hilt first, from his hand to hers. "Thank you, Lord Vladimer. I would feel better if you would let one of us deal with your wound. You would think more clearly if you were not in so much pain."

"That is not acceptable."

"No," she said with a sigh, checking the revolver's safety before slipping it into her own pocket. "I suppose not."

Should Telmaine mention that Lord Vladimer's cane was as lethal as a revolver in his hands? She had been there when he had killed a man with it. She found she didn't dare.

"What do you want us to do when we pull into the station?" the mage said.

"I would suggest you leave nonmageborn to the railway crew. You deal with mages. I would much prefer that you immobilize rather than kill them, since we need information. However, the magical aspect of this is your command; I cannot advise."

Arrival in Strumheller was a welcome anticlimax, in one sense. There was no Shadowborn ambush waiting for them. But in another, it was immediately apparent that this was no normal night. They disembarked into a cordon of railway workers and were promptly set upon by a brace of reporters from the local broadsheet and several officials from the railway. On the opposite platform, Telmaine could sonn a shifting crowd and the panting profile of a waiting train. Vladimer raised his voice over the racket to order Phoebe to secure carriages for their party to take them to the manor, and insisted on being taken to the telegraph office before he would answer any questions. The reporters descended upon Farquhar, demanding to know who they were and why they should be traveling with Lord Vladimer, and were they aware of what had happened to Stranhorne, and what were these reports of the archduke having been mortally injured. The strongest living Darkborn mage beamed at them, whipped four beanbags from his pockets, and began to juggle. Telmaine's momentary relief that he was not going to tell them anything swiftly passed when the reporters switched their attention to her; in a traveling dress made for an archduchess, she was the obvious anomaly amongst the plainly dressed mages. She backed up under their barrage; reporters were a species the sheltered Lady Telmaine had little experience of.

She was saved by an incursion of armed men. Farquhar Broome's beanbags swooped down into his hands—something hopefully not too conspicuous to the nonmages around—and she felt a surge of magic between the others, a massing of defensive powers. A man in railway uniform thrust himself between her and the reporters, setting his back to them and addressing her. "M'lady, we need t'clear the platform for an unscheduled train from Stranhorne. They've got wounded."

"Wounded?" she managed.

"Aye. There's bad trouble in Stranhorne."

Trouble . . . "What," she said, aristocratic accent to the fore, "is happening in Stranhorne?"

"Don't rightly know," said the station guard tersely. "If you'll go into th'concourse, you can talk to th'agent there—he'll tell you what's possible for getting y'back up the line. Excuse me." He shouldered past her.

"This is the second evacuation train," the younger of the two reporters said at her shoulder. "First one came through with the worst injured, children, physicians, the young baronet and baronette—"

"Physicians," Telmaine caught. "Where—where are they? Did you speak to anyone? Did you hear anything of a Dr. Balthasar Hearne?"

"Hearne? Wasn't he the man that—" She could not miss their suddenly keener interest. "Is he a relative of yours, m'lady?"

"Dr. Hearne is my husband," she said. "So if you would kindly tell anything you know, I would be much obliged."

"My colleague was going to say that a man by that name had been arrested by Lord Mycene and—taken off toward Stranhorne. Why was your husband—"

The train, reeking of smoke and burned *something*, drew into the station. The younger reporter said, "That engine's a Stotler nine-oh-four. What are they doing running a nine-oh-four on this line?"

"Best they had, likely."

In a long, expiring squeal of brakes, the train halted. The doors crashed open, swinging back to rebound off the train's flanks. Men jumped down, began lifting down children, women, injured men and women. Someone shouted, "Help here!" Telmaine, straining, sought any line of profile or plane of cheek that would identify Balthasar before extending her mage sense in desperation. The sense of pain, of panic, of grief, of terror, nearly made her cry out. Her knees buckled. Phoebe's voice in her mind said, <*Don't* open yourself!> and the shock of that intrusion jerked her rigid. She recoiled, both from the crowd and it.

Phoebe shouldered her way through the crowd, using deference to her femaleness, and where that failed, her height and elbows. She put her mouth close to Telmaine's ear. "Some of us are going to stay here, if they'll accept our help for the worst hurt."

"Mistress— Miss—," said the younger reporter.

"Magistra," growled Phoebe. "And if you don't want your beer to taste like horse piss for the next month, you'll keep your next words behind your teeth."

Vladimer, accompanied by a four-man guard, arrived before the reporter found a rejoinder. "We're leaving."

The guard swallowed up Telmaine and Phoebe; Phoebe attached herself to Lord Vladimer's side, hastily explaining the mages' deployment, while Telmaine wavered along behind. She did not know what had shaken her most: her sense of the refugees or having Phoebe address her so.

They arrived to be greeted by an argument in Borders accents so broad as to be unintelligible. The mages' end was being upheld by a fiery man in his late twenties; Telmaine remembered, from the flurry of introduction in Minhorne, that his name was Bryse, and that he came from Strumheller. Vladimer interrupted crisply, "I'll pay what they're asking. Let's get going."

The collective surprise over his ability to make sense of the argument was good enough to get them aboard; Vladimer, Telmaine, Phoebe, and Farquhar shared one carriage. Vladimer said, "They'll need something to make up their losses on the Stranhorne passengers. Horses have to eat, never mind men." With one of his thin smiles: "At one point in my misspent youth, I drove a cab for hire. Excellent way of gathering information." He paused; he did not need to be a mage to be aware of his companions' nervous anticipation of his next words. "Stranhorne Manor and the lands east of it have been overrun. Baron Stranhorne himself is believed dead. He and others used explosives to set fire to and collapse the manor to trap the Shadowborn who forced entry. My informants say that the explosions were probably premature, not entirely unexpected given the Shadowborn's casual way with fire. Ishmael, Ferdenzil Mycene, and the young Stranhornes led a fighting retreat to Stranhorne Crosstracks. Unfortunately, although Ishmael escaped with the others from Stranhorne, he made a bid to reach survivors from the baron's party, and has not been heard of since."

On an exhale, Phoebe Broome said, "No."

"And Balthasar?" Telmaine heard herself say in a thin voice.

"No one who knew your husband, or knew of him, had reported to the railway authorities. Perhaps we will learn more when we arrive at the manor."

Tam

Tam rolled on his side in the hard bed, trying to find a less painful position. He'd been born a peasant and spent his young-adult years one meal away from hunger and one mischance away from prison, so he wasn't soft, but the overreach had left him aching in bone, muscle, and joint. If he regained his former station, he was buying new mattresses for this household.

It wasn't his aching body that kept him awake. Nor had he retreated to bed purely because he felt awful. If he had stayed in the main room, either Jovance or Fejelis would have asked him what had happened between him and the high masters. Jovance, whatever her bitter differences with the Temple, was a high-ranked mage, and Fejelis had a keen eye for deception. They would realize very soon that what he had supposedly done was impossible.

He had already been exhausted when the high masters summoned him, exhausted by grief at Lukfer's death and from annulling the Shadowborn death magic that riddled the ruins of the tower. He had welcomed the masters' examination, desperate that they should know what he knew—until he realized that, horrific as the shattering of the tower had been for him, it had been far more so for them. Lukfer had warned him that the archmage and the oldest high masters—centuries old themselves—had received the memories of mages who remembered the first years after the

Curse. Only the earthborn's utter dependence on the lights they created had saved mages from extinction then.

I should have warned Fejelis, he thought, made him understand how their friends among the artisans threatened not only the Temple's current wealth and status by their experiments with generating light from electricity, but raised atavistic terrors in ancient minds.

He had struggled at the end, which had decided his fate. He still did not know who had sent Perrin running to warn Fejelis that the high masters planned to strip his magic and probably his mind from him. Perhaps she truly did not intend Fejelis harm, since she had tried to warn him when she realized the treachery planned in her name. By then it was too late. Tam had been bound, body and magic, able to hear everything and do nothing. He had heard Fejelis argue for Tam's life, heard him tell the high masters outright he knew about the Shadowborn and their powerlessness against their magic, and heard him appeal for the formation of an alliance. He had heard Prasav accuse Fejelis of conspiring to undermine the Temple, and offer Fejelis and Tam himself as scapegoats for the Shadowborn's crimes. He had realized, from the silence of the mage's spokeswoman—who with one touch could have confirmed Fejelis's innocence, and who *knew* Tam's—that Fejelis was about to die.

And then he felt the archmage's magic slip through the binding like a sharp knife, felt the archmage's strength extended for him to grasp. He had swatted aside the crossbow bolts, reared up, and seized and *lifted* Fejelis—and Orlanjis, too, apparently—and dropped them all here. Here in the Borders, where Lukfer had brought his granddaughter six years ago.

Once more he should be grateful for Fejelis's steadiness. If he'd been alone, he would have died at sunset, sprawled unconscious on the bracken beside the railway tracks.

Instead, he lay on a hard bed and waited for the high masters to find him. Or for Fejelis or Jovance to ask that question.

Overspent, aching, preoccupied, he missed the first

questing touch of magic. A newly familiar magic, tainted with the sense of their enemies, but fundamentally Darkborn.

He felt her sense him. <Telmaine.>

Telmaine

Without an introduction, Telmaine would never have known the woman who greeted them as Ishmael's sister. She was so unlike him: dainty, pretty, and fashionably dressed. But Noellene di Studier did have her brother's phlegmatic temperament; she received them—the archduke's illegitimate brother, Telmaine, and a posse of mages—without fuss or fluster, directed her housekeeper to find everyone suitable rooms, and escorted Vladimer, Phoebe, and Telmaine into a large, well-appointed apartment to meet the Stranhornes.

The apartment was kept at sickroom heat by a fire in the grate. A lanky young man, no more than a teenager, lay on a couch, his shoulder and chest heavily bandaged. A woman in her early twenties sat beside him, coaxing him to drink from a medicine glass. She wore a maternity dress—she was past the stage where it was proper for her to be out in society—and riding boots, her hair woven back in a simple braid. *Wife?* No, too close a resemblance; the two shared the same wide, slightly prominent brow, the same strong features.

"Lord Vladimer Plantageter," Noellene said. "May I introduce Baronette Laurel and Baronet Boris Stranhorne. My friends Lord Vladimer Plantageter, Mrs. Telmaine Hearne, and"—the barest hesitation—"Magistra Phoebe Broome."

Telmaine heard the baronette draw in her breath sharply, not at Phoebe Broome's name, but her own.

"As you are," said Vladimer firmly, as the baronet moved to push back his covers. "You will accomplish nothing by fainting at my feet." *You should know,* thought Telmaine, reproachfully. Had Vladimer not been faint with pain and blood loss when he first tried to convince the archduke of the emergency and Ishmael's innocence, Ishmael and Balthasar might be with them now.

Vladimer allowed Noellene di Studier to move a chair in place for him and sat down, leaving the baronette to seat the rest of them. Telmaine could not prevent herself wondering, albeit fleetingly, whether Noellene knew that Phoebe Broome had been her brother's mistress.

"Lord Vladimer," Laurel Stranhorne said, extending a hand to him. He took it, dipped his head, and released it, a sketch of courtesy. "It is an honor finally to meet you. Ishmael has spoken of you often. I can offer you a summary, and then explain more fully as you need. Ishmael preferred his reports that way—the essentials first, then action, if need be, and then the details." Her smile was almost too fleeting for them to catch the quiver at its corners.

"Ishmael always has a sound grasp of priorities," said Vladimer, with a suggestion of warmth. "Go on."

"Stranhorne Manor and, as far as we know, the villages to the south and west beyond, were overrun by the Shadowborn almost a full night ago," the baronette said. Her studied detachment was effortful. "We had scant warning, and still don't know the extent of the force against us—it consisted of Shadowborn, animals, and . . . ensorcelled Darkborn. The leaders were mages. We took in those of our people who had managed to reach us before we had to close the gates, and set to defend the manor. We had been stockpiling munitions in case the Isles asked for our help." Vladimer's expression did not change at that admission. "We tucked them away in the cellars of the manor when Lord Mycene arrived. When the manor came under heavy attack, our men moved the explosives to structural points within the manor. The plan was that if the Shadowborn forced entry, our father"—she stopped, pressed her lips together, and composed herself to go on—"our father and others were to fire the munitions while the rest of us broke out through the front gate and made a dash for the Crosstracks. Father and the others meant to get clear, but the Shadowborn were using fire. We think the explosions were premature." The baronet threw his undamaged arm over his face. His sister slipped her hand into his and squeezed. "We were attacked twice on the way to the Crosstracks and lost another twenty or thirty people. But they didn't move on us during the day, and we're evacuating as many as we can tonight. We've had to fight off raids on our trains, but we have succeeded so far."

"I now appreciate," said Vladimer, slowly, "why the Stranhornes have earned the respect of such very different connoisseurs of warfare as Ishmael di Studier and Lord Sachevar Mycene. What of Ishmael? Is he . . . ?"

She shook her head quickly, sparing Vladimer the word at which he had balked. "He left the manor with us, but he went back to try to find Father, and he has not returned."

Vladimer's expression turned bleak; if he called anyone friend, it was Ishmael.

"I wouldn't give up hope," Noellene di Studier said. "I've learned not to."

"Lord Mycene and his men are still at the Crosstracks. With Lavender—my sister. People are still filtering into the Crosstracks from the surrounding areas. You know how extensive the underground complex is, so now that we have reinforcements from Strumheller, we hope we can hold. But, not knowing the extent of the Shadowborn forces, we cannot promise."

"These reinforcements—I trust they do not represent a substantial portion of Strumheller's own defense." He sonned Noellene di Studier's scowl. "I have no wish to insult your brother, but by Ishmael's account, he does not have the experience—"

"His troop commanders do," the baronette said. "My brother—*both* my brothers—are the quintessence of Borders stubbornness when it comes to each other, but they know their duty to their people and they are neither of them fools."

"Please," Telmaine interrupted. "Where is my *husband*, Dr. Balthasar Hearne? Is he back in the Crosstracks?" She could not imagine, if he were already in Strumheller itself, he would not have come to find her. "Or did he . . . ?" She could not voice the thought that he might have stayed behind in Stranhorne. Or *died* in the manor. Hopeless as he was with a firearm, he would put himself between any patient, woman, or child, and the Shadowborn. He might even have volunteered—

"I am sorry, Lady Telmaine," Baronette Stranhorne said. "I am truly sorry. We don't know what happened to your husband."

She lies, Telmaine thought. "That is *not*—"

With an edge of desperation, the baronette said, to Vladimer, "Ishmael said that you knew about the Shadowborn, Lord Vladimer, that they can, apparently, change their form—"

"Yes, we know about them," Telmaine said, beyond courtesy. "Tell me about my husband!"

Vladimer, too, must have sensed something in Laurel's manner. He said, "Baronette, if you would."

"We had one of those Shadowborn in Stranhorne Manor," she said, slowly and unhappily. "We think it arrived with Lord Mycene, as one of his men. Dr. Hearne had been helping our surgeon, quite capably, so I didn't suspect him, but I caught him, or something in his shape, opening a side entrance to let in the Shadowborn."

"No!" Telmaine cried out. "Balthasar would *never* do that."

"Not willingly," said Vladimer in a tone that made Phoebe's head turn toward him.

"Whether it was or wasn't, your husband did not escape with us. I'm terribly sorry, Lady Telmaine."

Her ears were roaring. She heard Noellene di Studier say, "Put her head down." She would have welcomed fainting, welcomed escape from the terrible choice between Balthasar as betrayer, ensorcelled by the Shadowborn, and Balthasar left behind, living or dead, in the ruins of Stranhorne Manor. But someone—*Vladimer?*—pushed her head down to her knees and held it there.

Slowly her head cleared, and her wits and resolve returned. She would not believe it until she had sensed for herself that Balthasar was gone, that his essence was no longer in the world. She need not rely on others' reports or wait, perhaps in vain, for some relics of him to be returned to her. She could thank magic for that.

And she could thank it for something else, too: if Balthasar were dead, she would be able to do more about his death than weep for him. Unlike other wives, she would not have to beg others to punish or avenge his death . . . or beg them to do nothing, for their own lives' sake. She had power; *she* could deal with his murderers.

"Lady Telmaine!" hissed Magistra Broome. Farquhar Broome's softly scolding, <Tsk,> brushed her mind. Smelling burning, she reared up—Vladimer had removed his hand—but all that remained was a faint scent of smoke and a tingle of magic.

"Yes," Vladimer said. "There is that." He let a beat pass, but neither of the Stranhornes challenged that cryptic statement. "Thank you, Baronette Stranhorne; that was most succinct. Your father is a great loss, to Stranhorne and to the archdukedom as a whole. I will ask for further details in a moment, but first I owe you, I think, a summary of events in the city."

Telmaine realized he was going to begin with Balthasar's opening the door to Tercelle Amberley. He certainly would not begin with his own encounter with the Shadowborn. She did not want to hear her part of it again; she would surely scream or weep. She stood up. "Please excuse me. Hearing it again would only distress me."

The threat of magical vapors was even more potent than the threat of the ordinary kind. The door was well closed behind her before Vladimer said another word.

Out in the hall, she had nowhere to go; if she had been given a room, she did not know where it was. She did not want to join the mages; they might be her kind, but the train journey had amply demonstrated that they were not her class. She simply let her feet take her where they would, and when they led her through an unobtrusive door into a small library that smelled disquietingly familiar, she realized then that she had been guided by Ishmael's memory.

Centerpiece to the library was a molded relief of the region as large as a dinner table and surely as heavy. When she was much younger, her brothers had had such a relief in their part of the nursery, across which model huntsmen, soldiers, and rogues skirmished on those nights when winter weather barred them from outdoor make-believe. This had a far more serious purpose.

She paused before it. She could not imagine Ishmael being careless in the placement and orientation of something so essential to his planning. So if she stood thus, then Stranhorne should be . . . Cautiously, she extended her mage sense outward, seeking her husband's familiar vitality. It had never been a vibrant vitality—Balthasar lacked the brawny energy of her brothers and Ishmael—but it had a distinctive constancy and sweetness.

And then, out there, she brushed up against something potent and vile—Shadowborn magic, but so concentrated that she crumpled her magic back into her skin with such violence that, between the action and the Shadowborn magic, she found herself leaning over the table, fighting dry heaves.

<Telmaine?>

She nearly screamed, but the mental contact was not Shadowborn; it had a ground-glass abrasiveness that she had learned to associate with one Lightborn mage. <Magister Tammorn?>

<Thank the Mother,> Tammorn said. <Can you hold this contact? I'm—> But she already knew what he was; she had felt burnout before. He felt her recoil, read the memory that surged to the forefront of her thoughts. <No! Curse it, don't drop it. I'm not going to die on you!>

His exhaustion was even greater than his irritation, but she did not sense the excruciating pain she had sensed from Ishmael, or that terrifying sense of his life draining away. Cautiously, she assumed the burden of the contact. Immediately, he demanded, <What's happening? What are you doing in the Borders? How did you break my binding?>

The binding that he had imposed on her as the price of his help when she went to save the archduke. <I won't let you do that to me again.>

<Lady Telmaine, in my present condition, I couldn't bind dandelion fluff. What were you just doing?>

<I was trying to find my husband. I sensed>—she gagged, and managed—<Shadowborn.>

"Mother of All," he muttered aloud. <Could you *please* try to organize your thoughts? My head's about to split as it is.>

Control, she urged herself. Feeling her way, she moved hesitantly to the hearth and sat down on it, drawing her legs up beneath her. The slate was cold under her hips, even through the layers of fabric, but it was not combustible. <My husband, Balthasar, was in Stranhorne when the Shadowborn invaded. I thought I might be able to find him. Instead, I sensed Shadowborn—nothing but Shadowborn.>

"Shadowborn," Tam said, to whoever was with him. "Yes, I know we knew that, but she says strong mages. No, I promise, I won't try—" <Lady Telmaine, I'm in a railway man's hut on the Strumheller–Stranhorne line, half an hour's ride out of Strumheller Crosstracks. There's me and six others. We've already fought off one Shadowborn attack. We've no means of travel, not even one of the rolling platforms the railway uses for maintenance, and I'm flat-out spent getting down here. We need help.> The urgency wasn't for himself; she sensed that. Someone with him . . .

And the door to the library burst open, reminding her, terrifyingly, of the moment when the Duke of Mycene and his men invaded the archduke's bedroom with revolvers drawn and took her prisoner. Magistra Broome led with skirts flaring, Vladimer several limping strides behind her. Farquhar Broome followed, that familiar expression of impish fascination on his face.

"Lady Telmaine," demanded Phoebe, "what are you doing?"

"Speaking to Magister Tammorn," Telmaine said. Etiquette as taught a duke's daughter had no protocol for providing introductions by magic and across distance and sunrise. "He's . . . not an enemy." Which was as accurately as she could characterize him.

"Magister Tammorn?" said Vladimer sharply, thrusting past Phoebe Broome with little care either for propriety or his wounded arm. "Can you interpret for me?"

"You want to talk to him?"

Vladimer propped the cane against the hearth and gripped the mantel, standing over her. "I most certainly do."

<Vladimer?> Tammorn said, when she asked. A surge of emotion, foremost of which was rage, and memory of a beloved master and friend becoming a corpse under his touch, of the great, lifeless body in his arms, of the cold stour of Shadowborn magic from the ruins of the Mages' Tower. <The one that let them . . .> No word. No word, but impressions and emotion as dense as lead.

"He *didn't do it himself*!" she blurted in defense, not only of Vladimer, but of herself.

At Tammorn's end, someone had a hard grip on his shoulders. Someone was speaking to him in a tone of urgent concern, but no words penetrated through the mage's anger.

<I can't possibly think what he has to say to me,> Tam said, savagely. <I can't possibly think how he dares.>

"Telmaine," said Vladimer, looming over her.

"He's angry," she said up to him. "He's— He says he can't possibly think what you have to say to him."

Vladimer drew a sharp breath. "Please tell him . . . tell him that my failure to take action was the worst misjudgment—the worst mistake—of my life. It cost me my place at my brother's side, and his trust and high regard."

She relayed the message. And was promptly clubbed by the mage's rage, grief, and more memories, as by a wave that knocked her off balance, bowled her over, sucked her down. She was gasping, drowning in the undertow of his grief and her own. Vladimer suddenly released the mantel, seized her arm in a bruising grip, and shook her, an exertion more punitive to him than to her. "Tell the man he can have my life if he wants," he said into her face. "Tell him he can do with me whatever he cursed well wants—*after* he has listened to me."

She did. There was a long silence. Tammorn's anger receded, sinking in exhaustion. The someone with him—by the mage's emotional response, it was the young Lightborn prince himself. But what was the prince of the Lightborn doing in the Borders?—was supporting and steadying him. <What does he want?> Tammorn said, at last.

"He wants to know what you want," she said to Vladimer.

Vladimer released her, set his hand on the hearth, and buckled down onto the stone beside her. "An alliance," he rasped. "Between our mages and theirs."

"But the Lightborn cannot *sense* Shadowborn magic," Telmaine protested.

"Lightborn can speak to Darkborn using magic," Vladimer said, tersely. "As you are demonstrating right now. Darkborn can sense Shadowborn with magic. And Lightborn can destroy with magic. Darkborn perceptions can direct Lightborn force. Together, we can fight them." He paused. "*Tell him*, Telmaine."

She did. The connection popped like a soap bubble under harsh sonn.

"He's gone," she said.

"What do you mean *gone*? By the Sole God, woman, can't you use words properly, without all this genteel circumlocution?"

If the carpet ignited underfoot, it would be all *his* fault. "I mean *gone*. Broke the connection. Is not talking to me anymore."

"Contact him," Vladimer ordered.

"No," she said, more forcefully than she had ever spoken to him. "He heard. He understood." Vladimer drew breath, and she twisted to brace a hand on his chest, shocking herself more than she did him. "Lord Vladimer, *listen*. He's not in Minhorne; he's down in the Borders. He is badly overspent in his magic—bad enough to be ill with it. He says he's with friends in a railway hut. He needs transport out. When he speaks to me again, if I can say that a train will stop and collect them, I think it would help."

"This is more important than—"

"I think one of the people with him is the Lightborn prince himself." Deliberately, she said, "He did not tell me, but it's the way he feels. He thinks of Prince Fejelis as a beloved younger brother. When he tried to bind me, back in the city"—a circumlocution, if ever there was one—"it was because he thought I was Shadowborn and had hurt Fejelis."

His drawn face set in his old, calculating expression. "I'll order a train to pick them up. They can bring lights with them and ride in a closed carriage. I need those Lightborn here. I need that mage to listen to me. Unless"—he sonned Phoebe Broome, who had been standing very still—"unless you have a mental telegraph line to any other high-ranked Lightborn mage that I do not know about." His head turned slightly to expand his challenge to Farquhar, who shook his head soberly. "They're refusing to have anything to do with us, dear boy."

"Lord Vladimer," Phoebe Broome said, "before we take this any further . . . *Did* you know of the attack on the Lightborn Mages' Tower before it happened? Because that is what that sounded like."

The silence was long, and Vladimer's breathing quick and shallow.

"You referred to a misjudgment. A mistake that cost you your position and your brother's regard. May I know—as the person responsible for my people being here, as your ally in this, or so I believed—whether you knew, and, if so, why you chose not to warn the Temple or us?"

"Magistra Broome," Vladimer said, "you heard my offer to the Lightborn. It was meant. If he leaves any part of me, it's yours."

"What use is your life to me?" Her voice shook with distress. "Do you have any *idea* what this plan of yours will mean for us? We are mages, Lord Vladimer, and the one characteristic that is common to the lowest and highest of mages is that we sense vitality, which means we sense life, we sense death, and we sense suffering. And there are times when that pain is *unbearable*."

"Magistra," Vladimer said, coming to his feet. "The creatures that slaughtered us also appear to have magic, and no such fine sentiments as these."

"They are not fine sentiments to *us*, Lord Vladimer. They are the truths we live by. Before we accept your orders to do *anything*, did you stand by and permit the slaughter of the Lightborn mages? If so, *why*?" There was a long silence. "That's right, your *life* is easy for you to give up. But the *truth*, no."

Telmaine, rising, thought she had never seen Vladimer look so sick, not even when he learned of Casamir Blondell's death. She said, almost in a whisper, "There was more to his ensorcellment than coma."

"How so? The Shadowborn died; any ensorcellment was broken."

She wished Phoebe Broome were a woman of her own class, because there were ways of communicating the unsayable to those who understood the code.

"If it makes any difference to you," Vladimer said, starkly, "I realized my error when the relic of my loyal lieutenant, Casamir Blondell, was laid in my hands. He denounced my decision—in fact, he accused me of treason—and went on his own to investigate. He was caught and killed, or incapacitated and left for sunrise. But between my receiving his relic"—an amulet Blondell had worn to protect himself against magic—"and being rendered unable to act, was a span of minutes. I was on my way back to ask for my brother's ear when Magister Tammorn attempted to bind Lady Telmaine. In attempting to stop Telmaine's magical outburst, I shot the blameless Lady Sylvide, and was promptly overpowered and drugged into a stupor on the excuse of insanity."

"I thought . . ." Phoebe's hand moved slightly, the gesture as stillborn as her initial thought. "No matter the shunning, the denunciations from pulpits, the expulsion from work, from families, from society—no matter all of that—I thought there must come a time when we would by our virtue prove ourselves, *prove* that magic was not what the Sole God's Church said it was, what history said it was, what the slander in the broadsheets said it was. I thought there would come a time when you—all of you—would understand that all we wanted was to live and do our work as well as we were able. . . ." Her voice trailed away.

"Magistra Broome, I am truly sorry."

A half shake of the head, perhaps of negation, perhaps simply to clear her mind. "And you," she said to Telmaine. "Did you also know? Did you also keep silent?"

"I . . . ," she said, weakly, remembering listening to Mycene and Kalamay toying with Bal's life and her sister's happiness. Phoebe would never understand what had made her probe Mycene's thoughts. In a low voice she said, "I thought Vladimer would— "

"Vladimer," Phoebe Broome said, flatly, "but not you."

She shrank under that tone, and for a heartbeat hated her. What did *she* know of the stifling restrictions of society that punished the least initiative in a woman—she with her father and her brother and her commune? But in the shabby little boardinghouse where her flight had brought her, Telmaine had gathered both responsibility and power into her hands, despite the fact that by doing so, she had lost society, virtue, the self that was. She said, simply, "I did not know how then."

"Curse you. Curse you both," Phoebe said, and turned away.

"*Wait*," said Vladimer, in raw appeal. Phoebe halted, but did not turn. He spoke not to her, but to her father. "Magister Broome— " He choked to a halt.

Farquhar Broome tilted his head to one side, considering him. "Dear boy," he said gently, "we have built a tradition and earned trust by only practicing magic upon the willing. You are as far from willing as a man could be. And that is something I need no magic to know. "

"I do not *want*," Vladimer said harshly. "Indeed, this is the very last thing I want. But I *will* that it should be done. If this is what it will take for you to work with me, then *do it*."

Phoebe drew breath, her expression a mingling of outrage and protectiveness. But magic flowed, and she did not speak. The elderly mage smiled at Vladimer, the creases in his face falling into well-worn pleats. "I am quite old, dear boy, as I suspect you already know, given the dossier you will have compiled on me. Life was not always as kind to me as it has been in these last years, when it has given me a home, a community, and a son and daughter to cherish me. There is not much in the way of men's natures and conduct toward one another that I do not know. If you entertain some notion that I will be more forgiving, perhaps you are right. But I will remind you that it is the young ones, the ones like my daughter, you must also convince."

"You are their master, Magister Broome. If you accept, *they* will," Vladimer said, intensely.

"Oh, dear," Farquhar Broome said. "It is not quite like that, but, yes, I do have some influence. You *should* ask my daughter, but you find betrayal by a man the less painful to contemplate, for all you pretend such dislike of women." He clicked his tongue at Vladimer's recoil. "I have met it all before, as I said.... Shall I ask the others to leave?"

"No," rasped Vladimer. "Let them witness it done."

"Then sit down. I will be quick."

Vladimer did, lowering himself painfully onto the hearth again. Telmaine resisted the urge to move away. The mage took Vladimer's head between his hands, turning his face up with gentle pressure. The magic was no more than a breath, but Telmaine felt the healing in it. Then Farquhar Broome stooped and kissed Vladimer on the forehead. Unexpected as the gesture was, it was not theatrical or absurd. Telmaine's throat filled: she remembered her own father—not a demonstrative man—kissing her so, when he gave his last gift to her: permission to marry Balthasar.

"Dear boy," the mage said, "I dare not urge you to be easier on yourself. You are able—and you are willing—to do great evil. But you are equally able—and equally willing—to do immense good. Which you do is a choice you will make every day." He straightened, released Vladimer, and stepped back.

Vladimer's cane toppled slowly to the carpet as his hand went to his arm. His face and entire posture relaxed at the sudden release from pain. "What an extraordinary sensation," he murmured; Telmaine was not sure that he was aware he was speaking aloud. She felt a discreet nudge of magic, and the cane hopped upright again, coming to perch by Vladimer's knee.

Phoebe was standing with her hand pressed to her lips. With her attention on Vladimer, Telmaine had not sensed any exchange between Phoebe and her father, but obviously it had happened. "Lord Vladimer," Phoebe said, in quite a different tone, and her father tapped her arm. "We shall just let that settle a while, shall we?"

"No!" Vladimer said urgently, surging to his feet. His cane spilled again, but when Telmaine tried to pass it to him, he ignored it. Speaking quickly, overriding any question or offered sympathy, he said, "Notwithstanding their apparent magical strength, the thing—one of the things—that perplexed me throughout this is how capricious their actions have appeared, a mixture of the subtle use of ensorcellment and coercion and the gross manifestations of magic. It may be they are capricious by nature, but I have found the assumption of caprice rather than logic to be a dangerous one to make about one's enemies. We must think this through, and quickly. Was Stranhorne merely the first, geographically, or was there a reason why it should suffer the first mass attack?"

He started at a forcible knock on the door: Noellene di Studier, with Laurel di Gautier at her shoulder. "Lord Vladimer, excuse me. There's a telegram from Minhorne—"

He almost lunged at her, snatching it from her extended hand without a word of thanks. Telmaine sonned the momentary surprise on Noellene's face, and the more speculative attention on Laurel's, as he used both hands to tear it open. He dropped into an armchair, spreading the telegram on his lap to sweep his fingers over the text. They held their collective breath.

He lifted his head. "The Lightborn have delivered an ultimatum to my brother. They wish the city surrendered to them in reparation for the attack on the Mages' Tower. They rejected all arguments as to the existence of the Shadowborn. They gave this ultimatum at a meeting, and immediately prior to the meeting, the archduke's party came under attack from a boy of some fifteen or sixteen years, manifesting Shadowborn magic and purporting to be the son of Lysander Hearne—Balthasar Hearne's brother." To

Telmaine, he said, "I suspect this is the individual you and I encountered at the train station. . . . The Lightborn gave no indication they were aware of the incident. The Shadowborn was accompanied by Dr. Balthasar Hearne."

Telmaine heard Laurel di Gautier breathe, "Oh," but was too dizzy with relief to wonder why.

"Dr. Hearne managed to physically subdue the Shadowborn mage"—Vladimer's brows rose as he read—"using chloroform, but not before the Shadowborn had incapacitated Phineas Broome and killed the Duke of Mycene."

If the rumor that Sachevar Mycene had fathered Vladimer had any truth to it, no one would know from his manner. "Chloroform," Vladimer noted with approval, "is less flammable than ether. . . . Hearne claimed to have been ensorcelled by the Shadowborn, but the ensorcellment obviously had its limits. He also claimed the ensorcellment allows him to survive in daylight. He volunteered to offer himself to the Lightborn court in a living demonstration of the existence of Shadowborn magic."

"No," Telmaine breathed. *"Why?"*

"Despite considerable reservations that he is acting according to his own will, my brother decided he had no choice but to take the risk, in hopes that Hearne could provide the evidence needed to convince the Lightborn." To Farquhar Broome: "Can someone be ensorcelled to move during daylight?"

"Not by us," Farquhar said. "Nor, to my knowledge, by the Lightborn. How intriguing."

By his expression, "intriguing" would not have been Vladimer's word for it. To Telmaine, he said, "Your husband appears to have survived the transition. They were able to exchange words with him through the wall."

"Are they sure it is him?" Laurel said.

Vladimer nodded approval. "His sister—who is a mage—vouched for him, as did two members of the commune working at the palace who had no known contact with the Shadowborn. They all confirmed he was Darkborn, ensorcelled, and the man they had known in the past as Dr. Hearne. Which passes for certainty, I suppose, in these times.

"According to Hearne, there are two factions of Shadowborn, led by two very strong, rival mages. One goes by the name of Emeya; the other name Hearne could not learn. Their ambitions appear to be territorial, though Hearne could not say why they chose to act on them now." He refolded the telegram. "Admirably succinct. I owe Casamir Blondell another debt of thanks; he trained his successor well. What is unfortunately apparent is that we are unlikely to get immediate reinforcement from the north—"

"Did my husband know that I am still alive?" Telmaine interrupted. She would be *cursed* if she let this question go unasked. "Did anyone tell him?" If *only* she had made herself known to Olivede at the train station and not shirked that personal awkwardness. If only the—she could say this in the privacy of her own mind—*cursed* Lightborn were not obstructing the mages from speaking to their fellows in Minhorne. If only Balthasar had never opened his door to the pregnant Tercelle Amberley . . .

"If anyone did know to tell him," Vladimer said, "then my ruse with Blondell's ash and your jewelry was not nearly as convincing as I intended it to be."

Farquhar Broome was shaking his head at her with the expression of a benign tutor. His magic drizzled around her, dampening her fires.

"I will inform my brother of your survival when I telegraph in return." A wintry smile. "We did arrange that he lay the blame for your escape on me." To Noellene di Studier he said, "I need to speak with your brother and his advisers. This makes it exigent that we use every asset and advantage we have to keep up the pressure on the Shadowborn. . . ."

Telmaine hardly heard. Balthasar, gone into the light and ensorcelled by the Shadowborn. Ishmael, lost around Stranhorne. With tight fists and a tight throat she said, barely audibly, "Magister Broome . . . I retract all suggestion of impropriety around the request you made of me on the train. You had every right to ask, and I . . . have an obligation to answer."

He gave her a broad smile. "My *dear* girl."

Balthasar

The summons to the archmage's presence came a half hour later. By then, Floria had badgered him not only into self-possession, but into putting his appearance in order. She sent for a pair of eyeshades, two oval pieces of smoked glass held in a fine frame of wire, to cover his sightless eyes. His eyes disturbed Floria; it was plain. Lightborn were averse to physical infirmity, but he had never thought of himself that way.

He was glad she was at his side, though he had not expected to find her so disconcerting. In the sentimental manner of boy and youth, he had presumed she was beautiful, but it was a shock to find that she truly was, even with her hair scraped and netted back and that wary, hard expression. Hers was an elegant, bone-cast beauty that would last into old age. He knew women who had labored all their lives as domestics and at the factories, but he had never met one whose strength had been groomed like a fine racehorse. She asserted herself in space like a man—indeed, like a nobleman—expecting others to yield to her. Only her voice, familiar to him since early childhood, was the same.

Six vigilants, including Captain Lapaxo, escorted them. From Floria's descriptions of the palace, he knew that the walls had been painted by some of the finest artists in the land. He could even have said what the panels depicted, had he known exactly where he was, from her descriptions. But to sonn alone, they were featureless.

"Who?" Floria murmured to Lapaxo.

He replied, "Helenja."

The dowager consort, mother of the princess, and descendant of Odon the Breaker, a southern lord reviled in Darkborn history.

"Why?"

"Y'think she'd tell me?" Lapaxo said. And even lower, though not low enough to escape Balthasar's hearing, "You believe him, about Rupertis?"

So the captain of vigilants knows about the report, Balthasar thought. *Good.* The more who knew, the better.

"He hasn't been seen since, has he?"

They finished the walk in silence, passed by a wide double door, and were shown through—threaded through—a narrower side door into a suite of rooms even hotter than outside.

Helenja, dowager consort, was a heavyset woman with a broad, handsome face oddly enhanced by a once-broken nose. Perhaps among the southern clans, such an injury did not merit a healing. Perhaps it was even a mark of beauty or vigor. At her side was a lean man with a fine, crafty face and a caul marking him as one of the highest in the land. His clothing, though of Lightborn style, had panels of lace that Balthasar recognized as Darkborn work and that Telmaine would have priced to the penny. Balthasar suspected he could put a name to him: Prasav, Isidore's cousin and nearest rival. The young woman with him, whose resemblance suggested she might be kin, wore an expression of covert fascination, her face not quite turned toward him.

He swept sonn over the others, making himself pay attention to their positions, groupings, and alignments to try to distinguish advisers, attendants, and hangers-on. A few he recognized: Mistress Silver Branch, with her clerk, who was trying to make himself as small as possible. Balthasar hoped he had not endangered the man by making him record his testimony. The young mage who had tested him at the door, and—he realized this with a pang of visceral alarm—two of the group whom he had challenged on the streets.

Helenja waved them forward. "This is the one?" she said to them.

An unnerved silence. Then they tried to answer together. "Yes, Mistress Helenja." "But we—"

"'Yes' is sufficient." To Floria: "Why did you not bring him directly to me?"

"I was stopped at the door."

"Mmph," said the dowager, swinging across to stand in front of Balthasar, studying him up and down. "I admit, I expected something a little more impressive." Her head turned toward the door, then back to him, and she pointed to one side. "Over there."

He did as indicated. At a hand signal from Lapaxo, two of the vigilants joined him. Helenja did not object to them, but she stopped Floria as she made to accompany him. "I want you there."

On the opposite side of the room. Floria went, a threat in her expression.

Helenja returned to her place midway between them and waited. There were few chairs, which was in keeping with the Lightborn's aversion to showing infirmity. He should maybe have accepted Floria's offer of a stimulant, except he remembered too well the effect of her stimulants on the unaccustomed constitution. He hardened himself to endure.

Some minutes later, the double doors abruptly folded back. "The princess, Mistress Helenja, Master Prasav." Vigilants and mages filed in, followed by a tall young woman with an elaborately woven cap of hair who stopped three strides in and spun to face him with an expression of appalled revulsion.

"So," Helenja said, with a long sigh of satisfaction.

The newcomer controlled her face, though her throat worked involuntarily with nausea, and turned to face Helenja. "Your message said you needed to speak to me urgently."

"Princess," Helenja said, "I presume you have not yet had a copy of that extraordinary report prepared by Mistress Tempo's clerk. Meet Dr. Balthasar Hearne, Darkborn."

So this was the usurper princess. Floria had cast aspersions on her courage and honor, but Floria was a woman of slow-shifting loyalties, and one who preferred her world ordered, and all those in it predictable. The mage princess offended both loyalty and order, and no one could have predicted her ascent. To his sonn, the princess seemed far too young for her role, tired, nervous, and overburdened—another person rolled over and harried by events and others' wishes. He felt a great empathy for her.

She tried to recover her balance. "That's . . . not amusing, Helenja."

"No, it's not amusing at all that the Temple has lied to us."

"I don't know what you mean," she said on an exhale.

"Of course you do." Helenja's waving hand scattered hard echoes of metal and gems. "Fejelis claimed that lineage mages could not sense Shadowborn magic, but that sports could. For that, the Temple allowed his unrighteous deposition, because they could not afford to have us believe that they were unable to defend themselves or us against Shadowborn magic. You, however, are not a lineage mage. What do you sense about that man?"

"He cannot be Darkborn," the princess said, a little desperately.

"I have witnesses who found him walking the streets without lights," Helenja said. "Shall we try that?" she said to Balthasar. "Put him in a darkened room."

"If that is what you have to do," Balthasar said, "do it."

Helenja rewarded him with a smile. Floria's stance gave the impression of a cat about to pounce. "She"—Helenja gestured toward the young judiciary mage—"tested him at the door. She thought his mind had been broken by the horror of the tower's destruction. But you have another explanation, don't you?"

"Mistress Helenja, Mother, I can't—"

"You can't *what*?" The dowager's voice was a growl. "Two-thirds of the contracts held within this palace are contracts to protect us against hostile magic. If the Temple cannot protect us—as the attack on its own tower showed—then those contracts are invalid."

Balthasar drew a breath. "Princess," he said, "Mistress Helenja. Forgive me, but the integrity of your contracts is an internal matter between the Temple and you. I am here to prove the existence of the Shadowborn, and to assert Darkborn innocence in crimes you have held them responsible for."

Helenja's expression was one she would have turned on a potted plant that had rustled its leaves and spoken aloud.

"Princess," Balthasar pressed. "You may be the only person in this palace able to sense this ensorcellment, but you *can* sense it. Your reaction showed it."

"It was Floria—"

"You turned toward me, not Floria," he said gently. "My

ensorcellment is the more recent, and probably the stronger."

A shiver passed through her; her face changed. "Come with me," she said, in a voice deeper and more authoritative than before. He had taken a step forward before he recognized that there was magic behind it, magic working on him. In sudden panic, he struggled against it. From the far side of the room, Floria shouted, "Under whose contract do you use magic against us?"

The compulsion stopped. The princess said in her own voice, "The high masters will see you now. Please come with me."

"Take him," Prasav said swiftly. Helenja merely gave a sour smile at his preemptive gamesmanship. "We will speak again," she said to Balthasar, a statement that had the quality of a threat—though against whom, he could not tell. He forced himself to walk steadily forward and not even to turn his head toward Floria. Pride and honor precluded his taking her into danger with him. Then he found her at his side once more, her face showing something of his own panic and resentment at being overpowered so—when she shouted out, she had said "magic against *us*." He tried to take her hand, but she shook herself free with a frown and set her hand on the hilt of her rapier.

Three men and two women waited for them in an upstairs suite. The most remarkable of the men was a small, wiry man wearing nothing more than a loincloth and sandals. The less remarkable of the women was a plain, middle-aged woman in a featureless tunic that covered her to midshin.

He dipped a bow to the man in the loincloth, as though to the archduke himself, taking a bold guess at his identity. "Magister Archmage."

The high masters also regarded him as they might a speaking plant. There was no revulsion in their reaction, despite their far greater strength than that of the second-rank princess, further confirmation that they could not sense the Shadowborn ensorcellment. He felt a movement behind him, and Perrin passed by him, her face working, to stand between the archmage and Valetta. The archmage glanced aside at her, questioning; she gave a jerky nod. And then the nausea and the personality in her face simply drained out, and she stood silent, swaying slightly.

"Balthasar Hearne," Valetta said, "we wish to examine the magic that Magistra Viola—Princess Perrin—senses on you, through her. We will try to do you no harm, but we cannot promise that harm may not come to you."

"Magistra, this is what I came for, in expectation"—he stressed the word—"that my presence here, and the ensorcellment on me, would convince you that what the archduke said to you is true. I consent to your examination."

He had no sooner finished than a great, disorientating surge of magic rolled over him. He was aware of Floria first gripping his arm and then supporting him. <You did not tell us,> a voice said in his mind, <that you were mageborn.>

"I'm not," he gasped out. All he had ever had was the ability to sense concerted, powerful magic—like last night—and a diagnostic acumen that Olivede reckoned was due to a tenuous sense of the inner workings of the body that might, were it stronger, be magic. But otherwise, he could not even touch-read, could certainly not heal, and could anticipate no longer a life than any other earthborn. Conversely, he had been spared the stigma his sister lived under.

<For our law, what you are will be sufficient,> another voice intoned. <That will make this much easier.> Another wave of magic rolled over him and drowned his wits.

He came back to himself lying on a wide, comfortable bed of stretched netting. His sonn picked out a circular relief on the ceiling above him, a stylized sun whose rays extended to each distant corner. Many Lightborn rooms had such a device, and he remembered Floria telling him that it was a potent symbol even to those who did not associate it with any divinity. This one was as molded and detailed as any Darkborn ceiling decoration. He said, vaguely, "That would be painted gold, wouldn't it?"

Floria leaned over him, her expression anxious. "I'm all right," he said, and demonstrated so by sitting up. He didn't realize until he was upright that he had used his sprained wrist without pain, and that the bandage was gone from his other hand. He felt his face; the tenderness from the scoring was also gone; he could no longer feel the seams. And he did not ache. He felt astonishingly well.

They were not in a holding cell—his swift cast around the room showed a large, strangely furnished suite—but he would study his surroundings later. "What happened?" he said, urgently. "What did they say? What did they decide?"

"To me, nothing," she said, unhappily.

"I'm all right," he said again. "No more ill effects than a day of very disturbing dreams, and physically, very well. Did I pass out?"

"No," she said. "You stood, you walked, but you simply—like Perrin—seemed to disappear from inside yourself."

"Disturbing," he acknowledged for her; he would examine his own feelings later. "So you noticed a change in me, and then, even if they did not say anything, could you describe what happened? Were you also"—he could not, he found, say the word "ensorcelled," could not apply it the actions of those he hoped would be, needed to be, allies—"held as I was?"

"No," she said, frowning. "I was aware throughout. They were much more interested in you."

"They'd have had plenty of time to study your ensorcellment, if they'd wanted." He frowned in turn, a new thought occurring to him. "If the ensorcellment is still active, then it was not due to the Shadowborn Ishmael killed—Jonquil, they called him—or the one called Midora, who died in Stranhorne Manor." *Was that Sebastien, too? Or one of the others?* Was Floria's connection to his family the reason the Shadowborn had chosen her to carry the talisman to Isidore? A shudder of sheer rage went through him, unattenuated by the ensorcellment.

No, unattenuated by *any* ensorcellment.

"Balthasar?" she said, her tone wary, almost warning. She had advised him about keeping his composure. But how else should he react to these . . . atrocities now that he no longer needed to warp his own thoughts and emotions simply to survive?

He heard his voice, distorted by the intensity of his emotion. "They've annulled the ensorcellment on my will. They've left the ensorcellment protecting me against light, or they've assumed it—or I'd be dead by now."

He had to think. Why should they have lifted the ensorcellment? Why might they have assumed his protection? Was he their chance to practice with Shadowborn magic? Could they do so through the princess? Did that trace of magic in him mean that they cared about the ensorcellment on him? That they had healed him suggested it might. He wished he knew whether they had removed the ensorcellment on Floria. "Did you get any sense of what they might do now?" he asked her, desperate for *some* answer to any question.

She shook her head. "As I said, they exchanged not a word after you spoke."

But by the set of her shoulders, there was more. He was already learning to read her. "What is it, Floria? You said they mostly concentrated on me. What did they do to you?"

"Raised the memory of my ensorcellment," she said, rising to stand with her back to him.

He waited. "A lover?" he said, finding the question unexpectedly difficult to ask.

She turned, eyes narrowing.

"You are not the first," he said, turning his face a little to the side, so that he would not seem to be probing or challenging her. "It seems to have been the way they liked to turn people."

"Curse him," he heard her whisper.

Hands upturned on his lap, he sighed. "We can but hope."

She sat down beside him on the bed, the slump on her shoulders betraying her weariness. He remembered this was night for her and that she would not have shown her vulnerability to anyone. "He was one of the men in the companion house. I've always been so careful, as my father insisted. . . ."

It seems a bleak approach to intimacy, he thought, as he

had thought before. The promiscuity did not trouble him as much as the lovelessness. "I'm sorry," he said.

She gave a twisted little smile. "Nothing to do with you, Bal. You always urged me to find a true partner—a husband, in your terms. You could be quite insufferable on the subject."

He supposed he had been, happy as he himself was then. "You deserve to be loved, Floria," he said, quietly. "No doubt you will tell me that my Darkborn prejudices are showing, but what was right for a man is not right for a woman. What was right for your father was not right for you."

She turned her head, a smile gentling that hard, beautiful face. "You've said that to me before."

This close, he could sonn the slight thickening and change in texture of her skin, and realized that her face was bruised badly. Her voice had sounded husky, which he had put down to strain. "You're hurt," he said, shocked that he had not realized.

She shrugged. "Met with a mob outside Bolingbroke Station on the way back from the palace. Did something stupid and needed to be fished out of the fountain."

He touched her face gently, but the pretense that it was a clinician's touch failed as soon as he felt the silken warmth of her skin. There was no wall between them now. Their weight on the mesh of the bed created a subtle, in-falling force. It took no effort for him to tilt sideways, to close the distance between his lips and hers; the effort would have been in resisting. Her lips were cool and firm at first, then softened as they parted. Her breath stroked against his lip, quickening with her breathing. Her hand caught the back of his neck hard, and her fingers spread in his hair.

Then that moment of abandonment passed, and he pulled back. She held him briefly, and then yielded, her hand sliding away. His sensitized skin remembered the track; his sensitized mouth, her lips.

"I'm sorry, Floria," he muttered, deeply ashamed of his behavior. "This is not right."

"You'll notice," she said after a moment, "that you are

not sitting on the floor, wondering what hit you. Which you would be if I objected."

He opened his mouth to say "I'm sorry" again, and closed it. Nine years of marriage had taught him that a wise man did not apologize for doing something a woman wanted, no matter how foolish or wrong that thing might be.

"It would have been strange," she said, "if we had met and this had not happened."

"I'm not myself," he said, inadequately. "Everything that has happened . . . Telmaine . . ." Remorse mingled with his grief now, that he had come so near to betraying both the women he cared most for. "It's too soon. Maybe . . ."

"Yes," she said, in a tone he could not interpret. "Telmaine. I had a conversation with her just before I left the palace. She told me it was very important that I tell you we had spoken."

"Thank you," he whispered. "But I'm not . . . sure I'm up to hearing her message at the moment."

"That *was* the message. When Telmaine returned to the palace and was taken prisoner, it was night. When she spoke to me, it was daylight. Why would her jailors let her speak to me? Why would they let her release me when they'd shown no sign of caring that I'd have been dead when my light failed? Balthasar, she's a mage—a strong mage. Unless she *wanted* to stay in that cell and die, it would not hold her." She paused. "All she said was that it was very important that I tell you she and I had spoken, not *what* I should tell you. I did not make the connection immediately myself, and then I waited to tell you because I needed you to hold together before the court." She waited, stoically, for his response, her face like a carved mask.

So stupidly simple a chain of reasoning. He had held most of the links himself—he *knew* what Ishmael had told him about Telmaine's strength as a mage, and he *knew* she would not submit tamely to death. He should have connected them, would have connected him, but for the abomination of the ensorcellment. In a raw whisper, he said, "Floria, even if you'd told me before, I *couldn't* have believed you."

A moment for understanding to come, and then she swore, softly.

He put a hand over his face, dislodging the spectacles. If his loss of composure disturbed her, he was going to shock her now. "Could you please . . . give me a few minutes to myself?"

He felt her rise, the netting release. She touched his cheek, her fingertips calloused, scratchy, and warm—except for the warmth, unlike Telmaine's. To his lowered head, she said, "I would lie with you, Balthasar, for the asking. All these years demand more than a kiss. I would never have made you my enemy by deceiving you on something that important. . . . But I'll leave you now."

Eight

Tammorn

<Tammorn.>

He had known this contact would come ever since he spoke to Lady Telmaine. Indeed, he had known it would come since he recovered enough to think clearly. Though he had not expected the archmage himself, there was no mistaking that immense strength. The archmage's replenishing touch across distance had the healing warmth of sunlight. Tam all but groaned in relief as his pain and leaden exhaustion dissipated. He sat up: one did not address the master of the Temple while supine in bed.

<*Why?*> He cut to the essence. <*Why release me?*>

<Why not? You told us no more than the truth. You are not our enemy . . . and we need you to do something for us.>

<I won't leave Fejelis unguarded.> He put force of feeling, if not force of magic, into the statement. He showed the archmage a swift succession of impressions: waking to the reports of bullets, hearing talons scrape the metal roof overhead, sensing that vile aura, hearing Orlanjis cry out and Jovance shout, and then the painfully intense burst of matter manipulation. He was aware of the archduke's gratification at the last, but he could not have concealed Jovance's presence, even if he had tried. <The Darkborn are letting us ride one of their trains into Strumheller; we heard over the telegraph. Archmage, they are desperate for our help.>

He felt a moment's base relief that he could not conceal the information that Vladimer had known about Mycene's and Kalamay's plans, and done nothing to prevent it. He was glad not to be tempted.

<It is of no account,> Magistra Valetta said. Unlike the archmage, her magic stung like static sparks. <The earthborn have always hated us.> This close to her, he could tell that she returned their hatred in equal measure. <This is not the first atrocity they have committed, but we have determined it may be the last.>

<You can sense Shadowborn magic, and you are the strongest surviving mage who can,> the archmage said. <We want you to be our envoy to the Shadowborn.>

<To the *Shadowborn*?> he said in disbelief.

<They are mages, Tammorn,> Valetta said.

<They are *murderers*,> Tam said—and sensed Magistra Valetta's startlement at being so fiercely contradicted. <They—not the Darkborn, *they*—murdered *dozens* of us. They'd have murdered more, but for Lukfer sacrificing his life. How dare you darken his memory by pretending he lied about the Shadowborn?>

<The Darkborn were the ones who fired the cannon,> Magistra Valetta said. <We cannot know, until we speak to the Shadowborn, who was responsible by law.>

Were they really going to pretend that this had been done according to compact, to pretend that the Shadowborn had been working under the orders of the Darkborn and so were indemnified, even for *this*? <If you could have sensed what Lukfer and I sensed in the tower—>

<We did,> the archmage said. <Through you.>

<But Lukfer mastered that magic. Perhaps . . .> Valetta paused. <Perhaps it was his native form.>

He sensed the calculation in that thought, but even so, Lukfer had been born a sport, and his strength had been immense but dangerously uncontrolled. Ever since he had been received into the Temple's care as a young child, he had been the high masters' ward. He had used pain—mostly the pain of living in poor light—to bleed his energies in healing effort. Tam had assumed that he had achieved his final act of mastery because of his mortal injuries, but he remembered how even before, Lukfer had cast fire and effortlessly annulled an ensorcelled crossbow bolt that was killing Fejelis. If the high masters were right, there could be no crueler irony—

<If this magic is peculiar to sports, you have the potential for the same mastery. We know he *gifted* you at the last.>

He had had neither the time nor the heart to examine that gift yet. It was the gift of the master to his or her favored student—a distillation of the master's essential knowledge of magic, imparted magically as a nucleus of insight and memory. It was a precious, perilous gift. Given too soon, it could overwhelm the student and distort his maturation. Given maliciously, as the Shadowborn had done to Lady Telmaine, it could induce possession. She should be grateful for Ishmael di Studier's steady hand.

But given at the right time, the *gift* could accelerate a mage's realization of his full capacities. And that, he knew, was what Lukfer would have wished for him.

<You *know* how strong you are, Tammorn. We have felt how strong you are.>

<No!>

<Would you waste his *gift*, Tammorn?>

That was rich of her. The high masters would have burned out his magic, Lukfer's precious gift or no, for the impertinence of exposing their weaknesses.

<That was merely theater.>

What he had sensed, facedown on the floor within the circle of high masters, was not theater. He told them so.

<Tammorn, you broke the compact. And, yes, we remember all the justifications you offered, but you broke the compact. You intervened when Fejelis was poisoned, although you were not contracted to the palace—>

<Fejelis was *dying*. The contracted mages might not have reached him in time.> He had never said he was sorry and he never would, though they had bound his magic for five years after and seemed set on holding it against him indefinitely.

<You sheltered and encouraged artisans working to import Darkborn technologies—>

<Their work has nothing to do with magic! The compact—>

<*Enough,*> said the archmage. <Tammorn, you will do this thing, whether of your own free will or not. It is our best chance of a peaceful resolution.>

<*Peaceful*—with that?> He threw his impressions at them, of that swirl of violence outside the hut, of the corrupted vitality and magic of the Shadowborn.

<The compact reached seven hundred years ago has run its course,> the archmage said. Centuries whispered behind his voice. <We have damaged the earthborn; we freely acknowledge it, and they in turn have damaged us. It is time for us to seek the society of our own kind. We can offer them wealth and knowledge, and they can offer us land.>

<You'd have us move to the Shadowlands?>

<There are older, better names for it; it is time those were brought back into use. It seems a reasonable solution, does it not?>

Not for me, Tam thought. His heart and causes were here, with Beatrice and the children, with Fejelis, with the artisans, with the immigrants from the provinces who trod the road he had trodden a quarter century ago. <What of the people who depend on light?>

<We will make sure they have enough,> the archmage said. <It would be immoral to do otherwise. Perhaps the Darkborn might run one of their Borders trains into the Shadowlands. Or we could build one ourselves. Powering it would be simple enough.>

He was going to laugh or scream curses at them, both equally futile. <I *will not do it.*>

He could feel the weight of Valetta's magic, Valetta's will, readying to bear down on him. Others stood behind her. <You have no choice,> the archmage said, no gentleness in that ancient voice. <We must do what we must to survive.>

<*They*—>

<*Shhh.*>

<We will make sure your prince is safe,> the archmage

said into his stilled mind. <I promise. He makes me think . . . > of a striding man sweeping across a wide, tiled floor and turning to gesture, every long line of him radiating vitality. A chieftain or prince of an age remembered only by the high masters.

But remembered, Tam thought, *as I would have remembered Fejelis a hundred years after his death.*

<He would have caused us great trouble in the ordinary way of things, but he is what they will need; we will leave him as our gift to them.>

<It is *night* out there,> he said, a last, desperate objection. <If I take light with me into their camp, and they are Darkborn by lineage, they'll die. If I don't take light with me, *I* will die.>

<Not necessarily so.> He sensed deep satisfaction. <The Darkborn have given us the means.>

Ishmael

"You might as well wake up," a man's voice said. "I know you're faking; I'd do the same in your place."

He might have taken the voice for Balthasar Hearne's, except that it was crisper and more forceful in delivery, and slightly deeper in timbre. Without moving, Ishmael said, "Lysander Hearne, is it?"

He rolled over on the sheets, propped himself up on his elbow, and sonned the speaker. He perched on a stool well out of lunging reach, one foot hooked on the crossbar, revolver resting on his knees. The man's resemblance to Balthasar Hearne was notable, though he was sinewy rather than slight, and casually dressed in clothes that would let him move freely. There was about him no taint of Shadowborn, only the air of a man who lived hard and wary and on the edge of the law.

"So you've met my weakling brother," the man noted.

"'Twas your weakling brother set your plans in disarray."

Lysander Hearne snorted. "And which particular plans are those?"

Ishmael, reclining, spread his free hand. "Th'ones upset by the birth of Shadowborn-got sons to Tercelle Amberley."

Muscles tensed in Lysander Hearne's face, enough to be noticeable, not quite enough to constitute an expression. "It so happens," he said, levelly, "those weren't *our* plans." He paused. "You're very calm. Case you don't recall, you were dead as mutton back there."

As an effort to disconcert him, that missed its mark entirely, because he had just realized something far more disconcerting. Carefully, he turned his magic on himself, eased vitality from his bones to his tissues . . . and felt nothing. There was no breathtaking pain, no faltering heart, no sense of his life draining uncontrollably into his magic. He caught a breath, shaken with equal measures joy and fear. Not even Magister Broome had been able to undo the damage done to him. Now he had the measure of the mage who held him prisoner.

And something else was gone, as though it had never existed: the Call.

So he was where the Call wanted him. Nowhere he recognized, in a bedroom easily as large as the baronial suite in Strumheller, furnished with pieces whose style and materials he had met only in museums. There was not a join or a seam in them, not in the curving headboard, the rounded edges of the dressing table, or the bowed front of the wardrobe. *More to the point,* he thought, *none of them can be easily moved.* This was no travelling camp.

But the bite of the arid air on his throat had already told him he was no longer in the Borders.

He tossed the covers back, swung his legs over the edge of the bed onto solid floor, and stood. "Now what?"

Hearne jerked a thumb over his shoulder. "There's the wardrobe. Our lady wants you."

"Your lady?"

"Lysander's and mine," said a woman's voice from beyond the end of the bed. A long step carried him sideways, away from her, and his pivot placed both of them in front of him.

She came forward with no apparent embarrassment at his nakedness, a lovely, foul-tainted creature in a dress faithfully Darkborn. The gown covered her from high collar to cuffs to ankles in layers of silk and lace, and if he recalled his sister's digressions on fashion, she was at least a decade outdated. In the Darkborn manner of a mage, she wore gloves. Her face had a sculpted refinement, with full lips, a narrow, straight nose, wide brows, and distinct cheekbones. A face such as he had sonned on celebrated actresses and lords' mistresses, who were often one and the same.

"M'lady," Ishmael said, dipping his head.

"Charming," she said, "but insincere, Ishmael di Studier." Arms folded, head tilted, she added, "Given that you greeted me by firing point-blank at me."

He set his jaw, trying to hold his composure at the aura of magic around her. Its mere strength would have set his head spinning, even without the Shadowborn aura of it.

"I'd thank you for saving my life," he said at last, "if I thought I'd like what you mean me for."

"Ah, well, Ishmael. That's not for me to explain."

"And your name is, m'lady, since you make so free with mine?"

"Call me Ariadne." She turned her head toward Lysander Hearne. "Sander, if you would?"

Lysander frowned, but pushed himself off his stool and went to the wardrobe, producing from its depths an evening suit in the Darkborn style, more formal than Ishmael would have chosen for himself. "Put it on. Or we'll do it for you."

"Need t'relieve myself," he said, accepting it from Lysander's hand, and turned his back on them to walk, with studied steadiness, into the bathroom. As he expected, there was no way out, and no weapon more threatening than hard soap and a back brush. He'd go before their lady as stubbled as a vagrant.

He managed the suit, though not nearly as well as his manservant would have. It was tight across the shoulders, but otherwise a passable fit. He gave the cravat his best shot and then let it lie, returning to present himself for their inspection. Lysander Hearne passed him socks and shoes, and he sat down on the bed to pull them on.

"Are you hungry?" she said, the social hostess.

Not with that magic around him. "I'd sooner get m'fate settled, if you'd be so kind."

Lysander gave an odd smile. "Oh, she is that."

With Lysander at Ishmael's elbow and Ariadne at Lysander's, Ishmael left the room, finding himself in a corridor as wide and fine as any in the archducal palace. Except for one feature: windows with shutters turned back. He tried not to be disconcerted by the gusts of warm wind, and wrestled briefly with the urge to ask what time of night—or day—it might be, but pride precluded that. Lysander Hearne wasn't alone in his posturing. Otherwise, Shadowborn stronghold or no, it had the feel of any large household. Of all the perils he had associated with capture by the Shadowborn, being run over by a dashing housemaid with a stack of fresh-laundered towels was not among them.

Ariadne's magic thrust open a door, and they herded him into a wide receiving room. Lysander said, "Ishmael di Studier, my lady."

His sonn caught movement at the far end of the room. A harsher stroke outlined the woman standing on a raised dais. Her simple dress, a knee-length tunic and trousers suitable for this warmth, was far more revealing to sonn than a Darkborn woman's. His first absurd reaction was chagrin at the impropriety. He halted

Lysander Hearne tapped his elbow. "Go on."

"No need." The woman forestalled his response. "Thank you, Lysander, Ariadne. Please go now."

Lysander bowed and withdrew, as quietly as Ishmael himself might have. Ishmael heard a sandal brush tile and sonned the woman as she stepped down from the dais. She was small, her figure described by the straight lines of childhood or age. Her hair was short and untidy, a jumble of crisp curls; her mouth was generous and her nose, almost snubbed, no balance for it; her cheekbones were flat and indeterminate. An ordinary face with a winning smile. If it were her true face, any more than her apparent age were her true age.

"Ishmael di Studier," she said, pleasantly. "I've wanted to meet you for a very long time."

He had no sense of great strength about her, but that very absence was suggestive. He set his stance, hands relaxed and open at his side. "You'll pardon me if I say I've had no like wish."

"Apparently not," she said. "I've seldom known anyone to hold out against Ariadne's Call so long."

"Then that'll give you the measure of my will t'cooperate, if it's cooperation y'want, or submit, if it's submission y'want." For all the good it might do him.

"Come here and sit down," she said, "and we'll talk."

A quarter century of rough work had taught him to conserve his strength. He followed her out onto an open balcony, dense with plants in pots and planters, and took the chair she indicated.

"Have my people seen to you?" she said.

"Aye, as much as I'd allow," he acknowledged.

A feathery eyebrow lifted, but she did not inquire. They sat in silence, each waiting out the other.

"What is it y'want with me?" he said at last. "You've gone to some trouble, it seems, to get me."

"What do you think I want you for?" she said, temporizing.

Ishmael shrugged. "We've always thought th'ones who followed th'Call wound up in something's larder or someone's belly." She frowned, but did not contradict him. "It comes t'me now, meeting Hearne there, that you've another use for Darkborn. But I'll not serve you willingly, whatever it is you want of me."

"And who do you think I am?" she said.

He tapped his abdomen with a lightly closed hand, conveying part of his answer: a mage, and one powerful enough to pull him back from a death he thought assured. "I fought you for twenty-five years. I thought t'die fighting you."

"You would have. Does that not tell you something?"

"It's hardly worth you making a point of raising me only t'break me. My people will regret my fate, but nothing you do t'me will weaken them. And if you send me back to them ensorcelled, they'll know."

"Ishmael," she said, gently, "you fear all the wrong things

of me." There was something in her voice that chilled him—not merely that she deflected, but did not deny he had reason to fear. "My name, which you are too stubborn to ask for, is Isolde." She paused, waiting for recognition. Then with slight resignation, said, "My mother was Imogene."

As the name of the mage attached to the Curse, the supposed leader of those who had worked the great Sundering of peoples, it had not been used on either side of sunrise for eight hundred years.

"Think it through, Ishmael," she invited.

All he could think of was that Xavier Stranhorne had been right.

Yet he could hear Vladimer asking why, if the Shadowborn had such might, would they hide in the Shadowlands all these years. Why only now move against the north, and in such an oblique, chaotic way?

"I'm the younger sister. The one who did not make it into the history books."

"Aye, well, it's not usual that the living do," Ish said, still suspended between belief and disbelief. "And the Shadowborn. What are they t'you? Are they your making?"

"No."

"But th'Call. That was your handmaiden's. As I said, if th'Call's how you bring people t'serve you, I'm not minded to." Futile bravado; ensorcellment could make him serve, willing or no. He drew a deep breath and steadied his tone. "Explain t'me what you want, if y'would."

There was a silence. His sonn caught the small smile curling the corners of her mouth. His mother had smiled so when he pleased her. She had been a sensitive, sophisticated woman who had no patience with childishness.

That, too, she could no doubt pluck out of his mind, if so inclined.

"What do you already know about the Sundering, Ishmael?"

"I'm no scholar," he said. "A scholar I know"—no need to tell them that Xavier Stranhorne was dead, if they did not already know—"says th'final break had something t'do with geography or perhaps weather. But I've th'experience t'know it was probably nothing of th'sort at root. Factions, ambitions, rivalries; whether it's dukes or dockside gangs or market stallholders or mages, it's the same."

"Not *quite*, Ishmael."

"I'll have t'take your word for it. How long have I been here?"

"Less than a day, Ishmael. Be still." He was not aware of having moved, but inside, yes, he had reared up at the realization that time had passed without him. "They took Stranhorne Manor, but moved no farther yet."

"Not allies of yours?"

"Definitely not allies of ours."

"Do y'mean t'oppose them, or do y'mean just to stand by?"

"That," she said, "may depend on you."

"And how's that?" he fired back before he could think better of it.

She straightened up. "I'm afraid you will have to put up with some history. At the time of the Sundering," she said, in a voice that was clear and somehow younger, "I was a child of eight. Imogene and her followers knew that laying the Curse would burn them out, if not kill them. Yet for the Curse to survive them, it had to be anchored in vitality and magic. For the anchoring in magic, they chose nine of their children—younger brothers and sisters, children and grandchildren."

He could imagine what Phoebe Broome would have said to that. The Broomes were fiercely principled in their use of magic. "Y'make the distinction between vitality and magic," he said. It had been deliberate enough to catch his ear, whether she meant it to or not. "And th'vitality?"

"In everyone born into it. Could you imagine it being done any other way?"

If he considered only the execution, he could not. A mage, even a low-ranked mage such as he himself had been—was—could draw on another's vitality as well as his own, whether mage or nonmage. There was a cost; he was always laid up for days if he pushed himself into overreach. The Broomes' commune's code of contact prohibited them from doing so except when it made the difference between life and death, and all involved had given full, knowledgeable consent. The Lightborn Temple did not even allow that between mageborn and earthborn, although he had heard rumors of the practice behind mages. But a work of magic that drew on the vitality of all those living and yet to be born, with magic that was anchored in children . . . "And th'purpose of it." Ishmael growled. "Th'Curse."

"Revenge," the woman said, sounding slightly surprised. "Imogene's revenge upon everyone who failed her, betrayed her, let her daughter die."

"And was th'Curse meant to turn out this way?"

"Why do you ask that?"

"Because it makes cursed"—he caught himself too late to avoid the idiom—"little sense. Why, if they'd t'doom themselves in the setting of the Curse, not simply kill and be done with it?"

"You don't understand revenge, do you, Ishmael?"

His thoughts glanced off memories: his father's bitter words, sending him on his road; his words to his father, demanding his inheritance; his thoughts after Athelane had rescued him from the glazen and died in doing so; his realization that half a dozen men of his own barony had set out to murder him on his return for his father's laying out [illegible] a dozen other experiences to sear a man's heart and rouse his anger.

But he realized she was right. Anger he understood, not revenge. He'd always made sure of a merciful final shot, no matter how monstrous the enemy, and no matter the terms of his hire or mood of the mob. It was safer, but that had not been the entire reason. Killing didn't turn his stomach; torment did.

And surely the object of the Curse had been torment, to leave those who survived the first sunrise, the first sunset, living in dread of the next and the next and the next. He smiled grimly. He had no idea how many Darkborn had survived that first sunrise, or how many Lightborn that first sunset, but they and their descendants had lived to build twin civilizations on either side of sunrise.

He was a son of that civilization, and he was done with being toyed with like a mouse trapped by an overfed lap cat. What did it matter what Imogene's intent had been, or how she justified herself? She was eight hundred years gone. "I don't care about the history. What matters is now."

She rocked back ever so slightly at the change in his voice.

"If y'won't come to the point as to what y'want of me, then I'll tell you what I want of you: I want the Shadowborn—th'ones who have overrun Stranhorne, and all their ilk—turned back. I don't care if they live or die, as long as I never hear of them—claw, bristle, fang, wing, or Call itself—whether in the Borders, th'offshore waters, th'Isles, or the land itself, from this day onward. Do you have the strength and the will t'do that?"

"With your help," she said, and he thought he might hear a little caution entering for the first time.

He barked a laugh. "I'm a burnt-out, first-rank mage."

"But I'm not," she said, softly. The softness chilled him. "I'm not the mage Imogene was, and I'm not the mage my sister was. But with one exception, I may be the strongest living mage."

"Th'exception being your enemy, the Mother of Shadowborn."

"Mother of Shadowborn . . . no, you cannot blame her for them. But never mind. Emeya was a couple of years older than me. . . . Well, I don't suppose you would care what else she was. Her mind did not survive the Sundering. We were able, while more of us lived, to contain her. Now there is only me."

"And what killed the rest of you?"

"Time. Despair." Her narrow shoulders shifted. "If I were not Imogene's daughter, I would have succumbed centuries ago."

"What is it y'want from me?"

"I have borne nine children and outlived them all. They in turn fathered or bore children, none of whom survived."

"Survived Emeya and th'others?"

"Until Ariadne came to me, I had no other mage even

approaching my strength. I could not risk myself, because without me, there would be no one to stop her."

"Ariadne . . . came over?"

"She's Emeya's granddaughter. It was Emeya's great-grandson, Jonquil, you killed—though how you achieved that, I do not know. But it gave me even more hope of you."

"T'do what?"

"With Jonquil and Midora dead, she has only two mages as strong as Ariadne."

He waited.

"I need you as an ally," she said, simply. "You are a mage, experienced in fighting Emeya's monsters, and with abundant vitality. There is no one else quite like you."

"I'm first rank."

"Ariadne and I can augment your strength, Ishmael."

"That's not possible."

"Am *I* possible?" she said, distinctly amused. "Is the fact that you are able once more to use your magic possible? They told you it was not, didn't they? I can augment your strength."

He found himself standing, driven there by the urge to run from the greatest lure she could possibly cast before him.

She spoke as though she had not noticed his reaction, as though he were still sitting in the chair. "You're not much use to me as a first-ranker, that's very true. But I can augment your strength." She moved her hand; he sensed the first flicker of magic—Shadowborn magic—he had received from her. Out in the corridor, a bell chimed. "I'll have Lysander take you to get something to eat while you think about what I've said."

Floria

Voices woke Floria, voices from the sitting room outside. She rolled to her feet with revolver drawn and sighted through the open door of the bedroom, even as she recognized them.

Lapaxo sat at ease on a high-backed chair to one side,

wall at his back. Balthasar, on the couch, faced the outer door: that much of her instructions he had heeded. The corner of the low glass table was between him and the captain. Bal twisted to face her, and the shift in his expression made her aware that she was untucked and mussed, with her hair unraveling down her shoulders.

"Floria," he said. "It's all right. The captain had some questions for me."

"I told you to wake me if anyone came to the door." She had left him alone, as he asked, though she resolved she would find a way to tell him she did not despise him for the intensity of his emotion. So when he came back out into the sitting room, pale but in control of himself, she had honored his offer to take watch while she slept.

But she had *told* him to wake her.

"I would have, shortly."

"*Shortly* could have been too late," she said. The captain seemed entertained, which did nothing to reassure her; Lapaxo was the most serious man she knew. But she put up the revolver. Had Lapaxo meant harm, he would have acted as soon as he heard her stir. She could afford the two or three minutes it would take for her to tidy herself.

She listened through the door as Balthasar continued to describe how the Shadowborn had killed Rupertis, in detail that was brutally clinical even by a vigilant's measure. Not something she would have expected of Bal—though she would not have expected him to open the door, either, with her safety depending on it. She had to remember that Balthasar had his own purpose here.

As she returned, Lapaxo was saying, "We know Johannes. He was cousin to the servant we lost with Isidore, and to two or three others who work in the palace. He drinks their lager and talks revolution to anyone who'll listen, and Parhelion took him for a blowhard. But if he knew Rupertis, then that's my first choice for how Prasav knew that Fejelis had ties to the artisans. We'd had Isidore's orders to keep it close, just to those of us assigned to Fejelis." He pounded his thigh with a fist, his mouth grim. "If I'd had the least suspicion Rupertis was suborned, I'd never have left him in charge." He shook his head. "That mage, he's the one your father found, isn't he?"

"Yes." Tam had arrived in the city destitute, unaware that what had blighted his fortunes for a dozen years or more was poorly emerged magic. He might have struggled on for a dozen more years—if someone had not cut his throat first . . . had he not crossed paths with Darien White Hand.

"Darien thought it was hilarious that he'd see what a city full of mages could not. . . . You know where he'd go, that mage, when he took Fejelis? I heard you told Helenja west, over the border and into the mountains."

"Last place he'd go."

"You haven't switched sides?" the vigilant captain asked, bluntly.

He was entitled to the question, though it angered her to have him, too, question her loyalty. "I was Isidore's vigilant. His last orders to me were to look out for Fejelis."

He gazed at her; she returned the gaze levelly. A one-sided smile curled his lip. "I'll tell you now that my heart nearly stopped when Fejelis insisted on interviewing you alone. I'd have placed even odds you'd have put a knife in his heart."

"And five minutes later, I'd have been dead, and Fejelis already healed." If Fejelis had been responsible for Isidore's assassination, she would have set out to depose him, yes, but she would not have been stupid about it. "Fejelis did not succeed by unrighteous deposition; therefore he is the rightful and righteous prince, and I will do what I must to see him restored."

"And the Darkborn?"

She glanced at the listening Balthasar. "An old friend."

"Vigilants don't have old friends," Lapaxo said, citing a well-worn maxim.

"Vigilants don't have lovers, either," she returned, pointedly. Lapaxo had lived with the same woman for more than twenty years.

He signaled a touch over his heart.

She wondered why he had come. At forty-five, he was old for an active vigilant, and unlike her, had no long family tradition of service behind him. Twelve years ago, he had been a captain in the city watch, and even now he thought like a watchman, paying far more attention than most vigilants to the city outside the palace walls.

"Lapaxo, why are you here?"

Lapaxo turned to look at Balthasar, and Floria's hand shifted to her revolver as he slipped a hand into his waist pouch and drew out a printed sheet of paper. "Two dozen copies of this came in with the mail bag with the reports from the Darkborn public agents. Every other mail slot accessible to the night has them pushed through it, and I don't doubt that there have been hundreds more distributed overnight out in the city."

The sheet was printed in solid black type on thin white paper, Lightborn make—Darkborn paper tended to take ink poorly—but unmistakably Darkborn in content. Typesetting could be done by touch as easily as by eye. In plain language, it laid the responsibility for the burning of the Rivermarch, the murder of the prince, and the destruction of the tower on the Shadowborn, who had influenced people on both sides of sunrise to work for them. It accused the Temple of failing in its contracted duty to protect the earthborn, and their brightnesses of exploiting the disaster to demand that the Darkborn cede their rights to the city. It asked for the readers' support in resisting this injustice.

She read it aloud for Balthasar, slowly, so that Lapaxo could appreciate how he flushed with anger and then paled as he listened. Bal took it from her hand and ran his fingers over the featureless surface. "So that was what he meant."

"Who?" Floria and Lapaxo said together.

"The archduke spoke of other measures. What he meant, he would not say in front of me. But we know how restive some of your people are against their brightnesses and against the Temple. This aims to redirect their anger away from the Darkborn, toward older grudges—"

She remembered the mob she had confronted outside Bolingbroke Station and imagined them battering at the gates of the palace itself, howling for the blood of their brightnesses.

"They've forced his back to the wall," Lapaxo said, appreciatively, though whether his appreciation was directed at the Lightborn strategy or the Darkborn response, she could not tell. "This could be very effective. The spark's already been set to the tinder—we saw that yesterday. This will throw oil on it. Who will burn? We'll know after sunrise. Tell me, Hearne—and know that I can have it confirmed—were *you* sent as an agitator?"

"No," Balthasar said, forcefully. "I knew nothing of this, and if I had, I'd have wanted nothing to do with it. And I will so declare before Mistress Tempe, or anyone else you want."

She waited, ready to counter Lapaxo's first threatening move, and aware that he was aware of her readiness. But all Lapaxo did was sigh. "You'd better get him out of here," he told her. "He's a dead man otherwise."

"I am not going anywhere," Balthasar said.

Perceptive as he was, he had missed the meaning of Lapaxo's sigh. Balthasar himself was spark to the oil, living proof of the existence of Shadowborn. The more widely he spread belief in himself, the more widely he spread belief in the assertions in these papers. That he had persuaded Lapaxo of his innocence had done no more than make Lapaxo regret the inevitability of his death. Their brightnesses would not leave him alive to lend support to this.

Her eyes shifted to the back of his dark head. One blow would be enough, but, stunned, he would not be able to travel by himself, and she could not carry him out until sunrise. Though Lapaxo might help.

Then Bal's head came round, and she thought for an instant that he had somehow deduced her thought, but his attention moved beyond her to the door, his head angled, listening. She heard nothing—but he was Darkborn. She raised her hand to stop him from speaking and signaled to Lapaxo. The captain slid from his chair, moving to the door. She pulled Balthasar up, meaning to get him into the bedroom. Behind a wall, he'd be shielded—

She heard the lock turn. As the door burst open, she kicked Balthasar's feet from underneath him and dropped him into the shelter of the table, snagging the collar of his thick jacket to soften his descent. That consideration earned her a knife in the side and the sting of a second across her neck. Two more knives clattered off the table. She jerked the knife out of her side—a small throwing knife, not dangerous outside eye or throat—even as the mandala on the skin of her abdomen started to burn. Lapaxo flowed around the door with a sweetly economical slash that opened the nearest woman's body from rib to hip. A third pair of knives fell from her hands.

"Poison!" Floria grunted, half doubled over. If the poison was giving the asset this much trouble, Lapaxo or Bal could die of a scratch. Lapaxo shied from a blade, and two more assassins forced their way through the door. They wore light armor and were armed with rapiers. *"Bal, stay down!"* she barked, and leaped to straddle the arms of the chair, brazenly exposed—a flamboyant idiocy her father would have whipped her for, but one that kept their attention on *her*. A knife lodged in the muscle of her shoulder; a second, aiming to split her throat, hissed past her ear. She shot the man who had thrown them above the right eye. With a ceding parry and bind, Lapaxo slipped his blade neatly through the seam of the nearest man's armor. The downed woman twisted violently with a flash of bluish intestine, and lashed out. Floria's shout of warning came too late. As Lapaxo sprang clear, Floria shot the last assassin, and jumped down from the chair to land beside the table, revolver swinging from the fallen to the door and back. Her hands were slippery with cold sweat.

Behind her she heard a scrape and a scuttle, and movement caught the corner of her eye—Balthasar dropping to his knees before Lapaxo, who had backed to brace himself against the wall with one hand, rapier still raised, eyes still on the door. The fabric covering his right shin was bloody. Balthasar slashed a strip from his own jacket—Sweet Imogene, with one of those cursed poisoned knives!—and flipped the strip around the captain's leg below the knee, cinching it tight. "I need water," he said over his shoulder, to Floria. "Something to wash the wound. And a clean knife."

"Identify them," rasped Lapaxo.

There was only one identification she cared about: who was still a threat. Her eyes flicked over the assassins, taking in their attire: that of ordinary palace staff, complete to the red morning jackets, stained a much darker red with blood. Two of the four were dead, or indistinguishable from it. The woman was lying curled up around her spilled intestine. The fourth was sprawled on his back, gargling and trying spasmodically to roll over. The corridor outside was empty for now. She wondered what had become of the guards outside; nothing good, she expected. She flicked away all the knives she could see, and then risked leaning over the assassins to frisk them and strip them of other weapons. There were no apparent firearms, but the rearmost was carrying a rolled-up black tarpaulin. A quiet assassination, then—Balthasar with poison, Floria with poison assisted by steel, and her body, at least, quickly disposed of.

She whirled as Balthasar lunged for the table. Oblivious to her reaction, he caught up the carafe and a glass and smashed the glass and used the broken stem to open the poisoned cut, raising new blood. Lapaxo's face was gray and he was breathing heavily, but he was still standing, back flat against the wall. Balthasar, his fingers on the pulse at his groin, said, urgently, "Floria, I need some digitalis, some stimulant—"

"I've nothing with me." She would have, she *should* have, if she hadn't been knocked from crisis to crisis.

"Then *get me some*," Balthasar said, lurching out of his crouch to catch the captain as he began to slide down the wall. The rapier fell with a clatter. "*That* or a mage."

Arguing the matter was pointless if Bal couldn't see that moving them from a defensible position could kill all three of them more surely than lack of help would kill Lapaxo.

The sound of running footsteps from outside sent her back behind the table. She'd have grabbed Balthasar if she'd thought he would come, but—"Quiet!" she barked at him, and in a burst of adrenaline-fired strength, heaved the glass table on its side. It made an inadequate shield, but its crash was enough to command the attention of the new arrivals.

Who were half a dozen vigilants wearing judiciary

badges, with Tempe Silver Branch at their back. The lieutenant in charge swiftly assessed her and the casualties, and then directed two of his men to clear the way for Tempe and the young mage who had questioned Balthasar. Tempe walked, seemingly unaware, across the tacky floor, while the mage followed her with mincing step, her face working in horror and revulsion. Adamantly, Floria pointed to Lapaxo. Tempe said to the mage, "Him first," and the mage went. Balthasar ceded his place with profound relief, whispering urgently to her.

A ferocious cramp bent Floria over. Hands braced on knees, she grunted out an assurance that she'd be fine. Tempe scowled; she hated it when appearances contradicted the truth told her. "You're bleeding."

"Scratches," Floria rasped. Tempe took her arm, examining the wound, and unstuck the side of her tunic to check the other, carefully avoiding the blood. "*Bitch* of a poison." If it had come to her against the assassins, she'd have been fatally off form, even if no poison could kill her outright. She freed a hand to knead her abdomen, willing everyone to go away and leave her to her misery. Maybe she could deflect their attention. "You'd better get the mage on to them soon if you want answers."

"Helenja or Prasav? Take your pick. The two who were posted to guard you are dead." She put a hand on Floria's shoulder, knee behind her knee, and pushed her down onto the mesh couch. "We've been having an interesting night, while you two were snug in here." Her suggestive tone earned her a sour look, which she met with a quizzical expression. "Been two letters for him, heavily ciphered—and, yes, I know they've not been delivered. We want to know what's in them. Also leaflets"—she nudged the paper on the ground with a toe—"pushed through every available mail slot and newspaper drop in the civil-service sector and servants' quarters. Variety of texts, all the same theme—the Shadowborn are your enemy, we're not, their brightnesses and the Temple are obstructing our alliance. You can say this for the Darkborn: they're thorough. I'd venture to say this wasn't all thought up in a night; someone had it planned ahead of time."

"Lord Vladimer," Balthasar said, from beside Lapaxo. Lapaxo's eyes were closed, but his skin had already warmed several tones from death gray. Then Balthasar noticed Floria's hunched posture and came quickly to his feet. "Floria!"

"I'm *all right*!" she said, sharply. "The asset protects me." If he couldn't read her eyes, she willed him to read her expression: *Watch what you say*. Both for her sake and his.

He started around to the rear of the couch, but was intercepted by Tempe's outstretched arm. "You don't want to get behind a vigilant just coming off a fight." She looked him up and down. "Vladimer? Word came to us that he had lost it mentally."

Floria, craning her neck, saw him realize that he had spoken too freely, particularly to a woman with an asset of veracity. He said, "Lord Vladimer would have thought about the implications of tension between Darkborn and Lightborn before. He received the council's reports, and it is his job to assess and deal with threats to his brother's rule."

"I've read some of your council's writings. This isn't without precedent."

"We—the council—write leaflets when we feel we need to inform, not to agitate," Balthasar said, adamantly. "Floria, won't you let me—"

"There'll be poison mixed in with the blood," Floria said, straightening up. "No point having you poison yourself now."

The mage drifted over to them, leaving Lapaxo with two of the vigilants. Tempe glanced toward the door. "If you would see to the survivors, Magistra."

"I cannot, Mistress Tempe," she said, stiffly. "They attempted to harm a mage."

"A mage—," said Floria, baffled. Tempe said to Balthasar, "*Are* you?"

"Not by any useful measure," he said, quick mind visibly working. "I can sense anything on the scale of weather-working, but nothing smaller. I never thought it amounted to anything."

"It doesn't, ordinarily. Well, well, well. So now you're under *Temple* law." Tempe looked at the mage, a glitter in her eye. "Magistra, does this man look harmed to you?"

"No," the mage said, warily. Floria had heard that same tone in a junior vigilant greeting a veteran's invitation to play a friendly dice game or practice a no-fail fighting move.

"Exactly. The vigilants are the ones who are poisoned and bloody, while he hasn't a hair out of place." Not strictly true, but any further bruises and sprains were strictly Floria's doing. "How do you know their intent was to harm him?"

The mage opened her mouth. Closed her mouth. Said finally, "You want to know," and turned and picked her way across the tacky floor to the fallen.

"She'll go far," Tempe predicted. She glanced toward Lapaxo, who was being lifted to his feet by two of the vigilants. "Good not to lose another captain tonight. Nice work with the tourniquet."

"Yes," Floria said, obscurely resentful that she had not been allowed to say it first. "It was."

Tempe drummed her fingers on her knee. "So, did whoever ordered this do it before or after the Temple had laid claim?"

"I don't understand," said Balthasar, perching on the edge of the upturned table, his worried attention more on Floria than Tempe. She was irritated; she had survived much worse, and she needed him not to assume Tempe was an ally.

"Several possibilities. The Temple wants you completely under their control. Ordinarily, they don't bother themselves with less than first-rank mages, but you are unique."

Floria had a sudden, uneasy feeling that she did not want to hear the rest, not with a mage likely to lay a healing hand on her in the next few minutes.

"The compact prohibits mages from using magic to either benefit or harm earthborn, except under a negotiated public contract and at the request of an earthborn. You understand?"

"Yes." By the tight tendons in Balthasar's neck, he did not like the way this was going, either.

"The compact does not apply to *mages*, although there is governance on the use of magic by stronger against weaker mages."

Governance, Floria thought. *That depends upon strength.* She suddenly discovered an unwelcome sympathy for the princess, a mere second-rank mage in possession of knowledge that her superiors were determined to deny. Little wonder she seemed hardly more than a puppet.

The mage approached somewhat warily. "Two of my colleagues have arrived," she said, primly. "They're seeing to the prisoners."

"Was it Prasav gave them their orders?" Tempe asked the mage. "Or Helenja?"

"Sharel," said the mage, pointedly. "And they were to kill him, too."

"Of course," Tempe said, relaxing slightly. This was retaliation against Floria and Balthasar for that incident in the night, not some wider political scheme. Floria wondered if she could possibly cozen the Mother of All Things into letting her be there when Helenja found out that Sharel had ordered the assassination of a man claimed by the Temple. At the very least, there would be a substantial fine.

"Mistress Floria," said the young woman.

Floria, resenting the mood, gave the mage her best intimidating stare. Tempe scolded, "Don't bully the girl."

She was good for a third-ranker. She dealt with the trivial wounds and left the poison and the asset to fight it out without interference. Her eyes widened, though, at the strength of the asset. Neither of the mages maintaining it had been in the tower last night, or this skirmish would have had quite a different outcome.

"You can go and report now," Tempe said, watched the mage leave the room, then turned back to Floria.

"What are the other possible reasons for the Temple . . . adopting me?" Balthasar said.

Tempe smiled thinly. "Control, of you as a source of information and a source of disruption. Possession, of an example of some very interesting magic. I understand magic only as much as the next nonmage."

Disingenuous of her, in Floria's opinion, given her asset and her relentlessly inquiring nature.

"But I do know that until now, nobody has known how to keep a Darkborn alive in light, or a Lightborn in darkness. I don't think your archduke quite grasped the implications of this, for the Temple; if I had been him, I would not have let you come over. It may even have bearing on our understanding the nature of the Curse itself, a puzzle for eight hundred years. . . . Yes, I think they'd want you alive."

Assuming, Floria thought, *that the high masters have not already learned everything they needed from Balthasar.*

"That makes it less likely they'd use you as bait," Tempe added. "Though not inconceivable."

"Bait for whom?" Balthasar said with strain in his voice. "And for what?"

Tempe gestured suggestively toward the door. "Enemies of the Darkborn. Enemies of the Temple. Enemies of the status quo. This court is riven with factions, but in the main, enemies know each other; we exist in a balance of tensions and oppositions. We do not like them to be disturbed. Now Isidore is dead, Fejelis has vanished, and you have come in from outside, bringing with you rumors of unseen forces of unknown potential—This isn't a simple place you have come to, Balthasar Hearne."

"I've known Floria for decades," he said, by way of answer.

"Yes," she said, with that annoying glint of speculative amusement.

Floria bit her tongue; she did not want to invite Tempe's curiosity.

"It's different, being on the same side of the wall." He turned his face to her, then to Tempe—sonning, Floria realized. "Please advise me."

"Next time I say, 'Stay down,' *stay down*," Floria said. "Save me grandstanding."

He looked abashed. "I . . . understand."

But wasn't sorry; she heard that distinction. And she'd be

a hypocrite if she pretended she'd respect him more for cowering under the table.

The corner of Tempe's mouth drew down. "*My* advice: get out of here. The Temple's protection goes only so far, particularly now that they've torn up the compact. Tell your archduke this is not a good idea, trying to stir up the populace. Their brightnesses won't forget it."

"And the Shadowborn?" Nothing in Balthasar's face betrayed his feelings—so he could do it if he needed to.

"Are magical, yes? Therefore the Temple's problem. Or their brightnesses, should they choose to contract with the Temple to deal with them."

"That's not enough," Balthasar said.

Tempe sighed. "That man Johannes—his cousin was summoned to his bedside, found him raving about Shadowborn who could turn a man into a flare, burn him to char in seconds. Half the servants had heard that story, or versions of it, by the time we knew."

"Did he mention Balthasar?" Floria said.

"Not in any version I heard—but who's to know who else from that household will be talking—or the group he's part of?" She stood up and said, deliberately, "So take your lover home and leave him there, if you want him alive by tomorrow's sunset."

"We are not lovers," Floria said, not looking at Balthasar.

Tempe snorted. "Woman, I've an asset of veracity. Whether you've lain with him or not, you've loved this man as long as I've known you. While he was on the far side of sunset, you were safe to be the perfect vigilant. That kind of accommodation has the habit of breaking down, though seldom as spectacularly as this."

"Thank you for your counsel, Mistress Tempe, and for your intervention tonight," Balthasar said, steadily, though Tempe's words had brought a flush to his pale skin. "But until the Shadowborn are dealt with, I shall stay. May I have the letters addressed to me now?"

From his pocket, he slipped a cipher. Tempe's irritated glance at Floria rebuked their collective negligence in not finding it and questioning him for the key. He worked the cipher one-handed with some dexterity, reading the messages with the fingers of his left hand, lips moving slightly as he committed the translation to memory, and apparently quite oblivious to the activity around him as Tempe's people gathered up the dead and wounded.

He lacked most of the basic instincts of survival in the Lightborn court, she had to admit. She had to assume that was nurture, not nature: with the exception of his brother Lysander, his lineage was sound, producing generations of civic-minded, intelligent men. Quiet men, with the kind of courage that was proven only on testing, as Balthasar had proven his. The women were less distinguished, but she suspected the diminishing effects of Darkborn expectations of their sex; Balthasar's small daughters were promising enough.

A daughter of hers would be spared that impediment. Her lineage offered the health and athleticism and survivorship of ten generations of vigilants, plus her asset. The Mother of All determined how those offerings would be endowed—except the last—but at least they would be on offer. Even if a child inherited Balthasar's blindness, the example of Ishmael di Studier and the Stranhornes had proven that was no handicap. . . . Though if a child required an ensorcellment to live under light . . .

And there was Telmaine, and Darkborn expectation of sexual fidelity in marriage, which Balthasar, unlike many of his peers, practiced. She did not need Tempe to explain to her that in a court of alliances that formed and dissolved overnight, governed by contracts that could be torn up even before the signatures had dried, that she had learned to prize, even idealize, such loyalty. If she asked him, would it lessen her in his eyes . . . thoughts . . . or herself in his? *Think highly of yourself, don't you, woman? Assuming he'll be yours for the asking . . .*

His movement drew her eye as he returned the cipher back to his pocket, and folded up the letters. With a shake of the head in response to Tempe's extended hand, he pocketed the letters as well. As he drew breath, she converted the silent request into a staying gesture, and motioned forward the secretary who had just arrived. "I think it best we enter this into the record under a judiciary seal."

Balthasar began to explain how Lord Vladimer had taken the Darkborn mages—and Telmaine—south to the Borders to contend with the Shadowborn, and were requesting Lightborn assistance. Floria, listening, thought, *And first we all three have to survive.*

Fejelis

"Tam's gone *where*?" Fejelis demanded.

Jovance was a step behind him as he threw open the door to the small bedroom, on the empty bed and empty room. He turned to face her, and she put a strong hand on the center of his chest and firmly pushed him backward over the threshold. "Give us a moment," she said, over her shoulder. "Get everything together, and tell us as soon as you hear the train."

As she kicked the door closed, he seized her shoulders, answering her disrespectful handling of her person with his own. *"Where has he gone?"*

"He has been *sent*"—she laid stress on the word—"to negotiate with the Shadowborn."

He should not have such difficulty understanding simple words. He looked around at the bed, its covers trailing off the edge, the sheets still creased with Tam's restless movements. If he touched it, might it still be warm? ". . . I didn't even know he'd gone."

"You're not a mage, Prince Fejelis."

The title—reminding him who and what he was, and why this might be a disaster much larger than betrayal by a friend. ". . . Gone to the Shadowborn?"

"*Sent,*" she reminded him, forcefully. "It wasn't voluntary; that I can tell you."

"But Tam's— "

"Very strong. My grandfather said seventh-rank potential, sixth-rank fulfilled, fifth"—a sour expression—"acknowledged. But against the high masters, he had no chance."

". . . He got us away." He felt dazed and blundering, and knew it showed.

"Only with the archmage's help, he told me. They anticipated needing him to do this—and the archmage had taken a liking to you. You remind him of someone from his past."

". . . And the Shadowborn?" Fejelis said, disregarding anything else for the moment. "Has he a chance there?"

Her eyes asked him not to make her answer that question. "Not . . . if they're hostile. Tam . . . said to tell you goodbye, to give you his love, to give you his regrets. He made me promise I'd look after you. Said you'd look after me, Beatrice and his children, the artisans. . . ."

Fejelis felt his shoulders bow under the weight of all Tam's love and lost hopes.

She tipped her forehead forward, bouncing it lightly on his chest. With him pinning her arms, she could move neither forward nor back. "He didn't have a choice, Fejelis. If nothing else, you must understand that."

". . . Could we go after him?"

She lifted her head, honey-colored eyes narrowing. "*No*, Fejelis. He . . . gave me an impression of what he sensed just before he *lifted*. It's ugly and it's very, very strong."

"Where?"

"West of us. I'd say close to the Darkborn barony of Stranhorne. Directing or driving the force that overran Stranhorne. *No*, Fejelis."

Can I believe her? he thought, with a sudden and too-welcome suspicion. Suppose it was the Temple who had found Tam, seized him, and took him unwillingly—Fejelis believed that, at least—back to Minhorne? He'd rather have her a willing traitor and a liar than Tam a traitor, a tool of the high masters, and a prisoner of the very monstrousness that had produced the things they had fought.

She was still in his hands, and he realized that through his grip on her shoulders, through the coarse weave of her sleeves, she could know everything he was thinking. He let her go, like a coal that had fallen into his hand, and at the flicker of pained emotion in her eyes, promptly regretted that. ". . . I'm sorry."

"I know." She hesitated. "I should have cloaked my touch-sense, but . . . I had to peek."

His lips formed something that was not a smile. "Now you know."

She sighed. "I too wish it had been that way, Fejelis."

". . . Is there nothing—nothing we can do for him?"

"No. If the Shadowborn kill him, then we can try to avenge him. It didn't occur to him to veto that."

Her smile was wondrously cold, but in her eyes was the knowledge that death was not the worst that might await Tam. The silence was punctuated by a chime. "We need to go," she said quietly. "The train's coming."

He opened the door just as Jade was raising his fist to knock.

"We wait until they stop and blow the whistle twice," Midha said, as they gathered around the door. "That's the usual routine if we have to come down to a train in the night. Either the caboose will have been cleared for you, or someone in it will shout instructions."

They had Jovance's assurance that there was nothing living nearby except for those on the train and themselves, but Orlanjis was still shivering slightly at the thought of going into the night. Fejelis put a hand on his shoulder, drawing his gaze, full of unspoken questions and uncertainty. Fejelis managed, from somewhere, to summon a grin. "Have you ever actually ridden a Darkborn train?" His brother had shown a surprising—perhaps lifesaving—knowledge of the Darkborn railways, and admitted to a desire to escape court to the railways. "This'll be a first."

Orlanjis managed, from somewhere, to summon a pout. "Don't tease."

Then the whistle sounded, and Midha opened the door. They dropped a rope with lights down either side of the ladder and climbed down one at a time, with only Jade staying on guard above. Orlanjis suddenly blurted, "I have to get something."

Midha, frowning, nodded to Sorrel. "Make it quick."

Lights in hand, she flanked him on his dash underneath the platform to a tarpaulin that, from its profile, covered a stack of drums. He reached underneath and withdrew a bundle of red: Fejelis's ceremonial caul and jacket, which Orlanjis had hidden in a futile attempt to disguise their identities. He was sweating when he returned, his arm blanched with exposure to shadow.

Fejelis accepted the bundle and tucked it under his arm with a quiet "Thanks." He could feel the hard wire of the caul against his ribs.

The door to the caboose opened with a crack that made them all jump, and a great fan of light spilled across the gravel and scrub alongside the tracks. A man's huge silhouette waved at them and a voice barked from inside. "All aboard that's coming aboard. This train's got a schedule to keep." By its pitch it could be man or woman, aged but still strong.

"Les?" said Sorrel. "Les!" Their boarding was briefly obstructed as Midha and Sorrel crowded into the doorway to confirm and shout greetings; then the train whistle blew warning and Midha boosted Jovance aboard. Fejelis and Orlanjis scrambled after. Midha closed the door and bolted it behind them.

"They ordered me out because of this cursed hip," explained the railway legend in frank disgust to Jovance. "Put Lomand and his gang in place. Didn't know anything about it until the train stopped and they all got out. I'll skelp the lot of them if we don't find our hut entirely as we left it." She was a small woman whose weight made scarcely a bulge in the netting of the hammock slung for her. It seemed implausible that the deep, forceful voice could be hers, or that the hulking Nathan could be her son. He had an inch on tall Fejelis and at least half his weight.

Then again, Fejelis knew within two minutes of climbing into the caboose that if personality had mass, the engine would have been in for a hard pull on the hills. Celeste inspected them with pale blue eyes, unimpressed. "Who're these'uns? New blood? Look an unlikely pair. Pair of city lads run away from trouble?"

"In . . . a sense," Jovance said, with a quick, cautious glance at Fejelis.

Gently, so as to show he had taken no offense, Fejelis said, ". . . I am Fejelis Grey Rapids. This is my brother, Orlanjis."

She scowled. "If you're going to pull my leg, my laddie, pull the one that's not broke."

His thoughts seemed to hit an unseen obstacle—*thump*. At his side, Orlanjis started to quiver and sank down to rest against the rocking wall of the caboose. Fejelis realized his brother was laughing. Jovance said, tremulously, "It's so, Les," and undermined her assertion by collapsing, giggling, beside Orlanjis.

After that, Celeste could not be convinced, particularly since, when she chose to fire some testing questions at them, Orlanjis had the answers. "Why would a prince's son learn about trains?" she demanded. To that, Orlanjis had no response. To Fejelis he might confide his dream to flee court for a simple life as a railway engineer, but not to others. Fejelis left them to talk trains, glad to have Orlanjis distracted from the horrors of the night. He had heard the undertone of hysteria in his brother's laughter.

He had no such diversion. "What am I going to tell Lord Vladimer?" he murmured, as he and Jovance sat side by side on the floor, backs against the rough wall of the carriage.

She made a small hand gesture, one he knew from Tam when he sealed a conversation against eavesdropping. He had always thought it was a quirk of Tam's, but perhaps it was one they had both learned from Lukfer.

"What can you tell him?" she said, close-cropped head bent close. "He should know he's reaping what he sowed."

He twisted to face her. "The only thing he is guilty of, by Tam's testimony, is inaction. The rest was other men's doing."

A flash of yellow eyes, unreadable.

He took his best guess at an answer to that flash. ". . . Jovance, I'll treat with whomever I have to, to achieve my ends."

"Which are?" she said, neutrally.

He let out a breath. ". . . My position back, of course." He bounced the red bundle on his hand and had to snatch at it before it unraveled, sending the caul skittering across the cabin. "Unlike Jis," he said, "I've never given any thought to an alternative occupation." Then, more soberly: ". . . I have to speak to the archmage again. I'd like to be able to convince him that this is folly, but if it's not—if it's quite simply that the Shadowborn are too-strong mages and we have the choice of death, enslavement, or collusion—then I must know that. It may be"—he rolled his head on the rough wall to look at her—"that I too must treat with the Shadowborn, to try to secure the best possible terms."

"For whom? For you? Their brightnesses?"

". . . For myself, their brightnesses, the palace staff, the artisans and craftsman and merchants and indigents . . . for us, the Lightborn. I would count it my failure if Minhorne suffered what Stranhorne Manor has and I had done nothing to avert the stroke."

Jovance's hand opened and closed. Something moved in her face, something grim, powerful. Despite himself, he remembered the viscous red rain of a body ruptured in midair.

"Fejelis," she said, slowly. "If it's death or enslavement, I'll take death. I'll not have done to me what's been done to Tam."

He felt the words physically as a pang in his stomach or beneath his heart. He drew up his feet, bracing himself with his angled legs, and wondered what to say to her. Her determination would not change his decision—could not, even if he knew that by some choice or conciliation of his own, he could save her. Yet to say so aloud seemed cold, and he did not feel cold toward her fate.

She said, quietly, "I didn't tell you that to influence your decisions, or make what you have to do more difficult. It's difficult enough. I told you so you'd not be taken by surprise."

". . . 'Difficult enough'?" he picked up from that bleak tone. "Do you mean 'hopeless enough'?" A hesitation, longer than his usual. ". . . What do you sense?"

She shook her head. "I also told you," she said, "so we'd

not waste the time we have." She slid work-hardened fingers under his jaw, turned his head, and kissed him.

"That's playing dirty," he said, huskily, when she drew back.

"So it is."

"You're not going to tell me."

"No, I'm not. It's a matter for mages, and it would do you no good to know."

He chose to accept that, for now. At least she had not pointed out that none of the mages were under contract to him on this matter.

A far too few minutes later, the train drew into Strumheller, giving them no opportunity for more than that kiss, an interlude of the desultory, uncertain conversation between two people exploring a mutual attraction, and another kiss. Celeste gleefully observed, "That's no prince, though the lad's got taste." Orlanjis looked worried, as well he should. Neither tradition nor compact allowed for a mage consort to the prince, and the Temple would still want Jovance's strength for their lineages. Fejelis doubted he would meet the obscure fate of her first earthborn lover, though, who had been lost on his travels, possibly through the Temple's doing. Whatever Fejelis's fate was to be, it would not be obscure.

And if they escaped death or enslavement, the relations between princedom and Temple would change. He would see to that.

They listened as doors slammed open, so forcefully the train rocked, and the people inside spilled out. He heard bellowed orders from men, and shouts from men and women—if Darkborn women were submissive and meek, he did not hear much evidence of it—and children crying. At one point, there was a shot, followed immediately by a thoroughly profane rebuke from one of the voices in charge. Someone knocked hard on their door to tell them that they'd hear the bell when it was safe for them to come out. They waited more or less in silence. Talking was difficult with the racket outside, and flirting inhibited by tension, and by Orlanjis sitting on the floor on his other side. Though his young brother made a negligent chaperone, since by the time they heard the bolt slide back, Orlanjis had dozed off, propped against Fejelis's shoulder.

"Wait until y'hear the bell," the voice said from outside. "Lightborn quarters are off the west end of the platform—you'll know from th'signage, if y'haven't been here before. When you get inside and th'door shut and all, throw th'switch t'turn off the bell t'let us know. The baron and some'll be down to join y', very shortly." He rapped on the door again, and they heard his booted feet move away.

Nat helped his mother to her feet, and she tucked crutches under her arms. He could have carried her effortlessly, but Fejelis had no doubt, even on this slight acquaintance, as to how she would receive that. He prodded Orlanjis awake and resisted the temptation to tease him with the request that he witness the formalizing of a contract, less on Orlanjis's account than Jovance's. They heard the bell, and Nat opened the door on chill night air; shivering, they climbed down.

Strumheller Crosstracks Station was an open station. He did not linger to look around, aware of the courtesy their hosts were extending them, surrendering even so small a portion of their precious hours of darkness on a night like this. The Lightborn quarters were easy to identify, even without the painted sign. It was the one building where the paintwork was truly decorative, not merely functional, the door, trim, and mounted panels on the sides brightly painted in a rustic, slightly garish style. Ordinarily the mounted panels would have held posters, but there was no one to read them here.

They closed the doors behind them, gladly putting the stone walls between them and the night. The building was surprisingly large, accommodating a dozen people in three bedrooms and a six-bed dormitory, and very well lit. The lack of posters outside was more than made up for by the many sheets of notice and instruction inside, which Nat and Les completely ignored. They staked their claim to their favorite rooms.

Jovance threw the lever to turn off the bell, saying, "The

meeting room is through here." She steered them into a modest-sized room dominated by a long glass table and an equally long glass sideboard. Six chairs of Lightborn design were pushed in on one side of the table, so that the occupants would face what looked like a large watercolor painting on paper, with a fine silver mesh over it: the paper wall. The painting would be backed by several layers of opaque black. Orlanjis, who had not had many dealings with Darkborn, eyed it dubiously. It looked flimsy, but any breach would be more dangerous to the Darkborn than to themselves. Jovance said, "Shall I get you something to drink, your brightnesses?"

She was prompting him back into a role; he supposed he should be grateful. "I'm not sure my stomach is up for more bedeeth tea," he said, "but I need something to keep me alert. It has been a long night."

"I'll see what I can do," she said, and left.

Orlanjis said in a low voice, "Fejelis, she's a *mage.*"

". . . I'm fairly sure there's no ensorcellment involved," Fejelis said.

"That's not what I meant," Orlanjis said. "I mean, she's not eligible to be consort. And if you're not serious, I mean—" He flushed deeply, to Fejelis's well-hidden amusement. So his indulged younger brother had a sense of ethics in romance.

". . . I could be quite serious. And if it comes to that, we will deal with it then."

"But why should she—"

"Who's he insulting?" Jovance interrupted, coming into the room with a tray. "Me or you?"

She must have used magic to heat the water that quickly. She offered them their choice of cups and dispensed tea from the common pot. Orlanjis's scowl dissipated as he fell on the bannocks and cheese. Self-appointed food taster or ravenous adolescent? Finding himself in a losing race for the spoils, Fejelis concluded it was the latter. Jovance helped herself to a portion and then simply watched the scrum with a sisterly smirk. She never did get an answer to her question.

Fejelis was halfway through his second cup of bitter Darkborn tea and wondering if there was any more cheese in the stores when they heard the door open on the other side. He put down the bannock he had been holding, and, wanting a napkin, wiped his mouth on his sleeve.

Jovance leaned down to breathe in his ear. "Eight people. Three mageborn. Two pretty strong."

A voice from the other side of the wall said, "Your brightnesses?" A prompting murmur. "Magistra?"

"Yes," Fejelis said. He made himself speak steadily, without his habitual hesitation. "This is Fejelis Grey Rapids, prince of the Lightborn; my brother, Orlanjis; and Magistra Jovance." He realized he had no idea how she styled herself on such occasions. Earthborn Lightborn clung to a fashionable minimalism in using titles, although they were as prideful and hierarchical without them as the mages with their ranks, or the Darkborn with their layers of nobility. It did help, when dealing with either of those, to have a title to brandish, but he was not sure she would want to use her Temple rank, even if he knew it.

"I am Baron Reynard Strumheller," the Darkborn on the far side of the wall said, in an aggressive, light baritone, as though daring Fejelis to dispute his claim. "I have with me Lord Vladimer Plantageter, the brother of the archduke"—Jovance's face hardened at the name—"Baronet Boris Stranhorne, Baronette Laurel Stranhorne, Lady Telmaine—Mrs. Balthasar Hearne, formerly Lady Telmaine Stott." That a woman, but not a man, could gain or lose rank by marriage was one of those Darkborn nuances that had taken hours of study to understand. "Magister Farquhar Broome"—he saw Jovance nod in recognition—"and Magistra Phoebe Broome."

Jovance leaned over to whisper, and he pointed to his ear and the wall in warning, and indicated the paper and pens and ink laid out on the sideboard.

"My companions and I are deeply grateful to you for your timely retrieval and hospitality, Baron Strumheller," Fejelis said.

Jovance dealt out pens and paper. Orlanjis eyed his dubiously. Incongruously, the pen was of Darkborn manufacture, the wooden barrel carefully carved, with a metal nib and hidden bladder that stored ink. The first time one of these had been laid before Isidore, the prince had laughed himself breathless at the cheek of the Darkborn, out to best the Lightborn there as well.

Fejelis uncapped the pen, tapped it to start the ink flowing, and scribbled, *3rd mage lady T*. He had not named her when he told Jovance and her colleagues the background to Tam's, Orlanjis's, and his sudden arrival beside the railway tracks, and he did not think Jovance or Orlanjis would connect name and account now. Even so, Jovance gave him a searching glance.

Vladimer Plantageter said, "I expected that the mage—Magister Tammorn—would have been with you."

Straight to the heart of the sticky questions, Fejelis thought. "So did I," he said. At least he had had a chance to decide beforehand how to meet it. Which was directly. "Magistra Jovance tells me that he has been sent by the archmage and high masters to open negotiations with the Shadowborn."

There was a reverberating silence from the other room, no spurious or stalling questions as to his meaning.

"That is not news I wanted to convey," Fejelis said, "any more than it is news you wished to hear. Magister Tammorn did not go willingly—he is a sport, and able to sense Shadowborn magic in a way that lineage mages do not, and his sense of them was of something hostile and dangerous—but being under Temple law, and being fifth-rank, he had no choice. If he had defied the high masters' orders, he would have been coerced into it."

"Well," they heard the baron mutter, "that's that, then."

"That most decidedly is not that," Vladimer said, his voice gritty. "That is not welcome news, but not, perhaps, unexpected." And what exactly did he mean by that—that he expected treachery of the mages? Or the Lightborn? "However, Prince Fejelis, your being here in the Borders is unexpected. The report I had from Minhorne is that you had been deposed."

And in the usual course of such things, should have been dead, yes. "My survival was Magister Tam's doing. He *lifted* my brother and me out."

"Why bring you here?"

Despite himself, he hesitated a half beat. ". . . He brought me to someone he trusted—Magistra Jovance, granddaughter to his master, Lukfer. Magister Tammorn is more than a contracted mage to me. He is a good friend."

"That is not the usual relationship between earthborn and mageborn," Vladimer said, crisply. A slightly reproachful murmur from the other side. Jovance scribbled, *F Broome.*

"You're not the first to tell me that, Lord Vladimer."

A woman's voice spoke up, slightly hesitant but determined. "Lord Vladimer, neither my father nor I can detect any sense of Shadowborn about them."

P Broome, wrote Jovance. *Checking us.* Orlanjis shuffled his chair closer, craning his neck to see.

Fejelis decided that he would not acknowledge that they themselves lacked a similar advantage. He scratched, *Cn they tell yr lineage vs sport?* She squinted, deciphering, and shook her head.

He'd be better reassured if her expression were more certain, though if any of the Darkborn weren't Darkborn or were Shadowborn-held, he might be dead or ensorcelled before he knew he'd misjudged. The paper wall was a fragile thing. The vigilants would be disgusted with him for sitting still, so his voice could be placed, but instinct told him that he should stay where he was; the tension on the far side of the wall was palpable.

"And what do you plan to do now?"

Orlanjis was frowning at the other's tone. Fejelis wished he were able to signal that he was choosing to let the Darkborn have control for a while, to let them settle. "Get back to Minhorne," he said. "Hope to be able to influence the archmage—"

"To do what?"

That, too, he had thought through. ". . . To consider the interests of the earthborn as well as the mageborn in their actions. I don't know why the high masters have chosen the course they have taken. Perhaps it was anger for your people's attack on the tower." He'd get it said, rather than leave it leering through the silences. "For me, I don't think that in itself was enough, but if they felt themselves weakened by it, so that they did not feel they could fight . . ." *Assuming,* Fejelis said privately to himself, *that they wished to fight under any balance of powers.* His fear was that the Temple had decided that their loyalty lay with magic, whatever the nature of that magic. He could not say that to the Darkborn, and deepen their hostility against magic. Or was that what Vladimer had meant when he said that the Temple's move was not unexpected? ". . . I could continue to enumerate reasons, but won't know until I ask."

"Which may satisfy your curiosity, Prince Fejelis, a motive with which I find myself in sympathy. But what will you do when you know?"

Jovance's pen beat a soft staccato on her paper, leaving dots of ink. He quirked a smile at her; Lord Vladimer was obviously accustomed to provoking a reaction and letting others do the soothing. Sejanus Plantageter was superb at it. ". . . How is your brother the archduke, Lord Vladimer? I had had some bad news of him earlier."

"If you are asking as to whether I have power to negotiate," Vladimer said, "I do."

"I'm glad to hear it, but no. I was asking because, when I return to Minhorne, it will be reassuring to me to know that I have Sejanus Plantageter on the other side of sunset, rather than a regency council." *Composed,* he thought, *of bigots and old men.*

And are those in charge of the palace any better? queried an internal voice that sounded remarkably like his father's.

"You need not worry about Mycene anymore," the Darkborn said. "The telegram I had earlier said that he had been killed by a Shadowborn. The present Duke Mycene is fighting Shadowborn in Stranhorne Crosstracks. Kalamay continues alive, but I don't doubt Sejanus will deal with him. My brother is quite well."

Which was a relief, but left more than a little unsaid. Fejelis well knew that Plantageter was strongly opposed to having magic in his city, but despite his prejudices, the archduke insisted on scrupulous respect of Lightborn rights under the letter and the spirit of the law. Fejelis could only hope that had not changed. "The injury was magical, was it?"

"Yes . . . Shadowborn, indirectly."

Gracious—or politic—not mentioning Tam's part in it. Might Vladimer suspect that Fejelis already knew more than he was saying, from Tam?

Vladimer, suspect? With a name that was a byword for suspicion? Very well. He would put Vladimer's trust to the test. "What is your plan, Lord Vladimer?"

"To retake Stranhorne Manor and the territories on the far side," Vladimer said. "We have reinforced Stranhorne Crosstracks all night by train with troops and reserves from Strumheller and Telemarch, farther around the border, but, unfortunately, our ability to reinforce by day is limited by the design of this station. Stranhorne has also received further reinforcements from the estates and towns on the inner Borders, including Mycene lands, and they are close to the numbers that they can safely shelter."

Fejelis breathed out: Vladimer seemed prepared to treat him as an ally after all. "Both Magister Tam and Magistra Jovance warn me that these are very strong mages. If you come into contact with them, you will take high casualties, possibly to not much advantage."

"It has th'full support of the baronies," Baron Strumheller said—growled, rather.

"If it comes to that, we may," Vladimer said. "But that does not imply we will lose. Ishmael—the former Baron Strumheller—killed a Shadowborn mage at my bedside, admittedly with the help of Lady Telmaine here." *Rank?* he scratched, to Jovance, and she, *6?* "Baron Stranhorne's sacrifice stopped the advance across Stranhorne lands, and we have information that one of the mages present was killed. I ask you: if they are so potent, then why are they employing such familiar tactics of assassination and social disruption—earthborn tactics, not mageborn? Why use people, such as your Mistress White Hand, or the dukes of Mycene and Kalamay? Why take such care to turn us against each other before they emerged into the open?"

All good questions, Fejelis acknowledged. "You assume that you have seen their full strength."

"I assume nothing. But we have no choice but to fight or be overrun. By doing so, we may also ease the pressure on the city, which is no small concern of mine, and perhaps provoke your Temple to find its courage."

"You are not the one to judge the Temple's courage," Jovance said, sorely provoked.

"I may have no right, Magistra, but others do: my brother, the archduke, who knew nothing of this until after the tower was down; Baronet and Baronette Stranhorne, who both fought in the defense of their home, though the lady is with child and her brother not yet eighteen; Baron Strumheller and his brother and predecessor, who built much of the defense we are now mobilizing, and who is a mage himself."

A mage who knew Shadowborn . . . "Is the previous Baron Strumheller still alive?" Among Lightborn, he would almost certainly not be, but Darkborn convention allowed for the deposition of the living.

"Unknown," Vladimer said. "He was lost in the retreat, but I've learned not to discount his survival."

That sounded as though it was directed to someone else's address, likely the brother's. How much did he wish to risk alienating one or another of the Darkborn by inquiring further? And if the high masters would not listen to their own, why should they listen to a Darkborn sport mage? ". . . I will support you in any way I can," Fejelis said. He decided it was time for a little provocation of his own. ". . . Here we are, three Lightborn, essentially alone in the barony. Why not simply take us hostage?"

"I thought about that," the Darkborn spymaster said, unruffled. The muttering this time sounded as though it was coming from Baron Strumheller; Fejelis thought he heard the word "hospitality" in a resentful tone. "But who would ransom a prince they'd tried to depose, especially in the coin I needed? And the mage with you would be more trouble than you're worth."

Point to Vladimer. Jovance's smile showed teeth, and Orlanjis's eyes on the decorated paper wall were white ringed. Fejelis quickly sketched two stick swordsmen, the cauled one with arms outflung as he was impaled on the other's blade. As an artist, he would have starved on the street, but the sketch eased the tension along the glass table while leaving the Darkborn listening to silence for a little while. "... We will see which one of us is right about my importance," he muttered, knowing the Darkborn would hear. He raised his voice. "... I'll be leaving for Minhorne first thing in the morning, Lord Vladimer." And if he had any sense, he should have asked Jovance beforehand if she would take him. He had a mental image of himself riding in triumph into the city on a hay cart, but that was beyond his drawing skills. He corralled his wandering thoughts. "... The high masters are mine to deal with, but I'd appreciate any additional information you have on what has happened over the past day and night."

Ishmael

Lysander Hearne was waiting in the hall outside her room, lounging against the wall as though he had idled away hours there. He returned Ishmael's sonn and shrugged himself upright, then strolled over and fixed Ishmael's cravat with a few brisk tugs. There was something cheerfully brazen about him that Ishmael, in his shaken state, could not help appreciating.

"Ready to get something to eat?"

"As long as there's none of their magic close enough t'turn my stomach, or I'll get no good of it."

The corner of Hearne's mouth twitched slightly. "You're a rock-nerved bastard; I'll grant you that. I know what she just put to you."

He steered Ishmael into an interior room where the air was still and all walls sonned as solid. The hexagonal table in the center was large enough to seat twelve luxuriously, and eighteen at a pinch. Lysander directed the servant who arrived at the ring of a bell to set the table for two. He pulled out a chair for Ishmael. "Sit."

Ishmael sat. Hearne dropped into the nearest chair on the next edge of the hexagon. "So," he said, "any questions?"

"Aye," Ishmael said. "A few."

"And you're wondering whether you can trust me."

"No," Ishmael said; about that he was quite clear.

Unexpectedly, Hearne leaned back and laughed. Ishmael's sense was that the laughter was unfeigned, even pleased. "If you know my brat of a brother, I'm sure you're wondering how I came to be here."

Ishmael was entirely content to let him tell his story; he'd take what he would out of it. Servants set down fresh rolls, with pâté and preserves, fruit and cheese, and newly made tea.

"I was twenty-one years old," Hearne said, while Ishmael cut and spread a roll, "and a very bad little boy. I was clever, and I didn't care who I hurt, and I knew what I wanted. I was well on my way to wealth and I'd have found my way to power, for all there wasn't a title in the family. But I made a mistake. After that, if I didn't leave, I'd have to deal with the one person who knew what I'd done. I found I couldn't. I could make the brat's life a misery, but I couldn't kill him—not with the fresh feel of that girl's throat cracking under my hands. You ever felt that?" The question was rhetorical; he did not wait for an answer. "So I ran. Nowhere's far enough when a man's trying to run from himself, but I didn't know that then. Down at Odon's Barrow I crossed some of the local enforcers and was knocked senseless and dumped out in the middle of a field. They'd been feeding troublemakers to the Shadowborn."

"They were," Ish said. "We put a stop t'that."

"I woke up on the march to Emeya's midden, a prisoner. You'll hear more about Emeya presently. Over the centuries, she and our lady have pulled in tens of thousands, and those tens of thousands have begotten others. Emeya's—barony, I suppose you'd call it—is probably seventy, eighty thousand strong now. Earthborn here do what earthborn have always done: farm, hunt, spin, craft, flirt, gossip, intrigue, marry, breed, and die. I'd no desire to be a peasant groveling in the dirt, so I maneuvered my way into her stronghold itself."

His face was utterly devoid of expression. "I said I was a bad little boy, but that's all I was—a little boy. Though I expect I'd have grown up and made out all right—but for Ari.

"Besides Emeya, she had four strong mages—and I mean eighth-rank, if not more. That's the kind of power our lady's offering you, di Studier. There were Ariadne, Neill, Jonquil, Midora—all of Emeya's lineage, as mages reckon it. There'd been more, but a while back—a couple of hundred years—they tried to take over and lost. Ari was the youngest, and Neill was Emeya's favorite, then. Neill wanted to wait for Ari to come round to his wooing, but Emeya wouldn't have it. She set an ensorcellment on them, meaning to force them together. Ari had enough strength to bind another man in that ensorcellment—me. I could no more have refused her than I could have flown. It made me an enemy of Neill and a target of Emeya's anger, and I hated Ari for it."

If there was an ensorcellment of that sort on him now, Ishmael could not sense it. He certainly did not behave as though he hated her—not even counting the bullet he'd put through Ishmael. Head lowered, Hearne said, "That was the way we started, but along the way, something changed. I never thought I'd care about what someone else felt. And when the boy was born—well, I've a cur's way with the small and weak, but this one was different, too. This one was *mine.*" He sonned Ishmael with a harsh stroke, his expression defensive, and a warning. "I wanted her safe, I wanted him safe, and the only place to look for safety was here. It was cursed slow doing, convincing Ariadne to take the risk, and by the time I did, the boy had will and strength of his own, and Emeya had made a pet of him—they all had. He wouldn't come. He said he'd bring Emeya down on us. He forced me to choose, and I chose Ariadne."

There was a long silence. "Ariadne's strength and knowledge were gifts to Isolde. If the uprising hadn't reduced the numbers of Emeya's strong ones, not to mention made her so suspicious she put a choke chain on the survivors, Emeya'd already be the only one left."

"Emeya's got one less of the th'strong ones," Ish said. "I shot th'one called Jonquil at Lord Vladimer's bedside; two bullets in the body, one in the brain. It's possible that Stranhorne got others, including your Neill."

Lysander sonned him with that close attention he recalled from dealing with his brother, though it was plain the two were very different men. "Did you, indeed?" he said. "Frankly, that surprises me."

"I'd th'help of a brave mage. And"—before Lysander could ask who—"it's likely I met your son at Stranhorne."

The father leaned forward, ready, Ishmael thought, with any of half a dozen ordinary questions. *How did he seem? Was he all right?* But he eased back without speaking, his lips tight, his expression one of hard-schooled composure.

"I took him for your brother th'first time I sonned him. Seemed t'me as though he could do with steady feeding t'flesh him out, steady labor t'build him up, and no small amount of education. I've known street children less neglected. He's got th'one trick of fire down fine—nearly broiled me—and he's learned something of ensorcellment." He would hold back, for the moment, how Sebastien had used that skill, or how the near broiling had been provoked. "I also got th'sense that your leaving had lost him favor," he added.

"It would," Hearne said, taking the information straight.

"If Emeya were t'lose this war, you'd have your son."

"If he lived."

Ishmael chewed bread and considered. Lysander had all the characteristics of a virtuoso liar—someone who lied merely to keep in practice—but Ishmael could not tell which part of this might be fabrication. The one part he believed was Hearne's feeling toward his son. Briefly, he entertained the thought of asking the man if he could touch-read him. But he knew the answer, because as sure as sunrise killed, there were things that *none* of them were telling him.

"If she's got th'ability t'augment mages, where are th'others?"

Unease passed across Lysander's expression. "What do you mean?"

"Th'question's simple enough. If she can do this t'me, why not t'others?"

"It's . . . not exactly like closing a cut, di Studier. It's going to be very taxing for both of them."

"And?" said Ishmael. Lysander sighed and toyed with a fork, flicking the tines with a nail to make them chime. "They were children when this was done to them. They lost most of the higher knowledge of magic that existed from before the Curse."

"Seems t'me some things are better lost," Ish rumbled.

"Isolde knew it was possible; it was done to her, after all. But she did not know how. When Ariadne came over, it filled in what she did not know. Between them, they could do it."

"You're telling me I'll be th'first to have it tried on me," Ishmael said.

Lysander laid down the fork. "You're not exactly the usual low-rank mage. You've pushed your magic to its limits and beyond, you fought Shadowborn for some twenty-five years, and you held out against Ari's Call for nearly ten years. If anyone's got the constitution for this, you have."

And I'm not fool enough to be flattered into noticing you've not answered my question, Ishmael thought.

"Frankly, now, whether you do or don't do it, whether it succeeds or doesn't, if Isolde cannot take down Emeya, if she tries and loses, you're as dead as we are. And if you live, you're looking at a cursed lot of power. I'll not believe any man who tells me that makes no difference to him." He snorted. "I've been trying to persuade her to do it on me, but I've as much magic in me as a mud pat."

"So it's t'the death, her and Emeya. And after, if she wins, what then?"

He committed his attention not to sonn, but to his other senses, allowing Lysander to think himself unobserved, but listening hard for the change in Lysander's breathing, for the timbre of his voice as he answered. "Trust me, you *don't* want to live in a land ruled by Emeya."

That, at least, sounded sincere. "So th'choice is rule by one or rule by th'other, is it?"

"If it comes to that—and I'm not saying it will—"

"But y'think it likely," Ishmael interposed. He was in no mood to indulge prevarication. "I'll thank you for the feeding and the counsel, Hearne. I'm the better for th'one at least. And now I think I'd best have another word with the lady."

They found her not in her grand receiving room but on a small balcony that, like the other, was crowded with planters and pots. She was weeding. Ishmael, stepping firmly onto the balcony, suddenly felt a one-sided heat, like the heat of a fire, or the heat he felt through his day shade when he overnighted outside. He checked himself midstride. He had heard neither bells nor dawn chorus to mark the dawn, nor had he sensed his own ensorcellment in the miasma of Shadowborn magic. He did now.

"You'll get used to it," Lysander Hearne said with false cheer.

She circled a planter and shook her head reproachfully at her servant. "Shall we go inside?" she asked, gently.

In the cool of the interior, he recovered his equilibrium; there was nothing to do about the ensorcellment but be glad of it. "You'll do with me what y'want, m'lady, I've no doubt of that. But if it matters t'you that I'm willing, then let me have a sense of you." He jerked off his gloves, demonstrating, if not conveying, his meaning. It was ridiculous of him to propose this, to pretend that she would be unable to deceive him or suborn his will—but she need not touch him to do that. He said, "If the sense convinces me, then you can have me willing. If not, I'll fight you with all that I am, puny though that may be."

"Not so puny, Ishmael," she said. She extended her hand, as a lady might for a formal greeting. The hand was smooth skinned and evenly fleshed, younger than her face. Even so strong a mage had her vanities. Her hand did not tremble. His, he noted, did.

To have actually taken her hand would have seemed too

much an intimacy. He lifted his fingers, offering his palm. She turned her hand likewise, and set palm to palm.

Telmaine

"I shall want you with me" was all Vladimer said as they left the conference with the Lightborn. He had moved on before Telmaine understood what he meant: that he was taking her with him to war. She pushed after him, forcing her way through pressing lines and tight huddles of men, skirts snagging on stacked crates and heaped, stuffed bags.

She caught up with him as he intercepted the stationmaster, who had been trying to dodge him. Little wonder, given the way their last encounter had ended, with the stationmaster telling Vladimer there was no way on this cursed earth that he could convert an open platform into a covered station in the few hours remaining before sunrise, and Lord Vladimer must apply elsewhere for magic or a miracle. Vladimer said only, "Will this train be ready by sunrise?"

"Aye, it'll be ready," said the stationmaster, deflating from posture of war. "It'll leave within the half hour, if I've anything to say about it, and be into Stranhorne less than two hours after sunrise. It'll be stopping for lookouts; I don't want it traveling without a Lightborn guard."

"Good," Vladimer said. "Have someone call me when it's ready to leave."

"Aye," the stationmaster said, and, with no "excuse me" turned away to bellow, "No, you'll *not* load that in there, unless y'want to be blown t'very small pieces."

He sounded so like Ishmael, her heart hurt. She tried for imperious and failed. "Lord Vladimer, did I hear you correctly?"

"I regret you do not have time to send to the manor for luggage, but I am certain that if you use your charm, some of these gentlemen would be delighted to oblige you."

Given what she wanted at this *particular* moment, which had nothing to do with luggage, probably not. "Lord Vladimer, a *word*, if you would."

He did not so much find as clear a corner; the quartet of

men occupying it flowed out like putty. "Now," he said. "What is unclear about—"

"What could I possibly do in Stranhorne Crosstracks? The Broomes don't want me using magic, don't want me to be part of their group." Which had been more humiliating than she would have thought possible, given that she had had to be backed, resisting, into magic, and forced into their company. Given that she had let them into her mind, let them explore the Shadowborn *gift*. The worst of it was that she knew they knew how she felt, and she knew they were probably right. "I haven't the experience, and I'm too strong to be safe."

"So I am informed," he said. "I am willing to take that risk. I know you can communicate over distance without adverse effects on your contact, and it occurs to me that I might need that."

"You're not thinking to talk with the *Shadowborn*?" she breathed.

All expression left his face. "No."

There was a silence. She stood quivering slightly with the urge to apologize, even for a question that had to be asked in this night of betrayals. "If the Mages' Temple does not repent of its decision," Vladimer said, in a whisper like sand blowing through dry reeds, "then I shall unrepent of my silence."

She pressed her back against the wall, fighting the impulse to scramble away—like the nine-year-old Telmaine whom Vladimer had surprised in his private sanctum, years ago. He said in a slightly less deathly voice, "I trust that they will, for if not"—he raised his head, turned as though to cast, but in the end did not; his hearing would have told him everything he needed to know—"it is likely we are all going to death, ensorcellment, or enslavement."

"Does that not *bother* you?" she whispered. "All these people."

"I recall we had a previous conversation along these lines," he said. "And while things that have happened since have made me reconsider some of the things I said then, I do not believe that I have done anything to regret, here." His expression changed, disturbingly, at some thought. She would not have been surprised if he was remembering what Magister Broome had said to him; she certainly was. "If the Temple does repent its decision or find its courage, it will be immensely useful for me to be able to speak to Fejelis or his mage."

"I don't . . . think the Lightborn mages will be best pleased with me." Not if Tammorn was anything to go by. She tried not to sound as frightened as she felt.

"A risk we must both take." He turned his head, and this time cast over the platform. "They're nearly ready. You recall that I said—not very long ago, if one merely thinks in hours—that there might come a time to contact Ishmael. I may ask you to do that once we reach Stranhorne."

"I'd be glad to," she said. "I'd have done it already, but—"

"I will give you an order, if you wish," he said.

"I don't *need* an order," Telmaine bridled. "Ishmael may need help."

"Good." She expected him to move, aware that the crowd on the platform was thinning, that there was almost no one near them. Aware, too, of the presence of the Broomes and their commune: Farquhar Broome's vast, quiet power; Phoebe's tightly disciplined strain; the others she was learning to recognize. She could sense about them the foul taint of Shadowborn magic, from their hurried rehearsals. That sense of exclusion scraped her spirit, but shriveled into pettiness as she sensed something more about them: resolve, almost resignation. They had taken the measure of their enemy and their enemy's magic, and they did not believe they would be returning.

Then Vladimer said, "I have one more request of you, Lady Telmaine. I will not be made a slave to the Shadowborn again. If it comes to that—if I give you the order, or if I fall to their ensorcellment, I want you to kill me. Shoot me in the head, use your fires, do whatever you must to do it quickly and *thoroughly*. I will it, and I *wish* it."

Nine

Tammorn

He did not die. He stood on scrub and heather, in night's very heart, and did not die.

He did not realize until then how much he had wished the high masters had been wrong, even if it meant his death. But he could sense the protective ensorcellment on him, sheathing him but not caging him—he still had all his strength to answer his will—and they had somehow managed to make it feel more like an itchy suit of clothing than a coating of sewage. He would sense the strength and vitality of the high masters in it, but the guiding magic had been Perrin's, second-rank sport though she was.

Fejelis would chide him for not having paid better attention to what they had been doing, and he would accept the chiding, knowing that Fejelis would not have sunk into passive misery. He hoped Fejelis would understand, and that Tam could return something for his betrayal. The high masters had sent him to negotiate for themselves, for the Temple, and he had no choice in that—but he would also negotiate for Fejelis and the earthborn, if he could.

The thought made him look out of himself and around. His eyes seemed to be adjusting to the darkness, rendering it less absolute with every minute that passed. There was even a thin glaze of light on the barren hills around him, like the luster on one of Beatrice's pots, from a three-quarter moon rising to the east.

Beatrice . . . Years ago he had promised to protect her, promised her—standing amidst the shards of glazed crockery and tiles, the sticks left of shelving and workbenches—that she need never again fear the bullies of her own guild. She had come to him on that promise. In that, too, he had failed; the Temple would surely look again at his children, and if it chose, would take over their rearing.

He shivered. The night wind, sweeping in with the moonlight, was cold, and his clothing was styled for the heated interior of the palace and the Temple. He was standing on a dirt path on a barren heather and bracken slope. He knew such dirt paths—he had spent his boyhood driving herds along them, herds that dwindled year by year, sold off for the taxes. The soil here was even poorer than the soil in the foothills of the Cloudherds. But this scraped land was Darkborn; here the barons cared whether their people starved. He smiled bitterly into the darkness. If it were only their brightnesses suffering here, then he would do nothing for the earthborn, a peasant mage's revenge for the centuries of oppression.

The night seemed darker, now that he could see the moonlight, than it had before. Shadows cast by moonlight seemed far denser than those cast by sunlight. The shaded lee of the hills, the roots of the bracken, the sides of the path, all might have been folded out of the world. He shuddered and raised his eyes to a sky so filled with stars as to replete even a Lightborn eye. He had not looked willingly on the stars for more than thirty years, since his younger brother had been murdered, but even then, he had never seen their full plenitude. If Artarian had been here, he would have flung himself down on the night-damp bracken, green eyes huge with wonder, and not stirred until the sun came up.

Magic surged, sudden, close, and Shadowborn enough to make him swallow hard. Thirty yards down the path was the figure of a man, briefly dark and then radiantly illuminated. Tam stared, the light painful to his dark-adapted eyes, at his right hand, which seemed to be holding the light. Behind the light was great strength not entirely controlled. In the

Temple, with his training complete, the man might have been one of the high masters—a contender for archmage, even. He felt the magic rake his ensorcellment, and the man whistled. "Tammorn, I take it? I'm Neill. Emeya sent me to meet you."

Still staring at his hand, Tam said, "How do you do that?"

Neill turned up his palm, showed the coldly blazing stick within. "This. It's quite straightforward."

"Not for Lightborn, it's not," Tam said. "Our lights need recharging by sunlight."

"I'll show you when we get a chance." Neill looked like a man in his early twenties, but then so did Tam, who was nearly fifty. He was quite tall, with an underdeveloped build, as though unaccustomed to using his muscles when magic would serve. His face was angular; hollow-cheeked; and all brow, jaw, and nose, with a lupine cast to it. His dark hair was coarse, wavy, and windblown. His eyes were deep-set, and Tam could not tell their color. He wore a long, patchwork coat of hides and furs, open over a ruffled shirt and heavy trousers. There was an ensorcellment on him, a binding of the will. The invested vitality had the feel of the mage he had spoken to when he had reached into that roil of Shadowborn power south of Stranhorne.

He swallowed again and breathed slowly to calm his stomach and his nerves. "I am ordered by the archmage and the high masters to open negotiations with the Shadowborn."

"Then, first of all, don't refer to us as Shadowborn. Our home's Atholaya."

He had heard, or read, the name somewhere, but could not recall where—Lukfer had more than once had sharp words for him for his studied indifference to Temple history. If the dead could speak, it would be to say, "I told you so."

"Are you taking me there?"

"She sent me here to make sure you weren't a danger to her. We've been dealt a few unpleasant shocks of late." He did not sound as though he entirely regretted those shocks—but, then, would the Shadowborn archmage ensorcell a loyal follower so?

He felt Neill's magic playing around him, prying at his own ensorcellment. "How fascinating," he said. "How long have you known how to do that?"

The instincts of a tower-trained mage prevailed: above all, impress. "A few hours, since the Darkborn came with the ensorcellment on him."

"Darkborn . . . Ah, Sebastien, what have you done? Was this Darkborn named Hearne, by chance?"

"They didn't say." And to his regret, he had not asked.

"I am sure it was." He sighed. "Foolish boy. So the Temple sent you here with a just-learned, completely untried ensorcellment on you. To impress us, I presume, with their aptitude and the obedience they can command from a strong mage." A glint of tooth. "Are you expendable, Magister Tammorn?"

Tam matched that cynical smile with one of his own, but did not answer.

"So . . . the Lightborn Temple wants to treat with us. For what?"

"Should I not wait and take that up with your archmage?"

"You could. The problem is that Emeya is insane. Come at her direct, with reasoned argument, and you will meet only unreason. I know how to deal with her."

"Is that why she has you ensorcelled?" Tam said, coming at him direct.

The lantern sank in his hand, throwing angled shadows across his face. Of the deep-set eyes, only a hint of bluish sclera remained. "I failed to take Stranhorne, and a valued one of our number was killed. She does not think there is any such thing as failure, only willful defiance."

Tam lowered his voice. "You don't have to put up with that."

Neill lifted the lantern and held it out, almost between their faces. "Are you trying to suborn me? Better and more beloved than you have tried. But it's less a case of where the bread's buttered as who's holding the knife." Teeth showed in his smile, sharper than before. "But I suppose you've earned something for that. So I'll give you some advice: go back to your Temple; go back and tell them that Emeya recognizes no peers. If she did, she would have to recognize the one who surely is. If they don't agree, they can test themselves against her power. I expect they will lose, though I'd much prefer that they win. Oh yes, the ensorcellment only prevents me working against her will. It does not prevent me saying what I think."

There was another Shadowborn as strong, and an enemy of Emeya? "Emeya's presence was the strongest I sensed."

Neill's feral smile flashed. "You'll not get me to spill that way, Tammorn. If you're not going to go back to your Temple, then I suppose I'll just have to take you to Emeya. What are the Temple's terms?"

"I think I should best take that up with your lady."

"As opposed to a mere minion? On your own head be it." Magic surged, caught him up, and, despite his reflex resistance, *lifted* him.

His first sense was of magic all around him—hideous, tainted magic that reminded him of nothing so much as a slaughterhouse in high summer. If he could endure the assault of rotting blood and hot urine and manure on his senses then, he could endure the assault of this on his magic now.

"I don't know why it takes your kind that way at first," Neill said. "We've had the occasional mage follow our Call, though all have been low-ranked. The distress will pass, or you'll be past feeling it. This way. Stay close."

Tam followed at Neill's shoulder, stumbling despite the light the man carried. He had trodden rough ground before, but never by a single light, and he was repeatedly deceived by shadows and pits impersonating shadows. Some great violence had been done the land here, leaving it gouged, deeply scored, and stripped of scrub, bracken, grass, and tree. Only tussocks and fragments of root remained, barbs for the ankles and snares for the feet. He was aware they were on a downslope, but between trying to control his revulsion to Shadowborn magic and trying to keep his footing, he was not aware how the torn earth had been reshaped until Neill stopped moving and he looked ahead—up at a towering earthworks molded from the dirt and the embedded fragments of the plants swept up with it. His mouth fell a little open: he had a gift for inert-matter manipulation himself, but he could never have imagined having moved so much of it. . . . He could just see the top of the wall, and though the curve of it was perceptible, it must easily exceed the circumference of the tower. The slope they had just climbed down was the pit scoured to raise it. They reached an arch of earth that was not only packed but fused into clinker, and, passing through, entered a midden of sleeping animals.

Sleeping monsters—no farm animals these, brought into the village stockade for shelter. He could smell fur and urine and feces, and instead of grain or hay, the odor was of rotting meat and old blood, for real, this time. From a mound of gray pelt that was waist-high at its apex, a spear-shaped head rose on a long neck and four slitted eyes glared at the light. Neill murmured a word that seemed to carry as much affection as command, and the creature sighed and laid its head down once more.

A huge wolf shouldered past Tam to butt Neill's knees. Tam had had a herd dog who liked to do that, thinking it a merry joke if he could dump people on their rumps, but it had done it to Tam's father, and he had sold it at the lowlands fair. Neill crouched to fondle the wolf's ears, allowing it to nuzzle his face and chin as though those jaws could not have torn his throat out with a snap. "Hey, Mayfly, good hunting out there?"

Tam took one look at the dried blood on the beast's ruff and averted his gaze. Behind the beast—Mayfly—came several others, sizing up Tam for the eating and making up to Neill, whose magic spun out and around and through them. Their maker, perhaps, because Mayfly and several of the others were nearly twice the size of the foothills wolves Tam had hunted in his youth. Their master, certainly. Neill clucked at Mayfly like an old village wife feeding her chickens, gave it a parting pat, and led Tam to stairs that followed the inner shell of the earthworks upward. Tam could not help but look back, remembering Fejelis and the others talking after their defense of the railway hut and railroad, and measuring the numbers that might yet be turned against the Darkborn and against his own earthborn. And then up, apprehensively, toward the lair of the flying Shadowborn.

The stairs, like the arch, were built of clinkered earth, rough and uneven. Neill held the light at his side, showing him the edge, for which Tam was grateful. He wondered why, with such power as he clearly had, Neill did not simply let it carry him to the top. Unless that, too, was bound.

And then all speculation ended with an obliterating sense of Shadowborn magic, and only Neill's quick clasp saved him from a stumble and possibly a fall. "She's back," he said, quite unnecessarily. "And she wants you. Now."

He let Neill haul him up the last several yards, aware of the urgency in his manner. Yet at the top of the stairs, at the first sight of the person who stood there, he halted in commonplace shock.

She was a *child*, a fair-haired girl of no more than thirteen. No taller than his chest, her figure barely budding, her dress a simple blue frock with a pattern of rushes and dragonflies and grass stains over the knees, and a circlet of wilting purple daisies around her curling crown. Her skin was translucent in Neill's light, like his son's, who had inherited Beatrice's lovely complexion. Almost he might have believed that she was an innocent trapped at the center of this vortex of magic, rather than its focus, because no child commanded that kind of power. She peered up at him from beneath transparent lashes and smiled shyly.

Before her magic tore his mind apart.

He was not aware of falling to his knees and then to his hands and knees, but that was where he found himself when the magic let him go. Helpless, shaking, he vomited himself dry. In the one, two, three—however many infinite—minutes she had pillaged his mind, she had taken from him his past, his knowledge of the Temple, his knowledge of magic, and even—something the high masters had refrained from doing—Lukfer's last *gift*. His life had been pulled from him in a tumble of faces, places, experiences, emotions: his hardscrabble boyhood, his muddled youth, Artarian's death, his years of wandering, his rescue by Darien White Hand, meeting Lukfer, saving Fejelis and being punished for it, falling in love with Beatrice, finding a friend in Fejelis, his children's births, Isidore's death, Lukfer's death and the carnage in the Temple, rescuing Fejelis, the high masters' orders, the high masters' wishes, his own hopes . . . Knowledge and memory, she had taken it all.

He felt Neill's hands light on his forehead and the back of his head, but he barely felt the touch of the man's magic, except that his stomach finally stopped wringing itself out. The Shadowborn mage hooked his hands beneath his armpits and hauled him upright on his knees and then to his feet. "I warned you," he said, through set teeth. Angry, Tam realized, and on his behalf. The Shadowborn mage pulled Tam's arm across his shoulders and walked him around the curve of the earthworks. They were on an inner ramparts, with another level above them; there he sensed the presence of the flying Shadowborn.

Another earth wall loomed before them, with a smaller archway closed by a hanging. With a snap of the hand, Neill tossed aside the hanging to allow them through. Inside, another gesture lit several illuminated wands jammed into the walls. He dropped Tam into an armchair. The chair, the bed, the table—all were carved with a detail that any Darkborn would have coveted, though the wood was deep, even, rose brown, and highly polished. Except for its disturbing opacity, for its ability to cast dense shadows, it might have graced a bedroom in a guild master's house. "I refuse to sleep on dirt," Neill said, observing his interest.

In the corner, in a carved basket, tawny fur stirred. A small wildcat hissed at Tam from where she lay curled around her kits. "Where's your sister?" Neill said to her, and a thread of magic looped the room, drawing a second wildcat out from under the bed. Decades-old habit made Tam tally the bounty on the skins. Neill folded himself down on the floor, which he had covered with a camp mat in the southern style, allowing the cat to sprawl across his lap. Her flank bulged with her own unborn litter. "I'd best send you back, hadn't I?" the mage said to her. "Too many things with big teeth around. I'll do it as soon as she lets me." He looked up at Tam; in this light, his eyes were a deep blue. "Not much of a welcome for the emissary from the Temple."

"Why?" Tam said hoarsely.

"Her? Me? You? The world? Life?"

"She could have *asked*."

"Simplest answer: because she can, and now you and your Temple know she can." He shook his head. "You should have let me handle it."

"You're stronger than I am," Tam said bluntly, "but not that strong."

The corner of Neill's mouth tucked in. "And how, may I ask, did you survive in the Temple so long?" He met Tam's startled look with raised brows. "Did you think we didn't study our enemy?"

"We didn't sense your magic."

"We didn't send up fireworks. We knew the Darkborn could sense Shadowborn, even if we weren't aware that extended to Lightborn sports. We kept to the minor magic: shape-shifting when we had to"—*minor?* thought Tam—"ensorcellment of mind"—*Floria*—"some talismanic magic."

"The"—he cleared his throat—"the munitions that destroyed the tower?"

"Dealt with at the factory outside the city. All right," he said to the wildcat, who had taken his stroking hand in her jaws, teeth not breaking the skin. "I'll leave well enough alone." She heaved herself off his lap and squeezed back into her refuge under the bed.

"Who is Emeya? How did she get . . . the way she is? The strength she has."

Neill did not at first appear to hear the question, his eyes following the wildcat. But he let her go, rising to settle in the second chair. "How much do you know about the origin of the Curse?"

"Laid by the mage Imogene and her followers in revenge for the death of her daughter in a war between mages," Tam said, promptly.

"And why didn't it die with them?"

That was the subject of endless speculation amongst student mages, and like most such exercises in speculation, one Tam avoided. He was a peasant; what was, was. Magic was supported by the mage's vitality and will, and when those ceased, so, too, did the magic. The Curse was the exception. Those were the facts; speculation was specious.

Then he had a sudden, appalling thought. "Did *all* the mages who laid the Curse die?"

"The obvious question, but the answer is yes. All died, and more. If you think Emeya's a monster, you should have met Imogene . . . Be patient," he said in response to Tam's stirring. "I'll come to your answer. But first, Imogene, a monster beyond compare. She'd specialized for years—centuries, even—on ensorcellments of the will, and anyone who came within her reach was made subject or driven away, with the exception of her daughter Ismene, whom she doted on. Ismene took an earthborn lover—not by his choice, you understand. It meant nothing to her that he was plighted by custom and honor to another woman, or that he killed himself in shame when she cast him off. Earthborn law could not touch Ismene, and mage's law barely, but that man's betrothed—her name has not come down to us—did not forget. Thirty years it took her to have her revenge. How'd an earthborn kill a mage?" A smile, with sharp teeth. "The Darkborn seem to be learning the way of it. In this case, she found allies—many allies, who'd been injured by magic, who were jealous of magic, who feared magic—and what she couldn't find, she bought. She found ways of setting the mageborn against each other, made sure that Ismene had enemies enough among the mageborn that her magic was worn down—not that that was difficult—and finally lured her underground and dropped a mountain on her head. And *that* is why the Curse, why Imogene took such revenge upon the earthborn, for all those who were part of her daughter's murder. . . . I sometimes wonder what became of that lady after, though she probably did not survive too long."

"Did nobody try to stop her . . . Imogene?"

"Oh yes, and either joined her or died refusing. *That* was

the war between mages, there, between those who'd joined Imogene and those who opposed her. To ensure the Curse would survive them, Imogene anchored it in the vitality of everyone born into it, and made her and her followers' children the keystones of the magic. Of those, seven survived the first century. Six were alive at the end of the third. Four after the fifth. Two at the eighth."

Magic anchored in the vitality of another, one of the lost skills that the high masters had tried to retrieve for generations. He knew how the high masters would react to this, greedy as they were. "And those two are Emeya and . . ."

"Imogene's younger daughter, Isolde."

"And you are?"

"Emeya's great-great-grandson. *She* was so clearly deranged that even the other children knew it, so they kept her under ensorcellment. In the end, they were too few. Five hundred years had passed while she slept. You can imagine what that did for her. She let herself mature enough to bear a son, and then let others do the bearing for her."

Five hundred years and then five generations . . . This man might be older than the archmage's three hundred years. He had the strength for such longevity. "And Isolde?"

Neill released a long breath through his nose. "Imogene's other daughter, the one who was not the favorite, the one of whom nothing was expected. I'm sure her mother would have been surprised to find Isolde had outlived them all. I don't think she's sane, either."

And how much of that should he believe, given that between Emeya and Isolde there was at least rivalry and possibly outright war? He wished he had Fejelis here—the prince made a study of the ways people revealed themselves. Mages could grow lazy.

"Why, after all these centuries, should the two of you be looking north? Why attack the manor?"

"Emeya decided that Atholaya was too small for the two of them." The tone was easy, but the shift of his eyes in their deep sockets betrayed a lie. Then he sighed and leaned back on his hands. "Emeya is afraid of Isolde."

That might be truth, but the Temple mage distrusted

such a ready admission of vulnerability. What else did it disguise? "Has she reason to be? Is Isolde the stronger?"

"As to the manor, the Stranhornes and Strumhellers have been nothing but trouble for centuries. We wanted the manor. We'd have had *both* manors by now, but that we—*I*—got overconfident. Baron Strumheller, the man said, and I knew that name, but I've never sensed anything so weak and ripped up with overuse besides. So I was talking to him, waiting for Sebastien to join us, and he simply *shoots* me—calm as you please, with a bullet that would drop a scavvern. I suppose I should be glad he stopped at the one. And while I'm putting my viscera back together, Midora and the idiot boy start burning up the interior of Stranhorne, until—*boom.*" He gave Tam a dark look, then let out a sigh and snapped his fingers in the direction of the basket, following it with a prod of magic.

The wildcat hissed, but obediently caught up a kitten in its jaws and carried it, dangling, to Neill's knee. She crouched, glaring at him, while he examined it, inserting a finger into the small mouth, running a hand down the spine, testing the thrust of its hind legs. The diversion seemed to calm him, and he smiled engagingly at the angry cat as he handed her kit back. "She's a beauty, isn't she?" he said to Tam.

Her pelt certainly was thick and healthy, though small for full bounty. "The creatures—are they all yours?"

"They are now. I inherited them from Durran—my father—along with my bent toward fleshworking. He'd the original idea to use what the Darkborn call the Shadowborn to drive the Sundered out of Atholaya and keep them out. They were all terrified of what they'd do if they found us, he most of all."

"And . . . the transformed Darkborn?" Tam said. He'd been too overspent and sickened to characterize the magic around the flyers, but this man could rework flesh, so if any mage could . . .

A white glimmer in the shadowed eyes. "Ah, you realized that."

"Your doing?" he said, quietly.

"Emeya would not have let them live otherwise. Transformed, they're useful to her."

"Do *they* agree with you that life is worth accepting on any terms?"

"You don't have the slightest idea what you are talking about," Neill said, without temper.

"Do you not realize," Tam said, in a low voice, "that what you are doing is an atrocity?"

Neill tipped his head back, the light catching on the long, vulpine planes of his face. Its cast was not quite man, now Tam saw it fully in strong light, as though Neill had chosen to emulate one of his beloved animals. "I realize it. And I repeat: you don't have the slightest idea what you are talking about. Believe me, there are worse atrocities."

Tam was tired and sickened and ready to despair, but he struggled on. "And Sebastien?"

"My cousin Ariadne's son. Emeya wanted her mated—didn't matter to whom—but without waiting for them to find their way"—his eyes glittered with anger—"she set an ensorcellment on them. Ari was just strong enough to twist the ensorcellment toward another man, and just to add insult, she chose a new Darkborn slave, bound him to her and herself to him. The child born to them was mageborn, and strong, so Emeya let them live. But they were marked from that day. Hearne's a survivor, if nothing else. He persuaded Ariadne to make a run for Isolde. They'd have taken the boy, but he was Emeya's pet then, and he didn't want to go. Knowing what Emeya would do to her, I helped them get away." He grimly contemplated the pattern of the carpet. "If I'd known then what I know now, I wouldn't." He glanced up. "Emeya needs this Temple alliance; she just won't face the fact."

"Why?" Tam said.

The deep-set eyes looked directly at him, blue in their depths and calculating. Tam wished again to be Fejelis or one of the high masters, old and crafty, instead of a blunt, muddled peasant.

Neill said nothing; plainly, he was not going to answer that particular question, at least now.

"Why do you stay with her?" Tam said.

Neill said, "I'm a mage. I want knowledge. I *crave* the exercise of my power. That's what binds me. I couldn't live with all your Temple rules."

Tam knew that craving. At its best, that desire expressed itself as it had in Lukfer, in the long years of study and unceasing efforts to master his unruly strength, and in the generosity that had made him willing to offer his knowledge to anyone who would receive it from him. It was not his failing that so few had. At its worst . . . he thought he had taken his measure of it at its worst, when the high masters had him lying bound before them and ransacked his mind for his knowledge. But now . . .

Now he had met Emeya, he knew her strength exceeded that of the archmage, exceeded that of the archmage and high masters who had bound him—for all he might try to tell himself that she had taken him unawares and they had not. And if she knew magical protocols lost since the Sundering . . . the high masters would want those.

"You look quite horrified," Neill observed. "What are you thinking?"

"About magic. And your archmage. And the high masters."

"It's not an unendurable life, ordinarily. Just lately . . ." And then the color drained suddenly from his long face. "She wants me," he said. "Don't leave this room, whatever hap—" In a knot of Shadowborn magic, he was gone.

Tam gagged. "'Not an unendurable life,'" he quoted hoarsely, to the empty room. Hissing answered him, from the basket and from under the bed.

Could he escape, while Emeya was occupied with Neill? He might yet have the strength for a *lift*, drained though he was. He was desperate enough to try—to Stranhorne, even Minhorne. As Lukfer had repeatedly reminded him, distance was more a psychological barrier than a physical one; his body's memory of all those miles walked barefoot or in holed boots refused to yield to magic alone. But should he succeed in leaving, dared he take this information back to the high masters? Would it repel or entice them—all this power, all this knowledge? Would they believe him or think him mistaken about her strength? Would they send him back to accept her terms? And what hope for Fejelis and the earthborn then?

He had a dreadful vision of himself set up as master and protector of earthborn, as Neill was master and protector of beasts. Had his stomach not already been empty, he would have vomited. A voice insinuated itself into his thoughts. <No, then.>

The vision had not been his own temptation, but hers.

He extended his magic toward the archmage, the high masters; reached in blind desperation and met only her presence, her strength, pressing down. She said, <Be still, or—> and his sense of her magic reaching to twist the core out of his protective ensorcellment against darkness, of himself melting away, was so strong that for heartbeats he believed it had happened.

He fell back into the chair, feeling half dissolved. He did not sense the wolf enter the room, though he heard the wildcats hiss. He blinked tears from his eyes in time to see it regard the basket with intelligent yellow eyes, and lurched forward in his chair in an absurd protective reaction toward one predator against a greater. Then froze as the wolf turned its malign gaze toward him. It whined, padded forward, and, even as he mustered the magic he would need to defend himself, propped its jaw on his knee, its brows quirking, doglike, as it contemplated his face.

He was still sitting there, pinned in place by his guardian, when Neill reappeared. The mage landed on his feet and promptly dropped to hands and knees. Tam could see the stripes across his face and neck and arms, wheals like those he had seen on a man who had fallen into a swarm of skull jellyfish. Mayfly abandoned Tam to snuffle at Neill's ear. The mage slung an arm around his pet's neck and leaned against the shaggy shoulder. The wheals along his jawline seemed to bubble as magics battled within them, hers to hurt, his to heal.

Her magic intensified. The wheals suddenly split and the bubbling spread across his entire face, and he rolled away from the wolf, curling into a fetal ball. Far later than Tam would have expected, he screamed.

Her magic swirled away, and Neill slumped over onto his back, the blisters sealing themselves over, the raw flesh drying and dulling and going pink. He stared at the ceiling for several minutes, chest rising and falling, then worked a hand into the wolf's ruff and pulled himself up. "How d'you like that demonstration?"

"Not," said Tam.

"As you can perhaps gather," Neill said, sounding slightly breathless, "she is not receptive to the idea of an alliance. I think she mismeasures your high masters' strength, myself." His skin was as unmarked as it had been before, but Tam noticed that his face had lost the angularity and length of jaw and was now entirely a man's.

"Come outside," Neill said abruptly. "I know you'll never have seen this. I know I need to, just at the moment. It gives me strength."

In trepidation, Tam followed him outside, and with even more trepidation followed him up a final series of steps to the ramparts of the earthworks. He could see around him the crumpled mounds of sleeping Shadowborn, each one with a mat for a mattress and its folded wings for blankets. He could feel Neill's magic flickering around them, soothing. On the edge of the earthworks, not too close, Neill pointed east. The sky, so dark when they had met, had lightened along the horizon to the cobalt blue of a fine glass, draped with cloud. "Dawn," Neill said.

"I've seen dawn," Tam said. He would take no gifts from this cruel paradox of a man.

Neill glanced at him. "Not like this, I'll warrant. Enjoy it. It may be our last."

A wave of magic rose from beneath them. A boy's voice screamed rawly. Neill closed his eyes in sympathetic pain. "I have to go. You stay. No one will bother you. Mayfly." The wolf, summoned, pushed between them like a jealous child. "See no one does."

Neill was right; seen from this side of sunrise, daybreak was astonishing—the transparent yellow, the intense orange, the blinding break of sunlight. Artarian should have been here. Beatrice should have had these colors to glaze on her pots. Fejelis would have watched with his usual interest in the new. His son . . . would no doubt have tried to throw himself from the ramparts or down the gullet of a wolf. He wiped his face. How could a sight so beautiful elicit such despair?

Neill returned, climbing the stairs, looking weary beyond words, but with no physical hurt on him, to Tam's peculiar relief. The beast mage put a hand on Mayfly's back and leaned briefly. "She brought the boy back," he said. "She needs his strength. And he wanted healing."

He straightened and turned to face Tam, half his face brilliantly lit by the new, orange sun, half in shadow. "You asked why Atholaya was too small for Emeya and Isolde, why Emeya needed new territory. I told you that Imogene and the others anchored the Curse in children. So think about the fact that magic often doesn't mature until late adolescence or after. Even mageborn children wouldn't have had the strength to support magic like the Curse. Imogene changed those children. We think that Isolde is close to rediscovering how—with Ariadne's help. She may already have. Should she succeed, she will destroy Emeya."

"And why," Tam said, harshly, "would that be worse than allowing Emeya"—*and you*—"to continue unchecked?"

Neill gave him a very long look. "This: how do you think many of Isolde's own children and grandchildren died?"

Telmaine

Every train journey with Vladimer seems to take longer, Telmaine thought. They did not even have the compartment to themselves, she and Vladimer; the five officers of the Strumheller troop had been shoehorned into it. She ought to be grateful that, unlike Vladimer, she was sitting hip to hip with only two men, not three. The floor was muddy and sticky and littered with scraps of oiled cloth, odd bullets, and pieces of newspaper. As the train labored up a hill, a hip flask skidded out from under her seat and bounced off her foot before sliding under the opposite bench. At intervals it, or some other detritus, reappeared. The compartment was too crowded for anyone to grope after it. The air reeked of sweaty men, soap, old smoke, damp wool, oil, and ammunition. The carriage was not designed to travel by day, so all the vents had to be closed.

Vladimer and the men seemed unperturbed. They were planning, fighting verbal campaigns, just as her brothers and their friends had on those interminable summer journeys to and from the estate. All it wanted was her sister, Merivan, at her side, fingers poised to pinch should Telmaine try to join in the boys' talk.

Ishmael, Telmaine thought irritably, *would not spend all this time talking about it.* Ishmael was practical. Ishmael would prepare his weapons, settle his people, and then go to sleep. Let Vladimer work himself up to a pitch—she had the sense that this was the way he was—Telmaine would emulate Ishmael. She shifted until her head was more or less propped against the inner wall, shoulder hunched uncomfortably, and breathed slowly, remembering Balthasar's efforts at hypnotizing her before the girls were born. When this was over—and she must believe it would be over, somehow—she would delight in doing something as commonplace and removed from magic as having another child.

She became aware of the smell of lemon tea, drifting pleasantly through the reek of men going to war, though that was there, too, both in her dream and out of it. Ishmael was sitting on the floor of a train carriage, cleaning his weapons. She could sense great heat coming from him, furnace heat, as though he had been newly cast in clay and set out to cool. He was slow to lift his head when she spoke to him. And the weapons were strange. Was there such a thing as a two-barreled gun? It could not be safe, pointing both ways. He lifted his head, sonned her with a terrible regret, quite unlike any expression she'd known on his face, and pulled the trigger. She watched him fall away, as the man on the platform had fallen, the dart from Vladimer's cane in his belly. She touched her own abdomen and felt her hands sink into the wound he had made in her.

A man's voice said, "M'lady, are you all right?"

She was back in the carriage, her face wet with tears. One of the men handed her a handkerchief that was clean and well made, but had the smell of too much laundering. She nodded her gratitude nevertheless and dabbed her face. "Bad dream," she whispered. They murmured understanding, though she was sure they did not.

"We're nearly there," said the donor of the handkerchief. "It's gone sunrise."

After Ishmael had *gifted* her—tried, through mind-touch, to convey to her his accomplishment in magic, she had found herself dreaming his dreams, running through the Shadowlands, fighting remembered battles. But even when he was held in prison, in peril of his life, his dreams had not threatened her or himself, or despaired.

Or burnt so, with magic.

If she understood one thing, it was that he needed help. She could not endanger these men by using magic in such close confines and with only a train's siding between themselves and daylight, even if she was certain that this time, Vladimer would not miss his shot. Nor did she particularly want to die. She knotted her gloved hands, one in the other, and endured the last, interminable minutes as the train paused before Stranhorne Crosstracks to let their Lightborn guard disembark, listening to the shouted exchange between Lightborn outside and Darkborn inside. Balthasar would be heartened by the vulgar ease of it.

Unlike Strumheller, Stranhorne Crosstracks had an enclosed platform with doors that could be operated from safety. Vladimer, of all people, was the one to pause to help her down—only to lean close and say, "What do you sense?"

What she sensed was . . . overwhelming. People—Darkborn—closely packed on the platform, beneath the platform, outside, across the tracks. Thousands of them in the near vicinity, hurt, grieving, fierce, resolute, afraid, uncomprehending. She staggered, and he had to steady her. *"Shadowborn?"* he hissed.

"*No*, not that." In all that shocking miasma of Darkborn

emotion and suffering, there was no taint of Shadowborn. "Just Darkborn. Many, many people."

"Come with me, then. And tell the Broomes' party to follow."

Tentatively she did, knowing that Phoebe Broome definitely did not approve of either her presence there or her use of magic, but she drew no rebuke. Vladimer set out confidently across the warped and pitching boards of the platform, toward what proved to be a stair, metal steps laid over crumbling stone. He had been there before. He threw back over his shoulder, "One of the first settlements to reestablish itself after the Sundering. It has a number of underground warehouses and cellars, mainly used for storage and protection against raids before, that sheltered Darkborn immediately after."

She remembered his guided tour of the archducal palace in Minhorne, as they went together to interview Floria White Hand. She did not wish to be ungrateful, but she hoped this was not more of the same; Vladimer's choice of anecdote tended toward the macabre. "Did Ishmael tell you about these?"

"Maxim di Gautier, while raiding the palace's private libraries . . . After the Sundering, the Stranhornes extended the tunnels between the chambers and opened up more. It's quite extensive. If Stranhorne had to retreat, there'd be no better place to retreat to."

Telmaine, remembering Shadowborn fires, said nothing to that. She could sense the mages coming down quickly behind them. "Where are we going?"

"Where I expect we'll find whoever's in charge."

Planking and matting marked out a thoroughfare through the crowded underground space beneath the platform. Planks and stone blocks had been assembled into rough dividers and furnishings, allowing adults to sit and sick and tired people to lie, while children weaved and scrambled between the groups in a running game of troopers and Shadowborn. The clear thoroughfare was, of course, irresistible. Three urchins pelting along it would have plowed into Vladimer and Telmaine but for Farquhar

Broome's intervention. Deflected, they tumbled into the laps of a group of men playing cards, who reared up with roars and cuffs. In a belated flurry, sisters and mothers rushed to the rescue. Vladimer shamelessly left the altercation to evolve, and led them through a tunnel under the railway tracks.

Perhaps I do not need to worry about fire, Telmaine thought, smelling the damp.

They surfaced in a circular concourse like a smaller version of Bolingbroke Station in Minhorne, but Bolingbroke Station had been built in the last century, and this, by the rough stone and thick walls, much earlier. Most of the stalls along the outer and inner ring of the concourse were closed and boarded against the press of refugees, but some had had their boards and even their counters pried loose and carried away.

"Dear boy," Farquhar Broome hailed from behind. "Where are we going?"

Vladimer pointed. "Up." Overhead, Telmaine's sonn could pick out the edge of a balcony and the hard echo of iron railings.

They made their way around the perimeter to the ascending staircase with some difficulty, since not everyone respected the corridor. They did Vladimer, though, when he put into effect his declared intention to press into service anyone he found sprawled across his path, with no respect for excuses. After the first three, a wave of warning ran around the perimeter and trespassers scrambled clear.

On the balcony, they found the defenders, some of whom were already asleep, sprawled on mats and bags and bundles, weapons close at hand. Those who were awake were cleaning and repairing weapons and armor, playing cards, gossiping, sharing rations and flasks and pipes, and otherwise taking their ease. After the underground shelter and the concourse, pipe smoke was fragrant. As they climbed the next flight of stairs, onto the floor under the cupola, the officers stayed behind to arrange for places for their own men.

Under the domed ceiling of the cupola, they found fifteen

or twenty men around a round table where, in wet sand, someone had sculpted what Telmaine presumed was a relief of the land around Stranhorne, marked with a mixture of fine game pieces and roughly carved pegs. Lord Ferdenzil—no, Duke Ferdenzil Mycene—was leaning on the table with his elbows, and was short enough that it resembled a casual pose rather than a droop. He was haggard with exhaustion, something she could never have imagined possible. The tall young woman next to him, Baronette Laurel's twin, was frankly propped against the table and arguing with him in a voice that croaked with overuse. Both turned to sonn the arrivals with open relief, though Mycene's rapidly changed to sour amusement.

"Mycene," Vladimer acknowledged. "Baronette Stranhorne."

"Vladimer Plantageter," Mycene said. "This is a surprise."

"Indeed. A word, Mycene, if I may." He drew the other man off to the side. Telmaine felt a moment's sympathy for Mycene: Vladimer would not have been her choice to tell a man his father was dead, especially given the rumors about Vladimer's paternity and the enmity between Mycene and Vladimer. Her sonn caught Mycene's motion as he lowered his head into a gloved hand and turned away. Since he had been her suitor, and one her family heartily approved of, she had used her touch-sense to tell whether she could love him. So she knew the resentment he harbored toward his vigorous, intensely competitive father. But it is the people of great greedy vitality, who consume so much of those around them, who leave the greatest hollowness behind.

The baronette said, "What's happened?" To Telmaine's surprise, given the way they had been arguing, there was concern on her face.

"Vladimer is telling him that the duke, his father, is dead."

"Sachevar Mycene?" Lavender croaked. "How?

"Shadowborn," Telmaine said. At least here there would be no contesting their existence.

"In th'city?" one of the men said.

Vladimer, returning, saved her from questioning. Ferdenzil Mycene followed a step behind, though Telmaine wondered how much he would be hearing now. His expression was taut, dazed. She herself heard little of Vladimer's report to the Stranhornes, and only slightly more of the Stranhornes' report to Vladimer—given by a well-spoken man with a rogue's face, introduced as the Stranhorne lawyer—once she heard they had had no word of Ishmael. The Stranhornes and their reinforcements had spent most of the night sweeping the area, collecting survivors, and killing roaming Shadowborn. There were rumors that the main force had established a redoubt east of Stranhorne. *I might,* she thought, *have told them that.* And if they thought to ask the mages, Farquhar Broome certainly could. So there was no need for her to stay. Quietly, and, she hoped, unnoticed, she eased back from between Vladimer and Mycene, holding her skirts out to stop them from whispering. A light cast of sonn sketched in the space under the cupola. Two heavy, barred outer doors, flush with the curve of the cupola, must lead outside, but four seemed to lead into interior rooms. She tried a door and found it locked. She was well able to deal with locks, having freed herself from the execution room before Vladimer found her, but that would entail magic and draw attention. The next door was unlocked. She opened it and slipped inside, promptly stumbling on a heap of blankets on the floor, perhaps set aside from the baronette or the duke. The air was stifling; the wall hot. *With the sun,* she realized, shuddering slightly.

But it would do. The door was reasonably solid and she had to assume it was light-tight. In case. She sat down at the high writing stool before the desk, pushing the flammable papers on it aside with a grimace of unease. Quickly, before she could think better of this, she recalled the sense of her dream, the sense of Ishmael in it. She opened her senses and reached out with her magic, trusting the affinity between them to make the connection, as it had between her in the city, him on the train.

<Ishmael?>

The blast of heat brutally broke her from the trance. Groping and wild sonn found nothing alight, nothing smoldering, no smell of smoke. Panting, hands to her bodice, she fought to calm herself. The heat had been on Ishmael's end. Where his magic, and the vitality that fed it, had seemed like banked coals, now it seemed a furnace. It took all the love she had for him to open her thoughts once more. <Ishmael di Studier. Ishmael.>

Something stirred in the furnace, something familiar. She sensed it trying to articulate.

<Ishmael? What's happened to you?>

A cascade of impressions, and the heat of a monstrous magic, raging amongst those embers. <Ishmael,> she pleaded. <You're hurting me.>

The heat was instantly snuffed. She thought, for an instant of dread, that he had exerted himself magically and died. Yet she had felt none of the terrifying draining and pain that had ended their previous conversation.

<What are you doing?> Phoebe Broome, inevitably.

Her jaw set. How dared the woman, her social inferior, intrude.

<I may be your social inferior, *Lady Telmaine*—>

<I was speaking to *Ishmael*.>

<Ishmael? *That* was Ishmael?> She, too, broke the connection—mages, no manners. Then Telmaine felt the delicate touch of Farquhar Broome's magic, and a breath later, the man himself was standing in front of her, stooping beneath the curve of the cupola. "That was brave of you, dear girl, but not at all wise."

"What has *happened* to him? It *is* him, isn't it?"

"Of course; his presence is quite distinctive. But he must have undergone a remarkable transformation—"

<Telmaine.> Raw need reaching out from the furnace. She heard herself whimper with pain, despite her best resolution.

Farquhar Broome's hand descended lightly on her head; his magic veiled her, and the sense of heat and pressure lessened. <Dear boy,> he said, <be gentler to the lady, if you would.>

<Magister Broome?> That molten stream of impressions turned on the seventh-rank mage. Farquhar Broome

grunted, staggered back, and slid slowly down against the wall. Then Ishmael's presence was gone as abruptly as it came. "Oh, dear," the archmage of the Darkborn said, breathlessly. "That does present a problem."

She slid off the stool and onto her knees beside him. "Did he tell you what had happened to him?" she said urgently. "Can we help him?"

"Dear lady," Farquhar Broome said. She felt a twitch in her pocket, and the handkerchief she had borrowed jumped to his hand. He wiped his forehead with it and handed it back with his daft smile. All she could find to say was, "It's not clean."

The door flew open, and Phoebe Broome's sonn caught them. A moment of suffused silence, and then the mage said, in a controlled voice, "Father, what exactly was that?"

Farquhar's smile was suddenly much less daft and very unhappy. "That was our friend Ishmael, dear girl. As best I understand his situation, he is captive of one of two surviving mages from the time of the laying of the Curse—"

"That's—" The speaker thought better of "impossible."

". . . Who seems to have attempted, and succeeded, in augmenting Ishmael's strength." He reached up. "Help me up."

Phoebe, and the Borders-born mage who had argued with the coachman, lifted him between them. He said, shakily, "It was a rather brutal process, and would not have succeeded in someone less robust. And as you sensed, he has very little control."

"He studied wi'us," the Borders mage objected.

"Dear boy, all his efforts went toward *increasing* the effect of the little magic he had. Even under the best of all possible circumstances, it would take him time to adjust."

"Is he ensorcelled?" Phoebe said, horrified.

Her father turned to her. "I could not tell." Briefly, he supported himself on the lintel, and then handed himself through. Vladimer was waiting outside, Mycene and the baronette flanking him. "I think, Lord Vladimer," Farquhar said to Vladimer, "I will ask you to go downstairs, smartly now, and close off the space between the floors."

"What is it?"

"By your leave," the mage said, "it will be quicker if I simply show you."

Vladimer sonned him, taking in his manner, quite bereft of all eccentricity and whimsy. His shoulders tightened, and then he thrust his fisted hand at Farquhar. Farquhar's hand closed lightly around it. Vladimer's face registered his shock. *"Ishmael?"*

Farquhar squeezed his hand and released it. "I am afraid so, dear boy. Explain it to the others."

"Do you think you can—"

"Me? I think not. But I might be able to give Ishmael what he needs, with the help of my dear people here, and, perhaps, if they will permit me to speak to them, the Lightborn. It is probably safer for bystanders not to be too close. You do understand?"

Of course Vladimer understood, having been at the archduke's breakfast. "If you don't have the strength," Vladimer said, intensely, "then I order you to wait on making any move. There is no purpose to your risking yourselves. Fejelis will be in the palace by now. Give him a chance to get through to the high masters."

Farquhar gave him his wide smile. "I shall most certainly try. Now *please*, go downstairs."

"But—," began Lavender di Gautier, hoarsely.

"Shoo!" said Farquhar, with matching gestures.

Vladimer hesitated, his expression an odd mix of annoyance and helplessness. Then he said over his shoulder to the others, "Downstairs. I will explain." His sonn brushed Telmaine. "Lady Telmaine?"

Telmaine shook her head firmly, not trusting her voice. Ishmael needed her, and needed her all the more because the mages, whom he regarded as his own, seemed to have marked him as a danger, if not an enemy. He did not deserve that from them, too. She stood tensely, poised for argument, as Vladimer herded Mycene, the baronette, and their men down the stairs.

"My dear ones," Farquhar Broome began, and then stopped and spread his hands helplessly.

"It's all right, Father."

"It is *not* all right." Telmaine sensed the interplay of magic between them, swift and cryptic, excluding her again. But this time, she found herself measuring them, measuring their magic against that inferno she had felt from Ishmael. They could not match him—Farquhar Broome's manner told him that. But if he destroyed them, it might destroy him. She remembered that dream. A warning?

<Let us sit down,> Farquhar Broome said, and, with no deference to rank, they spread around the room, found chairs and stools and trunks, and sat, leaving her to perch on a stool with her skirts spread around her.

<I shall try one last time to reach Kadar,> he said, <but I shall not exhaust myself in the effort. If they have made their choice, so be it.> He was, she realized, speaking of the Lightborn temple. Was Kadar the archmage? <A moment, my dears.> So close to him, she could sense him gathering and shaping his magic, transforming vitality into energy, into a reach across distance, with an assured, delicate touch that wasted not a wisp of vitality. *How old is he?* she wondered. *A hundred years? Two hundred? More?*

He let out a breath and shook his head. <No, no use. One can only trust that they are also able to shield against the Shadowborn, or the effort would go for naught. Let us compose ourselves. And then, dear girl,> he said to Telmaine, <I will ask you to reach Ishmael once again. Of us all, I think he is least likely to harm you. Though that does not mean you will be safe.>

No one feeling that furnace of magic could make that mistake.

The thought leaked; Farquhar Broome's wizened-apple face creased in a smile.

Telmaine drew a deep breath to settle herself and then whispered, <Ishmael.>

The heat. The overwhelming heat. That she knew it was not physical made no difference to what she *felt*. But within the heat, she could sense his alertness, his listening presence. She concentrated on that. <Ishmael, it's Telmaine. What can we do to help you?>

No words, no attempt at conversation. Was he shying from injuring her? If only she could have pretended to be unaffected by his magic. <Ishmael, Magister Broome and your friends are here with me.> She hesitated, but this was Ishmael. He *could not* be their enemy. <We're in Stranhorne Crosstracks—we just arrived. Balthasar's still alive, but he was captured by one of the Shadowborn and taken up to Minhorne. He's gone to the Lightborn court as envoy. The telegram said he had an ensorcellment on him to protect him from the light.> He would surely sense how frightened she was for Balthasar, how desperately she wanted this over and him safe—them all safe. <Ishmael, this is important: the Lightborn Temple has sent a representative, Magister Tammorn, a strong sport mage. . . . Do you know lineage mages can't sense Shadowborn magic? They've sent Magister Tammorn to the Shadowborn. We think they're looking for an alliance.>

<What was that?>

That was not Ishmael. She recoiled quickly, but not quickly enough. Magic split her mind like the husk of a seed, spilling and raking through the kernels within: her encounters with the Shadowborn, with Tammorn, with Vladimer, Fejelis, the archduke, Ishmael. Vaguely she sensed the blaze of Ishmael's outrage, and even more vaguely, Farquhar Broome's efforts to reach her. The Shadowborn—it was a woman—said thoughtfully, <So he'll fight for you, will he? I can use that.>

And she felt Shadowborn magic drop over her like a great sheet, and *lift*.

Ten

Fejelis

"I need you to stay here, help the Darkborn. . . ." Fejelis glanced up from folding the princely mourning jacket around the caul, and found his brother staring at him in dismay. He measured the angle and color of the early-morning light, and stuffed the bundle into his borrowed bag with more urgency and less respect than it deserved. "You know the railway. You can talk to the railway people, get them what they need. You've my authority to overturn the day-night orders. . . ." Which he had remembered to scrawl. Celeste was translating it into Darkborn script on one of the clever Darkborn punch machines, still chortling at her own perversity in refusing to believe Fejelis's claim.

"But what are you going to do?" Orlanjis said. "And can't I come with you?"

Fejelis forgave him the plaintive tone. "Take my city back. . . . Find a way to get the Temple to see sense and work with the Darkborn mages. . . . Calm things down between Lightborn and Darkborn so the archduke of the Darkborn can see his way to reinforcing Strumheller and Stranhorne, and make sure he understands the need to . . . decide what to do *after* lunch." His brother did not react to the weak jest. "We simply can't take you with us, Jis. I need Jovance on her feet at the end of the *lift*, and I need you to hold together the alliance here."

"Why are you trusting me? I've only ever been your rival."

This was the heart of it, and no less than expected, since they'd been set up as rivals all their lives. Fejelis straightened to face his brother. He hated being hurried in a conversation of this importance, hated having to strip it down to its essence. ". . . Orlanjis, we are fighting for our lives against an enemy that few of us even recognize. I'm *trusting* you because you've seen exactly the same thing as I have, and come to the same conclusions. I'm trusting you because I watched you fight, come under attack, and not break. When we go back to the palace and all the usual problems and politics of a new reign, if I can keep you, I will. . . . You're not the boy you were even a few days ago." *Nor,* he thought, *am I.* He put his hands on his brother's shoulders and looked down into his eyes. "If I die doing this, all I ask is that you rule as you believe, not as anyone else tells you. Father didn't think that a prince's policy should survive the prince, and I agree. But try to be a good prince, and watch your back. I'll do my best to avoid leaving you quite as ghastly a mess as we have now, but if I fail, we will need as strong a relationship with the Darkborn—" He caught himself; shook his head. ". . . And here I said I wasn't going to try to influence you."

"That's not influence," Jovance interrupted from the door. "That's the verbal equivalent of sitting in a lather, tearing a piece of paper to bits. You're not telling him anything he doesn't already know. He's your father's son as well."

He gave her a grateful glance at that, then hugged Orlanjis quickly, thankful that when the Darkborn train had left with Lord Vladimer and his mages aboard, no one had suggested that Orlanjis travel with it. But the Lightborn railway workers were bringing in a day train with plans to press on to Stranhorne before sunset, and if Fejelis could not end this today, in the city, Orlanjis would go with them. "I'll give your regards to Mother, though I'd appreciate it if you sent a message to reassure her I didn't abandon you in the wilds."

Orlanjis watched from the doorway as they went down the steps of the small house and into the carefully tended garden. The perfume of the night-blooming flowers on the trellises lingered in the still morning air, though the flowers themselves were furled. A baffled bee was bumping gently against one as though trying to wake it. With the stillness and the early sunshine, and they being the only people moving in it, the world seemed new-made, free of Curse and Shadowborn.

"Nice pep talk," Jovance said in a low voice.

"I'm terrified for him," Fejelis admitted. "He's only fourteen."

"One thing reassures me," Jovance said. "I see no sign that he needs to do stupid things to prove his courage." She looked up at him, her skin warmed by the sunlight. "Nor do you; I don't think it *occurs* to you to be afraid." If she could feel his pulse, if she could touch him, she would know that was wrong. "Where do you want me to put us down? It needs to be somewhere I know, and it's best to be somewhere outside. I can sense and avoid living things more easily than inanimate objects."

". . . What do you say to the palace gardens, on the plinth of the sundial garden?"

Where, on certain ceremonial occasions, the prince would stand, his shadow marking a significant time. She stared at him, her lips parting, and then he remembered that one of those ceremonies was the public announcement of the contract between the prince and his chosen consort, and another, the sealing of the contract itself. His color mounted. "Jovance, I, um . . ."

She was still laughing when she landed them on the plinth above the sundial garden. The hour was a most unceremonial one, and their shadows tracked across the blue and silver border, outside time. She gasped as the effort of the magic caught up with her, and he got a hand around her back and guided her down to sit on the edge of the platform, all thought of his misstep slipping from his mind. "Sorry," she said, wanly. "Needed quite a punch to get through the Temple interference. It's a safe bet they know I've arrived."

"If they don't, tell them," Fejelis said. "I want to get their attention." He stepped from the platform down onto the ground. "Can you walk? I don't like us being exposed like this." He'd had one crossbow bolt through him already in his young reign. No sense inviting another.

"I'd like to say no," she remarked, gazing up under her lashes, "just to make you carry me." She slipped off the plinth onto her feet, and steadied herself with a grip on his arm, delighting him with the casual ease of the gesture. Of all the people he knew, only Tam and his father had ever touched him so easily. "No," she murmured, and he realized she was aware of his distracted thoughts. "Maybe not a good idea." Then she lifted her head. "Company, Prince."

Good company, he found, turning: Captain Lapaxo at the head of a flying wedge of palace vigilants, with a look on his face that promised a locked safe room for a feckless prince, and a fate worse than death for anyone who would think to harm him. Fejelis towed Jovance several yards down the path to get the flower beds off the line of the charge. He had enough civil wars on his hands without adding one between vigilants and gardeners.

Lapaxo halted in front of him, scowling. "Well, *curse it*, your brightness." Then the captain outraged protocol and endeared himself to Fejelis forever by clapping hands to his prince's arms and giving him a sharp shake. "Where'd you get to?"

"The Borders," Fejelis said. And could not resist adding, ". . . I'm glad to see you, too, Captain." He was; he had feared Lapaxo had been murdered to clear the way for Rupertis. He waved away Lapaxo's apology. "This is Magistra Jovance, who has been good enough to bring me back, and is under verbal contract to me." Fortunately for princely decorum, she did not respond to any double entendre. She still looked very pale.

"And Magister Tammorn?"

He started along the path, and when Lapaxo did not remonstrate, strode out. Jovance dealt stoically with the pace, following a few steps behind and stumbling only a little. "Whereabouts unknown at present, *not* by his own volition. What's been happening here?"

Lapaxo gave him a terse summary of events: the ultimatum to the Darkborn, the first signs of Darkborn retaliation, and then the arrival of the Darkborn envoy. "I knew about him," Fejelis said—it had been part of Vladimer's briefing. "What's he . . . Never mind. I want to meet him." Quite aside from the envoy's political importance, he was curious to meet anyone with that much crazy courage.

He felt Jovance's fingertips graze his wrist, as though by chance. <You realize that's how the Temple learned to send Tam to the Shadowborn at night?>

He managed not to gawk at her. Even Tam had never mind-touched him like that.

"He reacts well in a crisis," Lapaxo said, which was high praise from the vigilant. Explaining how the Darkborn emissary had already survived one assassination attempt carried them up the steps and into the vestibule. Servants and staff stared. A couple skittered through various doorways, while others sidled casually out, no doubt to scurry every bit as quickly to various masters. He found himself fighting a manic grin: he was home.

"Where are they?" he said.

He didn't need to explain who, not to Lapaxo. "Up in the archmage's suite."

"All of them?" Fejelis said. Either that indicated a shift in the balance of power or a refusal on the part of either his mother or Prasav to award the other the territorial advantage. "Tell them I want them down in the main receiving room, five minutes or sooner: the archmage, the high masters, Prasav, Helenja. The Darkborn envoy, too. Tell the high masters I know where they've sent Tammorn"—Jovance's golden eyes flashed alarm—"and tell Prasav I am not pleased with his suborning Captain Rupertis."

"It wasn't Prasav alone," Lapaxo said. "It was Shadowborn—I hadn't come to that yet. And Rupertis is dead."

Fejelis swallowed. His headlong pace was making him dizzy, yet he sensed that the only way to prevail here was to move fast. He'd worked hard at training speed and timing into himself on the piste; it was time to apply these lessons outside. "*Ten* minutes, then. I need a change of clothing."

He needed a bath, too, and several hours' more sleep, but he could whistle for those, prince or no.

Jovance touched his arm again, more deliberately, and mind-whispered, <Steady.>

Lapaxo gave orders; they collected and shed vigilants and servants and staff as they rolled down the corridors. He scanned faces, gauging mood. Jovance's touch said, <They seem pleased to see you.> He sensed pleasure and pride behind the words, and wished the touch had lingered.

His chief dresser and two assistants were already waiting in the main receiving room, one assistant with an armful of red fabric and the second with a steaming bowl, a razor, cloths, a towel. A mage vigilant nodded to Lapaxo from behind them: the bowl, towels, and dressers were safe. As the vigilants deployed to their posts at the doors and on the balcony, he dropped the shoulder bag on the dais with a quick "No, I'll need that" to the servant who would have swept it away, and let the dresser strip him to his underwear and swab him down with the brisk efficiency of a mother cat washing her kitten. He was glad he'd had the chance to shave in the railway house, because having a razor plied at that speed would have tried his nerves. He stepped into trousers and shoes, and stooped for a blouse and to receive a comb through his hair. No time for the ornate styling fashionable at court. Lapaxo stayed at his right shoulder, continuing his report in an increasingly distracted fashion as servants streamed into the hall, inspecting mirrors, dusting lights, straightening pictures, carrying more lights on stands, carrying flowers in transparent bowls, trying to do in five minutes what had taken them several days before his ill-omened coming of age. Fejelis was sure his orders had not included all this, yet it took very little reflection to decide that if he had thought to give these orders, he would have. Lapaxo, finally pressed beyond endurance, said, "What *is* this?"

Letting his intuition speak for him, Fejelis said, "Defiance."

Lapaxo's look demanded he make sense. ". . . Defiance of disorder," Fejelis said. "Defiance of change. Defiance of illegitimate authority." He pulled the wrapped caul from the Darkborn bag, giving the wincing dresser a penitent glance, and unwrapped it with more care and respect than he had rolled it up. He handed the red mourning jacket to the dresser for shaking out and brushing down, and cradled the caul briefly in his hands. A few strands of pale hair were snagged in the wire. His father's, or his own? The caul was still shaped to his father's head, but its fit was close enough. By sleight of hand, the dresser produced a mirror and held it at just the right angle with the precision of long practice. Fejelis was braced for the shock of his father's cauled face looking back at him, as it had the first time he donned the caul, but with a greater shock, he saw only his own. He felt Lapaxo's hand on his elbow; his eyes must have lost focus for a moment. "When did you last eat?" muttered the captain.

"Not that long ago." Bannocks and cheese before speaking with Vladimer, though he was having difficulty remembering when he'd last eaten a full meal. "Later," he said, as the door of lesser privilege suddenly opened on a phalanx of vigilants judiciar around a familiar fair woman in red, and a black-haired stranger whose eyes were masked by smoked lenses. "That's the Darkborn," Lapaxo said in a low voice. "Name's Hearne."

"Floria's friend?" Fejelis said, finally remembering where he'd heard the name.

He tried not to stare, but the Darkborn's very ordinariness made it difficult. That slim body and narrow, intense face could have belonged to one of the palace's archivists or librarians, except for the dark glasses and the heavy, unsightly clothing. The Darkborn seemed to be perspiring a little, which Fejelis would have taken for nervousness, except that his posture suggested determination more than nerves. Those thick clothes must be hot—of course, the Darkborn were used to the chill of night. As they approached, he noticed Floria's gliding step and ceaselessly moving eyes: Floria at her most dangerous. But when her eyes lighted on him, confirming the truth of rumor, they narrowed with glittering satisfaction, and she smiled.

At his side, Jovance was staring at the Darkborn, squinting slightly. He could see her hand working. Lapaxo had said the ensorcellment on Hearne was Shadowborn, and she was lineage.... "Magistra?" he prompted in a murmur.

Recalled to herself, she put her mouth to his ear. "He's got the archmage's touch on him. One *mother* of an ensorcellment. That's *exactly* what they did to Tam." She sounded angry. He felt angry. But he said, low voiced, "It's not his fault."

"If he hadn't come—" The party was nearly within earshot, and she bit back the rest of the statement. He waited, but she did not finish it, even silently.

Lapaxo muttered something at his other side, and Fejelis angled his head toward the vigilant. "Forgot to tell you," the captain said, sounding annoyed at himself. "Temple claimed them as one of theirs. Say's he's mageborn."

Says, Fejelis thought. *Mages don't need the Temple to say they're mageborn.* He exchanged glances with Jovance; she shook her head slightly. *Now what are they up to?* He gestured the new arrivals to wait a moment, and beckoned the dresser with the brushed-down mourning jacket to him, slipped his arms into the sleeves, was briskly tweaked and tugged. Nodded his thanks, and, with a deep breath, turned. With the party's entrance, the hall had begun to drain of servants, and now was almost empty of them, its hasty grooming and staging, like his, as complete as it was going to be.

He realized he didn't know the Darkborn's title, only that he was a physician and—no, he had met the man's wife already; he was untitled. "Dr. Hearne, I am Fejelis Grey Rapids, styled prince." He might as well test the man's mettle. "... I understand you have already received a traditional court welcome."

"Was *that* what it was?" Hearne's voice was a steady tenor.

That boded well. And because this was a Darkborn and Fejelis understood such courtesies were important, he said, "... I just recently—a few hours ago, in fact—spoke to your wife."

He had not realized that a man already so pale could go that much whiter. Floria instantly closed the step between them, but the Darkborn, holding on to his composure, said, "No, I'm all— Excuse me, Prince Fejelis, but when I came here, it was under the impression my wife was dead. Floria told me otherwise, but to hear that you have spoken to her . . . What did she say?"

"Strictly speaking, though I spoke to her, she did not get a chance to speak to me. But we were introduced, and Magistra Jovance"—he indicated her—"sensed both her presence and her magic. She was in good health."

"Thank you," the Darkborn breathed. Poise restored, he said a little hurriedly, "Prince Fejelis, the archduke will be delighted to know you are back. He has high expectations of your help in resolving the difficulties between our peoples."

Not a professional diplomat, Fejelis thought, *but in earnest.* And he had the delicacy of phrasing mastered already. *Difficulties, indeed.* He said, "I have equal hopes of his— "

Floria's head turned like a cat's. He hadn't been aware of the noise from outside, but that was surely his mother's voice. And then the door of greater privilege burst open before a roil of mages and vigilants. He caught sight of several he recognized as Prasav's, plus men and women in the dun and ochre of the southern contingent, plus the bright glitter of chains of rank around several throats. He realized he was on the brink of entertaining an unrighteous brawl for precedence.

"Excuse me," he said to the Darkborn envoy, and started to draw a breath, but stopped as he caught Lapaxo's headshake. He was glad of that a moment later, and gladder still that Lapaxo had the courtesy to take a step away before he thundered, "Order in the presence of the prince!"

He could have sworn he could hear the chime of shuddering glass in the silence that followed. The contested doorway cleared. Fejelis sprang onto the dais, which earned him a glower from Lapaxo as the vigilants scrambled to cover him. At his glance of appeal, Jovance tripped up the steps to stand where a contracted mage would be expected to stand.

There was a pause, then Perrin entered, flanked by mages and Temple vigilants, the archmage, Magistra Valetta, and the high masters—seven of them—following so closely on her heels that they seemed to be herding her. The change in his sister, since their meeting in the ruins of the tower, was appalling. No twenty-year-old should be that haggard. A sideways glance at Jovance, no partisan of Perrin's, showed her as disconcerted as he was. She wasn't close enough to tell him whether this was magical overreach, the burden of her awareness of Shadowborn magic, or the burden of being a usurper princess. At Perrin's first sight of him, her expression showed only relief, then guilt, and finally unease. He waited for her to draw closer, keeping a slight smile on his face all the time. "Hello, sister," he said. "Had enough of this job yet?"

Her breasts rose and fell beneath the thin, red vest and mourning jacket, reminding him how that first time they met after ten years, before he recognized her, she had demanded he mind his eyes. "Mother, *yes*," she said, strongly. "You want it back?"

The depth of his relief told him that he had not been sure that she would yield, or that the Temple would let her. She slipped through her honor guard and swiftly mounted the stairs. She turned toward their gathering brightnesses—Prasav and Helenja's retinues were in the room, and the rear was filling fast—and paused, and then pulled the blue pins from her hair that held it in its caul-like style, shaking out the braids with a vigor that was near violence. "I renounce all claim on my brother's title!" She turned to him, and Fejelis did not miss the tensing of the vigilants around him. With a silent apology to them, he held out his hand to her. And Jovance tensed in her turn, until she realized, as he had, that Perrin's hands were gloved, her touch safe.

"Fejelis, I'm so sorry," she said, so quickly her words slurred. "It happened so fast, and you were barely gone when I realized you'd been *right*, and the *Temple* was hiding from the truth—" He squeezed her hand, quieting her. Now to find out the price the Temple would extract for ceding his title back to him . . .

"Where is Orlanjis?" shouted Sharel from Helenja's side, and no doubt with Helenja's leave. His mother, true to nature, looked as disgusted at Perrin's ready surrender of her pretendership as she had at her assumption of it.

"He's in the Borders, helping the Darkborn defend themselves," Fejelis said. "And doing well at it, thanks to your teaching." She started to shout something else, but he was ready for her. He might not have Lapaxo's seasoning, but he had healthy lungs and a voice solidly past adolescence, and whether he liked it or not, the blood of generations of southern clan chiefs.

"This ends here!"

No shivering glass, but a gratifying silence. "This internecine warfare *ends here*," he said, less loudly but no less emphatically. "I pardon my sister for her offense against me. I left Orlanjis in the Borders with my full trust, knowing that he *would* fulfill that trust. I left him with instructions to support the Darkborn in every way he could—because having seen them fight, having spoken to them and heard their preparations, I'd much rather have them as friends than enemies. I *know and acknowledge* the outrage of the attack on the tower, but until we establish what part magical influence played in the decisions made by Duke Mycene, whom I am told died under magical attack by a Shadowborn"—Hearne, he saw, was surprised he knew that already—"and Kalamay, then by our own law, we cannot retaliate."

"And the Darkborn leaflets?" Prasav slipped in.

Darkborn leaflets? Ten minutes was not enough. But this was his court, not Prasav's. "I will *not* sign an order of eviction for the Darkborn from Minhorne. This city is theirs as much as it is ours.... But all of that is *irrelevant*. Your brightnesses, mages of the Temple: how much time have you wasted while the enemy—who murdered my father, who threatens all of us—advances? I tried to warn you not a day ago"—truly, was it only that?—"and got deposed for my pains, and nearly shot at the command of a captain of vigilants who had been suborned by the Shadowborn."

Prasav's expression was sweet revenge for those twisted

half-truths about Tam and the artisans; he didn't expect Fejelis already to know.

"But for the actions of Magister Tammorn, my mentor and my friend. Who is not here because he was sent, by his own superiors, the masters of the Temple, to the camps of the enemy. *Tell me,*" Fejelis fired at the high masters, "*that you did not send my friend to treat with the enemy!*"

In his peripheral vision, he glimpsed his sister's horrified face, Jovance's frozen stance, Lapaxo crouching to lunge, before it came to the captain that the one threat he could not protect his prince from was the prince's own madness.

"No," said a voice he had never heard before. "I did not send him to treat with the enemy."

It was the archmage, who had not been known to speak aloud in the hearing of earthborn—even Temple servants—in living memory. The small man clasped his hands and bowed over them to Fejelis, a gesture of respect from two centuries past.

Several heartbeats went by before Fejelis realized that the archmage was not going to elaborate on that statement. By then he had waited too long and lost the initiative for the obvious question. Then Jovance said from beside him, in a voice that sounded girlish but determined, "Magister Archmage, Tam explained to me before he left what you had asked him to do."

Magistra Valetta said, "That was what we had asked him to do." Hitherto the confident mouthpiece of the archmage, the one he spoke through, she suddenly had the air of a woman who no longer knew what would drop out of her mouth.

"Please do us the courtesy of explaining," Fejelis said, quietly.

"By their deeds," said the archmage, "we shall know them."

"You set Tam out," Fejelis said slowly, "as bait."

"With Lukfer dead, Tam is the strongest living sport," said Magistra Valetta, still with that expression of one about to go cross-eyed from watching her own lips. "We had no one better suited. But we could not tell him because we wanted to know . . . what they were."

They didn't tell you, either, Fejelis inferred. Plans within plans—he could almost feel sorry for her. He met the archmage's eyes, experience centuries deep in them. More than three hundred years old, he knew the man was. And the archmage's father—how old was he? How close was the archmage to a living memory of those who had laid the Curse?

He weighed what he should say next. He had been lucky and inspired to have come this far, but he had done so by outrunning the opposition. Now they were all standing still, listening.

Friendship demanded that he argue that Tam be spared, as he had done not a day ago, without a moment's thought—charging in to challenge the high masters, throwing himself into Prasav's trap. He had been lucky to keep his life, lucky to keep his brother, lucky to keep his sister, lucky to regain his caul. Lucky to have remained alive, so far. More than half that luck accrued from the luck of meeting Tam.

He remembered sharing breakfast with his father in the prince's private chambers, having one of their rare conversations about the costs and burdens of being prince. They rarely dwelt on it, as there seemed no purpose: as night followed day, as summer followed spring, Fejelis would be prince. But he remembered his father saying, eyes half closed against the early sun, *"And then there will be the first time you must sacrifice a friend. . . ."*

He could feel the quiet in the room, the expectation. He wondered what Jovance would think of him—but if she chose to remain with him, she would see him do worse than this, to try to make something of his reign, salvage earthborn and mage.

"And do you know yet?" Fejelis said, quietly

The archmage said, "Not yet."

Telmaine

She heard Ishmael's growled *"No,"* and felt magic grapple with magic, his great, unformed seething rising against the woman's. The *lift* suddenly released her and she swayed on her stool, and then reached down to grip it with both hands through the folds of her skirts. Sonn and magic intersected on her from her companions. The young Borders mage, Bryse, had come to his feet, inspired by an impulse of chivalry.

"Should I—?" she gasped to Farquhar Broome, though did not know what she wanted to ask. In the end, it was not for him or for anyone else to say. *I walked through the fire to rescue my daughter, and Ishmael went with me.* And when in distraction and weariness her concentration failed her, he had held back the inferno, though it had cost him his magic and nearly his life.

Now Ishmael was the one standing in the inferno, and she the one who must hold it back.

She felt their surprise, Ishmael's and the woman's, at her touch, and from him the same emotions he had felt as she went to rescue Florilinde: admiration and dismay and protectiveness. Whatever the Shadowborn had done to him, he was still Ishmael. They had no chance for any further exchange. Through him, she heard the woman say, <*Now,*> and felt her magic fasten on to Ishmael, spinning strength and vitality from him. He did not resist. Telmaine's resistance on his behalf had no more effect than a sparrow's pecks and fluttering wings on a boy stealing her eggs.

<Don't distract him,> ordered a woman whose presence she had not registered until then, distracted by Ishmael and the sorceress who held him. Ishmael braced himself at that voice. Not a flinch or a cringe, because Ishmael would never cringe, but he remembered what she had just done to him in making him a monster.

No matter her power, Telmaine would *not* cower before her. <Why *not*?>

<Because of this,> said the woman. Fleetingly, she thought that they were trying to *lift* her again, trying to carry her bodily away, and then she knew where she had felt this sensation before—fighting the Shadowborn beside Vladimer's bed, as he seized on her magic and vitality both and began to drag them from her flesh. <*Ishmael!*>

<Idiot,> said the woman, and *did* something to release

her. Magic reunited dramatically with flesh as she struck hard floor and sprawled, gasping, on it. She rose, dazed, smelling the smoky, sun-warmed air of the railway-station cupola. Her hip and shoulder and the side of her head hurt. Her companions were silent, motionless, their heads turned toward Farquhar Broome. She sensed the magic that knotted them together and excluded her.

She rose to elbows and knees, then hands and knees, in the billows of her skirts. A lady did not fight; that was one of the earliest lessons of the nursery. Any instinct for it she had as a small, unruly girl was whipped and shamed out of her. Denied the means to protect herself—physically, legally, or magically—she shied from dominant or cruel men, and so never learned how to fight as she had learned other things secondhand. She would have lost against the Shadowborn—lost magic, mind, and life—were it not for Ishmael. She would *not* abandon him.

But she could not fight his warder, and could not last against that terrible draining of vitality. She reached instead but for Ishmael's adversaries, the ones she had sensed beyond the ruined manor of Stranhorne. One, as monstrous as the ones preying on Ishmael, two, three; the third the boy she had met—and bested—in Minhorne. Let that give her hope. She could sense the weaker presence—weaker in comparison to *them*—of the Lightborn Tammorn, and sense his despair. What price the Temple's solicitations now?

None of them were paying attention to lesser beings. She knew about *that* as a great lady among servants. Crouching, grinning savagely, she gathered her will, gathered her magic, and aimed it at the distant trio.

Burn, Telmaine willed. *BURN.*

She poured her magic across the miles between them, poured it into the place where he and his mistress were, igniting mats and drapes and clothing. The boy screamed in terror. She sensed the woman's magic welling up inexorably to quench the fires, stoke them though Telmaine might with vitality and will. In doing so, the woman was killing Tammorn. Strong as he was by himself, in this company, he was the weakest of them all. She must not waver, for Ishmael's sake.

Then the Lightborn mages stooped upon them, seizing Isolde, Ishmael, Ariadne, and Telmaine. Her skirts ignited and flame leaped up her bodice; she threw out arms and magic, trying to push away the flames from her shriveling flesh. Across her awareness came a great gust of magic—Ishmael's magic—snuffing them out and sending her to the floor again. She curled up there, clad only in rags and cobwebs of burned lace, and choking on smoke and ash.

Phoebe Broome screamed, *<Kadar, listen to me!>* The mesh of magic between the commune mages hummed and pulsed. She lifted her head and sonned Farquhar Broome's wizened face working with effort as he exerted himself, a seventh-rank mage, to the fullest.

It would not be enough. She pushed herself up on shaking arms and dragged a rag of skirt around her body, a scant but necessary gesture toward decency. Sweet Imogene, but it *hurt* to reach outward, hurt as much as it had bearing her children, hurt as much as it had those last dozen steps carrying Florilinde out of the inferno. Yet she pushed away the storm of magic around her, moved in a self-created void through it, toward the inferno that had Ishmael in the heart of it. This time she would not falter; this time there could be no lapse. She reached out her hand and touched not the chilled metal of a doorknob, but a broad, fever-hot hand.

Had this been the living world, clothes and skin and their own solidity would have constrained their embrace, but this was some domain of magic alone. She passed through and into him like vapor mingling with vapor. She could feel the beat of his heart behind her own ribs, the heave of his breathing in her own chest, the ache of his effort behind her own forehead. She—he—*they* were sitting in a small room, the warm wind from the open doors to a balcony on Ishmael's sweating face. Seated to their left was a small old woman whose magic was one of sickly, draining cold. Behind them she could sense another woman, his warder, Ariadne, leaning with her hands on Ishmael's shoulders, her magic caging him. The magic of the Lightborn wheeled around them, swift striking and merciless—still air turned suddenly to gales, bare tile raged with flame, bone cracked, scars split, flesh turned to rot. . . . She found herself suddenly, urgently, called to heal as Ishmael's lungs began to bleed.

<*Kadar,*> Farquhar Broome cried out. <*They are not the enemy.*>

All the bones in Ishmael's right hand shattered. Reeling with his agony, Telmaine wrapped them with her magic, started to mold them whole. Ishmael said, <That'll not kill me. Ignore it. Save yourself for what will.> The woman's hands tightened spasmodically on his shoulders, and Telmaine could hear her choking. A man's voice—Balthasar's? No, not possible—cried, "Ariadne—"

<*Ishmael.* What's happening?>

<Usual muddle when a skirmish goes sour,> Ishmael said, but she could sense his struggle for breath. <They take us for th'enemy. The strength's on this side, but the Lightborn have the knowledge—and they're cursed inventive.> A vertebra in his spine split like a rotten log; he groaned aloud and braced himself against falling as his legs lost all strength. In his memory two revolvers cracked together and he slid limply down a wall into the mud and surrendered himself to death. Frantically, Telmaine poured her magic over the damage, repairing bones, nerves . . . <Can't fight the magic,> Ishmael explained. <Can *hurt* the bodies . . . Steady; you'll overreach.>

<What does that matter if we lose?> This. *You.*

<No . . . > The Lightborn assault abruptly ceased. Ishmael coughed to clear his windpipe, leaned over to spit blood, coughed again, and swiped his sleeve across his mouth. He sonned right and left, checking around him by ingrained habit—checking *on* those around him by ingrained habit. Fleetingly, he noted the humor of it, those reflexes expressing themselves in these circumstances. It was an amusement she did not share. From the floor, from where he crouched cradling the fallen woman, another man sonned back. He had Balthasar's narrow face and fine features, but, as he wiped froth from the woman's lips, there was a helpless ferocity in his expression that was quite alien to Balthasar's face. This had to be Lysander Hearne. But the

woman, though she was dressed in Darkborn fashion, was pure Shadowborn.

On the other side, the older woman's head turned toward Ishmael. Telmaine's perception of her was overlaid with Ishmael's knowledge. Isolde, daughter of Imogene herself, last but one survivor of that cursed generation, who had killed most of her descendants in trying to create another mage as powerful as she, and had finally succeeded in Ishmael.

<Best go back,> he said.

<And leave you alone here? Never.>

She could sense his struggle with himself, conveyed in impressions rather than words, and it was all the stronger for that. He had no hope for himself: his strength was beyond his control and barely in Isolde's. He was no more than a reservoir for Isolde to tap, a weapon for her to aim. Before Telmaine touched him, he had not even been a thinking weapon. <You *need* me, Ishmael.>

<It's likely t'kill you, Telmaine.> She might overextend herself, she might be killed by the Lightborn or the other Shadowborn, or drained to death by Isolde or Ariadne . . . or by Ishmael himself.

But all the love he had never declared had been in her name. She might tell herself that she was staying for Balthasar, for her children, for Sylvide's widower and son, for Vladimer and the archduke, even. That was all true enough; if they did not, somehow, turn this battle, then all of them would suffer. But even if there had been no one else, she would have stayed for him.

<Ishmael?> Farquhar Broome said. <Dear boy, can you hear me?>

Telmaine felt him hesitate, and answered for him. <We can hear you.>

<Dear lady . . . this is admirable, but not at all wise; you do not know what you are doing.> Fortunately for decorum, he did not give her an opening to rejoinder. <We have an understanding with the Lightborn now, though I do wish that had come sooner. But whatever you do, you will have all the help we can give.>

<Pass my thanks,> Ishmael said. <Though I doubt there's much for them t'do.>

<There *must* be something,> Telmaine said. Involuntarily, she remembered her dream, his double-ended gun, and sensed his stillness, the forming of a plan. <*No,*> she insisted, appalled. <Ishmael, there has to be a better way.>

An eerie sense of touch, like a warm hand brushing her face. <Not that, but—>

Isolde spoke: "Again."

From the floor, Lysander Hearne said, "No," as the woman struggled free of his embrace, rising on her knees.

Isolde disregarded him, and Ishmael did not react, did not resist, as her magic fastened upon his magic, his vitality, once more. Telmaine reared up, raging, but Ishmael said, <Wait.>

<You can't just—>

<*Wait.*> That was Ishmael the Shadowhunter, Ishmael the veteran, alarming and reassuring both. She had trusted him then; she had to trust him now, even though the last thing she wished was to sit passively while Isolde bled him cold of magic and vitality. He said, <It has t'be between them.>

<What has to?> But he did not answer, not directly. Instead he fed her what he had taken from Isolde's mind when he set his hand to hers: Imogene, monstrous in power if not in character; Ismene, monstrous in power and character; Isolde, the denigrated younger child pinned between worship and resentment. Child enough to be bewildered and terrified when Ismene died—mages were not supposed to *die*. Child enough to be flattered when Imogene proposed making her part of her vengeance, making her a keystone of the Curse. Child enough to believe that if she did this for Imogene, Imogene would come to care for her as she had for Ismene. <How could a mother?> Telmaine demanded, but the demand went unanswered. And she had known mothers as cruel on the earthborn scale . . . Too young to endure the horror of the aftermath of the Curse, watching the mages around her warring and dying, the earthborn who had served or befriended them burning at

sunrise or melting away at sunset. Too young to endure the isolation and hatred of the others for being Imogene's daughter.

I might pity her, Telmaine thought, *but for what she has done to Ishmael.*

She could feel the strain on him as the vessels in his lungs began to ooze again, his legs went numb, his hand ached with crumbling bones, and magic drained him. She pinched off those vessels, eased pressure on those nerves once more, but it was a shocking effort now. <*Ishmael,*> she whispered. <I can't—>

<Hold a little longer. They have to exhaust each other before—>

<Before?>

<Shh.> A whisper in her mind, shockingly weak. He let her feel Isolde as he felt her, the great, thrumming rope of magic stretching out between the Shadowborn, dragging on Emeya's vitality and magic as Emeya dragged on hers. She remembered how the Shadowborn at Vladimer's bedside had sought to uproot her own magic and her life. <All I can think t'do—> Ishmael's heart suddenly stuttered.

<*Ishmael!*>

He took a terrifying moment to answer her. <Aye, I'm out of time. Tell Magister Broome I mean t'try to bind them both together. Cage them, so they finish each other. It may not go well—>

She pummeled his stalling heart, frantic. <We don't have time to think about that! Magister Broome!>

<Yes, dear girl.>

<Help us!> She threw open her mind, let him have Ishmael's intention, Ishmael's knowledge, her determination to stay, her reasons for staying—little caring anymore about propriety.

<*Kadar,*> Broome said. <Let us try young Lord Vladimer's idea, shall we?> And the harsh, sharp-edged Lightborn magic, expertly shaped and deftly wielded, severed the magic binding and drawing on Ishmael. Farquhar Broome said, with an incongruous, childlike glee, <It worked!>

Ishmael's heart steadied to its powerful beat. <Aye, it

dlu.> He pulled himself forward in the chair, oblivious to his damaged hand, and sonned Isolde, whose face was strained with hatred, oblivious now to anyone but her nemesis. <Don't know how long that'll pertain.> Swiftly, he sonned the two on the floor. Hearne was alert; the woman in his arms staring. Ishmael ground out, "Are y'with us, or not?"

Lysander Hearne said, quickly, "With you. Don't hurt her. Ariadne." He turned her face to him, kissing her forehead gently. "Ariadne, it's over."

A grim smile pulled Ishmael's scar at such a presumptuous promise. <Telmaine, mind them. I trust them far as I could throw them—yesterday, not today. Magister Broome . . .>

<*Tammorn now*,> said the Lightborn archmage. Far to the northeast, on the summit of an earthworks, the Lightborn mage slumped to the ground, semiconscious but free. There was a brief, forceful interchange between the archmage and the other Shadowborn mage present, his mind as half tamed as his magic, his thoughts evasive and wary.

The boy cried out, <Emeya, they're trying to—> Suddenly decisive, the stronger mage smothered his warning.

Isolde's head turned toward Ishmael. Ariadne sat up suddenly, her mouth gaping in shock or on a cry.

<*Mine*,> Ishmael said. His power suddenly surged around them, a wall of furnace flame. On the far side of it, Farquhar Broome's magic played around it like a flute around thunder, coaxing, guiding, swift and deft in its touch. The Lightborn mages were there—several of them—lending their guidance to Farquhar's. She could sense the structure of the binding, like the one Tammorn had worked on her, but that seemed no more than a cobweb in comparison to this. She could feel Isolde begin to struggle, heard her cry out to Emeya to cease and join with her. If Emeya heeded her, Telmaine was not aware of it; her attention was fully on Ishmael, on the heart and lungs and bones and muscles striving to sustain such massive, magical effort, despite their burden of a lifetime's injury and hard use. He could not last . . .

Isolde, her energies divided, died first. Briefly, furiously, Emeya's ferocious energies turned on Ishmael's. Telmaine wrapped her magic around Ishmael's faltering heart, wrapped her will around Ishmael's life. And then, suddenly, Emeya fell away, her last scream—that of a young child—reverberating through the link between them.

Ishmael went limp in his chair, drawing huge, gasping breaths. She thought for a moment he was going to black out, but he stayed her efforts to lend him strength. <Thank you,> he said at last. <Now you'd best get back. You're about spent yourself.>

At first she could not remember where she might get back to, that she had existence herself, a body, magic, separate from his. She could feel him pushing at her, untangling her like a twining vine. <I don't want to,> she pleaded.

<Telmaine, I've more left now than you.>

<What are you going to do?> she demanded, clutching.

He sighed. <The first thing is t'get control, if I can. I've wished all my life t'be stronger, but there should be limits t'wishing.>

<That was clever of you, dear boy,> Farquhar Broome said, a gentle imposition.

Ishmael sonned Isolde, who had slumped sideways in her chair, one arm trailing, with no sense of life or magic about her whatsoever. Sonned Lysander Hearne, who sat supporting—indeed wrapped around—his Shadowborn lady.

Lysander breathed, "You did it." Then, his face hardening, said, "Leave her alone. Do you understand? You'd not have done that without her."

He does not understand at all. Ishmael and Telmaine shared the same thought, his one of weary amusement, hers of exhausted outrage. <Nothing else t'do,> Ishmael said—answering Farquhar Broome more than Lysander. <A sad thing, though. They'd this done t'them as children, and no choice t'be other than they were.>

<There's much about magic that's sad, Ishmael,> said the strongest living Darkborn mage.

<Lucky to bring it off, we were. . . . I'm going t'need your help. I'm no child, but—>

<*Sebastien*, don't!>

Raw strength of magic and rage of defeat, transmuted to fire and death, hurtled across the distance between the Shadowborn redoubt and Ishmael. Sebastien held back nothing of his magic or his furious young vitality. Ishmael was exhausted and unguarded, against them and against his own strength. Telmaine felt Sebastien's fires roar up around him, the death magic batten onto him.

She responded without thought, tendering her vitality to sustain his once more. Magic seized on hers, as the Shadowborn's had, but this time it was his—all his. She began to struggle, as she had struggled then, but she was completely overmatched. She felt his vitality resurge against the death magic, and felt the heat of his power mount, but there no longer seemed to be anything familiar about it, any part of the man she loved. She remembered again his face in her dream, with its terrible regret.

Tammorn

Neill closed Emeya's staring eyes and smoothed her dress down over her thin, childish knees. Her circlet of flowers had tumbled from her head and made a pale smudge in the shadows. Neill scooped it up, hesitated, and then bent his head to kiss it. He glanced toward Sebastien, who lay on his side, head propped on outstretched arm, eyes half closed, tears seeping from them, lips trembling. Neill's face was almost devoid of expression, his eyes dark. He sighed, spilled his handful of wilting flowers onto Emeya's chest, stood, and came back to Tam, who sat in the entrance, clinging to the sunlight.

"I'll be going now, I think," Neill said, conversationally. "I'd rather not wait for that"—he gestured south with a thumb—"to get organized and come looking for me." A wry, humorless smile. "Emeya wanted him dead from the start, but I could never see bothering about a first-rank mage, even one so adept at killing my creatures. We had bigger threats to worry about." He glanced over his shoulder at the dead, eight-hundred-year-old child. "She couldn't have known, any more than I. It was just that she liked my beasts."

Tam said nothing. He felt hollowed out, too numbed by horrors to feel glad or grateful for his life. He didn't have the strength to hold Neill, even if he could have found the resolution.

"I won't take the boy," Neill said. "If either of his parents survived this, they'll be looking for him. And if they didn't, there's still the uncle. I'd rather not give anyone more reason to come after me. Try to see he's treated decently, would you?"

"Where will you go?" Tam said. "The Temple—"

"Will . . . ?" prompted Neill, with a lift of an eyebrow, as Tam paused to muster his weary thoughts.

"There are provisions in our laws—"

"The ones that dealt so fairly with you?" said Neill, ironically. "Thank you, but no. I cannot claim to be only a boy. I'll just be going—my creatures here will follow me. I'll make no trouble if I'm left alone. I'm no Emeya. Maybe I'll drop by for a beer, in a century or two."

"Traitor," whispered Sebastien.

Both men looked at him. He levered himself up on his elbow and spat in Neill's direction. "Traitor," he said, louder.

"Yes, I am," Neill said. "And because of that, we're all still alive. Do you want to come with me?"

The boy did not answer. He was staring at Emeya's body, his thin chest rising and falling erratically. Neill said, "They'll be looking for you soon, Ariadne and Lysander. Or you could go to them. I'd suggest, though—"

Sebastien's head swung like a lodestone findings its pole. His face twisted with hatred.

Neill's "*Sebastien*, don't!" was late—how late, Tammorn would never know. The boy's magic blazed out. Tam recognized in it the annulment of life that he had almost lost Fejelis to, and that his master Lukfer had died while undoing in the ruined tower, driven not at Neill, but into the vortex of unstable strength far removed from them. Tam had known magic that unstable. He had loved the man who possessed it, but he had always known that, were he not himself a mage of considerable potential, he could not have been Lukfer's friend. Had he ever achieved control, Lukfer would have been eighth rank. Tam had no idea how the tower might rank Ishmael di Studier.

He had time to recognize disaster, time to extend a hand toward Neill, time to draw breath to speak a useless warning, before Ishmael di Studier's unwilled retribution reached them, his inchoate power finding shape in the form that Sebastien had thrown at him. Neill threw his own strength between it and Sebastien. Tam felt him reaping vitality from the creatures around him. Mayfly lunged past Tam, snarling at a threat he could not see. Neill caught the brindled pelt as he slid to his knees. "Get out," he gasped to Tam.

It was already too late. Di Studier's raging magic engulfed him, too.

Balthasar

"It's over," Perrin breathed.

Balthasar, leaning against Floria, turned his head to sonn in the direction of the voice. He was still off balance from the flux of magic around him. Perrin was speaking to her brother; the young Lightborn prince was crouched on the platform at Jovance's side, one hand spread on the floor to steady himself, the other gripping his knee in painful self-containment. Jovance sat cross-legged and unresponsive, her expression one of intense, pained concentration. Despite his obvious concern for her, Fejelis's face was turned toward the circle of high-ranked mages in the middle of the room. Like Jovance, they were sitting on the floor. Unlike Jovance, they were ringed by a guarding circle of mid-ranked mages and vigilants contracted to the Temple, and who held back any threat from the earthborn around them.

The prince said, quietly, "What's over? Can you tell me what happened?"

Perrin's face turned briefly toward the high masters, but no guidance came from there. "There were two very strong—very, very strong—mages. Shadowborn," she said with an undertone of defiance. Fejelis nodded impatiently. "And a third, Darkborn, almost as strong, and unstable. The two fought each other. And the third—the Darkborn—

bound them together until they died. With the help of the Darkborn and the high masters."

"The Darkborn was Magister Broome?" said Fejelis, frowning.

"No. One by the name of Ishmael di Studier."

"Ishmael?" said Balthasar, involuntarily.

"You know this man?" Fejelis said, head turning swiftly.

"I mentioned him in the account I gave the judiciary." Which Fejelis would not have had time to read. What were the essentials? "He's—was; I'll explain later—Baron Strumheller of the Borders."

"They told me in Strumheller Crosstracks he had been lost during the retreat. They told me he was a mage, but not that he was high ranked." His voice was edged with strain and suspicion.

"He's not. He's first rank, and he'd taken an injury that left even that unusable. Something must have happened to him. He trained with the Broomes—follows their codes."

Jovance lifted her head. "We must bind him," she said in that strangely hollow, uninflected voice that told them the archmage and high masters were speaking through her. Fejelis's shoulders tensed. He stood up to his full height, looking down at her. "Why?"

"His magic is unstable; he's a danger to us all." Jovance's voice shifted to a normal, young woman's alto. "Fejelis," she said, urgently, "this man is even stronger than my grandfather was, and has no more control. It's not punitive; it's for all our safety."

The Lightborn prince was young; he could not entirely hide his thoughts, though Balthasar did not know him well enough to guess what they were. But if the Temple's handling of Balthasar himself were any measure, there would be layer upon layer of motivation for this, and one of the layers would be power.

Jovance tendered, softly, "Fejelis, Tam's still alive."

Fejelis blinked a couple of times, facing over their heads, but chose not to answer her. To Balthasar, he said, ". . . How will the Darkborn react to this?"

"Farquhar Broome will understand the necessity," Magistra Valetta said. "The rest . . . are not strong enough to trouble us."

Balthasar only half understood this, but what he understood did not sound good. "Baron Strumheller is a nobleman of the Darkborn realm. Please don't underestimate the reaction of the archduke and the aristocracy." Which was stretching it, considerably, in one direction, and not at all in another. The aristocracy might not care what became of Ishmael, but they would care intensely about the principle, the trespass against the boundary of sunset.

"Envoy Hearne," Magistra Valetta said. "This is a matter of magic."

Floria's hand closed firmly on his arm. He knew a warning grip when he felt one. Nevertheless, he said, "Knowing the man as I do, if he truly is a danger to you all, he would willingly let you bind him until he achieves control. He is highly principled, deeply loyal, and has used his magic solely to heal and protect."

"It is not a matter of the man's intent—" She broke off suddenly.

Jovance gave an urgent shout of, *"Fejelis!"* The prince whirled and dropped down beside her and caught her as she pitched backward. Balthasar felt magic surge around him, roiling and chaotic, and redolent of the death that Sebastien had carried in his touch.

"Come with me," said Floria, harshly, to him. On the far side of the prince, Lapaxo raised his head; Floria, ever alert, answered his stare. "If that ensorcellment comes off him, he's a dead man." She didn't wait for leave, but three vigilants caught up with her in the doorway. Floria said, "Carry him," and he felt himself caught up and lifted off his feet by two taller vigilants.

"Where?" one said.

"The training room."

Hallways, stairs, at a sprint, Balthasar pinned between them, his sonn making scant sense of anything he passed. Smells of fresh bread, laundry, old socks. They skidded to a halt in front of a door; Floria wrenched it open, and they threw him in. He landed badly, painfully hard, on bare floor. The door slammed on him. He heard her shouting his name, but all he was aware of was the magic, deathly and incoherent, as it tore at the life of every magical entity within the city, from the strongest to the least significant. His last conscious thought was, *Telmaine* . . .

Eleven

Telmaine

"Well" was the first thing Telmaine heard. "Words quite fail me."

The voice was that of Telmaine's imperious elder sister, Merivan. But Merivan was in the city, where Telmaine had left her. Merivan could not be here.

"That'd be a first," whispered Balthasar, breath stirring Telmaine's hair.

She turned her head toward his voice, sensing even as she did the presence of magic encasing that familiar vitality. What was Balthasar? "Bal?"

His answer was to draw her to him, bedcovers and all, tucking her head against his neck, mind open to her in utter abandonment and an incontinence of thought uncharacteristic of him. She mumbled protest, both at that and the force of his embrace.

"I shall tell Mother that she appears to be awake," Merivan said over their heads. "Assuming," she added, "you do not smother her in the meantime, and add to the scandal the two of you have visited on our family."

She left in haste. Merivan never liked to be around people when she cried.

"Bal," Telmaine mumbled, "I have to breathe."

His grip eased, and she abruptly changed her mind and put her arms around him. "I thought you were gone," he whispered against her neck. Through her touch-sense, like a spill of gaming chips, came the memories: that ghastly boy insisting she was dead, the archduke failing to contradict it, crossing to the other side of sunrise, Floria . . . She caught her breath in jealous shock. "Why didn't the archduke *tell* you?" she demanded. "Vladimer said he was acting on *his* orders. Wasn't he?"

"He was. He simply did too thorough a job of making it appear you had died, using the ash, having you leave your jewelry—"

"Oh, do you have it?" It seemed of paramount importance that his silver love knot once more be resting in the hollow of her throat, that his rings be circling her fingers, all recovered from the ash of her false death. He produced all from his breast pocket and silently fastened the chain around her neck, and slid the rings onto her fingers. She remembered how cold his hands had been during their wedding ceremony, the high-society wedding an ordeal for the shy, young physician. They seemed little warmer now. They also reeked of Lightborn inks. His thoughts were troubled and complex and scarcely coherent—but she did sense his joy and profound relief at having her *back*. "What have you been *doing*, Balthasar, and why do you have that ensorcellment on you?"

"Acting as the archduke's personal envoy to the Lightborn court. It's likely to become a long-term position—"

Before she could question the thoughts behind his words, the doors swung open on a chorus of "Mama, mama, mama!" Balthasar intercepted their daughters' charge long enough to rescue Amerdale's kitten before Florilinde, with Amerdale two hands and a knee behind, threw herself on Telmaine.

Amerdale got the first words in. "Mama, you slept through my *birthday*!"

Florilinde corrected, with all the authority of her year's seniority, "She wasn't sleeping; she was *very ill*."

"Did you have a baby?"

"Amerdale!" That was Merivan, shocked.

Telmaine abandoned her maternal responsibility to correct and guide, and forgot her concerns about her husband,

and simply shook with laughter. Balthasar remained straight-faced, cradling the kitten in one hand and stroking it with the other. Its tiny mouth opened and closed, mewling unheard over the rumpus. The room filled: Merivan; the dowager Duchess Stott, who had last sonned her daughter being led to her execution; her stodgy elder brother, the current Duke Stott; her flighty younger sister, Anarysinde; her other brothers . . .

"I haven't the stamina to be an invalid," Telmaine complained, after the dowager had finally shooed them all out—knowing her family, just before celebration turned to recrimination. "I couldn't entertain all these *visitors*." Getting out of bed was easier announced than achieved; she was shocked to find how much support she needed simply to reach the armchair. Balthasar succeeded in tucking in the corners of his smile at her affront, but not the smile itself.

"And how *many* kittens did Amerdale cozen you into allowing into the household?" she said, once settled.

"Only three. One for her, one for Flori, and one for me." The rhythm was that of a six-year-old piously enumerating fair-shares. "There'll be one for you, if you want it. Of course, if we take that one, we'll not be able to leave the last of the litter behind."

"Mother of All, we'll be overrun with cats." She put her hands out, decently gloved again, and he took them tightly in his. "There were times I never thought we'd . . . Bal, what happened? After I . . . after—"

He released a hand to touch her lips, gently; behind the touch was the memory of retrieving her from the Borders and bringing her home. "You've been unconscious for nearly three weeks; that's why you're so weak, in part. Olivede thinks your magical strength will come back, given time. I must let her know. You mustn't try to use it yet, and you shouldn't try at all unless there are one or more other mages around."

"I would be happy never to use it again," she said, with feeling. "Oh, Balthasar, *who*?"

She hated that guarded professional expression that told

her he was weighing how much to tell her. "Balthasar, please. I *know* people died. Just tell me who." *Ishmael . . .*

He sighed. "We lost Farquhar Broome. The Lightborn archmage and two of the high masters. Magister Tammorn. Neill of the Shadowborn. Between the six of them, they managed to shield the rest of you, to some extent. Magistra Phoebe is still unconscious—she was most closely linked to her father. I'd have been dead, too, but for Floria. She realized what would happen to the ensorcellment on me if anything happened to the high masters. She got me into a dark room just in time."

"I will thank her for that." She breathed into her hands. "But Ishmael. Is he . . . ? Where is he?"

"My brother, who turned up in Isolde's service, told me that Ishmael simply disappeared. *Lifted*, to where, we don't know. Olivede tells me that she thinks both Magister Broome and the archmage of the Darkborn *gifted* him—as Ishmael did you—with as much of their knowledge of magic as they could. This was in the last moments of their lives, and quite possibly a sacrificial move. It may have helped him regain control. In any case, none of the surviving mages have been able to sense him. As far as I know—and I think I am close enough to both the archduke and the prince now that I would be told—no one else knows where he is, either."

"He could be dead," she whispered.

"I don't think so. If he were, and assuming we understand the situation correctly, the Curse would have failed. We are still Lightborn and Darkborn, and still alive."

"Still . . . alive?"

"A rather chilling speculation that came up in the aftermath: given Imogene's nature, would she permit release of her curse without consequences?"

"You've been spending *far* too much time around Vladimer."

He gave a rueful smile and a slight headshake. "Not Vladimer; Lysander. He was captured outside Stranhorne, searching for his son."

"And the boy?" she said, tight-lipped.

"He lived," Balthasar said. "In poor shape, but expected to recover eventually. He's with the Temple. They'll be able to train and discipline him; they've still got enough mages of sufficient strength to control him. And he's safer under Lightborn law. His twins are with the Broomes still, which is where I'd sooner they stay."

She sat straighter in her chair, the better to give force to her assertion. "If either that boy or your brother does the least thing to hurt you—"

"Lysander went south—to Isolde's stronghold—as soon as he was certain the Temple would look after the boy. I think his Shadowborn lady—Ariadne, the boy's mother—came through, but I don't know how well. I offered to help, if he needed it, but I don't believe he will take me up on that. It was a strange meeting. I suspect he might try to come to an arrangement with Vladimer. I think they might understand each other quite well."

"Vladimer," Telmaine said, suspiciously. "Why Vladimer?"

"The archduke signed an order of exile on Lord Vladimer four days ago."

"That's not fair!"

Balthasar smiled at her swift reversal. "Political necessity, given the mood in the Lightborn court. And Sylvide's death."

She chewed her fingertip. How could she have neglected Sylvide? Yet Vladimer's public trial and punishment—possibly even execution—would achieve . . . what?

Politics, she thought. When had affairs she disdained as not seemly for a lady's attention come to define the fates of people she cared for? *Despite* herself, in some cases.

Balthasar continued, thoughtfully. "I also suspect that Sejanus is using this to place Vladimer in Atholaya. Ferdenzil Mycene will surely take an interest in the choice parts, though the archduke may regard that as preferable to his interest in the Islands. Though I think his relationship with the Stranhornes will not be the same as before, which is all to the good."

"Might Mycene marry Lavender? They seemed to be getting . . . on in Stranhorne Crosstracks." He'd laugh at her if she had to admit that she'd concluded it from an argument and Lavender's concern for Mycene's bereavement. At least, she hoped he would laugh at her. She hoped he was still capable of laughter.

"Too early to say," Balthasar said. "Mycene came back to the city only a week ago to settle his father's affairs; he'd been helping the Stranhornes deal with the survivors of the Shadowborn's army." His expression was suddenly stark, haunted—remembering what? She thought of what she had sensed from him when he said he had gone to the Borders to find her. Find her amongst the dead and senseless, the dead and the hideously mutated.

She swallowed. "I . . . Could they be changed back?"

"Not and live," Balthasar said bleakly.

He drew a breath and resumed, with a self-possession she was beginning to find eerie. "The mages are interested in those territories as well, though Prince Fejelis is working hard to try to prevent the Temple from moving out of Minhorne. They're feeling vulnerable, I think, and—" He checked himself and left that thought unspoken—*for the moment,* she resolved. "Long-term, I think Sejanus would rather like Vladimer for governor of the Darkborn aspect of the territory."

"You're very free with the archduke's name, all of a sudden," she observed.

"I've got to know him better. He's a good man. He asked me to offer you his apology for what he put you through, and his thanks for everything you have done. He will, of course, offer you his thanks in person and in public, when you are fit."

"I'll forgive him what he did to me, but not what he did to you. He should have *told* you *immediately* that he hadn't had me executed."

"In the circumstances, he didn't know that Vladimer had, in fact, carried out his orders. So what could he say—that he'd tried to save you, and failed?"

There was obviously no use arguing, but she would have the matter out with Sejanus Plantageter. "This envoy post," she prompted. "That's why you have *that* ensorcellment on you."

"Yes," he said. "By contract with the Lightborn Temple, the first ever arranged between Darkborn and Lightborn. How much do you know about what happened in Stranhorne, about Sebastien—"

"I know you *beat* him," she said, fiercely. "I know you freed yourself and saved the archduke. That's *all* I need to know." Which was ridiculous of her, she knew, because as they shared a bed, she would have no choice but to know everything, but she would not let him condemn himself for weakness. "And then you went over to the Lightborn side, to prove—" A sudden, frightening thought came to her. "Are you *staying* there? Is that what you're trying to tell me?"

"No," Balthasar said, emphatically. He took her hand, turned it up, cradled it between his hands. "I did not want to get to this until you were stronger, but I suppose it is inevitable ... given that you can't help knowing what I think. Telmaine, we—Darkborn and Lightborn, earthborn and mage—came closer to disaster over this than I ever want us to come again. Without Ishmael and you and Vladimer and the Stranhornes, the Shadowborn would have overrun us all."

And without you as well, she thought.

"Without the mages, Ishmael's magic might have destroyed dozens, if not hundreds, more, and perhaps even himself. If Ishmael had died, the Curse would have failed, and we have no idea what the consequences would have been. The best outcome may have been for us to survive, but in a state of civil war."

"What has *Ishmael* to do with the Curse?"

"As best I understand it, from Olivede and others, Ishmael has inherited the sustaining of the Curse. Which means it lives as long as he does, if he cannot find a means of either sharing or releasing it. I believe we must work to bring our people to a point at which we can release the Curse. Which won't happen overnight; I don't expect it to happen in my own lifetime, but it is what I will be working toward."

"But you're not a diplomat, Balthasar. You're a physician."

He started to say something; stopped. The animation left his face. "Gil di Maurier died."

Who? The young Borders nobleman whom Balthasar had been treating for his addictions, and whom Ishmael had set to finding out where the kidnappers had taken Florilinde. He had succeeded, too, but in doing so had been badly wounded. She had done what she could to tip his chances toward survival, but covertly and timidly, still trying to protect her social position. Which she had probably lost. And Gil di Maurier was dead. "Balthasar, I'm so sorry. If I had done more—"

"I'm told he just gave up," Balthasar said, his voice clear with pain. "A version of recent events made its way into the broadsheets, of course, and no one would have thought to restrain their tongues around him. I'm sure he heard his survival being called a miracle. He wasn't a stupid man. He might have thought it was you; equally, he might have thought it was me. I'd been having some success, after all, when others had given up on him. He had a pathological aversion to magic and mages. In his weakened condition, it was too much for him to suspect that magic had kept him alive."

Telmaine began to cry. "I meant to help him."

He drew her against him, tucking her head against his cheek. "I know. So did I. But the wound and the cure were equally mortal." She could feel his grief, read his memories of the laying-out service. When everyone else had taken shelter at the tolling of the sun bell, he had waited outside by the bier as the sun came up and turned the body of Gil di Maurier to ash.

He seemed to have momentarily forgotten she knew what lay behind his words as he said, "Unfortunately, others feel and will feel as he did. I have already had letters declining my services. So I will think of this envoy post as an extension of my work with the Intercalatory Council—which it is—and know it is something that desperately needs doing. . . . And, Telmaine." He rested his forehead against hers. "Others lost far more."

She wanted to cry out the protest that he would not give up so readily, but she sensed, too clearly, that he did not want that. He had changed. He had always been dutiful and intensely civic-minded, but there was a new hardness and purpose to him.

"What will they do to Ishmael if they find him?" she whispered. "Try him for murder and sorcery?" She heard the edge to her voice as she named the charges, false when they had been laid, but now, in a cruel, twisted way, *true*.

"*Shh,*" Balthasar said. "We'll find a way. The archduke signed a formal pardon for the original charges, and we're working on preventing any more from being laid. When it's safe, we'll find him. Vladimer's started working on it already." He kissed her, a light brush of the lips, and she was not displeased to sense the claim in it. "I could use your help with the Lightborn Temple. You've at least had some contact with them, and your being a mage is more than a convenient fiction. They regard women differently on the Lightborn side."

And he had been spending entirely too much time in their company. "I am *not* a Lightborn woman," she reminded him, dangerously.

"I know that. But you're also one of the strongest surviving Darkborn mages. If the Darkborn mages had a representative in the courts—"

"I'd rather have a baby," she muttered. *I'd rather have my ordinary life back*. Unlike Merivan, she enjoyed the months in confinement, when it was not proper to be in society—assuming, of course, that society would ever admit her again. It was cowardice—she knew it was cowardice—but she could long.... Abruptly, through the touch of his skin on hers, she read his thought and reared back. *"Floria?"*

His expression was far less penitent than it ought to have been. Alas, surging to her feet and stalking out of the room needed more energy and muscle tone than she had. She started to rise and fell back. "Balthasar," she protested, detesting the waver in her voice.

"I did hope to wait until later, but yes. Floria has made a

request of me, which I am considering honoring." She snatched her hands pointedly away from his touch; he was lucky her magic was spent. "I love you, Telmaine," he said. "It tore the heart out of me finding you in Stranhorne, and hearing what you and Ishmael had done. I don't want you ever to go through that again."

She pushed down the thought of her and Ishmael's intimacy. Nagging conscience refuted her argument that it was *not* the same. "What does your being unfaithful to me have to do with that?"

That made him flinch, as he deserved. "Perhaps it doesn't, but a child born across sunrise will be one more tie between Darkborn and Lightborn. I owe her my life, three times over, already. I . . . We'll have to talk about this. . . . I don't love Floria, not as I love you; I am sure of that now, but I am, and probably always will be, her friend." He paused. "You'll know that I'm telling the truth."

And you're still *a rat bastard, Balthasar Hearne,* she thought. "And what about when we find Ishmael?" she flung back at him. "What if *he* still loves me?"

"Telmaine," he began, and stopped, and for the first time since she had awakened, that composure of his wavered and she realized how tired he was. How much rest had he had, as envoy between Darkborn and Lightborn courts, and then worrying about her? "You *know* how I feel about you," he said in a low voice.

Which was true, *curse* him.

"I will take you on *any* terms," he said, softly. "Because, even without magic, I know you. I know that, angry as you are, you wouldn't do anything that would truly break my heart."

"But you would break mine." She growled.

"No . . ."

There was a long silence. "Do you realize," he said, slowly, "that as a sixth-rank mage you might outlive me by one or two centuries? And Ishmael by even more. Isolde and Emeya were eight hundred years old when they died."

"I don't *care* about centuries." What mattered was the here and now. If she could learn how to turn him into a—a *cat*, then she need never worry about Floria White Hand again. But what use would he be as a husband then? If she could turn *Floria* into a lizard, now . . . Poor Farquhar Broome would have been appalled. Or maybe not, if he had all the experience he claimed.

"Telmaine?" he said, sounding uncertain.

She didn't have to explain what she was thinking, or what she felt, or why she had stifled a giggle, or why she was now starting to cry. She did not want to think about living without Balthasar. When he gathered her against him, she let him.

Eventually he said, "That young man who was working for you and Vladimer, Kip— "

"Kingsley," she muttered, rubbing her cheek against his collar. She would not permit the ex-prison apothecary to flaunt his dubious birth in her service.

"I think I can use him as a secretary. He's very sharp."

He was that. And impertinent, telling her that the Rivermarch would receive her, if society turned her out. "He's not trained as a secretary."

"I'm not trained as an envoy," Balthasar pointed out. "And I do need someone who is, even if they won't take the ensorcellment. I thought about speaking to Daniver di Reuther—I know he has been looking for a post—but given the circumstances of Sylvide's death, I don't know."

She would have to visit Sylvide's widower, express her regrets, try to explain if she could, let him hate her if he must. She remembered Sylvide at the archduke's breakfast, talking about visiting an aviary with her young son, spending the day there, to the horror of Daniver's dictatorial mother. She remembered Sylvide throwing her arms around her, understanding nothing except that Vladimer was threatening her dearest friend.

Others had lost more, Balthasar said. Sylvide, Gil di Maurier, Farquhar Broome, Tammorn, the Lightborn high masters she had never met, Tercelle Amberley . . . Ishmael. She had her life and her magic, and the loss of her reputation was a much smaller thing than she had ever imagined it would be, when she was desperately trying to protect it.

She had her children and her husband. As he said, she could be sure of that, even if he was no longer as entirely hers as he had been. She would learn how to maintain that ensorcellment on him herself; she was not leaving it to the Lightborn. She would help him with the Lightborn mages. And she probably wouldn't turn Floria White Hand into a lizard, no matter the temptation.

But she wouldn't tell Balthasar that quite yet.

Epilogue

Ishmael

No relief map carried the island, or none that he had ever laid hand or sonn on. It was a crumb of rock dropped from the land's table and forgotten, far to the southeast of the mainland. He supposed, when he regained enough of his reason to do so, that Isolde must once have visited here. Or perhaps one of the others. He must have taken the knowledge from someone.

He did not remember how he found the cave. It was deep enough to escape the sun, had he needed to. From an unknown predecessor he inherited a battered cooking pot and a bent ladle, a small poke of coin, and a blanket gone mildewed and rotten in the damp. The coin suggested that the previous tenant had not simply moved on. He turned it over in his fingers, trying to remember why he would think it at once insignificant and of great importance.

He had not much time for wondering, that first year. He had to survive, which he did by foraging, hunting for anything edible on the scrubby hillsides, under the rocks, and amongst the tide pools. He improvised a hook and a line and he fished, with admittedly mixed success. With a strip torn from his increasingly ragged clothes, he fashioned a slingshot and taught the greedy seagulls to be wary of him.

He knew from the first that there were Darkborn on the island, a village saved from dire inbreeding by the sea and its well-traveled pathways. When the wind was right, he could hear the bells on the buoys rocking in the swell outside the bay, and in the stillness around sunset and dawn, he could hear the sour note of their cracked warning bell. Sometimes he heard their voices as they emerged for their night's fishing. He did not realize they knew about him until, returning from the rocky beach with his thin pickings, he found a wrapped parcel laid across his threshold: a new-caught fish. Subsequent gifts contained more fish, potatoes, better fishhooks and twine, a knife, a rusty ax, a length of cloth, and even an unsigned note telling him where he could find a derelict dory, his for the mending. The kindness, the knowledge that he was not completely outcast, was the greatest gift of all. There was nothing he could give his benefactors in return but his thanks, not even a name.

Until early in the second year, when he heard the village bell ringing an alarm. He was running down the path toward the village before he knew it, knife on belt and ax in hand. The villagers gathered on the beach were too distraught to notice his sudden arrival among them, a gaunt figure with knife-barbered hair and beard, and ragged clothes covered by a length of plaid. Something had come from the sea and seized two of the children collecting crabs and clams on the water's edge. Something . . .

He strode to the edge of the sea, hand coming across to unsling his rifle, sonn hammering the water . . . but only the waves moved, and he had no rifle. . . . He felt some new force spread out from him, vastly more powerful than sonn, thrusting across the waves, down through the water, along the bed of the bay, finding the fading vitality of a child, and beside it, something hungry. Not all Shadowborn were sustained by magic and had died with their makers. He raised his ax and brought it down to cleave sand, and felt the magic cleave water and bone. The smell of brine and blood rolled in with the wind, and with a heave of its skin, like an obedient dog, the sea laid two small bodies onto the packed sand at his feet.

After a few weeks, the rumors died down, the village sages agreeing that the children's lives were a gift of the Mother. But now when the children foraged, one or more of the women or old men stood guard; they knew not to presume on the Mother's generosity. It was a pitifully weak guard, had there been anything dangerous in the bay—which he knew there was not—but he did not interfere. He was too busy. The islanders might give charity to a hapless madman washed up on their shores, but a grown man with some of his wits come home must make shift to feed himself. So he was busy learning how to make his dory watertight, how to braid a line that would not break, how to choose bait, how to weave and repair a net, and how to cast the net from a boat without following it into the water. And how to put up with being teased for getting seasick on waves gentle enough—so they said—to soothe a baby in its cradle. He found their mockery as welcome as their kindness. He also found a name to give them: Ish.

He did not leave his cave to move into the village. He trusted himself to work around them, but not to sleep, not to dream. He took to storing his supplies and provisions outside after once too often finding them strewn around him when he woke. He had too little to break it carelessly. He refused all offers to help him make the cave more livable, to enclose it, for instance, or build furniture. He would not be able to explain a splintered wall, shattered furniture—or, rather, he would not have wanted to find an explanation for such violence. And he needed time alone for the exercises that, years ago, he had learned to focus his small strength, and now had to find a way to apply to the mastery of more power than any sane man could want. The magic seemed bent on emerging, no matter how firmly he tried to sit on it.

Though he supposed he would not be considered sane by most measures, while scratching out an existence on a crumb of rock on the borders of the known world, learning to fish and taking lessons in magic from dead men, bringing to mind everything that the archmages of Darkborn and Lightborn had tried to *gift* him as they died. If he did not master this strength of his, he would be the one breeding monsters and sending out his Call.

In the third year, during the quiet seas of midsummer, he let himself be talked into crewing for a visit to the mainland.

By then he rarely woke in a shambles, and he had been able to equip his cave with a bed and a table and a chair, build a fireplace and chimney, and start on a curved stone wall to enclose the mouth of his cave before winter. He thought he dared risk leaving the island. He needed to risk leaving the island. He was half delirious with island fever. Since his sixteenth year, he had been constantly on the move, and now his world was circumscribed by the shores of one small island and the unfriendly sea. He needed off the island, whose every crack and crevice he knew, and he needed to taste and smell something other than fish. He needed news from the north, needed to know that those who had fought and lived had won what they deserved. He wanted to buy spice seeds, remembering how far to the north and long ago, he had sat in a prison cell and told Lady Telmaine that he wished to retire and grow spices on a remote island.

He needed to know that he had not killed her, too.

So he took ship to the mainland. The port was a third the size of Stranhorne Seaport, but still seemed so crowded to senses and magic after the island that he spent the first day in the fisherman's inn, sleepless, afraid he had made a serious mistake. The second night he forced himself into the market to bargain for seeds, and for the herbs for a recipe against seasickness he'd learned years ago. No surplus of magical strength seemed to suppress his body's conviction that it did not belong on water. After that, he found his way to a sailors' bar and used some of the small stash of coin to order a plate of lamb stew and start a round of drinks and gossip. The north was at peace, he learned as he nursed his beer. The mages had gone south into exile, like the archduke's half brother. Always trouble when two brothers shared the same dam but not the same sire . . . Heads nodded complacently—as if all the men in the room were the sons of the fathers they claimed. There was talk of a railway line running all the way from north to south, crossing the Shadowlands, to terminate a mere two hundred miles along the coast. A new type of steam-driven ship was being built in Minhorne. Ishmael sighed, regretting the want of sailors' wives. The one accomplishment Vladimer had ever conceded women as a sex was their effectiveness as gossips. If Ishmael wanted to know more, know about the people, he would have to go north.

He was not ready. He went back to the island instead, to fish and plant spices in the salt-soaked, barren earth, and then to learn to read the soil and change it. That autumn, the island had its best-ever potato crop, and Ishmael his first meal of seasoned sole. He wondered if he could grow lemons.

The following year, he went again to the mainland, though his purse could not produce lemon trees, and he had greater concerns than farming. The coast had suffered a summer of raids by a lawless band that had established itself in a village to the west. Ishmael, listening with a veteran's ear to the accounts of their atrocities, agreed that the raiders needed to be cleaned out before their numbers and ambition swelled further, but was appalled at the proposed tactics. With considerable bellowing and a show of his marksmanship, rusty as it was, he gained a hearing, and more roaring and storming got him time to start training the scratch troop they mustered. Not to mention to recover some of his old form. But if he could win arguments with men, he could not win them with the seasons; the onset of winter forced their attack long before he felt prepared. Fighting men was grisly, sickening work, and they took far too many casualties for him to call their success a victory. The worst was that he could neither help the wounded nor escape their pain. He stayed awake three days and nights straight, until he was staggering with exhaustion and could sleep like the dead.

The next summer he kept to the island, fished, planted spices and potatoes, guarded the bay, and built the wall that might eventually enclose an orchard. He told himself he might be wise to be circumspect, in case a report had traveled up the coast. He remembered Vladimer saying, "If a man truly intends to disappear, he must give up his old habits." He healed a seagull's broken wing, and then the gashes to his hands from the bird's beak, and stroked away a cancer that was slowly killing the village-hall cat. *Sheep,* he thought. He should keep sheep. If the shepherds in Strumheller were to be believed, sheep were susceptible to every ailment known. Sheep would give him practice.

He was sitting on a barrel outside his cave one night in late summer, mending a net. Though the night was still clear, a gale was rising in the west, and only the hardy and hungry had gone far beyond the bay. He was neither, but he was keeping vigil over those flecks of vitality in the cold sea. So it was that he sensed the ship running before the wind, even before he heard its passing bell. Sensed the ship, its living crew, and its two passengers, and that familiar, magical touch, gloriously matured and refined.

He stood up, the net sliding unnoticed from his hands. He drew a deep breath of the storm-heavy wind, aware of the sudden cessation of pain from a wound that had not closed until now.

<Lady Telmaine. How good it is t'speak to you again.>

About the Author

Alison Sinclair is the author of *Legacies*, *Blueheart*, and *Cavalcade* (which was nominated for the Arthur C. Clark Award), as well as *Darkborn* and *Lightborn*. She lives in Montreal.

Connect Online

www.alisonsinclair.com

twitter.com/alixinc

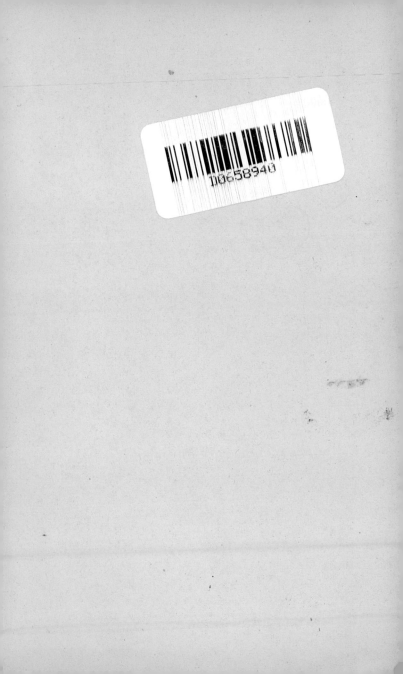

NET FORCE 3

Paru dans Le Livre de Poche :

LE CARDINAL DU KREMLIN

CODE SSN

DANGER IMMÉDIAT

DETTE D'HONNEUR

JEUX DE GUERRE

NET FORCE
1. Net Force
2. Programmes fantômes

OCTOBRE ROUGE

L'OURS ET LE DRAGON

POWER GAMES
1. Politika
2. Ruthless.com
3. Ronde furtive
4. Frappe biologique

RAINBOW SIX

SANS AUCUN REMORDS

LA SOMME DE TOUTES LES PEURS

SUR ORDRE

TEMPÊTE ROUGE

Tom Clancy et Steve Pieczenik présentent

TOM CLANCY

Net Force 3

Attaques de nuit

ROMAN TRADUIT DE L'AMÉRICAIN PAR JEAN BONNEFOY

ALBIN MICHEL

Titre original :

TOM CLANCY'S NET FORCE
NIGHT MOVES

Ceci est une œuvre de fiction. Les personnages et les situations décrits dans ce livre sont purement imaginaires : toute ressemblance avec des personnages ou des événements existant ou ayant existé ne serait que pure coïncidence.

L'histoire de l'épée se confond avec l'histoire de l'humanité.

Richard BURTON.

Chausser les lunettes de la science dans l'espoir de découvrir la réponse à tout ce qu'on observe est synonyme d'aveuglement intérieur.

J. Frank DOBIE.

Prologue

Vendredi 1er avril 2011, 2 : 15
Faubourgs de Sahiwal, Pakistan

Le milieu de la nuit, et la température flirtait encore avec les trente-deux degrés. L'humidité était si élevée que la sueur ne s'évaporait pas et, faute de pouvoir s'évacuer, l'âcre transpiration imbibait les uniformes noirs des hommes. Avril seulement, et déjà un nouveau record de chaleur au Pendjab, presque quarante-six degrés, avec en gros des prévisions identiques pour le lendemain. Beurk.

Trois des hommes en treillis trempé étaient tapis dans l'ombre un peu plus profonde d'une rangée de broussailles rabougries, à quelques dizaines de mètres de la voie ferrée. Ils attendaient.

Au loin, un sifflement annonça l'approche du train.

« Ça ne devrait plus être long », observa Bhattacharya. À cause de son obésité, les autres le surnommaient parfois entre eux Ganesha, du nom du dieu-éléphant, mais sans jamais oser le lui dire en face. Nonobstant sa corpulence, Bhattacharya était aussi coléreux qu'agile, et une fois mis en branle, il s'avérait être un formidable adversaire. Il y avait deux ans encore, il était officier dans l'armée, avec le grade de colonel. Mais, lors d'une garden-party à Panipat, il avait poignardé un officier de même rang au prétexte qu'il l'avait insulté, et seule la présence bienvenue d'un médecin également invité avait sauvé le gros homme d'une inculpation pour meurtre. Toujours est-il que cela lui avait suffi pour être arrêté et dégradé sur-le-champ avec le choix d'une alternative simple : la prison ou l'unité spéciale.

Comme d'autres formations clandestines de par le monde, l'unité spéciale n'avait aucune existence officielle. Aucun des hommes ne portait d'armes ou d'équipement de l'armée régulière. Les fusils d'assaut étaient des AK de surplus chinois, les pistolets étaient allemands, les poignards japonais. Leur matériel de transmission venait de Nouvelle-Zélande, leurs bottes d'Indonésie et leurs tenues d'Australie. Aucun ne portait sur lui le moindre article susceptible de l'identifier, et encore moins de l'identifier comme un soldat indien. Et lors d'une opération, aucun homme ne devait se laisser capturer. Si l'éventualité devait se présenter, on escomptait un prompt suicide par balle ou à l'arme blanche. Le geste n'était pas aussi héroïque qu'il pouvait le paraître. Quiconque refusait d'accomplir son devoir n'avait de toute façon pas longtemps à vivre : avant d'embarquer pour cette mission, chaque homme avait dû absorber un poison à action lente. S'il en revenait, on lui fournirait l'antidote, et il s'en tirerait juste avec quelques jours de grippe carabinée. Si, en revanche, il ne revenait pas pour telle ou telle raison, il mourrait au bout de longues et atroces souffrances en comparaison desquelles le suicide était une promenade de santé. Bref, s'il fallait en arriver là, mieux valait choisir la sortie rapide.

En Inde, dès qu'il s'agissait d'opérations militaires secrètes, on faisait appel à l'US. Une majorité de pays disposaient d'unités équivalentes, même si presque tous se seraient empressés de nier pareille allégation.

Cette mission était tout aussi secrète que les autres. Se glisser furtivement au Pakistan pour effectuer une opération clandestine était une entreprise pour le moins risquée. C'est que les Pakistanais étaient gens susceptibles – compte tenu de la situation politique, on pouvait aisément le comprendre.

Rahman était allongé au sol près de Ganesha. Originaire de New Delhi, la quarantaine, l'homme n'était pas issu d'une caste particulière. Grand et mince, c'était tout l'opposé de Bhattacharya. Rahman connaissait bien cette région du Pakistan, ayant naguère appartenu aux gardes-frontières de l'armée indienne, les fantassins placés en première ligne face aux gardes pakistanais stationnés de l'autre côté des barbelés au poste de Wagah. Là, chaque soir, les adversaires se jouaient le rituel d'agression stylisé qui ponctuait le lever quotidien des couleurs et la sonnerie cérémonielle du clairon. Les foules convergeaient de kilomètres à la ronde pour assister à ce simulacre de bataille, acclamant chaque camp comme s'il s'agissait d'un match de foot.

Le troisième homme de la bande était Harbhajan Singh et, comme de juste, on l'appelait le Sikh. Bien que Singh fût un nom sikh relativement répandu, ses compagnons l'avaient en fait baptisé ainsi en hommage au soldat qui était parvenu au *moksha* – l'illumination – alors qu'il patrouillait dans les montagnes près de Nathu-La, le long de la frontière chinoise, dans les années soixante. Tout ce qu'on avait retrouvé de lui, c'était ses lunettes d'alpiniste, son fusil et son casque. Aujourd'hui encore, le fantôme de Singh continuait à errer dans le secteur : les Chinois le voyaient souvent faire le guet au sommet d'une montagne ou traverser à pied sec un torrent. L'armée s'était longtemps refusée à croire de telles balivernes, jusqu'à ce qu'un général en tournée d'inspection se montre irrespectueux envers le fantôme et, en guise de châtiment, se fasse prestement tuer dans un accident d'hélicoptère au retour dans ses quartiers. À dater de ce jour, tous les nouveaux commandants de la région avaient pris grand soin d'y envoyer leur voiture personnelle une fois l'an, afin de conduire Singh jusqu'à la gare pour sa permission annuelle. Et on ne manquait pas non plus de louer au fantôme une place dans le train. Ça ne devait pas être inintéressant d'être le chauffeur d'une telle équipée, même si aucun n'avait jamais prétendu avoir vu de ses yeux Singh monter en voiture ou dans le wagon.

Tout cela était sans aucun doute fascinant mais ne contribuait guère à réduire l'inconfort que Singh éprouvait sous sa barbe et son turban, dans la touffeur de la nuit tropicale. Même si son trisaïeul avait vécu près de Lahore, quelques kilomètres à peine un peu plus au nord, Singh avait passé l'essentiel de son existence à Madras, dans le golfe du Bengale ; la température était certes élevée à longueur d'année, mais au moins la brise de mer rendait-elle la chaleur supportable. Il avait certes également passé plusieurs années à Calcutta, où il faisait encore plus chaud qu'à Madras, mais même Calcutta n'était pas une étuve comme le Pendjab. L'endroit le plus torride de la planète, à ce qu'on racontait. Il voulait bien le croire.

« Le voilà, dit Bhattacharya. Vous voyez les phares ? »

Singh et Rahman acquiescèrent dans leur barbe. Le

long de la voie, les autres « mercenaires » devaient déjà se préparer à l'assaut. Ils étaient soixante en tout, et alors que certains allaient sans doute y laisser leur vie, ils ne seraient regrettés que de leurs camarades. Vous n'intégriez l'US que si vous étiez seul au monde, sans femme ni famille, ni lien d'aucune sorte. Bref, uniquement si on pouvait se passer de vous.

Le train siffla de nouveau, plus proche.

Agrippant son clone d'AK-47, Singh aspira l'air nocturne fétide et chaud. Il n'était pas un très bon Sikh, il n'avait plus pratiqué les rites depuis de longues années, mais cela ne l'empêcha pas de répéter à plusieurs reprises le nom de Dieu. Ça ne pouvait pas faire de mal.

Le train apparut. Invisibles du mécanicien, les sabots inclinés de deux taquets dérailleurs [1] avaient été soudés aux rails, juste à la sortie d'une courbe en devers sur la gauche.

Le train spécial Multan-Lahore allait marquer sous peu un arrêt aussi brusque qu'imprévu.

Singh retint son souffle lorsqu'il entendit l'engin haletant heurter les taquets. Le *clang !* sonore fut aussitôt suivi d'un crissement de métal. La loco dérailla, creusant un profond sillon dans la terre du talus. Un concert de craquements assourdissants emplit l'air, tandis que la machine se couchait et continuait de labourer le sol.

Les cinq ou six premières voitures du convoi

---

1. Coins métalliques posés ou boulonnés sur les rails d'une voie de garage, avant son branchement sur une voie principale et destinés, comme leur nom l'indique, à protéger celle-ci en faisant dérailler tout wagon parti accidentellement en dérive (*N.d.T.*).

déraillèrent à leur tour, culbutant les unes sur les autres comme un train miniature. De nouveaux craquements sinistres montèrent dans la nuit, accompagnés d'un épais nuage de poussière et de fumée.

Singh s'était déjà relevé et courait vers le convoi encore lancé sur son erre. Plusieurs wagons étaient restés sur la voie ; l'un d'eux, un fourgon aux portes fermées, se trouvait juste devant lui. La porte coulissa et cinq gardes-frontières pakistanais sautèrent à l'extérieur.

Singh les cueillit d'une rafale. À ses côtés, Rahman avait également fait parler les armes, tout comme Ganesha : les Pakistanais s'effondrèrent, hachés par une grêle de balles chemisées.

Désolé, les Paks, vous ferez mieux la prochaine fois.

On entendit d'autres coups de feu. La nuit était illuminée par les éclairs des tirs et des explosions de grenades. Éclat blanc aveuglant du phosphore, rouge des torches... Un spectacle haut en couleur.

Attaquants et défenseurs étaient en nombre égal, mais les troupes de l'US avaient l'avantage de la surprise et de la catastrophe ferroviaire. En quelques minutes, tout était fini. Plusieurs blessés hurlaient de douleur, mais quelques coups de feu mirent rapidement fin à leurs cris. Singh, Bhattacharya et Rahman se rendirent au fourgon qui leur avait été désigné. Il était vide mais ce n'était pas un problème. Ils posèrent les explosifs, réglèrent les détonateurs.

« On dégage ! s'exclama Rahman. Vite ! »

Tous trois rejoignirent prestement le reste de la troupe. Ils n'avaient que quelques secondes pour décamper. Personne n'aurait le temps de trouver les charges et de les désamorcer – quand bien même il y aurait encore un survivant pour y songer.

Un coup de feu claqua sur la gauche. Singh pivota, arrosa l'endroit où il avait repéré l'éclair de la détonation, lâchant de courtes rafales de trois balles. Il entendit un cri. Un des Pakistanais qui avait fait le mort. Il l'était pour de bon, maintenant.

Mais son ultime coup de feu avait fait mouche.

Bhattacharya s'effondra.

Singh freina des quatre fers. Courant toujours, Rahman ne l'attendit pas.

Le gros avait reçu la balle en pleine poitrine, légèrement de côté, sa tenue camouflée était déjà imbibée de sang, tache noire et luisante dans la nuit. Il leva les yeux sur Singh. « Je suis touché... Tire-moi de là, le Sikh. »

Singh hocha la tête. « Bien sûr. » Il pointa le fusil d'assaut sur le front de Bhattacharya, pressa la détente, tira une balle. Le corps de l'homme eut un spasme et retomba, inerte.

Pas le temps de s'attarder à faire des prières. Singh prit ses jambes à son cou.

Quelques secondes plus tard, bruit et lumière déchirèrent ce qui restait de calme dans la touffeur nocturne. L'explosion du train avait dû être visible à des kilomètres à la ronde.

Et elle devait être ressentie, d'une autre manière, sur la planète entière.

1

Vendredi 1er avril 2011
Hampton Court, Angleterre

Le palais dont le premier occupant royal avait été Henri VIII, au XIVe siècle, était immense. Les bâtiments de pierre couvraient plus de trois hectares, et dix fois plus si l'on comptait les pelouses et jardins clos entourant les corps de logis. Les chambres étaient immenses, hautes de plafond, dotées de vastes fenêtres, et d'âtres en pierre si vastes qu'on pouvait se glisser sous le manteau de cheminée sans se cogner la tête. La plupart des salles étaient vides, à l'exception de quelques tentures gigantesques et de lustres baroques. Quelques chambres étaient meublées de monstrueux lits à baldaquins ou de bureaux et de chaises. Il y avait des galeries de tableaux où étaient accrochées des toiles ternies par les ans. La plus grande partie de l'aile où ils se trouvaient présentement, celle des appartements du roi, avait brûlé dans un incendie accidentel au milieu des années quatre-vingt. On l'avait restaurée depuis pour lui redonner l'aspect qu'elle était censée avoir au XVIIIe siècle.

Alex Michaels était impressionné par les lieux. Difficile d'imaginer que quelqu'un ait pu réellement vivre dans un endroit pareil.

Il leur avait coûté quinze euros chacun pour visiter

le château, après le voyage en métro depuis Londres. Ils avaient traversé à pied la Tamise sur le pont d'Hampton Court pour accéder à l'entrée principale. Au cours des ans, Michaels avait pas mal bourlingué, surtout depuis qu'il était devenu commandant de la Net Force, l'unité spéciale du FBI[1], mais il avait réussi à n'être encore jamais venu en Angleterre. Toni et lui avaient donc décidé d'ajouter quelques jours de vacances à la semaine qu'on leur avait allouée pour assister à la Conférence internationale sur la criminalité informatique. Ils avaient besoin de souffler un peu ; leurs relations personnelles étaient en effet devenues quelque peu chaotiques ces dernières semaines.

Et c'est pourquoi ils se retrouvaient ici, dans l'immense palais des têtes couronnées, mais si vaste fût-il, Hampton Court n'était pas assez grand pour contenir la colère bouillonnante de Toni Fiorella. Michaels s'attendait à la voir exploser d'une seconde à l'autre, et les réduire en cendres, lui et la salle où ils pourraient se trouver à ce moment. Ils n'étaient pas mariés mais il semblait bien que la lune de miel était finie, malgré tous ses efforts pour éviter une telle issue.

Quinze euros, c'était une jolie somme pour avoir le droit de déambuler deux heures dans un vieux château moisi. S'il n'avait pas eu la calculette intégrée au virgil*[2] accroché à sa ceinture, il aurait été

1. Cf. *Net Force 1* et *Net Force 2, Programmes fantômes*, Albin Michel, 1999 ; Le Livre de Poche, n°s 37018 et 37019.

2. Pour les termes techniques, néologismes et sigles signalés par un astérisque, on se reportera au glossaire en fin de volume (*N.d.T.*).

bien en peine de savoir combien cela représentait au juste. Les conversions monétaires n'avaient jamais été son fort.

Il indiqua à Toni le générateur du faisceau de sécurité, encastré dans le potelet où était accrochée la lourde cordelière de velours censée dissuader les touristes d'aller s'asseoir dans les sièges d'époque. « Avance un peu et je parie que tu vas déclencher toutes les sirènes d'alarme. »

Toni demeura coite.

Seigneur, qu'est-ce que j'ai bien encore pu faire ?

« Tu vas bien ?

– Je vais très bien. »

Michaels inspira lentement avant de pousser un long soupir tandis qu'ils poursuivaient leur visite en silence. Un type en costume qu'on aurait pu croire sorti de la cour du roi Henri se tenait sous le portrait d'un couple hideux flanqué de deux chiens bien plus beaux qu'eux, et décrivait à un groupe de touristes la signification du tableau. L'homme en costume avait ce que Michaels appelait un accent de la haute, une voix aux intonations snobs, très classe.

Avant le début de sa liaison avec Toni, Michaels avait été marié. Il avait divorcé depuis. Les femmes avaient une façon de dire « Je vais très bien », sur un ton sec et brusque, qui signifiait tout le contraire. Il avait appris à ne pas approfondir la question tant qu'il n'était pas vraiment prêt à savoir ce qui clochait – et à l'apprendre parfois avec un nombre de décibels équivalant au niveau sonore d'un concert de death metal quand on est installé debout au premier rang face aux enceintes. Est-ce que Toni allait lui gueuler dessus dans la grande salle d'apparat ? Ou préféreraitelle attendre qu'ils se retrouvent dans l'une des petites salles Tudor où le cardinal Wolsey avait jadis entrepris ses études ? Pour l'heure, si Michaels se hasardait à la toucher, il était à peu près certain de se brûler les doigts. Elle était en rogne, et il était presque sûr que c'était après lui.

Pourquoi la vie ne pouvait-elle pas être simple ? Deux êtres s'aiment, ils se mettent ensemble et vivent heureux jusqu'à la fin de leurs jours...

C'était sans doute ce qu'avait cru Anne Boleyn quand elle s'était mise en ménage avec l'autre gros barbu, tu te souviens ? lui serina sa petite voix intérieure.

Il dit à sa petite voix intérieure de la boucler.

Elle attendit qu'ils fussent dehors, au milieu d'une pelouse humide et froide en direction des jardins nord avec leur labyrinthe de buis entretenus avec soin, pour enfin daigner lui adresser la parole. Il l'observait du coin de l'œil, admirant sa démarche athlétique, ses traits et sa silhouette magnifiques. Elle était son assistante depuis son entrée à la Net Force, et c'était une excellente collaboratrice. Elle avait également une douzaine d'années de moins que lui et c'était une Italienne du Bronx, belle, intelligente, coriace, adepte d'un art martial indonésien appelé le *pentjak silat*. Elle le lui avait enseigné et il faisait des progrès, mais si jamais il avait fallu en venir aux mains et qu'elle soit pour de bon en rogne, elle aurait pu l'étriller sans peine, les doigts dans le nez. C'était une sensation bizarre de savoir que la femme que vous aimiez était à tout moment capable de vous flanquer une raclée.

Quand elle parla, ce fut d'une voix calme, égale,

sans colère apparente. « Pourquoi as-tu envoyé Marshall à la réunion du CICO à Kaboul ? »

Nouveau soupir de Michaels. Oui, pourquoi ? Parce que l'Afghanistan n'était pas vraiment un endroit où il avait envie de savoir Toni. C'était un pays arriéré, les femmes y étaient des citoyennes de quatrième catégorie, passant après les hommes, les garçons et les chevaux, où l'on comptait de fréquents attentats terroristes contre les étrangers, surtout les Américains. Il n'avait pas envie de lui faire courir de risque. Mais il ne pouvait pas le lui avouer de but en blanc. Alors, il répondit : « Marshall voulait y aller. Je ne savais pas que toi aussi tu en avais envie.

– Pas particulièrement, répondit-elle.

– Eh bien voilà, ça c'est fait comme ça. Tu n'y étais pas obligée. C'est pas un problème, si ? »

C'eût été trop beau. Elle insista : « J'étais prête. J'aurais dû y aller.

– Mais tu viens de me dire que tu n'en avais pas envie. »

Elle s'arrêta pour le regarder. Bon sang, c'est vrai qu'elle était superbe, même quand elle était en rogne contre lui. Peut-être même plus encore quand elle l'était.

« Là n'est pas la question. J'étais prête, tu aurais dû m'envoyer, que je le veuille ou non. Pourquoi ne l'as-tu pas fait ? »

Il avait une excellente mémoire, qualité indispensable pour se livrer aux tergiversations, et pourtant, en définitive, Michaels ne savait pas trop bien mentir. Oh, bien sûr, il pouvait dire à une fille qu'elle était bien coiffée même si c'était faux, ou sourire en faisant mine d'apprécier le mauvais goût vestimentaire d'un supérieur sans mettre les pieds dans le plat, mais au-delà de ces mensonges tout bêtes destinés à ménager les susceptibilités, il n'avait pas de goût foncier pour la tromperie. Elle l'avait coincé, il avait essayé d'esquiver sans succès, alors il n'était plus question désormais de biaiser. Il hocha la tête et décida de jouer franc-jeu : « Parce que je ne voulais pas t'envoyer dans un endroit où tu aurais pu courir des risques.

– Ça, c'était ton opinion. » Et elle se remit en route.

Il la rattrapa. « Écoute, Toni. Je t'aime. Quel mal y a-t-il à vouloir t'éviter le danger ?

– Pour un amant, aucun. Je trouve même ça plutôt agréable. Mais pour un collègue dans le renseignement, non, ce n'est pas bien. Tu sais pertinemment que je peux me débrouiller toute seule.

– Certes », admit-il. Il le savait, il l'avait vue à plusieurs reprises en faire la brillante démonstration. Elle était même plus douée que lui en cas d'épreuve de force ; n'empêche, ce n'était pas non plus Superwoman.

« Je veux que tu me traites comme n'importe lequel de tes gars. »

Il sourit. « Ça serait tricher. Je ne peux pas t'imaginer ainsi et même si je le faisais, ma foi, ça ne m'intéresserait pas. J'aime bien les filles. Surtout toi. »

En réponse, elle lui adressa un tout petit sourire, presque imperceptible, elle n'était donc pas si fâchée que ça. « Enfin, je parlais du bureau. J'apprécie tout à fait d'être traitée en femme quand on est entre nous.

– Je comprends.

– Vraiment ? C'est important pour moi, tu sais. Je veux bien que tu me prennes par la main quand on marche au clair de lune, mais pas quand on est au boulot. Tu dois savoir faire le clivage entre vie privée et vie professionnelle, Alex.

– D'accord, je vais le faire. La prochaine fois que tu es prête, tu pars, où que ce soit. »

Son sourire s'agrandit. « Impec. À présent, est-ce que tu crois qu'on pourrait se trouver du chocolat quelque part ? »

Tous deux éclatèrent de rire ; Alex éprouva un immense soulagement. C'était leur premier voyage en Angleterre à tous les deux, et l'un des détails qu'ils avaient remarqué dès leur arrivée était la présence, partout, de distributeurs de chocolat : dans les boutiques, sur les quais de gare et jusque dans les cafés. C'était devenu une blague entre eux : trouver du chocolat. Ils s'attendaient l'un et l'autre à prendre quinze kilos et revenir aux États-Unis lestés de bajoues.

Le virgil d'Alex joua les premières mesures de la *Fanfare For A Common Man* d'Aaron Copland : une communication pour lui. Il décrocha l'appareil de sa ceinture, consulta l'afficheur : l'appel émanait du bureau directorial du FBI.

« Sympa », nota Toni, faisant allusion au thème musical. Elle agita le doigt comme un chef d'orchestre.

« Jay a encore dû se glisser dans mon bureau et reprogrammer la sonnerie. Enfin, c'est toujours mieux que la dernière fois, où il n'avait rien trouvé de plus malin que de me mettre le *Bad to the Bone* de George Thorogood.

– Ta-da-da-da-da-doum ! chanta Toni.

– Tous les gens autour de moi ont un sens de l'humour particulièrement tordu », observa-t-il avant de prendre la communication : « Alex Michaels.

– Ne quittez pas, je vous passe le directeur », répondit une secrétaire.

Toni le regarda et il plaqua la main sur le micro de son virgil. « La boss...

– Comme je peux regretter que Walt Carver ait eu cet infarctus, observa Toni.

– Moi, je pense au contraire qu'il n'est pas mécontent. Ça lui a donné une excuse pour prendre sa retraite et partir à la pêche. Ça ne fait jamais qu'un mois, on devrait lui donner une chance...

– Commandant, ici Melissa Allison. Désolée d'interrompre vos vacances, mais nous avons ici une situation dont vous devez prendre connaissance. »

Le visage de la nouvelle patronne du service apparut sur l'écran à cristaux liquides. Alex pressa aussitôt la touche du mode visuel tout en élevant le virgil jusqu'à découvrir en incrustation au coin de l'écran la vignette de sa propre image prise par la caméra de l'appareil.

Âgée de quarante-six ans, Allison était une rousse mince, à la voix et l'attitude froides pour ne pas dire glaciales. Sa nomination avait été politique. Avocate de formation, elle n'avait aucune expérience de terrain mais une connaissance encyclopédique du contenu de dizaines de placards politiques... La rumeur voulait que certains membres influents du Congrès aient fait pression sur le président pour qu'on lui offre la direction du FBI, laissée vacante après le léger accident cardiaque de Walt Carver, aussi s'était-elle bien gardée de faire du zèle. En dehors de deux réunions et de quelques notes de service, Michaels n'avait pas encore eu l'occasion de se frotter à elle.

« Allez-y.

– Il y a quelques heures, un commando armé non identifié a attaqué un train pakistanais près de la frontière indienne, tuant une douzaine de gardes avant de faire exploser le convoi. Celui-ci transportait une cargaison ultra-secrète de composants électroniques destinés au programme nucléaire militaire pakistanais.

– Je croyais que les deux pays avaient signé le traité de non-dissémination.

– Certes, mais aucun n'en tient le moindre compte. Le gouvernement pakistanais est convaincu que l'agression terroriste est l'œuvre d'une unité spéciale de l'armée indienne.

– Ont-ils une preuve de cela ?

– Pas suffisante pour déclencher une guerre. Jusqu'ici... mais ils font tout pour en avoir une. »

Michaels regarda l'image minuscule de la directrice. « Sauf votre respect, madame, en quoi cela nous regarde-t-il ? N'est-ce pas une affaire pour le contre-espionnage ?

– Ils sont dessus, mais s'il faut en croire les Pakistanais, il était rigoureusement impossible que qui que ce soit ait pu connaître le contenu du convoi. Or, les terroristes ont eu tout le temps de prendre position pour leur embuscade et les Pakistanais soutiennent que ce n'est pas possible.

– Et pourtant, ça l'a bien été, observa Michaels.

– Leur agent de liaison avec la CIA leur a signalé qu'il n'y avait que quatre personnes en tout et pour tout au courant du chargement et de l'itinéraire emprunté. Les caisses étaient anonymes, manutentionnaires et cheminots ignoraient tout de leur contenu.

– Une coïncidence, peut-être ? Une attaque menée au hasard ?

– Dix-neuf trains sont passés au même endroit au cours des vingt-quatre heures qui ont précédé l'attentat. Un seul convoi transportait du matériel d'une importance stratégique.

– Alors, quelqu'un aura vendu la mèche.

– Les Pakistanais jurent que non. Personne n'a eu l'occasion de les informer ; une fois l'opération lancée, trois des quatre individus qui étaient au courant se trouvaient ensemble ; quant au dernier – qui se trouve être le chef de la police secrète –, il n'a réussi à décoder le message électronique annonçant l'envoi qu'une heure seulement avant l'attaque. Une histoire de panne informatique sur son système. Même s'il avait voulu balancer l'information, il n'aurait pas eu le temps.

– Alors, quelqu'un aura intercepté le message et craqué le code.

– Et c'est là que nous intervenons, expliqua Allison. Le problème est que le logiciel de chiffrement était censé être à toute épreuve, une combinaison de nombres premiers de plusieurs centaines de chiffres. D'après la CIA, il faudrait faire tourner un Super-Cray à plein temps, jour et nuit, pendant un million d'années, pour casser le code. »

Formidable, songea Michaels. Il répondit :

« Je vais demander à mes gars d'y jeter un œil.

– Parfait. Tenez-moi au courant. »

Son image disparut de l'écran comme elle coupait la communication.

Toni, qui avait entendu leur dialogue, hocha la tête. « Im-pos-sible, fit-elle.

– Exact. Le difficile, on s'en occupe tout de suite. L'impossible prend un peu plus de temps. Allez, viens, on va voir ce labyrinthe.

– Tu n'appelles pas Jay ?

– Ça peut bien attendre encore quelques minutes. »

2

Vendredi 1er avril 2011
Londres

Le garçon arriva avec le gin-tonic qu'il posa sur la table près du profond fauteuil en cuir capitonné où Lord Geoffrey Goswell était assis, absorbé dans la lecture du *Times*.

Les marchés japonais faisaient le grand plongeon, la Bourse américaine se tenait bien et le métal jaune était en hausse.

Les prévisions météo sur Londres annonçaient de la pluie pour le lendemain.

Bref, rien de bien renversant.

Goswell leva les yeux. Il regarda le garçon qui était resté attendre une éventuelle requête et lui adressa un salut militaire. « Merci, Paddington, ce sera tout.

– Milord. »

Le serveur s'éclipsa sans bruit. Un type bien, ce brave vieux Paddington. Cela faisait combien de temps qu'il livrait les journaux et servait à boire au club ? Trente, trente-cinq ans ? Un homme poli, efficace, sachant se tenir, toujours discret. Ah, si tous les domestiques pouvaient avoir ne fût-ce que la moitié de ses manières. S'il y avait quelqu'un à ne pas oublier pour les étrennes, c'était assurément Paddington.

Installé à l'autre bout du tapis d'Orient ovale sombre

et élimé, Bellworth grommela derrière son journal en exhalant un nuage embaumé de cigare cubain. Il abaissa le quotidien – encore un de ces torchons à scandale : – le *Sun* ou le *New York Times* – et regarda Goswell par-dessus la feuille : « Je n'arrive pas à croire ce que vient d'annoncer le président américain. Qu'ils s'entêtent à ce point avec ces fadaises, ça me dépasse. Si notre Premier ministre se comportait de la sorte, il se retrouverait éjecté vite fait, et ce serait amplement mérité. »

Sir Harold Bellworth, quatre-vingt-deux ans, était de la classe 47, et donc de huit ans l'aîné de Goswell.

Ce dernier sourit poliment au vieillard. « Ma foi, c'est tout à fait typique des Américains, ça, n'est-ce pas ?

– Arrumph, oui, évidemment. » Telle était la remarque de circonstance qui permettait de répondre une bonne fois pour toutes à tant et tant de questions. Il y avait la manière britannique, et puis il y avait toutes les autres. Ma foi, c'est tout à fait typique des Américains, n'est-ce pas ? Ou des Français, des Allemands, ou, à Dieu ne plaise, des Espagnols. Franchement, que pouvait-on espérer, venant d'étrangers, sinon ce genre d'agissements ?

« Arrumph. » Harry releva son journal et poursuivit sa lecture.

Goswell avisa la grosse horloge au-dessus de la bibliothèque. Cinq heures et demie, déjà. Il aurait dû sans doute demander à Paddington d'appeler Stephens. Le trajet jusqu'aux Ifs allait prendre du temps, surtout un vendredi soir, avec toute la populace prête à se ruer hors de la capitale pour le sacro-saint week-end, mais on n'y pouvait rien. En temps normal, il restait à

Portman House, en ville, jusqu'au samedi, puis gagnait tranquillement sa résidence secondaire dans le Sussex, mais avec cet ami scientifique, Peter Bascomb-Coombs, qui débarquait pour dîner à vingt et une heures trente, il n'avait guère le choix. Compte tenu des embouteillages, il pouvait encore s'estimer heureux s'il arrivait à l'heure. Il replia les pages financières et les déposa près de son gin-tonic, saisit le verre, but une grande lampée. *Ah !* Il le reposa.

Quelques instants plus tard, Paddington apparut à l'improviste. « Milord ?

– Oui ? Demandez à Stephens de m'amener la voiture, voulez-vous ?

– Bien sûr, milord. Voulez-vous du thé et des sandwiches pour le trajet ?

– Non, j'ai un dîner prévu à la campagne. » Il congédia le domestique d'un geste un peu las.

Paddington sortit pour trouver le chauffeur. Goswell se leva, sortit la montre du gousset de son gilet, en compara l'heure avec celle de l'horloge du club.

Harry quitta de nouveau des yeux son quotidien. « Alors comme ça, sur le départ ?

– Oui, un rendez-vous avec mes scientifiques, à la campagne.

– Des scientifiques... » Dans sa bouche, le terme résonnait comme s'il avait dit « des voleurs » ou « des putes ». Il hocha la tête. « Eh bien, bon vent, dans ce cas. Au fait, vous êtes-vous décidé à abattre ce sacré bon Dieu d'if qui pousse derrière la serre ?

– Sûrement pas. Je compte bien d'un jour à l'autre lui donner comme engrais votre vieille carcasse. »

Harry partit d'un rire sifflant de fumeur. « C'est moi qui danserai sur votre tombe, jeune parvenu. Et en me réchauffant les mains à ce satané bois d'if, que je me ferai un plaisir de brûler dans ma cheminée. »

Les deux hommes échangèrent un sourire. C'était une vieille blague entre eux. Les ifs étaient souvent plantés dans les cimetières, et comme ils paraissaient toujours y prospérer, la légende voulait que les sels minéraux des corps en décomposition leur procurent un excellent engrais. Le grand if derrière la serre du domaine de Goswell faisait bien vingt-cinq mètres de haut, et il était sans doute âgé de quatre siècles. Depuis des années, Goswell menaçait de l'amender avec les cendres de son vieil ami.

Goswell nota que sa montre avançait d'une petite minute. C'était une Waltham en or, sans grande valeur, mais elle avait appartenu à son oncle Patrick qui était mort durant le Blitz, et il en avait hérité étant adolescent. Il en avait de meilleures qui marchaient à la perfection, des Cartier et des Rolex, sans compter deux petits bijoux suisses faits main, qui coûtaient chacun le prix d'une voiture neuve. La Waltham était un modèle tout simple, elle n'indiquait ni la date ni les infos financières, on ne pouvait pas non plus la porter à son oreille et s'en servir comme téléphone. Ce n'était qu'une montre toute bête, et c'est ce qu'il aimait.

Il remit la Waltham dans son gousset et se dirigea vers la sortie. Le temps de regagner la rue, Stephens aurait amené la Bentley 54. Dans le même ordre d'idées, il préférait la Bentley à la Rolls. C'était foncièrement la même voiture, mais sans la calandre ostentatoire, et un véritable gentleman se devait de fuir toute marque d'ostentation, n'est-ce pas ?

Il écouterait les infos de la BBC dans la voiture. Pour voir si les basanés d'Inde et du Pakistan avaient déjà commencé à se taper dessus à la suite du petit... intermède qu'il leur avait concocté. Ce serait vraiment chouette si, à force de se bombarder mutuellement, ils en revenaient au bon vieux temps du Raj de l'Empire, qu'on puisse leur enseigner à nouveau les bienfaits de la civilisation.

Ce ne serait que justice, non ?

Vendredi
Dans le Raj britannique, aux Indes

Jay Gridley surfait sur le Net, maître de tout ce que son regard embrassait.

Pour l'heure, il était dans un scénario de RV* – de réalité virtuelle – qu'il avait conçu tout spécialement pour la nouvelle mission qu'Alex Michaels lui avait confiée. Dans le MR* – le monde réel – il était assis devant sa console informatique au QG de la Net Force, à Quantico, Virginie, les yeux et les oreilles recouverts de capteurs, les mains et le torse bardés de câbles afin que ses plus imperceptibles mouvements puissent être retranscrits en impulsions de contrôle. Mais en RV, Jay portait un casque colonial, un short kaki et une chemise kaki amidonnée, avec des chaussettes montantes, de gros godillots, et un revolver Webley Mark 3 calibre 38 accroché à la ceinture. Il était juché sur le dos d'un éléphant d'Asie, assis sous un dais près du rajah local. Au-dessus de leur tête, le soleil de l'après-midi carbonisait les alentours, ratatinant à égalité hommes, bêtes et végétation sous le poids de sa chaleur torride. Devant eux, des autochtones basanés vêtus de simples pagnes tapaient sur des plaques métalliques à coups de bâton, agitaient des boîtes de conserve remplies de cailloux et chantaient à tue-tête pour chasser et rabattre hors des hautes herbes le tigre qui pouvait s'y être tapi.

Jay sourit de cette image, conscient qu'elle n'était pas politiquement correcte, mais c'était bien le cadet de ses soucis. Il n'avait guère de chance de tomber sur quelqu'un pendant qu'il se jouait ce scénario, et puis après tout, il était quand même à moitié thaïlandais ! Jadis, l'un de ses arrière-arrière-grands-pères ou grands-oncles avait dû sans doute se balader pieds nus là-bas dans la savane de ce qui était encore le Siam, à faire du ramdam et prier le panthéon local que le tigre détale dans la direction opposée. Tout bien considéré, il valait encore mieux être à l'ombre de la cabane posée sur le dos d'un éléphant de trois mètres, avec un fusil à double canon Nitro Express à portée de main, que de se trouver au sol à frapper un bout de tôle à coups de bâton. Sans compter ce petit supplément sympathique, un gamin juché sur la croupe de l'éléphant qui agitait des palmes fixées sur une longue perche pour vous éventer, vous et le rajah, d'une brise certes tiède mais néanmoins bienvenue.

Première classe de bout en bout. La seule vraie façon de voyager.

Ce que Jay traquait en fait, c'était de l'information, mais entrer au clavier ou par voxax* des requêtes de paquets de données en hexadécimal codé binaire, c'était quand même nettement moins jouissif que de traquer un tigre du Bengale mangeur d'hommes.

Bien sûr, ils n'avaient toujours pas vu le grand

fauve ; cela faisait pourtant un bon moment que les rabatteurs agitaient leurs bâtons et leurs crécelles, relativement parlant. Le rajah se confondait en excuses : « Moi vraiment désolé, Sahib », mais ce n'était pas de sa faute. Vous ne pouviez pas débusquer un tigre s'il n'y en avait pas.

Oh, certes, des gibiers de moindre envergure fuyaient devant les rabatteurs. Jay avait vu des daims, des cochons et toutes sortes de reptiles, dont deux cobras de deux mètres cinquante, et même un bébé tigre – mais pas le grand fauve qu'il avait espéré trouver. Le tigre était venu et reparti, peut-être en coup de vent... toujours est-il qu'il n'avait laissé aucune piste manifeste : il avait éventré sa proie et disparu. La proie virtuelle était en l'occurrence une chèvre enfermée dans une cage en inox aux barreaux de titane gros comme des cuisses de culturiste. Un tyrannosaure n'aurait pas pu les cisailler, même s'il avait eu des crocs en diamants, impossible, totalement exclu. La chèvre – en réalité, un fichier crypté donnant l'heure, la position et d'autres détails sur un convoi ferroviaire traversant le Pakistan un peu plus tôt dans la journée – aurait dû être à l'épreuve de n'importe quel monstre. Et pourtant, quelque chose avait réussi à écarter les barreaux comme de vulgaires nouilles trop cuites, pénétrer dans la cage, et la chèvre était désormais de l'histoire ancienne.

Au début, Jay n'avait pas voulu y croire, il était convaincu que quelqu'un avait sans aucun doute réussi à récupérer une copie de la clé à usage unique – puisque c'était ainsi que fonctionnait ce système de cryptographie – mais après avoir jeté un œil sur la cage – l'algorithme de chiffrement – il avait pu constater qu'on avait forcé celle-ci en recourant à la force brute, sans user de la moindre clé. Aucun rapport avec un banal logiciel de cryptage comme pouvait en utiliser un gamin pour dissimuler des fichiers pornos à ses parents, il s'agissait bel et bien d'un module de qualité militaire : même s'il n'était pas à 100 % inviolable, à condition d'y mettre le temps, celui qui avait réussi à le craquer y était parvenu en moins d'une journée.

Et ça, bien sûr, c'était tout bonnement impossible. Aucun ordinateur sur terre n'était capable d'un tel exploit. Une douzaine de Super-Cray fonctionnant en parallèle auraient pu y parvenir en, mettons, dix bons milliers d'années, mais en l'espace de quelques heures entre la réception du message et son décryptage, c'était rigoureusement IM-POS-SIBLE. Terminé. Point suivant. Tiens, justement, j'en ai une bien bonne à vous raconter...

Jay ôta son casque colonial et effaça d'un revers de bras la sueur qui lui coulait sur le front. Il faisait torride au Pendjab et malgré l'éventail, le dais fixé sur le dos du petit éléphant n'avait pas la clim. Il aurait pu bien sûr l'en équiper, mais quel intérêt ? N'importe qui pouvait concocter un scénario bancal rempli d'anachronismes ; les vrais artistes se devaient d'entretenir un minimum de pureté. Enfin, au moins de temps en temps, juste histoire de prouver qu'ils en étaient capables.

Comment une telle intrusion avait-elle pu se produire ? C'était impossible, en tout cas avec les données physiques qu'il connaissait.

Cela lui fit penser à cette vieille histoire remontant aux tout débuts de l'aviation. Certains ingénieurs avaient fait des études sur le bourdon. En se basant sur la surface alaire de l'insecte, son poids et sa morphologie, et en tenant compte de sa masse musculaire et de la force qu'il pouvait mobiliser, lesdits ingénieurs avaient déterminé, après moult manipulations de leur règle à calcul, qu'il était tout bonnement impossible qu'une telle créature puisse voler.

Bzzz ! Oups, en voilà encore un qui passe !

Cela avait dû être terriblement frustrant de considérer une feuille remplie de calculs mathématiques précis sur les flux aérodynamiques, la traînée, la portance, en ayant acquis la certitude que les bourdons ne pouvaient pas voler, et de les voir néanmoins butiner de fleur en fleur, oublieux de l'humaine certitude qu'un tel acte fût mathématiquement impossible.

La déduction logique était que les chercheurs avaient dû omettre un élément. Ils reprirent donc leur règle à calcul et leur porte-mine, poursuivirent leurs observations, remplirent des dizaines de calepins, et réussirent au bout du compte à découvrir comment opérait la synergie du vol du bourdon.

Si vous possédiez déjà la réponse, vous deviez à tout le moins être capable d'en inférer la question. Les bourdons vaquaient à leurs occupations aériennes depuis des millions d'années, nonobstant le fait qu'on pût penser le contraire, et c'était là un facteur qu'il convenait de prendre en considération...

Donc, Jay se retrouvait avec un fichier qui ne pouvait être ouvert par la force brute, or il avait été craqué comme une vulgaire coquille d'œuf serrée dans la main d'un géant. Quelle était déjà la formule de Sherlock Holmes ? « Quand vous avez éliminé l'impossible, ce qui reste, si improbable fût-il, doit être la vérité. »

L'intrusion n'avait pu être effectuée par aucune

méthode connue de Jay Gridley et, toute modestie mise à part, il estimait toucher sa bille en matière de piraterie informatique. Mais puisqu'elle avait été réalisée, c'est donc qu'il y avait un autre tigre tapi dans les hautes herbes. Tout ce qu'il lui restait à faire, c'était de savoir à quoi il ressemblait, de le retrouver et de le capturer. Sans se faire bouffer.

Il sourit à nouveau. Cela lui avait fait songer à un autre adage de chasseur. La recette du civet de lièvre ? Commencer par attraper un lièvre...

Vendredi
Stonewall Flat, Nevada

Mikhaïl Roujio plissa les yeux sous le soleil du désert. Bien que de teint plutôt clair, il avait bronzé depuis qu'il s'était installé dans la région, et désormais, il avait la peau tannée comme le cuir, le visage creusé de rides, des veines en saillie sur ses bras nus. Le temps n'était pas encore aussi torride qu'il le serait d'ici deux mois, les nuits étaient encore frisquettes, mais il faisait déjà pas mal chaud.

Roujio se tenait devant la caravane en alu Airstream qu'il avait achetée et installée au milieu des vingt-cinq mille mètres carrés de sable et de broussailles épineuses dont il s'était également porté acquéreur. Le vent chaud lui caressait le visage. Il était quasiment seul. Sur les cinq autres « lots » de deux hectares et demi, un seul était occupé par un bâtiment, en l'occurrence un simple dôme de plastique vert renforcé avec ce qui ressemblait à des feuilles d'alu, et rempli de rations lyophilisées, comme celles qu'utilisent campeurs ou randonneurs. Roujio n'avait eu aucun mal à en forcer le cadenas pour y jeter un œil dans les premières heures qui avaient suivi son emménagement. Tous les deux mois, un vieux type arrivait avec un gros pick-up GMC, il s'arrêtait devant le dôme, déchargeait de nouveaux stocks de rations lyophilisées et les entreposait dans le bâtiment, puis il le cadenassait de nouveau et repartait. Roujio se demandait pourquoi il amenait tous ces vivres. Les stockait-il en prévision d'une catastrophe imminente ? Redoutait-il une guerre ? Une épidémie ? Ou bien s'agissait-il d'un commerce quelconque ?

Les motivations des Américains étaient parfois difficiles à cerner. Chez lui, en Tchétchénie, et même en Russie, il n'avait jamais vu de vieillards amasser ce type de nourriture. Évidemment, c'était peut-être aussi parce que personne ne jugeait que ça en valait la peine. Et quand bien même, on n'en aurait pas trouvé en stock.

Roujio haussa mentalement les épaules. Peu importait. Le dôme était l'unique bâtiment aux alentours ; au-delà, près de cinq kilomètres plus loin, il n'y avait guère qu'un cabanon situé au bord d'une petite rivière à sec les trois quarts de l'année. Le cabanon appartenait à une église méthodiste, mais depuis l'installation de Roujio, il n'avait été utilisé qu'à trois reprises par des campeurs, et jamais pour plus de deux nuits. Et aucun de ces campeurs n'était passé assez près pour lui adresser la parole.

Il était ravi de cette solitude. Depuis qu'il avait quitté

le service actif, il n'avait eu que de rares occasions d'adresser la parole à des gens, et encore moins d'avoir à les tuer. Il avait mis de l'argent à la banque, qu'il pouvait utiliser à sa guise, avec sa carte à puce. Environ une fois par semaine, il se rendait en ville – deux heures de route – pour faire ses courses dans un de ces vastes supermarchés où il était totalement anonyme ; il ne discutait pas avec les caissières au moment de payer. Il faisait le plein à la pompe et s'en retournait chez lui. Il longeait par l'ouest la vallée de la Mort et quittait la route nationale pour emprunter une piste en terre jusqu'à sa caravane. La ville la plus proche – si on pouvait l'appeler ainsi – était Scotty's Junction. Un polygone de tir de l'armée dominait le terrain vers l'est.

Roujio avait payé sa voiture en liquide, un 4×4 Toyota, d'occasion mais pas trop vieux ; et il avait procédé de même pour la caravane, l'un et l'autre véhicules ayant été dénichés grâce à des petites annonces dans un journal de Las Vegas. Le terrain, il l'avait acheté en recourant à l'une de ses identités d'emprunt, afin d'éviter d'éveiller la curiosité ; il avait donné une avance substantielle au vendeur et réglait depuis ses échéances mensuelles, par prélèvement automatiquc sur le même compte, le premier de chaque mois. On n'aurait guère pu faire plus discret.

La caravane était pourvue d'un groupe électrogène et de batteries, elle avait même la climatisation, mais il l'utilisait rarement. Il appréciait la chaleur.

Il n'aurait pas pu dire qu'il était heureux – il ne l'avait plus été depuis le cancer qui avait emporté Anna, et il n'escomptait plus l'être à nouveau – mais il s'estimait satisfait. Sa vie était simple, ses besoins limités. Le plus grand projet inscrit à son programme était l'édification d'un mur de pierre sèche pour délimiter le périmètre de sa propriété. Ça lui prendrait peut-être dix ans, mais ce n'était pas un problème.

Du moins s'était-il estimé satisfait jusqu'à aujourd'hui. En parcourant du regard le terrain rocailleux, les collines au loin noyées dans une brume de chaleur et de poussière, il sut que quelque chose ne collait pas.

Aucun signe tangible ne révélait l'origine du problème. Pas d'hélico dans les airs, pas de nuage de poussière signalant l'approche d'un véhicule. Il saisit ses grosses jumelles et parcourut lentement les alentours. Ses deux hectares et demi étaient situés sur une éminence, en léger surplomb de la plupart des autres parcelles, ce qui lui procurait une bonne vue. Il distinguait le dôme du vieux, depuis l'avant de sa caravane. Il y jeta un œil. Rien.

Il gravit les quelques mètres de pente derrière la caravane, jusqu'à ce qu'il puisse apercevoir le toit du cabanon des méthodistes et le lit de la rivière à sec. Pas d'activité non plus de ce côté-là.

Il abaissa les jumelles. Rien de particulier, aucun motif d'inquiétude, mais il sentait malgré tout viscéralement qu'il y avait quelque chose d'anormal. Il retourna vers la caravane. Il avait entreposé son arsenal dans une caissette cachée sous le plancher de la chambre – le moment était peut-être venu de sortir son artillerie pour l'avoir sous la main.

Non. Pas encore. Il n'avait aucune cible sur quoi tirer. Peut-être son instinct le trompait-il ; peut-être son malaise ne provenait-il que d'un truc mal digéré ou d'un parasite quelconque.

Il esquissa un petit sourire crispé. Il n'avait pas

survécu jusqu'à aujourd'hui en se livrant à de vaines spéculations. Au mieux de sa forme, il s'était toujours comporté comme un cafard dérangé en pleine nuit par une lumière soudaine : d'abord fuir, s'inquiéter ensuite. Ça lui avait permis de rester en vie quand une bonne partie de ses collègues étaient morts. Avec les années, il avait appris à se fier à ses intuitions. Non, décidément, il y avait quelque chose d'anormal. Quoi que ce puisse être, ça allait se manifester tôt ou tard. Il s'en occuperait à ce moment-là.

Il réintégra la caravane.

3

Samedi 2 avril
Las Vegas, Nevada

Deux surprises attendaient à l'aéroport le colonel John Howard, commandant du bras armé de la Net Force, quand il descendit de l'un des vieux Learjet reconditionnés que le service utilisait pour les sauts de puce à l'intérieur du territoire américain. La première était que l'USAT, le Service de surveillance tactique satellitaire de l'armée – qu'on surnommait également parfois en privé le Gros Loucheur – avait formellement identifié leur cible : il s'agissait bien de l'homme recherché par la Net Force.

Ce n'était pas franchement une surprise, puisque le service le soupçonnait déjà – sinon, il n'aurait pas demandé à l'USAT de dérouter un de ses satellites pour pister le bonhomme. C'était malgré tout réconfortant d'avoir une confirmation.

La seconde surprise, toutefois, était plus qu'inattendue : Howard allait bénéficier d'une promotion.

La hiérarchie militaire était pour le moins bizarre au sein de la Net Force. Officiellement, tous les hommes ou officiers sous son commandement étaient détachés de la Garde nationale, quel qu'ait pu être leur service d'origine. Cette organisation n'existait en fait que sur le papier ; refuge pour caser scribouillards et autres clique-souris, elle était en réalité totalement déconnectée de la Garde ou de l'armée américaine. Son rôle essentiel était d'utiliser des troupes militaires dans des affectations civiles, en général hors du territoire métropolitain, mais elle devait également son origine à une bizarre loi fiscale issue d'une récente révision du code des impôts. Il n'en comprenait pas les arcanes, son patron ne semblait pas les comprendre non plus, pas plus que leur chef-comptable, mais le résultat était là.

Bref, pour toutes ces raisons, les grades au sein de la Net Force étaient plus ou moins figés. En tant qu'officier supérieur, il pouvait promouvoir les simples soldats mais uniquement jusqu'au rang de sous-off. Howard savait qu'il aurait dû rester dans l'armée régulière, ce qui lui aurait permis, même en temps de paix, de prendre sa retraite avec un grade d'officier de réserve supérieur à celui qu'il avait dans l'active. Le fait d'être noir jouait du reste en sa faveur, à cause des restes de culpabilité qu'entretenaient encore les Blancs dans l'administration. Il n'avait jamais envisagé d'aller au-delà du grade de colonel d'aviation quand il avait pris sa retraite pour intégrer la Net Force, même si la solde et, surtout, les possibilités d'action étaient plus intéressantes. Son supérieur direct était un civil, de sorte qu'en matière de galons, il était le mieux placé.

Julio Fernandez, son ordonnance au sein de la Net Force, et ce bien avant déjà qu'il n'intègre le service, lui annonça la nouvelle avec une allégresse manifeste.

« Redites-moi ça, sergent ! »

Fernandez, qui se tenait à l'ombre de l'avant-toit du hangar privé, sourit : « Quelle partie au juste vous a échappé, mon colonel ?

– Laisse-moi reformuler la question et tâche d'être

bref, il commence déjà à faire bougrement chaud : de quoi est-ce que tu me parles, sacré nom d'une pipe ? »

Les deux hommes se dirigèrent vers le hangar.

Fernandez rit de bon cœur. « Eh bien, il semblerait que le colonel doive se voir offrir, dans un délai de trente jours à compter du 1er avril, le grade de général de brigade. C'est un grade supérieur à celui de colonel et inférieur à celui de général de division, mon colonel, dans cette saleté d'organisation de la Garde nationale dans laquelle je me suis retrouvé embringué.

– Sous la menace de mon arme, sergent ?

– Si ma mémoire est bonne, mon colonel. »

Howard sourit. « Allons, Julio, qu'est-ce que tu me serines encore ? Jamais entendu parler d'une quelconque promotion, pas le moindre murmure. » Il essaya de dominer son excitation. Fernandez savait se montrer taquin, mais jamais il n'aurait plaisanté sur un sujet pareil. Howard avait toujours voulu être général, bien sûr, mais il avait tiré un trait dessus en quittant le service actif.

« C'est parce que vous n'êtes pas fiancé à la femme la plus belle et la plus intelligente de tout l'hémisphère occidental (ou oriental du reste), John. Une femme capable de dresser un ordinateur à chanter, danser et faire des sauts périlleux arrière sans même lever le petit doigt. J'ai vu de mes propres yeux l'ordre de promotion et il m'avait tout l'air d'un document officiel. »

Malgré le brusque afflux d'adrénaline, Howard remarqua : « Le lieutenant Winthrop n'est pourtant pas censée fureter dans certains domaines ? Détrompe-moi. »

Fernandez ouvrit les mains, écarta les doigts, en un geste d'impuissance. « Que puis-je y faire ? Je ne suis qu'un pauvre sergent, elle est mon supérieur hiérarchique. Mes connaissances en informatique tiendraient sur un timbre-poste, et encore, avec de la place pour y mettre le tampon. Du reste, quel intérêt à faire partie du meilleur groupe de fureteurs de la planète si on ne peut pas fouiner de temps en temps à sa guise ? Non, c'est tout ce qu'il y a de véridique. Félicitations, John.

– Merci, mais je le croirai quand je le verrai. » Il sentit son humeur passer au beau fixe. Le *général* Howard. Ça vous avait quand même une sacrée gueule.

Fernandez gloussa, comme s'il venait de lire dans ses pensées.

Howard se reprit, tâcha de modérer son excitation et son ego. « Et comment va Joanna ?

– Enceinte jusqu'aux yeux. La naissance n'est prévue pourtant que pour septembre et je dois bien vous avouer, j'ai dans l'idée que je n'y survivrai pas. À un moment, je suis comme un ange incapable de faire le mal, l'instant d'après, elle me vole dans les plumes sous prétexte que je respire trop fort... Elle tartine sa purée de ketchup, saupoudre de sel les glaces à la vanille. Et elle se lève quarante-neuf fois par jour pour aller pisser. »

Howard rit. « Bien fait pour toi. Quand vas-tu te décider à en faire une femme honnête ?

– Le 1er juin, à ce qu'on m'a dit. Elle aurait volontiers attendu un an, paraît qu'il faut bien tout ce temps pour organiser un mariage, même si pour moi, c'est de la daube. Toujours est-il qu'elle veut se marier avant la naissance du bébé, et qu'elle ne veut pas ressembler à une truie gravide, bref, c'est la date butoir. Je n'ai pas mon mot à dire, après tout, je ne suis que le futur époux.

– Les mariages et les grossesses, c'est ainsi, Julio.

– Il faut encore que je me trouve un témoin. Ça vous branche ? »

Howard secoua la tête. « Tu plaisantes ? Pour rien au monde je ne voudrais rater le moment où le tristement célèbre sergent Julio Fernandez se passe la corde au cou. Ce sera une fille ou un garçon ?

– Un garçon. »

Julio sourit.

« Déjà choisi un prénom ?

– Quatre : Julio Garcia Edmund Howard Fernandez. »

Howard s'arrêta pour considérer son ami. « Je suis flatté.

– L'idée ne vient pas de moi, faut vous en prendre à Joanna. Il y a également deux grands-pères dans le lot. Si ça n'avait tenu qu'à moi, je l'aurais appelé Bud, point final. Ah, et puis aussi, vous allez être le parrain, encore une de ses idées branques. »

Howard sourit. Il allait être le témoin du mariage de son meilleur ami, le parrain d'un garçon portant un de ses prénoms, et pour couronner le tout, promu général dans la version Net Force de l'armée américaine. Non, vraiment pas une journée comme les autres.

« Je ne voudrais pas gâcher l'ambiance, mais où en est-on avec notre fugitif ?

– Pas de lézard, mon colonel. Il vit dans une roulotte perdue au milieu de nulle part, tout seul, même pas un clebs. Sa plus grande ambition semble être de vouloir border un côté de son terrain d'un muret de pierre. La discrétion totale, il ne se lie avec personne, ne parle à personne, pour autant qu'on puisse en juger. Non, il se contente d'amasser des cailloux. Difficile de croire qu'on a affaire à un ancien des services secrets soviétiques, un spécialiste de l'action violente avec quarante-quatre éliminations à son crédit.

– Ma foi, s'il faut en croire Vladimir Plekhanov – et le psy qui a supervisé l'interrogatoire m'assure qu'on peut –, l'homme qui se fait appeler Mikhaïl Roujio est un individu dont les talents ne se limitent sûrement pas à entasser des cailloux dans le désert. Il faut qu'on opère dans les règles, vite fait, bien fait, qu'on arrive à le récupérer suffisamment en douceur pour qu'il reste en vie et soit en mesure de répondre à quelques questions.

– Pas de problème, ça devrait être du gâteau. Quoique... je pensais que les Russes étaient nos potes, désormais.

– J'imagine qu'il s'agit là d'un commentaire facétieux, sergent. Vous le savez aussi bien que moi, plus on en sait sur ses amis, mieux on se porte.

– Bien parlé.

– Parfait. Voyons voir ce que le Gros Loucheur nous a trouvé.

– Le poste de commandement est l'endroit le plus frais que j'ai pu nous dégoter, mon général.

– Pour la promotion, on attendra que je l'aie vue par écrit, sergent. » Howard sourit.

« Quelque chose de drôle, mon colonel ?

Je vous imaginais juste avec les galons de lieutenant.

– Vous feriez pas ça !

– Si j'étais général, il faudrait bien qu'ils m'écoutent... »

L'inquiétude qui se peignit sur les traits de Fernandez valait son pesant d'or.

Samedi
Les Ifs, Sussex, Angleterre

Près de la serre de Lord Goswell, derrière le corps de logis principal, le commandant Terrance Arthur Peel – « Tap » pour ses compagnons – regardait arriver l'antique Volvo noire. Les trois chiens du gardien – deux colleys et un berger allemand – se mirent à aboyer.

Peel aimait bien les chiens. À tout prendre, il aurait choisi d'avoir ce genre de bête auprès de lui sous la tente dans le bled plutôt que le plus perfectionné des systèmes d'alarme. Un chien vous prévenait dès que vous aviez de la compagnie, et une bête dressée savait faire la différence entre vos amis et vos ennemis. Et surtout, elle était capable d'égorger ledit ennemi si vous l'aviez dressée pour. Au contraire des humains, les bons chiens restaient toujours fidèles.

La Volvo s'arrêta et la portière droite s'ouvrit en couinant, livrant passage à un grand type dégingandé, la cinquantaine, cheveux gris, encore plus typé même que son nom ne pouvait le laisser entendre : Peter avait lui-même vérifié ses antécédents familiaux.

Bascomb-Coombs était vêtu d'un costume crème coûteux mais mal ajusté, d'une chemise de soie jaune avec une cravate bleue, et chaussé de souliers italiens en cuir gris perle. Rien de tout cela n'était donné. Les chaussures à elles seules avaient dû lui coûter trois ou quatre cents sacs. Monseigneur ne regardait pas à la dépense en ce qui concernait ses employés favoris, et Bascomb-Coombs était du nombre, ascendance juive ou pas.

Même si les origines ethniques du scientifique n'avaient guère d'importance, elles n'affectaient en rien ses capacités intellectuelles, et quels que soient ses autres traits de caractère, Bascomb-Coombs était tout ce qu'il y a de brillant. Un authentique génie, tellement en avance sur ses pairs qu'il avait quelque chose d'un Einstein ou d'un Hawking : il jouait dans une classe à part, excepté que le bonhomme n'était pas fichu de se conformer aux putains de règles du savoir-vivre. Il aurait dû être là pour dîner la veille au soir, or il s'était tout bonnement trompé de jour. Et ce détail mis à part, il avait quand même toujours une demi-heure de retard.

Le stéréotype du professeur étourdi avait certainement du vrai, si l'on s'en référait au cas de Bascomb-Coombs. Pour sa part, Goswell avait écarté ce travers d'un haussement d'épaules. On devait souffrir ce genre d'inconvénient – que pouvait-on espérer d'un prolétaire, génie ou pas génie ? Goswell n'était pas entièrement idiot (si l'on exceptait sa fixation sur l'Empire britannique), et il avait sans aucun doute assez de jugeote pour savoir que Bascomb-Coombs était trop précieux pour être largué à cause d'une simple erreur de date.

Peel sourit et rajusta le 9 mm SIG noir dans l'étui Galco fixé à sa hanche droite. Il avait une carrure assez imposante pour que le pistolet se dissimule sans peine sous son blazer en lin blanc de Saville Row. Un mètre quatre-vingt-cinq pour quatre-vingt-dix kilos et quelques, avec toujours la forme d'un soldat d'active. Naturellement, monseigneur n'était pas le genre de personne à s'entourer de gorilles en tenue camouflée armés de mitraillettes et menaçant ses hôtes. Bien que retraité des services secrets de Sa Majesté, Peel demeurait présentable. Bon régiment, bonnes écoles, toujours fière allure à quarante-cinq ans, et capable de ne pas s'emmêler avec les couverts lors d'un dîner officiel. En homme cultivé et civilisé, il savait bavarder avec les gens riches et célèbres sans jamais paraître déplacé. Il aurait dû être colonel à présent, s'il n'y avait pas eu cette affaire... désagréable en Irlande du Nord lors de son ultime mission. Foutu pays rempli de foutus sauvages sanguinaires.

Le petit com* glissé dans sa poche de blazer pépia. Ce devait être Hawkins à la grille, pour confirmer l'arrivée de la Volvo et s'assurer qu'aucun terroriste n'avait surgi du coffre pour dégommer Peel.

« G1 en fréquence. Le colis est livré ?

– Bien compris, G1. Tout est au vert à la maison.

– Bien copié, tout est au vert. Idem de ce côté. »

Peel regarda sa montre, un modèle à aiguilles et cadran noir des forces spéciales, avec des incrustations phosphorescentes en tritium, cadeau de ses hommes pour sa retraite. Aucun n'avait été ravi de le voir partir. Le reste de l'équipe de sécurité devait se pointer d'ici... maintenant.

– M1. Pas d'activité de notre côté.

– M2. J'ai deux des vaches du gros qui broutent du foin par ici, à part ça, rien de spécial.

– Mobile 3. L'enceinte est dégagée du point 4 au point 7.

– Grille 2. C'est mort comme un week-end de Toussaint. »

Peel accusa réception des messages de chacun des gardes en faction ou en patrouille. Il avait dix hommes, tous anciens militaires, répartis sur l'ensemble du périmètre. Des effectifs insuffisants pour une couverture efficace en situation de tir, mais la plupart des ennemis de monseigneur n'étaient pas du genre à prendre d'assaut les Ifs pour l'agresser physiquement. Ils seraient plutôt enclins à lui faire des crocs-en-jambe à coups d'OPA hostiles ou de prises de bénéfices.

Il sourit. Évidemment, monseigneur avait des ennemis qui ignoraient qu'ils étaient eux aussi sur sa liste, des ennemis dont il fallait de temps à autre... *s'occuper*, en toute discrétion, bien entendu. Raison qui avait conduit Tap Peel à entrer à son service. C'était en fait parce que Lord Goswell et son père avaient fait leurs études ensemble à Oxford et que Peel Senior avait réussi à acquérir des titres de noblesse de son cru avant de passer l'arme à gauche. C'était le genre de privilège qu'on gardait pour les membres de la famille, ou, faute de mieux, pour les copains.

Apparemment, on annonçait de la pluie dans le nord du pays. Alors qu'elle avait été prévue pour la région de Londres. Enfin, une petite averse ne ferait pas de mal à la végétation, même si les troupes allaient sans doute râler. Mais c'était le lot des soldats, non ? Quand on s'engageait, on s'engageait qu'il pleuve ou qu'il vente, qu'il fasse chaud ou froid, point final. Et Dieu sait qu'il avait eu son content de cataractes, de flotte qui vous ruisselle dans le cou tandis que vous maudissez les officiers qui vous ont assigné à ce poste.

Il sourit à nouveau. C'était quand même une

chouette vie que celle de soldat. Dommage que les occasions se fassent rares de nos jours. Enfin, à moins d'accepter d'aller traîner ses guêtres dans quelque république du tiers monde pour y jouer les mercenaires. Très peu pour lui. Du temps de son grand-père, soldat de fortune était encore un métier à peu près honorable ; mais aujourd'hui, n'importe quel crétin sans la moindre formation militaire pouvait répondre à une petite annonce dans un magazine américain et se retrouver bombardé gorille d'un potentat au fin fond de la jungle africaine. Non merci. Les combattants britanniques étaient des types un peu spéciaux, d'accord, mais merde, ils étaient quand même d'une autre classe que les zozos qu'on pouvait recruter dans les pages emploi d'un magazine.

Il était sans doute temps de rentrer. Le dîner n'allait pas tarder à être servi, et il allait y avoir d'abord l'apéritif. Bascomb-Coombs était plutôt vin blanc, et monseigneur ne se sentait pas à l'aise en compagnie d'invités qui ne buvaient pas. Peel s'autoriserait donc un whisky symbolique.

Monseigneur détestait boire seul.

Donc, un petit scotch, deux doigts, pas plus, pour être sûr de garder les idées claires.

Il sourit encore. Pas de doute, il avait connu des missions plus difficiles.

4

Samedi 2 avril
Washington, DC

Les épreuves de qualification du championnat national de boomerang avaient lieu sur le stade du lycée Clinton, et Tyrone Howard était tout ému de se trouver là, mais ce n'était rien en comparaison du plaisir extatique d'y être au titre de concurrent. Certes, il était dans la section cadets novices, et il n'était inscrit qu'à une seule épreuve, le temps maximal de vol, mais c'était quand même incroyable. Après tout, il ne pratiquait sérieusement la discipline que depuis six mois [1].

À côté de lui, Jimmy-Joe, son meilleur ami, lorgnait derrière ses gros verres de myope la brochette de concurrents en train de s'échauffer. « Waouh, dis donc, c'est pas comme qui dirait... dangereux ? Imagine que tu te prennes un de ces trucs sur le coin de la tronche ! On n'est pas en RV, c'est du vrai de vrai... »

Jimmy-Joe était branché 100 % réalité virtuelle, comme Tyrone encore quelques mois plus tôt, mais Tyrone avait pensé qu'il se ferait sans trop de peine à cette... activité de plein air. Même s'il lui avait fallu quand même une semaine pour convaincre son pote de quitter son ordinateur pour venir assister à une véri-

1. Cf. *Net Force 2, Programmes fantômes, op. cit.*

table compétition. « Eh bien, tu te fais assommer et tu te réveilles avec une bosse sur le front. Je te ferai dire que tu pourrais aussi te payer un court-circuit avec une interface et te cramer les neurones, hé, pauvre naze...

– Oh, bien sûr que je pourrais. Malgré une triple sécurité matérielle et quelque chose comme un demi-milliampère d'amplification ? Même pas de quoi se faire un putain d'œuf de puce sur le plat... Rien à voir avec se prendre un bon gros bâton au coin du cigare, mec. » Jimmy-Joe hocha la tête. Il luisait au grand air. Chaque matin, il devait mettre de l'écran total rien que pour gagner l'arrêt de bus, et il lui fallait quinze jours au soleil pour que son hâle passe du blanc au crème. Un léger contraste avec Tyrone qui exhibait un magnifique teint chocolat, même s'il restait enfermé toute la journée. Ce qui n'avait guère été le cas ces derniers temps. Lui aussi, il était un informazoïde de première – et plutôt doué dans son domaine, qui plus est –, jusqu'à ce que cette histoire avec Bella l'éjecte de la RV pour le replonger dans le monde réel. Sans parler que se faire larguer par la donzelle l'avait également pas mal secoué. Sa treizième année n'avait pas été de tout repos, et ce n'était pas peu dire, Casimir.

« Bon, très bien, tu m'as traîné ici », poursuivit Jimmy-Joe comme son ami se gardait de répondre. « File-moi le mode d'emploi, mec. D'où tu les sors au juste, tes drôles de bâtons tournoyants ? »

Grand sourire de Tyrone. « OK, je t'explique : il y a en gros deux grandes catégories de boomerangs. Les premiers sont ceux qui reviennent quand on les lance. Ils peuvent également décrire tout un tas de figures à l'aller et au retour, selon leur forme. Ça va du modèle de base qui ressemble à une banane vue en coupe à des espèces de rotors d'hélico à six ou huit pales.

« La seconde catégorie dérive des bâtons de guerre aborigènes. Ceux-là ne reviennent pas, ils continuent de voler jusqu'à ce qu'ils tombent – ou heurtent le crâne de quelqu'un. Un boomerang de combat peut aller plus loin que n'importe quel objet de même poids. Il vole en exploitant la précession gyroscopique due à l'asymétrie de la poussée sur sa face inférieure ; la portance est en fait engendrée par la combinaison des deux mouvements : rotation et progression linéaire.

– Stop ! La transmission a provoqué une erreur de protection générale, mec ! Tu peux me recopier ça en langage clair ?

– Il vole parce qu'il se transforme en hélice en tournoyant ; et il revient parce que l'angle d'attaque varie à mesure de la progression. »

Une femelle de berger allemand noir et feu passa au galop, lancé à la poursuite d'un Frisbee Jackarang en PVC rigide.

Tyrone se délesta de son sac à dos et en sortit son Wedderburn, un modèle de base. « Tu remarques l'arrondi du bord de ce côté, sur la face interne ? De l'autre, en revanche, l'extrémité est effilée. Quand il tourne dans le vent, la poussée varie à chaque tour, ce qui arrondit la trajectoire. Tu le lances de la main droite, comme ceci... (Tyrone lui montra comment le prendre, la face concave orientée vers l'avant, l'extrémité relevée) et il se redresse à l'horizontale avant d'obliquer sur la gauche. »

Jimmy-Joe considéra le boomerang, le soupesa. « Hum. Je pourrais coder un programme, intégrer les divers paramètres... poids, vitesse de rotation, vitesse linéaire, poussée aérodynamique, tout le bazar, et parvenir exactement au même résultat en RV.

– Trois TGV de retard, mec. Tous les lanceurs sérieux ont déjà leur scénario personnel depuis l'époque des Pierrafeu. J'en ai moi-même un pour chacun de mes modèles. Mais le programme, ce n'est jamais que la carte. Ici, t'es sur le territoire. » Tyrone ouvrit complètement son sac à dos pour dévoiler à son ami sa collection de boomerangs. Il en avait trois de forme classique et trois modèles en L. Moulés en résine armée, ultra-minces et ultra-légers, ils étaient conçus pour avoir un temps de vol maximal. Son préféré était le modèle « Océan Indien » de Möller, qu'il avait à présent assez bien en main.

Il l'indiqua. « C'est celui que je vais utiliser pour mon épreuve.

– Hmph. Ça me paraît moins difficile qu'une partie de Dinowarz.

– Le temps réel analogique, c'est autre chose que l'univers numérique, tête de nœud. Moi, je te parle de facteurs comme les réflexes, l'estimation de la vitesse du vent, de la température, et ainsi de suite... »

Jimmy-Joe n'était pas impressionné. « Je pourrais également programmer tout ça. C'est l'affaire d'une minute.

– Ouais, mais tu pourrais toujours pas aller là-bas, lancer le truc et le faire voler. »

La chienne revenait au galop, le Frisbee dans la gueule, qu'elle déposa aux pieds de son maître, un grand escogriffe aux cheveux teints en vert. « Bonne fille, Cady ! Encore une fois ? »

La chienne aboya en bondissant.

« Et c'est quoi, ton épreuve ?

– Temps de vol maximum. Tu lances, le boomerang part en tournoyant et le juge démarre son chrono. Chacun a droit à un lancer, celui qui tient le plus longtemps remporte l'épreuve. Tu dois le rattraper au retour ou ça ne compte pas, et il faut qu'il se pose à l'intérieur du cercle de cinquante mètres. On a intérêt à en prendre un léger avec la sustentation maximale. Le record actuel est d'un peu plus de quatre minutes...

– Merde ! Quatre minutes à tournoyer ? Et sans moteur ? À d'autres !

– Véridique. Et ça, c'est que le record homologué. Il y a des gars qui ont réussi à le maintenir en l'air pas loin de dix-huit minutes, officieusement.

– Tu blagues ? Ça me paraît impossible.

– Je te jacte que non. »

Tyrone soupesa le Möller. « Mon record personnel avec celui-ci est d'un peu plus de deux minutes. Si j'arrivais à réussir le même temps aujourd'hui, je pourrais sans doute intégrer l'équipe nationale junior.

– Ça, ce serait super-CPI*. »

Sourire de Tyrone. Ouaip, *ça passe impec*. Pas de veine que son vieux ne soit pas là pour le regarder. P'pa lui avait été vachement utile quand il avait débuté, Tyrone avait même retrouvé son vieux boomerang dans la maison de sa grand-mère. Bien sûr, p'pa n'était plus au niveau, à présent, mais pas de problème. Il était loin d'être nul, pour un père.

La sono se manifesta bruyamment. Le concours de Tyrone était annoncé.

Tyrone déglutit, il avait soudain la bouche sèche. L'entraînement était une chose, la compétition une autre. C'était sa première et il éprouva une brusque envie de pisser, alors qu'il y était allé à peine dix minutes plus tôt.

Malgré sa pâleur de joueur en salle, Jimmy-Joe semblait avoir chopé le virus. « Hé, dis donc, mec, c'est quand, ton tour ?

– Je passe en dix-huitième. Il y a une trentaine d'inscrits dans ma catégorie. Certains ont traversé tout le pays pour y participer, et plusieurs sont de vrais champions.

– Tu vas regarder lancer les autres ?

– Bien sûr. Ça peut toujours être utile. Et puis, je veux savoir quel est le temps à battre.

– De savoir qu'un cador a réussi, mettons, trois minutes, ça va t'aider ?

– Exactement comme de connaître le meilleur score à Dinowarz.

– Bien copié. »

Plusieurs épreuves se déroulaient en simultané : temps maximal, distance, précision, australienne... Tyrone et Jimmy-Joe se trouvèrent un coin à l'ombre sous le parasol d'un vendeur pour assister au début du concours des juniors.

Le premier candidat était un grand type mince au crâne rasé. Il avait opté pour un tripale rouge – pas le meilleur choix pour ce type d'épreuve – et Tyrone déclencha son chrono. Quarante-deux secondes. Nul.

Le suivant était un petit bonhomme râblé, avec un modèle en L vert fluo – apparemment un Bailey MTA Classic, ou peut-être un Girvin « Pendez-les haut et court ». À moins que ce soit une de ces copies taiwanaises, on ne pouvait jamais savoir à cette distance.

Tyrone chronométra le jet à une minute douze. Le gars ne risquait pas de décrocher le titre. La brise était faible, du nord-est, il n'aurait donc pas besoin de lester les pales en y scotchant des pièces de monnaie pour empêcher le vent de rabattre son boomerang.

Le troisième concurrent était une fille, aussi noire de peau que Tyrone, à peu près de son âge, et elle avait un Möller, du même modèle que le sien. Elle avança de deux pas, se pencha, lança.

Le boomerang partit vers les cieux, toujours plus haut, et parut vouloir y rester à demeure, glissant et tournoyant avant de revenir. C'était un jet superbe et un vol exemplaire. Tyrone détacha ses yeux du projectile pour contempler la fille. Elle avait le regard qui passait alternativement du boomerang au chrono et elle arborait un large sourire.

Elle pouvait. Quand l'oiseau redescendit enfin après son vol interminable, la fille avait un jet de deux minutes quarante-huit à son crédit. Un temps qui n'allait pas être facile à battre.

Les deux garçons regardèrent huit autres candidats, dont aucun ne parvint à moins de trente secondes de la concurrente numéro trois, puis il fut temps pour Tyrone d'aller s'échauffer pour son propre jet. Il avait la bouche sèche comme un désert, les boyaux noués, et le souffle court. Il n'avait pourtant aucune raison d'avoir le trac, c'était un exercice qu'il pratiquait tous les jours quand le temps le permettait : lancer son boomerang, des dizaines de fois. Oui, mais pas devant des centaines de spectateurs, et ce coup-ci, il n'aurait droit qu'à un seul essai...

Faites que je dépasse au moins les deux minutes... songea-t-il en s'approchant du cercle de lancement. *Ça ne suffira pas à m'assurer la victoire mais au moins je ne serai pas le dernier et je n'aurai pas l'air ridicule. Deux minutes, d'accord ?*

Il sortit de sa poche une petite pincée de poudre magique et la frotta entre trois doigts, la saupoudrant pour estimer la direction du vent. Dans leur chute, les paillettes étincelantes lui indiquèrent que le lit du vent avait dévié d'un poil vers le nord, mais était toujours en gros du nord-est. Il laissa tomber le reste de poudre, sortit son chronomètre et le cala dans sa main gauche, puis de la droite, il saisit le Möller. Il inspira à fond, trois fois de suite, exhala lentement, puis adressa un signe de tête au juge posté près du cercle. S'il en sortait, il était disqualifié. Le juge acquiesça et leva son propre chronomètre.

Vas-y, Tyrone.

Il prit encore une grande inspiration, avança d'un pas, se pencha, ramena le poignet en arrière et donna au boomerang le maximum d'impulsion possible. Il prit garde toutefois à ne pas trop lui donner d'effet à droite et à le maintenir au plus près d'un angle d'attaque de quarante-cinq degrés.

Il déclencha son chrono.

Deux minutes quarante et une secondes plus tard, son engin déclara forfait. Il le récupéra sans problème, à deux mains, et voilà, c'était terminé.

Tyrone avait le sourire. Il restait encore une douzaine de candidats, mais il avait battu son record personnel de plus de trente secondes, et il était second. Quoi qu'il advienne, il était satisfait de ce jet.

Alors qu'il s'apprêtait à rejoindre son ami, la jeune Noire qui avait remporté l'épreuve s'approcha. Elle avait une carrure athlétique avec une tenue – T-shirt, cuissard cycliste et chaussures de foot – qui mettait en valeur sa musculature. Elle était plutôt quelconque. Rien à voir avec le style canon d'une Belladonna.

« Joli jet, commenta-t-elle. Tu aurais appuyé un poil plus à gauche, tu aurais gagné dix, douze secondes et tu m'aurais battue...

– Tu crois ?

– Sûr et certain. Le Möller est donné pour six minutes, à ce qu'on dit. J'ai déjà réussi trois cinquante et une à l'entraînement. Mais je me présente... Nadine Harris.

– Moi, c'est Tyrone Howard.

– T'es d'où, Ty ?

– D'ici. De Washington.

– Eh, c'est vrai ? Moi aussi. Je viens juste d'emménager. J'arrive de Boston. Je suis au collège Eisenhower. Enfin, j'y serai la semaine prochaine. »

Tyrone la regarda, les yeux écarquillés.

« Sans blague ?

– Sérieux. Tu connais ?

– Un peu. C'est mon bahut.

– Waouh ! Ça alors, pour un hasard ! Dis donc, on pourrait s'entraîner ensemble. Le dernier collège que j'ai fréquenté, j'étais la seule à pratiquer le boomerang.

– Je veux bien te croire... Ouais, exemplaire. Je vais te filer mon mail. »

Quand Tyrone rejoignit Jimmy-Joe, son ami était en train de regarder par terre. « T'as perdu quelque chose, blondin ?

– Non, je cherchais juste un gros bâton.

– Un gros bâton ?

– Ouais, mec, pour toi. Pour t'aider à chasser les meufs. » Il indiqua d'un signe la jeune Noire qui s'éloignait, et fit mine de la frapper avec un bâton imaginaire.

« Allez, arrête ton char, pauvre noix, c'est juste une concurrente.

– Ça, j'ai pu noter.

– Tu passes trop de temps sur des sites pervers, JJ. Tâche un peu de t'ouvrir à la vraie vie.

– Et pourquoi ? C'est vrai que la tienne a l'air tellement plus marrante. »

Tyrone voulut lui balancer une gifle, mais l'autre esquiva. C'est qu'il était agile, mine de rien, ce petit con.

Plus tard, quand l'épreuve des juniors fut achevée, Tyrone contempla le tableau électronique installé pour afficher les résultats. Officieusement, il savait déjà qu'il était troisième – un Portoricain débarqué de nulle part l'avait en effet coiffé sur le poteau pour trois malheureuses secondes. Malgré tout, troisième sur trente-quatre dans un concours national, pour un bleu, c'était plutôt pas mal. Il était assuré d'intégrer l'équipe des États-Unis.

Le tableau se mit à clignoter, puis s'éteignit. Une seconde plus tard, l'image d'une espèce de drapeau apparut, oscillant dans la brise virtuelle.

Tyrone regarda son pote. « Allons bon, ils se sont fait pirater. Pourquoi t'irais pas leur proposer ton aide ? »

Le regard de Jimmy-Joe se mit à pétiller. « Tu crois ? »

Tyrone rigola.

Samedi
Las Vegas, Nevada

« On a un problème, mon colonel », annonça Fernandez.

Ils se trouvaient dans la zone de préparation et chargeaient les camions pour la traversée du désert. Une douzaine d'hommes et de femmes transportaient l'équipement, prêts à se lancer à l'attaque.

« Nous n'avons pas encore établi le contact avec l'ennemi, sergent. Ce n'est pas la police du coin, quand même ? »

Parfois, ils faisaient appel aux forces locales, parfois non, cela dépendait de la situation. Cette fois, il n'y avait pas de flics à proximité pour leur faire redouter qu'ils aient déjà localisé la cible, et les services du shérif du comté de Clark n'avaient pas besoin d'être mis au courant, puisque l'affaire se passait largement en dehors de leur juridiction.

Fernandez haussa les épaules. « Non, c'est l'ordinateur. Jetez donc un coup d'œil. »

Howard s'approcha de l'ordi tactique devant lequel un technicien du nom de Jeter était en train de pester.

« Apparemment, je vois flotter le pavillon britannique, observa Howard.

– Affirmatif, mon colonel, dit Jeter. C'est bien le drapeau anglais. Sauf qu'on était censés recevoir le faisceau du Gros Loucheur, avec l'affichage en 3 D de la position de la cible. » Jeter tapota d'une main le capot du moniteur. « Voilà ce qui arrive quand on s'approvisionne en électronique auprès de ces foutus Néo-Zélandais... sauf votre respect, mon colonel. »

Howard sourit. « Je compte sur vous pour nous régler ça avant notre départ.

– Affirmatif, mon colonel. »

Howard détourna les yeux, inspira un grand coup, expira. Il regarda sa montre. Il se demanda comment Tyrone s'était tiré de sa compétition de boomerang. Il fut tenté d'appeler, mais se ravisa. Transmissions cryptées ou pas, il était imprudent de dévoiler sa position en situation tactique, et ce n'était pas une habitude à prendre. Il appellerait son fils dès qu'ils auraient acquis et neutralisé la cible. Son Tyrone était un gentil garçon, mais c'était aussi un adolescent. La vie commençait à devenir compliquée pour lui, et ça n'allait pas s'arranger. Comment un père pouvait-il protéger son fils contre de tels aléas ? C'était impossible, et c'était cela le plus pénible. Le temps où papa était un sage tout-puissant était révolu. Howard n'y avait jamais prêté vraiment attention mais il fallait bien qu'il se rende à l'évidence : son fils grandissait, il changeait, et s'il voulait garder le contact avec lui, il allait devoir changer lui aussi. Ça lui faisait tout drôle.

« Ça y est, annonça Jeter. On a retrouvé le faisceau. »

Bon, les problèmes d'éducation, on verra plus tard, John. Concentre-toi plutôt sur les affaires en cours.

« Parfait, continuez. »

5

Samedi 2 avril
Londres

Toni Fiorella gravit l'escalier étroit aux marches grinçantes pour gagner le premier étage du petit immeuble qui en comptait quatre. C'est là qu'elle désirait se rendre, juste au-dessus d'une petite boutique d'électro-ménager, dans le quartier de Clapham, entre un restaurant indien de brique rouge et une boutique de troc dont la devanture était obturée par des feuilles de contreplaqué. Presque tous les bâtiments du secteur étaient délabrés. Peut-être pas autant que dans les pires coins du Bronx, mais ce n'était pas l'endroit où l'on aurait eu l'idée d'aller balader sa grand-mère la nuit tombée. À moins que ladite mamie soit trafiquante de drogue et armée jusqu'aux dents.

En arrivant sur le palier, Toni décela des odeurs de sueur, rance et fraîche mêlée.

La lourde porte en bois n'était pas verrouillée.

De l'autre côté se trouvaient quinze ou seize hommes et cinq femmes, tous en pantalon de survêtement noir, chaussures de sport et T-shirt blanc. Les T-shirts portaient au dos un sigle noir et blanc, reproduit en plus petit au-dessus du sein gauche : un kriss – le couteau ondulé javanais – incliné à trente degrés, encerclé par les deux mots : PENTJAK SILAT.

La vingtaine de personnes pratiquait des *djurus*.

Toni sourit. Les postures différaient des siennes, puisque cette version de l'art martial indonésien n'était pas le serak mais une variante du tjikalong – un style pratiqué dans l'ouest de Java – mais elle était suffisamment semblable pour qu'on ne risque pas de confondre les djurus avec des *katas* de karaté.

L'école proprement dite n'avait rien de bien folichon, aucun rapport avec les superbes gymnases du FBI. La salle était haute de plafond, cinq mètres peut-être. Le plancher de bois sombre était usé mais propre. Pliés dans un coin de la vaste salle, on voyait d'épais matelas de mousse bleue, eux aussi bien fatigués, ainsi que deux gros punching-balls garnis de plusieurs couches de ruban d'électricien. Une porte de bois marron exhibait une plaque indiquant qu'elle menait aux toilettes. Des tuyaux apparents, d'eau ou de chauffage, couraient le long du mur du fond à trois mètres de hauteur environ, et le métal des tubulures avait été peint de couleurs alternées, bleu, blanc et rouge. En plein milieu de la salle, un gros poteau de soutien était apparemment protégé par un vieux matelas fixé à l'aide d'une demi-douzaine d'élastiques de saut rouges et bleus. Deux rangées de tubes fluorescents ornaient le plafond. Intégré dans une des fenêtres, un extracteur électrique ronronnait, chassant à l'extérieur les odeurs de transpiration.

Bref, l'archétype de la salle de gym de bonnes dimensions, sans fioritures.

Un grand type passait entre les élèves, vêtu comme eux, surveillant les exercices, corrigeant les postures, distribuant les compliments lorsqu'ils étaient mérités. Sans avoir une musculature de culturiste, il était large d'épaules avec un bassin étroit. Ses cheveux gris taillés en brosse avaient encore quelques reflets bruns. L'homme portait des lunettes d'aviateur. Au premier regard, on lui aurait donné la trentaine, mais Toni supposa qu'il devait être quinquagénaire, à en juger par les mains fripées et les petites rides au coin des yeux.

« Bonsoir, lança-t-il avec un accent britannique un peu sec. Que puis-je pour vous ?

– Bonsoir. Je suis Toni Fiorella. C'est moi qui vous ai appelé un peu plus tôt.

– Ah oui, l'Américaine en visite. Bienvenue ! Je suis Carl Stewart et voici mes élèves. » Il les embrassa du geste. « On terminait nos djurus.

– Que je ne vous dérange surtout pas. Je vais rester là à regarder, si c'est possible.

– Mais, bien sûr, je vous en prie.

– Merci, gourou. » Toni alla se poster près de la pile de matelas.

« Bon, très bien, dit Stewart en s'adressant à la classe. Des questions sur les djurus ? »

Quelques mains se levèrent. Stewart répondit à la curiosité des élèves concernant les diverses postures. Il se montrait patient, sans condescendance, et décomposait chaque fois le mouvement correct.

L'homme était souple, équilibré, nerveux. Au silat, même si la capacité à exécuter un djuru avec précision n'était pas toujours l'indicateur d'une bonne aptitude à se battre, l'observation des mouvements d'un individu n'en demeurait pas moins fort révélatrice.

Les mouvements de Carl Stewart dénotaient une aisance rare. Et pourtant Toni en avait vu, des pratiquants de silat, depuis des années.

Intéressant.

Durant la demi-heure qui suivit, Stewart fit travailler les techniques d'autodéfense, montrant comment les mettre en pratique contre un agresseur, puis il répartit les élèves par paires pour qu'ils s'entraînent à leur tour. Même sans ceinture pour identifier le niveau de chacun, quelques minutes d'observation suffisaient à différencier les élèves avancés des débutants.

Toni savait que c'était là sa faiblesse. Elle avait un bon entraînement grâce à son gourou (c'était ainsi que les Indonésiens appelaient leur maître), mais elle manquait de pratique de groupe, que ce soit comme élève ou comme instructrice. Gourou lui avait toujours dit qu'il lui faudrait enseigner pour tirer le plus grand profit du silat. Et elle venait juste de s'y mettre.

Au bout d'une trentaine de minutes, Stewart fit effectuer à ses meilleurs élèves des séries de duels en style semi-libre. Chacun jouait tour à tour le rôle de l'attaquant et du défenseur. Les attaquants avaient le droit de lancer coups de poing et coups de pied, mais en visant exclusivement le torse ou la cuisse, endroits où un blocage raté faisait juste un peu mal, sans plus.

Elle regarda le premier duel s'engager. Le défenseur était un grand maigre aux longs cheveux bruns, l'attaquant un petit rouquin râblé. Le grand maigre présenta son flanc droit à l'attaquant, adoptant une posture les pieds largement écartés ; sa main gauche était levée à hauteur du visage, l'autre abaissée pour protéger le bas-ventre.

Poil-de-carotte tapa dans son poing droit, pour indiquer qu'il allait s'en servir pour mener son attaque. Placés à deux mètres l'un de l'autre, les deux hommes se tournaient autour avec lenteur.

Poil-de-carotte plongea, le poing tendu vers le centre

de la poitrine de Maigrichon. Ce dernier pivota légèrement, bloqua l'attaque et riposta du revers de la main droite, puis il enchaîna avec une prise et un *sapu*, qui renversa Poil-de-carotte et le jeta à terre.

Pas mal.

Poil-de-carotte se releva, salua Maigrichon en plaçant le poing dans sa paume opposée, puis les rôles s'inversèrent.

Maigrichon attaqua. Poil-de-carotte esquiva par en dessous, enfonça son épaule droite dans l'abdomen de Maigrichon, s'avança et effectua un *biset*, une prise à la cheville, qui jeta Maigrichon au sol.

Pas mal, pas mal du tout. Il devait s'agir des deux meilleurs élèves, estima Toni.

Stewart les congédia d'un geste puis, se tournant vers Toni : « Nous avons ce soir parmi nous une pratiquante américaine de silat. Peut-être aimerait-elle nous faire une démonstration ? »

Toni sourit. Elle s'y était plus ou moins attendue. Comme elle était en jean, tennis et pull de coton à manches courtes, elle n'avait pas besoin de se changer. « Volontiers.

– Joseph, si tu veux bien ? dit Stewart avec un signe de tête à Poil-de-carotte. Joseph est mon plus ancien élève. »

Toni hocha la tête et salua tour à tour Stewart et l'élève, en fermant le poing contre la paume de l'autre main. Position détendue, les mains baissées.

Poil-de-carotte passa sur sa gauche. Elle recula en croisant les pieds, pivotant pour le suivre.

Poil-de-carotte plongea, le poing droit en avant, le poignet serré par la main gauche, prêt à effectuer un balayage latéral en cas de blocage.

Toni se laissa choir au sol, intercepta Poil-de-carotte en lui expédiant sèchement un coup de pied en plein abdomen, passa l'autre pied derrière le genou droit de son adversaire tout en lui assenant un nouveau coup du pied gauche.

Poil-de-carotte bascula en arrière en même temps que Toni exécutait un roulé-boulé, tout en projetant ses pieds joints au-dessus de la tête de son assaillant, marquant le coup en claquant le sol de la main gauche pour indiquer qu'il avait porté.

Poil-de-carotte attendit pour s'assurer qu'elle avait terminé et lorsqu'il la vit s'effacer pour lui montrer que c'était bien le cas, il se releva à son tour, arborant un large sourire. « Joli mouvement ! »

Stewart aussi était souriant. La prise avait certes été spectaculaire, mais elle l'avait pratiquée contre son meilleur élève, il était donc en droit d'être impressionné.

« Très bien, mademoiselle Fiorella.

– Toni, je vous en prie, gourou.

– Oserai-je vous demander si vous vous sentez en forme pour effectuer un *kembangan* ? »

Toni acquiesça. Bien sûr. Le kembangan était la « danse des fleurs » et, contrairement aux postures ou katas de la plupart des arts martiaux, c'était l'expression spontanée de l'art du pratiquant de silat, sans aucune figure préétablie. Un expert ne reproduisait jamais deux fois les mêmes. À l'opposé du *buah*, danse où l'on déployait le maximum de force et de vitesse, le kembangan adoucissait les mouvements ; il se pratiquait les paumes ouvertes plutôt que les poings fermés, et il enchaînait les figures en une chorégraphie adaptée aux circonstances – mariages ou autres célébrations.

Si vous vouliez réellement évaluer la qualité d'un pratiquant de silat, il fallait le voir effectuer le kembangan. Dans l'ancien temps, quand un combat était imminent mais que les adversaires ne voulaient pas se tuer ou s'estropier, il leur arrivait de recourir plutôt au kembangan. Les experts étaient capables de discerner le vainqueur par la maîtrise dont il faisait preuve lors de la danse, évitant ainsi d'en venir aux coups. Si vous étiez battu au kembangan, vous présentiez vos excuses ou régliez le différend éventuel, et la cause était entendue. Il était déshonorant de vouloir s'acharner contre un adversaire de force inférieure, et stupide de s'entêter à défier celui qui de toute évidence vous surpassait. Bien entendu, les meilleurs danseurs introduisaient parfois de propos délibéré d'infimes erreurs dans leur chorégraphie pour tromper l'adversaire en lui faisant croire qu'ils étaient moins doués qu'ils ne l'étaient en réalité. Lors des compétitions de kembangan, il n'y avait que lorsque les concurrents s'estimaient de valeur équivalente que le jeu progressait jusqu'au niveau des coups de poing ou de pied.

Toni inspira profondément, souffla avec lenteur. Elle s'inclina cérémonieusement devant le gourou, se vida une deuxième fois les poumons, puis une troisième, et enfin commença.

Il y avait des jours avec et des jours sans. Aujourd'hui, son influx était bon, elle sentait l'énergie la traverser et elle savait qu'elle pourrait réussir une danse correcte sans erreur grossière. À mi-parcours, elle fit délibérément un léger faux pas, avant de se rattraper au dernier moment. Il convenait de ne pas embarrasser le gourou responsable de l'école qu'on visitait en lui offrant une prestation trop parfaite. Cela aurait risqué de le mettre en porte à faux vis-à-vis de ses élèves, ce qui était malséant.

Une minute devait suffire. Elle acheva sa danse, fit une nouvelle révérence. C'était une de ses meilleures prestations, elle le sentait. Son gourou pourrait être fière.

Les élèves applaudirent spontanément.

Toni rougit, gênée.

Stewart lui sourit. « Superbe. Un kembangan remarquable. Merci... gourou. »

Toni s'inclina légèrement. Il avait reconnu son talent en l'appelant « maître ». Et à présent, elle était curieuse. C'était un rien effronté, mais elle demanda : « Je serais ravie d'apprécier à mon tour votre kembangan, gourou. »

Le silence se fit parmi les élèves. Ce n'était pas un défi direct, mais le message était clair : je t'ai montré mes capacités, à ton tour de me dévoiler les tiennes.

Le sourire de Stewart s'élargit. « Bien sûr. »

Il lui adressa une révérence, différente de la sienne, mais l'intention était identique, il vida ses poumons et son esprit, puis commença. Ses meilleurs jours devaient être derrière lui. À cinquante ans et quelques, il était sans doute déjà sur la pente descendante. Telles étaient les lois de la physiologie humaine. Son savoir était peut-être supérieur, mais son corps aurait toujours un temps de retard et, même si c'était progressif, il allait perdre chaque jour un peu plus de terrain. La femme qui avait été le gourou de Toni était une femme extraordinaire, incroyable, mais elle était déjà âgée quand Toni avait débuté, et certaines choses lui étaient impossibles. Même si Stewart était apparemment encore en bonne forme physique, sûrement bien meilleure que chez la majorité des hommes de son âge, il devait néanmoins avoir déjà perdu une bonne partie de son tonus. Elle estima qu'elle aurait pu commettre une ou deux fautes de plus dans sa démonstration.

Dès la première série de mouvements de Stewart, Toni saisit l'étendue de son erreur.

Quand on était un guitariste honorable et qu'on regardait une cassette d'Andrés Segovia faisant ses exercices, on avait envie de pleurer. Parce qu'on comprenait que jamais on ne lui arriverait à la cheville.

Stewart était pour les arts martiaux l'équivalent de Segovia.

Toni l'observa, fascinée. L'homme évoluait comme s'il n'avait pas de squelette, comme s'il était une goutte d'huile bouillante roulant sur une glace propre, lisse, sans effort... un spectacle ahurissant. Elle n'avait jamais vu personne effectuer le kembangan avec un tel talent.

À peu près au même moment que Toni, Stewart eut une légère hésitation. Son pied redescendit un tantinet de travers, et il dut prestement se pencher pour retrouver son équilibre.

Toni n'y crut pas une seconde. Cet homme qui était assez vieux pour être son père n'aurait jamais commis une telle erreur. Il la lui avait offerte pour que ce ne soit pas elle qui perde la face.

Elle était ébahie. Il n'y avait pas à tortiller : Stewart la surpassait, et de loin. C'était l'adversaire parfait, celui que son gourou l'avait toujours entraînée à affronter : plus grand, plus fort, sans doute plus rapide, et avec une technique supérieure. Au silat, on ne s'entraînait pas à battre des adversaires sans talent, on s'efforçait d'apprendre à vaincre ceux qui étaient aussi bons, voire meilleurs que vous. Si vous parveniez à garder le dessus en de telles circonstances, vous aviez saisi l'essence de l'art indonésien.

Si elle se battait contre Stewart, c'est lui qui gagnerait. Pour elle, ça ne faisait pas l'ombre d'un doute.

Dès qu'elle en eut pris conscience, Toni n'eut qu'un seul désir : l'affronter, le mettre à l'épreuve, se faire battre afin d'en tirer la leçon.

Stewart acheva sa danse et s'inclina. Les élèves étaient prêts à manifester bruyamment leur enthousiasme mais il leva la main pour les réduire au silence. Il s'inclina devant Toni avec une sécheresse toute militaire et un lent hochement de tête.

Toni lui dit alors : « Je compte séjourner ici une semaine ou un peu plus, et je serais honorée si vous m'acceptiez dans votre classe, gourou.

– Tout l'honneur serait pour moi », répondit-il.

Oh, Seigneur !

Samedi
Dans le Raj britannique, aux Indes

Jay Gridley se servait d'une grosse machette en argent pour se frayer un passage au milieu des lianes épaisses qui traînaient jusqu'en travers de la piste. La tâche n'était pas facile, chaleur et humidité l'enveloppaient d'une brume pestilentielle qui le laissait trempé de sueur. La poignée de bois lui donnait des ampoules et la puanteur des branches et des treilles coupées avait des relents douceâtres... d'une telle intensité qu'elles semblaient déborder de sève.

Cela n'avait rien d'une partie de plaisir, cette traversée de la jungle, mais il n'y avait aucun moyen de faire de ce scénario de pistage une promenade de santé. Quel que soit celui qu'il pouvait inventer, la tâche ne lui serait pas facilitée pour autant. Qu'il opte pour une meule de foin, et l'aiguille serait microscopique ; qu'il crée une plage, et sa mission serait d'essayer de trouver une *tache* couleur sable sur un grain de sable particulier. Bref, la mission était difficile, point final, inutile de tourner autour du pot, circulez, y a rien à voir.

Mais il se rapprochait du but. Malgré tout.

Un énorme python albinos se chauffait au soleil sur une grosse branche loin à sa gauche, à l'écart de la piste, aucun danger. Gridley sourit. C'était le chien qui n'aboyait pas la nuit qui lui avait indiqué la bonne direction. Le joueur qui avait craqué le code secret au Pakistan était bien meilleur que tous ceux que Gridley avait déjà pu affronter, aucun doute. Meilleur encore que le paysan de Georgie, meilleur encore que le Russe fou, et malgré ses réticences à l'admettre, bien meilleur que lui. Ce gars était un maître, obligé, pour réussir ce qu'il avait fait, et sans laisser la moindre trace.

Enfin, pas exactement. Le tigre avait quand même laissé une nouille, ou si l'on préférait, une *Piste EN Négatif* dont l'acronyme était PENNE*, d'où cette... « nouille », par assimilation plaisante avec un autre terme argotique. Le concept était impossible à transmettre à quiconque ne connaissait pas le domaine de la RV sur le bout des doigts, et d'une difficulté extrême à appréhender, même lorsqu'on le connaissait. Par son aspect contre-intuitif, c'était en gros comme de vouloir saisir les arcanes de la physique quantique. Le tigre qui avait bouffé la chèvre était passé par ici parce qu'il n'avait laissé aucune piste... et surtout, parce que personne n'aurait pu passer par ici.

Gridley tailla une branche aux feuilles en cœur grosses comme des assiettes à soupe. La branche tomba. Le poids du fusil à canon double posé sur son épaule était oppressant, l'étui du Webley à sa ceinture lui rentrait dans les côtes. Il n'y avait aucune piste visible mais Jay était sûr et certain que le tigre était passé par ici. Il coupa une autre branche, s'en débarrassa...

Il avait raison. Il était bien passé par ici.

C'est à peine s'il l'entrevit au moment où il bondissait. Un éclair orange et blanc, des dents énormes, une patte aux griffes de dragon.

Puis le tigre lui donna sur la tête un coup de cette griffe monstrueuse, et pour Jay Gridley, le monde vira soudain au rouge et disparut.

6

Dimanche 3 avril
Londres

Alex Michaels fut tiré d'un rêve agité au son de la fanfare d'Aaron Copland jouée par son virgil. Il s'assit et fusilla du regard l'appareil posé près du lit, dans son chargeur. Ce qui était encore marrant l'après-midi ne l'était plus du tout à deux heures du matin, même pour vous tirer d'un cauchemar impliquant votre ex-épouse.

À côté de lui, Toni se retourna.

Michaels se leva, empoigna le virgil, coupa la sonnerie, puis se précipita vers la salle de bains. Sitôt entré, il ferma la porte et mit en route le circuit vocal. Après s'être vu dans la glace, il décida de laisser coupé le mode vidéo. À poil, les yeux chassieux et les cheveux en bataille, il n'était pas à son avantage.

L'appel provenait du bureau d'Allison.

« Alex Michaels...

– Ne quittez pas, je vous prie, je vous passe le directeur. »

Bon, d'accord, elle le réveillait au beau milieu de la nuit, mais elle n'allait quand même pas s'abaisser à l'appeler en personne...

Elle fut presque aussitôt en ligne.

« Michaels, nous avons un problème ici. Un de vos garçons, Jason Gridley... c'est ça ?... a eu semble-t-il une sorte d'accident cérébral. Il est actuellement à l'hôpital.

– Quoi ?

– On l'a trouvé lors du changement de poste, aux commandes de son ordinateur.

– Un accident cérébral ? Mais comment ? C'est un gosse ! Il n'y a aucun antécédent de ce type dans sa famille.

– Il faudra que vous demandiez aux médecins. » Elle marqua une pause. « J'ai cru comprendre que Gridley était votre homme de confiance pour les scénarios de réalité virtuelle.

– Effectivement. » Bon sang, une attaque cérébrale ? Jay ? Il n'arrivait pas à se faire à l'idée. Jay n'avait que vingt et quelques années.

« Est-ce que cela pourrait avoir un rapport quelconque avec notre enquête sur l'incident survenu au Pakistan ? »

Mais de quoi parlait-elle ? « Non, non, en aucun cas. Il est impossible d'être blessé par un ordinateur en mode virtuel, même avec le niveau de la connexion d'interface réglé au maximum, il n'y a pas assez de courant. Pourquoi même poser une telle question ?

– Parce qu'un informaticien du renseignement britannique ainsi qu'un de ses collègues au Japon ont subi le même accident cérébral, l'un et l'autre au cours des dernières heures.

– Pas possible. Je veux dire, il est impossible qu'ils aient été provoqués par leur machine.

– Il n'empêche, commandant, que cela me fait l'effet de coïncidences surprenantes. Et on m'a fait comprendre – de manière tout officieuse – que ces deux agents informaticiens enquêtaient eux aussi sur la situation au Pakistan.

– Bon Dieu !

– Peut-être que vous pourriez envisager d'abréger vos vacances...

– Je... oui, bien sûr, vous avez raison. Je réserve une place sur le premier vol pour Washington.

– Parfait. Tenez-moi au courant. »

Michaels contempla son reflet dans la glace. Jamais une seconde d'ennui...

« Alex ? »

Il ouvrit la porte. Toni, tout embrumée de sommeil, se tenait devant lui, nue et superbe. « À qui parlais-tu ?

– À la patronne. »

Et il lui annonça aussitôt la mauvaise nouvelle concernant Jay.

Dimanche
Las Vegas, Nevada

« Nom d'un fils de pute !

– Dois-je prendre cela pour moi, sergent ? »

Howard sourit à Fernandez mais c'était un sourire crispé, forcé. Il comprenait sans peine la frustration de son ami – lui aussi, cette histoire le faisait chier.

L'ordinateur tactique était en rideau. Par deux fois, il avait repris son fonctionnement normal après avoir affiché le drapeau britannique, et puis il avait perdu le signal satellite et n'avait jamais réussi à le récupérer.

Les techniciens avaient bidouillé dans tous les sens, et il était apparu que la panne ne provenait pas de chez eux, mais du système satellitaire de l'armée. Howard s'était aussitôt entretenu avec l'officier responsable de leur côté, mais ça n'avait pas avancé à grand-chose. Le commandant Phillips s'était montré poli mais sec : leur système faisait des siennes, et si le colonel voulait bien l'excuser, il était dans la merde jusqu'au cou pour essayer de s'en dépêtrer, alors s'il était possible qu'on le rappelle dans les plus brefs délais...

Cela remontait à plusieurs heures déjà, or le faisceau n'était toujours pas accessible.

Howard regarda sa montre, puis Fernandez. « Bon, d'accord, c'est râpé. On est baisés. Dis-leur de décrocher. »

Comme de juste, son fidèle lieutenant n'était pas ravi de la nouvelle. « Mon colonel, on n'a pas besoin du faisceau de Gros Loucheur. Ce type est perdu au beau milieu du désert. On peut le repérer en visu.

– Négatif, sergent, ce n'est pas la procédure.

– Mon colonel, les armées ont conquis des territoires depuis des milliers d'années sans couverture satellite. C'est un gars tout seul dans une putain de caravane, on a deux pelotons et assez de matos pour remplir un wagon de marchandises ! Je ne vois pas où est la difficulté.

– Allons, Julio, tu connais les règles. On n'a aucune marge de manœuvre en cas de pépin. Tu l'as dit toi-même, ce gars-là est tout seul. Il est ici depuis des mois, il ignore notre présence, on couvre toutes les voies d'accès et de sortie. Il n'a aucune intention de filer et même s'il le voulait, il ne pourrait pas. Comme cas d'école, on ne peut pas rêver mieux. »

Fernandez grommela dans sa barbe.

« Pardon, sergent ?

– Mon colonel, sauf votre respect, c'est de la daube. Si vingt hommes ne peuvent pas s'emparer d'un homme seul sans l'aide d'un satellite, on ferait aussi bien de raccrocher l'uniforme, partir à la pêche et attendre que vienne la mort. Sauf votre respect, mon colonel. »

Cette fois, le sourire d'Howard était sincère. « Tout à fait d'accord, Julio, mais c'est le protocole imposé pour cette situation opérationnelle. Les gars de la reconnaissance satellite vont bien finir par réparer leur système. Dis aux hommes de se prendre leur soirée. Allez faire la tournée des casinos, voir les spectacles, profiter des néons de Vegas. Et soyez de retour à six heures pile, qu'on reprenne à zéro. »

Fernandez haussa les épaules. Une permission surprise était toujours la bienvenue et puis, après tout, c'était Las Vegas. Un homme avec trois sous en poche y avait l'occasion de se créer toutes sortes d'ennuis sans trop de difficultés. « Ma foi, mon colonel, puisque vous le prenez comme ça, j'imagine qu'il va nous falloir prendre notre mal en patience.

– Et souvenez-vous, sergent, vous êtes quasiment marié, dorénavant.

– Oui, mon colonel, bien sûr. Quasiment marié, certes, mais pas encore mort. Je n'ai pas mes yeux dans la poche. »

Les deux hommes se sourirent.

Howard se dirigea vers le motel proche réquisitionné par la Net Force pour loger ses troupes. Ça faisait toujours bizarre de bivouaquer, non pas dans une tente sous les étoiles mais dans un hôtel climatisé. C'était plus logique, bien sûr. Un campement militaire en rase campagne avait plus de chances d'attirer l'attention que si véhicules et matériel étaient rangés au garage et les troupes planquées hors de vue.

Il comptait appeler chez lui et parler à sa famille, prendre une douche pour se décrasser et tenter de se rafraîchir, puis peut-être se trouver un bon restaurant. On mangeait bien à Las Vegas, surtout dans certains casinos, et qui plus est, pour pas cher. Les gens du coin devaient se dire qu'ils allaient plumer le client, entre les tables de jeu et les machines, ils avaient donc tout intérêt à le garder en lui rendant le séjour et la chère agréables. Et on pouvait jouer au kéno tout en cassant la graine. La plupart des établissements servaient petit déjeuner, déjeuner et dîner vingt-quatre heures sur vingt-quatre. Une fois que vous aviez mis les pieds au paradis du jeu, le temps s'arrêtait. D'ailleurs, les pendules y étaient bannies, pour ne pas vous rappeler qu'il était temps de plier bagage.

Cela faisait déjà pas mal d'années qu'il n'était pas revenu, mais Howard avait l'impression que l'endroit n'avait guère changé. On pouvait laisser les gosses dans une crèche gratuite, ou bien les lâcher à Warner Bros World ou au Hard Rock Café, pour qu'ils aillent claquer l'argent de leur bourse scolaire. C'était le triomphe du loisir familial, bien loin du temps où la Mafia régnait ici en maître.

Le motel était discret et surtout bon marché ; de ce côté, la Net Force ne différait pas des autres agences gouvernementales. Les fonctionnaires n'avaient pas besoin de descendre dans les meilleurs hôtels aux frais du contribuable. Ça faisait toujours mauvais genre, surtout en période électorale.

Un antique bandit manchot trônait près du distributeur de Coca ; Howard le contempla avec un hochement de tête. Il n'était pas joueur. Oh, bien sûr, il achetait un billet de loterie de temps en temps, voire pariait cinq dollars sur un match de foot ou de baseball, mais on ne pouvait pas dire qu'il avait la fièvre du jeu. Les statistiques étaient toujours en faveur de la banque et, à ses yeux, le mieux était de voir les jeux de hasard comme un loisir. Vous vouliez jouer au casino, vous preniez quelques dollars et vous alliez les claquer, exactement comme si vous vous étiez rendu au restaurant ou au spectacle. Une fois l'argent dépensé, terminé, vous quittiez la table, et basta. Vous ne vous creusiez pas les poches pour essayer de récupérer les sommes perdues, et si jamais vous aviez gagné plus avant le délai que vous vous étiez imparti, vous rentriez vite fait mettre l'argent à la banque.

C'est son père qui lui avait enseigné ça. Quand on jouait selon les règles d'un autre, la plupart du temps, c'était lui qui gagnait. Mieux valait consacrer son argent à des choses plus utiles.

La chambre d'Howard était petite mais propre, et, miracle, il y avait de la pression à la douche. Après s'être décrassé, il ouvrit son sac, enfila un pantalon kaki en toile et une chemisette, retrouva des chaussettes propres et chaussa ses vieux mocassins. Ça payait toujours de prendre avec soin une tenue de pékin quand on travaillait à proximité d'une ville. À un moment, on était soldat, l'instant d'après, on était civil. Et de nos jours, la coupe de cheveux n'était plus un critère.

Donc, appeler à la maison, faire le tour de la famille, puis sortir grignoter un petit quelque chose. Et après ? Peut-être rentrer et lire. Après tout, il allait devoir se lever tôt, et même s'il s'était remis de l'infection qui l'avait mis à plat dernièrement [1], l'époque où il pouvait faire la fête toute la nuit et enchaîner sur le boulot sans débander était depuis longtemps révolue. S'il voulait être debout et opérationnel à six heures pétantes, il allait devoir se coucher à une heure décente.

Il se sourit dans la glace. Peut-être que Fernandez avait raison ; peut-être qu'il ferait mieux de prendre sa retraite et de partir à la pêche.

Non. Pas encore.

Dimanche
Quantico, Virginie

Quand Jay Gridley s'éveilla, il connut un moment de panique : où était-il ?

Il avait une perfusion dans la main gauche, un tube qui lui sortait du pénis pour s'introduire dans une poche attachée sur le côté du lit, et des capteurs sans fil collés sur le torse et le crâne. Un brassard ceignait son biceps gauche. Il était vêtu d'une de ces chemises de nuit courtes ouvertes dans le dos.

Un hosto. Bon, d'accord. Et il avait dû lui arriver quelque chose pour qu'il se retrouve ici. Mais quoi ? Un accident ?

Impossible de se souvenir. Il entreprit d'examiner ses membres avec plus d'attention, pour voir si quoi

---

1. Cf. *Net Force 2, Programmes fantômes, op. cit.*

que ce soit manquait ou était endommagé. Non, ils étaient bien là tous les quatre et il ne ressentait aucune douleur...

Une grande brune à cheveux courts en blouse verte apparut près de son lit. Elle lui saisit le poignet droit tout en consultant sa montre. La trentaine, très séduisante. Elle lui sourit. « Hé », fit-il.

Il ne sentait pas les doigts de la jeune femme sur son poignet. À vrai dire, il ne sentait plus du tout son bras droit. Il n'avait plus aucune relation avec ce membre. Comme s'il avait appartenu à une autre personne. Que... ?

Elle l'interrompit : « Vous êtes au service neurologique de l'hôpital de la base. Vous avez eu un AVC, un accident vasculaire cérébral. Une attaque. Je m'appelle Rowena, je suis l'infirmière de garde. Est-ce que vous comprenez ? »

Une attaque ? Comment était-ce possible ? Il répondit : « Je comprends. »

Mais ce qui sortit alors de sa bouche était une espèce d'horrible baragouin empâté : « gne tompian ».

Sa panique latente se mua en terreur explosive.

L'infirmière lui posa la main sur le torse, du côté gauche. Ça, il le sentit. « Du calme. Le médecin qui s'occupe de vous arrive, elle vous expliquera tout. Mais écoutez-moi : vous n'avez pas à vous inquiéter. Vous avez une paralysie transitoire du côté droit. Elle va disparaître. L'accident que vous avez subi était mineur. Le traitement qu'on vous administre va régler ça. Cela prendra quelques jours, deux semaines peut-être, d'accord ? Mais vous allez vous en tirer sans aucune séquelle. »

Gridley sentit sa panique s'apaiser un peu. Il allait

s'en tirer sans séquelles. Il s'accrocha à cet espoir, de toutes ses forces. Sans séquelles.

À moins qu'elle te raconte ça pour t'empêcher de perdre complètement les pédales, lui dit sa petite voix intérieure.

Une autre femme pénétra dans la chambre, une petite boulotte aux cheveux blond décoloré. Elle aussi était en blouse verte et elle était munie d'un écran-plat*. Elle attaqua sans préambule : « Je suis le Dr West. Dans le courant de l'après-midi d'hier, vous avez eu un léger AVC. Une attaque. Il n'y a eu ni caillot ni hémorragie importante visible à la tomographie ou au scannographe et la cause est idiopathique, ce qui veut dire que nous en ignorons l'origine. Vos signes vitaux sont normaux, pression artérielle, respiration, pouls, et votre bilan sanguin reste dans les limites normales. En dehors de l'AVC, vous vous portez à merveille. Vous avez ce que nous pensons être une hémiplégie transitoire ou hémiparésie, et nous escomptons sa résorption totale. Vous me suivez ? »

Gridley hocha la tête en silence, répugnant à entendre le son de sa propre voix.

« Bien. Vous allez rester ici un jour ou deux, ensuite on vous laissera retourner chez vous. La kiné commence cet après-midi. Quelqu'un viendra vous montrer les exercices à faire. »

La toubib regarda sa montre. « Faut que j'y aille. Je repasserai vous voir un peu plus tard, avec une escouade d'étudiants en médecine. Vous allez avoir d'autres visites, pour des prélèvements de sang, la prise de médicaments... D'ici là, tâchez de vous reposer un peu. »

Le Dr West tendit à Rowena l'écran-plat et ressortit de la chambre.

Se reposer ?

Ouais, d'accord. Une partie de sa cervelle venait d'exploser et il était censé se *reposer* ?

Pas question. Totalement exclu. Il n'avait pas non plus envie de rester là étendu à se ronger les sangs, mais quel choix avait-il ? Il était intubé, câblé et branché de partout, il ne risquait pas de filer quelque part.

Seigneur ! Comment cela avait-il pu arriver ?

7

Dimanche 3 avril
Les Ifs, Sussex, Angleterre

Applewhite apporta le plateau de Goswell et le déposa sur la table. De la vapeur s'échappait du bec de la théière – il faisait un peu plus frais ici dans le jardin, mais c'était une fraîcheur vivifiante. Goswell hocha la tête. « Merci, Applewhite. »

Le maître d'hôtel servit une tasse de thé, ajouta un morceau de sucre et une rondelle de citron. « Je vous rapporte des pains au lait, monsieur ?

– Je pense que ça ira. Mais allez me chercher un téléphone, je vous prie.

– Certainement, milord, tout de suite. »

Applewhite avait sorti un portable de sa poche de jaquette avant que Goswell n'ait eu le temps de boire une gorgée de thé. Il hocha la tête. La technologie... Un progrès discutable sans aucun doute, mais qui lui avait été bien utile, à tous points de vue, financier, entre autres.

« Et comment s'appelle déjà notre ami scientifique ?

– Peter Bascomb-Coombs, milord.

– Ah oui, bien sûr. » Goswell répéta le nom de l'homme devant le micro, puis il porta le combiné à son oreille. L'appareil sonna trois fois.

« Oui, qui est à l'appareil ? » La voix paraissait

irritée. Enfin, rien d'étonnant, les spécimens dans son genre l'étaient toujours.

« Geoffrey Goswell à l'appareil.

– Oh. Lord Goswell. » Cela lui fit bien vite changer de ton. Non, mais ! « Que puis-je pour vous ?

– Pas grand-chose, mon garçon. Je vous téléphonais pour prendre des nouvelles de... eh bien... de la petite affaire dont nous avons discuté récemment à dîner.

– Ah oui, ma foi, cela se présente bien, monseigneur. Il y a eu un ou deux petits pépins mineurs, mais je les ai réglés et nous devrions d'ici peu être à nouveau dans les temps. »

Il manifestait une prudence louable, le scientifique. Même si Peel l'avait assuré que son téléphone mobile et celui de son interlocuteur étaient protégés contre toute écoute intempestive, Goswell détestait voir les choses de cette nature exprimées tout haut hors des murs de son domicile.

Il acquiesça, puis se rendit compte que l'autre ne pouvait pas le voir puisque l'appareil n'était pas équipé d'une caméra ni d'un quelconque dispositif de visée. « Eh bien, c'est parfait. Et ces... euh..., ces curieux dont vous m'avez parlé ?

– Ils ont cessé de l'être, monseigneur. Ils ont d'autres soucis en tête à l'heure actuelle.

– Eh bien, à la bonne heure. Je m'en vais vous quitter maintenant. »

Applewhite réapparut pour récupérer le mobile et le ranger. « Aurez-vous besoin d'autre chose, milord ?

– Oui, voyez si vous pouvez me dénicher Peel, voulez-vous ? J'aimerais lui toucher un mot s'il est disponible.

– Tout de suite, milord. »

Applewhite s'éclipsa pour aller chercher le commandant. Cela allait au moins laisser à Goswell un peu de temps pour déguster son thé avant qu'il ne refroidisse.

Goswell avisa un mouvement du coin de l'œil. Il se tourna et découvrit un lapin dans un parterre, en train de grignoter des pousses. Le petit salopiot ! Il n'était pas à quinze mètres ! Bien sûr, ces satanés rongeurs ne se manifestaient pas quand il avait son fusil, c'est qu'ils étaient malins ! Il n'avait plus ses yeux de vingt ans, mais sacrebleu, il était encore capable de dégommer un lapin qui osait le narguer à quinze mètres de distance avec son Purdey de chasse à double canon, Dieu merci ! Il songea un instant à appeler Applewhite pour lui dire d'aller chercher son arme afin qu'il puisse régler son compte à l'effronté, puis il se ravisa. C'était une matinée trop radieuse pour être gâchée par une détonation, si satisfaisante que puisse être la perspective d'enseigner à Jeannot Lapin les bonnes manières. Mieux vaudrait demander au jardinier de lâcher ses chiens sur lui. C'était rare qu'ils réussissent à en attraper, mais ça leur faisait tellement plaisir, et puis ensuite les lapins avaient tendance à se tenir à carreau pendant un certain temps.

Il dégusta son thé. Et quand Peel arriva, le rongeur décida de s'éclipser. Peut-être avait-il pressenti que l'homme était excellent tireur avec le pistolet qui ne le quittait jamais et qu'il était par conséquent plus sage de prendre congé.

« Monseigneur ?

– Bonjour, commandant. Asseyez-vous et prenez une tasse de thé.

– Merci, monseigneur. » Peel s'assit. Un type bien,

l'image de son père, le vieux Ricky. Il se servit une tasse de thé, sans sucre.

« J'ai réfléchi au sujet de notre ami scientifique.

– Bascomb-Coombs.

– Lui-même. J'ai pensé qu'on aurait peut-être intérêt à le tenir à l'œil, si vous voyez ce que je veux dire. Le bonhomme est précieux, mais avec ce qu'il a dans la tête, nous ne voudrions pas le voir nous faire faux bond, n'est-ce pas ?

– Je ne pense pas que l'hypothèse soit vraisemblable, monseigneur.

– Certes, certes. Mais sait-on jamais, on ne saurait être assez prudent, n'est-ce pas ?

– Je comprends tout à fait. Il se trouve justement que j'avais prévu votre inquiétude et c'est pourquoi j'ai fait mettre notre M. Bascomb-Coombs sous surveillance.

– Pas possible ? Excellent. Vous êtes un brave gars, Peel.

– Merci, monseigneur. J'apprécie votre confiance. »

Goswell sourit en buvant son thé. Il était bon d'être entouré d'hommes comme Peel, des hommes qui savaient prendre des initiatives sans qu'on ait besoin de les tenir par la main. Des hommes d'extraction assez convenable pour ne pas commettre d'impair ou se livrer à des actes inconsidérés. Eussent-ils été un peu plus nombreux que l'Empire ne serait pas tombé aussi bas.

« Que M. Bascomb-Coombs s'avise de devenir un problème, monseigneur, et nous sommes bien entendu prêts à nous occuper de lui... de manière, disons, expéditive.

– Ah, ma foi, voilà qui est excellent. Prenez donc un petit pain. »

Peel sourit. Oui, vraiment un brave gars. Quel

dommage, vraiment, cette histoire en Irlande. Malgré tout, la perte du régiment était un gain pour Goswell. Il aurait bien voulu en avoir douze comme lui. Il était si dur de s'entourer d'éléments de valeur, de nos jours.

« Excellents, ces petits pains, monseigneur.

– Je dirai à Applewhite de transmettre vos compliments au chef. »

C'est dans ces conditions qu'un gentleman était censé prendre son petit déjeuner. Par une belle journée de printemps, installé dans son domaine campagnard, avec du thé et de succulents pains au lait, en compagnie de gens agréables. Oui, absolument.

Dimanche
Londres

Attablés dans un petit restaurant près de leur hôtel, Alex et Toni prenaient leur petit déjeuner. Toni expliqua : « Nous avons un vol qui décolle d'Heathrow à midi. Je n'ai pas pu nous avoir de place sur le Concorde ou sur un vol direct, il faudra donc changer à Kennedy pour rallier Dulles avec un petit coucou. »

Alex but une gorgée de son café avant de remarquer : « Tu pourrais rester ici. Tu n'es pas obligée d'écourter tes vacances.

– Rester ici toute seule ? Quel intérêt ?

– Eh bien, ce cours de silat que tu as trouvé m'a l'air intéressant.

– Juste deux heures en soirée. Non, si tu pars, je pars. Tu auras besoin de moi au boulot. »

Il touilla ses œufs avec sa fourchette, pas vraiment affamé. « Trop cuits... Un poil de plus, et on aurait pu jouer au hockey avec.

– Je suis désolée pour Jay.

– Les toubibs ont dit qu'il allait s'en sortir très bien. Sans doute sans séquelles.

– N'empêche.

– Je n'arrive pas à croire qu'il ait été blessé par un truc survenu en RV. » Alex fixait ses œufs sur le plat tout desséchés.

« Tu as vu les rapports des Britanniques et des Japonais. Le même accident est arrivé à leurs hommes, et eux aussi furetaient dans le même secteur que Jay.

– Malgré tout, ça paraît impossible.

– Craquer le code de l'itinéraire du train pakistanais aussi. Celui qui y est parvenu a sur nous plusieurs métros d'avance. Il sait des choses que nous ignorons.

– Que voilà une pensée réconfortante. »

Elle le regarda. Il semblait terriblement lugubre. « T'as un autre souci en tête, Alex ? »

Il touilla ses œufs une dernière fois, puis reposa sa fourchette. « Eh bien, oui. Mais je ne voulais pas t'importuner avec ça.

– Vas-y, importune-moi. C'est quoi ?

– J'ai reçu un mot des avocats de mon ex, ce matin, par fax électronique.

– Et... ?

– Megan me poursuit pour obtenir la garde intégrale de Susan.

– Oh, non.

– Oh si. Peut-être que je n'aurais pas dû mettre un pain à son nouveau mec[1].

– Tu m'as dit toi-même qu'elle préparait déjà le coup.

– Oui. Mais ça n'a certainement pas dû aider. Pas plus que d'avoir dit que s'il dormait un jour de plus chez Susie, j'attaquerais celle-ci pour adultère.

– T'étais vachement remonté.

– Mouais. Et stupide. Ce n'est pas une méchante femme, c'est juste qu'elle a le don de me mettre en rogne.

– Ne lui trouve pas des excuses. C'est une salope. »

Il sourit. « Malheureusement, il se trouve que cette salope est la mère de mon seul enfant, et elle veut m'enlever ma fille. Pour que ce prof barbu lui serve de père.

– Qu'en dit ton avocat ?

– Ce que les avocats disent toujours. De ne pas s'inquiéter, qu'il va s'en occuper, que Megan ne gagnera pas. »

Elle tendit le bras au-dessus de la table pour lui prendre la main. « Ça va marcher. Tu es un homme trop bien, n'importe quel juge pourra le constater. »

Il sourit encore, retourna la main pour serrer la sienne.

« Merci. Je t'aime.

– C'est pour ça que je suis ici. »

Elle aimait Alex depuis un bon bout de temps, et même s'il avait parfois le don de l'exaspérer, avec sa manie de mettre le couvercle sur ses émotions et de vouloir absolument la protéger, ce n'était là que

1. Cf. *Net Force 2, Programmes fantômes, op. cit.*

broutilles. Qu'ils finiraient bien par surmonter, à la longue. Elle en était certaine.

Dimanche
Las Vegas, Nevada

Malgré sa résolution de se coucher tôt, il était minuit quand John Howard se retrouva, au bout d'une longue promenade, en train de contempler le ciel au milieu du parking de l'hôtel-casino Luxor. Un vent sec et mordant tourbillonnait entre les voitures en soulevant des nuages de poussière. L'aire de stationnement était entourée de palmiers et de végétation exotique. Les étés du Nevada étaient assez chauds pour convaincre les arbres qu'ils pouvaient prospérer, à condition de leur procurer suffisamment d'eau, mais les palmiers n'avaient pas l'air de se plaire au ras du bitume et ils oscillaient dans la brise, comme s'ils se sentaient déracinés.

Au sommet de l'immense pyramide noire que formait le Luxor, était disposé un mince anneau de projecteurs qui braquaient à la verticale leur faisceau puissant. La chaleur émise par cette colonne lumineuse évoquant un rayon laser était assez intense pour aspirer l'air et la poussière, les projetant vers les cieux au milieu de leur fontaine de photons. La nuit ne pouvait contempler Las Vegas que de loin : la ville interdisait tout accès aux ténèbres.

Howard observait ce faisceau lumineux bouillonnant. Un papillon de nuit qui s'aventurerait trop près de cette colonne blanche se retrouverait illico rôti et propulsé vers la lune.

Toute cette ville avait quelque chose d'incroyablement décadent, et le Luxor en était le symbole. Plus de quatre mille chambres, une bonne demi-douzaine de restaurants, un casino qui ne fermait jamais, une piscine olympique, plus un voyage au pays des Morts, dès le hall d'entrée. C'était l'Égypte ancienne vue par Disney, et contre un dollar, on pouvait tirer le bras d'une divinité antique et tenter la fortune. Faites vos jeux, mesdames et messieurs, faites vos jeux...

Il était entré, avait regardé autour de lui, ébahi mais aussi écrasé par l'ensemble du spectacle. Ici, à l'extérieur du bâtiment massif dont l'entrée était marquée par un obélisque géant qui eût ridiculisé celui de la Concorde, et gardé par un sphinx en bien meilleur état que son grand frère d'Égypte, Howard pouvait toucher du doigt l'ampleur de la richesse des États-Unis. Un pays capable de réaliser des lieux pareils, uniquement conçus pour le loisir, la distraction des millions de touristes qui avaient les moyens de venir y jouer... voilà qui en disait long. Il ne pouvait guère le reprocher aux organisateurs dont l'objectif était de délester les gogos de leurs économies : ils avaient accompli un boulot remarquable, mais si séduisant et impressionnant que soit le résultat, il avait en même temps quelque chose d'un peu... répugnant.

Las Vegas faisait appel au côté fêtard, jouisseur, cigale, insouciant du lendemain qui existe en chacun de nous. Mais aussi au côté sombre, avide du joueur invétéré. C'était le symbole de tout ce que l'Amérique incarnait de toc et de tape-à-l'œil. Mais c'était malgré tout le pied.

Howard étouffa un rire ironique et se décida à regagner sa chambre de motel. Eh bien, John, deviendrais-tu philosophe avec l'âge ? Si tu n'y fais pas gaffe, tu vas te retrouver dans une cellule de moine à contempler ton nombril.

Il rit à nouveau. Allons bon. Enfin peut-être pas tout de suite.

Dimanche
Stonewall Flat, Nevada

Roujio s'éveilla d'un sommeil agité, aussitôt aux aguets, comme il en avait pris l'habitude bien des années auparavant dans les services secrets soviétiques. Il tendit l'oreille mais ne releva rien d'anormal. Au bout de quelques minutes, il se leva, se rendit aux toilettes, puis se dirigea vers la porte de la caravane et l'ouvrit. Tout nu, il contempla le désert.

La nuit était claire, cloutée d'innombrables étoiles scintillantes. Hormis la brise qui agitait le sable et les broussailles, rien ne bougeait. Pas le moindre signe de vie.

Il se frotta le menton. Il ne s'était pas rasé depuis plusieurs jours, il serait peut-être temps...

Quelques instants après, il refermait la porte. Quelque chose clochait. Le danger menaçait derrière sa porte, même s'il ne pouvait le voir ou l'entendre, il sentait qu'il était là.

Soupir. Le moment était venu pour lui de sortir son arsenal et de se préparer. Il avait d'autres détails à vérifier, bien sûr, certains préparatifs entrepris dès son installation. Si l'heure de la Faucheuse était enfin venue, il n'éprouverait aucun regret, mais s'il devait perdre l'ultime bataille, au moins aurait-il fait le maximum pour la gagner. Il se sentait un peu rouillé, faute d'entraînement, et tout ce qui lui restait, c'était son astuce. Il comptait bien l'exploiter au mieux.

Roujio retourna dans la salle de bains. Il allait se débarbouiller et se raser, puis se vêtir pour s'apprêter au combat.

8

Dimanche 3 avril
Londres

Michaels et Toni réglaient leur note d'hôtel avant de monter dans un taxi pour gagner l'aéroport quand le réceptionniste remarqua : « Il serait peut-être judicieux que vous appeliez votre compagnie aérienne, monsieur.

– Oh ?

– Oui, monsieur. Nous venons d'apprendre qu'il y avait comme un problème avec les horaires de vol au départ d'Heathrow. Ainsi que de Gatwick, du reste, j'en ai peur. »

Il s'avéra que le réceptionniste était le roi de la litote. Les multiples tentatives de Michaels pour contacter British Airways se révélèrent en effet infructueuses. Toutes les lignes étaient momentanément occupées et on lui conseillait de rappeler plus tard, merci.

Alors que c'était justement ce qu'il s'apprêtait à faire, Toni le prit par le bras pour l'attirer devant un téléviseur installé au bar de l'hôtel. La BBC venait d'interrompre ses programmes pour diffuser un bulletin spécial : apparemment, les réseaux informatiques de tous les grands aéroports internationaux avaient pété les plombs. La panne affectait non seulement les ordinateurs de réservation et de délivrance des billets, mais aussi les systèmes de contrôle aérien et les balises de navigation et d'atterrissage automatique. Un rapide tour d'horizon révéla que les problèmes touchaient Los Angeles, New York, Dallas-Fort Worth, Denver, Sydney, Auckland, Djakarta, New Delhi, Hongkong, Moscou, Francfort, Paris et Londres. Le trafic aérien civil sur toutes les grandes plates-formes aéroportuaires internationales avait été pour ainsi dire gelé en l'espace de quelques minutes. Le personnel aérien essayait de gérer la crise, mais sans ordinateurs, la tâche était quasiment insurmontable. En bien des endroits, il vous était impossible d'acheter un billet ou une réservation. Quand c'était le cas, vous n'aviez guère d'espoir de trouver un avion prêt au départ – et encore, à condition d'avoir repéré la bonne porte – et si, par miracle, vous réussissiez à en dénicher un, il était hautement improbable qu'il puisse décoller dans un délai prévisible.

Pour aujourd'hui, en tout cas, l'homme semblait interdit de ciel.

« Nom de Dieu ! s'exclama Michaels.

– C'est effectivement le bordel. Et tu sais quoi ? »

Alex hocha la tête, amer. « Ouais. Quelque part, ça va nous retomber dessus. »

Il savait qu'il n'aurait pas dû dire ça, savait que le dieu las qui surveillait les imbéciles était toujours aux aguets de ce genre de remarque. La réaction ne fut pas longue à venir.

« Commandant Michaels ? »

Michaels se retourna pour découvrir une belle et grande femme aux yeux verts. La trentaine, cheveux blond délavé taillés court, elle était vêtue d'une tenue sombre, discrète, la jupe descendant presque aux genoux, et chaussée de souliers à talons plats. Quand elle avança vers lui, il se fit l'observation qu'elle devait être gymnaste. Ou peut-être danseuse. Très mignonne en tout cas...

« Oui ?

– Je m'appelle Angela Cooper, je travaille au MI-6. » Elle sortit un portefeuille et lui exhiba une carte holographique attestant de son appartenance aux services de renseignements extérieurs britanniques. « Auriez-vous l'obligeance, mademoiselle Fiorella et vous, de m'accompagner ? Le ministre Wood et le directeur général Helms aimeraient beaucoup s'entretenir avec vous.

– Nous étions censés prendre un avion », nota Michaels.

D'un signe de tête, Cooper indiqua la télévision avant de lui adresser un petit sourire. « J'ai bien peur que ce soit hors de question dans un avenir proche, monsieur. Et si nous devons régler ce problème, votre aide nous sera bien utile. Nous en avons déjà informé votre directeur. »

Michaels regarda Toni. Elle haussa les sourcils, l'air interloqué.

Eh bien, pourquoi pas ? Ça serait sans doute toujours plus amusant que de poireauter dans une aérogare bondée. Par ailleurs, il avait beaucoup entendu parler du bâtiment où logeait le MI-6 ; faute de mieux, ce serait intéressant de le visiter.

Il y avait quelque chose chez Angela Cooper qui agaçait Toni. Alors que la jeune Anglaise les pilotait dans le dédale des rues de Londres à bord de sa grosse Mitsubishi jusqu'à Vauxhall Crossing, Toni essayait de mettre le doigt dessus. La jeune femme était séduisante, polie, bien élevée. Elle avait sans doute son âge, à un ou deux ans près, et si elle travaillait au MI-6, les deux jeunes femmes devaient sans doute avoir pas mal de points en commun. Tout bien considéré, elle ne semblait pas avoir la moindre raison de détester Mlle Cooper. C'était peut-être une question d'alchimie personnelle. À moins que ce ne soit à cause de ce qu'elle avait cru lire dans le regard d'Alex quand la jeune femme les avait accostés : cette brève étincelle d'intérêt masculin prestement étouffée. Il lui avait dit qu'il l'aimait et Toni le croyait, mais les hommes étaient parfois difficiles à cerner. Si elle n'avait pas été là, quelle aurait été la réaction d'Alex devant cette grande bringue aux cheveux blond filasse ? Aurait-il flirté ? Poussé le jeu plus loin ?

Elle se haïssait de manifester une telle jalousie. Rien ne l'autorisait à croire qu'Alex fût infidèle, même en pensées, mais c'était ce qu'elle ressentait d'instinct. Personne n'avait jamais dit que l'amour était logique. Ou si c'était le cas, c'était un mensonge.

« Nous voici sur Vauxhall Bridge Road, annonça Cooper. À présent, c'est tout droit jusqu'à l'autre rive de la Tamise. Vous n'allez pas tarder à voir apparaître notre immeuble, sur votre gauche. Juste après la bouche de métro. » Elle tendit le doigt et Toni s'avança sur la banquette arrière pour mieux voir.

Le siège du MI-6 était un bâtiment imposant et assez inhabituel pour une ville comme Londres. Il était revêtu de pierre de taille crème, avec de vastes surfaces vitrées aux reflets verts.

Assis à l'avant à côté de Cooper, Alex observa : « Je

pensais que la sécurité intérieure était l'affaire du MI-5. Que le MI-6 ne s'occupait que de l'étranger.

– Un peu comme le FBI et la CIA ? répondit Cooper. Ma foi, jusqu'à un certain point, c'est vrai. Mais leurs attributions se recouvrent plus ou moins. Au cours des dernières années, le MI-5 s'est défait d'une bonne partie de ses ressources pour se recentrer sur l'Irlande du Nord, la lutte contre le crime organisé et la fraude fiscale. Au siège, tout le monde s'accorde à estimer que cette menace informatique émane sans doute de l'étranger, ce qui nous offre une certaine marge de manœuvre pour intervenir. Après tout, nous faisons tous cause commune. »

Alex sourit. « Ça, c'est une différence avec le couple FBI-CIA. »

Cooper lui rendit son sourire, exhibant une dentition parfaite. « Oh, bien sûr, nous avons nous aussi nos rivalités entre services. Et le MI-5 – entre nous, on l'appelle le SS, le Service de sécurité – hausse parfois le sourcil quand on a tendance à venir marcher sur ses plates-bandes. Mais au gouvernement, nos ministres de tutelle semblent passablement démunis devant toute cette affaire et c'est pourquoi ils ont demandé au SIS – le *Secret Intelligence Service*, c'est-à-dire nous, au MI-6 – de filer un coup de main aux gars du renseignement intérieur. En fait, notre système informatique est plus performant que celui du SS, ce qui nous place idéalement. Cela dit, je vous soupçonne, outre-Atlantique, d'être plus avancés que nous. Nous avons eu d'excellents échos du travail de votre organisation. Vous êtes une émanation du CITAC, n'est-ce pas ? »

Elle faisait allusion au *Computer Investigations and Infrastructure Threat Assessment Center* (le Centre d'évaluation des menaces et d'enquête sur la criminalité informatique) que le FBI avait créé au milieu des années quatre-vingt-dix pour traiter ce problème.

« Pas exactement, répondit Alex. Mais il y a en effet un rapport. Je constate que vous avez bien révisé vos fiches. »

Nouveau sourire Colgate de Cooper.

Décidément, Toni n'aimait pas du tout cette fille, et si Alex n'arrêtait pas de sourire comme un idiot à chaque remarque de Mlle Cooper, il courait au-devant de gros ennuis.

Bien révisé ses fiches. Tu parles, Charles.

Dimanche
Stonewall Flat, Nevada

La préférence de Roujio allait aux armes de petit calibre, comme celles auxquelles il s'était habitué dans les Spetsnatz. En fait, elles étaient tout aussi efficaces que les gros flingues qu'aimaient tant les Américains – à condition de viser juste. Une balle de 22 dans l'œil faisait plus de dégâts qu'une de 357 Magnum dans la poitrine. Par ailleurs, il était bien plus facile de tirer correctement avec un petit calibre : il n'y avait presque pas de recul, la détonation et l'éclair restaient discrets, sans compter que le canon plus long accroissait la précision du tir.

On enseignait en général aux Américains à viser le centre de masse, et dans ce cas, une balle plus grosse était un avantage, compte tenu du relatif manque de puissance des armes de poing, mais de ce côté ils auraient pu prendre exemple sur les agents israéliens ou soviétiques. Avec un minimum de pratique, viser la tête devenait un réflexe.

Quand il était venu s'installer dans ce désert, Roujio avait acheté deux armes, toutes deux d'occasion. La première était un pistolet d'exercice, un Browning Silhouette IMSA, dérivé du modèle Buck Mark du même fabricant. C'était un semi-automatique à chargeur de dix projectiles, muni d'un canon de 22,5 centimètres surmonté d'une lunette Tasco ProPoint. La visée était électronique, engendrant dans le champ visuel un minuscule point rouge sans défaut de parallaxe. Le maniement était simple : on chargeait une balle, on allumait le viseur, on alignait le point sur la cible et si l'on pressait la détente avec précaution, la marque rouge correspondait au point d'impact. À dix mètres, on pouvait faire un trou dans une pièce de dix cents. À cent, le canon bien calé sur un appui, Roujio était capable d'atteindre à tous coups une cible grosse comme la main. À l'entraînement, il avait déjà touché une cible de la taille d'un homme à près de trois cents mètres de distance – une fois estimées correctement la dérive et la trajectoire de la balle. Même un projectile ridiculement petit comme celui du Browning pouvait méchamment vous surprendre s'il vous atteignait de plein fouet, y compris à cette distance. Ce n'était peut-être pas le meilleur choix pour le tir de loin, mais en théorie, les munitions qu'il utilisait (des CCI Minimag) avaient une portée de deux mille quatre cents mètres. Un fusil restait bien sûr une arme supérieure mais on pouvait toujours planquer un pistolet sous un par-dessus, si la nécessité se faisait sentir, tout en l'utilisant pour atteindre un homme en pleine tête à des distances bien supérieures à celles où savaient opérer la majorité des utilisateurs d'armes de poing.

La seconde arme de son arsenal réduit était un Savage modèle 69 série E. Un fusil à pompe de calibre 12. Acheté lui aussi sur le marché clandestin, mais dans une autre ville que le pistolet, il n'était pas aussi perfectionné que les modèles plus coûteux qui utilisaient un mécanisme à double glissière : avec un seul pontet asymétrique, il se révélait moins efficace en cas d'enrayage. L'arme avait une capacité de cinq cartouches – pour sa part, il affectionnait la chevrotine n° 4 – mais avec une configuration à canon court, ce que les Américains appelaient un mousqueton, et correspondait à peu près à ce qu'il avait cherché au départ.

Il aurait certes pu se procurer un bon fusil de chasse avec lunette pour gagner en portée. Si toutefois quelqu'un avait l'intention de l'assassiner à cinq cents mètres de distance à l'aide d'un fusil à grande puissance, il avait pour régler la question un moyen plus efficace que le duel façon western. Il avait fait le tour de sa roulotte et inspecté tous les endroits d'où un tireur pouvait l'atteindre, et il n'y avait qu'un nombre réduit d'emplacements où l'on avait une bonne ligne de mire. Une fois ces derniers repérés, il y avait installé certaines défenses de son cru. Évidemment, on pourrait toujours l'abattre quand il était loin de la caravane, mais on ne pouvait jamais se prémunir contre tous les aléas.

La veille au soir, il avait nettoyé et huilé les deux armes avant de les charger de munitions neuves. Il avait en outre garni quatre autres chargeurs pour le pistolet et, pour le calibre 12, il avait glissé douze projectiles supplémentaires dans la cartouchière qu'il pouvait se fixer autour de la taille. S'il devait recourir au fusil à pompe pour se défendre, c'est que la situation serait devenue délicate : il n'aurait sans doute guère de chances de recharger ; malgré tout, on ne pouvait jurer de rien. S'il en arrivait à ce stade, il était prêt à vendre chèrement sa peau. Il était toujours possible qu'il perde, mais même dans ce cas, le vainqueur ne s'en tirerait pas indemne.

Il avait fait le maximum. Il aurait pu tenter de fuir, mais il était sans doute déjà trop tard. Quoi qu'il advienne, il n'y pouvait plus rien, et il était prêt à toute éventualité. Désormais, ce n'était plus qu'une question de patience.

Et la patience, ça le connaissait. En attendant, il allait essayer de dormir un peu. C'était peut-être la dernière fois avant un bout de temps. Ou avant le sommeil éternel.

Il se dirigea vers son lit, déposa le fusil et le pistolet par terre à portée de main, et juste à côté, un petit émetteur de radiocommande. Il s'étira, inspira profondément à plusieurs reprises, se relaxant au maximum et, en quelques minutes, sombra dans le sommeil.

Il rêva d'Anna.

9

Dimanche 3 avril
Las Vegas, Nevada

« C'est loin d'ici ? s'enquit Howard.

– Une vingtaine de minutes, répondit Fernandez.

– Baisse la clim d'un poil, il ne fait pas si chaud.

– Mais mieux vaut ne pas laisser la température monter dans l'habitacle, John. D'ici midi, il va sans doute faire trente-cinq et vous savez à quel point ces bahuts absorbent la chaleur.

– Si tout se passe comme prévu, à c'te heure-là, on sera déjà dans l'avion pour Washington.

– Ça ne fait jamais de mal de parer à toute éventualité », nota le sergent.

Howard hocha la tête. Ils roulaient seuls dans le command-car, un Humvee* modifié couleur sable. « Transmission automatique, direction assistée, climatisation, et tu t'inquiètes d'avoir chaud ? Tu te fais douillet avec l'âge, mon petit Julio.

– Peut-être que le général voudra plutôt prendre sa calèche, la prochaine fois ? Je suis sûr que la vieille Nelly serait plus à son goût...

– Eh bien, au moins elle ne se plaindrait pas de la chaleur, elle.

– Et dans le cas contraire, vous pourriez toujours

manier votre fouet de postillon. Je parie que vous en avez plein votre penderie. »

Sourire d'Howard. « Bon, d'accord. On se refait un topo de la situation ? »

Fernandez leva brièvement les yeux au ciel. « Mon général, nous avons trois équipes de deux hommes – enfin, de deux personnes – postées en surveillance à Cow Scull Gulch. Si jamais l'ami Ivan s'avise de pointer le nez dehors, on peut à tous les coups le dégommer aussi facilement que Davy Crockett un écureuil. On passe sous la couverture satellite du Gros Loucheur dès huit heures du matin ; par ailleurs, un hélico de la Garde nationale sera à tout moment à notre disposition, prêt à décoller de Nellis, si besoin est, ce qui ne sera pas le cas. On aura enfin, de part et d'autre, deux escouades de fantassins motorisés, prêts à intervenir... et tout ça pour un ex-espion soviétique bouclé dans une roulotte Airstream perdue au milieu de nulle part, sans aucune possibilité de fuir ou de se planquer. »

Howard acquiesça. « Très bien. »

Fernandez décela néanmoins chez lui comme une pointe d'inquiétude. « Ben quoi, John ? On pourrait très bien aller tous les deux alpaguer ce connard – sans même que vous ayez à descendre de voiture. Si bon que soit ce mec, c'est jamais qu'un type isolé...

– Les Allemands pensaient sans doute la même chose du sergent York[1], observa Howard.

---

1. York, Alvin Cullum (1887-1964). Ce natif du Tennessee s'engage en 1917 dans l'armée américaine et devient sergent au 328e régiment d'infanterie, 82e division. Le 8 octobre 1918, dans la forêt d'Argonne, il capture à lui seul un bataillon de mitrailleurs allemands qui tenaient une position fortifiée. À cette occasion, il

– Bon Dieu, chef, vous vous faites bien trop de mauvais sang. » Fernandez réduisit de deux crans le réglage de la clim. « Ou alors, c'est vos neurones qui s'engourdissent... À part ça, comment s'est débrouillé le fiston avec son concours de boomerang ? »

On avait vu plus subtil pour changer de sujet, mais sans doute Julio n'avait-il pas tort, il n'aurait pas dû se tracasser autant pour un malheureux type perdu dans le désert. Se conformer à la procédure, atteindre leur cible, bref, rien de bien folichon, on récupérait le sujet et on le refilait aux psys pour qu'ils le cuisinent. « Tyrone ? Il a fini troisième.

– Vrai ? Plutôt pas mal pour une première fois, non ?

– Oui, tout à fait. En plus, il a battu son record personnel, et ça l'a rendu encore plus fier que de monter sur le podium.

– Je le comprends. Vous savez, vous n'êtes pas un si mauvais père, pour un vieux... Il faudra que je vous pose deux-trois questions quand je vais rejoindre le clan. »

Howard sourit. Il imaginait d'ici la première fois que le bébé de Joanna et Julio leur ferait une poussée de fièvre, leur vomirait un machin verdâtre ou se choperait la colique. Il se souvenait de quelques coups de fil nocturnes affolés à sa mère quand Tyrone était encore un nourrisson.

---

tue 25 soldats ennemis et fait 132 prisonniers. Ce fait d'armes exceptionnel lui vaut de se voir décerner la médaille d'honneur du Congrès et la croix de guerre française... Exploit d'autant plus remarquable pour un homme qui n'avait endossé l'uniforme qu'à contrecœur, puisqu'il était à l'origine objecteur de conscience (*N.d.T.*).

« Quelque chose de drôle, John ?

– Ouaip. Ta tête à deux heures du matin avec un bébé qui chiale. Faudra que je demande à Joanna de sortir le caméscope. »

Il inspira à fond et souffla lentement. C'était son trac habituel en opération, ça lui prenait toujours juste avant d'ôter le cran de sûreté. Sans doute que s'il s'était trouvé sur un vrai champ de bataille avec un minimum d'expérience du combat, il aurait réagi différemment. Il en était sûr.

Dimanche
Quantico, Virginie

Assis dans un fauteuil roulant électrique, Jay Gridley regardait deux patients jouer au ping-pong. Son idée qu'on devait flemmarder deux-trois semaines à l'hôpital au moindre pépin grave datait visiblement un max. Vous aviez des mecs opérés à cœur ouvert de la veille qui étaient sur pied le lendemain, arpentant les couloirs d'un bout à l'autre en traînant leur perche à perfusion.

Apparemment, il valait mieux se remuer que rester au lit, pour régler les problèmes des suites opératoires. En partie, du moins.

Ses parents devaient passer le voir, ils seraient là dans l'après-midi, une perspective qui l'enchantait modérément. Ils seraient contrariés, ils voudraient s'occuper de lui alors que lui, euh, eh bien...

Allons bon, à quoi pensait-il, déjà ?

Un nouvel accès de panique le submergea, le recouvrant d'une nouvelle pellicule de sueur moite. L'aspect physique, c'était déjà pénible, d'accord, mais enfin, on l'avait assuré qu'il réagirait au traitement et que d'ici quelques semaines, il aurait retrouvé l'intégralité de ses capacités antérieures : il pourrait marcher, parler, déconner comme avant ; son esprit, en revanche, ne semblait pas tourner rond, il n'arrêtait pas de ruminer des idées qui se mélangeaient en tous sens, un vrai pastis, avant de lui échapper complètement.

Ce truc lui flanquait une trouille bleue. Il pourrait toujours s'interfacer en RV avec un bras coupé ou une jambe de bois, et merde, même manchot ou cul-de-jatte, mais si son cerveau ne... si son cerveau ne...

Ne quoi ?

La panique le saisit et, durant un instant, il ne sut plus pourquoi, et puis ça lui revint. Son esprit. Son cerveau. Ses idées dont il perdait le fil. C'était comme d'essayer de faire du calcul mental au moment de s'endormir : on n'arrivait pas à se concentrer, à suivre le fil de son raisonnement, impossible... impossible de... de s'y accrocher !

Il fallait qu'il mette la main sur une machine à RV et se connecte en ligne. Qu'il vérifie s'il était encore en mesure de faire ce qui lui importait plus que tout au monde. Ce n'était pas seulement son boulot, c'était sa vie. Il n'arrivait pas à s'imaginer dans l'incapacité d'accéder à des ordinateurs.

Il héla une des infirmières qui passaient dans la salle de loisirs. Il ne chercha pas à parler – ça aussi, ça lui flanquait encore la trouille – et se contenta de mimer un casque à réalité virtuelle : les deux index devant les yeux, les pouces sur les oreilles.

Elle acquiesça. « Bien sûr. Au bout du couloir sur votre gauche. Si vous voulez, je vous y emmène. »

Il la congédia d'un geste, puis, de sa main valide, actionna la manette de commande du fauteuil. Il trouverait l'ordinateur tout seul. Il comptait se connecter et voir ce dont il était capable.

S'il était capable de faire quoi que ce soit...

Dimanche
Les Ifs, Sussex, Angleterre

Le commandant Peel se carra dans le fauteuil devant son plan de travail, dans le bureau que lui avait alloué monseigneur dans ce qui était naguère le logis des gardiens. Quatre siècles plus tôt, au moment de la Réforme, l'édifice était une église catholique. À cette époque, alors que l'Église d'Angleterre montait en puissance, on risquait sa vie à pratiquer la religion catholique dans certains coins d'Angleterre, c'est pourquoi les fidèles assez fortunés se faisaient bâtir de petits sanctuaires privés à l'abri des murs de leur manoir où ils se réunissaient en secret avec quelques élus pour pratiquer leur culte. Tant qu'ils se montraient discrets et tant que le maître des lieux restait assez riche et influent, les autorités locales détournaient les yeux.

Le fait que le roi ait voulu divorcer n'était pas une raison suffisante pour, sur un coup de tête, abjurer sa foi et renoncer à des rites pratiqués avec ferveur depuis des générations.

La fenêtre devant Peel n'était pas un vitrail, mais elle avait cette découpe trilobée symbolisant la Sainte-Trinité ; quant au bureau, il était disposé à l'endroit même où jadis se dressait un autel.

Assis devant le moniteur, Peel regardait la vidéo, tout en écoutant le rapport du lieutenant Wilson, l'un de ses meilleurs hommes. Wilson dirigeait l'équipe qui avait surveillé Bascomb-Coombs.

« Vous êtes certain qu'il ne se doute pas qu'il est observé ?

– Absolument certain, monsieur. Il est peut-être plus malin qu'un amphi bourré de diplômés d'Oxford, mais il n'est pas trop connecté à la réalité. On s'est bien gardé de bidouiller son matériel et ses programmes – il les a équipés de tout un tas de protections auxquelles on préfère ne pas toucher – mais on a malgré tout réussi à installer des caméras cachées partout dans sa maison et son bureau. Il y en a au plafond au-dessus des stations de travail dans son labo et chez lui, braquées sur son clavier et son moniteur. Son système a beau être protégé par les meilleurs dispositifs de sécurité existant, on n'a qu'à le regarder taper ses codes ou l'écouter les énoncer en vocal. Sans compter qu'on a sur vidéo tout ce qu'il voit sur écran.

– Et malgré tout, on ne peut pas remonter la piste de ces piratages des aéroports ?

– Non, monsieur. Impossible de retrouver la trace d'aucune de ses manipulations en ligne. Ce type a trouvé le moyen de saturer un casque de réalité virtuelle, on ne sait toujours pas comment, grâce à quoi il a réussi à expédier à l'hosto un certain nombre de petits curieux. Attaque cérébrale.

– Vraiment ?

– Oui, monsieur. On a du reste un petit souci à ce sujet. Il semble que le MI-6 ait contacté le patron de l'unité du FBI de lutte contre la criminalité informatique, la Net Force. Il est ici à Londres, pour collaborer avec eux.

– Déjà ? Rapide !

– Apparemment, il se trouvait déjà sur place, pour participer à un congrès ou je ne sais quoi.

– Hmm. Ça vaut le coup d'aller vérifier. Tenez-moi au courant.

– Bien, monsieur.

– Autre chose ?

– Rien pour ce qui concerne le projet. Mais il y a un détail qui pourrait vous intéresser. Vous vous souvenez de Plekhanov ?

– Le Russe qui a failli s'emparer de l'Asie ? Bien sûr. » Ils avaient fait une assez jolie opération financière en participant à l'entraînement d'un des groupes de Plekhanov.

« Après sa capture, il y a eu quelques bavures, poursuivit Wilson. La plus notable étant l'agent traitant des Spetsnatz. Roujio[1].

– Ah oui. Pas joli-joli, effectivement. Il a disparu de la circulation, c'est ça ?

– Selon toute apparence, ce n'était que temporaire, d'après ce qu'a pu apprendre Bascomb-Coombs. Il semble qu'ils soient sur le point de récupérer ce M. Roujio, quelque part dans l'Ouest américain.

---

1. Cf. *Net Force 1, op. cit.*

– Pas de veine pour lui.

– Je pensais que ça pourrait vous intéresser, monsieur.

– Oui, eh bien, prévenez-moi dès que vous avez du nouveau. »

Dès qu'il eut raccroché, Peel leva les yeux vers la fenêtre. Tout cela s'annonçait des plus prometteurs. En dehors du régiment, il n'y avait pas de quoi s'ennuyer. Aucun doute là-dessus.

Dimanche
Stonewall Flat, Nevada

« Tout est prêt ?

– Affirmatif, mon colonel, répondit Fernandez. Les tireurs d'élite sont en position, les troupes au sol également. Le site est bouclé et, à l'heure où je vous parle, le commando fait route vers sa caravane. En passant hors piste, au cas où il aurait miné la route d'accès. » Fernandez sourit, pour bien montrer qu'il blaguait.

Les deux hommes se tenaient prêts du Humvee, vêtus de leur Intellicombi*. Ils s'étaient garés à huit cents mètres en retrait sur la grand-route – la seule, du reste – qui conduisait à la caravane de Roujio. Howard avait relevé sa visière et, les yeux rivés à ses jumelles Leupold grossissement 10 – le modèle de campagne à blindage silicium –, il balayait lentement les alentours, cherchant à localiser la cible. « Pas trace du bonhomme. Ça doit pas être un lève-tôt.

– C'est son problème. Nos gars seront sur zone dans une minute... deux-trois flash-bang*, quelques grenades de gaz émétique, et monsieur l'assassin se réveillera à moitié aveuglé, dégobillant son repas de la veille, et le cul dans la merde. Vous auriez dû me laisser diriger le commando, c'est con qu'on rate le spectacle.

– Tu es sur le point de devenir père de famille, Julio, et si tu me crois capable d'annoncer un jour froidement à Joanna qu'il t'est arrivé malheur, tu rêves, mon gars. Non, tu ferais mieux de t'habituer à la perspective de bosser derrière un bureau.

– Manquerait plus que ça !

– Plus vite que tu ne penses, sergent. »

Il contempla la roulotte. Jusqu'ici, ça allait.

Roujio était déjà réveillé quand il entendit approcher le véhicule. Il se leva, boucla la cartouchière autour de sa taille, puis empoigna la carabine et se l'accrocha à l'épaule. Il récupéra le pistolet et le boîtier de radiocommande, puis s'approcha de la fenêtre au-dessus de l'évier. Il reposa le Browning, fixa le boîtier à sa ceinture, regarda dehors.

Un camion trapu, anguleux, de couleur beige, arrivait dans sa direction à bonne vitesse, remontant la pente douce, progressant parallèlement au chemin, à dix mètres sur la gauche. Un nuage de poussière grise tourbillonnait dans son sillage.

Un assaut par l'armée ? Avec un chauffeur qui choisit de ne pas emprunter la route pour éviter des mines ? Pas con. Si c'étaient des militaires, ils seraient sans doute équipés de tenues pare-balles, donc ses munitions risquaient de ne pas leur faire grand mal, sauf à viser avec une extrême précision. Un point à ne pas oublier.

Il inspira puis expira lentement à deux reprises, prit un verre, l'emplit d'eau, se rinça la bouche, cracha dans l'évier. Il reposa le verre, glissa le pistolet dans sa ceinture, gagna la porte.

Des invités s'annonçaient, il était temps de leur dérouler le tapis rouge.

Il dégrafa le boîtier de radiocommande. Il était doté de quatre boutons, chacun émettait un signal focalisé par la parabole installée sur le toit de la caravane.

Avec un soupir, il appuya sur le premier bouton.

« Merde, c'est quoi, ça ? » s'écria Howard.

Une muraille grise circulaire s'éleva du sol autour de la caravane, montant en volutes dans l'air encore frais du matin. La roulotte disparut derrière le nuage gris foncé en l'espace de quelques secondes.

« Il a des fumigènes », crut bon d'annoncer Fernandez dans le micro du LOSIR* intégré à son casque. « Ralentissez.

– Pas possible », répondit, narquois, le leader du commando.

Howard avait perçu l'échange dans son propre casque, mais déjà il avait rabaissé la visière et commuté celle-ci en vision infrarouge.

Sans grand succès. Quel que soit le produit fumigène employé, il dégageait également de la chaleur : impossible de voir au travers.

Il visionna l'empreinte satellitaire du Gros Loucheur, mais l'image, même retraitée par ordinateur, ne dévoilait rien non plus à l'intérieur de l'anneau de fumée, hormis la roulotte.

« Il est toujours dedans, annonça Howard. Avancez avec précaution.

– Bien reçu », répondit le leader du commando.

Roujio regarda par la fenêtre surmontant la porte. Les bombes fumigènes avaient masqué sa caravane. D'ici quelques secondes, elles finiraient de dégager leur produit pour exploser dans un éclair aveuglant qui devrait finir de perturber les capteurs certainement pointés sur lui.

Il regarda le deuxième bouton. Hocha la tête. Il n'avait plus tué personne depuis un bail, mais cette attaque était à l'évidence due à des militaires, et tous ces tireurs embusqués devaient être des soldats prêts à l'abattre sur ordre. Ils connaissaient les risques du combat. Et sinon, ils n'allaient pas tarder à les découvrir.

Aux neuf emplacements d'où un tireur embusqué était susceptible d'embrasser parfaitement sa caravane, il avait enterré vingt-sept mines antipersonnel, dissimulées sous des grosses soucoupes en papier retournées et recouvertes d'une fine couche de terre et de sable. Les mines étaient des variantes de la bonne vieille Bouncing Betty, « Betty la bondissante » : une petite charge de gaz comprimé propulsait un premier élément pas plus gros qu'un paquet de cigarettes jusqu'à une hauteur d'un mètre vingt environ, où une seconde charge, plus puissante, détonait en répandant une gerbe de fragments d'acier meurtriers. Tout homme non protégé situé dans un rayon de quelques mètres autour de la charge explosive serait fauché par les éclats, tué ou sérieusement blessé. Même avec une armure, une partie des fragments pouvait s'introduire par une couture ou toucher un endroit non protégé et occasionner des blessures graves, voire fatales.

Il appuya sur le bouton.

Le LOSIR d'Howard résonna de cris et de hurlements affolés, bien vite noyés sous le bruit de petites explosions captées par les écouteurs puis, une seconde ou deux plus tard, retentissant sur le terrain.

« Au rapport !

– On s'est chopé une mine, mon colonel ! Spalding est touché ! Il saigne de partout !

– On s'est fait arroser au point S2, chef, on est couverts de poussière, mais pas de blessé !

– Reader est à terre, elle a le visage maculé de sang !

– John... là ! »

Howard regarda la fumée, vit des éclats lumineux transpercer le brouillard. Bon sang, qu'est-ce qui se passait ?

Quand les premières bombes fumigènes eurent fini de brûler leur charge de magnésium, Roujio ouvrit la porte de la caravane et bondit à l'extérieur. Il n'avait que quinze mètres à parcourir, mais il devait être planqué avant que son signal thermique ne reste le seul détectable dans le secteur. Au cas où ils auraient mis en place une surveillance par avion ou par satellite.

Il se dépêcha.

La planque était masquée par une feuille de

contreplaqué, entourée de bandelettes de matériau réfléchissant la chaleur. Il avait pris soin de coller de la terre et des herbes sur le dessus de la planche : une fois celle-ci en place, elle était virtuellement invisible et assez résistante pour supporter le poids d'un homme. Le réduit ne faisait que deux mètres sur un, mais il n'avait pas l'intention d'y moisir longtemps.

Une fois dans le trou, il plia un bâton luminescent qui lui procura assez de lumière pour y voir et allumer le petit moniteur sur accus. Une caméra sur le toit de la caravane – elle aussi dissimulée à l'intérieur d'une antenne parabolique – et une seconde planquée dans la décharge au fond du terrain lui donnaient une image noyée de fumée, granuleuse mais exploitable, de la roulotte et des alentours, y compris son 4×4.

La voiture était déjà chargée de tout le matériel nécessaire à l'achèvement de son plan.

Le temps, d'ici quelques secondes, que la fumée se dissipe.

« La fumée se dissipe », entendit Howard dans son LOSIR.

– Allez-y avec un maximum de précautions, répondit-il.

– Vous le voulez toujours vivant ? »

Howard crispa les mâchoires. Il avait jusqu'ici quatre blessés – et d'après le toubib, deux en état assez grave pour être conduits aux urgences. L'hélico de la Garde était déjà en route.

« Affirmatif. Vivant, si possible. Mais protégez-vous au maximum. Je ne veux plus de pertes, compris ? Si vous devez tirer, vous tirez.

– Bien reçu, mon colonel. »

Maintenant, se dit Roujio. Il appuya sur le troisième bouton de sa télécommande.

« Là-haut ! » s'exclama Fernandez.

Howard regarda. Un véhicule jaillit de la fumée, remontant la route. Le 4×4 de Roujio.

« Il prend la fuite ! »

Une mitraillette crépita. Howard leva ses jumelles pour cadrer la voiture qui s'éloignait. Il vit des traces d'impact apparaître sur la tôle. Quel idiot ! Est-ce qu'il espérait sauter comme ça dans sa bagnole et filer au volant ?

Roujio appuya sur le dernier bouton.

Avant qu'Howard ait pu ajuster la mise au point pour distinguer le chauffeur, la voiture sauta. Le sol trembla sous leurs pieds et l'onde de choc déferla sur eux avec un bruit de fin du monde. Une boule de feu s'éleva sous un champignon de fumée qui évoquait une bombe atomique miniature. Ce n'était pas le réservoir qui explosait : la voiture avait été piégée.

« Bordel de merde ! s'exclama Fernandez. Qu'est-ce qu'il avait foutu là-dedans ? »

Quand la fumée commença de se dissiper, il ne restait plus rien du véhicule, sinon un bout de châssis et deux pneus en train de brûler. L'essentiel des débris enflammés avait été projeté dans un rayon de plusieurs centaines de mètres.

Howard écarquilla les yeux. Dieu du ciel ! Quel merdier !

« Il semble en définitive que vous ayez eu raison de vous inquiéter, mon colonel. Je révise mon opinion. »

Howard se contenta de hocher la tête.

10

Dimanche 3 avril
Lhassa, Tibet

Jay Gridley était assis par terre en tailleur, drapé dans une robe safran, enveloppé de l'odeur tenace de patchouli qui imprégnait l'air frais. La natte mince sous ses fesses avait du mal à empêcher le froid des dalles glacées d'irradier ses reins, et son crâne rasé était frigorifié. Par la fenêtre ouverte, il apercevait la neige accumulée en un tapis de trois mètres d'épaisseur qui recouvrait tout le paysage d'une croûte resplendissante. Une litanie sans paroles résonnait en fond sonore et des centaines de chandelles répandaient leur lumière à travers la salle imposante.

Tout au bout, assis en lotus sur une petite plateforme de bois qui ne le plaçait que quelques centimètres au-dessus des autres moines, le grand bonze, Sojan Ripoche. L'homme était chauve lui aussi, septuagénaire, avec des petites rides de sourire au coin des yeux qui ne le quittaient jamais. Gridley comprit pourquoi après avoir écouté le gourou parler pendant quelques minutes. Il souriait sans arrêt.

En cet instant, le vieillard évoquait une divinité du panthéon bouddhiste : « En sanskrit, il s'appelle Yamantaka. Les Chinois l'appellent Yen-an-te-chia. Au Tibet, nous le connaissons sous le nom de

Gshin-rji-gshed. Partout ailleurs, il est Celui-qui-conquiert-la-mort, l'un des Huit Terribles, le *drag-shed*, gardien de la foi et saint patron du *Dge-lugs-pa.*

« Terrible à contempler est cette manifestation du Mañjusri bodhisattva. Il y a bien longtemps, lors d'une grande bataille au Tibet, Gshin-rji-gshed a pris cette forme pour affronter et défaire Yama, déesse de la mort. Il avait neuf têtes, trente-quatre bras et seize pieds. C'est l'horreur incarnée, la terreur toute-puissante, le Piétineur de Démons.

« Bref, poursuivit le vieillard, tout sourire, c'est le genre de personnage à qui l'on n'a pas intérêt à chercher des crosses. »

À retardement, Gridley eut une réaction de surprise en entendant cette dernière phrase. Elle paraissait un rien déplacée dans la bouche d'un saint homme tibétain.

Jay soupira. C'était le scénario du vieux – si même c'était bien un vieux et pas quelqu'un simulant la vieillesse – et il l'appréciait modérément. Trop austère. Et maintenant qu'il était dedans, il ne savait plus trop ce qu'il était venu y faire. Qu'avait-il espéré trouver ?

L'infirmière. L'infirmière lui avait suggéré d'aller consulter ce type. Après qu'il eut arraché et jeté à terre le casque de RV, parce qu'il n'avait pas été capable de se concentrer sans perdre le contact. Oh, certes, il pouvait toujours utiliser la RV, mais uniquement de manière passive, en mode client. Il était désormais incapable de la créer. De la manipuler. Ça partait toujours bien, mais au bout d'une minute ou deux, il se mettait à dériver, et l'imagerie s'évanouissait.

Un informaticien pas foutu de piloter un ordinateur.

Un créateur de réalité virtuelle infoutu de faire marcher la RV. Il était fini. Sa vie était fichue.

Mais l'infirmière – c'était une espèce de bouddhiste, quelque chose comme ça – lui avait donné l'adresse web de ce type, et conseillé d'aller y faire un tour. Il en avait déjà aidé d'autres, avait-elle ajouté.

N'ayant plus rien à perdre, Gridley y était allé. Mais sans trop voir en quoi ce Gshin-rji-machin-truc-chouette pourrait lui être d'une quelconque utilité.

Comme s'il avait lu dans ses pensées, le vieillard tapa une seule fois dans ses mains et tous les moines, Gridley excepté, se volatilisèrent. La pièce autour de lui se mit à tourbillonner et se transformer, et Jay se retrouva assis dans un fauteuil confortable face au gourou, assis lui aussi. Finies les robes safran : Jay était en pantalon de velours, pull et bottes de moto, tandis que le vieux était en jean et chemise de toile. Le Tibétain se tenait les jambes croisées au niveau des chevilles, il était chaussé de Nike, mais arborait toujours son sempiternel sourire. Il avait la dégaine d'un vieil oncle en visite.

« C'est mieux comme ça ? »

Gridley cligna les paupières. « Euh, ouais, j'imagine...

– Des tas de mecs préfèrent l'imagerie monacale. Ça leur donne l'impression d'avoir découvert la vérité. Ce Tibet-là, hélas, n'existe plus aujourd'hui que dans les films. »

Il fixa Jay droit dans les yeux. « Toi, mon garçon, tu as un problème.

– Ouais.

– Ton aura est fracturée. »

Allons bon, s'il lui faisait le coup de l'aura, il était peut-être temps de décroch...

– Ce que je veux dire, c'est que tu me sembles éprouver quelque difficulté à te concentrer. Drogue ? Problème médical ? Tumeur ? Attaque ? »

Comment diable pouvait-il deviner une chose pareille ? Rien ne transparaissait en RV !

« Euh...

– Prends tout ton temps. Si tu préfères te déconnecter et revenir un peu plus tard, pas de problème. »

Jay fit non de la tête. « Vous n'avez pas vraiment l'air d'un gourou.

– Tu veux de nouveau le monastère ?

– Non, c'est juste que...

– Les préjugés, coupa le vieillard. C'est toujours catastrophique. Tu avais une idée préconçue de mon apparence, et dès que je me manifeste et que mes actes ne correspondent pas aux attentes, on est perturbé. Or, tu l'es déjà bien assez, n'est-ce pas ?

– Euh, ouais, effectivement.

– Eh bien, on va régler tout ça. Mais chaque chose en son temps. Comment dois-je t'appeler ?

– Vrai nom ou pseudo ?

– Peu importe, pourvu que tu réagisses.

– Jay.

– D'accord. Moi, appelle-moi Saji. Tu es venu chercher la lumière, c'est ça ?

– Je... euh, je ne suis pas sûr. »

Rire de Saji. « Ce que je veux dire dire, c'est que tu n'es pas du tout venu pour ces conneries bouddhistes, démons, Dharma et tout le bataclan. Mais tu veux quand même faire la lumière.

– Ouais.

– Eh bien, être bouddhiste n'est pas du tout un obstacle dans cette voie, en fait, ça aide. Mais ça aussi, on y reviendra plus tard. Chaque chose en son temps. La nature de ton affection ?

– On m'a parlé d'une sorte d'attaque cérébrale.

– Parfait, nous pouvons arranger ça.

– Vous m'en voyez ravi.

– Pas moi, Jay, *nous*. » Il tapota de l'index sa tempe droite. « Nos cerveaux disposent de quantités de redondances intégrées. Tu souffres d'un court-jus quelque part, mais il est parfaitement possible de dérouter le signal vers un endroit où le câblage est de meilleure qualité. Il se peut que ce soit inutile, mais on verra bien. Je m'en vais te poser une série de questions, tu répondras comme ça te chante.

– D'accord.

– Combien font quatre-vingt-sept moins treize ? »

Allons bon, du calcul mental ?

« Oui, du calcul mental. Pour commencer. » Grand sourire.

Jay soupira. Quand vous touchiez le fond, le seul choix était de remonter.

« Soixante-quatorze.

– Et qui est l'actuel président des États-Unis... ? »

Dimanche
Stonewall Flat, Nevada

« Qu'est-ce qu'on a, Julio ?

– Pas grand-chose, chef. On a récupéré quelques éclats d'os carbonisés et tachés de sang, des bouts de machins qui ressemblent à des cheveux brûlés, et deux dents. J'ignore quel truc il avait mis dans sa bagnole, mais ça ne l'a pas raté. Je doute qu'on arrive à récupérer tous les morceaux. »

Howard soupira. Oui, pas de doute. Il appréhendait déjà la rédaction de son rapport.

« Très bien. Terminez la fouille de la caravane, laissez deux hommes en faction sur le site, et on fait venir les gars du labo. Puis on remballe et on rentre.

– Entendu, chef. »

Howard contempla le cratère où le véhicule de la cible s'était volatilisé dans l'explosion. Ce n'était pas le plan prévu, mais au moins l'avait-il éliminée. L'homme était un tueur professionnel. Sans parler de ses exploits passés, Reader se retrouvait en sale état, et trois autres de ses gars avaient été amochés au point de se retrouver à l'hosto. La cible aurait méritée d'être interrogée et bouclée pour mille ans, mais ça n'arriverait pas. La justice avait été expéditive, Howard n'en mourrait pas.

Il se détourna pour rejoindre le Humvee. Julio avait eu la bonne idée de laisser tourner la clim. Dehors, il faisait de plus en plus chaud.

Bon Dieu, ce qu'il détestait ça.

Coincé dans sa planque, Roujio essayait de dormir. Il faisait chaud, il était crevé, mais il était incapable de se relaxer suffisamment pour décrocher. Il avait envisagé de piéger également la caravane pour qu'elle saute en même temps que la voiture, puis il s'était ravisé. Peut-être que quelqu'un pourrait la récupérer. Tout compte fait, elle lui avait procuré un toit. Et, plus important, celui qui resterait éventuellement en faction sur place allait sans aucun doute s'abriter du soleil torride à son ombre, voire y pénétrer et profiter de la clim.

De l'intérieur, il n'y avait aucune fenêtre qui donnait sur sa planque, il s'en était bien assuré.

À l'heure qu'il était, ils avaient dû trouver les restes de ce qu'il avait laissé exprès dans un emballage plastique stérilisé et fermé sous vide : cheveux et poils récupérés dans la poubelle d'un coiffeur ; quelques os, de la viande crue et du sang de porc mélangé d'anticoagulant à base de mort-aux-rats. Et, touche finale, un crâne humain piqué au squelette d'une classe de sciences de lycée, puis introduit sous la peau du crâne du porc et rempli avec la cervelle de ce dernier. Autant d'éléments qui ne tromperaient pas une seule seconde un médecin légiste, mais quiconque aurait vu le véhicule pulvérisé par l'explosion avait des chances de prendre ces débris d'os, de chair et de sang pour des restes humains. Assez longtemps en tout cas pour lui laisser le temps de s'échapper.

Rien n'était moins sûr, mais c'était un coup à tenter.

Les caméras montraient des hommes montant dans les véhicules pour repartir. Ils allaient laisser des gardes en faction, sans doute pas plus de deux ou trois soldats. Il allait faire chaud, les hommes allaient ôter leur casque et une partie de leur armure ou se réfugier dans la caravane. Dès cet instant, il serait prêt. Ayant fouillé la roulotte à la recherche d'explosifs et n'ayant rien trouvé, ils se croiraient en lieu sûr.

La main posée sur son pistolet, Roujio essaya encore de dormir. Même quelques minutes, ce serait déjà bien. Il était tellement fatigué.

Dimanche
Londres

À l'intérieur, le siège du MI-6 n'était pas différent de n'importe quel immeuble de bureaux moderne. Michaels ne savait trop ce qu'il avait escompté, d'autant que le QG de la Net Force évoquait lui aussi un banal siège de société ; malgré tout, il s'était plus ou moins attendu à voir James Bond ou Q ou quelque autre figure mythique arpenter les couloirs, tout affairée à servir Sa Majesté.

Ils étaient installés dans un divan confortable dans le bureau de Matthew Helms, le directeur général. Avec lui, Angela Cooper et Clifton Wood, député et ministre chargé des relations avec le Parlement. Toni était ressortie pour appeler le directeur du FBI.

« ... serait de notre intérêt réciproque de résoudre cette affaire au plus tôt, était en train d'expliquer le ministre.

– Entièrement d'accord, dit Michaels, même si je ne vois pas trop en quoi je puis vous aider. Vous disposez de vos propres agents. »

Wood et Helms échangèrent un regard à la dérobée. Helms se racla la gorge : « Ma foi, oui, mais voyez-vous, c'est un aspect du problème. Le MI-5 comme le MI-6 veulent l'un comme l'autre sauter sur l'occasion et il y a comme qui dirait... une certaine rivalité entre services. »

Cooper gratifia Michaels d'un bref sourire. Au temps pour son goût de la litote.

« Notre idée est qu'en réunissant nos effectifs sous l'égide la Net Force, on irait peut-être un peu plus vite. Ni la sécurité intérieure ni le renseignement ne veulent renoncer à une once de leur autonomie, mais avec l'intervention d'un tiers allié... » Il laissa la phrase en suspens, haussa les sourcils et écarta les mains.

Michaels hocha la tête. Politique politicienne... Comme de juste. Mais ce n'était pas tout. S'ils étaient prêts à faire intervenir un service étranger pour calmer le jeu, c'est qu'il y avait autre chose encore. Il avait du mal à imaginer le FBI et la CIA laisser le renseignement britannique s'immiscer dans leurs affaires et participer à une opération commune. Non, il s'en passait ici bien plus qu'ils ne voulaient en dire.

La porte s'ouvrit et Toni revint dans la pièce. Michaels la vit raccrocher son virgil à sa ceinture tandis qu'elle lui adressait un petit signe de tête.

Donc, le directeur les avait embarqués dans cette histoire.

Il hocha la tête à son tour avant de se retourner vers Helms. « Nous serons bien entendu ravis de vous apporter toute l'aide possible. »

Ce qui suscita les sourires des trois Rosbifs.

Michaels aurait aimé être aussi ravi qu'eux. Alors que son plus cher désir était de rentrer à la maison. Il avait son fils à l'hôpital, des problèmes juridiques avec son ex, et Dieu sait ce qui pouvait encore lui tomber dessus en son absence.

Son virgil pépia. Michaels fronça les sourcils. L'appareil était réglé pour refuser tous les appels sauf ceux de priorité maximale. Il le dégrafa de sa ceinture et regarda l'afficheur : le colonel Howard. « Messieurs, si vous voulez bien m'excuser un instant... »

Le ministre et le chef du MI-6 sourirent à nouveau avec un hochement de tête.

Michaels sortit dans le couloir. Qui sait, c'était peut-être enfin des bonnes nouvelles.

11

Lundi 4 avril
Washington, DC

Tyrone Howard se dirigea vers son vestiaire, redoutant de croiser Essai, la terreur du lycée. Depuis que Bella l'avait plaqué, ses rapports plus ou moins amicaux avec Presse-Purée LeMott, le malabar gentil copain de classe de Bella, étaient devenus incertains. Essai savait que ses chances contre Presse-Purée étaient nulles, aussi pour l'heure, se retrouver pote avec l'ami de Bella avait conféré à Tyrone une certaine immunité contre les initiatives de ce crétin patenté [1]. Essai – pour S.E., alias « Sinistre Énormité », l'individu ayant la carrure et l'intellect d'un brontosaure – était en effet prêt à vous ratatiner à la première occasion, et les chances de Tyrone contre lui dans une bagarre étant également nulles, mieux valait donc rester sur ses gardes.

Il réussit à gagner les vestiaires sans avoir aperçu Essai. Peut-être qu'il s'était fait virer de ce cher vieux collège Eisenhower pour avoir été surpris à fumer. Ça serait bonnard.

Ty déposait son sac à dos dans le vestiaire sans plus faire attention quand une voix lança : « Hé, Tyrone ! »

---

1. Cf. *Net Force 1, op. cit.*

Il se retourna. C'était Nadine Harris, la championne de boomerang.

« Hé, Nadine ! »

Elle se laissa couler au milieu de la cohue, glissant avec grâce, telle une nageuse fendant les eaux. « T'as cours ce matin, toi aussi. Exemplaire.

– Ouais. C'est qui, ton tuteur ?

– Peterson.

– Il est cool. Je l'ai eu en Médias, niveau un. T'as eu quoi, comme notes ?

– Anglais, deux, maths, trois, biologie, un, médias, deux, physique, trois, histoire, deux.

– Pas mal, pour le trimestre », observa-t-il.

Elle haussa les épaules. « Pas si mal. Je m'en suis bien sortie parce que le dernier établissement que j'ai fréquenté avait un niveau assez élevé. Et toi ?

– Anglais, deux, maths, trois, médias, trois, dissert, quatre et, euh, HM, un...

– Tu peux t'extasier sur ma moyenne, Ty ! Dissert, quatre ? Je pensais qu'on ne pouvait pas prendre cette option avant le lycée. Et HM ? C'est histoire militaire, non ? »

Ce fut à son tour de hausser les épaules. « Mon père est dans l'armée. J'ai pensé que ça valait le coup de le tenter... il m'a pas mal tuyauté. Tu sais qu'il lançait, dans le temps, et il y a une section lancement dans ma classe.

– Sans charre ? Waouh ! Un vieux qui lance ! Et il est bon ?

– Ben... pas vraiment. Il faisait ça quand il était gosse, il a même eu deux boomerangs en bois, des machins d'entrée de gamme, en contreplaqué. Mais il sait tout un tas de trucs sur leur utilisation au combat, tout ça, comment les Aborigènes les utilisaient dans les guerres tribales.

– Exemplaire ! »

Alors qu'ils bavardaient, Tyrone éprouva une sensation bizarre, comme s'il était... observé. Il regarda alentour, en prenant soin de le faire avec discrétion. Peut-être qu'Essai était dans les parages et l'avait dans le collimateur.

Belladonna Wright arrivait du bout du couloir, accompagnée de deux copines, et son regard était braqué droit sur lui.

Tyrone sentit ses épaules se raidir, ses joues devenir cramoisies, ses boyaux se liquéfier. Il avait envie de fuir se planquer sous un rocher.

Elle était plus belle que jamais, la Belladonna, et le souvenir d'être assis sur son lit à l'embrasser, de se mettre à la peloter...

T'embarque pas sur cette pente glissante, Tyrone. Ça va se voir. Ce serait gênant puissance dix.

Mais il était déjà trop tard. Il dégrafa la courroie de son sac à dos pour le laisser pendouiller, vite fait, devant son bas-ventre.

« Tu te sens bien, Tyrone ? s'enquit Nadine. On dirait que tu viens d'avaler une mouche ou je ne sais quoi.

– Ah ? non, enfin, je veux dire, si, je me sens bien. Je... euh, je viens juste de me rappeler un truc que j'ai oublié. Une corvée. À la maison. »

Nulle, Tyrone, nullissime, ton excuse complètement faiblarde !

Bella passa en coup de vent, comme un cuirassé accompagné de ses deux escorteurs, belle à tomber par terre. Elle ne daigna pas détourner les yeux vers lui.

Nadine avait dû remarquer quelque chose sur les traits du garçon car elle se retourna pour regarder.

« Waouh ? C'est qui, celle-là ?

– Belladonna Wright », répondit Tyrone, en essayant d'éviter de prendre une voix de canard. Il réussit presque.

« On joue pas dans la même catégorie, observa Nadine. C'est le genre papier peint qui tue.

– Papier peint ?

– Ouais, enfin tu vois : elle a rien d'autre à faire qu'être jolie à regarder. J'parie qu'on l'invite partout, rien que pour le plaisir de la mater. Tu la connais ?

– Pas vraiment. » Il avait *cru* la connaître, mais il s'était trompé, c'était sûr. Elle l'avait laissé choir comme une vieille chaussette.

« Quand on est belle, tout vous tombe rôti dans le bec. Quand on est comme moi, faut se décarcasser.

– Comment ça, "comme toi" ? T'es pas si moche, quand même ! »

Elle eut un autre petit haussement d'épaules, détourna les yeux. « Mets-moi à côté d'elle (d'un signe de tête, elle indiqua Bella) et y a pas photo. »

Tyrone ne répondit rien, mais elle n'avait pas tort.

« J'espère qu'elle n'a pas de la cervelle, en plus. Ça serait le pompon... Canon *et* intelligente. »

De ce côté, elle n'avait pas de souci à se faire, Tyrone le savait. Bella n'était pas totalement idiote, mais ce n'était pas non plus une lumière. Il n'avait pourtant pas envie de l'avouer. Même après ce qu'elle lui avait fait, ça avait quelque part un petit côté... déloyal. Et puis, si jamais Presse-Purée venait à apprendre que Tyrone cassait du sucre sur le dos de Bella, ça risquait de chauffer pour son matricule. Elle avait peut-être une demi-douzaine de mecs sur sa liste d'attente, mais Presse-Purée faisait partie du lot. Tyrone préférait donc se tenir à carreau. D'autant qu'on ne l'avait pas baptisé « Presse-Purée » pour des prunes.

« Bon, dis donc, faut que j'y aille, dit Nadine. On garde le contact, OK ? On tâche de se voir pour lancer ensemble, un de ces quatre.

– Ouais, d'accord. Faut qu'on se fasse ça. »

Il la regarda s'éloigner. Elle avait la démarche athlétique, à la fois musclée et gracieuse, mais c'est vrai qu'elle ne jouait pas dans la même catégorie que Bella, question allure.

Eh bien, tant pis. Pour lui, Bella, c'était de l'histoire ancienne, fini, terminé, affaire réglée, et il n'était pas à la recherche d'une remplaçante. Peut-être que Nadine et lui pourraient se retrouver pour lancer ensemble le boomerang, impec. Elle savait y faire, et il pourrait apprendre quelques trucs avec elle, peut-être. Ça serait pas si mal d'avoir quelqu'un comme elle pour s'entraîner, même si elle était plutôt quelconque. Elle avait le coup de main, elle savait faire voler un boomerang, c'était l'essentiel. Il n'avait pas besoin de lui rouler un patin.

Lundi
Virginie

« Mon colonel ? » C'était Julio.

Howard quitta des yeux l'image d'holoproj* surmontant son bureau, qui affichait le rapport sur lequel il trimait. Pas moyen de présenter sous un jour favorable le compte rendu des événements survenus là-bas dans le Nevada. Sa seule consolation était de n'avoir perdu aucun homme. Reader allait devoir subir une intervention de chirurgie faciale réparatrice, mais elle s'en sortirait. Au moment de la première détonation, elle était penchée, le dos tourné ; malheureusement, elle s'était retournée pour regarder. Sa visière était certes abaissée, mais hasard malencontreux, deux éclats avaient réussi à se glisser par en dessous. À un ou deux centimètres près, le Lexan aurait stoppé les shrapnels. Elle avait déjà eu la chance que les fragments n'aient pas pénétré plus loin dans le crâne. Le cerveau était intact...

« Ça m'embête à dire, John, mais on a un sérieux problème.

– Pire qu'hier ?

– Oui, chef, j'en ai peur.

– Merveilleux. Accouche.

– Lindholm et Hobbs sont morts, l'un et l'autre descendus à bout portant par des balles de petit calibre.

– Quoi ?

– Leur véhicule a disparu. On a fait décoller des équipes, la police locale et la police d'État font des recherches au sol, mais aucun indice jusqu'ici. »

Howard le dévisagea. Comment était-ce possible ?

« Les médecins légistes disent que les dents et les fragments de crâne que nous avons rapportés sont bien humains mais proviennent d'un homme décédé depuis longtemps. En revanche, le sang et les autres débris osseux, de même que les fragments de cerveau, proviennent tous d'un membre de la famille des suidés... en clair, d'un porc. »

Cette révélation, et ses conséquences, fut un choc sévère pour Howard. « Alors il est vivant. Il n'était pas dans la voiture.

– Affirmatif, mon colonel, c'est la seule conclusion logique. Il a dû se planquer quelque part – j'avais demandé à une équipe de passer la zone au peigne fin... il a attendu que nos hommes relâchent leur surveillance, puis il les a éliminés et a dérobé leur véhicule.

– Quelle merde...

– Vous l'avez dit. On a sous-estimé le bonhomme. Grandement sous-estimé, John. Il nous a baisés.

– Pas “nous”, Julio. Moi. C'est ma faute. »

Fernandez regarda la pointe de ses chaussures. Il savait.

Howard regarda dans le vide. Ce qui venait d'arriver était terrible. Au cours des années, depuis qu'il commandait le bras armé de la Net Force, il avait eu plusieurs blessés dans des escarmouches, mais jamais un seul tué. Et aujourd'hui, parce qu'il avait merdé, deux de ses hommes avaient été abattus. Bordel !

Et le pire, c'est que l'auteur de ces meurtres avait filé.

Allons bon, que pouvait-il faire ?

Lundi
Londres

« Tu es sûr que tu ne veux pas m'accompagner ? demanda Toni.

– J'aimerais bien. Franchement, dit Alex, mais il

faut absolument que je récapitule tout ce merdier. » Du geste, il indiqua l'ordinateur portatif posé sur la table de nuit.

« Je peux rester t'aider.

– C'est gentil, mais tu ne peux pas lire à ma place, autant que tu te détendes tant que tu en as la possibilité. Vas-y, entraîne-toi, évacue un peu de cette tension. Tu te sentiras mieux, et tu pourras toujours me refiler un coup de main par la suite. Je sais que ce cours est important pour toi. J'ai vu ton visage quand tu en es revenue. Va. Éclate-toi. »

Elle acquiesça. Elle voyait la pertinence de son argument. Elle avait vraiment envie d'aller à ce cours de silat et Alex avait raison, elle avait toujours les idées plus claires après s'être dépensée physiquement. « D'accord, dit-elle enfin. Je serai de retour dans trois heures environ. »

Il se pencha pour effleurer ses lèvres d'un baiser avant de lui sourire. « Prends ton temps. Je ne vais nulle part. »

Le trajet en taxi dans les rues de Londres jusqu'à la salle de Clapham était une aventure en soi, et le temps que Toni y parvienne, la nuit tombait. Mais elle avait quand même un quart d'heure d'avance, ce qui lui laissait le temps de se changer et de s'échauffer un peu avant le début du cours.

À l'intérieur de la salle, une dizaine d'élèves s'échauffaient déjà, pratiquant des djurus et des exercices à deux. Elle se rendit aux vestiaires, passa un pantalon de survêtement, une brassière, un T-shirt et des chaussures de boxe, puis les rejoignit pour commencer une séance d'étirements. Même si elle était encore capable de faire le grand écart, il lui fallait plus longtemps pour s'échauffer que lorsqu'elle avait quinze ans. De la souplesse dans les jambes était bien utile – pas autant que pour le *bukti*, mais c'était un avantage indéniable au serak. Le mouvement de rotation de base exigeait de se baisser en même temps que l'on pivotait, et plus on descendait bas, mieux c'était. Autant avoir les tendons du jarret en bon état.

Gourou Stewart arriva, déjà en tenue d'exercice. Il aborda Toni. « Heureux de voir que vous avez pu vous libérer, gourou. Je suis sûr que nous aurons beaucoup à apprendre l'un de l'autre. »

Sourire de Toni. « Je ne sais pas trop ce que je peux vous enseigner, gourou, mais je sais que j'ai beaucoup à apprendre de vous. »

Il lui rendit son sourire et elle ressentit un fugitif moment de triomphe pour avoir réussi à le dérider.

Stewart gagna le devant de la salle avant de se retourner.

« Bon, très bien. Est-ce qu'on peut commencer ? »

Penché sur les images holographiques de son petit écran-plat, Michaels épluchait les comptes rendus, parcourait les fichiers en rapport avec l'enquête britannique sur l'attaque du pirate. C'était une besogne ennuyeuse, compliquée par cette étrange façon qu'avaient les Anglais d'orthographier les mots. Il ne pouvait s'empêcher de les rectifier mentalement, ce qui ralentissait encore son rythme de lecture.

Son virgil annonça un appel.

« Une télécom d'Angela Cooper », émit la puce vocale. Il avait réglé l'appareil pour remplacer le jingle musical de Jay par la voix synthétique. Entendre la fanfare était au-dessus de ses forces maintenant qu'il avait appris que le jeune homme était à l'hôpital.

« Connexion, dit Michaels.

– Commandant Michaels ? Angela Cooper à l'appareil. J'ai un certain nombre d'éléments ultra-confidentiels à ajouter à votre liste de lecture. Vous voulez que je vous les apporte ?

– Volontiers. Je reste ici toute la soirée.

– Ça ne devrait pas prendre aussi longtemps. Je suis à la réception. »

Il sourit. « Montez donc. »

Deux minutes plus tard, on frappait à la porte de sa chambre d'hôtel. Michaels l'ouvrit et découvrit que Cooper était également capable de s'habiller en décontracté. Elle portait une paire de jeans collants, des bottes Doc Martens sang-de-bœuf, et un corsage noir à col pelle à tarte. Elle était équipée elle aussi d'un écran-plat, mais si elle était armée, il ne voyait pas où elle aurait pu planquer un taser* ou un flingue sous une tenue pareille. Très séduisante.

« Commandant...

– Entrez. »

Ce qu'elle fit, en lui présentant aussitôt l'écran-plat. « Ce n'est pas grand-chose, mais il y a deux trucs refilés par les Pakistanais qui valent sans doute le coup d'œil. »

Il prit l'écran. « Quelle nouvelle de la pagaille aérienne ?

– Il y a du mieux. La plupart des ordinateurs affectés ont pu être relancés. Toutefois, je ne vous conseillerais toujours pas de prendre ce soir un vol pour Rio, à moins d'avoir un pilote hyper-compétent, mais la situation s'est améliorée. Ils ont perdu un avion-cargo à Auckland International, trois morts, mais jusqu'ici, aucun crash d'avion civil ayant entraîné des pertes en vies humaines. »

Il hocha la tête.

L'agent du MI-6 regarda autour d'elle. « Sympa, la chambre. Mlle Fiorella est ici ?

– Non, elle est à un cours d'arts martiaux.

– Ah. Rappelez-moi de ne pas la mettre de mauvais poil. Bien, il faut que j'y aille, je ne veux pas vous retarder dans votre travail. Nous avons été très heureux de vous avoir avec nous, monsieur.

– Je vous en prie, appelez-moi Alex. Tous ces "commandant" et ces "monsieur", c'est pour le bureau.

– D'accord. Mais dans ce cas, il faut m'appeler "Angela". »

Elle consulta sa montre.

« Un rendez-vous urgent ? »

Elle plissa les paupières. « Pardon ? Oh non, pas du tout. Je me demandais juste si j'avais le temps de manger un morceau sur le pouce avant de filer chez ma frangine. Je suis censée garder ma nièce ce soir. Elle a huit ans. »

Michaels sourit à nouveau. « Presque l'âge de ma fille.

– Je ne savais pas que vous étiez marié.

– Divorcé, en fait.

– Désolé.

– Il n'y a pas de quoi. Ce fut un soulagement. Excepté pour Susan – c'est ma fille –, c'est mieux pour tout le monde.

– Je comprends. J'ai moi-même été mariée. Brièvement. Une expérience pénible, à la fin surtout. Par chance, on n'a pas eu d'enfants, bien que je les adore.

Une veine pour moi, ma sœur s'est tapé le boulot à ma place. Se retrouver dans le rôle de la "Tatie Angie" qui apporte les cadeaux et gâte le mioche, c'est tellement plus marrant. Dites, on mange bien, dans votre hôtel ?

– Ils font d'excellentes viandes rôties, et ils servent des sandwiches au bar. » Michaels regarda les deux portables à écran tactile contenant les informations secrètes. « Je ferais bien moi-même une pause. Ça vous dérange si je vous tiens compagnie ?

– Pas du tout, au contraire. »

Elle sourit et, l'espace d'une seconde, Michaels éprouva un sentiment de gêne. Toni était sortie et voilà qu'il s'apprêtait à dîner avec la séduisante Mlle Cooper.

Enfin, ce n'était pas comme s'il allait se taper la belle. Ils allaient juste manger un sandwich ensemble, point final. Un homme devait bien manger, non ?

Ben tiens. Cause toujours.

Il récupéra le second écran-plat. Il préférait ne pas les laisser traîner dans la chambre, même si les deux appareils étaient protégés par des mots de passe. Vu le genre de bandits sur qui la Net Force était déjà tombée, la protection semblait assez illusoire.

Angela se dirigea vers la porte, l'ouvrit, lui sourit à nouveau. Un sourire qui lui parut chaleureux.

Juste un sandwich, et basta. Il avait Toni, une fille qu'il aimait, il ne lui fallait rien de plus, merci bien.

12

Mardi 5 avril
Londres

Peel s'arrêta devant une sandwicherie d'Oxford Street. L'établissement restait ouvert jusqu'à pas d'heure, ce qui vous permettait de déjeuner à minuit, si ça vous chantait. Quand on avait goûté aux rations de combat, n'importe quoi sur une tranche de pain relativement frais soutenait à l'aise la comparaison, et il adorait la salade aux œufs mimosas qu'on servait ici.

Il emporta le sandwich, un paquet de chips et une boîte de Coca, jusqu'à l'une des petites tables circulaires près de la fenêtre. Il mangea en observant les passants, en majorité des civils vaquant à leurs affaires. Les nanas étaient chouettes, avec leurs chaussures à semelle compensée qui semblaient apparemment être revenues en vogue. Certaines des adolescentes qui passaient devant la devanture de la sandwicherie avaient des pompes dont les semelles devaient faire quinze bons centimètres d'épaisseur. Incroyable ce que les meufs arrivaient à s'infliger au nom de la mode.

Peel ne crachait pas sur le sexe, même s'il n'était pas trop du genre à s'attarder avec les nanas par la suite. Ou avant, d'ailleurs. Il y avait toujours des belles de nuit aux alentours des lieux de permission, et si vous preniez soin de vous protéger des maladies, vous pouviez vous en taper autant que le permettaient vos finances. Avec son boulot actuel, il n'était pas limité de ce côté-là, ce qui se traduisait par des séances d'une heure environ, une ou deux fois par semaine. Une nana différente à chaque fois, des call-girls provenant de divers services, pour éviter d'instaurer une routine susceptible d'être repérée par un ennemi. Quand on se laissait mener par sa queue, on risquait d'y perdre la tête.

Alors qu'il entamait la deuxième moitié de son sandwich, distrait par des pensées vaguement érotiques, il eut une surprise fort désagréable : Peter Bascomb-Coombs se matérialisa près de lui. L'homme lui dit, tout sourire : « Ça ne vous dérange pas si je m'assieds à côté de vous, n'est-ce pas, commandant ? »

Sans attendre une réponse, le scientifique se glissa sur un des tabourets de plastique à dossier chromé. Il indiqua du geste le sandwich. « Il est mangeable ? »

Eh bien, pour une coïncidence fâcheuse... Comment Bascomb-Coombs avait-il eu l'idée de se pointer ici ? Il ne s'y était pas rendu depuis que le bar était sous surveillance, ce qui remontait déjà à plusieurs semaines. Enfin, bon, très bien, Peel pouvait mettre ça sur le compte du hasard...

Comme s'il avait lu dans ses pensées, l'autre dit : « Non, je ne me suis pas pointé par hasard, vieux. Je suis venu vous voir.

– Vraiment ? À quel sujet ? » réussit à articuler Peel. Il posa le reste de son sandwich, l'appétit soudain coupé. Il s'essuya les lèvres avec une serviette. Son sens du danger était en éveil. Comment ce type avait-il pu savoir qu'il était ici ?

« Au sujet d'un profit mutuel, dit Bascomb-Coombs.

– J'ai peur de ne pas vous suivre.

– Allons, allons, Peel. Vous êtes-vous réellement laissé prendre par mon numéro de savant distrait ? Je parie que non. Tout comme j'ai toujours su depuis le début que vous me faisiez surveiller.

– Professeur, j'ai peur de ne pas savoir ce que vous êtes en train d'insin...

– Épargnons-nous la séance d'esquive, voulez-vous ? Combien ?

– Je vous demande pardon ? » biaisa Peel, qui cherchait toujours à discerner les raisons de cette apparition par trop soudaine. Comme dans un mauvais film d'espionnage.

« Pour vous avoir dans *mon* équipe, commandant. Vous et moi savons pertinemment que Goswell a perdu les pédales avec son plan délirant pour ressusciter le temps glorieux de l'Empire. Il s'imagine vraiment que faire s'affronter les métèques du tiers monde et monter la pression entre Américains, Chinois et Russes suffira à ramener la Grande-Bretagne sur le devant de la scène. Mais, vous, franchement, vous ne pouvez pas croire à de telles fadaises ? »

Peel n'était pas idiot. Les fondements de son boulot venaient simplement de basculer, ébranlés par un séisme aussi formidable qu'imprévu, et tout d'un coup, la situation venait de changer. Il était pragmatique : mieux valait voir sur quoi tout cela pouvait bien déboucher. Il répondit : « Non, bien sûr que non. »

Grand sourire de Bascomb-Coombs. « Je savais bien que vous étiez plus malin que ça. Voyez-vous, monseigneur m'a classé dans cette jolie petite niche, celle de l'idiot savant, du jeune génie étourdi qui oublie de remonter sa braguette en sortant des pissotières, et il faut qu'il continue d'y croire. Pour l'heure, il contrôle toujours mon projet, même si je ne vais pas tarder à remédier à cela. Tôt ou tard, votre équipe de surveillance aurait risqué de me mettre des bâtons dans les roues, c'est pourquoi j'ai décidé de traiter directement avec vous. Vos hommes sont loyaux, n'est-ce pas ?

– Ils le sont, confirma Peel.

– Bien, bien. Donc, la seule question reste : qu'est-ce que vous demandez pour continuer à raconter à Goswell quel pauvre crétin je fais dès que je ne suis plus devant un ordinateur ? Ce petit jeu de dupe n'a plus besoin de durer bien longtemps, mais pour l'heure, le délai reste critique. »

Peel était un officier de l'armée, il avait déjà participé aux combats. Il y avait des moments où l'on pouvait se permettre le luxe de prendre le temps de méditer, d'élaborer des plans d'attaque et de défense, et des moments où l'on visait et tirait d'abord et où l'on réfléchissait ensuite. Il prit sa décision sur-le-champ : « Ce que je demande ? De participer à l'action », répondit-il.

Le scientifique arbora un nouveau sourire Colgate. « Ah, vous êtes effectivement plus malin que je ne l'imaginais. Vous ne savez même pas en quoi consiste mon "action". »

Quand le vin est tiré... Il répondit : « Peu importe, n'est-ce pas ? Goswell me paie bien, mais mon genre d'activité a une durée de vie réduite. Je ne vais pas dire que j'envisage de prendre ma retraite d'ici une vingtaine d'années dans une petite ferme à la campagne, pour finir mes jours à entretenir mon jardin et tailler mes rosiers... C'est ce que Goswell me promet.

Je compte sur vous pour m'offrir mieux, si je bosse pour vous, non ?

– Oh, sans aucun doute, commandant Peel. Je peux faire beaucoup mieux que ça, beaucoup mieux. Je peux vous offrir assez d'argent pour vous bâtir tout un complexe de fermes, une pour chaque jour de votre existence. Et vous offrir une armée de domestiques pour vous tailler vos rosiers.

– Vous piquez ma curiosité, dit Peel. Je vous en prie, continuez. »

Mardi
Jackson, Mississippi

Assis sur le lit dans la chambre d'un Holiday Inn, Roujio regardait la télévision. Il n'y avait rien sur lui, ni sur le décès des deux soldats dans le désert du Nevada. C'est ce qu'il avait prévu. L'organisation responsable de l'attaque contre sa caravane allait tout faire pour dissimuler son échec, du moins à l'égard de l'opinion publique. De ce côté, les Amerloques étaient bien comme les Russes. Tout ce que l'opinion ignorait ne pouvait causer de problème. Il y aurait des recherches, bien sûr, et ils voudraient le capturer vivant, pour lui faire payer ses actes. Ils s'en étaient pris à lui parce qu'ils savaient qui il était. Peut-être aurait-il mieux valu pour lui qu'il abatte le commandant de la Net Force quand l'occasion s'était présentée ?

Non, vu les circonstances, cela eût dénoté un

manque de professionnalisme. Plekhanov s'était fait prendre, et éliminer l'auteur de sa capture n'aurait servi à rien. De toute manière, le défunt aurait été promptement remplacé et cela aurait donné à son organisation des raisons supplémentaires de traquer l'assassin d'un des leurs... plutôt que de s'en prendre à l'un des hommes de main du Russe, susceptible en outre de ne pas moisir aux États-Unis.

Résultat, une fois encore, il se retrouvait en cavale, avec un temps d'avance sur ses ennemis, sans aucun doute déjà lancés sur sa piste. Il se sentait las.

Mais il éprouvait également comme un sombre plaisir. Il n'avait pas entièrement perdu la main, loin de là. Lorsqu'il le fallait, il avait encore une certaine maestria. Il n'était peut-être plus aussi bon que cinq ou même simplement deux ans plus tôt, mais, il n'y en a pas beaucoup qui auraient pu rivaliser avec lui. Même diminué, il faisait mieux que la plupart. Ce n'était pas de la vantardise, mais la simple vérité.

Il soupira. Il lui restait encore plusieurs identités, de l'argent planqué en divers endroits, en liquide comme en monnaie électronique. Que faire à présent ?

Peut-être s'en retourner chez lui. En Tchétchénie. Revoir sa vieille datcha avant de mourir.

Il y avait songé, mais sans jamais le faire. Le désert américain semblait mieux lui convenir. Mais il sentait l'imminence de la fin, et si tous les endroits se valaient quand l'heure de la Faucheuse avait sonné, il était peut-être dans l'ordre des choses de se retrouver en cet instant auprès d'Anna. Alors, pourquoi pas la datcha, en définitive ?

Le bercail. Il retournerait au bercail. Et s'ils le retrouvaient là-bas, eh bien, c'en serait fini.

Mardi
Le sol lunaire

« La lune ? fit Jay. Vous m'avez amené sur la *lune* ? »

Saji rit, exploit peu commun si l'on songeait qu'il n'y avait ici nulle atmosphère pour y respirer ou transmettre les sons. Dans le MR en tout cas. Il lui répondit : « Je ne connais guère d'endroit plus tranquille. J'ai besoin que tu ne sois distrait par aucun signal sensoriel. Pourquoi ? Tu aurais préféré l'obscurité d'une caverne ? Ou un caisson d'isolation sensorielle ? »

Jay fit un signe de dénégation. « Non. Je suppose que c'est sans importance.

– Tout juste. Trouve-toi un coin confortable, assieds-toi, on va commencer. »

Jay dodelina de la tête. Un endroit confortable sur le sol lunaire. Ben voyons.

Mais il arpenta la poussière grise en rebondissant dans les airs – enfin, ce n'était pas vraiment le terme approprié – à chaque pas, jusqu'à ce qu'il trouve un promontoire rocheux qui avait une étonnante ressemblance avec un siège. Il s'assit.

Saji avait disparu mais en laissant derrière lui un sourire de chat du Cheshire qui s'évanouit sur cette ultime remarque : « Souviens-toi simplement de ce que je t'ai dit. »

Jay se retrouva seul, sur la lune, dans un silence

absolument total. L'idée était de rester assis en laissant ses pensées divaguer, puis de recourir à la technique de méditation enseignée par Saji pour les contrôler. Une technique qui n'avait rien de bien sorcier en apparence : il lui suffisait de compter ses respirations. Plus simple même, il n'avait qu'à compter ses expirations. Une fois parvenu à dix, on repartait à zéro. Plus facile, il voyait mal.

Jay ferma les yeux. Une... deux... trois...

Il se faisait vraiment l'effet d'un idiot. Saji n'aurait-il pas pu inventer un meilleur scénario que cette putain de surface lunaire ? C'était tellement... oups... il était en train de dévier. Saji l'avait bien mis en garde contre ça. Quand une pensée parasite s'insinuait, il était censé faire le ménage avec une inspiration profonde, la mettre gentiment de côté, puis reprendre son décompte. D'accord, d'accord. Ça, c'était dans ses cordes. Vas-y, mec.

Une... deux... trois... quatre... cinq...

Qu'est-ce qu'il espérait avec ça ? Rien qu'à rester assis à compter ? Quel intérêt, franchement ? Ça ne pouvait rien donner de... et merde, c'était reparti.

Une... deux... trois...

Jay vit le tigre, éclair fugitif, et il cessa de compter parce que l'expiration suivante ne se produisit pas... bon Dieu, le tigre !

Il rouvrit les yeux. Rien de visible... hormis le paysage lunaire morne et désolé, rien d'audible, hormis les battements de son cœur. Qui, remarqua-t-il, s'étaient accélérés. Bigre. L'exercice s'avérait plus difficile que prévu.

Ping ! Une note unique, cristalline.

Il avait un appel, et qui ne pouvait émaner que de trois personnes : sa mère, son père ou son patron.

Le paysage lunaire s'évanouit. Jay était assis dans le fauteuil de sa chambre d'hôpital. Il tendit la main vers le com.

Mardi
Londres

« Comment ça va, Jay ? demanda Michaels.

– Je me sens mieux, chef », répondit la voix. Mais elle était pâteuse, presque inintelligible. Les effets de l'attaque cérébrale.

Michaels avait activé le mode visuel et le com de la chambre d'hôtel lui procurait une image correcte du jeune homme. Il n'avait pas l'air si différent, à part peut-être un léger relâchement des traits sur un côté du visage.

« Désolé de n'avoir pas appelé plus tôt. Toni et moi, on s'est retrouvé engagés par le MI-6 pour leur filer un coup de main sur cette histoire. T'es au courant que d'autres agents ont été blessés comme toi ?

– J'en ai entendu parler.

– Concernant ta façon de procéder, tu te souviens de quoi que ce soit qui pourrait nous servir ?

– Désolé, chef, mais non. Je ne me souviens que d'un tigre. » Il secoua la tête. « J'arrive même pas à me rappeler avec certitude si ça a un rapport quelconque avec l'enquête.

– D'accord, t'en fais pas pour ça.

– Je veux bosser sur cette affaire, patron, mais...

– Quand t'iras mieux, si on n'a pas coincé le mec d'ici là. On a mis toutes les forces du monde civilisé à ses trousses. On l'aura.

– Je ne crois pas, chef. Je n'ai... jamais... vu... quoi que ce soit de semblable. »

Le simple effort de cette brève conversation l'avait épuisé, Michaels le voyait bien. « Repose-toi, Jay. On te tiendra au courant. »

Il coupa la communication. Seigneur, quel merdier.

Son virgil annonça un appel. Il regarda l'écran. Cooper.

« Oui, allô ?

– Commandant. Euh, Alex. Juste un coup de fil pour vous mettre au fait. Nos techniciens ont élaboré un scénario qui pourrait expliquer comment un casque de RV pourrait provoquer des dégâts cérébraux.

– Vraiment ?

– Oui. Apparemment, c'est en théorie possible. Je n'ai pas les connaissances électroniques ou mathématiques pour piger, mais pour faire simple, il semble qu'on pourrait programmer certains composants des circuits intégrés pour qu'ils se comportent comme des condensateurs. Ils pourraient stocker de l'énergie, un peu comme un flash qui se recharge, avant de la relâcher d'un seul coup. En disposant d'un moyen quelconque pour focaliser cette micro-décharge électronique, on pourrait effectivement provoquer un court-circuit des liaisons neuronales. En théorie, précisent-ils, parce qu'ils sont incapables de le réaliser.

– Quelqu'un aurait-il une telle avance sur le reste de la communauté informatique ?

– Apparemment, oui.

– Tout ça ne me dit rien qui vaille.

– Moi non plus. Et nous n'avons toujours pas le moindre indice sur l'auteur de ces actes. Nous espérons que votre expertise nous éclairera. »

Soupir de Michaels. Ouais, c'est ça. Son meilleur expert avait la cervelle cramée par le mystérieux agresseur qu'ils recherchaient. Sûr que ça n'allait pas leur faciliter la tâche.

« Eh bien, discom*, dit Cooper. On se revoit tout à l'heure au QG ?

– Ouais, j'y ferai un saut. »

À peine avait-elle coupé la connexion que le virgil se remit à sonner. Seigneur, ça n'arrêtait pas. Cette fois, c'était Melissa Allison. Comme s'il avait besoin de ça.

« Commandant ?

– Madame la directrice...

– Du nouveau ? »

Eh bien, au train où vont les choses, on serait pas foutu de reconnaître une vessie d'une lanterne. Mais il répondit : « Non, m'dame, rien de concret jusqu'ici. Le MI-5 et le MI-6 ont mis leurs moyens informatiques à notre disposition et on rattrape le terrain perdu.

– Tenez-moi informée de vos progrès.

– Bien entendu. »

Il reposa le virgil sur son chargeur au moment où la porte de la salle de bains s'ouvrait et Toni, drapée dans un peignoir, sortait de la douche, dans un nuage de vapeur. « Ai-je entendu le téléphone sonner ?

– Ça, ouais, pour sonner, il a sonné. » Puis il la regarda, sourit : « Mais on en recausera après. »

Elle lui rendit son sourire. Défit le peignoir et le laissa tomber. « Après quoi ?

– Viens voir.

– C'est quoi, la formule magique ?

– Viens voir, vite ! »

Elle éclata de rire.

Dès qu'elle fut à sa portée, il la prit dans ses bras, et dans les minutes qui suivirent, toutes les autres idées qu'il aurait pu avoir disparurent comme par enchantement.

13

Mardi 5 avril
Quantico, Virginie

Il n'y avait pas foule sur le parcours d'obstacles et après une centaine d'extensions, cinquante pompes dont douze claquées, John Howard n'avait pas encore évacué toute sa frustration, mais, malgré tout, il ne se sentait pas vraiment d'humeur à effectuer le parcours. Il se sentait trop tendu, trop agacé, trop... il ne savait quoi. Il avait envie de tabasser quelqu'un, de lui défoncer la gueule et de faire gicler le sang, puis de le voir s'effondrer, de préférence sur une surface dure et tranchante. Ça lui faisait une belle jambe que son ire soit surtout dirigée contre lui. Il avait merdé, dans les grandes largeurs, et cette promotion dont il s'était permis de rêver avait toutes les chances d'être annulée avant qu'il en ait vu la couleur.

Pas de pot, mais en définitive, c'était infiniment moins important que les deux soldats tués. Perdre des hommes au combat, dans une escarmouche, c'était une chose. Les perdre sur une zone réputée sûre, abattus par un type seul qui vous faisait passer pour un con, ça craignait un max. Enfin, les perdre, tout simplement...

Et c'est pourquoi il restait planté là, à regarder les

quelques Marines et jeunes recrues du FBI le dépasser, se sentant impuissant.

Jusqu'ici, on n'avait plus eu la moindre nouvelle de Roujio depuis sa disparition. Certes, ils avaient retrouvé le camion, garé devant un supermarché à Las Vegas, les vitres descendues, la clé encore sur le contact. À l'heure qu'il était, il pouvait être n'importe où dans le pays... voire même n'importe où sur cette foutue planète. La Net Force avait les meilleures bécanes du monde pour traiter l'ensemble des données disponibles : réservations aériennes, horaires de cars et de trains, agences de location automobile, ventes d'autos et de motos, et jusqu'aux vols de véhicules à Las Vegas et dans la région, mais pour l'instant, ils n'avaient rien qui corresponde de près ou de loin au signalement du fugitif.

Il voulait ce type, il le voulait comme rarement il avait voulu quelque chose depuis une éternité. S'il arrivait à le dénicher, il comptait bien sauter dans un avion, mandat officiel ou pas, et, quoi qu'il en coûte, lui faire sa fête, à ce connard.

« Mon colonel ? »

Il se secoua pour évacuer les pensées morbides qu'il avait laissées l'envahir et se retourna. Julio.

« Je pense avoir trouvé un truc intéressant. »

Il était tout sourire.

Bigre. Enfin, de bonnes nouvelles. Pas trop tôt.

Mardi
Les Ifs, Sussex, Angleterre

Les infos télévisées étaient, comme cela semblait devoir être désormais la règle de nos jours, écœurantes. Le président américain était reparti sur la « fibre morale », un sujet qu'il n'était certainement pas le mieux placé pour traiter. Les présidents américains avaient toujours été réputés pour leur manque de contrôle de soi, de Warren G. Harding à Bill Clinton en passant par Kennedy. L'idée même qu'un dirigeant aux valeurs spirituelles et morales à ce point élastiques puisse donner à quiconque des leçons de moralité était d'un ridicule achevé. Surtout quand le susdit dirigeant était connu pour avoir l'éthique sexuelle d'un vison en chaleur. L'actuel président des États-Unis ne valait pas mieux que ses prédécesseurs... simplement, il n'avait pas encore été pris en flagrant délit.

Goswell regarda l'écran en hochant la tête. Eh bien, oui, il allait bien être obligé d'y mettre bon ordre, non ? Il comptait passer un coup de fil à son homme de confiance, afin de voir s'il n'y avait pas moyen d'utiliser son nouveau jouet pour découvrir ce que tramait le président. S'il existait des traces enregistrées sur un ordinateur quelque part – et ce devait certainement être le cas –, le scientifique pourrait mettre la main dessus. Que les Américains puissent se repaître d'un nouveau scandale et que le salopard soit tellement occupé à défendre son prétendu honneur qu'il n'ait plus le temps de fourrer son nez ailleurs.

En attendant, il avait un autre coup de fil à passer.

« Applewhite ?

Le majordome se matérialisa près de lui. « Milord ?

– Un téléphone, je vous prie. Et un à cadran, si ça ne vous dérange pas.

– Bien, milord. »

Le domestique alla chercher le téléphone. Goswell détestait ce genre d'affaires, mais la réalité exigeait parfois qu'un homme soit contraint de faire des choses qu'il aurait préféré éviter, ne fût-ce que pour se tenir la tête hors des flots lors d'une tempête...

Applewhite revint avec le téléphone. On aurait dit un de ces vieux modèles en bakélite à cadran circulaire qu'il avait connus étant gosse, mais ce n'était qu'une réplique. Le boîtier était tout aussi bourré d'électronique que n'importe quel autre combiné moderne et aucun gros cordon noir et torsadé ne pendait au bout. C'était un sans-fil.

Tout en prenant l'appareil, il s'enquit : « Pas trace de notre lapin ?

– La cuisinière dit l'avoir aperçu quand elle est descendue au potager ce matin, milord.

– Ah, fort bien. Dans ce cas, allez me chercher mon fusil de chasse. Et on ira voir si on ne peut pas lui mettre un peu de plomb dans la tête, à ce bougre.

– Oui, milord. »

Tandis que le domestique allait ouvrir le meuble où étaient rangés les fusils, Goswell composa le numéro de l'homme qu'il désirait contacter. Il n'y eut qu'une seule sonnerie avant qu'une voix bourrue ne réponde :

« Ouais, kicé ? » Le ton trahissait un manque d'éducation certain.

« Goswell à l'appareil. Vous avez des informations pour moi ?

– Tout juste, chef.

– Dans ce cas, rendez-vous à l'endroit habituel. Disons... sept heures ?

– Ça marche. »

Goswell reposa le combiné sur sa fourche, soupira, hocha la tête. Il était désolant d'avoir à passer par de tels individus, mais c'était une tâche qu'il ne pouvait déléguer.

Applewhite revint, le fusil cassé posé au creux du bras, deux cartouches artisanales, culot de cuivre et chemise en carton vert, dans la main. Goswell ne s'autorisait jamais plus de deux coups. S'il ratait sa cible, eh bien, le lapin aurait droit à un jour de plus pour saccager le potager. Ce n'était que justice.

L'arme était un fusil de chasse Rigby Bros fait main. Sans nul doute approprié pour tirer le lapin, avec son double canon pour cartouches de 16. Son acier gravé de volutes était de toute beauté, mais il n'était pas adapté aux munitions modernes, si bien qu'il faisait fabriquer par son armurier des cartouches que le fusil pouvait digérer sans lui péter à la figure. Les amorces dégageaient pas mal de fumée avec une forte odeur de poudre. George Walker, l'armurier, affirmait pouvoir remplacer la poudre noire par du Pyrodex, ce qui réduirait le dégagement de fumée, mais ça ne dérangeait pas Goswell outre mesure. Deux bonnes giclées de chevrotines de 8 suffiraient à expédier Jeannot Lapin *ad patres*, pour peu qu'il arrive à l'aligner dans son viseur, car le rongeur semblait deviner quand Goswell était armé et quand il ne l'était pas.

Applewhite lui tendit une paire de tampons acoustiques. Goswell fusilla du regard son majordome.

« Votre médecin insiste, milord. »

Goswell dodelina de la tête. « Très bien, donnez-moi ces fichus tampons. » Mais en secret, il n'était pas contre. Il s'agissait de protections électroniques fabriquées par une de ses sociétés installées en France – le diable emporte ces bouffeurs de grenouilles – et il devait bien convenir qu'elles étaient efficaces. Le circuit intégré aux écouteurs détectait le bruit ambiant et l'annulait aussitôt par un bruit équivalent mais inversé en phase, réduisant la détonation à un imperceptible *plop !* En revanche, tant qu'il ne détectait pas de détonation, le casque amplifiait les sons normaux, permettant d'accroître la perception auditive. Et Goswell devait admettre que son ouïe n'était plus ce qu'elle était. Du reste, il envisageait sérieusement de se faire poser des implants qui lui rendraient sa capacité à suivre les conversations normales, laquelle s'était récemment détériorée de manière notable. Les implants avaient apparemment une durée de cinq ou six ans grâce à leurs micro-accumulateurs qui se rechargeaient avec l'énergie des vibrations sonores perçues. Plusieurs bonshommes et une vieille lady de sa connaissance avaient subi l'intervention chirurgicale et tous s'étaient montrés enchantés des résultats. Peut-être sauterait-il le pas, lui aussi. Il avait déjà eu les yeux traités au laser et pouvait désormais se passer de ses lunettes de lecture, sauf quand il était trop fatigué. La technologie était un bienfait discutable, mais de temps à autre, elle avait malgré tout ses avantages.

« Une fois que j'aurai réglé son affaire à ce lapin, demandez à Stephens de m'amener ma voiture. Je vais descendre faire un tour au club.

– Bien, milord. Et bonne chasse. »

Sourire de Goswell. « Merci, Applewhite. Je l'aurai, ce petit vaurien, je vous le garantis ! »

Mardi
Londres

Peel se rendit en voiture au lieu de rendez-vous indiqué par Bascomb-Coombs, encore quelque peu secoué par le tour inattendu qu'avait pris sa destinée. Pas de doute, la fortune lui souriait. Bascomb-Coombs avait déclenché ce matin même l'ouverture d'un nouveau compte dans une banque indonésienne, un compte numéroté sur lequel Peel pouvait tirer à sa guise, un compte sur lequel se trouvait l'équivalent en roupies indonésiennes d'un million d'euros.

D'un claquement de doigts, Peel se retrouvait millionnaire, et avec la promesse de bien plus à la clé, s'il se conformait convenablement à ses nouvelles obligations.

Le petit immeuble de bureaux était situé un peu à l'écart d'Old Kent Road, pas très loin des vieux gazomètres de la South Eastern. Ce n'était pas l'endroit qu'il aurait personnellement choisi, mais c'était peut-être aussi bien, puisque même au cours de ses recherches, il n'avait pas spécialement remarqué cet immeuble.

Il se gara au parking, coupa le contact et se dirigea vers le bâtiment gris et trapu d'un seul étage. Les fenêtres étaient munies de barreaux et un vigile était installé derrière un comptoir dans le hall. L'homme vérifia sur son écran d'ordinateur que les traits et le nom de Peel correspondaient, puis il ouvrit une gâche électrique qui le fit accéder à la cage d'escalier.

Peel escalada rapidement les marches et emprunta le couloir du premier jusqu'au bureau situé tout au bout. En passant devant les autres portes, dont certaines étaient vitrées, il nota que presque tous semblaient vides.

La dernière porte sur la droite n'était pas verrouillée. Il l'ouvrit et pénétra dans la pièce.

« Ah, commandant, toujours ponctuel. C'est une qualité que j'apprécie. Entrez, entrez, que je vous fasse faire le tour du propriétaire. »

De fait, il n'y avait pas grand-chose à visiter. Dans un angle, une console d'ordinateur, un holoprojecteur et une station de travail, et devant, un fauteuil à roulettes. Un petit frigo et un mini-four étaient installés dans un coin, avec, juste à côté, un lit pliant. Une pancarte apposée sur la porte adjacente indiquait les toilettes.

Peel haussa le sourcil, comme pour dire : voilà tout ce que vous avez à me montrer ?

Bascomb-Coombs sourit. « Ça ne paie pas de mine, n'est-ce pas, mais la véritable installation se trouve ailleurs, bien entendu, dans la salle informatique de Lord Goswell, à Chelmsford. Nous y sommes reliés téléphoniquement et pour répondre à la question que vous ne manquerez pas de me poser, oui, la ligne est protégée. D'ici, je peux faire tout ce que je fais à Chelmsford sans que personne en sache rien.

– Pardonnez-moi mon ignorance, monsieur Bascomb-Coombs, mais que faites-vous au juste ? Je veux dire, je connais le dispositif, du moins ce qu'a bien voulu m'en dire Goswell, et j'ai pu constater les résultats, qui sont sans aucun doute impressionnants, mais du diable si je sais comment ça fonctionne au juste. »

Rire du scientifique. « Et je doute fort d'être capable de vous l'expliquer. La devise de Turner est qu'on ne peut expliquer les choses de manière simple que si celui qui les explique les a bien comprises, or je ne suis pas certain de les saisir entièrement moi-même. Et, sans vouloir vous vexer, je doute que vous ayez le bagage mathématique et physique suffisant pour les comprendre. À ce stade, mon ordinateur n'est guère que l'équivalent d'une allumette : bien pratique pour allumer un feu, mais ce n'est pas pour autant que j'appréhende le détail des réactions chimiques à l'origine du processus...

Il sourit et Peel lui rendit son sourire. Le bonhomme ne venait-il pas de le traiter de crétin ?

« Je peux toutefois vous apporter quelques éléments de base, si vous le désirez. Vous êtes plus ou moins familiarisé avec les ordinateurs traditionnels ?

– Plus ou moins.

– Dans ce cas, vous devez savoir que la plupart des ordinateurs sont des machines de Turing qui exploitent la logique booléenne fondée sur l'arithmétique binaire. Vous avez des zéros et des uns – des bits quantiques d'information qu'on appelle des Q-bits – et ce sont les seuls choix possibles. C'est soit zéro, soit un, point final. Dans un ordinateur quantique, toutefois, on peut avoir une superposition simultanée des deux états. Cela semble *a priori* déraisonnable, mais en parallélisme quantique, on peut utiliser simultanément toutes les valeurs intermédiaires possibles de tous les registres d'entrée. »

Peel acquiesça, comme s'il comprenait un mot du putain de charabia que lui débitait son interlocuteur.

L'autre poursuivit : « Si l'on recourt à l'algorithme de factorisation quantique de Shor, on peut voir qu'un OQ* – un ordinateur quantique – est capable de factoriser un grand nombre en une infime fraction du temps nécessaire à la même opération avec une machine à l'architecture traditionnelle. Un problème sur lequel un Super-Cray devrait mouliner plusieurs millions d'années peut être résolu en quelques secondes avec mon OQ. De sorte que pour des problèmes concrets tels que le déchiffrement, ma machine s'avère infiniment supérieure. »

Peel hocha la tête. « Dans ce cas, pourquoi tout le monde n'utilise-t-il pas ces fameux OQ ? »

Bascomb-Coombs rit. « Oh, ils aimeraient bien, mais ce n'est pas le genre de truc qui s'improvise comme ça. La difficulté est que l'état cohérent d'un ordinateur quantique est en général détruit sitôt qu'il est affecté par l'environnement ambiant. En clair, dès qu'on le met en route et qu'on essaie d'y accéder, on le détruit. Un problème pour le moins épineux. On a tenté toutes sortes de moyens pour contourner cet obstacle au cours des années : lasers, excitation photonique, pièges à ions, pièges optiques, RMN, polarisation et même résonance de spin... c'est la dernière tentative en date.

« Wineland et Monroe ont travaillé sur la porte quantique unique en piégeant des ions de béryllium. Kimble et Turch ont polarisé des photons pour aboutir au même résultat. NTC a obtenu quelques résultats encourageants avec la résonance magnétique nucléaire, tandis que Chuang et Gerschenfeld ont appliqué l'algorithme de Grover à un modèle biquantique, en utilisant les atomes de carbone et d'hydrogène d'une molécule de chloroforme. Mais le problème a toujours été celui de la reproductibilité et de la stabilité. Jusqu'à ma machine.

– Et comment y êtes-vous parvenu, si c'est si difficile ?

– Parce que je suis plus intelligent qu'eux. » Dans sa bouche, cela ne résonnait pas comme une vantardise, et au vu des résultats, ce n'en était pas une.

« Je vous ai largué dès que j'ai parlé de Q-bits, pas vrai ?

– Déjà avant, j'en ai peur », avoua Peel.

Bascomb-Coombs sourit. « Ne faites pas de complexe, commandant. Les physiciens dans le monde capables de comprendre ce que j'ai fait se compteraient sur les doigts d'une main, même si je leur mettais sous le nez le modèle opérationnel. Non, vos talents résident ailleurs. Je n'aimerais pas avoir à vous assommer dans une ruelle sombre, ou vous affronter sur un champ de bataille. »

Peel accepta le compliment avec un hochement de tête. « Certes.

– Toujours est-il que tout cela revient au fait que je dispose d'un ordinateur capable de faire des prodiges, et forcer des serrures vient en tête de liste. Sauf à les débrancher et les déconnecter complètement, pas un système sur terre n'est inviolable pour ma machine. L'argent ne signifie rien quand on peut s'introduire à sa guise dans n'importe quelle chambre forte. Les secrets militaires sont à notre disposition. Personne ne peut nous dissimuler quoi que ce soit.

– Vraiment ? Dans ce cas, pourquoi n'êtes-vous pas maître du monde ? »

L'homme partit d'un nouveau rire. « Vous me plaisez bien, Peel, c'est tellement rafraîchissant de vous entendre après avoir subi pendant des années le discours pesant de scientifiques imbus de leur personne. La réponse est que mon ordinateur n'est pas encore parfait. Il a encore quelques petits défauts et, de temps à autre, il plante. À vrai dire, il est opérationnel à peu près la moitié du temps. De sorte que je suis condamné à gâcher mes heures de loisir à des considérations frivoles comme l'argent et le pouvoir... du moins tant que je ne serai pas arrivé à le rendre plus stable. C'est à cela que je consacre l'essentiel de mon énergie, à l'amélioration du système. Parce que Goswell est le propriétaire de la machine et la maintient sous bonne garde, je suis bien obligé d'accéder à ses requêtes. Mais l'heure est proche. Et à ce moment-là, j'aurai besoin à mes côtés d'hommes de votre trempe. »

Peel se mit à songer au million d'euros dans la banque indonésienne. Il était déjà plus riche qu'il ne l'avait jamais rêvé. Son père, en dehors de son titre, n'avait été qu'un pauvre hobereau qui avait tout perdu avant sa mort. Un million d'euros, c'était loin d'être négligeable, mais s'il restait aux côtés de ce drôle de loustic, il pouvait espérer bien plus !

« Je suis entièrement à votre service, monsieur Bascomb-Coombs.

– Oh, je vous en prie, appelez-moi Peter, Terrance. Je suis sûr que nous allons parfaitement nous entendre. »

14

Mercredi 6 avril
Seattle, État de Washington

Roujio emprunta le métro qui passait sous l'aérogare de SeaTac pour rejoindre sa porte d'embarquement. Il avait une place sur le vol BA 747 de Londres. Il avait pris un car du Mississippi à La Nouvelle-Orléans, puis de là, un 727 rallongé pour rallier Portland, Oregon, et enfin un Dash 8 jusqu'à Seattle. Si quelqu'un avait réussi à le filer jusque dans le Mississippi, il aurait noté un cheminement similaire de Las Vegas à Jackson : il avait d'abord loué une voiture pour se rendre à Oklahoma City, puis de là, enchaîné trois vols sur court-courrier, toujours vers le sud ou vers l'est. Un éventuel poursuivant se serait attendu à le voir continuer dans cette même direction, en gros vers Miami, alors qu'il avait rebroussé chemin. Une fois à Londres, il se rendrait en Espagne ou en Italie et de là, s'envolerait pour l'Inde et la Russie, et enfin, son pays natal.

Quand vous étiez pourchassé, il était déconseillé de fuir en ligne droite – surtout quand les chiens étaient plus rapides que vous.

Le train était bondé et lorsqu'il s'arrêta pour embarquer de nouveaux voyageurs, Roujio se leva de son siège pour offrir sa place à une jeune femme enceinte jusqu'aux yeux et lestée de deux sacs de voyage. Anna et lui avaient toujours voulu des enfants, mais cela n'avait pas pu se réaliser.

La femme le remercia et s'assit. Il se retint à la main courante et regarda, derrière les vitres, défiler la paroi du tunnel.

Le train s'arrêta, les voyageurs descendirent, et Roujio se dirigea vers sa porte d'embarquement. Il avait plusieurs heures d'avance, mais nulle part où aller d'ici là. Il trouverait bien une sandwicherie ; des toilettes en cas de besoin ; un endroit où s'asseoir et peut-être faire un somme. Dans l'armée, on apprenait à dormir n'importe où, et on avait vite fait de s'assoupir dans un siège confortable.

Le vol pour Heathrow était direct, neuf ou dix heures tout au plus, et il avait réservé une place dans la cabine centrale, comme s'il était en voyages d'affaires. Il était vêtu d'un complet discret, d'une chemise bleu ciel avec cravate, et il portait une mallette remplie de magazines et d'une ramette de papier blanc pour renforcer cette image. Il n'était qu'un pion de la grande machine industrielle, sans rien de remarquable.

British Airways valait bien d'autres compagnies, et elle était sans aucun doute supérieure aux lignes intérieures russes ou chinoises. Son dernier vol sur un avion de ligne britannique s'était déroulé sans encombre, hormis à l'atterrissage. Le gros-porteur avait touché la piste avec suffisamment de violence pour déclencher le déploiement des masques à oxygène et noyer les passagers sous le contenu des porte-bagages. Personne n'avait été blessé mais la surprise avait été de taille. Peut-être qu'ils avaient confié le manche à l'hôtesse, pour qu'elle s'entraîne... À moins que le pilote ne se soit endormi...

Il haussa mentalement les épaules. Il avait connu des atterrissages plus rudes. Une fois, pendant une mousson, son vol JAL s'était posé à Tokyo avec une telle rudesse que le train avant s'était affaissé, engendrant une pluie d'étincelles visibles par les hublots de la cabine malgré le tarmac détrempé. Une autre fois, lors d'un vol vers Moscou, l'antique appareil russe à turbopropulseurs s'était posé normalement mais avait heurté un camion-citerne lors du roulage, tuant le chauffeur et jetant à terre une demi-douzaine de passagers trop pressés qui avaient débouclé leur ceinture et quitté leur siège. Ce coup-ci, on avait dû déplorer plusieurs fractures. Enfin, sur un terrain de campagne au fin fond de la Tchétchénie, le petit Cessna d'où il venait de débarquer rejoignait la piste d'envol et avait roulé sur une soixantaine de mètres à peine lorsqu'il s'était désintégré en sautant sur une mine.

Cela faisait un bail qu'il avait cessé de se tracasser pour si peu. Si votre numéro devait sortir, vous n'y pouviez rien. D'ici là, le vieux dicton restait vrai : tout atterrissage dont on se tirait sur ses deux jambes était un atterrissage réussi.

Une des buvettes du terminal vendait des sandwiches à la viande et il en commanda un, arrosé d'une bière. La télévision était allumée sur une chaîne de sports. Des femmes hideuses, boursouflées comme des crapauds humanoïdes, la peau tannée comme du vieux cuir, paradaient sur une estrade en faisant jouer leurs muscles. On aurait dit des mecs en bikini. Dans les coulisses, un de ces spécimens se faisait interviewer et lorsqu'elle parlait, sa voix était plus grave que celle d'une basse d'opéra.

Incroyable ce que les gens arrivaient à s'infliger. Roujio avait eu brièvement l'occasion de s'entraîner avec les athlètes de l'équipe olympique russe, et il savait tout des substances chimiques qu'ils ingurgitaient pour améliorer leurs performances. Les androgènes utilisés par ces femmes provoquaient des altérations irréversibles : voix grave, acné, pilosité corporelle et faciale, hypertrophie des organes sexuels. La gonflette, c'était parfait pour s'exhiber à vingt-cinq ans sur une scène, mais dans quel état seraient ces pauvres femmes à quarante ou cinquante ans ? Si même elles atteignaient cet âge... Il hocha la tête. Ça s'appelait ne pas voir plus loin que le bout de son nez.

« Bon Dieu, vous pouvez pas couper cette merde ? » lança au garçon un des clients du bar. Plusieurs autres levèrent leur verre pour signifier leur approbation. Le loufiat haussa les épaules et changea de chaîne.

Roujio termina son sandwich et sa bière.

Mercredi
Londres

Le MI-6 avait alloué à Toni et Alex un bureau de bonne taille équipé de tous les moyens d'accès à son réseau informatique. Du moins, dans les limites de ce qui concernait ce problème précis. Toni s'était déjà heurtée à quantité de fichiers non accessibles.

Alex était au bout du couloir et discutait avec Helms. Restée seule dans le bureau, Toni effectuait des corrélations entre divers fichiers informatiques de compagnies aériennes, quand Angela Cooper tapa à la porte ouverte.

« Entrez, dit Toni.

– Désolée de vous déranger, mademoiselle Fiorella, mais Alex se demandait si vous ne voudriez pas les retrouver, le directeur général et lui, ils ont un mot à vous dire. »

Alex ? Elle l'appelait « Alex » ?

« Bien sûr », répondit Toni. Elle se déconnecta de la station de travail. Cooper attendait, tout sourire, mais avec un soupçon d'impatience.

« Par ici, je vous prie. »

Toni se sentait pataude et engoncée à côté de cette blonde en corsage vert sombre, la jupe coupée trop haut au-dessus des genoux, avec ses chaussures à talons de cinq centimètres. Elle avait toutefois de jolies gambettes et peut-être que si Toni avait été grande et tout en jambes, elle aussi les aurait exhibées, au lieu de porter un chemisier de soie bleu passe-partout, un jean et des chaussures de marche. D'un autre côté, en faisant ses valises, elle n'avait pas prévu qu'elle allait travailler. Après la conférence, où elle avait mis les deux ensembles qu'elle avait amenés pour le voyage avant de les donner à nettoyer, il ne lui restait plus guère que des tenues décontractées. Après tout, ils étaient censés être en vacances, non ? Mais elle allait devoir appeler le pressing pour récupérer ses fringues. Pas question de laisser Mlle Cooper la faire passer pour une godiche.

« Désolée d'avoir ainsi interrompu vos vacances. »

Toni abandonna ces considérations vestimentaires pour revenir aux problèmes du moment. « Comment ? Oh, enfin, ce n'est pas de votre faute. On a quand même eu le temps de visiter un peu votre pays.

– C'est autre chose que les États-Unis, n'est-ce pas ?

– Vous y êtes déjà allée ?

– Mais oui, bien sûr. Plusieurs fois, pour raisons professionnelles. Et j'ai passé un été à l'UCLA du temps où j'étais étudiante. Merveilleux, le climat de Californie, c'est la première fois que j'ai vraiment bronzé. »

Je veux bien le croire. Toni imagina Cooper en bikini. Elle devait être canon. La file des prétendants avait dû s'allonger au soleil de Los Angeles. Elle la voyait d'ici manier le bâton pour éloigner les importuns – à moins qu'elle n'ait au contraire préféré attirer leur attention, ce qui avait dû être le cas. C'était le genre...

« Alex dit que vous êtes du Bronx ? »

Allons bon, qu'est-ce qu'il était encore allé lui raconter !

« Oui. Et j'ai bien peur que New York ait peu de rapport avec la Californie.

– J'ai déjà eu l'occasion de passer une semaine à Manhattan, fin août. La chaleur et l'humidité étaient assez épouvantables.

– Et c'est pire en septembre. »

Elles parcoururent une dizaine de mètres sans ajouter un mot. Le silence commençait à se faire pesant lorsque Cooper observa : « J'ai cru comprendre qu'Alex était divorcé et avait une petite fille. Est-ce que vous la connaissez... sa fille ? »

Seigneur, quelle mouche avait piqué Alex d'aller lui raconter tout ça ? Et quand avait-il eu l'occasion de le faire ? S'il continuait sur sa lancée, il allait lui refiler des photos d'eux deux en train de s'ébattre au lit ! Elle répondit : « Non, je n'ai pas eu l'occasion de la rencontrer. Je lui ai parlé deux ou trois fois au com. J'ai vu des photos d'elle. Elle vit avec sa mère dans l'Idaho.

– C'est loin dans l'ouest du pays, n'est-ce pas ?

– Oui. Loin dans l'ouest.

– Ah... eh bien, vous voici arrivée. » D'une main, elle indiqua la porte.

« Vous n'entrez pas ?

– Je crains que non. D'autres obligations m'appellent. Mais je vous verrai plus tard. »

Cooper tourna les talons et s'éloigna, en ondulant légèrement des hanches.

La salope.

Dans la pièce, Alex était debout devant une table avec Helms et tous deux examinaient des tirages photographiques sous un projecteur. Alex leva les yeux à son entrée. Il ne souriait pas. « Toni. Viens donc voir ça. »

Elle s'approcha. Les clichés étaient apparemment des vues d'installations militaires prises par un satellite espion et retraitées en fausses couleurs par ordinateur. Toni crut deviner deux missiles balistiques intercontinentaux sur leur rampe de lancement à une extrémité du complexe. « Qu'est-ce que je regarde ? »

Ce fut Helms qui répondit. « Il s'agit d'une base de lancement expérimentale située à Xinghua, près de la côte de la mer de Chine orientale. C'est là que les Chinois mettent au point un nouveau type de missile nucléaire à longue portée. »

Il tapota sur le missile de la photo. « Hier soir, un ordinateur a mis en alerte deux des prototypes opérationnels et entamé les quatre-vingt-dix minutes du compte à rebours de lancement. Les missiles étaient braqués sur Tokyo.

– Seigneur ! souffla Toni.

– Tout juste. L'ordinateur était verrouillé, ils étaient dans l'impossibilité d'interrompre la séquence. Heureusement, les deux têtes étaient factices, et chance supplémentaire, les techniciens ont pu annuler manuellement la procédure. Les Chinois, pourtant toujours discrets en la matière, s'avouent terrifiés. Quelqu'un a réussi à contourner leurs protections et leurs codes pour déclencher l'allumage de l'extérieur. Les satellites-espions américains qui surveillent en permanence la base ont vu les préparatifs de lancement et l'aviation américaine a aussitôt fait décoller en urgence les chasseurs bombardiers basés sur l'île sud-coréenne de Cheju-do. Si les missiles chinois avaient été lancés, les avions furtifs auraient essayé de les abattre, et ils auraient sans aucun doute bombardé la base pour empêcher tout lancement ultérieur. »

Toni dévisagea Alex. Il avait un air sinistre.

« Même sans charge nucléaire, deux engins de ce gabarit arrivant en plein centre de Tokyo auraient provoqué des dégâts considérables.

– Et c'est encore notre pirate aérien ?

– Ou un de ses émules. Mais j'ai du mal à croire qu'il y ait deux spécimens de ce genre. »

Toni hocha la tête.

« Il faut qu'on neutralise ce type, en vitesse. Or notre as de la traque, Jay Gridley, est HS.

– Un malheur n'arrive jamais seul, c'est ça ? » nota Helms.

Toni le regarda, avant de se retourner vers Alex. C'était mal barré. Très mal barré.

Mercredi
Washington, DC

Tyrone avait calculé que s'il se rendait sur le terrain de foot juste après la sortie de ses cours, il serait libre une quarantaine de minutes avant l'arrivée des autres élèves. Quarante minutes, c'était largement suffisant pour effectuer une bonne douzaine de jets.

Il se plaça près de la ligne médiane, pour tâter d'un doigt humecté la direction du vent. Il y avait une bonne brise qui soufflait du nord, et il décida de scotcher des pièces de monnaie à son MTA pour l'empêcher de se faire embarquer par les rafales. Cela ne lui prit qu'une minute.

Il se positionna dos au vent, prit deux profondes inspirations et secoua l'épaule pour détendre les trapèzes. Il avait envisagé de faire des haltères – les meilleurs lanceurs avaient tous une forme athlétique – et se muscler un peu les bras n'aurait pas été du luxe. L'équilibre était délicat. Trop de mollesse dans le jet, et l'engin ne décollait pas, trop d'énergie et le boomerang piquait du nez à coup sûr. Mais il y avait des moments où on avait besoin d'un petit supplément de forces, maintenant par exemple ; quand le vent soufflait en rafales, et compte tenu de son gabarit, Tyrone était un peu limite. Sans pour autant être un hercule, un léger surcroît de masse musculaire ne lui aurait pas fait de mal.

Il effectua son premier jet, pour vérifier l'angle des pales et s'assurer du bon équilibre des pièces servant de lest. Le modèle « Océan Indien » se mit à tourbillonner, formant une tache rouge floue, mais bientôt il vacilla et prit de l'angle trop vite. Tyrone récupéra le boomerang et rectifia l'inclinaison des pales en les tordant délicatement vers le haut. Il déplaça de quelques millimètres la pièce scotchée sur le bras long, la fixa de nouveau, puis fit un nouvel essai.

Déjà mieux, mais un poil déséquilibré. Bon, il pouvait passer la journée à régler le truc, surtout avec du vent, et il était à peu près au point pour une séance d'entraînement.

Il en était à son septième lancer, ayant enfin réussi à dépasser la minute de vol, ce qui n'était pas si mal vu les conditions atmosphériques, quand il entendit Nadine le héler.

« Salut, Ty ! »

Elle traversa le terrain, se délesta de son sac à dos et en sortit son MTA personnel, un grand modèle en L à rayures bleues et blanches. C'était un Quark Synlin. Il n'en avait jamais vu de près mais il les connaissait par les holos, et il avait pu en apercevoir deux, de loin, lors du tournoi, aussi le reconnut-il d'emblée.

« Merde, comment t'as pu mettre la main dessus ? Je croyais que Quark avait cessé la fabrication.

– Effectivement, mais il en reste encore quelques-uns en stock. Ma mère m'a dit que si je lui prouvais que j'étais capable de manier les modèles de compétition, elle me prêterait l'argent pour me l'acheter. Quand j'ai gagné le concours, elle a estimé que j'étais prête. Il est arrivé par colis exprès aérien ce matin. » Elle brandit le boomerang. Tyrone le lui prit comme si c'était un nouveau-né, avec une infinie délicatesse.

« Et il donne quoi, au lancer ?

– J'en sais rien, j'ai pas encore eu l'occasion de le tester. Si tu l'essayais ? »

Il la regarda, éberlué. « C'est à toi de commencer, c'est le tien.

– Non, non, vas-y. T'es déjà échauffé.

– Ouais ?

– Sûr. »

Il humecta son doigt, vérifia la direction du vent.

« Moyen à fort, cinquante degrés vers le haut, et traîne pas. Mieux vaut accentuer la dérive verticale. Entre cinq et dix face au vent. »

Il acquiesça. Se mit en position. Inspira un grand coup, prit son élan et lança.

Le grand Quark fila sur une cinquantaine de mètres avant de se mettre à pivoter et gagner de la hauteur, beaucoup de hauteur, trente, trente-cinq mètres avant de basculer de la perpendiculaire en vol horizontal. Puis il ricocha à deux reprises sur un courant ascendant.

« Mince, non mais t'as vu ça ! »

C'était un vol superbe... l'engin donnait l'impression de vouloir rester à jamais dans les airs, avant enfin de redescendre à moins de vingt mètres de l'endroit d'où il était parti, légèrement sous le vent. Tyrone n'eut aucun mal à le récupérer au vol.

Il n'avait pas de chrono mais Nadine avait pris le sien.

« Deux minutes cinquante et une. Pas mal du tout.

– Ouais, tu parles ! Ça bat mon record personnel ! » Avec un temps pareil, il l'aurait battue elle aussi lors du tournoi. Mince alors !

Il contempla le boomerang, puis sourit à Nadine. « Merci. » Il lui rendit l'engin. « À ton tour. On a encore une vingtaine de minutes avant d'être envahis par les maniaques du ballon rond.

– De quoi lancer encore deux fois, tu crois pas ?

– Je veux, mon neveu. » Ils rirent tous les deux.

Nadine était extra. Surtout pour une fille.

15

Mercredi 6 avril
Monts Alamo Heuco, Nouveau-Mexique

Debout sur un bout de sol désertique, Jay Gridley écoutait le silence au milieu de la rocaille et des épineux. Le soleil était un marteau aveuglant qui écrasait tout ce qui se trouvait en dessous de lui. On se serait cru au milieu de nulle part, et si on filait droit vers l'est, l'ouest ou le sud, on quittait les États-Unis pour se retrouver au Mexique ; du point où il se trouvait, la frontière la plus proche n'était qu'à deux ou trois kilomètres.

Saji se tenait près de lui. Il avait plus la dégaine d'un Indien que d'un Tibétain. Il portait jean délavé, bottes de cow-boy, chemise de toile à manches longues, et il était coiffé d'un haut chapeau blanc, ceint d'un bandeau en peau de serpent à sonnette.

« Tu sens la présence d'eau ? » dit Saji.

Jay, qui était vêtu à peu près comme lui, mais coiffé d'un sombrero mexicain plus foncé à large bord, hocha la tête.

« Tout ce que je sens, c'est le désert. La poussière, le sable, le roc chauffé à blanc, un point c'est tout. »

Et c'est vrai qu'à chacun de leur pas, ils soulevaient un nuage de poussière ocre rouge, fine comme du talc. Elle recouvrait ses bottes et ses habits, lui piquait les yeux et le nez, rendait la respiration difficile. Il n'y avait pas de vent, ça permettait au moins à la poussière de retomber vite. Un scénario fort réaliste, et il était de Saji... ce genre de création dépassait les capacités de Jay.

« D'accord, voyons voir si on peut déceler un signe quelconque. »

Jay hocha la tête. « Comment avez-vous appris toutes ces techniques de pistage ? »

Saji lui servit son sourire niais. « Jerry Pierce, un pote navajo, est un Fils des Loups de l'Ombre. Pisteur pour les gardes-frontières. C'est lui qui m'a tout appris. En échange, je lui ai enseigné la Voie du Milieu.

– Un Navajo bouddhiste ?

– Pourquoi pas ? Le bouddhisme n'interfère pas avec la plupart des autres croyances religieuses – du moins, pas avec celles qui ne professent pas un monothéisme militant. Allez, viens. »

Tous deux avancèrent avec précaution sur le terrain sablonneux. Au bout de quelques pas, Saji s'arrêta et dit :

« Stop ! Tu l'as vu ? »

Ils étaient peut-être à trois mètres du rebord d'une falaise abrupte, un à-pic de vingt à vingt-cinq mètres. « Vu quoi ? Le bout du monde ?

– Rien d'aussi spectaculaire. Juste là, sous ton nez. »

Jay se dévissa les yeux et s'accroupit pour examiner le sol. Il distinguait trois choses : une croûte de terre, un unique brin d'herbe coupée vert pâle, et un caillou usé, rougeâtre et poussiéreux. La nature du sol l'empêchait de retenir la moindre empreinte. « Je vois rien du tout.

– Rien du tout ?

– Bon, d'accord. Je vois effectivement quelque chose. Un bout de terre racornie, un caillou et un brin d'herbe coupée. C'est tout.

– Regarde autour de toi. Vois-tu d'autre végétation ? »

Jay se releva, contempla le paysage alentour. « Il y a quelque chose qui ressemble à un buisson de créosote, à une dizaine de mètres par là-bas. » Il s'approcha du rebord de la falaise, regarda en contrebas. Rien ne poussait de ce côté.

« Je vois rien à proximité. Il y a un grand cactus, tout là-bas, à perpète... C'est le désert avec un grand D.

– Très bien, réfléchis-y une minute.

– Sans vouloir vous vexer, Saji, mais si j'étais capable de réfléchir plus de trente secondes sans que mon cerveau se ramollisse, j'aurais pas besoin de vous !

– Ferme les yeux, compte tes respirations ! »

Jay soupira. Mais il obéit.

Une... deux... trois... qu'est-ce... que... j'ai... vu... ?

Il rouvrit les yeux. « L'herbe. »

Saji hocha la tête. « Qu'a-t-elle de particulier ?

– Elle n'a pas sa place ici. Comment est-elle arrivée ? Il n'y a rien alentour qui y ressemble.

– Bien. Pourrait-elle avoir été apportée par le vent ? »

Jay fit un signe de dénégation. « Il n'y a pas un poil de vent. Et si elle était là depuis longtemps, elle serait sèche comme un os blanchi au soleil, or elle est encore verte.

– Ce qui signifie ?

– Quelqu'un l'a déposée ici. Elle s'est peut-être

détachée d'une semelle ou elle était collée à une jambe de pantalon.

– Très bien. Et ensuite ? »

Jay réfléchit. Saji le lui avait dit, mais il n'arrivait plus à s'en souvenir. Bon, d'accord, pense avec logique, Jay. C'était dur, mais quand même pas comme s'il avait dû élaborer un programme complexe, il suffisait d'avancer pas à pas. Oui, mais dans quelle direction... ?

« S'écarter en spirale, chercher au sol les endroits qui auraient pu retenir des traces éventuelles ?

– Bien. Voyons voir ça. Fais attention, il ne s'agirait pas d'effacer une piste. »

Jay s'éloigna en spirale du brin d'herbe, progressant avec lenteur, guettant des traces. Il n'en repéra pas la moindre dans un rayon de quinze mètres alentour. Il s'avoua vaincu.

« Aucune piste.

– Tu es sûr ?

– Merde, oui, j'en suis sûr ! »

Saji attendit quelques secondes.

« Désolé. Je suis à cran.

– Pas de problème. Regarde plutôt par ici. » Saji le mena vers une plaque de sable, pointa le doigt. « Là.

– À d'autres. Ce sable est parfaitement lisse, sans la moindre marque, vous allez pas me raconter que vous y voyez une piste !

– Les traîne-tapis, dit Saji.

– Pardon ?

– Ils attachent à leurs pieds des bouts de tapis coupés, passés par-dessus leurs chaussures, qui ne laissent pas de traces. Si tu vois un endroit parfaitement lisse en plein désert, méfiance. Regarde plutôt juste à côté. Tu vois les ondulations laissées par le vent ? Le piqueté des gouttes de pluie ? Les inégalités sur le sable, là, et encore là. À présent, examine de nouveau cet endroit précis. »

Jay regarda. Effectivement. Le sable était absolument lisse.

« Accroupis-toi au ras du sol, en te plaçant de biais par rapport au soleil. »

Jay obéit. Oui, il pouvait distinguer autour de la partie lisse un léger ressaut qui décrivait grossièrement un ovale. « Ça y est, je l'ai vue !

– Parfois, ce que tu dois chercher, c'est l'absence d'une chose qui devrait être là. Parfois, ce sera très subtil, comme cette empreinte en négatif. Notre gibier est passé par ici, cheminant vers le nord, au ras de la falaise. Un homme qui le pisterait à cheval ne s'approcherait pas autant, de peur de chuter, même si sa monture le laissait faire. Ce grand cactus dont tu as parlé tout à l'heure, très loin par là-bas ?

– Ouais, eh bien ?

– Je parie qu'il a fait halte au pied pour se reposer à l'ombre.

– Comment diable pouvez-vous savoir une chose pareille ?

– Il est au nord d'ici. Il n'y a pas le moindre abri à des kilomètres à la ronde. Si tu avais marché sous ce soleil torride pendant deux heures, les pieds à moitié cuits sous les bouts de tapis enveloppant tes bottes, en progressant le plus lentement possible pour ne pas soulever la poussière, tu ne crois pas que tu t'arrêterais à l'ombre pour boire un coup ? »

Saji s'éloigna à grands pas en direction du cactus géant.

« Euh... Saji ? On ne devrait pas prendre garde à ne pas effacer des traces ?

– Non. S'il s'est rendu au cactus, on n'a pas besoin de savoir par quel chemin. Il n'a pas basculé par-dessus la falaise, sinon on aurait aperçu les vautours tournant autour du cadavre. Il n'a pas rebroussé chemin dans notre direction. Donc, il s'est rendu au cactus. On reprendra la piste à partir de là.

– D'accord, admit Jay. C'est vous le chef.

– Non, Jay, c'est toi le chef. Moi, je ne suis qu'un guide. »

Il repartit. Jay le suivit.

Mercredi
Jackson, Mississippi

John Howard contemplait la chambre de l'Holiday Inn où Roujio avait passé la nuit précédente. La femme de chambre n'avait pas encore fait le ménage ; Roujio avait réglé deux nuits d'avance et accroché à la porte la pancarte « Ne pas déranger » avant de quitter les lieux. Et pourtant, on avait du mal à croire qu'elle avait été occupée. Le lit était fait, la seule serviette utilisée avait été repliée avec soin et replacée sur la pile avec les serviettes propres. Le verre de la salle de bains avait été rincé, séché et remis à sa place initiale, dans son étui en papier. Et s'il avait utilisé les chiottes, l'homme avait poussé le vice jusqu'à resserrer le rouleau de PQ comme s'il était neuf.

« Pas la moindre trace d'impact sur l'environnement, commenta Fernandez. Je rêve d'avoir une épouse aussi méticuleuse. »

Howard se mordilla la lèvre inférieure. « J'imagine que ce serait trop espérer qu'il nous laisse une carte avec sa destination cerclée de rouge, son numéro de réservation et les horaires de la compagnie aérienne.

– On va bien finir par le choper, mon colonel. On a réussi à retrouver sa trace jusqu'ici, eh bien, on va continuer à suivre sa piste. Il semble bien qu'il allait vers l'est.

– Peut-être.

– Peut-être qu'il allait vers l'est ou qu'on va bien finir par le choper ?

– Les deux. »

Mercredi
Les Ifs, Sussex, Angleterre

Peel se tenait devant la vieille chapelle qui lui tenait lieu désormais de bureau et il regardait Lord Goswell. Ce dernier était encore en train de battre la semelle, armé de son antique pétoire, cherchant à débusquer un de ces lapins qui ravageaient régulièrement son potager.

Le vieux cinglé se prenait pour un authentique Nemrod. Peel avait déjà entendu une bonne douzaine de fois ses récits de chasse. Dans les années soixante du siècle passé, quand ce genre d'activité était encore de pratique courante, Goswell avait effectué un safari en Afrique. À cette occasion, il avait abattu un éléphant, un lion et un léopard, plus un assortiment d'antilopes, gazelles et autres gibiers de moindre importance. Certes, les yeux et les oreilles de monseigneur étaient alors plus acérés et d'un demi-siècle plus jeunes, et il disposait d'une armée de porteurs pour trimbaler son matériel, sans oublier un chasseur blanc du pays pour lui débusquer ses cibles. Avec ce genre de traque, on n'avait qu'à pointer son fusil et presser la détente au signal, et si jamais vous manquiez votre coup, le chasseur blanc était là pour vous sauver la peau. Rien de comparable assurément avec le pistage d'un buffle blessé au milieu d'une forêt de bambous...

Juste à cet instant, le vieux cinglé, qui était à moitié sourd et aveugle, devait sans doute être un plus gros risque pour ses pieds que pour d'éventuels lapins en goguette. Cela faisait des mois qu'il les traquait à l'occasion et s'il avait pollué l'air un nombre incalculable de fois avec sa satanée poudre à canon, il n'avait jusqu'ici réussi à toucher que le sol ou, une fois, l'angle de la cabane à outils.

Goswell n'était pas un mauvais homme, juste un exemple caricatural des individus de sa classe. Né riche, éduqué dans les meilleures écoles, jouissant des bonnes relations, il n'avait jamais eu à désirer quoi que ce soit. Il avait fait un bon mariage, avait comme de juste la progéniture de crétins habituels, qui avaient eux aussi fait de bons mariages. L'un ou l'autre venait de temps en temps lui rendre une petite visite, plus souvent apparemment depuis la disparition de leur mère, quelques années plus tôt. Même un couple de petits-enfants faisaient l'effort de passer voir le vieux, qui les avait bien sûr couchés sur son testament. L'adage disait vrai : les riches étaient différents, surtout dans les vieilles familles. Ils considéraient certains avantages comme leur dû, n'avaient jamais envisagé les choses autrement.

Le vieux leva sa pétoire, visa mais s'abstint de tirer. Il la rabaissa en marmottant.

Peel sourit. Enfin, il n'allait pas tarder à savoir comment ça faisait d'être riche. Il avait un million en banque, il pouvait décrocher désormais, faire des placements de père de famille, et vivre dans l'opulence jusqu'à la fin de ses jours, sans même toucher au capital. C'était la sécurité, surtout pour lui qui avait toujours été persuadé de mourir au combat. Mais il pouvait faire encore mieux, rien qu'en se contentant de continuer à bosser pour Goswell. Seul petit changement : la nature de ses rapports sur Bascomb-Coombs. Ses hommes continueraient à filer l'expert en informatique, sauf à certaines périodes bien déterminées. Un guetteur serait relevé, pensant être remplacé par un collègue, sauf que les choses ne se passeraient pas ainsi : il subsisterait un trou, aussi long que voulu par l'informaticien, que Peel comblerait en rédigeant son rapport. Juste quelques lignes à modifier... pas mal pour un boulot payé un million.

Le vieux disparut au coin du bâtiment et Peel se fit la réflexion qu'affublé de son gros casque suppresseur de bruit, il avait des allures de géronte extraterrestre.

Peel consulta sa montre. Bientôt l'heure pour ses hommes de se pointer.

Bien entendu, le marché avec le savant juif n'allait pas toujours se limiter à laisser monseigneur dans le brouillard, il le savait. On allait sans aucun doute franchir une nouvelle étape, qui allait à coup sûr impliquer une tâche un peu plus pénible que l'altération d'un journal informatique. Et tandis que Bascomb-Coombs semblait convaincu de son invincibilité lorsqu'il s'agissait de ses Q-bits et autres délires quantiques, si jamais un zigue défonçait la porte et se mettait à tirer dans le tas, il faudrait en face quelqu'un qui sache répliquer s'il voulait sauver son cul de petit génie.

Enfin, Peel connaissait la musique, il l'avait fait longtemps, d'abord pour la reine, puis pour sa grande bringue de fils, et pour bien moins d'argent qu'aujourd'hui...

Une bombe explosa. Suivie, une demi-seconde plus tard, d'une autre détonation.

Peel s'accroupit, cherchant à localiser le danger ; sa main s'était automatiquement posée sur la crosse de son pistolet. Puis il se détendit en apercevant le nuage de fumée grasse passer en volutes devant lui, avant d'entendre le vieux se mettre à pester : « Ah, le vaurien ! Le sale petit vaurien ! »

Peel sourit. Encore un de raté. Il se redressa, s'épousseta, et alla s'assurer que le vieux n'avait rien. Ce n'est pas parce qu'il trahissait sa confiance qu'il ne devait pas se montrer courtois.

16

Jeudi 7 avril
Londres

Michaels décida d'accepter l'invitation de Toni et de l'accompagner à son cours de silat. Il aurait dû s'entraîner, il avait négligé ses exercices ces derniers jours, et Dieu seul savait quand ils pourraient rentrer chez eux et reprendre le train-train habituel. Jusqu'ici, ils étaient toujours au point mort dans l'enquête sur cette nouvelle menace. Il se sentirait sans doute bien plus détendu s'il pouvait se dépenser, suer un bon coup.

« Toi, tu as ton air des mauvais jours », constata Toni.

Elle était assise en face de lui à l'arrière du taxi et il lui adressa un sourire machinal. « Désolé. J'ai passé le plus clair de l'après-midi pour ainsi dire à compter des trombones... Je ne suis pas plus avancé qu'au début. Je me fais l'effet d'un con.

– Pourquoi te sens-tu personnellement responsable de la capture de ce pirate cinglé ? Des dizaines de services gouvernementaux de par le monde sont à ses trousses, et aucun n'est plus avancé que nous.

– Ouais, peut-être, mais moi, je trône au sommet de la pyramide aux États-Unis. Personne n'a dans le collimateur les Portugais ou les Tasmaniens en comptant sur eux pour coincer notre bonhomme. On est la dernière superpuissance qui reste.

– Hé, ho, Silver ! »

Il plissa les yeux, ahuri : « Hein ?

– C'est comme ça qu'il est devenu le Ranger solitaire. Tonto l'avait soigné après l'embuscade de la bande à Bush Cavendish. Quand il reprend ses esprits, il demande des nouvelles des autres. Alors Tonto lui répond : “Lui mort, eux tous morts. Toi... seul Ranger qui reste... Toi... Ranger solitaire.”

– Vraiment ?

– Oui. Et tu sais ce qu'il y a d'écrit sur le canon de son pistolet ?

– Quoi donc ?

– “Ne me force pas à te faire mal.” »

Il lui sourit. « Comment tu sais tous ces trucs ?

– Une jeunesse mal employée. Des grands frères qui collectionnaient tout et n'importe quoi, des voitures aux vieux 78 tours. Je peux tout te dire sur Hopalong Cassidy, Roy Rogers et Gene Autrey, si ça t'intéresse. Tu veux en savoir plus sur le fidèle compagnon de Red Ryder ?

– Pas spécialement.

– Pas intéressé non plus par les mésaventures de Li'l Beaver ? » Elle battit des paupières et lui sourit.

« Euh... ouais, peut-être... mais pas devant le chauffeur de taxi. »

Ils éclatèrent de rire tous les deux.

Le cours de silat était installé dans un quartier sordide et miteux qui faisait regretter à Michaels de n'avoir pas emporté son taser. L'intérieur toutefois était propre et les élèves se montrèrent polis quand Toni les lui présenta.

L'instructeur, un certain Carl Stewart, arriva et Michaels fit également sa connaissance. Le type avait l'air assez sympa, de quelques années plus âgé que Michaels, et plutôt bien conservé. Un peu plus grand, les cheveux un peu plus gris, un peu plus large d'épaules, les biceps plus développés. Il portait des lunettes d'aviateur à double foyer et Michaels se demanda pourquoi il n'utilisait pas plutôt des verres de contact ou des lentilles jetables.

« Toni me dit que vous vous êtes mis au silat, dit Stewart. Allez-vous vous joindre à nous ce soir ?

– Si ça ne vous dérange pas, volontiers.

– Pas de problème. » Il sourit à Toni, elle lui rendit son sourire et Michaels ressentit un brusque accès de... de quoi ?

De jalousie ? Non, bien sûr que non. Il avait confiance en elle.

Le cours débuta et Alex s'avança sur le tapis pour répéter docilement les deux djurus qu'il avait appris. Il jetait à la dérobée des regards sur Toni et nota ses mouvements de pieds : le *tiga*, puis le *sliwa* – le triangle et le carré – qui accompagnaient ses djurus. Elle semblait en pleine possession de ses moyens.

Stewart s'arrêta devant Alex. « Vous me semblez un tantinet distrait, monsieur Michaels. Il vaudrait mieux que vous vous concentriez sur vos mouvements. »

Alex rougit, acquiesça, s'excusa : « Désolé, gourou. »

Stewart hocha la tête, sourit et passa à l'élève suivant.

Encore heureux qu'il ne s'agisse pas d'exercices de méditation zen : il aurait eu droit à un bon coup de badine. Il se concentra de nouveau sur ses mouvements, mais il se sentait emprunté. Il ne pratiquait que depuis quelques mois et la plupart des mouvements lui semblaient encore être anti-naturels, aller contre l'intuition.

Au bout d'un quart d'heure de djurus, Stewart interrompit la séance pour répondre aux questions. Même si les élèves pratiquaient des mouvements différents de ceux de Michaels, les remarques sur l'équilibre et l'importance d'un bon positionnement du bassin lui rappelèrent des points que Toni avait également soulignés.

« Bon, très bien. Nous allons à présent travailler les enchaînements, annonça Stewart. Toni ? Tu veux bien me servir de partenaire ? »

Toni lui fit une brève salutation. Quand Stewart lui rendit son salut, la position de ses mains était légèrement différente. Le poing droit de Toni était serré au niveau de la poitrine, la main gauche le soutenant en coupe par en dessous ; alors que les phalanges de Stewart étaient tournées vers le creux de la paume de l'autre main.

« Un direct du droit, s'il te plaît, ici. » Il effleura l'arête de son nez.

Toni s'avança et lança le poing. Si le coup avait porté, il lui aurait certainement brisé le nez. Il bloqua le bras de la jeune femme à deux mains, projeta le coude dans ses côtes, pivota, fit un pas, frappa de nouveau les côtes, puis avança le pied et la renversa. Il la retint d'un bras autour du torse avant qu'elle ne tombe. « Ça va ?

– Oui.

– Encore une fois, s'il te plaît. Lentement. »

Toni répéta son attaque et Stewart réitéra son enchaînement – blocage des mains, coup de coude et rotation –, l'empêchant à nouveau de tomber en lui passant un bras autour de la poitrine.

Pile en travers des seins, nota Michaels non sans une légère irritation. Était-ce franchement nécessaire ? Toni pouvait tomber sans se faire mal, il l'avait déjà vue choir sur un sol dur et rebondir comme une balle en mousse. Or ici, il y avait des matelas partout.

Toni sourit à Stewart et son visage exprimait une joie sans mélange. Michaels avait déjà vu plusieurs fois chez elle cette expression, en général juste après un orgasme...

Il n'appréciait pas du tout de lui voir cet air en ce moment...

Il se tança mentalement : *Tâche un peu de faire marcher ton ciboulot, mon garçon ! Il s'agit d'un cours d'arts martiaux, nom d'une pipe ! Il n'est pas en train de la peloter, il lui fait une démonstration de la méthode pour tabasser le crétin qui ferait l'erreur de l'attaquer !*

Ouais, bon, d'accord.

« Des questions ? »

Michaels décida de se lancer. « Pourquoi ne pas l'avoir frappée au visage plutôt que dans les côtes ? »

Stewart sourit – comme du reste la majorité des étudiants. Michaels le nota, mais ne dit rien. Stewart avait toutefois remarqué son regard.

« Désolé, monsieur Michaels, mais j'ai expliqué aux

élèves qu'on pouvait la plupart du temps amocher tant qu'on voulait un adversaire en le travaillant au corps. Les Indonésiens attaquent rarement au visage ; les grands spécialistes du coup de boule sont plutôt les... Occidentaux. »

Michaels acquiesça. Toutefois son hésitation avant de mentionner les « Occidentaux » indiquait que Stewart avait failli dire autre chose et Michaels était prêt à parier que ce devait être les « Américains ».

« Très bien, mettez-vous par deux et on essaie. Toni, tu veux bien m'aider à surveiller ?

– Oui, gourou », répondit Toni.

Michaels se retrouva devant un gamin dégingandé, cheveux en brosse et deux anneaux dans le nez, qui devait avoir dans les dix-sept ans. L'ado se présenta : « Giles Patrick.

– Alex Michaels.

– Vous commencez en défense ?

– D'accord. »

Le jeune homme s'avança vers lui au ralenti, le poing flottant dans la direction de Michaels à une vitesse d'environ le huitième de la vitesse normale.

Michaels bloqua l'attaque, avança le coude, puis eut un trou. Qu'est-ce qui venait ensuite ?

« Direct du gauche dans les côtes, là, souffla le gamin.

– D'accord, d'accord. Laissez-moi recommencer. »

L'autre réitéra son attaque mollassonne et cette fois, Michaels bloqua, lança le coude, puis le poing, mais lorsqu'il voulut pivoter, il était en déséquilibre et le pied du jeune resta collé au sol.

« Il faut bien positionner vos hanches, indiqua le

gamin. Pivotez vers l'intérieur, les épaules et le bassin dans l'alignement.

– D'accord.

– Encore une fois ?

– Oui. »

Ce coup-ci, Michaels réussit la décomposition de la séquence et le gamin alla au tapis sur son mouvement pivotant. Parfait ! Il se sentait plutôt fier.

Toni s'approcha de lui. « Pas mal du tout, Alex, mais quand tu bloques le coup, fais-le en remontant, comme ceci. Giles ? »

Tout sourire, l'ado s'en prit à Toni, mais cette fois, à la bonne vitesse.

Évoluant avec aisance, la jeune femme dévia le coup vers le haut, s'ouvrant ainsi une voie royale pour enfoncer le coude dans l'aisselle de son adversaire.

« Merci, Toni. »

Il crut la voir froncer le sourcil, mais elle opina avant de reporter son attention sur le couple d'élèves suivant.

Froncer le sourcil ? Pourquoi ? Parce qu'il l'avait appelée « Toni » ?

« Je peux refaire un essai ? demanda Giles.

– Euh, bien sûr. »

Michaels se mit en position et passa à l'attaque. Le gamin enchaîna un-deux-trois-quatre et Michaels heurta rudement le tapis. Il se releva aussitôt.

« Ça va bien, monsieur Michaels ?

– Ouais, ouais, très bien. Et appelle-moi Alex. » C'était déjà pénible de se prendre une peignée ; il n'avait pas besoin en plus d'avoir l'impression d'être son grand-père.

Il se prépara pour une nouvelle attaque. C'était sympa de pouvoir évacuer un peu sa tension, mais jusqu'à présent, il ne pouvait pas dire que le cours était une partie de plaisir. Loin de là.

Lord Goswell se tenait devant l'immense marine qui avait toujours décoré le mur est du petit salon de son club depuis qu'il le fréquentait. C'était une huile de deux mètres quarante de haut sur trois mètres quarante de large, dans des tons gris et bleus, représentant un voilier ballotté par les vagues au milieu d'un orage. Les éclairs illuminaient les marins cherchant désespérément à maintenir à flot l'embarcation. La scène était très spectaculaire et d'un rendu quasiment photoréaliste.

Goswell fit tourner le glaçon dans son verre de gin-tonic presque vide et fut aussitôt récompensé par l'apparition de Paddington avec son plateau. « Un autre, milord ?

– Pourquoi pas ? Dites-moi, savez-vous qui est l'auteur de cette toile ?

– Oui, milord. Elle a été peinte par Jeffrey Hawkesworth en... 1872, si je ne me trompe.

– Elle est tout à fait remarquable. Est-ce un peintre que je devrais connaître ?

– Non, milord. Ce fut un des rares civils tués par les Zoulous à Rorke's Drift en Afrique du Sud lors de la guerre des Boers, en 1899. Il n'a réalisé que fort peu de toiles. Le club est tombé sur celle-ci quelques années après sa mort ; une donation de son frère, Sir William Hawkesworth, anobli par Sa Majesté la reine Victoria pour services rendus aux Indes. »

Goswell opina. « Intéressant.

– Puis-je aller chercher votre apéritif, milord ?

– J'imagine que vous n'envisageriez pas de quitter le club pour entrer à mon service ?

– Vous me faites là un grand honneur, milord, mais je me verrais forcé de le décliner. Ce ne serait pas convenable.

– Non, bien sûr que non. Faites, je vous en prie, faites. »

Il regarda le domestique s'éclipser. Diable. C'était le genre de loyauté qui ne pouvait s'acheter. Dommage. La plupart du temps, on faisait toujours une bonne affaire.

Paddington revint, portant sur son plateau un nouveau verre, idéalement glacé.

« Il y a un appel pour vous, milord. » Un téléphone mobile était posé sur le plateau à côté du verre.

Goswell prit les deux. Il hocha la tête. « Merci, Paddington. »

Acheter la loyauté... d'autres avaient moins de scrupules. Dès que Paddington se fut éloigné, Goswell activa le combiné. « Vous avez ce que je vous ai demandé ?

– Ouaip, j'l'ai.

– Rendez-vous à l'endroit habituel, dans ce cas. Dans une demi-heure. » Il coupa le téléphone.

Goswell se remit à contempler la toile en sirotant son gin-tonic. Dommage que l'artiste ait été emporté par ces foutus sauvages. Il aurait sans aucun doute fait du grand art. Certes, l'armée royale avait donné une belle leçon à ces moricauds à la bataille de Rorke's Drift. Une poignée de soldats contre mille indigènes, et les troupes avaient su, grâce à Dieu, leur tenir tête et défendre chèrement leur peau ! Ces hommes avaient appris à ces foutus nègres ce qu'était la détermination britannique, nom d'une pipe !

Il leva son verre devant la toile, en guise de salut. « À la tienne, mon vieux. »

17

Jeudi 7 avril
Londres

Physiquement, Toni se sentait super bien après les exercices, même si elle était un rien irritée par la façon qu'avait eue Alex de vouloir se montrer par trop familier avec elle devant les autres élèves. Il se sentait mal à l'aise, elle le sentait bien, aussi n'avait-il cessé de l'appeler « Toni » au lieu de « gourou », et à deux ou trois reprises, il lui avait souri ou caressé l'épaule, histoire de faire comprendre à tout le monde qu'ils étaient un peu plus que maître et élève. Elle n'y voyait pas d'inconvénient quand ils étaient seuls au gymnase, entre eux, mais ici, c'était déplacé. Il y avait là-dedans un petit côté « elle peut me botter le cul, elle a le droit, elle est à moi ! » que Toni goûtait très modérément. Elle l'aimait, mais parfois, Alex avait des côtés tellement... enfantins.

Cela dit, la plupart des hommes de sa connaissance étaient ainsi, et lui l'était plutôt moins que la moyenne. Et surtout, il l'aimait sincèrement, aussi pouvait-elle passer l'éponge pour cette fois.

Mais ce n'était pas tout. Il y avait un autre truc qui la travaillait, elle n'aurait su dire quoi. Ce pouvait être à cause de toutes leurs tuiles au boulot, mais ça n'en n'avait pas l'air.

Il fallait qu'elle évoque ces deux problèmes... Le plus dur étant de les aborder sans déclencher une scène de ménage.

Avoir un amant qui était à la fois votre patron et votre élève pouvait parfois s'avérer compliqué. Elle n'y avait jamais réfléchi avant qu'ils ne se mettent ensemble. Sans doute parce que, dans son for intérieur, elle n'avait jamais vraiment escompté vivre avec lui. Elle l'avait désiré, plus que tout au monde, mais cela n'avait pas semblé destiné à se concrétiser. Et pourtant si, et ç'avait été merveilleux, mais pas idéalement parfait.

Il était toujours plus simple de fantasmer sur quelque chose que de le posséder « en vrai ». Tous les couples avaient leurs problèmes : ses parents s'étaient mariés juste après la Grande Inondation, ils étaient toujours ensemble et s'aimaient toujours autant, mais même eux connaissaient les scènes de ménage. L'inverse eût été malsain. Malgré tout, Toni n'avait jamais connu jusqu'ici de relations vraiment durables, et chaque fois qu'Alex et elle avaient une prise de bec, elle le supportait très mal. Elle avait toujours peur de le perdre. Peur qu'ils se détachent l'un de l'autre. Peur d'avoir entretenu trop d'illusions sur leur couple, et que la réalité ne soit pas à la hauteur de ses attentes.

Cela dit, le cours s'était bien passé. Gourou Stewart était aussi bon enseignant que pratiquant. Il prenait le temps, pendant que les élèves s'exerçaient entre eux, de montrer à Toni tel ou tel mouvement. Leurs techniques étaient suffisamment proches pour qu'elle puisse voir l'intérêt de ses conseils et elle lui en était reconnaissante.

Alors que le gymnase se vidait, Stewart avait

remarqué : « On devait s'entraîner ensemble, soit avant, soit après les cours réguliers, avant que tu repartes. Nous aurions tant de choses à nous enseigner mutuellement si tu pouvais t'y consacrer. »

La proposition l'avait enthousiasmée. « Ce serait avec grand plaisir », avait-elle répondu.

Et maintenant qu'elle se retrouvait avec Alex dans le taxi pour regagner le nouvel hôtel que le MI-6 leur avait réservé, Toni se rendit compte à quel point elle avait apprécié ces séances d'entraînement. Le silat était simple, direct, sans détours. On exerçait le corps en même temps que l'esprit, en gardant l'un et l'autre concentrés sur des choses simples : frapper ici, esquiver là, garder une bonne assise, exploiter l'angle et l'effet de levier.

Bien moins complexe que de gérer les émotions des individus, et même ses propres émotions. Surtout peut-être ses propres émotions.

Alors qu'ils descendaient de taxi devant l'hôtel, Michaels remarqua : « On nous file, as-tu remarqué ? »

Elle ne se retourna pas mais le regarda. « Quoi ?

– Il y a un type dans une Toyota grise garée de l'autre côté de la rue, une trentaine de mètres en retrait. Il était derrière nous quand on s'est rendus au cours de silat. Je suis à peu près sûr qu'il était également derrière moi quand je suis descendu à pied chercher un sandwich, ce midi. Ce serait une fantastique coïncidence que le même type se trouve là chaque fois que je mets le nez dehors.

– Les services secrets britanniques ? »

Il salua d'un signe de tête le portier en uniforme

lorsque celui-ci leur ouvrit les portes de l'hôtel. Il se sentait sale et collant de sueur après son entraînement, mais il lui sourit comme si Toni et lui se rendaient à un mariage princier.

« Ça se pourrait, j'imagine. Si l'un des leurs devait venir fouiner autour de nos petits secrets à Quantico, je lui mettrais moi aussi le FBI au cul, pour m'assurer que personne ne l'intercepte pour lui extorquer des renseignements.

– T'as pas l'air convaincu.

– Ma foi, si on faisait filer un de leurs hommes, je m'arrangerais pour que l'agent chargé de la filature ne se fasse pas repérer... à moins de chercher délibérément le contraire. Les Rosbifs devraient avoir des gars aussi pointus que nous pour effectuer une surveillance discrète. Ils sont chez eux, ils connaissent les lieux. Non, en toute hypothèse, je n'aurais pas dû le remarquer. »

Ils traversèrent le hall et gagnèrent l'ascenseur. Toni le devança pour appuyer sur le bouton.

« Peut-être qu'ils voulaient justement que tu le remarques. Pour te faire savoir que nous sommes sous leur protection.

– Ça serait quand même plus simple de me le dire, non ?

– Et nous, on le leur dirait ?

– Peut-être. Surtout si on pensait qu'ils vont s'en douter, de toute manière. »

Un tintement annonça l'arrivée de la cabine et les portes de bronze moulé s'ouvrirent avec une grâce pesante. Le liftier leur sourit. Une veine que le nouvel hôtel où on les avait transférés fût subventionné par les Britanniques... sinon, leur patronne aurait eu une attaque en découvrant la note.

« Un test amical ? T'as été agent traitant, toi aussi.

– Ouais. Mais j'ai perdu pas mal d'habitudes, depuis. Oh, je regarde toujours deux-trois fois dans le rétro quand je conduis, et je jette de temps en temps un coup d'œil alentour. Je ne suis pas totalement assoupi depuis cette histoire avec Selkie[1], mais je ne fais pas non plus de zèle. Pas autant qu'il faudrait. Non, ce type n'est pas un bon, c'est tout. Je n'arrive pas à croire que le MI-5 ou 6 m'assigne un mec pareil et s'imagine que je ne le remarque pas.

– Peut-être qu'ils ne veulent pas gâcher un élément de valeur rien que pour toi. Qu'ils ont envoyé la seconde équipe parce qu'ils s'imaginent que tu es un affreux Amerloque trop imbu de sa personne pour remarquer quoi que ce soit. » Elle sourit. « Il se pourrait qu'ils aient raison. Mais je pense quand même que je vais passer un coup de fil à Angela Cooper, voir de quoi il retourne. »

Ils entrèrent dans la cabine. Le liftier leur demanda l'étage.

« Quatre, je vous prie », dit Toni. Au lieu de son vague accent du Bronx, elle s'était fendue d'une imitation passable d'accent britannique snob. Cela donnait quelque chose comme « quââtre ». Michaels la regarda, légèrement interloqué.

Dès qu'ils furent dans leur suite, Michaels sortit son virgil pour appeler Cooper. Toni fit couler l'eau sous la douche et il la regarda se déshabiller tandis que Cooper prenait la communication. Il l'avait surprise chez elle et elle avait activé la caméra. Le peu qu'il voyait lui révéla qu'elle portait un petit truc rouge et

---

1. Cf. *Net Force 1, op. cit.*

soyeux. Le cadrage s'arrêtait juste au ras des épaules. Il activa lui aussi sa cam.

« Alex, que puis-je faire pour vous ?

– Me répondre honnêtement à une question.

– Bien sûr.

– Est-ce vous ou le MI-5 qui me fait suivre ?

– Certainement pas nous. Je doute que ce soit le Service secret, mais je peux vérifier. Ne quittez pas. » L'image se figea et la mention « En attente » s'inscrivit en incrustation sur le minuscule écran.

Toni ôta sa culotte, fit passer la brassière de sport par-dessus sa tête. Elle se retourna, s'offrant à lui dans toute sa splendeur, puis, avec un petit signe de main, elle s'éclipsa sous la douche et fit coulisser la porte.

Il décida d'abréger l'entretien. Il avait grande envie d'entrer sous la douche avant que Toni n'en ressorte. Il s'était senti déjà pas mal excité tout au long du cours de silat, et cela n'avait fait que croître et embellir lors du retour en taxi.

« Alex ? Le MI-5 dit qu'ils ne vous ont pas mis sous surveillance. Auriez-vous remarqué quoi que ce soit d'anormal ? » Cooper souriait.

Il réfléchit promptement. « Non, je pense que ce doit être la parano due au grand âge.

– Vous n'êtes pas si vieux.

– Je vous vois demain. Désolé de vous avoir dérangée chez vous.

– Appelez quand vous voulez. Ça ne me dérange pas. » Elle s'appuya au dossier de son siège et la robe ou le corsage de soie rouge s'entrebâilla légèrement, révélant l'amorce du décolleté.

Il discommuta* et, aussitôt, son radar masculin crut avoir capté un signal. Était-ce... de l'intérêt ? Il n'avait fréquenté qu'un nombre réduit de femmes. Depuis son divorce, Toni était la seule à avoir sérieusement éveillé son intérêt. Il manquait peut-être de pratique en la matière mais de toute évidence, Cooper n'avait pas l'air de le trouver bon à jeter. Loin de là.

Intéressant. Sympa pour son vieil ego de savoir qu'une femme intelligente et superbe pût éventuellement s'intéresser à lui. À supposer qu'il ait bien décodé le signal.

Même si cela n'avait pas grande importance. Il avait bien plus intéressant sous la main. Il se dirigea vers la douche, ôtant un à un ses vêtements trempés de sueur.

« Qu'est-ce qu'elle a dit ? lança Toni, de sous le jet.

– Que ce n'était pas quelqu'un de chez eux.

– Alors, il faut qu'on découvre qui c'est. »

Il ouvrit la porte de la cabine, fut récompensé par un nuage de vapeur brûlante qui embua aussitôt les miroirs derrière lui.

« Demain. Tu me fais un peu de place ? »

Son regard s'abaissa. « Si tu restes devant moi. Je n'ai pas envie d'être poignardée dans le dos. »

Il sourit. « Ça alors. Voyez-vous ça. Je me demande bien d'où ça vient.

– Un cadeau de Mlle Cooper, peut-être ? »

Il fronça les sourcils. « Quoi ?

– Eh bien, tu ne l'avais pas avant d'avoir décroché ton virgil, pas vrai ? »

Est-ce qu'elle cherchait à le taquiner ? Elle souriait, mais il n'était pas si sûr.

Autant de considérations qui eurent le don de... refroidir ses ardeurs.

Toni le remarqua. « C'était une blague, Alex. »

Il était au comble de l'embarras. Il s'empara du

savon et du gant de toilette. « Tourne-toi. Je vais te laver le dos.

– Alex...

– Je suis vraiment fatigué. C'était crevant, cet entraînement, j'ai pas l'habitude. Il faut que je dorme. » L'excuse paraissait bancale et il savait qu'elle n'était pas dupe. Il fit mousser le savon sur le gant, Toni se tourna et il lui récura le dos. Peut-être avec plus d'énergie qu'il n'eût été de mise.

Quelque chose se passait entre eux, une chose qu'il ne comprenait pas. Quoi que ce puisse être, ça ne lui disait rien qui vaille. Absolument rien.

Toni n'insista pas, toutefois, et il lui en fut reconnaissant. Il n'avait pas du tout envie de se lancer dans une querelle d'amoureux. Il était réellement vidé.

Il était crevé mais, au contraire de Toni qui s'endormit quelques minutes après être sortie de la douche, il resta à bouquiner pendant une heure. Il se décida enfin à se coucher, éteignit la lumière, essaya de dormir. Après avoir vainement cherché le sommeil pendant encore une heure, il comprit qu'il n'y n'arriverait pas de sitôt : il était trop énervé, trop crispé pour se détendre.

Il sortit du lit avec précaution, se rendit dans la salle de bains, passa un jean, un T-shirt, des tennis. Il sortit le kick-taser* de son étui et en vérifia la batterie. La petite arme sans fil utilisait comme propulseur une cartouche de gaz comprimé. Non létale, elle tirait une paire de fléchettes porteuses d'une charge à haute tension – de quoi estourbir n'importe quel agresseur, même tirées à travers des vêtements. La portée efficace n'était que de quelques mètres, mais c'était la distance où se produisaient la majorité des fusillades. La vieille maxime des tireurs du FBI à ce sujet restait toujours valable : « Trois pieds, trois balles, trois secondes. » Si un mec se trouvait à cinquante mètres de vous en train de détaler dans la direction opposée, il n'était pas vraiment dangereux. L'armurier de la Net Force lui avait dit que quelqu'un avait inventé un gilet tissé d'une résille électromagnétique capable de neutraliser une charge de taser. Mais un gilet n'était pas une armure intégrale, on pouvait toujours viser les jambes ou la tête. Et l'appareil était simple d'emploi grâce à son viseur laser. On plaçait le minuscule pointeur rouge sur la cible, calibré pour tenir compte de la légère dispersion des deux fléchettes avec la distance, et c'était l'emplacement qu'elles atteindraient une fois le bouton pressé. À la seule condition de ne pas être trop loin. Et de ne pas avoir la main qui tremble. Il n'avait eu à tirer qu'une seule fois pendant le service, et les résultats avaient été plutôt concluants.

Il glissa le taser dans sa poche arrière, enfila un coupe-vent pour masquer le tout et sortit discrètement de la chambre.

Alex Michaels quitta l'hôtel par la porte de service, contourna le pâté de maisons et s'approcha par l'arrière de l'endroit où s'était garée la Toyota grise.

Et où la Toyota était toujours garée, le même type installé au volant. Il avait descendu sa vitre et fumait un cigare. L'odeur était décelable à quinze mètres.

Le commandant de la Net Force contourna la voiture au moment où un bus passait, le courant d'air renvoyant la fumée à l'intérieur de l'habitacle. Le type à l'intérieur eut un mouvement de recul.

Michaels sortit son taser, se précipita vers le côté droit, celui du conducteur dans ce pays, et s'accroupit le long de la portière en plaçant l'arme sur le rebord de celle-ci.

« Salut ! Alors, on s'amuse bien ? »

Le gars, maigre, calvitie naissante, dans les trente-cinq ans, faillit en avaler son cigare.

« Seigneur Dieu ! Faites pas ça ! Vous m'avez flanqué une peur bleue ! »

Américain, l'accent ne laissait planer aucun doute. Un « Occidental ».

Posé à l'avant sur le siège voisin, Michaels remarqua un petit ordinateur à écran plat, une caméra numérique et une paire de jumelles. Il y avait également une bouteille isotherme et un sac en papier taché de graisse, sur lequel était posée une barquette en carton contenant les reliefs de son repas : friture de poissons et pommes frites. Et sur le plancher, un vase à large bec. Vide. En vue de satisfaire un besoin naturel.

Si Michaels avait encore eu le moindre doute, ce dernier élément finit de le dissiper. L'homme au cigare assurait une planque.

« Très bien, mec, alors qui es-tu et pourquoi est-ce que tu me files ?

– Merde, mais de quoi parlez-vous ? J'ignore qui vous...

– Écoute, on peut faire ça gentiment ou adopter la manière forte. Tu peux me parler... ou je peux appeler mes copains du renseignement britannique, te faire arrêter pour espionnage et boucler dans un cachot si profond qu'il faudra un mois au soleil brumeux de ce pays pour y parvenir.

– Hé, je suis citoyen américain, j'ai des droits...

– On est en Angleterre, l'ami. Ici, ils ne jouent pas selon les mêmes règles. À toi de choisir... »

L'homme au cigare réfléchit quelques secondes. Il était grillé et il n'allait pas s'en sortir en parlementant. Il haussa les épaules. « Je suis un détective privé de Boise. »

Michaels plissa les paupières. Un privé ?

« Qui vous a engagé ?

– Je sais qui vous êtes. Je sais que vous pouvez me créer un monceau d'emmerdes. Vous pouvez me coller au trou si ça vous chante, mais je ne peux pas vous dire pour qui je travaille. Que ça se sache, et ma carrière professionnelle est fichue. Mais vous êtes un type malin, devinez vous-même. »

Boise. Et merde...

Megan. Mais enfin... pourquoi ?

Michaels rangea le taser. Il se releva. « Je ferais mieux de rentrer. Si jamais je vous revois dans les parages, je vous promets que je demande aux flics de vous faire déguerpir. »

Il s'écoula un long moment, puis l'homme au cigare démarra. Michaels regarda sa voiture s'éloigner.

Il sortit son virgil. Ici, on était au milieu de la nuit, il y avait... quoi... sept-huit heures de décalage horaire avec l'Idaho...

Peu importait l'heure là-bas. Tant pis s'il tombait sur elle à son travail. Il pressa la touche mémoire, cliqua sur le numéro de son ex.

« Salut, Alex », fit-elle. Réfrigérante. Sa voix était un entrepôt de glace en plein hiver au pôle Nord. Et à l'ombre. « Quitte pas une seconde, le temps de trouver un coin tranquille où l'on puisse parler. »

Elle reprit la communication au bout de quelques secondes, puis alluma sa caméra. Elle était en tenue professionnelle, les cheveux coiffés en chignon. L'air en pleine forme, comme toujours.

« Megan. Comment va Susie ?

– Elle va très bien. Tu m'appelles au boulot pour me demander ça ?

– Non. Je viens juste d'avoir des mots avec un privé au crâne dégarni et fumeur de cigares, lança-t-il, se contrôlant avec difficulté. Pourquoi me fais-tu suivre ?

– Autodéfense.

– Bon sang, mais de quoi parles-tu ?

– Après avoir tabassé Byron le soir de Noël, tu m'as menacée, au cas où tu aurais oublié[1] ! » La glace dans sa voix se mit à fondre. À présent, c'était plutôt un volcan qui grondait, prêt à entrer en éruption. « Tu m'as dit que si jamais il avait le malheur de passer une nuit sous mon toit – je dis bien *mon* toit, Alex, pas le tien et le mien – tu me ferais légalement déchoir de mes droits maternels !

– Je n'ai jamais dit ça. Je n'ai jamais dit que tu étais une mère indigne !

– Tu me fais marrer, tiens ! Tu as dit que tu m'enverrais Byron dans ma gueule de pute et réclamerais la garde exclusive de notre fille. Eh bien, mon petit bonhomme, on sera deux à jouer ce petit jeu. Byron va passer ce soir la nuit sous mon toit, tout comme il l'a fait la nuit dernière, et celle d'avant, et comme il le fera encore la nuit prochaine ! Et autant de putains de nuits que je voudrai le garder auprès de moi ! Et tu sais quoi ? En me baisant à me rendre folle, en plus ! »

Comme elle avait toujours su si bien faire, elle réussit à le mettre en rogne. Incapable de se maîtriser,

1. Cf. *Net Force 2, Programmes fantômes, op. cit.*

il rétorqua, du tac au tac : « Ça devrait pas être trop difficile, t'as déjà de bonnes bases. »

Elle rit, consciente d'avoir réussi à le mettre en colère. Quand elle reprit la parole, elle était redevenue la reine glacée : « Très drôle. Mais tu peux bien rire, moi, je sais tout de tes petites coucheries. De cette petite mijaurée de Toni Fiorella. Au moins, Byron est de mon âge, je ne l'ai pas pris au berceau. On verra bien comment le tribunal apprécie que tu tringles une de tes employées ! »

Et merde !

« Oui, mais moi je ne fais pas ça devant Susie. » Il aurait pu trouver mieux comme repartie.

« Bref, ce que tu es en train de me dire, c'est que tu peux baguenauder comme un prêtre défroqué avec des putes, mais que s'agissant d'un couple fiancé sur le point de convoler t'es plus d'accord ! Je doute que le juge de Boise se laisse vraiment émouvoir par ce genre d'argument. Mais tu as toujours eu le chic pour déformer la réalité afin de la plier à ta définition de la morale, pas vrai ? »

Il aurait dû s'excuser, il le savait. Verser une barrique d'huile sur ces eaux troubles, l'apaiser. Lui dire qu'il avait perdu son sang-froid quand il s'était jeté sur son petit ami (qui avait quand même commencé, ne pas l'oublier) et dit des choses qu'il ne pensait pas. Le seul problème est qu'il les avait pensées. Et qu'il les pensait toujours, même si désormais l'affaire se présentait sous un nouveau jour. Elle avait raison. Aucun juge n'allait ôter à Megan la garde de Susie, à moins qu'il puisse prouver qu'elle était une mauvaise mère, or la vérité l'obligeait à reconnaître que c'était une mère formidable. C'était déjà son opinion quand ils étaient ensemble, et il n'en avait pas changé. Et surtout, il n'avait pas envie de perdre sa fille. S'il se retrouvait cantonné à des visites annuelles ou bisannuelles durant les vacances, leur relation serait condamnée. Elle grandirait en considérant Byron comme son vrai père. Ce serait lui qui la conduirait à l'école ou au centre commercial, lui qui l'aiderait à faire ses devoirs et tout ce dont Michaels aurait dû s'acquitter à sa place.

Il aurait dû s'excuser, tenter de rattraper le coup. Mais il tergiversa trop longtemps.

« Au revoir, Alex. Tu peux toujours appeler Susie, je ne veux pas qu'elle s'imagine que je te chasse de sa vie, mais toi et moi, nous n'avons plus rien à nous dire. Et salue de ma part ta jeune dulcinée. »

Elle coupa la communication.

Michaels plissa les yeux. Planté au milieu du trottoir d'une rue du centre de Londres en pleine nuit, il avait l'impression de s'être fait plaquer par un trois quarts adverse. Son ex-épouse était au courant de sa relation avec Toni – pour une jeune dulcinée, elle n'avait quand même que douze ans de moins que lui ! – et c'est le genre d'argument qu'on allait lui renvoyer dans les gencives au tribunal si jamais il contestait la garde de sa fille. Toni et lui étaient l'un et l'autre majeurs, mais il était son patron. Bref, ça s'annonçait mal. Le FBI voyait d'un très mauvais œil ce genre de relation et puisqu'il n'avait aucune expérience avec la nouvelle directrice, il était douteux qu'elle soit prête à se mouiller pour lui sauver la mise si jamais le scandale éclatait.

Pour dire les choses crûment, il s'était fait baiser.

18

Jeudi 7 avril
Walworth, Londres

La première véritable mission de Peel pour son nouveau boss était une opération sur le terrain, parfaitement dans ses cordes. Autre chose que de rester planté dans cette espèce de vieille chapelle pleine de courants d'air, à regarder des colonnes de statistiques défiler sur un holoproj informatique. Aucun doute, tout vaudrait mieux que ça.

Il semblait qu'un scientifique, l'un des anciens professeurs de Bascomb-Coombs à l'université, aujourd'hui retraité de l'enseignement et devenu consultant, était en train de bidouiller dans un domaine informatique réservé... Or ce brave vieux BC était sur le point de lâcher sur le monde une de ses nouvelles diableries électroniques, et il n'avait pas envie de voir son ancien prof marcher sur ses brisées. Et sans avoir l'intention de blesser sérieusement son vieux mentor, il avait tout de même l'intention de le mettre hors circuit pendant deux ou trois jours. Est-ce que Peel pouvait s'en occuper ?

« Niveau deux, dit Peel aux trois hommes dans la voiture. Tout le monde est paré ? »

Le trio installé à l'arrière (Peel était assis derrière le volant de la grosse berline Chevrolet à conduite à droite) répondit comme un seul homme : « Oui, monsieur. » C'étaient les plus jeunes de ses hommes, Lewis, Huard et Doolittle, déguisés en loubards – Doc Martens à bouts ferrés, jean ample, chemise noire découpée pour exhiber de faux tatouages sur les bras et le torse. S'y ajoutaient faux percings au nez, boucles d'oreilles et perruques de skinhead pour masquer leur coupe en brosse militaire.

Bref, trois zonards baraqués, prêts à la bagarre, prêts à faire un mauvais coup. Le tableau idéal, propre à faire réagir illico presto n'importe quel représentant des forces de l'ordre. De ce côté, les flics étaient champions : vous leur envoyiez une image bien stéréotypée, ils ne cherchaient pas plus loin et s'empressaient de tomber dans le panneau.

Niveau deux. Le code venait d'un commando en Afrique du Sud, du temps où il avait participé à un séminaire d'entraînement, trois ans plus tôt. Pour les actions physiques directes, sans recours à l'arme blanche ou aux armes à feu, il existait cinq niveaux opérationnels :

Le niveau un était le plus bas, se limitant aux menaces et aux bourrades, bref à l'intimidation, sans atteinte à l'intégrité physique du sujet.

Le niveau deux impliquait des dégâts faibles à modérés : bleus, éventuellement quelques côtes cassées, l'équivalent d'une bonne rixe dans un bar. Deux ou trois points de suture, quelques calmants, un jour ou deux jours de repos, et vous étiez frais comme un gardon.

Le niveau trois était assez sérieux pour entraîner un séjour à l'hôpital et exiger plusieurs semaines, voire plusieurs mois de rétablissement. Ça ne rigolait plus.

Le niveau quatre signifiait que vous gardiez des séquelles de l'agression jusqu'à la fin de vos jours : invalidité du genou ou de la cheville, mains écrasées, perte d'un œil ou de l'ouïe, bref, vous en ressortiez estropié. Le rétablissement était long et douloureux et jamais total.

Le niveau cinq était... terminal. Le sujet était censé endurer une souffrance extrême, pour qu'il sache ce qu'il avait fait et qu'il ait tout le temps de le regretter avant de décéder.

Les Sud-Africains nieraient bien sûr l'existence d'un tel code. Ils n'y avaient plus eu recours depuis la fin de l'apartheid... officiellement, du moins. Et bon nombre de services secrets civils et militaires de par le monde continuaient de recourir à de telles pratiques quand il fallait s'occuper d'adversaires un peu trop curieux. Peel avait le souvenir d'un homme politique israélien, quelques années plus tôt, qui s'était étendu publiquement sur la politique officielle du gouvernement en matière de torture. Expliquant que, dans certaines circonstances extrêmes, elle se justifiait. Qu'est-ce que les juifs n'avaient pas entendu quand la nouvelle avait fait le tour des médias ! Bien entendu qu'ils recouraient à la torture, si nécessaire. Un fou d'Allah pose une bombe et se fait arrêter avant qu'elle n'explose... Seul un imbécile irait lui demander poliment : *Excuse-nous, Abdul, mon garçon, mais sans vouloir abuser de ta patience, pourrais-tu nous révéler, comme ça, où se trouve la bombe, qu'on puisse la désamorcer ? Au fait, veux-tu encore une tasse de thé à la menthe ?*

Quoi qu'on puisse penser des Israéliens, c'étaient des survivants. Si vous aviez le malheur de salir leurs chaussures, ils vous balançaient une montagne sur la tête en guise de représailles. Ce genre d'attitude ne désarmait peut-être pas les fanatiques prêts à mourir au nom du Coran, mais les gouvernements un peu plus sensés gardaient la menace en tête avant de se hasarder à contrer Israël. La technique du talion multiplié par trois restait toujours fortement dissuasive dans certaines régions. Et les Israéliens ne laissaient jamais rien passer, jamais. Vous leur crachiez dessus et en moins de deux vous vous retrouviez avec une lance à incendie en pleine tronche avant d'avoir eu le temps de piger ce qui vous arrivait.

Si vous vouliez que votre pays survive à ses ennemis, vous agissiez en conséquence. Et personne n'avait besoin d'aller bavasser devant les caméras de CNN sur la façon d'introduire des épingles sous les ongles d'un terroriste pour sauver de la mort des citoyens innocents, pas vrai ? Ça faisait partie du jeu. Quand on se faisait piquer, il fallait en assumer les conséquences. C'était hélas ainsi que Peel avait été contraint de démissionner... pour excès de zèle avec les terroristes irlandais – ce qui, à son humble avis, relevait du pléonasme. Quels que puissent être les accords de paix signés, ces foutus rouquins d'Irlandais n'étaient pas prêts à se calmer et à se conduire en êtres civilisés. Mais certains étaient morts durant ses interrogatoires, la nouvelle avait gagné les échelons supérieurs de la hiérarchie, et voilà le résultat.

Enfin, bon. De l'eau avait coulé sous les ponts. C'était encore au temps où il était commandant dans l'armée britannique, servant avec honneur le roi et la couronne. Désormais, il était au service d'un autre maître, un homme qui comprenait la réalité des choses, avec pour conséquence immédiate qu'il avait déjà amassé un joli magot. L'un dans l'autre, il n'avait pas perdu au change.

La cible émergea du pub, dans un concert de vivats chaleureux et imbibés d'alcool. BC voulait le voir avec quelques bleus, mais sans plus, juste de quoi le mettre HS durant quelques jours, après quoi, cela n'aurait plus d'importance. Il ne devait pas être trop sorcier de neutraliser un vieux professeur d'université.

« Et c'est parti, les enfants. Faites vite... et soyez prudents. »

La cible, un sexagénaire bedonnant vêtu d'un costume de tweed vieux de vingt ans et coiffé d'un feutre assorti, exhibait une barbe presque entièrement blanche et tenait à la main un parapluie roulé.

« À vos ordres, commandant », lança Lewis, tout sourire. Il dirigeait le petit groupe. « Ce brave vieux mandarin. Comptez sur nous pour lui témoigner nos marques de respect. »

Huard et Doolittle éclatèrent de rire. Ils descendirent de voiture.

Leur plan était de calquer leur pas sur celui du professeur et, une fois assez près, de lui bondir dessus, de lui assener quelques bons coups, puis de filer avec son portefeuille. La police n'y verrait qu'un nouvel exemple déplorable de jeunes qui ont mal tourné et dirait au vieil universitaire qu'il pouvait s'estimer heureux de s'en être tiré à si bon compte. Ils rechercheraient le trio de skinheads, mais comme ces derniers auraient cessé d'exister d'ici une heure, déguisements ôtés et détruits, leur quête resterait infructueuse. La voiture d'un complice attendait au coin de la rue pour les récupérer : une camionnette volée, aux plaques échangées avec celles d'un fourgon garé devant un cinéma proche. Une opération simple et indétectable.

Le commandant lança le moteur de la Chevrolet, prêt à démarrer dès qu'il se serait assuré que l'agression se déroulait comme prévu.

Les trois prétendus skinheads s'approchèrent, riant et parlant trop fort, pour intercepter le professeur. Lewis, qui avait en main une cigarette non allumée, fut le premier à atteindre la cible. Il agita sa clope en demandant quelque chose au vieux. Peel était trop loin pour entendre mais il connaissait le truc : *Hé grand-père, t'aurais pas du feu ?*

Huard et Doolittle se coulèrent à ses côtés, pour encercler le vieux.

Peel embraya. Tout se déroulait comme à la parade. Un, deux, trois...

Puis, soudain, le décompte sauta de trois à dix-sept... Le professeur bondit comme un émule de Zorro, piqua Lewis du bout de son parapluie, le frappant avec violence au plexus. Le chef de la bande en perdit le souffle et sa cigarette, tandis qu'il reculait en se tenant le ventre. Le professeur pivota sur la gauche, maniant le parapluie comme une hache, qu'il expédia en travers de la figure de Huard. Sous le choc et la surprise, ce dernier recula à son tour.

« À l'aide ! glapit le vieux à barbe blanche, d'une voix à réveiller les morts. À l'assassin ! À l'aide ! »

Doolittle plongea pour lancer un coup de poing à l'épaule du vieillard. Le vieux pivota et le frappa de son parapluie, ne le manquant que parce que le faux skinhead eut le réflexe de reculer avec la grâce de Nijinski dans le *Lac des Cygnes*.

« À l'aide ! À l'aide ! Au secours ! »

Plusieurs clients se ruèrent hors du pub et virent ce qui se passait.

Magnifique ! Vraiment magnifique !

Lewis se ressaisit, repartit à l'attaque, esquiva un nouveau coup d'estoc du parapluie et réussit à flanquer un bon coup de poing sur le nez du vieil excité. Le professeur tituba et chut rudement sur le trottoir, mais sans pour autant lâcher son arme. Il la balança dans les jambes de Doolittle, le parapluie heurta un mollet avec un claquement que Peel entendit à trente mètres de là. Il continuait de faire des moulinets avec, ne ratant sa cible que parce que Doolittle réussit un nouveau petit pas de danse pour se dégager.

Quel sacré foutu gâchis !

Fini de jouer. Les trois loubards prirent leurs jambes à leur cou alors qu'une foule grandissante de clients du pub s'apprêtait à leur faire un mauvais sort. Les garçons étaient jeunes et en forme, ils ne fumaient pas, contrairement à cette bande de pédés, et ils ne devraient avoir aucune peine à distancer un ramassis de bonshommes d'âge mûr lestés d'une pinte ou deux. Sinon, ils n'auraient que ce qu'ils méritaient. Les idiots.

Peel fit démarrer la voiture et tourna au coin de la rue en jetant un dernier regard au professeur. Il n'avait pas l'intention de relater exactement les faits, ni comment l'attaque avait mal tourné. Le vieux s'en tirerait sans doute avec une fracture du nez, ce qui devrait lui suffire – même si c'était sans doute moins que ce qu'avaient prévu les trois loubards qui s'étaient jetés sur lui.

Salut les mecs. Que je vous présente mon pote, le sergent catastrophe.

Enfer et damnation ! Il les avait pourtant bien mis

en garde, mais ils étaient jeunes et trop imbus de leur personne pour envisager une seule seconde qu'un vieux bonhomme pût constituer la moindre menace. Ils ne s'attendaient sûrement pas à se retrouver devant John Steed avec son chapeau melon et son parapluie de samouraï, pas vrai ?

Enfin, ça leur servirait de leçon pour la prochaine fois. Et les leçons vexantes et douloureuses étaient celles qui se gravaient le mieux dans la mémoire.

Sacré nom de Dieu.

Vendredi
Dans le Raj britannique, aux Indes

Jay Gridley se tenait immobile, la machette dans une main, le revolver dans l'autre. Il n'avait pas encore bougé, et déjà, il dégouttait de sueur. La jungle s'étendait devant lui, formant un épais lacis de feuilles et de lianes, trop verdoyant, et certainement par trop vivace. Son cœur battait la chamade, il avait du mal à respirer. Il devait mobiliser toute son énergie pour maintenir l'image de la jungle, et malgré tout, elle oscillait sur les bords, menaçant de se dissoudre d'une seconde à l'autre.

Ce n'était pas un simple problème de concentration mentale. Certes, les exercices de Saji l'avaient aidé – respiration, méditation et tout le tremblement. Et puis, son grand-père avait été bouddhiste, il en connaissait pas mal, donc, il n'était pas complètement dépaysé. Non, le gros problème, c'était que...

Jay Gridley avait peur. Pis, il était terrifié. C'était la jungle où rôdait le tigre, d'où le fauve avait jailli du couvert pour se jeter sur lui toutes griffes dehors et lui lacérer le cerveau au point de l'empêcher de penser. Peut-être même de lui ôter à tout jamais la faculté de surfer sur le web, et si c'était le cas, il avait signé son arrêt de mort.

Il n'avait pas besoin d'être ici. Personne ne le forçait à retourner dans la jungle. Mais s'il ne pouvait plus jouer avec des ordinateurs, alors autant mourir tout de suite.

Il inspira de nouveau. Sa petite arme de poing ne ralentirait même pas le tigre, il le savait, mais il ne pouvait pas manier la machette et pointer à la fois son gros fusil à canon double. Si le fauve se jetait à nouveau sur lui, il serait à nouveau blessé, plus gravement peut-être que la dernière fois.

Il pouvait demander de l'aide. Saji s'était dit prêt à l'accompagner. Il n'aurait pas d'arme, puisqu'il se refusait à tuer même une créature virtuelle, mais il pourrait lui offrir son soutien moral. Et il y avait d'autres agents, appartenant ou non à la Net Force, susceptibles de se connecter avec Jay et de partager le scénario, dont plusieurs seraient ravis d'amener avec eux un mortier et de tirer sur tout ce qui bouge. Mais ce n'était pas la bonne méthode. Jay ne pouvait pas passer le restant de ses jours à réclamer de l'aide. S'il était incapable d'évoluer seul dans la vallée de l'Ombre, alors il ne pourrait s'acquitter de sa tâche, et s'il ne pouvait plus accomplir ce qu'il aimait plus que tout au monde, quel intérêt ?

Il inspira encore, exhala très lentement. Il allait y aller. Si le tigre le chopait, eh bien tant pis, mais il comptait bien manier son gros couteau et presser la détente du Webley, il n'avait plus rien à perdre.

Il éleva la machette. Le mur de végétation virtuel ondula et vacilla. L'image commença à s'effacer. Zut !

Il retrouva ses esprits chez lui devant sa station de travail ; il était trempé d'une sueur malodorante, et son cœur continuait de battre à tout rompre.

Il avait été prêt. Pas de problème. Il voulait y aller.

Simplement pas assez pour maintenir la cohérence du scénario.

Il poussa un soupir. D'accord. Il n'avait plus qu'à y retourner. Remettre ça.

Dans un petit moment. Quand il aurait eu le temps de reprendre son souffle, de se reposer un peu. Oui, promis, il reviendrait. Juré.

19

Samedi 9 avril
Londres

Mikhaïl Roujio, désormais l'allure d'un touriste ordinaire, déambulait en direction de l'Imperial War Museum, le musée de la Guerre. Le bâtiment, avec son dôme et sa façade à colonnes, aurait presque pu passer pour une église italienne, n'eût-il été gardé par deux canons de 375, venant, à en croire le panonceau apposé à proximité, des vaisseaux *HMS Resolution* et *HMS Ramillies*.

Les églises avaient été les témoins de violences au cours des siècles mais il n'avait jamais entendu parler de tels édifices gardés par des pièces d'artillerie navale disposés sur leur parvis.

D'un côté du passage, une haute dalle de béton se dressait, fragment du mur de Berlin provenant des alentours de la porte de Brandebourg. Il était encore adolescent en 1989, quand les gens s'étaient mis à démolir le mur, et le symbole, à l'époque, lui était passé au-dessus de la tête. Ce qu'un président américain avait jadis surnommé l'« empire du mal » avait été simplement pour lui sa patrie. À l'époque, il ne connaissait pas grand-chose du monde en dehors de sa terre natale. Il en avait appris un peu trop à son goût depuis.

Le fragment du mur de Berlin avait été peint pour

évoquer un personnage de BD géant, bleu et noir, la bouche grande ouverte. Jaillissant de ce gosier rouge sombre, étaient inscrits les mots : « Changez de vie. »

Facile à dire, pour vous.

Roujio était venu plusieurs fois à Londres, le plus souvent en transit, une fois en mission pour effacer un collègue devenu incontrôlable ; et il avait déjà visité plusieurs sites touristiques : le palais de Buckingham, le monument à Wellington, Abbey Road. Anna et lui avaient même failli un jour passer leurs vacances en Angleterre, avant qu'elle ne tombe malade, mais un imprévu les en avait empêchés. Depuis la mort de son épouse, il n'avait guère eu l'occasion de faire du tourisme. Anna ne se serait guère plu ici, mais aujourd'hui, les musées étaient plus au goût de Mikhaïl.

À l'intérieur, la galerie principale était encombrée de vieux chars d'assaut et de pièces d'artillerie, tandis que plusieurs avions étaient suspendus au plafond. Il passa devant un char Mark V, un mortier de 225, une Jeep. Les gris verdâtres étaient les couleurs dominantes.

La pièce la plus spectaculaire de l'exposition était une fusée géante allemande, un V2 coupé dans le sens longitudinal pour exhiber son moteur. Le missile, imposant, était peint en vert foncé. Pointu comme un cigare avec ses ailerons de queue, on aurait dit une fusée de bande dessinée.

Roujio contempla le V2. Il imagina la terreur qu'avaient dû éprouver les civils en voyant ce monstre dégringoler du ciel durant le Blitz. D'après la pancarte explicative, plus de six mille cinq cents de ces engins étaient tombés sur Londres et le sud-est du pays, avec leur équivalent en plus petit, les V1, tempête de grêle explosive qui avait entraîné la mort de huit mille neuf cent trente-huit personnes.

Il se demanda comment ils avaient pu arriver au chiffre exact des tués... Huit mille neuf cent trente-huit ?

Si les Allemands étaient parvenus à doter ces monstres d'un système de guidage efficace, ils auraient tué bien plus de monde. Mais si redoutables que fussent ces engins, leur utilisation revenait à balancer des pétards. Qu'ils aient réussi à toucher Londres relevait plus du hasard que de l'habileté. Une grande majorité de V1 et de V2 s'étaient perdus en mer ou en rase campagne. Et dans un conflit, neuf mille civils ne représentaient pas grand-chose dans le décompte total des victimes. Quelques gouttes dans un océan de sang.

Ce que les hommes savaient le mieux faire, c'était tuer leurs semblables. Surtout, comme à la guerre, quand on leur donnait quartier libre.

Roujio passa devant un projecteur, encore un modèle militaire peint en verre camouflage ; il contempla un de ces petits chalutiers en bois, à la peinture écaillée, utilisés lors de l'évacuation de la poche de Dunkerque ; examina le char d'assaut de Monty – un de ceux de la campagne d'Afrique contre Rommel, quand Montgomery était encore un général anonyme et pas encore le célèbre maréchal.

Des reliques à la gloire de la tuerie.

Il y avait également, dans des salles latérales, des équipements de cryptographie avec lesquels pouvaient jouer les visiteurs et, à l'entresol, une simulation de la Grande Guerre, conçue pour évoquer les tranchées. À ce niveau, il y avait également une exposition sur le

Blitz, ainsi qu'une zone consacrée à la Seconde Guerre mondiale, de même qu'à des conflits plus récents : guerre de Corée, guerre froide, Viêt-nam, Malouines, Bosnie, Kosovo, Moyen-Orient... Roujio passa sans s'attarder devant les présentations contemporaines ; elles n'avaient guère d'intérêt pour lui. Il connaissait toutes ces guerres. La Tchétchénie et son invasion par les troupes russes restaient dans sa mémoire comme si elles dataient de la veille, et non pas de presque douze ans.

Même si les tranchées de Verdun en 1916 avaient été un océan de bouc, les combats avaient été infiniment plus propres qu'au temps où Roujio appartenait aux Spetsnatz. Plus propres au sens où vous saviez qui était l'ennemi, où il se terrait, et où les choses étaient expliquées noir sur blanc. Attaquer ici, tirer là, vivre ou mourir en cours de route. Il n'y avait guère d'états d'âme à avoir, il n'était pas question d'abattre des gens assis derrière leur bureau ou couchés au lit avec leur femme ou leur maîtresse. Quand tel avait été son lot. Ce genre de combat, il connaissait.

Non, ils n'avaient rien de gratifiant, ces monuments à la guerre, mais quelque part, ils semblaient appropriés. Il comptait prendre son billet d'avion et partir dès aujourd'hui, si possible. Peut-être avec un détour par l'Espagne, en utilisant une autre identité. Il devait déjà faire bon à Madrid à cette époque, et les odeurs de l'Espagne étaient plus agréables que celles de l'Angleterre.

Samedi
Quantico, Virginie

Il aurait dû être chez lui, avec sa femme et son fils, John Howard le savait, mais il ne pouvait pas se relaxer suffisamment. Il serait resté planté là à ruminer ses idées noires, les siens l'auraient senti, et cela n'aurait été agréable pour personne. Alors, autant qu'il soit au travail, même s'il n'y avait apparemment pas grand-chose à faire ici non plus.

Il songea à Roujio, s'interrogea sur l'individu. Comment un homme pouvait-il devenir un tueur de sang-froid ? Il avait débuté comme simple soldat, et tuer était parfois inévitable, mais à un moment donné, quelqu'un l'avait recruté pour des missions d'élimination physique. Il avait cessé d'être un soldat pour devenir un assassin, une créature de l'ombre. Howard pouvait encore comprendre qu'une bouffée d'adrénaline pouvait vous amener à vous faufiler dans une ruelle sombre en gardant deux pas d'avance sur votre poursuivant, mais exécuter des meurtres de sang-froid ? C'était quand même différent...

« On rumine, John ? »

Howard sourit à Fernandez. « Je pensais juste à notre gibier.

– Vous aimeriez bien savoir où il crèche ?

– Ça aussi. Mais je me demandais surtout comment il peut agir comme il le fait. » Il s'expliqua, espérant que Julio partagerait son opinion.

À sa grande surprise, son ami hocha la tête. « Pour moi, je ne vois guère de différence.

– Abattre des hommes d'une balle dans la nuque ? Tu ne vois pas de différence ?

– Seraient-ils moins morts s'ils avaient été tués de face ?

– Comment ça ?

– Ces deux hommes qu'on a perdus étaient des soldats, ils étaient de garde. Le risque accompagne le boulot. S'ils avaient été plus prudents, ils seraient sans doute encore en vie... ou à tout le moins, ils auraient eu l'occasion de riposter. Mais quand on s'en tient simplement aux faits, quelle différence, franchement ? Qu'on vous tire dessus au nom du mal et du pouvoir ou au nom du bien et du bon droit, de toute façon, vous êtes refroidi. Peu vous importe le motif, pas vrai ? Vous êtes mort et bien mort. »

Howard dévisagea Fernandez comme si le sergent s'était mué en une grosse chenille extraterrestre tirant sur un narguilé : *quiii eees-tuuuu ?*

Fernandez nota le regard et sourit. « Vous n'aimez ni les espions ni les assassins, mais ils ont toujours fait partie des armées. Aujourd'hui encore. Quand on se lance dans la bataille, on tient à avoir tous les atouts de son côté, ou du moins, pas contre soi. Alors on envoie un espion dans le camp adverse pour découvrir les plans de l'ennemi. Comme eux font pareil, c'est le plus rapide qui prend l'avantage : les espions les plus vifs ont une avance sur le camp opposé. Ce petit jeu est aussi vieux que la guerre, vous ne croyez pas ?

– Les espions ne sont pas des assassins, rétorqua Howard.

– Ouais, c'est vrai. Mais laissez-moi vous poser une question rhétorique, mon colonel. Imaginons que vous puissiez remonter le temps jusqu'à l'Allemagne des années trente...

– Et que j'assassine Hitler ? » termina pour lui Howard. Il avait déjà entendu cet argument.

« Ouais. Vous le feriez ?

– Sans hésiter. C'était un monstre. Cela sauverait des millions de vies innocentes.

– Alors, vous seriez malgré tout un assassin, d'accord ?

– Oui, mais dans ce cas, la fin justifierait les moyens. C'est parfois le cas, Julio. Je serais prêt à assumer les conséquences morales.

– Pas de question là-dessus, et j'aurais fait de même à votre place. En revanche, comment savons-nous quels étaient les objectifs de notre gibier ? Et pourquoi il s'est lancé dans ce qu'il a fait ? Et réfléchissez à ce que vous auriez pu faire à sa place, là-bas, dans le désert. On est allé le capturer et s'il avait riposté en nous tirant dessus, on l'aurait aussitôt aligné, pas vrai ? Abattu froidement.

– Oui.

– Donc, d'un point de vue tactique, il était encerclé, en infériorité matérielle et numérique. De notre point de vue, il devait se rendre ou mourir.

– C'était notre point de vue. On s'est trompés.

– Affirmatif, mon colonel. Il nous a battus à plate couture, et il l'a fait en utilisant les instruments en sa possession. Je n'aurais pas été capable de faire ce qu'il a fait. Vous non plus, j'imagine ?

– Non.

– Vous vous seriez fait descendre, les armes à la main.

– Sans doute.

– Moi aussi. Et à l'heure qu'il est, on serait morts. Roujio, non. Et c'est lui qui est en cavale.

– Non, mais je rêve... tu admires ce mec ?

– Quand un type me bat à mon propre jeu, ça oui. Je me crois bon dans ma branche, vous aussi. Ce gars, c'est un ennemi formidable, et si l'on regarde les choses en face, ce sont justement ceux-là qu'on doit affronter, pas vrai ? Vous vous rappelez, la fusillade à Grozny[1] ? »

Howard acquiesça. Il s'en souvenait.

« Ces révolutionnaires qu'on a abattus ne jouaient pas dans la même catégorie que nous. Ils n'avaient pas la moindre chance dès l'instant où on avait décidé de les neutraliser. Marqués, foutus, sans rémission. Vous avez même fait part de votre déception lors du vol de retour. Tellement cela vous avait paru... facile.

– Je m'en souviens.

– Eh bien, ce livreur de glace après lequel nous courons, il n'a rien d'une proie facile. Il joue dans la même division que nous et, bon sang, il est peut-être même meilleur. L'attraper, ça va être quelque chose, vous ne croyez pas ?

– Foutre oui.

– Ce n'est pas la guerre, John, mais ce n'est pas non plus une promenade de santé. Vous êtes en rogne parce que le gars nous a nargués, pas parce qu'il a tué des gens. Les samouraïs ont tué infiniment plus de monde que n'importe quel ninja. La question n'est pas le bilan en morts, mais la victoire. »

Howard ne put cacher l'esquisse d'un sourire.

1. Cf. *Net Force 1, op. cit.*

« Comment es-tu devenu ce... philosophe taoïste, Julio ?

– Je suis sur le point de me marier et d'avoir un enfant. Ça donne à réfléchir.

– Eh bien, rentre vite chez toi t'occuper de ta future. Pour l'instant, ici, tu ne sers à rien. »

Le carillon d'avertissement de l'ordinateur d'Howard retentit. Indiquant un sujet indexé.

« Vas-y, ordinateur, dit Howard.

– Sujet A-1 localisé », répondit la machine.

Howard se pencha. Merde ! Ils le tenaient !

Enfin, à condition d'y débarquer assez vite. Où que ce puisse être.

20

Samedi 9 avril
Old Kent Road, Londres

Peel observait Bascomb-Coombs, une fois encore sans savoir le moins du monde ce que faisait le bonhomme. Mais BC aimait avoir un public, aussi avait-il droit à un commentaire en direct.

« Et c'est parti. Nous introduisons le mot de passe que nous avons dérobé aux portiers... et voilà... nous sommes dans la place. On file droit sur les portes intérieures, qu'on ouvre également sans le moindre effort... »

Il tapait en même temps sur son clavier, ses doigts dansaient comme autant de petits elfes. Il fredonnait dans sa barbe en riant doucement.

« Les pauvres. Ils ont reconstruit leurs murs deux fois plus hauts et deux fois plus épais, mais ça ne sert à rien, vous voyez. Il doit encore rester des passages... et qu'importe la résistance des portes, si vous avez les clés, rien ne peut vous arrêter. *Et voilà*[1] !

Il se détourna du moniteur dont l'écran était constellé de lignes complexes, de suites de chiffres et de lettres auxquelles Peel ne comprenait rien. « Quelle est l'intensité de votre désir de pouvoir, Terrance ?

---

1. En français dans le texte (*N.d.T.*).

– Je vous demande pardon ? »

Bascomb-Coombs indiqua le clavier. « Venez voir ici et pressez cette touche : pendant quelques millisecondes, vous serez l'homme le plus puissant du monde. Vous aurez plus d'influence sur l'existence des gens que quiconque sur la planète. »

Peel fixa l'homme, sans bouger.

« Ah, on hésite. Vous devez connaître le dicton : "plus on a de pouvoir, plus on a de responsabilités".

– C'est de Churchill ? »

Sourire du scientifique. « Spiderman, en fait. Je parie que vous ne voulez pas sauter le pas. »

Peel fit non de la tête.

« Eh bien. En route. Toujours plus haut. » Il tapa sur une touche, d'un doigt décidé. « Voilà qui devrait leur donner matière à réfléchir. »

Samedi
Siège du MI-6, Londres

« Commandant Michaels ? »

Alex Michaels leva les yeux de son bureau. Il ne reconnaissait pas l'homme qui se tenait devant lui, encore un de ces jeunes gens bien de leur personne qui grouillaient dans le service, en costard-cravate. Il aurait aussi bien pu être agent du FBI, sauf que ses fringues étaient mieux coupées. « Voui ?

– Le directeur général Helms m'a demandé de vous confier ceci, monsieur. »

Il lui tendit un disque argenté de la taille d'une pièce de monnaie. « Si vous voulez bien apposer votre pouce, je vous prie. » En même temps, il lui avait tendu un lecteur d'empreintes. Michaels appuya le pouce droit sur la petite surface grise de l'appareil. Le messager lut l'afficheur et fut apparemment satisfait du résultat. « Merci, monsieur. »

Michaels contempla le minuscule disque informatique. Quand on redoutait un piratage de son système et qu'on n'avait qu'une confiance modérée dans les protections électroniques, il existait des moyens de contourner ses craintes. La méthode la plus sûre était d'isoler son ordinateur de tout contact avec d'autres machines, de supprimer toute voie de communication matérielle. S'il n'était pas branché sur le secteur, ni relié par aucune connexion optique ou numérique à un réseau interne ou externe, on était tranquille.

Personne ne peut s'introduire chez vous si votre maison n'a ni portes ni fenêtres.

Bien entendu, vous ne pouvez pas non plus sortir, et c'est là où le bât blesse.

Donc, lorsqu'on s'isole, on n'accepte l'entrée de données que par le truchement de disques protégés et contrôlés. Et si on doit se connecter à une autre machine, on lui transmet par porteur un disque-mémoire. C'est lent, ce n'est pas pratique, mais c'est sans risque.

Michaels introduisit le disque dans son lecteur et le fit analyser par son logiciel antivirus. Même s'il était censément garanti contre tout virus*, on le vérifiait malgré tout. Toujours.

Le logiciel – c'était le meilleur programme du genre disponible au MI-6 – indiqua consciencieusement que le support mémoire était propre, sans la moindre trace de virus, vers ou autres gâteries indésirables.

Michaels lut le disque. Il y avait du nouveau sur plusieurs fronts. Les ordinateurs de contrôle aérien et de réservation de billets étaient, dans l'ensemble, de nouveau opérationnels et tournaient normalement. Ça, c'était la bonne nouvelle.

La mauvaise, c'était qu'ils n'avaient toujours pas réussi à déterminer l'origine du piratage qui avait engendré le problème. La trace disparaissait purement et simplement après un certain nombre de pare-feu* et de trappes logicielles.

« Bon après-midi, Alex. »

Il leva les yeux, découvrit Angela. Elle portait un T-shirt vert, un jean serré délavé, des tennis. Sa surprise devant sa tenue devait être visible. Elle sourit et précisa : « Samedi décontracté.

– Ah.

– Du nouveau ?

– J'ai bien peur que non. J'étais juste en train de parcourir le disque que m'a fait parvenir votre patron. Les lignes aériennes sont de nouveau opérationnelles. »

Elle s'approcha d'un pas traînant, se pencha pour regarder par-dessus son épaule.

Il sentit son sein droit lui caresser le dos.

Apparemment, samedi décontracté signifiait également pas de soutif.

Bigre.

Elle se recula prestement. « Eh bien, voilà au moins une bonne nouvelle. »

Le jeune homme qui avait apporté le disque revint dans le bureau, pas au pas de course, mais presque.

« Commandant... le directeur général Helms voudrait vous toucher un mot. Vous aussi, Cooper.

– Des problèmes ?

– Je ne peux rien dire, monsieur. »

Des problèmes.

Samedi
Les Ifs, Sussex, Angleterre

Assis dans son bureau, Lord Goswell sirotait un gin-tonic en regardant dehors par les portes-fenêtres. Il semblait bien que la pluie menaçait à nouveau. Qui sait, l'averse serait peut-être suffisante pour noyer ces satanés lapins ; en tout cas, sa partie de chasse n'avait guère été fructueuse. Peut-être devrait-il au bout du compte se faire opérer des yeux plus tôt que prévu.

Il entendit l'une des domestiques piailler après quelqu'un dans le hall. Il sourit en sirotant son gin. Puis il sortit sa montre à gousset et regarda l'heure.

« Quel est le problème, Applewhite ? »

Le majordome entra, l'air contrit. « Désolé pour cette agitation, milord. Mais la bonne et le chef sont tout retournés.

– Allons bon, et pourquoi ?

– Il semble que la télé soit en panne. Et les téléphones aussi.

– Pas possible ?

– Si, milord. On n'arrive même plus à capter la

plupart des stations sur les postes à transistors ou sur l'autoradio.

– Ma foi, on serait retourné à moins, vous ne croyez pas ? Vous pensez que ce sont les Russes qui nous lâchent des bombes ?

– J'en doute fort, milord.

– Eh bien, je suis certain que le gouvernement de Sa Majesté veillera à régler le problème dans les plus brefs délais.

– Oui, milord. »

Applewhite retourna apaiser la femme de chambre et le cuisinier, tandis que Goswell faisait cliqueter ses glaçons dans son verre. Il devait reconnaître cette qualité à ce jeune prodige, il était bougrement bon en informatique. Non seulement les lignes aériennes étaient de nouveau en rade, mais l'ensemble des communications mondiales étaient tombées en rideau et la plupart des satellites étaient déconnectés. Résultat, les signaux de radio et de télévision par lesquels ils transitaient étaient coupés, en même temps que les réseaux de téléphone. Une sacrée secousse ! Et, bien entendu, la situation redeviendrait normale au Royaume-Uni bien plus vite que partout ailleurs sur la planète, si les calculs du jeune Bascomb-Coombs étaient corrects, ce qui, jusqu'ici, avait toujours été le cas. Oui, un jeune homme brillant, sans aucun doute.

Dommage qu'il doive mourir. Le personnel de valeur était toujours si rare à trouver.

21

Samedi 9 avril
Au-dessus des côtes de Virginie

Le bras armé de la Net Force avait remis en route un de ses vieux 747 retapés pour le vol vers l'Angleterre, et John Howard, installé dans la cabine, regrettait de ne pas être à bord d'un supersonique. Plus vite ils seraient rendus au Royaume-Uni, mieux ce serait. Bien entendu, il aurait aussi bien pu souhaiter disposer d'une machine à remonter le temps pour y arriver la veille. Les services officiels alternaient régimes de vache grasse et de vache maigre au rythme d'un anorexique en traitement, et le Congrès se trouvait dans une phase de serrage de ceinture modéré lors du financement de la Net Force. Enfin, cela aurait pu être pire. Ils auraient pu se retrouver avec de vieux bimoteurs DC-3 confisqués à des trafiquants par le service des douanes plutôt qu'avec une flotte de 747.

Il aurait voulu mettre tout de suite la main sur Roujio mais enfin, il était déjà en route. Dès son arrivée, il allait devoir travailler la logistique avec les Rosbifs, mais ils avaient déjà un accord avec le gouvernement de Sa Majesté et la présence sur place de Michaels serait un atout supplémentaire. Howard n'imaginait pas que les Anglais leur chercheraient noise s'ils récupéraient sur leur territoire un ancien tueur des services spéciaux soviétiques.

Bien entendu, ses hôtes n'appliquaient plus la peine de mort et s'ils engageaient une procédure officielle d'extradition, cela risquait de poser un problème. De nombreux pays étaient montés sur leurs grands chevaux à cause de cela, refusant de livrer leur racaille aux Américains, à moins que ceux-ci ne promettent de ne pas les passer sur la chaise électrique.

Enfin, bon. On n'aurait pas à en venir à cette extrémité. Il n'y aurait pas la moindre paperasse officielle pour encombrer les juridictions de Sa Majesté. Si le bonhomme ne revenait pas avec eux pour se présenter devant la justice des États-Unis, ce serait à coup sûr parce qu'il ne serait plus là pour affronter la justice des hommes.

On ne tuait pas impunément des membres de la Net Force. Pas tant qu'Howard serait à la tête du service.

Il était en tenue civile, mais il avait l'essentiel de son matériel de campagne dans le sac posé sur le siège vacant à côté de lui. Il entreprit de fouiller dedans. Il avait tendance à vérifier régulièrement le contenu de son barda dès qu'il partait en mission, même s'il avait peu de chances d'avoir changé depuis son dernier examen cinq minutes plus tôt. C'était un tic nerveux, il en avait pris conscience depuis longtemps, aussi n'y prêtait-il plus attention. Deux précautions valent toujours mieux qu'une.

Il regarda autour de lui et vit que Julio était parti tout au fond, près de la queue, direction les toilettes. Bien. Mieux valait que Julio n'ait pas vu ce qu'il avait fait à son talisman ; pas tout de suite, en tout cas.

Il retira son porte-bonheur du paquetage et l'examina encore une fois. « Talisman » était un drôle de terme pour qualifier une arme de poing. Mais c'était un antique Smith & Wesson 357 modèle 66, en inox, bien différent des H&K tactiques en polymère équipant le reste de son unité. Cela faisait des années qu'il gardait ce revolver dans son état d'origine, à l'exception d'un léger rodage du mécanisme par l'armurier et la pose de prises ergonomiques sur la crosse. Bref, un banal six-coups à barillet, guidon et cran de mire en tôle, sans gadgets superflus. Il se sentait à l'aise avec, il l'avait eu sur la hanche chaque fois qu'il avait dû faire le coup de feu, et comme la vieille mitraillette Thompson dont il avait hérité, il en émanait une espèce d'énergie. Howard n'était pas superstitieux, il n'évitait pas les chats noirs, se fichait pas mal des échelles et des miroirs, mais il croyait fermement que le Smith possédait une sorte de pouvoir magique. Cela tenait en partie au fait que c'était un objet fiable, bien conçu, fonctionnel, sans bidules complexes susceptibles de s'enrayer. Sans être technophobe, sans se prendre pour un luddite[1], quand il s'agissait de machines, Howard avait toujours privilégié la simplicité. Les commandos d'élite et les forces spéciales de l'armée et de la marine, les Rangers, les SEAL, les Bérets verts avaient tous un arsenal personnel assisté par ordinateur. Des trucs comme des carabines dotées de caméras de télévision pour pouvoir tirer dans les angles sans se démasquer ; des équipements avec détecteurs, lasers, lance-grenades et tout le bordel intégré, qui coûtaient la peau du cul... il aurait pu leur demander ce genre de matos,

---

1. Du nom de N. Ludd, qui à l'époque de la révolution industrielle, prônait la destruction des machines (*N.d.T.*).

mais les forces d'intervention d'Howard se contentaient de banales mitraillettes de 9mm, même s'il s'agissait de modèles haut de gamme. Des trucs qui faisaient *bang !* quand on pressait la détente, qui avalaient n'importe quel type de munition où qu'on se trouve sur la planète, puisque la balle de 9 était la plus répandue dans toutes les forces armées. Et Howard estimait qu'il revenait au servant de l'arme de s'assurer qu'il avait bien visé sa cible. Certes, ils disposaient d'Intellicombis modifiées, équipées de tout un tas d'ordinateurs tactiques, de LOSIR pour communiquer, de GPS* pour se repérer, d'affichage tête haute et tout le bataclan, mais quand un de ces gadgets tombait en panne, on avait toujours le recours de tirer à la main. Le principe de simplicité maximale avait toujours eu sa faveur en ce qui concernait les armes létales, et il ne s'était jamais privé de le faire savoir.

Aussi, quand il considérait son fidèle six-coups avec ce viseur électronique Tasco Optima 2000 monté à la place du cran de mire habituel, ça lui faisait, comme qui dirait, tout drôle. Et après avoir passé des années à considérer d'un air dubitatif ces armes de poing en résine synthétique qu'il affublait du sobriquet de « flingues Tupperware », sa nouvelle acquisition avait toutes les chances de le faire passer pour un hypocrite aux yeux de ceux qui le connaissaient bien.

D'un autre côté, le viseur électronique n'avait rien de si complexe. Il consistait en une simple fenêtre de plastique transparent disposée trois centimètres environ devant une petite diode électroluminescente qui projetait dessus un minuscule point rouge. Sauf quand le bouchon de protection était posé sur l'objectif, le viseur était toujours en service, la consommation étant infinitésimale. Pour éteindre le dispositif, il suffisait de remettre le capuchon et l'ordinateur de calcul intégré se mettait en veille. En pratique, le maniement était tout aussi simple : il suffisait d'ôter l'embout de protection, de lever l'arme et de viser les deux yeux ouverts, et aussitôt le petit point rouge flottait dans les airs devant vous au-dessus du canon. L'endroit où se plaçait le point, une fois qu'on avait visé, correspondait à celui où arrivait la balle, à condition de ne pas trembler au moment de presser la détente. Aucune parallaxe. Et contrairement au viseur laser, ni faisceau ni point lumineux pour révéler à l'ennemi votre présence : la tache rouge était invisible côté canon, et même si ça n'avait pas été le cas, elle se réduisait à une imperceptible tête d'épingle de sept minutes d'angle d'ouverture[1].

L'ensemble ne pesait guère plus qu'un chargeur, ne déséquilibrait pas l'arme et était infiniment plus facile à régler qu'un viseur classique à guidon et cran de mire. En outre, il était presque indestructible, d'après les essais effectués. Alors qu'Howard n'avait pas encore besoin de lunettes pour lire son journal, le guidon de son pistolet à canon court commençait à lui paraître flou depuis quelques mois. Quand le maître d'armes lui avait présenté ce nouveau petit joujou sur un de ses pistolets d'exercice, il l'avait essayé, ça n'engageait à rien.

Et il avait eu des résultats de 15 % supérieurs dès le premier chargeur.

---

1. Le dispositif est le même que celui du viseur Telrad, bien connu des astronomes amateurs, utilisé pour le pointage de leurs instruments (*N.d.T.*).

Pour un soldat, améliorer de 15 % son efficacité au combat avec une arme de poing était loin d'être négligeable. Au bout de deux chargeurs supplémentaires, il avait encore bonifié de deux points ses performances.

Au début, il avait essayé d'ignorer le dispositif. Mais lors de ses visites ultérieures au stand de tir, il l'avait à nouveau utilisé. L'armurier lui avait expliqué qu'il pouvait démonter le cran de mire, meuler le guidon, puis sabler l'extrémité du canon, monter à la place le viseur électronique, le tout en l'espace de deux ou trois jours. Bon sang, avait-il ajouté, et sans vouloir offenser le colonel, avec une antiquité pareille, il ne se serait de toute façon pas servi du guidon en combat rapproché, et au-delà de six ou huit mètres, le point rouge allait améliorer sa précision de tir. Alors, franchement, où était le problème ?

Howard n'avait pas répondu, mais le problème était le qu'en-dira-t-on.

Julio ne lui passerait jamais ça.

Il avait bien hésité un bon mois, mais une fois qu'on y avait pris goût, il était impossible de faire machine arrière, et les chiffres étaient indiscutables : même arme, mêmes munitions, et il était plus rapide et plus précis avec le viseur électronique. Bref, l'affaire était entendue, il allait faire monter cette merveille technologique sur le canon d'une arme dont le dessin initial remontait aux premiers modèles conçus par Samuel Colt, quelque part aux alentours des années 1830... Même le mécanisme à double détente n'était pas une nouveauté, les jeunes recrues de Robert Adams l'employaient déjà quinze ou seize ans après les premiers revolvers du père Samuel. Le viseur et le Smith constituaient donc un mariage intéressant : la technologie du XVIIe siècle avec celle du XXIe.

Mais c'était le mariage de la carpe et du lapin et Howard préférait le révéler à son sergent le plus tard possible. Dans une situation d'urgence telle qu'il pourrait alors se passer d'explications...

Il leva les yeux et vit Julio revenir des chiottes. Il planqua de nouveau le revolver dans son sac. Au même moment, l'un des membres d'équipage, le navigateur en l'occurrence, arrivait par l'autre côté : « Colonel ? »

Il regarda l'aviateur. « Oui ?

– Nous avons... euh, un problème, monsieur. »

Samedi
Johannesburg, Afrique du Sud

Le nouveau train automoteur léger, emportant six cent soixante-quatorze voyageurs de Pretoria à Johannesburg, brûla l'arrêt prévu en gare de Tembisa à près de cent quarante kilomètres/heure. Le mécanicien bascula en manuel pour reprendre les commandes à l'ordinateur de pilotage, enclencha le freinage d'urgence et le convoi se mit à ralentir. Tout se serait bien passé...

... si un second train de voyageurs n'avait pas été à l'arrêt juste à la sortie sud de Tembisa.

Le train automoteur roulait encore à plus de quatre-vingt-dix quand il vint s'encastrer à l'arrière du convoi arrêté qui était censé le précéder de dix minutes.

Les deux trains basculèrent et plus des deux tiers des voitures sortirent des voies, pliées en accordéon comme des jouets brisés par un enfant gâté.

La moitié des occupants de la voiture de queue du convoi immobilisé furent tués sur le coup. D'autres furent éjectés et moururent peu après.

Un certain nombre furent électrocutés par les caténaires abattues.

Le mécanicien du train percuteur, resté à son poste, était mort dans la collision, en même temps que des dizaines de voyageurs paniqués installés dans la voiture pilote juste derrière lui. Ses derniers mots, enregistrés par la boîte noire, furent : « Oh, merde... ! »

Un incendie, déclenché par les étincelles dues à l'impact ou peut-être à un court-circuit, embrasa les aménagements intérieurs de l'une des voitures du train arrêté. Une épaisse fumée envahit la scène, la recouvrant d'un nuage noir.

Le bilan, provisoire, faisait état de plus de deux cents morts. Mais de nombreuses victimes allaient sans doute décéder lors du transfert à l'hôpital ou des suites de leurs blessures.

Personne ne songea un seul instant au troisième train de voyageurs qui suivait sur le même itinéraire à dix minutes d'écart. On aurait dû. Le mécanicien de ce dernier convoi s'inquiéta de constater que ses appareils de transmission étaient hors service alors que sa machine abordait l'avant-gare à trop grande vitesse.

Le temps qu'il réussisse à reprendre la main à l'ordinateur, il était déjà trop tard.

Nul ne sut quelles furent ses dernières paroles, car l'impact fut assez violent pour détruire la boîte noire en cabine, ne laissant qu'une masse informe et carbonisée.

Samedi
Kona, Hawaii

La balise s'éteignit à l'instant même où le gros-porteur L10-11 C3 arrivant du Japon se présentait pour l'atterrissage à Kona au beau milieu d'un orage tropical. Le pilote réagit apparemment de manière excessive quand l'appareil fit une embardée et le jumbo-jet de la JAL toucha avec assez de violence pour provoquer l'affaissement de la partie arrière du train droit. Le gros appareil dévia aussitôt sur la droite, se mit en crabe et glissa en travers de la piste, pour aller percuter un MD-80 d'Hawaiian Air qui attendait le décollage pour effectuer son saut de puce pour Maui. Le petit appareil répandit son kérosène qui s'enflamma et la boule de feu entraîna à son tour l'incendie du gros-porteur. Il y eut une terrible explosion. Des touristes qui attendaient dans l'aérogare furent tués, fauchés par les fragments d'alu qui s'abattirent en grêle comme des éclats d'obus en traversant les larges verrières du terminal, lacérant tout sur leur passage.

Des fragments de carlingue et de corps humains retombèrent en pluie jusqu'à plus de huit cents mètres à la ronde.

Quatre cent quatre-vingts personnes avaient péri dans l'accident, quatorze autres furent tuées sur le coup dans le terminal et sur les pistes, et cinquante-six autres furent sérieusement blessées.

Samedi
Perth, Australie

Malgré des mesures héroïques, dix-huit jeunes poliomyélitiques installés dans des poumons d'acier du Memorial Hospital de Dundee moururent par suite de la défaillance des groupes électrogènes après une coupure de courant qui avait touché toute l'agglomération. Une tragédie d'autant plus terrible qu'il faisait si sombre dans le bâtiment dépourvu d'éclairage de secours qu'on ne put localiser certaines des victimes que près d'une heure après leur décès.

Samedi
Siège du MI-6, Londres

« Oh, mon Dieu, s'exclama Alex Michaels. Il est en train de massacrer des gens. »

La vidéo de la catastrophe ferroviaire en Afrique du Sud provenait d'une caméra de surveillance installée dans la gare de Tembisa. La catastrophe aérienne avait été filmée par un touriste qui attendait un passager embarqué sur le vol JAL. Le reportage sur les morts en Australie était uniquement audio, sans images.

Tant mieux, songea Michaels. La simple idée de voir près de vingt personnes mourir lentement en essayant désespérément de respirer aurait été insupportable. Au moins, lors des deux autres accidents, la plupart des victimes avaient-elles connu une mort rapide.

« Oui, confirma Cooper, il a planté des dizaines de systèmes informatiques névralgiques. Je ne vois pas comment une telle chose est possible. »

Michaels non plus, mais comme pour la fameuse autruche avec la tête dans le sable, se boucher les yeux n'éliminait pas le danger. Les communications, les transports, et même les feux de circulation étaient en rade. Mais qui était ce type ? Comment pouvait-il déclencher *simultanément* de tels incidents sur toute la planète ?

Ils se trouvaient dans le bureau que leur avait fourni le MI-6, et tout le bâtiment autour d'eux bruissait d'une frénésie qui reflétait la leur. Il regarda Toni : « Il faut qu'on parle à nos gens chez nous.

– À moins que tu aies un pigeon voyageur rapide, bonne chance, observa Toni. Les lignes terrestres qui transitent par le câble transatlantique sont brouillées, et tout ce qui passe par les satellites de communication ne donne plus que du charabia.

– J'arrive pas à y croire. Il a réussi à couper virtuellement tout ce qui peut être lié à un grand réseau informatique. Le pouvoir qu'il maîtrise dépasse tout ce qu'on a vu jusqu'ici », nota Cooper.

C'était incontestable. Mais surtout, pourquoi le pirate faisait-il une chose pareille ? Qu'avait-il à y gagner ? Était-ce un terroriste ? Michaels savait qu'il devait faire quelque chose. Oui, mais quoi ? Que pouviez-vous faire quand tous les outils que vous utilisiez normalement étaient cassés ?

Débrouille-toi pour en dénicher d'autres, mon petit Alex, ou ce gars va nous paralyser toute la planète vite fait. Peut-être qu'il l'a déjà fait... vu que tu n'as plus de renseignements fiables – comment savoir ?

« On reçoit ces vidéos et ces rapports grâce à nos lignes protégées et durcies, expliqua Cooper. On essaie de récupérer le maximum de données par leur truchement. Je vais voir si on peut obtenir du temps sur une de celles-ci pour contacter votre agence aux États-Unis. »

Elle ressortit et Michaels contempla son bureau. « Il faut qu'on fasse quelque chose.

– Je sais. »

Mais quoi ?

22

Samedi 9 avril
Londres

Roujio se trouvait devant la poste en face de la cathédrale de Westminster. Il avait noté l'agitation frénétique autour de lui. Il s'était apparemment produit une panne électrique et informatique généralisée. Il était en train d'acheter des timbres quand le courant s'était coupé et que la machine s'était bloquée en avalant sa monnaie. En ressortant du bureau de poste, il avait remarqué les feux de circulation éteints et comme une inquiétude perplexe planant autour de lui. Des policiers étaient bientôt apparus pour régler la circulation au carrefour. En surprenant des bribes de conversations, il put déceler ce que les gens croyaient savoir et s'interrogea dessus. Mais tout cela ne l'avait pas distrait au point de l'empêcher de remarquer l'homme qui se dirigeait vers lui en hâte en arrivant par la gauche, slalomant entre les voitures pour traverser Victoria Street.

Que cet homme en eût après lui, c'était certain. Il était jeune, athlétique, souriant, mais cela ne voulait rien dire, Roujio avait souri à certains des sujets qu'il avait supprimés. C'était toujours désarmant, un grand sourire, ça levait les soupçons. Quel danger pouvait représenter un individu souriant ?

Un danger mortel, Roujio le savait. Mais était-ce le cas, en l'occurrence ?

Bien que fringué comme un jeune oisif, jean et blouson de cuir, le type avait une dégaine de soldat. Son port avait incontestablement quelque chose de militaire. Ce gars-là avait passé un certain temps sous l'uniforme, aucun doute là-dessus. Ou alors, c'est qu'il portait un corset.

Roujio envisagea les différentes options.

Que faire ? Détaler ? Faire front ?

Un coup d'œil alentour. Personne d'autre ne s'intéressait à lui. Apparemment, en tout cas. Si ce type était seul, qu'est-ce que ça signifiait ? Le mec souriant n'exhibait aucune arme visible, et même s'il pouvait avoir planqué un flingue sous son blouson, il avançait les bras ballants, sans faire mine de vouloir dégainer.

Roujio, quant à lui, n'était pas armé, à l'exception d'un canif, une arme pas spécialement redoutable. Certes, dans un corps à corps, il était capable, si nécessaire, de tuer avec ce couteau, mais s'il fallait en arriver là, c'est que la situation serait critique.

Si jamais il était pris en sandwich par un commando chargé de l'enlever ou de l'éliminer, des types assez bons pour qu'il ne repère que celui qui ne faisait aucun effort pour se cacher, alors il était déjà mort. Les autres devaient calquer leurs mouvements sur le type souriant qui avait désormais presque entièrement traversé la rue : au premier geste de sa part, les jeux seraient faits.

Roujio glissa la main dans sa poche droite de pantalon et tâta le canif. Il avait une lame de sept centimètres qu'il pouvait ouvrir d'un coup de pouce, aussi vite qu'un couteau automatique. Néanmoins, s'il était bien leur cible, et s'il sortait la main de sa poche avec une arme, il serait sans doute mort avant d'avoir pu ouvrir le couteau. S'il avait été le tireur d'élite du commando d'élimination, il aurait visé la tête : atteindre le système nerveux central était le seul moyen d'immobiliser à coup sûr l'adversaire. Une balle traversant le crâne, et on pouvait en général écrire le mot fin.

Le réticule était-il déjà centré sur son front ? La tache d'un pointeur laser dansait-elle déjà sur sa nuque ?

Il regarda encore une fois autour de lui, mais sans réussir à localiser le tireur. Ni du reste qui que ce soit dans la rue d'autre. Où se planquaient-ils ? Se faisait-il si vieux qu'il avait perdu sa faculté de repérer la mort aux aguets ? Ou le type en blouson était-il seul ?

Alors qu'il était prêt à s'avouer vaincu par des joueurs meilleurs que lui, ce scénario le gênait aux entournures. Il n'avait jamais imaginé qu'ils auraient la tâche si facile. Il avait espéré faire meilleure figure pour sa sortie. Peut-être était-il trop usé, peut-être avait-il trop tiré sur la corde, peut-être était-ce le dernier acte.

Le type souriant gagna le trottoir et s'immobilisa à trois mètres de lui, hors de portée d'un assaut avec son malheureux canif.

« Monsieur Roujio ? » Ce n'était pas une question. La main droite du type avait glissé vers le revers du blouson contre la hanche. Une arme était planquée là, couteau ou arme à feu.

« Oui. » Inutile de nier. On ne lui ferait pas le coup de l'erreur sur la personne. Si Roujio avait déjà eu le temps de sortir et d'ouvrir son canif, les jeux eussent été déjà faits : même à cinq ou six mètres, il était capable de fondre sur un type muni d'un pistolet dans un étui caché et de le poinçonner avant qu'il ait pu dégainer son arme. Cela n'avait rien d'un exploit : n'importe qui, pourvu qu'il soit doué à l'arme blanche, pouvait faire ça. C'était une simple question de vitesse de réaction. Mais avec le couteau dans la poche, c'était une tout autre affaire. Il avait une chance sur deux. Peut-être qu'à tout le moins, il réussirait à entraîner son meurtrier dans la mort. Mais si un tireur planqué dans une voiture ou dans un immeuble voisin l'avait déjà mis en joue ? Eh bien, dans ce cas, au premier geste inconsidéré, Roujio se retrouverait le nez sur le bitume, et sans doute déjà mort avant d'avoir atteint le sol. Une fin rapide, sans bavure. C'était tentant de vérifier.

« Bonjour, monsieur. Je suis le caporal Huard. Le commandant Terrance Peel vous adresse ses respects et se demandait si vous seriez libre pour dîner ce soir avec lui ? »

Peel ? Comment diable savait-il qu'il était à Londres ? Et que lui voulait-il ?

Le jeune sous-off tendit à Roujio une carte. Une adresse était inscrite dessus.

« Vers dix-neuf heures, d'accord ? » dit Huard.

Roujio acquiesça.

« Voulez-vous l'itinéraire ? Doit-on passer vous prendre ?

– Non

– Eh bien dans ce cas, parfait. À plus tard. »

Huard sourit, fit demi-tour, s'éloigna d'un pas décidé. Roujio l'observa jusqu'à ce qu'il le perde de vue. Personne ne le rejoignit. Il fut quelque peu rasséréné de constater que Huard semblait avoir été seul. Il n'empêche, il aurait dû le repérer plus tôt.

Roujio examina la carte de visite. Peel. Intéressant. Cela faisait près de deux ans qu'il avait fait sa connaissance. Le commandant entraînait alors une des unités paramilitaires de Plekhanov, après s'être fait virer de l'armée britannique pour... quoi donc, déjà ? Avoir torturé à mort un prisonnier de l'IRA ? Que faisait-il à présent ? Et surtout, comment était-il au courant de sa présence ici ? À ce coin de rue, à cette heure précise ? Il avait dû le faire suivre. Mais pourquoi ?

Et pourquoi Roujio n'avait-il pas remarqué plus tôt cette filature ?

Il glissa la carte dans sa poche, ayant déjà mémorisé l'adresse. Il se rendrait au rendez-vous pour en avoir le cœur net.

Samedi
Dans le Raj britannique, aux Indes

Cette fois-ci, Jay n'était pas seul. Il s'était fait accompagner par un guide autochtone pour faire le guet. Enfin, c'était en réalité un programme « détecteur de mouvements », qui se mettrait à piailler dès que qui (ou quoi) que ce soit débarquerait dans son scénario à l'improviste, pour l'avertir à temps de fourbir son arme. Enfin, il espérait que ce serait à temps. Le fait que le programme eût l'aspect d'un guide indigène enturbanné n'était pas un inconvénient. Et il avait rajouté une autre petite modification au scénario : il n'avait plus avec lui l'antique fusil à éléphants à canons superposés, manufacturé avec amour par un armurier de l'Angleterre victorienne. L'arme qu'il portait désormais suspendue à l'épaule et qui lui battait la hanche était un fusil de chasse ultra-moderne : c'était un Streetsweeper de fabrication sud-africaine, un semi-automatique de calibre 12 à barillet et canon court, chargé de douze cartouches à gros gibier double zéro alternant avec douze balles, plus une engagée dans la chambre. Au moindre mouvement suspect devant lui, il n'avait qu'à pointer l'arme et presser la détente pour faire jaillir une grêle de métal capable de tout broyer sur son passage. Aucun être vivant ne pourrait digérer une telle quantité de plomb. Le flingue était lourd, mais c'était une masse réconfortante pesant sur la bandoulière qui s'enfonçait dans son épaule.

« Tâche d'ouvrir l'œil, avertit Jay.

– Oui, Sahib. »

Jay se pencha pour examiner le sol, utilisant les talents nouveaux enseignés par Saji dans le scénario de la montagne et du désert du Nouveau-Mexique. Repérer des traces et chercher aussi bien ce qui était absent que ce qui était là. Il savait que le tigre avait dû passer par là, parce que, selon la logique perverse de la réalité virtuelle informatique, il n'aurait pas pu passer par ce chemin. Et sachant cela, Jay devrait être en mesure de repérer sa piste. Impossible de traverser ce genre de fouillis végétal sans laisser de trace.

L'odeur pestilentielle de la jungle torride l'avait recouvert comme le dernier souffle d'un mourant, collante et nauséabonde, mais il l'ignora. Il aurait pu choisir un scénario plus agréable, un refuge douillet pour skieurs dans les Alpes, une plage ensoleillée à Malibu avec vols de mouettes et déambulation de starlettes en bikini, mais c'était le terrain sur lequel l'avait mené le tigre, et c'était là qu'il devait, pour ainsi dire, enfourcher son cheval de bataille. S'il refusait l'obstacle, il savait que sa peur ne le quitterait plus. Et pas question de surfer sur le web quand on avait la pétoche, on y rencontrait trop de scénarios à vivre, trop de jungles à éviter.

La terreur avait dans sa bouche un goût de métal chaud. Il transpirait, il tremblait, il sentait des sanglots s'étrangler dans sa gorge presque à chaque inspiration. En un temps bien lointain, il avait été Super-Jay, plus rapide qu'une balle de fusil, plus puissant qu'une locomotive, capable de se rire de tous les dangers tapis dans les recoins sombres du Net. Mais plus maintenant. La griffe monstrueuse du tigre lui avait ôté son invulnérabilité. Elle lui avait révélé l'empire des ténèbres au bout de la route. Les ténèbres dans lesquelles chacun finissait par pénétrer, un fait dont il était conscient intellectuellement, mais auquel, dans son for intérieur, il n'avait jamais vraiment cru.

Il y croyait désormais.

Et c'est pour cela qu'il haïssait le tigre. Pour lui avoir fait connaître la terreur. L'avoir forcé à admettre ce que chacun savait sans jamais réellement oser en parler. Jay ne croyait pas en un Dieu bienveillant prêt à l'accueillir aux portes de quelque paradis mythique, pas plus qu'il ne croyait en quelque entité diabolique et malfaisante régnant sur un enfer éternel. Jusqu'ici, il n'avait eu foi qu'en lui-même, en ses propres capacités, or le tigre l'en avait dépouillé. Les enseignements de Saji sur le bouddhisme l'avaient aidé et cette religion l'attirait par son pragmatisme et son aspect terre à terre, mais elle n'avait pas pour autant effacé sa peur.

Il vit une trace sur le sol de la jungle : une légère dépression sur un carré de brindilles et de feuilles mortes depuis longtemps transformées en tapis d'humus. Il leva les yeux vers le guide, qui surveillait toujours la forêt, puis examina de nouveau la marque au sol. Guère profonde pour un tigre de ce gabarit, mais c'était une piste, il en était sûr. Le fauve était passé par là.

Ce qui voulait dire que Jay devait y passer à son tour.

Il se redressa. « Viens, Mowgli. Par ici.

– Bien, Sahib. »

Jusqu'ici, le scénario restait stable, c'était déjà ça.

Il se demanda combien de temps il réussirait à maintenir le décor environnant si jamais il apercevait le tigre. Il avait l'impression que ça ne durerait pas longtemps.

Jay inspira un grand coup, rajusta la bandoulière de son arme, et se mit en route.

Peel sourit à Huard. Dans cette ancienne chapelle transformée en bureau, le jeune homme semblait quelque peu déplacé. Sans doute n'était-il plus entré dans un lieu saint depuis son enfance – même si Peel n'était pas le mieux placé pour lui donner des leçons. En dehors des mariages et des funérailles officielles, la religion n'avait jamais été son fort.

« Et l'impression que vous a donnée le bonhomme ?

– Ma foi, mon commandant, il ne m'a pas paru si vif que ça. Je veux dire, il ne m'a pas aperçu avant que je sois devant lui, presque sous son nez, et il est resté planté là, la main dans la poche, comme s'il se branlait. M'est avis qu'il a dû sérieusement perdre la main depuis le temps où il était avec les Russes... Si tant est qu'il l'ait jamais eue. Mon commandant. »

Peel hocha la tête. « Vous avez l'enregistrement ?

– Ici. »

Huard lui tendit une infosphère* de la taille d'une bille.

Peel introduisit celle-ci dans le lecteur de l'ordinateur et d'un clic, activa la machine. La projection holographique se matérialisa à l'échelle 1/6, au-dessus du bureau. L'image de Roujio prise par la caméra miniaturisée intégrée à la boucle de ceinture de Huard était remarquablement stable et nette. Valait mieux, vu le prix que leur avait coûté ce foutu gadget. L'ancien agent soviétique était sur le trottoir opposé, masqué alternativement par le passage des véhicules, alors que le caporal s'apprêtait à traverser la rue.

« Ordinateur, grossissement deux fois. »

L'holoproj clignota et doubla de volume. Roujio se tenait à l'angle du trottoir, le regard perdu dans le vide. Effectivement, il n'avait pas l'air bien réveillé... quoique ?

« Ordinateur. Pause. Retour arrière cinquante images, lecture, grossissement trois. »

Huard, qui n'avait toujours pas bougé, fronça les sourcils :

« Mon commandant ?

– Regardez, Huard. Et prenez-en de la graine. »

La projection clignota et la séquence reprit, agrandie, en plan plus serré. Là. Juste à l'instant où l'image vacillait légèrement, ce devait être au moment où Huard descendait du trottoir, le regard de Roujio se tourna.

Peel sourit. « C'est là qu'il vous a repéré, caporal.

– Mon commandant ?

– Il vient de vous apercevoir de l'autre côté de la rue. Et sans trop bouger la tête, il est en train d'inspecter les alentours. D'en chercher d'autres avec vous. »

Huard hocha la tête. « Je ne vois rien, mon commandant.

– Non, bien sûr que non. Ordinateur, image de taille normale. »

Nouveau changement de vue, au moment où Roujio glissait la main dans sa poche.

Peel expliqua : « Il y a planqué une arme. Un couteau ou peut-être un de ces petits pistolets sud-américains taille porte-clés.

– Comment pouvez-vous dire ça, mon commandant ?

– Parce que c'est ce que j'aurais fait si je vous avais vu vous diriger vers moi de l'autre côté de la rue. Au moindre geste brusque de votre part, il vous aurait tranché la gorge ou vous aurait expédié deux balles de petit calibre.

– J'étais armé, mon commandant !

– Huard, cet homme tuait des gens quand vous étiez encore en culotte courte. Que vous n'ayez pas remarqué qu'il vous avait repéré et se préparait à vous accueillir, ça n'a rien de surprenant. Si vous aviez tenté de dégainer votre arme, je doute que nous ayons eu cette conversation. »

Huard n'en croyait rien mais il répondit : « Si vous le dites, mon commandant. »

Peel sourit. Ces jeunes... ils ne savaient que gaspiller leur jeunesse. Convaincus d'avoir toute la vie devant eux ; c'était même incroyable qu'ils soient aussi nombreux à vivre aussi vieux. Si Huard survivait, il finirait bien un jour par comprendre.

« Eh bien, ce sera tout, caporal. Continuez.

– À vos ordres. » Huard se mit au garde-à-vous, fit demi-tour et quitta le bâtiment.

« Ordinateur, repasse la séquence. »

La machine obéit. Peel regarda. Il appréciait le spectacle d'un vrai professionnel dans ses œuvres. Il avait hâte de retrouver Roujio. Les éléments de valeur se faisaient si rares de nos jours.

23

Dimanche 10 avril
Londres

Toni n'avait guère de temps disponible, surtout avec une crise comme celle qu'ils vivaient, mais elle s'était depuis longtemps rendu compte que si elle ne s'entraînait pas, elle ne valait plus rien dans une situation de stress intense. Elle devait avoir une soupape pour évacuer la pression, et si elle passait un jour ou deux sans pratiquer le silat, ou du moins sans une sérieuse séance d'étirements, elle devenait capricieuse et stupide. Aussi, quand ses journées étaient vraiment chargées, quand tout le monde se retrouvait débordé et qu'elle n'avait plus une seconde à elle, elle trouvait du temps autrement : parfois elle sautait le déjeuner, parfois, le dîner. D'autres fois encore, elle prenait sur son sommeil. Elle pouvait sauter un repas ou une heure de repos et rester opérationnelle, alors que sans exercice, elle était revêche et mal fichue. Elle faisait des erreurs stupides, ronchonnait après les gens, était incapable de se concentrer ou de se motiver.

C'est pourquoi, ce matin, l'entraînement devait avoir la priorité. Il n'était pas cinq heures qu'elle était déjà levée, se débarbouillait, porte de la salle de bains fermée pour ne pas réveiller Alex, et passait un survêtement pour descendre à la salle de gym de l'hôtel.

D'accord, ce n'était peut-être pas la meilleure heure pour s'échauffer, mais c'était toujours mieux que rien. Ce n'était pas par désir de se payer une bonne suée dès avant l'aube, c'était une nécessité. Une dépendance, peut-être, mais c'était comme de placer de l'argent à la banque : le dépôt d'aujourd'hui ne serait peut-être pas aussi gros que voulu, mais au moins cela lui donnerait-il de quoi tirer un peu plus tard, si nécessaire. Et vu comme les choses tournaient, elle allait en avoir besoin. Au temps pour leurs vacances.

Mais en vérité, elle était également un peu excitée : Carl Stewart devait venir la rejoindre à la salle de gym de l'hôtel. Quand elle était passée à son cours pour lui expliquer que son boulot allait l'empêcher de venir tous les soirs, il lui avait proposé de la retrouver pour des séances particulières, et il s'était trouvé que c'était également un lève-tôt.

Ça l'avait même fait rire : « Ah, comme ces gens qui sautillent devant leur fenêtre en respirant à fond, tout sourire au soleil du petit matin.

– Dieu merci, non, c'est juste une question d'horloge interne. J'ai toujours été ainsi. Debout à quatre heures, couché à neuf ou dix, je n'y peux rien. Alors, j'ai appris à faire avec. Mais il est vrai que je pratique l'essentiel de mon entraînement le matin. Il n'y a pas grand-chose d'autre à faire quand le reste du monde est encore en train de pioncer.

– Eh bien, dans ce cas, je serais ravie qu'on s'entraîne ensemble.

– Il y a une salle de gym correcte dans ton hôtel, avait-il alors remarqué. Ça t'économisera une course en taxi.

– Et ça vous en coûtera une.

– Pas vraiment. Je suis en voiture. Et ce n'est pas si loin d'où j'habite. J'ai un appartement à Knightsbridge.

– Knightsbridge ? Plutôt chouette comme quartier, non ? On y est passés en arrivant. C'est à côté de Hyde Park ? »

Il prit un air gêné. « Oui, enfin mes parents ont fait un petit héritage du côté maternel, et ils ont une petite affaire familiale qui tourne assez bien. »

Alors qu'elle descendait vers la salle de gym en parcourant les halls déserts à cette heure, Toni ne put retenir un sourire. Avant que les ordinateurs ne perdent le nord, elle avait regardé le marché immobilier dans le quartier de Knightsbridge. Le prix des appartements y atteignait l'équivalent du demi-million de dollars. Quant aux maisons particulières, ça commençait à trois millions. Et l'on proposait des maisons jumelées de quatre pièces pour sept millions. Et la plupart de ces offres avaient déjà trouvé preneur.

Apparemment, la petite affaire de Stewart tournait plutôt rond.

Carl l'attendait dans la salle de gym, détail révélateur en soi, puisque l'accès était censément filtré par un badge électronique. Toni introduisit sa propre carte dans la serrure et franchit les lourdes portes vitrées. Il n'y avait qu'eux seuls.

« Bonjour. » Il semblait trop allègre, trop éveillé pour une heure pareille.

« B'jour. »

Il s'échauffait déjà avec des étirements et elle se joignit à lui. La salle était équipée de plusieurs presses, d'un stepper, d'une piste elliptique et d'un tapis roulant, tous dotés des toutes dernières interfaces de RV. Une zone réservée à l'aérobic occupait le fond de la salle devant une grand miroir, sur une quinzaine de mètres carrés. Pas de tapis, mais la moquette était assez épaisse et l'espace était amplement suffisant pour que deux personnes pratiquent le silat.

Dix minutes plus tard, ils étaient prêts à commencer. « On se fait quelques minutes de djurus ? » proposa Stewart.

Elle opina. C'était toujours ainsi qu'elle entamait ses séances. Les petites danses étaient la base de tout le reste. Toutes les postures de combat se retrouvaient dans les djurus, si on savait bien regarder.

Pendant longtemps, Toni avait pratiqué les danses du bukti, les huit djurus de base simplifiés, avant de passer aux postures du serak ; depuis peu, toutefois, elle était passée directement à la forme générique de cet art martial. Dans bien des endroits, le bukti negara était encore pratiqué comme une sorte de test, pour vérifier si un élève s'entraînait sérieusement. Si, après avoir passé deux années à effectuer les mouvements de base, il ne s'était pas découragé, alors il pouvait accéder à des postures plus complexes, plus exigeantes. On racontait que le serak avait été inventé par un individu éponyme, en Indonésie. Serak ou Sera, également connu sous le nom de Ba Pak – « le Sage » –, était un Javanais, connu pour être un combattant formidable, bien qu'il fût manchot et affligé d'un pied bot. Que cet homme fût ingambe était déjà remarquable ; qu'il ait pu développer un art martial faisant de lui l'égal ou le meilleur face à des adversaires pourvus de leurs quatre membres était proprement incroyable.

Après dix minutes de djurus, Carl s'arrêta. « Tu veux enchaîner quelques combinaisons ?

– D'accord. »

Une fois encore, Toni était frappée de constater la supériorité de Carl sur le tapis. Aucune de ses attaques ou contre-attaques ne réussit à passer. Il les bloquait apparemment sans effort, restant toujours bien dans l'axe. Elle dut s'échiner à empêcher ses deuxième et troisième séries de ripostes au pied et au poing d'arriver dans le vide – surtout les uppercuts, des coups délicats qu'il fallait faire passer sous une ligne de défense haute mais par-dessus un éventuel blocage bas. Elle réussit toutefois à l'empêcher d'arriver au contact, même s'il parvint une fois à lui effleurer la poitrine et une autre à lui toucher le menton. Pas assez fort pour faire mal mais assez pour lui faire comprendre qu'il aurait pu l'amocher s'il avait voulu.

Génial. Exactement ce qu'il lui fallait.

Il lui montrait une prise qu'il affectionnait, ils étaient collés l'un à l'autre, elle avait l'entrejambe plaqué contre sa cuisse, la main droite de Stewart posée sur ses fesses, en appui pour une rotation du bassin quand elle avisa du coin de l'œil que quelqu'un les observait du hall. Elle n'eut pas le temps de regarder mieux car Carl achevait sa prise d'un ciseau à la jambe qui la jeta au tapis, enchaîné avec un coup de pied et un coup de poing.

Quand elle se releva, le témoin dans le hall avait disparu. Sans doute un chasseur qui servait un petit déjeuner.

« Encore une fois ? demanda Carl.

– Oui. » Elle avait le sourire. C'était vraiment génial.

Elle attaqua, au poing.

Alex ressentait une douleur sourde au creux du ventre, une douleur qui lui nouait les entrailles. Il l'avait déjà ressentie auparavant et la reconnaissait : la jalousie. Il les avait vus tous les deux dans la salle d'exercices, Toni et son instructeur de silat, cet Anglais, il les avait vus collés l'un à l'autre, la main du type posée sur son cul. Ouais, d'accord, ça faisait partie des mouvements, il connaissait assez les prises du silat pour le savoir, n'empêche, ça le faisait chier et il pressa le pas pour regagner leur chambre. Elle ne l'avait pas vu et il n'avait surtout pas envie qu'elle ait vent de sa présence. En temps normal, il aurait dû encore être au lit à cette heure, mais il s'était réveillé au moment où elle fermait la porte et il n'avait pas réussi à se rendormir. Alors il s'était levé, habillé en vitesse pour descendre les observer s'entraîner. Peut-être que ça lui apprendrait quelque chose, après tout.

Ouais, eh bien, il avait appris comment on vous pelotait le cul.

Il savait qu'il se montrait déraisonnable. Mais c'était moins les mains du type sur les fesses de Toni qui le gênaient que le fait qu'elle ait eu visiblement l'air de prendre son pied. C'était sans doute juste le silat, le plaisir d'avoir le privilège de s'entraîner avec un gars du niveau de Stewart. Sans doute. Mais il ne pouvait se départir de cette idée obsédante : et s'il y avait autre chose ? Tous les deux, ça n'allait plus très fort depuis une quinzaine, avec cette querelle sur son refus de l'envoyer en mission et tout ça. Peut-être que son intérêt pour le grand Anglais baraqué dépassait celui de simple partenaire d'entraînement ?

Ouais, bon d'accord, elle lui avait dit qu'elle l'aimait. Mais son ex-femme aussi avait dit la même chose. Son prétexte pour divorcer tenait à la carrière de Michaels, à ses absences répétées, au fait qu'il n'était plus là pour s'occuper d'elle et de leur fille, mais elle l'avait aimé avant et aujourd'hui elle ne l'aimait plus. Elle le haïssait, même, qui sait, après qu'il eut arrangé son petit ami.

Il arriva devant la chambre, mit la carte dans la serrure, entra.

Il n'avait vraiment pas besoin de ça, surtout pas maintenant, avec tout le merdier qui leur tombait sur la tête. Pourquoi l'existence ne pouvait-elle pas être simple ? Pourquoi chaque fois que tout semblait tourner rond, il fallait qu'un obstacle imprévu surgisse sur la route, qu'un pneu éclate et l'envoie valser dans le décor ?

Et pourquoi, nom de Dieu, fallait-il toujours qu'il réagisse de façon aussi émotionnelle ?

Pourtant, avec l'éducation qu'il avait reçue, un homme ne passait pas son temps à s'épancher et geindre sur ses problèmes personnels. Son père avait été officier de carrière et Michaels ne l'avait jamais vu pleurer, même pas quand leur chien s'était fait écraser. Son vieux n'était pas du genre loquace, mais une de ses seules conversations vraiment sérieuses avec lui avait traité de ce que les hommes devaient et ne devaient pas faire : quand tu prends un coup, tu l'encaisses et tu continues. Ne jamais laisser paraître qu'on a été touché. Si tu souffres le martyre, tu souris. Ça déstabilise l'adversaire.

Ayant été élevé dans un milieu où les émotions autres que le rire ou la colère étaient interdites aux mâles, Michaels savait qu'il n'avait pas besoin d'être aussi rigide, que ce n'était pas un péché d'éprouver des sentiments, mais il était difficile de s'affranchir de ces vieilles habitudes héritées de l'enfance. Savoir intellectuellement qu'on a le droit de se laisser aller n'était pas la même chose que d'en être capable en pratique.

Ce n'était pas seulement sa carrière qui avait tué son mariage. Cette habitude de cacher ses émotions avait constitué, il en était conscient, une partie de ses problèmes conjugaux. Et il semblait que cela devait recommencer aujourd'hui avec Toni.

Qu'y faire ?

Il hocha la tête. Pour l'heure, il n'avait pas le temps de s'en occuper. Il avait un boulot, un cinglé doté d'un matériel informatique incroyable qui était en train de tuer des gens, ajoutant encore à la misère du monde. Il devait régler ce problème à la façon professée par le guerrier samouraï Musashi : quand on est confronté à dix mille ennemis, on les combat un à un, en commençant par le plus dangereux.

Évidemment, il fallait être bougrement rapide pour battre dix mille adversaires, et il avait donc tout intérêt à s'y mettre tout de suite. Sa vie sentimentale devrait attendre.

Il laissa un mot à Toni, puis appela un taxi pour le conduire au MI-6.

24

Dimanche 10 avril
Washington, DC

C'était un superbe matin ensoleillé, pas un poil de vent, une journée idéale pour lancer. Dix heures du matin. Où était Nadine ? Elle devait le retrouver sur le terrain de foot. Mais voilà qu'elle arrivait, au détour du gymnase, un sac à dos passé à l'épaule. Elle le vit, sourit, lui fit signe.

« Hé, Tyrone ! »

Il répondit à son signe de la main.

Il y avait deux types qui s'entraînaient au tir au but de l'autre côté du terrain, aussi s'installèrent-ils du côté de la cage nord pour déballer leur matériel. Tyrone avait apporté quatre de ses boomerangs préférés, avec un sachet de poudre métallisée et son minuteur ; Nadine avait trois boomerangs, se fiait manifestement à ses doigts pour vérifier le vent et elle s'était munie d'un chronographe.

Un drôle de modèle, ce chrono : analogique, rond, imposant, argenté.

« Waouh ? Où t'as trouvé ça ?

– Mon père l'a acheté lors d'un voyage en Russie. Tu presses ce bouton pour le faire démarrer, idem pour l'arrêter ; la grande aiguille te donne les secondes, les petits cadrans intérieurs affichent les minutes. Ça marche sans pile. »

Elle lui tendit le chrono et il l'examina.

« Batterie solaire ? » Il ne voyait pas de cellule.

« Non, non, c'est un mécanisme à ressort. Ça donne une autonomie de, disons, plusieurs heures, après quoi on le remonte.

– Exemplaire ! J'ai une radio comme ça : on tourne la clé, elle marche une heure, jamais besoin de la recharger.

– Mon vieux dit qu'on pourrait gagner vachement de place dans les déchetteries si on utilisait un peu plus de mécanismes à ressort ou à gravité au lieu de piles.

– Ouais. C'est la prochaine tendance. »

Ils s'échauffèrent, roulant des épaules, faisant des moulinets de bras, secouant les mains, autant de gestes que Tyrone avait appris en observant les autres lanceurs. Il y avait aussi des étirements spécifiques, pour accroître la souplesse des muscles des épaules et du dos. Il avait vu sur le Net des articles sur des pros qui s'étaient déchiré des ligaments ou provoqué des tendinites en lançant avec trop d'intensité sans échauffement préalable et il n'avait aucune envie de récolter la même chose. Bien sûr, la plupart des types qui se blessaient étaient des vieux – vingt, trente ans ou plus...

Nadine s'essaya à quelques jets qu'il observa avec attention. Elle était en excellente condition – ça se voyait aux veines saillantes sur son biceps – et elle avait un style parfait quand elle lançait – utilisant tout son corps et pas seulement le bras, comme il convenait de le faire. On pouvait apprendre beaucoup en regardant quelqu'un travailler.

Ils s'entraînaient depuis bientôt une demi-heure et

s'apprêtaient à passer aux choses sérieuses quand Tyrone avisa trois ou quatre personnes qui les observaient depuis l'autre bout du terrain, à l'ombre d'un sycomore près de la barrière. C'était fréquent quand il lançait et en temps normal, il n'y prêtait guère attention, puisqu'il suffisait de détourner son regard du boomerang une seconde pour le perdre de vue. Il connaissait trop d'exemples de gars qui avaient perdu un boomerang orange fluo sur une pelouse tondue ras, *pouf !* disparu comme par enchantement... Parfois, ils piquaient du nez et réussissaient à s'enfouir juste assez dans l'herbe pour être invisibles ; parfois, ils se volatilisaient purement et simplement. Il avait ainsi perdu un quadripale rouge sur un parcours de golf où l'herbe ne faisait pas un demi-centimètre de hauteur... incroyable mais vrai.

Il ne lui fallut qu'un bref coup d'œil pour voir que parmi les spectateurs se trouvait Belladonna Wright.

Il reporta aussitôt son attention sur son boomerang et découvrit qu'il revenait, à une trentaine de mètres de lui ; il ne le quitta plus des yeux jusqu'à ce qu'il soit assez proche pour être récupéré. Il réussit à l'intercepter sans le laisser échapper, mais il était tout de même ébranlé.

Même s'il faisait de son mieux pour ne pas regarder Bella, Nadine ne fut pas dupe de son manège.

« Tiens, tiens. On dirait que cette vieille flamme n'est peut-être pas tout à fait éteinte, pas vrai, Ty ?

– Quoi ?

– Toi et ce cher cœur, là-bas sous l'arbre. À te voir, on pourrait croire que c'est une inconnue pour toi, mais d'après ce que j'ai pu entendre, vous vous êtes quand même payé du bon temps tous les deux...

– Et alors, et même si c'était vrai ?

– Rien, rien, c'est pas mes oignons. C'est juste que j'ai horreur de te voir te faire mener par le bout du nez, c'est tout.

– Comment ça ?

– Allons, Tyrone, me prends pas pour une pomme. Les petits lots dans son genre usent les mecs comme du PQ. On s'en sert, on les jette, il en reste toujours sur le rouleau... Elle a tout une file de types qui attendent dans son sillage et baisent le sol où elle vient de passer, rien que pour profiter de la vue.

– Ouais ? Et comment tu sais ça, toi ? »

Nadine regarda le bout de ses souliers. « On entend raconter des choses.

– T'as entendu d'autres trucs intéressants ?

– Je cherche pas à m'engueuler avec toi.

– Ah bon, j'aurais cru ! »

Elle leva les yeux, soupesa son modèle MTA. « Je suis venue m'entraîner. Ça t'intéresse toujours ? Ou tu préfères attendre que Miss America te siffle pour accourir comme un gentil toutou ?

– Ça risque pas. Pour ta gouverne, j'te t'apprendrai que c'est moi qui ai décidé de rompre avec Bella. » Enfin, ce n'était pas la stricte vérité, mais il avait lancé la conversation qui avait mené à la rupture. Et quand il s'était vu offrir le choix, il lui avait répondu qu'il n'était pas intéressé. Plus ou moins.

« À la bonne heure. Bon, alors tu vas lancer ? »

Tyrone regarda Bella, puis Nadine. « Ouais, je vais lancer. Prépare-toi à déclencher ton chrono, je sens que je vais te DÉ-PO-SER.

– Dans tes rêves ! »

Elle lui lança un petit sourire, qu'il lui retourna, mais

dans le même temps, il songeait à ce qu'elle venait de dire. Et si Bella le sifflait ? Si elle lui faisait signe, lui disait qu'elle avait envie qu'il passe la voir, s'asseye avec elle sur son divan et qu'elle l'embrasse comme elle l'avait déjà embrassé ? Est-ce qu'il accourrait ?

Pas question. Totalement exclu. En aucun cas. Merde.

Facile à dire quand il était quasiment certain que ça ne se produirait pas. Mais dans l'hypothèse opposée, est-ce qu'il laisserait tout tomber pour accourir ?

Question délicate. À laquelle il n'avait pas trop envie de réfléchir.

Il se concentra pour le jet. Trois pas, un, deux, trois... !

Le boomerang s'éleva dans les airs, tel un oiseau artificiel montant vers le soleil. Et pas prêt à redescendre de sitôt. À coup sûr. Voilà qui ferait taire les sarcasmes de Nadine.

Dimanche
Au-dessus de l'Atlantique

Manœuvrer le jumbo-jet n'était pas un problème pour le pilote de la Net Force et le poser en manuel non plus, à condition que la météo en Angleterre ne soit pas pourrie au point d'exiger une balise au sol pour localiser l'aéroport. Les instruments embarqués sur le 747 n'étaient pas affectés par la panne généralisée qui avait bloqué les principaux systèmes informatiques. Néanmoins, tenter de se poser au milieu du trafic dense régnant au-dessus d'Heathrow ou de Gatwick sans l'aide de contrôleurs au sol n'était pas vraiment la priorité pour un pilote.

« Non, absolument pas question, monsieur », avait-il répondu à Howard.

Par chance, il y avait des bases militaires autonomes au Royaume-Uni, du moins en ce qui concernait les opérations de vol, et ils pourraient y poser leur gros zinc, malgré le délai d'attente non négligeable. La plupart des bases encore opérationnelles avaient guidé des appareils civils affectés par la pagaille, ou autorisé décollages et atterrissages pour les vols impossibles à différer : évacuations sanitaires, transferts d'organes, déplacements de chefs d'État. Bref, ils risquaient de tourner pas mal avant d'être autorisés à se poser.

Enfin, ce ne serait pas la première fois, songea le pilote.

Heureusement, la plupart des organisations militaires étaient, par leur nature même, paranoïaques, et rares étaient celles à mettre tous leurs œufs dans le même panier. Que la moitié des réseaux informatiques de la planète soient tombés en rideau était un handicap, mais pas aussi grand que si la panne avait affecté l'ensemble des forces armées terrestres et maritimes. Tout bon soldat redoutait ce genre d'incident, et tout bon soldat savait en général convaincre les imprévoyants d'appliquer l'un ou l'autre plan de secours. Il semblait du reste que la corvée avait désormais des chances de s'avérer plus facile à l'avenir.

Ils auraient pu faire demi-tour et se reposer aux États-Unis, mais Howard n'avait aucune intention de laisser à nouveau sa proie lui échapper, pas s'il pouvait l'éviter. Le point positif était que s'ils avaient des problèmes de déplacement, Roujio devait être dans le même cas. Et il n'avait pas l'impression que l'assassin irait bien loin à pied. Même si le pister sans ordinateurs risquait de s'avérer coton, ce serait toujours moins compliqué s'il pouvait rester tranquille un moment.

Julio redescendit la coursive pour s'arrêter près de son siège.

« Mon colonel...

– Sergent ?

– Vous pensez toujours qu'on pourra récupérer notre bonhomme ?

– Oh, on finira bien par l'avoir. » Et Howard justifia son raisonnement.

Rire de Fernandez. « Sauf votre respect, mon colonel, mais c'est de la daube. S'il n'a pas avalé son bulletin de naissance à l'atterrissage, notre zigue est assez futé pour trouver le moyen de louer une voiture, un bateau, voire un zinc, et se tirer d'Angleterre. Il lui suffit d'agiter une poignée de leurs euros sous le nez d'un gamin désargenté, d'un pêcheur au chômage ou d'un pilote d'ULM sans le sou pour se retrouver avec un moyen de transport. Je parie que les Français ou les Espingouins seront pas mal débordés à essayer de surveiller la mer pour empêcher attaques ou détournements divers pendant que tous les ordinateurs sont en rade. Ses chances de se faire pincer dans ce bordel général sont quasiment nulles.

– Tu crois vraiment qu'il est si pressé de se barrer d'Angleterre ? Pour quelle raison ? Il ne sait pas qu'on est à ses trousses. Il est sans doute persuadé de s'en être tiré sans accroc.

– C'est ce que vous croiriez, à sa place ? »

Sourire d'Howard. « Bon Dieu, non.

– Moi non plus.

– Peut-être qu'il ne voudra pas prendre le risque.

– Je ne pense pas que ce gars redoute vraiment la prise de risque, vu son comportement jusqu'ici, John. »

Howard opina. Ce n'était pas faux. Et ils n'y pouvaient pas grand-chose.

Julio reprit : « Mais, merde, on pourrait avoir du bol. Il pourrait tomber du toit et se faire rouler dessus par un bus londonien, ou je ne sais quoi... Nous attendre quelque part sur un lit d'hôpital, sans rien de plus méchant qu'un abaisse-langue pour nous affronter quand on se pointera. 'Videmment, vu notre bol jusqu'ici, il serait foutu de nous tuer avec. Je vois d'ici la page nécrologique : "L'assassin liquide le personnel de la Net Force ! D'après les témoins, le sergent Julio Fernandez s'avouait déprimé."

– Z'avez toujours eu le chic pour me remonter le moral, sergent.

– Je fais ce que je peux, mon colonel. »

Dimanche
Siège du MI-6, Londres

Penché sur une pile de sorties d'imprimante, Michaels lisait les feuillets plutôt que de consulter les documents à l'écran. Une tâche de longue haleine. Toni était arrivée mais elle était repartie récupérer elle-même les données d'un satellite de reconnaissance depuis une station terrestre dont la liaison montante était encore opérationnelle. Ils ne voulaient pas courir le risque de faire transiter des informations, même par lignes terrestres sécurisées. Il était plus fiable d'aller les récupérer soi-même.

Alex avait des courbatures dans le dos et la nuque. C'était en partie dû au fait d'être resté assis à lire pendant des heures ; mais aussi à la tension engendrée par toutes les merdes qui lui déboulaient dessus. Megan et son détective privé, Toni, et la pagaille généralisée avec l'autre cinglé qui foutait le bordel partout.

« Toc, toc ? »

Angela Cooper entra, en même temps qu'elle frappait au battant de la porte ouverte. Elle portait un blazer bleu marine et une jupe courte assortie, avec un corsage bleu plus clair. Elle referma la porte sur elle. « Quelles sont les nouvelles du front, Alex ?

– Notre camp continue de perdre.

– On a réussi à relancer un paquet de systèmes. On reprend le dessus. Jusqu'ici, pas de dégâts irrémédiables sur des systèmes sensibles.

– C'est déjà ça. »

Elle s'approcha pour passer derrière lui et regarder par-dessus son épaule.

« Des analyses statistiques des transmissions téléphoniques transcontinentales ? Bigre. Voilà qui doit être fascinant.

– Mouais, à peu près autant qu'une thèse de philo sur les existentialistes allemands rédigée en chinois par des étudiants bantous. »

Elle lui posa la main sur l'épaule. « Mon pauvre ami. Vous êtes tout crispé.

– J'avoue avoir été plus détendu, admit-il.

– Vous devriez me laisser vous masser. » Et, joignant le geste à la parole, elle entreprit de lui dénouer les muscles. Il eut un instant d'inquiétude. Il ne pouvait pas la laisser faire ça. Mais, hmmm, ce que c'était bon. Elle avait les mains plus vigoureuses qu'il ne l'aurait imaginé.

« Vous n'avez pas besoin de faire ça. » Faiblard, comme protestation.

« Ça ne me gêne pas. C'est un de mes rares talents. Ma mère a été kiné, à une époque. Elle connaissait certaines des techniques de massage parmi les plus ésotériques – reiki, shiatsu, Aston-Patterning. J'en ai profité. »

Bon Dieu, ce que ça pouvait faire du bien. Il sentait fondre les nœuds dans tous ses ligaments. Il avait l'impression aussi que sa tête allait finir par se décoller si elle continuait à ce train-là. Cela n'avait rien de sexuel, mais c'était sensuel, à coup sûr.

« Vous savez, vous devriez vous étendre pour en profiter au maximum. » Elle continuait de lui palper le cou et le haut du dos, enfonçant les pouces, travaillant en spirales elliptiques.

« Seulement, le divan est trop mou, le bureau est trop court. Mais la moquette est propre. Allongez-vous par terre, sur le ventre, là, près du bureau. »

Alex obéit avec la docilité d'un homme en transe. Il ne se serait pas cru crispé à ce point. Elle trouvait dans ses muscles des nœuds tellement durs qu'on aurait cru des billes de roulement.

Allongé, le nez dans le tapis, il sentit qu'elle l'enfourchait, et du coin de l'œil, il vit sa minijupe remontée et ses genoux pressés contre ses flancs. Il sentait ses fesses effleurer ses reins.

Oh, oui...

« Ce serait plus facile si vous ôtiez votre chemise, mais peut-être que le lieu ne s'y prête pas vraiment. On pourrait jaser... »

Dans l'état où il se trouvait, Michaels se fichait comme d'une guigne que l'ensemble du MI-6 puisse jaser. Il laissa échapper un gémissement, quand sa paume s'enfonça dans la chair au-dessus de son omoplate droite.

Ça faisait mal, mais c'était un mal qui faisait du bien, il se sentait progressivement ramollir.

Elle se coula vers l'arrière, se tint en équilibre au-dessus de ses jarrets et posa les mains au creux de ses reins. Les pouces bien appuyés sur les fesses, elle lui caressa les hanches en mouvements tournants.

Ouf ! Sacrebleu, c'est qu'il y prendrait vite goût.

Y prendre goût ? Ça pourrait bien finir par devenir une drogue.

Il se rendit compte au bout d'une dizaine de minutes que ce serait le moment le plus mal choisi pour le retour de Toni. Il aurait bien du mal à se justifier. Il ferait mieux d'arrêter les frais. Maintenant.

Mais il n'en fit rien.

Et Toni ne revint pas et, au bout de vingt minutes de massage, Angela remonta vers le haut de son corps, lui fit encore un truc à la nuque, puis enfin le libéra et se remit debout.

C'est à peine s'il pouvait bouger. Il réussit tant bien que mal à se redresser.

Angela était toute rouge, le visage luisant de sueur, mais radieuse.

« Merci, vous venez de me sauver la vie.

– Ce n'était pas grand-chose, vraiment. Pour bien

faire, il aurait fallu une heure, une heure et demie, et en travaillant des deux côtés, face et dos. J'ai une table de massage à la maison. Peut-être que vous pourriez passer un de ces jours, que je vous fasse bénéficier du traitement complet. »

Une alarme se mit aussitôt à clignoter dans son cerveau : *Attention ! Danger ! Mauvaise idée !*

Puis il repensa à Toni et à son entraînement de silat. Stewart l'avait copieusement papouillée, non ? Alors, où était la différence ? Ce n'était pas du sexe, c'était innocent. C'était... thérapeutique.

« Ouais, ça pourrait se faire », s'entendit-il répondre.

Elle lui sourit et il lui rendit son sourire.

« Je dois être affreuse, genre vieille vache en sueur. Faut que j'aille me refaire une beauté. À plus tard. »

Après son départ, il constata qu'une partie de sa tension était déjà revenue, malgré l'intense séance de massage qu'il venait de subir. Et cela n'avait rien à voir avec le boulot.

Dans quelle galère es-tu encore allé te fourrer, Alex ?

25

Dimanche 10 avril
Les Ifs, Sussex, Angleterre

Installé à son bureau, dans le grand fauteuil de cuir, Goswell sirotait son gin glacé. Avec un soupir, il contempla les photos pour la dixième fois peut-être. À l'heure des miracles informatiques, il était sans aucun doute possible de truquer ce genre de documents, il le savait. Un expert pouvait sans peine placer le visage d'un homme sur le corps d'un autre, effacer ou ajouter des éléments qui n'avaient jamais existé. Il avait le souvenir d'un film montrant Winston Churchill – un sacré parlementaire, s'il devait en croire les confidences paternelles – bavardant assis aux côtés d'Abraham Lincoln, quand en fait, ce dernier avait été assassiné huit ou dix ans avant que naisse Churchill.

Il tria les photos. Oui, ce devait être réalisable, mais en l'occurrence, il était à peu près certain que ça n'avait pas été le cas. Ces clichés étaient tout ce qu'il y a d'authentique car l'homme qui les avait pris n'avait aucune raison de les trafiquer. On y voyait Peel, assis avec Bascomb-Coombs dans quelque gargote, et discutant avec lui. Bien sûr, Peel était son chef de la sécurité et Bascomb-Coombs l'un de ses employés, et un employé de valeur, du reste, on pouvait donc arguer à juste titre qu'une telle rencontre entrait parfaitement dans les attributions de Peel. C'était après tout son boulot de surveiller de tels individus, et s'entretenir avec eux n'avait rien de déplacé.

Goswell but une autre gorgée de gin et jeta un œil sur le carillon Westminster. Presque sept heures, le dîner serait bientôt prêt.

Non, Peel pourrait sans peine justifier son entretien avec Bascomb-Coombs. L'ennuyeux, c'est qu'il s'en était abstenu. Nulle part dans ses rapports il n'était fait mention d'une telle rencontre. Ni des rencontres ultérieures. Même si tous ces événements n'avaient pas été effacés du recueil de ses actes et observations, certains avaient assurément dû l'être. Il y avait d'autres photos.

Goswell hocha la tête. Pas très bon, tout ça. Fallait-il croire que la mémoire jusqu'ici sans faille de Peel avait commencé à défaillir ? Et de manière sélective, au sujet de Bascomb-Coombs ? Quel monde terrible que celui où on devait se résoudre à faire surveiller son plus fidèle surveillant...

La question demeurait bien sûr de savoir ce que tramaient ces deux-là. Qu'ils complotent ensemble devait sans nul doute révéler quelque chose.

Bon. Il n'était pas devenu capitaine d'industrie sans apprendre à déjouer ce genre de piège.

Il fit résonner bruyamment les glaçons dans son verre désormais presque vide.

« Milord ? Un autre gin ?

– Oui, je vous prie. Oh... et, Applewhite ? Voyez si vous pouvez trouver le commandant Peel, voulez-vous, et demandez-lui de passer me voir après dîner.

– Certainement, milord. »

Goswell contempla les glaçons qui finissaient de fondre tandis qu'Applewhite allait chercher la bouteille de gin. Il allait bien falloir qu'il coince ce faux-jeton de Peel d'une manière ou d'une autre. C'était quand même dommage. Une bonne chose que son père ne soit plus là pour voir ça. Cela lui aurait brisé le cœur de voir son fils ainsi trahir sa confiance.

Dimanche
Londres

Un léger crachin s'était mis à tomber et Roujio estima que cela ferait un prétexte idéal.

On était dimanche et, dans bien des villes, cela voulait dire que la majorité des commerces étaient fermés, mais pas à Londres. Il héla un taxi près du British Museum et donna au chauffeur l'adresse de sa destination, pas très loin d'une boutique située dans une petite rue à proximité de Regent's Park. L'échoppe, étroite et tout en profondeur, était spécialisée dans les cannes et les parapluies de fabrication artisanale. On pouvait aisément y dépenser deux cents livres pour un article fait main, et même beaucoup plus si l'on voulait. Il faut dire que le riflard était une spécialité nationale, le symbole du gentleman britannique, et il n'était pas douteux que la seule vente des pépins aurait suffi à assurer la rentabilité de l'établissement ; toutefois, la boutique avait d'autres articles en stock pour les clients bien informés.

Le taxi le déposa une rue avant le magasin. Roujio régla la course, puis, se ravisant, rajouta un pourboire suffisant pour que le chauffeur ne puisse se souvenir de lui ni pour sa pingrerie ni pour son extravagance, et il descendit. La pluie tombait un peu plus dru à présent, et Roujio fit mine de ne surtout pas remarquer l'homme qui l'avait pris en filature. Même si le type n'était pas complètement nul, il en aurait fallu un d'une autre carrure pour le filer incognito.

Dès qu'il fut à proximité de la fameuse boutique, il joua le passant irrité par les conditions météorologiques, s'ébroua ostensiblement et, comme pris d'une idée soudaine, décida d'entrer dans la place.

Tout ce petit jeu eût été vain si Peel avait été au courant des articles qu'on pouvait y trouver, mais sauf changement récent, les Rosbifs ne se doutaient toujours de rien.

La rencontre avec Peel avait été fort instructive. Qu'il prétende avoir repéré Roujio en corrélant les photos des passeports de tous les étrangers entrés dans le pays à une liste d'agents identifiés semblait à tout le moins excessif, mais toujours est-il qu'il avait réussi à le repérer. Et à lui coller un chaperon. Peut-être n'était-ce qu'un coup de pot. Ou peut-être qu'après tout, Peel disait vrai. Dans un cas comme dans l'autre, l'offre d'emploi était la bienvenue. Roujio n'était pas foncièrement intéressé par le boulot, mais encore une fois, il n'y avait pas péril en la demeure, et Peel pouvait lui faciliter la tâche, surtout avec tous les problèmes d'informatique survenus ces derniers temps. Qui sait si une petite escale ne lui serait pas profitable. La mission – se tenir prêt à éliminer éventuellement un lord anglais qui se trouvait, pur hasard, être l'employeur de Peel – piquait sa curiosité, même si

Roujio doutait d'avoir à concrétiser cette « neutralisation ».

L'explication bancale de son interlocuteur pour justifier son incapacité à s'acquitter lui-même de cette mission ou à la déléguer à un de ses sbires ne trompait personne. Il était évident qu'il cherchait un bouc émissaire, un agent étranger sur qui faire retomber l'assassinat ; et qui était mieux placé qu'un ancien tueur des services secrets soviétiques, qui plus est en fuite ? Un gars qui, sa mission accomplie, avait de bonnes chances de se retrouver truffé de plomb alors qu'il tenterait de s'enfuir, ce qui réglerait définitivement la question...

Roujio esquissa un sourire quand l'employé de la boutique lui adressa un discret signe de tête. À la place de Peel, c'est ainsi qu'il aurait préparé son coup : louer les services d'un tueur à gages, puis l'éliminer une fois la tâche accomplie, vite fait, bien fait, même si ce n'était pas terriblement futé. Tôt ou tard, quelqu'un finirait bien par venir demander pourquoi un type fuyant la justice américaine serait venu faire étape au Royaume-Uni pour exécuter quelqu'un, ce genre d'activité exigeant tout de même un motif. Et même ces balourds de policiers britanniques ne manqueraient pas de retourner chaque pouce de terre pour retrouver la trace de l'assassin d'un homme aussi estimé. C'est qu'ils avaient encore la conscience de classe chevillée au corps, dans ce pays. Mais dans certains domaines, les Rosbifs avaient toujours été affligés d'une certaine myopie. S'ils s'étaient montrés plus attentifs, sans doute seraient-ils restés la première puissance de la planète. L'excès de prétention pouvait faire s'écrouler un empire. Un défaut qui devait sans aucun doute affecter en partie le commandant Peel.

« Puis-je vous être utile, monsieur ?

– Je cherche un parapluie particulier. Un peu plus... costaud que les modèles ordinaires. »

L'employé ne se départit pas de son sourire. « Ah oui, je vois. Je vais tout de suite aller chercher le directeur, M. O'Donnell. »

L'employé s'éclipsa par une porte derrière le comptoir. Roujio fit mine d'examiner les modèles exposés. Le travail sur les poignées de plusieurs cannes et parapluies était fantastique, avec leur ivoire ou leur bois exotique sculpté de toutes sortes de formes extravagantes : ici un tigre, là un serpent, là encore une femme nue arquée en un demi-cercle plein de grâce.

« Bon après-midi, monsieur. Je suis M. O'Donnell. J'ai cru comprendre que vous recherchiez un modèle spécial ? »

Roujio acquiesça. L'homme était blond, de haute taille, portant costume sombre. « Oui.

– Puis-je vous demander qui vous a recommandé notre établissement ?

– Ce doit être le colonel Webley-Scott.

– Ah, je vois. Et comment se porte le colonel, ces derniers temps ? »

Le code de reconnaissance était manifestement le même. Roujio répondit, sans se démonter : « Toujours mort, aux dernières nouvelles. »

Le gérant sourit et opina. « Si vous voulez bien venir par ici, monsieur ?

– Je suis filé. Aucun rapport avec vous.

– Ne vous inquiétez pas. Il ne verra rien à travers la

devanture, à moins d'avoir un œil de lynx. Est-il susceptible d'entrer ?

– Je doute qu'il soit stupide à ce point.

– Eh bien, s'il l'était, il vous verrait ressortir de la porte des toilettes. »

Roujio suivit O'Donnell dans les W-C dont le fond était pourvu d'une porte dissimulée donnant sur une petite pièce discrète. Dans un angle trônait un antique coffre-fort aux pieds en fonte moulée, de couleur verte. Tout en ouvrant le coffre, le gérant demanda : « Cherchez-vous une arme de jet ou de poing ?

– Auriez-vous un modèle à projectiles multiples ?

– Tout à fait. Un cinq-coups. Petit calibre, j'en ai peur : seulement du 22.

– Cela fera l'affaire.

– Eh bien, voilà. »

L'article qu'il lui présenta avait toutes les apparences d'un parapluie classique, sinon que la poignée de bois en forme de J était peut-être un peu plus épaisse et massive que la normale.

« La poignée se dévisse ici... à l'intérieur, vous noterez l'arrière du barillet. C'est un revolver, comme vous pouvez le constater. »

Roujio avisa les cinq petits trous au fond du minuscule barillet à l'intérieur du manche. La gâchette et le reste du mécanisme étaient encastrés dans la poignée amovible. Ingénieux.

« On introduit ainsi les balles comme ceci, on revisse la poignée jusqu'au déclic, comme cela. On libère la détente de cette manière, en jouant sur ce discret poussoir, un peu comme avec un petit couteau automatique... »

D'un mouvement du pouce, il fit apparaître la queue de détente.

« Le mécanisme n'est qu'à double effet, bien sûr, et il n'y a pas de viseur, mais un bon tireur n'a aucun mal à viser de manière efficace. Le tube est en acier rayé, d'une précision équivalente à celle de n'importe quelle bonne carabine du commerce. L'embout est en caoutchouc mou et n'entrave en rien le passage de la balle si jamais vous n'avez pas le temps de l'ôter ; du reste, il joue le rôle de silencieux, même s'il faut le remplacer après plusieurs coups. Nous fournissons bien entendu des embouts de rechange. »

Roujio saisit la carabine camouflée, la soupesa. En temps normal, il n'aimait pas se balader avec une arme s'il n'en avait pas spécifiquement l'usage. Mais on n'était pas en temps normal.

« Vous avez déjà tiré avec ?

– Tout à fait.

– Et y a-t-il un endroit où je pourrais l'essayer ? »

O'Donnell acquiesça. « Cette caisse que vous voyez là : elle est remplie de matériau amortisseur et le fond est une plaque d'acier. » Il n'était pas du tout vexé. Seul un imbécile confierait son existence à une arme qu'il n'a pas lui-même essayée pour s'assurer de son bon fonctionnement.

« Les munitions ?

– J'ai des Stinger, pleines ou à pointe creuse.

– Excellent. Vous me le faites à combien ?

– Deux mille.

– Topez là ! »

O'Donnell sourit.

L'homme chargé de le filer s'était installé dans une sandwicherie de l'autre côté de la rue, et il l'observait derrière une vitrine en partie masquée par la buée. Un jeune homme aux cheveux courts qu'on aurait pu prendre pour le frère de Huard. La pluie tombait toujours à verse, aussi Roujio dressa-t-il à la verticale sa carabine neuve et chargée, l'employant pour sa fonction annexe. La toile de soie noire se déplia sèchement, entraînée par ses baleines de titane, et se verrouilla en place. L'arme avait tiré cinq balles sans aucun problème. Et, de toute évidence, c'était en plus un excellent parapluie. Un jouet superbe et meurtrier. Peu de gens se doutaient qu'une balle pleine à haute vélocité tirée avec un 22 long rifle pouvait transpercer un gilet pare-balles en Kevlar comme le classique modèle classe 2 protégeant les flics. On comprenait pourquoi les services de police aimaient mieux rester discrets sur la question.

Roujio sourit dans sa barbe en s'éloignant de la boutique.

Peel lui fournirait des armes, bien entendu, mais il valait toujours mieux garder un atout caché dans sa manche, au cas où...

Mieux valait l'avoir sans devoir s'en servir, que l'inverse...

26

Dimanche 10 avril
Dans le Raj britannique, aux Indes

La chaleur et l'humidité étaient oppressantes, et l'odeur âcre des fumées du tigre imprégnait l'air plombé. Le fauve était proche, et l'odeur de ses excréments se mêlait à celle de la peur de Jay.

Jay et son guide indigène suivaient les empreintes sur une zone de terrain dégagé. Elles étaient maintenant bien visibles dans la terre meuble. Pas de doute, plus d'erreur possible. La piste traversait la clairière pour s'enfoncer dans un épais fourré composé d'arbres aux troncs larges, de petits buissons denses et bordé d'une haie de bambous.

D'une main moite, Jay assura sa prise sur le Streetsweeper, inspira avec difficulté, expira avec lenteur. Le tigre était entré dans ce fourré et si Jay voulait l'avoir, il allait devoir y pénétrer à son tour. La perspective l'emplissait d'une crainte glaciale comme une cuve d'azote liquide, une frousse qui confinait à la terreur panique.

Il s'immobilisa. Ce qu'il aurait voulu, c'est décrocher de ce scénario, ôter son attirail, éteindre son ordinateur. Il avait envie de se trouver une île dans les mers du Sud quelque part en temps réel, pour filer y lézarder tout un mois sur une plage déserte, sans rien faire d'autre que se dorer au soleil en buvant des trucs avec du rhum et de la noix de coco. La dernière chose dont il eût envie, c'était de plonger dans cette muraille végétale pour pister ce truc qui avait planté son programme et lui avait flanqué la trouille de sa vie. Et s'il devait malgré tout le faire, cela risquait d'être la dernière de toute son existence.

Mais il n'avait pas le choix. Sinon, il avait aussi vite fait de raccrocher les gants ; s'il ne retrouvait pas la bête pour la détruire, il ne valait guère mieux qu'un encéphalogramme plat.

Il prit encore une grande inspiration, expira. « On y va. »

Ils étaient à la lisière du bois quand son guide indigène s'exclama : « Sahib ! Derrière nous ! »

Jay pivota et vit le tigre qui les chargeait, à une vitesse incroyable.

Il avait peut-être une demi-seconde devant lui et il comprit que ce ne serait pas suffisant. « On décroche ! » hurla-t-il.

Dimanche
Washington, DC

Jay sortit de RV pour retomber dans son appartement, paniqué, le cœur battant à tout rompre. Le tigre ! Le tigre ! Il n'arrivait même plus à respirer.

Dans son for intérieur, il savait qu'il devait y retourner. Avant que le fauve ne s'échappe. Il fallait qu'il y retourne. Il avait envie de crier, de pleurer, de fuir, n'importe quoi plutôt que ça.

Et pourtant il lança : « Reprise ! »

Dimanche
Dans le Raj britannique, aux Indes

Jay arriva juste à temps pour voir l'énorme tigre enfoncer ses formidables griffes dans son programme de détection – le guide indigène – et le réduire en débris sanguinolents.

Pauvre Mowgli.

Jay brandit sa carabine : le tigre s'était aperçu de son retour. Le grand fauve toussa, rugit, pivota pour lui faire face. Sans hésiter, il chargea...

Sans reculer d'un pouce, Jay visa...

Quinze mètres, douze, dix...

... Il pressa la détente... Le recul lui enfonça la crosse dans l'épaule. Il fit feu de nouveau, trop vite, trop haut...

... mais la première décharge avait touché le monstre. Il poussa un hurlement de douleur et de surprise, coupa court et détala vers la forêt. Jay aperçut du sang sur une épaule du fauve au moment où il faisait demi-tour pour s'enfuir.

Il l'avait eu ! Il fuyait ! Il n'était pas invincible !

Un éclair de triomphe balaya sa peur. Il avait affronté le monstre, il lui avait tiré dessus, l'avait mis en déroute !

Sa victoire toutefois ne fut que de courte durée.

Il se retrouvait désormais avec un mangeur d'hommes blessé, planqué dans la jungle. Cela n'allait pas lui faciliter la tâche.

Tant pis. Il devait se lancer à ses trousses, et il n'avait pas le temps de charger un autre programme de surveillance, il devait foncer tout de suite.

Jay plongea dans la jungle.

Dimanche
Les Ifs, Sussex, Angleterre

Debout près de la serre, Peel regrettait de ne pas avoir de cigarette. Cela faisait des années qu'il avait cessé de fumer, question de discipline avant tout, une façon de mettre sa volonté à l'épreuve. Tout le monde savait que c'était mauvais pour la santé, mais tant qu'il avait été soldat, il avait toujours pensé mourir les armes à la main ; il n'avait jamais cru vivre assez longtemps pour se faire rattraper par la nicotine. Du reste, son grand-père maternel avait fumé deux paquets par jour jusqu'à près de soixante-dix ans et il était mort à quatre-vingt-quatorze des suites d'une chute, donc tout cela était surtout une histoire de gènes. Et tous les jours jusqu'à sa mort, il s'était bu son whisky.

Non, Peel avait arrêté de fumer parce qu'il voulait se prouver qu'il en était capable. C'était quoi, déjà, la blague : arrêter de fumer ? Facile, je le fais vingt fois par jour.

La pluie avait cessé, il y avait un bout de ciel dégagé juste au-dessus de sa tête, et dans l'obscurité qui gagnait, on distinguait quelques étoiles. Tout était calme, tranquille, rien n'indiquait le moindre problème parmi ses hommes qui montaient la garde sur le domaine. Goswell l'avait invité à lui rendre visite, ils allaient boire un coup, partager une soirée agréable. Il avait son joli magot qui l'attendait à la banque. Bascomb-Coombs vaquait à ses affaires et si tout continuait de se passer aussi bien, Peel serait riche et puissant au-delà de toute imagination dans un avenir proche. D'autant qu'une fois réalisés les plans du scientifique, Peel avait bien l'intention de se débarrasser de lui pour prendre tout seul le relais.

Bref, il voyait mal comment la situation aurait pu mieux tourner pour lui. Malgré tout...

Ça coinçait quelque part.

Il n'aurait su dire où, mettre le doigt sur un point précis, il n'avait rien pour cerner son malaise, mais instinctivement, il le sentait. Un danger planait quelque part. Une cigarette ne l'aurait peut-être pas aidé à le découvrir, mais fumer lui avait toujours éclairci les idées, en lui donnant le temps de peser les problèmes. Comme Sherlock Holmes avec sa pipe, peut-être.

Enfin. Pas question non plus de sonner le branle-bas à cause d'une vague inquiétude. Un simple petit tour du propriétaire devrait suffire à apaiser ses craintes et c'est ce qu'il faisait, mais jusqu'ici, rien de concret ne s'était manifesté. Le danger, si danger il y avait, se matérialiserait bien le moment venu. C'était toujours comme ça. Et la question serait alors de savoir s'il aurait le temps de fourbir ses armes...

Lundi
Washington, DC

Tyrone descendait le couloir pour se rendre à son premier cours de la journée, bousculant les autres lycéens, chacun se hâtant comme lui vers son rendez-vous avec l'éducation.

« Hé, Ty ! »

Il s'arrêta, se retourna, reconnut la voix rien qu'à ces deux mots.

Belladonna Wright.

« Salut, Bella. »

Elle portait une robe bleue ajustée qui lui collait au corps comme de la peinture en bombe et s'arrêtait trente centimètres au-dessus du genou ; la robe était assortie à des sandales à semelles compensées de vingt centimètres, et elle avait remonté ses longs cheveux en une espèce de choucroute qui la faisait paraître encore plus grande. Elle n'était qu'à deux pas de lui.

« Comment va ? »

Il haussa les épaules. « Pas mal. Et toi ?

– Impec. Je t'ai vu avec ton boomerang, l'autre jour.

– Ouais. » Pourquoi lui parlait-elle ? Après qu'il l'eut vue embrasser l'autre crétin dans la galerie marchande et traitée de tous les noms, elle l'avait plaqué comme une vieille chaussette[1]. Ils ne s'étaient pas

1. Cf. *Net Force 2, Programmes fantômes, op. cit.*

reparlé depuis. Et voilà qu'elle se pointait comme une fleur, l'air de rien.

« On t'a pas revu au centre commercial depuis un bail, remarqua-t-elle, tout sourire.

– Non, j'y vais plus trop.

– Tu devrais faire un tour au nouveau resto-rapide. Il est hyperméga-cool.

– Ouais, peut-être un de ces quatre. »

Elle lui adressa encore un de ses sourires Colgate. En inspirant un grand coup pour mettre en valeur ses nibards. Fabuleux, superbes, à croquer, les nibards. Il déglutit, la gorge sèche.

« Bon, ben, alors à plus.

– Ouais, c'est ça », parvint-il à coasser.

Elle s'éloigna, avec une démarche de reine. De dos, elle était tout aussi fabuleuse.

Tyrone avait la cervelle douloureuse. C'était quoi, ce plan ? Elle lui souriait, l'invitait quasiment à sortir, se comportait comme si elle était positivement ravie de le voir ! Alors que la dernière fois qu'ils s'étaient causé (ça remontait à plusieurs mois), elle lui avait verbalement enfoncé le genou dans les parties quand il l'avait accusée d'avoir un autre petit copain, avant de lui conseiller d'oublier son existence ! Merde, qu'est-ce que ça voulait dire ?

La cloche retentit et Tyrone se força à sortir de sa transe pour se hâter de gagner sa classe. Il aurait bien voulu que son père soit à la maison. Peut-être qu'il aurait su lui expliquer tout ça.

Lundi
Siège du MI-6, Londres

Michaels prit soudain conscience du calme qui régnait dans les bureaux et il consulta l'horloge de son ordinateur. Merde, presque minuit !

Il était cassé. À force de rester penché sur la machine toute la journée, il avait de nouveau des courbatures et l'esprit dans le brouillard. La plupart des systèmes informatiques du Royaume-Uni avaient redémarré mais les autres pays européens connaissaient toujours de gros problèmes. Toni avait pris l'Eurostar pour Paris, afin de coordonner avec les autorités françaises la circulation des données. Elle ne devait pas revenir avant mardi soir. Depuis une heure, il commettait des erreurs stupides, les textes défilant sur l'holoprojecteur s'emmêlaient, devenaient incompréhensibles. Il était plus que temps de tout arrêter et de regagner son hôtel.

Il enfila son imper et quitta le bureau. À cette heure, il risquait d'avoir du mal à trouver un taxi en bas de l'immeuble. Il sortit son virgil pour en appeler un tout en se dirigeant vers la sortie.

« On fait des heures sup ? » s'enquit la voix d'Angela dans son dos.

Alex se retourna. « Ouais, mais apparemment, je ne suis pas le seul, pas vrai ?

– J'allais partir. Je vous dépose quelque part ?

– J'appelais un taxi. » Il brandit le virgil. « Je ne voudrais pas vous contraindre à un détour.

– Pas de problème, vous savez. C'est quasiment sur mon chemin.

– Dans ce cas, volontiers. »

Londres était une grande métropole qui ne dormait jamais, et même à minuit, les rues étaient encore encombrées. Combien de gens vivaient ici ? Douze, quinze millions ? Trop en tout cas pour cet espace confiné.

« Vous avancez dans votre enquête ? demanda-t-elle alors qu'ils passaient devant un café dégorgeant ses clients hilares sur le trottoir.

– Pas trop.

– C'est pareil pour nous, convint-elle. La plupart des réseaux britanniques semblent de nouveau en service, mais le reste du monde en est encore à recoller les morceaux. » Du geste, elle indiqua les joyeux fêtards à la sortie du pub. « Ça vous dit de boire une pinte et de grignoter un bout ? »

Alors même qu'elle posait la question, Alex se rendit compte qu'il avait l'estomac dans les talons ; il n'avait pris qu'un sandwich à midi, et rien depuis. « Ce ne serait pas de refus.

– Je connais un coin tranquille pas très loin de chez moi. Ils y servent d'excellents fish and chips. »

Une fois encore, il entendit dans sa tête pépier le petit signal d'alarme mais il était crevé, affamé, et il ne se sentait pas d'humeur à en tenir compte. Quel mal y avait-il à manger une friture arrosée d'une bonne bière ?

« Volontiers. Pourquoi pas ? »

Le pub était presque plein, mais comme promis, assez tranquille. Ils commandèrent des fritures et des pommes-frites, puis allèrent s'installer avec leurs chopes en attendant qu'on leur serve leur repas.

Alex but deux gorgées de sa bière, une brune forte

– de la Terminator Stout. D'un signe de tête, elle indiqua son verre. « À l'origine, elle vient d'Amérique. »

Il regarda la bière. « Pas possible ?

– Tout à fait. Une minuscule brasserie sur la côte Ouest. Un Londonien de passage y a goûté, ça lui a plu, il s'est mis à l'importer. Il ne vous a fallu que deux siècles pour que vous commenciez à produire des bières buvables. Encore une centaine d'années et vous pourriez bien fabriquer un roadster présentable.

– Là, je vous demande pardon. Chevrolet l'a fait avec la Corvette dès 1953.

– Vous vous y connaissez en bagnoles, pas vrai ?

– Un peu, oui.

– Eh bien, il ne leur a pas fallu longtemps pour la gâcher, leur Corvette, vous ne croyez pas ? Elle avait peut-être commencé sous de bons auspices, mais à la longue, elle s'est enflée comme un ballon pour se transformer en monstre boursouflé. Carrosserie plus grosse, moteur plus gros, de l'électronique à tout va, jusqu'à ce qu'elle ressemble à une berline et coûte plus cher qu'une Cadillac. »

Il sourit. « Ma foi, c'est un peu vrai.

– Alors que si vous prenez une MG des années cinquante ou soixante... »

Il la coupa, sarcastique : « Là, je vous arrête. Votre tire, c'est une poubelle. Ils auraient dû songer à les fournir avec un mécano en équipement de série. Votre MG d'époque passait plus de temps à se faire régler en atelier qu'à sillonner les routes.

– Bon, d'accord, je vous accorde que certains modèles étaient un rien capricieux, mais c'est un bien maigre prix à payer pour avoir le plaisir de la conduite.

– Ah, vous voulez dire le plaisir du remorquage. Dites à l'Automobile Club que vous avez une MG, et ils ne prendront même plus vos coups de fil. »

Elle lui sourit.

Leurs plats arrivèrent et l'odeur du flétan grillé et des frites chaudes l'enveloppa de son arôme succulent. Bon sang, c'est vrai qu'il crevait de faim !

Au bout de dix minutes passées à faire honneur au repas, et après la deuxième tournée de bière, Michaels se sentait nettement mieux. C'était sympa de pouvoir souper et d'avoir une conversation tranquille sans rapport avec le boulot. Ils discutèrent des mérites comparés des petits cabriolets japonais et coréens, du nouveau Trekker fabriqué en Afrique du Sud, et il lui parla de la Prowler et de la Miata qu'il avait restaurées.

Mine de rien, il était déjà deux heures du matin.

« On ferait peut-être bien de rentrer. On a du boulot, demain.

– Comment va cette tension musculaire ?

– Il y a du mieux. »

Elle lui posa la main sur la nuque, la fit glisser légèrement jusqu'à l'épaule. « Vous êtes encore tendu comme une corde de violon. » Elle marqua un temps, poursuivit d'une voix douce : « Mon appartement est juste au coin, en haut de la rue. Ça vous dirait que je vous fasse un massage ? »

C'était peut-être l'épuisement. Ou bien les deux bières et le bon repas. Ou encore parce qu'elle était une femme vraiment belle et intelligente, qui de toute évidence appréciait sa compagnie.

Toujours est-il que Michaels acquiesça. « Oui. Très volontiers. »

27

Mardi 12 avril
Dans le Raj britannique, aux Indes

Jay progressait avec un maximum de discrétion. Avec des résultats mitigés compte tenu de sa nervosité et du terrain sur lequel il évoluait. Traquer le fauve n'était toutefois pas un problème : les fourrés étaient piétinés et maculés de sang, et la piste était rectiligne, signe manifeste de la panique de la bête. Le tigre filait tout droit, sans chercher à se cacher.

Ou du moins, c'est l'impression qu'il donnait. Il avait déjà réussi à se faufiler derrière Jay et ce dernier n'avait pas l'intention de se faire avoir une deuxième fois. Aussi restait-il constamment aux aguets, tournant la tête sans cesse, comme s'il assistait à un match de tennis.

À la base de ce qui évoquait un énorme baobab, la piste s'évanouissait soudain.

Jay leva les yeux.

Dix mètres au-dessus du sol, le tigre gronda et se mit à charger en dégringolant le long du tronc, courant collé contre celui-ci comme s'il se jouait de la gravité !

Jay ne réfléchit même pas. Il leva d'un coup la carabine, la plaqua contre sa joue et fit feu. Mobilisant toutes ses forces pour résister au recul, il tira de nouveau.

Le tigre dégringola de l'arbre. Jay fit un écart à droite assorti d'un mouvement pivotant pour plaquer son arme au niveau de la hanche, et pressa la détente, alors que le fauve heurtait rudement le sol. Le choc fut avec assez violent pour ébranler le jeune homme, tapi à moins de deux mètres de là, le doigt toujours crispé sur la gâchette.

Il perdit le compte du nombre de coups tirés, il avait l'impression d'une salve continue. L'odeur cuivrée du sang du tigre vint se mêler à celle de la poudre brûlée et quand Jay cessa enfin de tirer, le sol était jonché de douilles en plastique rouges ou vertes, une douzaine au moins, peut-être plus.

En tout cas, le fauve ne tressaillait même plus.

Tremblant de tous ses membres, Jay laissa enfin échapper un grand soupir en expirant lentement, pour la première fois depuis de longues secondes.

La bête qui lui avait déchiqueté le cerveau de ses griffes acérées était enfin morte. Il l'avait tuée.

Mais alors qu'il se penchait pour examiner le cadavre, il comprit que ce n'était pas ce qu'il avait cherché. Oh, bien sûr, la bête l'avait attaqué et blessé, mais à présent qu'il l'avait tuée, il devenait conscient qu'il ne s'agissait là que d'un programme de sécurité, pas de la mystérieuse créature qui avait, dénotant une force incroyable, fait sauter les cages réputées inviolables des systèmes informatiques les plus perfectionnés de la planète. C'était peut-être ce qu'il avait rencontré de plus dangereux jusqu'ici en RV, mais ce n'était jamais que l'équivalent d'un chien de garde, lancé dans la jungle pour s'occuper des petits curieux comme lui, et sans commune mesure avec la puissance de son maître, l'entité inconnue qui l'avait ainsi placé en protection.

Non, le véritable monstre rôdait toujours. Et Jay savait que ce n'était pas sa pétoire qui pourrait le ralentir, si jamais il devait tomber dessus.

Bigre.

Mardi
Paris

Il était trois heures du matin et Toni n'arrivait toujours pas à trouver le sommeil. Son grand lit était pourtant confortable, sa chambre bien isolée et située à un étage assez élevé pour que le bruit de la circulation dans la rue en bas de l'hôtel ne soit qu'un murmure assourdi.

Elle avait eu une journée relativement tranquille, durant laquelle elle avait pu collecter et trier pas mal de données, avant de terminer en s'offrant un dîner aussi délicieux que copieux. Elle avait même pu s'entraîner un peu dans la salle de gym dont disposait l'hôtel avant de passer une demi-heure à se relaxer dans l'eau brûlante d'un bain bouillonnant. Elle aurait dû dormir comme un chérubin.

Et pourtant, elle avait l'esprit agité ; certes, l'inquiétude qu'elle ressentait aurait pu être due au boulot, mais non. C'était Alex. Il y avait un problème entre eux et elle ignorait lequel. Il était fâché après elle, elle le sentait bien malgré ses dénégations, et elle ne savait pas quoi faire.

Oh, elle avait bien tenté d'avoir une explication :

Alex ? Est-ce que tout va bien ?

Ouaip. Tout baigne.

T'es sûr ? Ai-je dit ou fait quoi que ce soit pour te contrarier ?

Non, Toni, je te répète que tout va bien. Je suis juste fatigué, c'est tout.

Puis il lui avait adressé un sourire crispé, sincère en apparence, mais sans grande conviction.

Comment vouliez-vous surmonter ça ? Combien de fois reposer la question sans paraître entêtée ? Et une fois obtenue une réponse, jusqu'à quel point s'y fier ? N'était-ce pas sa responsabilité ? S'il disait que tout allait bien, ne devait-elle pas l'accepter ?

Eh bien, avec les hommes, non. C'est en tout cas ce que lui dictait son expérience. Ils n'avaient pas le cerveau câblé comme les femmes. Ils disaient une chose mais ce qu'ils voulaient dire était tout différent.

À qui pouvait-elle s'en ouvrir ? Elle avait bien des copines aux États-Unis, prêtes à l'écouter et à la conseiller. Ou alors, elle pouvait peut-être appeler sa mère. Quel était le décalage horaire entre Paris et le Bronx ? Six heures ? Il devait donc être neuf heures du soir, là-bas. En ce moment, maman somnolait sans doute devant l'écran géant à plasma. De toute manière, ce n'était pas vraiment le genre de sujet dont on discutait volontiers avec une mère comme elle. Cela faisait si longtemps qu'elle supportait son père qu'il n'y avait pour elle qu'une façon d'aborder le problème, et du reste, Toni doutait que papa eût jamais, de toute son existence, exprimé tout haut devant quiconque une émotion un peu complexe : *Comment ça ? Une espèce de femmelette qui vient geindre et se plaindre de tes sentiments ? Dehors !*

Non, il fallait d'une manière ou de l'autre qu'elle arrive à se débrouiller toute seule. Dès son retour à Londres, elle essaierait de trouver le temps – elle le prendrait – d'avoir une discussion à cœur ouvert avec Alex. Ils trouveraient bien une solution. Elle l'aimait, il l'aimait, le plus dur était fait, non ?

Mardi
Londres

L'appartement d'Angela était situé dans une rangée de petits pavillons mitoyens sur Denbigh Street. Pas grand, mais propre et bien tenu, séjour, cuisine, chambre et salle de bains. Et elle avait effectivement une table de massage installée dans le tout petit salon. Michaels lui en fit la remarque : en pratiquait-elle tant qu'elle dût laisser la table à demeure ?

Non, elle venait juste de la sortir et de la monter le jour même.

Un petit déclic résonna dans la tête d'Alex : *Oh-oh.*

Elle lui tendit un drap. « Déshabillez-vous et allongez-vous sur le ventre. Couvrez-vous avec ça. Je vais ôter ma tenue de travail pour passer quelque chose qui m'engonce un peu moins. »

Elle s'éclipsa dans la chambre et Michaels se retrouva seul dans l'appartement d'une femme séduisante qu'il connaissait à peine, un drap plié entre les mains, et avec la perspective de devoir ôter ses vêtements.

Ce n'était peut-être pas une bonne idée.

Et puis, encore une fois, elle avait bien une table de massage et elle semblait effectivement s'y connaître en techniques de décontraction.

Il laissa échapper un gros soupir. Et puis merde.

Il se dévêtit pour se retrouver en sous-vêtement – un minislip de soie noire, cadeau de Toni –, s'allongea sur la table, à plat ventre, se recouvrit du drap.

Quand Angela revint dans le séjour, elle portait un cuissard en Elastiss gris et un caraco.

Sympa, le cuissard collant.

« Prêt ?

– Prêt ! »

Elle commença par lui enfoncer le coude dans les dorsales, et au bout de deux minutes, il commença à se relaxer. Quelque part, il était un peu déçu, après tout, ça n'allait être qu'un banal massage, mais pour l'essentiel, c'était le soulagement qui dominait. C'était une femme intelligente et belle, mais sa vie était déjà bien assez compliquée.

Elle consacra une demi-heure à travailler l'assouplissement des vertèbres. Puis elle passa aux cuisses et il sentit qu'il se crispait un peu, mais Angela restait pour sa part toujours aussi décontractée ; elle lui pétrissait les jambes avec assez d'énergie pour que ce soit presque douloureux, découvrant chaque jambe tour à tour avant de reborder le drap pour lui couvrir le reste du corps.

Puis elle s'attaqua aux pieds et aux chevilles avant de remonter vers les fesses, en glissant cette fois les mains sous les draps. « Ça ne va pas, comme ça », nota-t-elle avant de lui ôter prestement son slip en le faisant glisser sur les jambes et les pieds.

« Euh... Angela... ?

– Relax, Alex. Je ne peux pas travailler convenablement le muscle s'il n'est pas découvert. »

Il essaya bien de se relaxer, mais avec les doigts de la jeune femme qui lui pétrissaient allégrement le cul, ce n'était pas évident du tout. C'était même plutôt dur.

Et malheureusement, il n'y avait pas que ça de dur chez lui. Mais il était sur le ventre, ce n'était donc pas gênant... juste un tantinet inconfortable.

Après cinq minutes passées à se laisser masser les fesses, il commençait à se détendre à nouveau quand elle lança tout de go : « Parfait. À présent, retournez-vous !

– Pardon ?

– Le dos, voyez-vous, ce n'est que la moitié de votre anatomie. J'ai besoin de travailler aussi le devant. »

Fichtre. Comment allait-il pouvoir expliquer ça ? Sa... hum, *condition* présente ?

« Euh, c'est-à-dire que... enfin... voyez-vous, me retourner pourrait s'avérer comme qui dirait, eh bien, enfin, euh...

– On est un peu excité ? Vous en faites donc pas pour ça, Alex. Ce ne sera ni la première ni la dernière fois. Ça arrive tout le temps. »

Elle souleva le drap. « Tournez-vous, je vais vous le tenir. »

Il n'était pas enthousiasmé à la perspective de rouler sur le dos et ainsi lui révéler où son esprit était descendu se nicher – dès qu'elle allait relâcher le drap, il allait évoquer une tente de camping – mais enfin, bon, à la guerre comme à la guerre. Il garda les yeux fermés et se retourna.

« Mon Dieu, s'écria-t-elle. Comme c'est charmant. »

Il rouvrit les yeux au moment où Angela laissait tomber le drap à terre et grimpait sur la table pour l'enfourcher.

Son cuissard avait également disparu – comment s'en était-elle débarrassée ? Mystère. Et elle n'avait rien enfilé dessous. Encore une seconde, et c'était elle qu'il allait enfiler, et il sentait que si jamais cela devait se produire, son esprit partirait en roue libre. Il serait fichu.

« Hé, Angela ?

– Hmmm ?

– Écoutez, je ne peux vraiment pas.

– De toute évidence, si. Et ce n'est certainement pas l'envie qui vous manque. Je le vois bien. » Elle indiqua l'objet du délit.

« Certes, mais le problème est que je ne peux pas. Je suis pris.

– Ce n'est pas moi qui irai le lui raconter. Personne n'en saura rien. »

Alex secoua la tête. « Moi, si. »

Elle se recula, le toisa. « Vous en êtes sûr ? »

Soupir. « Ouais. »

De retour dans sa chambre, Michaels s'éveilla d'un sommeil agité au son du virgil jouant *Bad to the Bone* – « Mal jusqu'au bout des doigts ». Putain, ce que ça pouvait être vrai.

Toni !

Bon Dieu.

Il n'était pas dans la merde, à présent.

Le virgil s'entêtait à lui seriner qu'il était mal, mal, mal, et il se leva pour dénicher le satané bidule. Ouais, bon, d'accord, il n'avait rien commis de répréhensible, mais il n'aurait jamais dû se rendre chez Angela, il avait tout de suite su que c'était une erreur, pourtant il y était allé quand même. Et si l'on pouvait vous pendre pour vos pensées, alors il devrait déjà se balancer au bout d'une corde. En tout cas, la dernière chose dont il avait envie, c'était d'en parler à qui que ce soit, surtout à Toni.

Il s'abstint d'activer l'écran. « Allô ?

– Salut, patron ! »

Jay Gridley. Dieu soit loué. « Mon petit Jay. Comment va ?

– Nettement mieux. J'ai réussi à coincer le programme de sécurité qui m'a niqué le crâne et cramé les neurones.

– Félicitations.

– Ça, c'était le b-a ba de l'opération, chef. Le plus dur à présent, ça va être de retrouver le gars qui l'a concocté. Mais ça devrait toujours être plus facile qu'en partant de zéro.

– Bien.

– Et, euh... est-ce que Toni est près de vous ? »

Michaels sentit une poigne glaciale lui étreindre le cœur. « Euh, non, elle est à Paris. Elle doit rentrer cet après-midi.

– Alors, je lui repasserai un coup de fil. Il y a dans ses fichiers certains éléments auxquels j'aurais besoin d'accéder.

– Très bien.

– Au fait, comment ça se passe, à Londres ? Vous vous amusez bien ? »

Bonne question. Eh bien non, pas vraiment. Il s'échinait à devenir le plus grand salopard de menteur infidèle qu'ait connu la planète. D'accord, d'un strict point de vue technique, il n'avait pas commis d'infidélité, mais à coup sûr, c'était ce qu'il ressentait. Il avait l'impression d'avoir frôlé le carton rouge.

« Ouais, répondit-il néanmoins. Super. Bon, on en recause plus tard, Jay. Tiens-moi au courant. »

Il coupa son virgil. Bon Dieu ! Comment avait-il pu se montrer aussi con ? Deux ou trois verres, un bon repas, une séance de massage, cela n'avait tout de même rien de si méchant. Et puis, il avait quand même la nuque douloureuse, non ? Se déshabiller devant une toubib ou une kiné, il n'y avait pas de mal à ça. Mais l'idée de pouvoir aller plus loin lui avait traversé l'esprit, il était bien forcé de l'admettre. S'il pouvait se targuer d'une quelconque victoire, ce n'était que d'un cheveu, et encore celle-ci avait-elle comme un goût de défaite.

Il allait falloir de toute manière qu'il en parle à Toni.

La question était : comment s'y prendre ? Oh, au fait, pendant que tu étais à Paris, eh bien, tu sais, je suis passé chez Angela, je me suis déloqué, je l'ai laissé me masser le dos, et elle a bien failli passer de l'autre côté...

Quand diable allait-il pouvoir amener ça avec diplomatie dans le cours de la conversation ?

Bigre.

28

Mardi 12 avril
Londres

Goswell leva les yeux par-dessus son exemplaire du *Times* pour regarder Sir Harold Bellworth, assis à mâchouiller le cigare que, par négligence, il avait laissé s'éteindre. Le vieux garçon avait demandé à Paddington d'aller lui chercher une autre allumette et Goswell jugea le moment propice pour aborder le sujet qu'il avait en tête.

« Je pensais à quelque chose... Harry ? »

Bellworth quitta des yeux son cigare éteint. « Hein ? Quoi ?

– Vous vous rappelez sans doute cette histoire que vous avez eue avec cet... Arménien, si je ne me trompe, il y a quelques mois ? »

Bellworth renifla avec dégoût. « Un peu, que je m'en souviens ! Un sacré filou, ce gaillard, à venir oser ainsi fouiner dans mes affaires !

– Eh bien, j'ai appris qu'il avait eu un... accident malencontreux[1].

– Ça, on peut le dire. Tombé d'un quai de métro et écrasé par une rame. Bien fait pour lui. Enfin, ce n'était

1. Cf. *Net Force 1, op. cit.*

pas une grande perte, ça fera toujours un de ces fichus étrangers de moins. »

Goswell attendit le retour de Paddington. Ce dernier craqua une allumette, attendit que la flamme s'élève, puis se pencha pour permettre à Bellworth de rallumer son barreau de chaise cubain. Un nuage de fumée odorante s'éleva tandis que le vieux garçon tirait sur le cigare pour lui redonner vie.

« Vous êtes bien aimable, Paddington. »

Le majordome rapprocha imperceptiblement le cendrier. Bellworth avait la triste réputation de secouer ses cendres sur les tapis... « Ce n'est rien, sir. Voudrez-vous autre chose ?

– Non, non, ça ira comme ça.

– Très bien, sir. »

Paddington s'évanouit comme une ombre.

Bellworth reporta son attention sur Goswell. « Pourquoi diable mettez-vous sur le tapis un sujet aussi peu ragoûtant, Gossie ?

–Ma foi, ça me gêne de l'admettre, mais j'avoue connaître moi aussi un problème similaire. Je crois bien que j'aurais besoin de l'aide de quelqu'un de... discret pour me le régler. »

Bellworth tira une bouffée du cigare, puis le retourna pour en contempler le bout incandescent, avant de hocher la tête, abrité derrière le nuage de fumée grise. « Vous avez certainement sous la main du personnel pour prendre ce genre de disposition, sans aucun doute ?

– Justement, j'ai bien peur que le problème ne vienne de l'un d'eux. Et charger de la besogne un de ses subordonnés ne serait certes pas la solution idéale, n'est-ce pas ?

– Dieu du ciel, non, très mauvais pour le moral des troupes, j'en conviens. Eh bien, dans ce cas, voulez-vous que je passe un coup de fil à mon ami, pour lui dire de vous appeler ?

– Si ce n'est pas trop vous demander, Harry.

– Mais pas du tout, pas du tout, considérez que c'est une affaire entendue. À présent, que pensez-vous de la proposition de Lord Cleese de relancer les chantiers pour nécessiteux ? J'ai trouvé pour ma part l'idée fort astucieuse... »

Goswell sourit. Voilà un sujet sur lequel ils pouvaient s'accorder sans conteste. Remettre au boulot les pauvres plutôt que de leur verser des allocations chômage... Ces fichus socialistes allaient bien finir par signer la mort du pays si personne ne les empêchait de nuire et, de l'humble avis de Goswell, les suggestions de ce genre étaient frappées au coin du bon sens. Ça ne se réaliserait pas, bien sûr, ces diables de socialos feraient jouer leurs foutues relations si jamais quelqu'un s'avisait de déposer un texte en ce sens, mais malgré tout, cela ébranlerait toujours l'opinion si le Parlement devait être amené à discuter un tel projet. Sans aucun doute.

Il semblait condamné à mener sa petite guerre personnelle contre l'absurdité du monde, vu la façon dont ses instruments initiaux avaient été pervertis. Il soupira. Compte tenu de l'époque, on devait s'y attendre, mais cela restait quand même toujours une surprise. On ne pouvait tout bonnement plus compter sur personne de nos jours, en tout cas, plus comme dans le temps.

Affligeant !

Mardi
Londres

Toni ne s'était pas attendue à voir Alex le guetter dans la cohue à l'arrivée de l'Eurostar, mais il était pourtant bien là pour l'attendre à la gare. Son déplacement à Paris l'avait fatiguée et l'air dans le long tunnel sous la Manche lui avait paru bien confiné, même si ce n'était sans doute que psychologique... Toute cette masse d'eau qui pesait, invisible, au-dessus de votre tête. Encore heureux qu'elle ne soit pas claustrophobe.... Elle se sentait abattue mais son moral remonta aussitôt qu'elle l'aperçut.

« Alex ! Qu'est-ce que tu fais ici ? »

Ils tombèrent dans les bras l'un de l'autre. Il prit son sac et répondit : « Je m'ennuyais de toi. Bienvenue au bercail, chou. Alors, comment ça s'est passé ?

– Pas mal du tout. La plupart des Français savent très bien se tenir. C'est uniquement de la faute de quelques énergumènes s'ils ont aussi mauvaise réputation. Et tant qu'on ne fait pas semblant de comprendre leur langue ou de vouloir s'entêter à la parler, même les garçons de café finissent par ne pas être trop insupportables.

– Et puis, tu as toujours eu un faible pour les gens qui appréciaient Jerry Lewis, remarqua-t-il.

– C'était un génie du comique. Savoir faire des simagrées, c'est un art, tu sais. »

Il rit. C'était devenu une blague récurrente entre eux. Mais Jerry Lewis était incontestablement drôle : il avait su créer ce personnage de pitre, il lui avait donné ses lettres de noblesse et, sur la fin de sa carrière, plusieurs de ses rôles avaient été tout à fait remarquables. C'était un comédien sous-estimé.

« Du nouveau, ici ?

– Non... pas vraiment. Enfin, excepté que j'ai reçu un coup de fil de John Howard. Il vient de se poser sur une base aérienne au nord de Londres.

– Le colonel ? Qu'est-ce qu'il vient faire ici ?

– Le tueur à gages de Plekhanov, ce Roujio... eh bien, ils ont retrouvé sa trace en Angleterre.

– Formidable. Un pavé de plus dans la mare. »

Il ne releva pas.

« T'as l'air crevé, remarqua-t-elle.

– Je n'ai pas trop bien dormi.

– Je parie que je peux y remédier ce soir...

– Je te crois volontiers. »

Elle lui étreignit le bras. Il lui sourit. Leurs voies avaient eu tendance à diverger ces derniers temps. L'heure était sans doute venue pour eux de faire à nouveau route ensemble. Elle reprit : « T'as parlé à Jay ? Il m'a appelée. Il va mieux.

– Ouais. Je suis content de l'apprendre.

– Selon lui, il ne serait plus loin de démasquer notre pirate.

– Eh bien, enfin une bonne nouvelle sur ce front. Il était temps. »

Il semblait un rien crispé, mais il n'y avait qu'à voir sa mine, il était crevé, c'était sûr. Une bonne douche chaude et un gros câlin sous la couette leur feraient le plus grand bien à tous les deux. Elle avait hâte de faire l'amour avec lui. Et elle devait bien l'avouer, elle commençait à se sentir excitée à force d'entraînements avec Carl. Mieux valait pour elle évacuer au plus vite ce trop-plein de tension.

Mardi Cambridge

Howard était assis sur la banquette de la Ford, derrière Julio et le chauffeur que leur avait prêté la RAF. Ils descendaient vers Londres sur la M11. Ils dépassèrent des pancartes annonçant les sorties de Bishops Stratford et Sawbridgeworth, et n'eussent été la couleur et le lettrage des panonceaux, ils auraient pu se trouver sur n'importe quelle autoroute américaine traversant la campagne new-yorkaise ou nord-californienne. La végétation était similaire, les traces d'urbanisation pas si différentes. À ceci près qu'ils roulaient du mauvais côté de la chaussée.

Julio était assis à la place dévolue d'ordinaire au chauffeur et il semblait un peu plus détendu que quelques minutes plus tôt, lorsqu'ils avaient emprunté des artères à double voie de circulation. Sitôt quittée la base, chaque fois qu'ils voyaient débouler un véhicule au sortir d'un virage, Howard l'avait vu se crisper et son gros pied écraser une pédale de frein imaginaire. Il comprenait ce réflexe, ayant eu à plusieurs reprises exactement le même.

Pourquoi, au nom du ciel, les Britanniques avaient-ils choisi de conduire du mauvais côté de la route ?

On devait bien finir par s'y habituer mais Howard n'était pas pressé de tenter l'expérience.

Ils étaient encore à quarante-cinq kilomètres du centre de Londres, leur annonça le chauffeur, mais ils filaient à près de cent vingt à l'heure. Ils se rendaient au MI-6 retrouver le commandant Michaels pour l'informer des derniers développements de leur traque du « Fusil » – puisque telle était la traduction de son pseudonyme russe : le bonhomme était doté en plus d'un sens de l'humour assez particulier.

« Tout va bien, là où vous êtes, sergent ?

– Affirmatif, mon colonel. Je suis idéalement placé pour profiter du paysage. »

Leur chauffeur, un aviateur, sourit. « J'ai eu l'occasion de rendre visite à mon oncle qui habite New York. Eh bien, j'ai cru devenir cinglé la première fois que je suis monté en voiture avec lui. Pourquoi vous autres Yankees avez-vous décidé de conduire du mauvais côté de la chaussée ?

– Erreur, l'Angliche, protesta aussitôt Fernandez. C'est quoi, déjà, la marque de cette tire ? FORD, F-O-R-D, non ? C'est nous qui avons inventé les voitures, alors c'était à nous de choisir de quel côté rouler.

– Sans vouloir vous offenser, sergent, d'où tenez-vous cette idée saugrenue ? Henry Ford n'a jamais été qu'un pâle imitateur. Les fabriquer comme des petits pains, ce n'est quand même pas la même chose que d'avoir construit la première, vous ne croyez pas ?

– Vous n'allez tout de même pas me sortir sans broncher que c'est aux Anglais qu'on doit l'invention de l'automobile ?

– C'est pourtant la stricte vérité, sergent.

– Mon cul, oui. »

Le sourire du chauffeur s'élargit. « Bon, je vous l'accorde. Chacun sait que ce sont les bouffeurs de grenouille qui ont inventé le premier engin automobile à vapeur, avec le fardier tricycle du Français Nicolas-Joseph Cugnot, en 1769. Mais dès les années 1830, quantité d'inventeurs en Angleterre et sur le continent avaient fabriqué et commercialisé des engins de traction à vapeur... Vous en aviez même aux États-Unis dès la fin de la guerre de Sécession. Mais je suis bien d'accord avec vous, on ne parle pas ici de locomotives en réduction se traînant sur des chemins de terre... Mais d'automobiles, des vraies.

« Eh bien, la première vraie voiture, dotée d'un moteur à combustion interne, aurait été construite par Sam Brown. Avec son engin qui fonctionnait au carbure d'hydrogène, il aurait gravi Shooter's Hill, à Londres, entre 1823 et 1826, selon ses propres dires, ce brave vieux Sam n'étant pas trop précis sur les dates. Toujours est-il que c'est quand même un poil plus tôt que John Lambert, qui a assemblé la première voiture d'Amérique en 1891 seulement... Coiffant ainsi de près de deux ans les frères Duryea, traditionnellement considérés comme les premiers inventeurs... mais enfin, ce n'est qu'une goutte d'eau comparé à près de soixante-dix ans, non ?

– Formidable, grommela Fernandez. Bien ma veine de tomber sur l'historien patenté du royaume en guise de chauffeur. »

Rire de l'intéressé. « On doit toujours connaître son outil de travail, pas vrai ? Puisque je conduis une voiture, autant que je sache à peu près de quoi il retourne, non ? »

Ce fut au tour de Fernandez de rigoler. « Un point

pour vous. Une question, tout de même : de quel côté on conduit en France ? Hein ?

– On s'en fout, répondit l'aviateur britannique. D'abord, ce sont de foutus Français, alors ! »

Cette fois, même Howard dut en rire.

Mardi
Londres

Roujio retrouva Peel au pied d'une gigantesque réclame Coca-Cola qui scintillait de milliers d'ampoules blanches et rouges. Ils devaient discuter de sa mission mais, interrogé à ce sujet, Peel se contenta de hocher la tête. « Laissons ça de côté pour l'instant. J'ai autre chose à vous demander. »

Roujio haussa un sourcil. « Ah bon ? »

Des touristes se bousculaient sur les trottoirs. Un groupe de pensionnaires en uniforme, marchant deux par deux, main dans la main, se faufilait au milieu de la cohue, chenille blanc et bleu.

Peel avait l'air nerveux : il ne cessait de surveiller les alentours, discrètement mais avec insistance, comme s'il se sentait observé. « J'ai besoin de quelqu'un pour couvrir mes arrières, expliqua-t-il. J'ai dans l'idée que j'ai dû écraser les arpions de certains. »

Roujio acquiesça. « D'accord. On sait qui ?

– Pas avec certitude. J'ai bien une idée, mais il faudra que je la creuse.

– Pourquoi moi ? »

La véritable question était : *Pourquoi me faire confiance* à moi *? On ne se connaît quand même pas si bien que ça. Et tu dois déjà avoir tes hommes de main.*

Peel répondit à la partie non formulée de la question : « Parce que vous n'avez aucune raison de vouloir ma mort. »

Roujio demeura impassible. « Pas que je sache, en effet. »

Petit sourire crispé de son interlocuteur. « Vous avez une arme ?

– Pas encore », mentit Roujio, d'une voix neutre.

Peel sortit alors de son blouson une pochette de nylon bleu marine dotée d'une fermeture à glissière qu'il lui tendit : « Beretta, modèle 21A, calibre 22. Italien, mais celui-ci a été fabriqué en Amérique. Six balles dans le chargeur, une dans le canon. Double détente au premier coup, si on le désire, barillet à mécanisme basculant.

– Je connais ce modèle.

– Vous avez deux chargeurs supplémentaires, déjà garnis. Avec des Minimag CCI, à âme pleine. J'aurais pu vous avoir une arme plus conséquente, mais j'ai cru comprendre que les agents des Spetsnatz affectionnaient les petits calibres.

– On fera avec. Et sinon, il tire comment ? »

Peel hocha la tête, comme s'il avait anticipé la question, mais était néanmoins ravi de l'entendre. « Je n'ai pas eu le temps de demander à mon armurier de le roder, donc la double détente est sans doute un peu raide, réglée dans les dix-douze livres. En simple détente aussi, ça doit tourner autour de cinq livres, mais avec un peu plus de répondant. La hausse est réglée pile pour sept mètres, sinon, à vingt-cinq, le tir dévie de cinq centimètres au-dessus et d'un poil sur la droite.

– Pigé.

– Bref, j'aimerais que vous le gardiez sous la main. Et si jamais vous deviez voir quelqu'un me surprendre par-derrière avec une arme à feu ou un couteau, vous me le descendez, voulez-vous ? »

Roujio lui adressa un bref salut militaire, glissa dans son blouson la pochette, et une fois celle-ci planquée dans la poche, en ouvrit la fermeture Éclair. Il retira le pistolet et du pouce, à tâtons, ôta le cran de sûreté. Avec son canon court, le Beretta ne serait pas aussi précis que sa carabine-parapluie, mais c'était toujours ça en plus. Et Peel ne tarderait pas à en voir la couleur.

Le Russe se perdit dans la foule derrière lui, touriste parmi d'autres muni d'un parapluie, pour protéger ses arrières de tout danger potentiel. Peel se sentait un peu mieux, un peu plus en sécurité. C'était peut-être entièrement dans sa tête, un simple fantasme, cette certitude d'être filé, mais s'il avait survécu jusqu'ici, c'était parce qu'il s'était toujours fié à son instinct. Certes, il se trompait de temps en temps, mais il valait mieux une fausse alerte que prendre des risques...

Un jour, il bivouaquait avec un commando parachutiste en stage d'entraînement dans les bois, quelque part en Nouvelle-Galles-du-Sud. Ils avaient déjà progressé, sac sur le dos, sur plus de vingt-cinq kilomètres de pistes défoncées, au pied des collines. Ils n'étaient qu'à six cents mètres d'altitude, en terrain aride, une épaisse poussière rouge recouvrait tout et s'élevait en nuages denses chaque fois qu'ils mettaient le pied dehors. Ils avaient dressé leur camp dans une petite clairière entourée d'un maquis si dense qu'on aurait dit une muraille végétale.

La nuit tombait et les hommes s'apprêtaient à préparer le dîner quand la panique l'envahit. Une terreur soudaine, absolue, si prompte et si intense qu'il n'avait eu qu'une envie : fuir sur-le-champ, détaler à toutes jambes.

C'était parfaitement irrationnel. Il n'y avait aucune menace à proximité, pas un chat à des kilomètres, pour autant qu'ils le sachent. Il essaya de se raisonner. Merde, lui, un agent entraîné, un lieutenant qui avait fait ses classes au combat, jeune, brave, armé jusqu'aux dents, accompagné de six rudes gaillards, des durs à cuire dotés de la même artillerie... et il n'y avait rien dans ce foutu maquis qui pût constituer une menace sérieuse. Mais peu importait, il ne pouvait se départir de ce mauvais pressentiment. Sans la moindre explication, et en faisant comme si c'était prévu dans l'exercice, il ordonna à ses hommes de rempaqueter fissa et d'être prêts à lever le camp dans les cinq minutes. Il leur en fallut presque sept, mais dès qu'ils furent prêts, Peel les fit s'éloigner à marche forcée sur près de dix kilomètres avant que ce sentiment de danger ne le quitte. Ils plantèrent à nouveau leurs tentes, établirent un tour de garde.

Aux petites heures du matin, la sentinelle réveilla Peel en lui indiquant une lueur orangée qui envahissait le ciel. Un feu de forêt.

Plus tard, en vérifiant, Peel constata que le départ de feu s'était produit juste en contrebas de leur camp initial. Le front de flammes avait progressé avec une telle rapidité que des chevreuils s'étaient fait surprendre en pleine fuite : s'ils étaient restés là-bas, lui et ses gars, pas un n'aurait survécu.

Ses hommes s'étaient montrés impressionnés.

Comment avait-il su ? Une vague odeur de fumée indécelable par quiconque d'autre que lui ? Des animaux pris d'une frayeur si intense qu'ils auraient réussi à la lui transmettre ?

Il y avait longtemps réfléchi, sans jamais parvenir à une réponse satisfaisante. Mais plus essentiel que le « comment » restait le fait concret qu'il ait réussi. Un sens inconnu l'avait averti de l'imminence de la mort, et il avait eu le bon sens de se conformer à cet avertissement.

Depuis, la chose s'était reproduite à l'occasion de plusieurs feux de brousse au cours de patrouilles, quoique jamais de manière aussi spectaculaire que lors de cet incident en Australie, et chaque fois qu'il avait senti le doigt froid de la mort sur son épaule, il avait obéi à l'injonction. Plus d'une fois, une telle attitude lui avait sauvé la vie.

Il n'y avait aucun ennemi en vue ici mais la peur était bien là. La seule cause possible était le scientifique. Personne à part lui n'était au courant de ce qu'il tramait et le bonhomme avait sans nul doute quelque chose à cacher. Sinon, ça ne tenait pas debout : ce million que lui donnait Bascomb-Coombs, et cette proposition d'en faire pour ainsi dire un associé dans son plan, mais qui d'autre à part lui ?

Cela dit, il devait bien admettre qu'il n'avait pas eu ce magot sous les yeux... L'intégralité de la somme n'était garantie que par la signature d'une banque indonésienne ; en temps normal, cela aurait dû suffire, seulement Bascomb-Coombs était à la fois le propriétaire et l'opérateur du système informatique le plus vicieux qu'on ait jamais conçu... Nul doute qu'il était à même d'entuber quiconque n'avait pas la capacité de voir clair dans son petit jeu, si tel était son désir.

Mais pourquoi désirerait-il faire une chose pareille ?

Peel n'en avait pas la moindre idée, mais il sentait planer la menace et n'avait aucune envie d'en être la victime. Mieux valait prendre des mesures pour le découvrir, et surtout, faire vite. Et si l'auteur était Bascomb-Coombs, eh bien, tout son génie ne le protégerait pas d'un poignard entre les côtes ou d'une balle dans la nuque. S'il fallait en venir là, l'épée s'avérait une meilleure arme que la plume, pas de doute.

Peel se rendit à pied à la gare, quelque peu rasséréné maintenant qu'il avait décidé d'agir.

29

Mardi 12 avril
Washington, DC

Sojan Ripoche devait passer voir Jay. Il venait chez lui, en chair et en os, et le jeune homme n'était pas peu nerveux.

L'avantage de la réalité virtuelle était qu'on pouvait se fabriquer l'image de son choix. Certes, Jay avait tendance à conserver son aspect habituel dans la majorité des scénarios, parce que cela ne valait pas vraiment la peine de se fatiguer à inventer un personnage pour le seul plaisir d'impressionner les gens. Bon, d'accord, il s'améliorait un poil sur les bords : il avait l'air un peu plus grand, un peu plus musclé, avec des traits un rien plus virils, mais pas au point d'être méconnaissable quand on le croisait dans le MR. De toute façon, passé un certain nombre d'années à surfer en RV, on ne faisait plus trop attention à la dégaine adoptée par les autres joueurs. Vous les retrouviez hors connexion à l'occasion de telle ou telle conférence et vous aviez du mal à associer la personnalité réelle au personnage virtuel. Dans bon nombre de cas, ils se fabriquaient une image d'allure entièrement différente mais sans prendre la peine d'altérer leur voix et entendre celle-ci jaillir d'un corps totalement méconnaissable faisait parfois un effet bizarre. Ou bien, cas inverse, ils modifiaient leur voix mais pas leur visage, et ça aussi, ça faisait drôle.

Bref, la vérité était un domaine éminemment subjectif en réalité virtuelle. Le terme par lui-même avait quelque chose d'un oxymore...

Saji avait dit à Jay sur le Net qu'il devait passer une quinzaine à Washington, aussi lui avait-il demandé s'il avait envie d'une rencontre en temps réel. Jay avait accepté, non sans quelques réserves, malgré tout. Saji lui avait certes sauvé la peau, et il lui devait une hyper-BSFC – « Bougre de Sacrée Fière Chandelle » – mais quelque part, une vague inquiétude le rongeait : celle que le Saji réel ne fût pas à la hauteur de sa version virtuelle. Parfois, on répugnait à faire la connaissance de quelqu'un pour qui on éprouvait le plus grand respect, par peur que la réalité ne soit pas à la hauteur de votre imaginaire. Une fois – il était tout gosse –, Jay avait croisé par hasard l'animateur d'une émission télévisée qu'il adorait. À l'antenne, le type était tout sourire, bienveillant, le genre d'homme que tout gamin aurait rêvé d'avoir pour père. À l'époque, c'était son héros. Or, quand l'animateur en question avait repéré Jay, les premiers mots à tomber de ses lèvres divines avaient été : « Bon Dieu, qui m'a laissé entrer ici ce petit connard ? »

Au temps pour les héros de l'enfance.

Jay avait tué le tigre, mais comparé à ce qu'il lui restait à faire, il avait mangé son pain blanc. Désormais, il chassait le tyrannosaure, il traquait un dragon et il allait avoir besoin d'une arme de plus gros calibre. Et d'un peu plus de culot. Saji allait l'amener à sortir ses tripes, à faire le point sur sa condition actuelle, et il n'allait sûrement pas être à la fête. Par certains côtés, ça s'annonçait encore plus terrifiant que la chasse au lézard-tonnerre. Qui avait dit qu'une existence passée sans interrogation n'était pas digne d'être vécue ? Platon ? Aristote ? Ouais, peut-être, mais si on perdait trop de temps à s'examiner le nombril, ça finissait par flanquer la trouille. Peut-être qu'un excès d'interrogations rendait la vie invivable.

Avec la voix rauque et sensuelle de Lauren Bacall, l'ordinateur domestique annonça : « Jay, tu as un visiteur. »

Saji était ici.

Il était prêt à tout. Jay inspira profondément, se dirigea vers la porte. Et l'ouvrit.

Une petite brune toute menue, cheveux courts, blue-jean, T-shirt noir et bottes de cow-boy, se tenait devant lui. Elle avait l'air d'avoir vingt-cinq ans, devait faire un mètre cinquante même avec ses bottes, et arborait un sourire superbe entouré de larges fossettes... Elle aurait bien sûr pu être d'origine tibétaine, mais n'avait vraiment rien d'oriental dans les traits.

« Salut, Jay. »

Eh ben merde alors... Il se rendit compte qu'il avait été prêt à tout sauf à ça.

« Saji... », fit-il. Ce n'était pas une question. Putain de merde. Non seulement Saji était une femme mais elle était jeune et belle. C'était vraiment pas juste !

Putain de merde.

Mardi

Les Ifs, Sussex, Angleterre

« Un coup de téléphone pour vous, sir », dit Applewhite. Il entra dans la pièce avec le combiné. « Un dénommé... Pound-Sand, milord. Il dit que vous attendiez son appel. »

Goswell marqua un temps d'arrêt alors qu'il mirait les canons qu'il était en train de nettoyer. Pound-Sand ? Il ne connaissait personne de ce nom... Quelqu'un avait dû faire une blague à son majordome. Il souffla de toutes ses forces dans un des canons, provoquant un son creux, et un nuage de peluches de la lingette en coton dont il s'était servi pour le nettoyer s'envola pour retomber paresseusement dans les rayons du soleil de l'après-midi.

« Il précise que le conseil de vous appeler lui a été donné par un vieux gentleman amateur de cigares cubains... »

Ah, c'était donc ça. Il saisit le téléphone et fit signe au majordome de se retirer.

« Allô ?

– Lord Goswell ?

– Oui. Lui-même.

– Un instant, je vous prie, sir. » La voix paraissait cultivée, de bonne famille. Un bip électronique l'interrompit momentanément. « Excusez-moi pour ce retard, expliqua l'homme, mais on n'est jamais trop prudent, n'est-ce pas ?

– Vous venez de procéder à une analyse de spectre vocal ?

– Oui, monseigneur. Et la ligne est sécurisée. Cette conversation est intégralement cryptée. J'imagine que personne ne nous écoute sur un autre poste de votre côté ? »

Goswell hocha la tête, songeur. Excellent numéro. « Non, nous sommes parfaitement seuls, monsieur... euh, Pound-Sand, n'est-ce pas ? »

L'homme étouffa un rire. « J'espère que vous pardonnerez cette petite... plaisanterie, monseigneur. Sir Harold m'a dit que vous aviez comme un problème... délicat ?

– J'en ai peur, oui.

– Préféreriez-vous voir ce problème réglé de manière temporaire ou définitive ?

– Définitive, je le crains.

– Je vais m'en occuper de ce pas.

– Vous aurez besoin de précisions.

– Un simple nom me suffira, monseigneur. Je peux déduire le reste. »

Sourire de Goswell. Impeccable !

Il indiqua le nom de Peel à son interlocuteur.

« Merci, monseigneur. Je m'en charge. Eh bien, au revoir. »

Goswell raccrocha. Aucune discussion d'argent ou de détails sordides. Magnifique. Il se sentait déjà mieux. Il restait donc encore quelques hommes de valeur.

Mardi
Londres

Alex Michaels arpentait les berges de la Tamise près des jardins du Jubilé, regardant passer les bateaux-mouches et regrettant de ne pas pouvoir remonter le cours du temps. Sa vie était devenue un putain de feuilleton télévisé. Son enquête était au point mort. Son ex-épouse réclamait la garde exclusive de leur fille. Il avait une aventure avec sa principale subordonnée. Et pour couronner le tout, il avait bien failli coucher avec une autre, ce qui n'aurait jamais fait que la troisième femme en une douzaine d'années. Comment l'expliquer à Toni ? Que pouvait-il lui dire ? Oh, tu sais, pendant ton absence, j'ai été effectivement à deux doigts de m'envoyer en l'air avec la superbe espionne britannique Angela Cooper. Désolé.

Ouais. Il se retrouvait avec ce fardeau sur le dos, un fardeau si lourd qu'il pouvait à peine bouger. Jamais de sa vie il ne n'était senti écrasé par un tel sentiment de culpabilité. Il ne s'était jamais non plus trouvé dans une situation analogue. Comment avait-il pu se montrer si stupide ? Comment diable allait-il pouvoir rectifier le tir ?

D'ailleurs, était-ce même possible ?

Il ne pouvait supporter l'idée de perdre Toni. Mais s'il lui avouait ce qui s'était passé – rectification : quand il le lui avouerait –, c'était bien ce qui risquait d'arriver. Elle pouvait fort bien lui mettre deux claques et tourner les talons. Elle pouvait aussi lui rompre les os et tourner les talons, même s'il redoutait moins cette perspective que celle de contempler son visage blessé par cette révélation.

Enfin, merde, où donc avait-il eu la tête ?

Bien sûr, il pouvait toujours faire porter le chapeau à Angela, elle avait tout fait pour l'amener chez elle, c'est elle qui lui avait fait le coup du massage et tout ce cinéma, mais il n'était pas dupe de ces prétextes *a posteriori*. Elle ne lui avait pas non plus plaqué un canon sur la tempe. Ce petit jeu se jouait à deux. Il aurait fort bien pu décliner poliment sa proposition et rentrer se coucher.

Tant va la cruche à l'eau...

Bon, d'accord, il n'y avait pas eu de casse, mais enfin, ç'avait été limite-limite. Ah, nom de Dieu de nom de Dieu.

Un groupe de touristes japonais embarqués sur un bateau-mouche recouvert d'une grande bâche multicolore lui sourit en agitant les bras au passage. Ils devaient sans doute le prendre pour un Londonien en balade sur les quais.

Les touristes ne se doutaient pas que l'idée de se jeter dans la Tamise et d'y rester avait pour lui en cet instant même un attrait certain.

Il leur rendit leur salut. « Allez tous vous faire foutre », grommela-t-il avec un grand sourire de faux-jeton.

Comment des hommes pouvaient-ils faire des trucs pareils – tromper leur femme ou des personnes de confiance, comme il l'avait fait ? Enfin, presque fait. Un jour, il avait bu l'apéritif avec un avocat rencontré durant son travail. Un grand gaillard, beau et riche, marié à une femme superbe. Ils avaient trois enfants, une maison immense en Virginie, de l'argent, des chiens, des chats, bref, tout pour être heureux. Ils s'étaient mis à parler. Au bout de deux verres, l'avocat s'était confié à Michaels. Quelques jours plus tôt, il se trouvait à un petit déjeuner de bienfaisance dans la capitale. En dehors de son épouse, il y avait quatre autres femmes très séduisantes à sa table, certaines mariées, d'autres célibataires, entre vingt-deux et quarante ans. L'avocat avait précisé qu'il avait couché avec les cinq au cours de l'année écoulée, et qu'il comptait bien ne pas en rester là. Aucune n'était au courant pour les autres. Et d'ajouter qu'il considérait cet instant comme un summum dans son existence.

Michaels avait failli s'étrangler avec son verre. Ce type devait être cinglé. L'idée même d'être assis à table avec cinq femmes avec lesquelles il aurait couché l'emplissait de terreur. Dans une telle situation, il serait tombé raide mort de peur, aucun doute là-dessus. La tension aurait été insurmontable. Il sentait déjà son crâne... exploser, comme un pétard au réveillon de Jour de l'An.

Son expérience en la matière était limitée, mais il était convaincu que les femmes avaient une sorte de sixième sens pour ce genre de situation. Un regard insistant, une parole imprudente d'Angela, et Toni saurait tout de suite. C'était bien la dernière chose qu'il désirait – qu'elle l'apprenne par quelqu'un d'autre que lui.

L'avant-dernière étant qu'elle l'apprenne de lui.

Oh, Seigneur ! Mais qu'est-ce qu'il allait bien pouvoir faire ? Quelle que soit la manière d'envisager la situation, il était dans une impasse.

T'aurais peut-être dû y penser avant de te déloquer et de t'allonger sur la table de massage, mec. T'aurais peut-être dû enclencher l'ordinateur de bord avant de mettre en pression le circuit hydraulique...

Roujio suivait Peel, en s'arrangeant pour laisser deux ou trois véhicules entre lui et sa voiture de location. Il ne s'estimait pas un expert ès techniques de surveillance – il avait connu des agents capables de suivre un client jusque par-delà les portes de l'Enfer sans même que le Malin s'en aperçoive – mais la tâche était bien plus aisée quand le sujet était non seulement au courant de votre présence mais l'avait désirée. Certes, il avait déjà filé des individus – en général, juste avant de les éliminer. Et certes, il connaissait les principes de base de la surveillance en mouvement, les techniques de couverture, les méthodes pour se fondre dans le paysage, les moments où s'éclipser et laisser échapper la proie pour ne pas risquer de se faire brûler. Ce genre de talents faisait partie du métier, et sans être un expert, il en connaissait les ficelles.

Au passage, Roujio lorgna du coin de l'œil la plaque d'une rue. Old Kent Road. Et un peu plus sur la droite, il avisa un bâtiment industriel baptisé « Usine à gaz du Sud-Est ». Il nota mentalement ces détails.

L'un des trucs qu'omettaient les agents débutant dans la filature était de prêter attention à l'endroit où ils se trouvaient. Ils avaient tendance à se polariser sur le sujet, à l'exclusion de tout autre chose. Dans ces conditions, on risquait de ne pas apercevoir son comparse, aux aguets pour surveiller justement quelqu'un comme vous. Ou bien vous pouviez coller au sujet malgré ses tours et détours, parfois même alors qu'il était assez malin pour faire comme s'il ne s'était pas aperçu qu'il était filé, mais faute d'une attention suffisante, dès qu'il s'arrêtait, vous aviez beau lever les yeux, vous ne saviez plus où vous étiez. Dans une ville familière, ce n'était peut-être pas un problème, mais dans un endroit inconnu, cela pouvait créer des difficultés. En l'absence d'une carte détaillée ou d'un GPS, retrouver le chemin de la base pouvait se révéler une vraie galère. Et il y avait pire. Dans toutes les villes, il y avait des secteurs où il était impensable de rester garé plusieurs heures à attendre que le sujet daigne reprendre son véhicule et repartir. Une artère résidentielle dans un quartier huppé n'était pas un endroit recommandé pour s'attarder. Les gens fortunés avaient des biens auxquels ils tenaient et ils jugeaient également que la protection policière leur était un dû. Même s'il ne s'agissait pas d'une voie privée et qu'aucune loi ne vous interdise d'y stationner, si jamais le potentat local jetait un œil par la fenêtre de son hôtel particulier et vous apercevait garé en bas de chez lui, il ne manquerait pas de prévenir les flics qui s'empresseraient de venir contrôler votre identité. S'ils n'avaient pas été précédés par sa milice privée.

De même, rester garé un long moment devant une banque n'était pas non plus recommandé.

Si vous vous aventuriez dans un quartier inconnu et vous retrouviez dans les parages d'une école primaire, assez près pour être vu des gamins dans la cour de récré, vous pouviez parier tout ce que vous vouliez que la police ne tarderait pas à débarquer pour s'assurer que vous n'étiez pas quelque pédophile sadique n'attendant que l'instant propice pour vous livrer à des pratiques exhibitionnistes (voire pires) devant les chères têtes blondes. Si vous n'aviez pas une excellente raison pour justifier votre présence – et il n'existait aucune raison suffisante pour convaincre la police qu'un homme devait surveiller des enfants du haut d'un perchoir, sauf à les convaincre que vous étiez un des leurs chargé justement de surveiller celui pour qui ils vous prenaient –, on vous convaincrait avec fermeté de quitter les lieux.

Dans une telle situation, il était conseillé d'avoir prévu un autre point de chute pour poursuivre la surveillance...

Peel s'engagea dans un parking devant un petit bâtiment gris d'un seul étage.

Roujio passa devant et avisa une place libre dans la rue, quelques mètres plus loin, sous les branches d'une espèce de marronnier. Il sourit. La première règle de la surveillance automobile telle qu'énoncée par Serge, le vieil agent russe qui lui avait enseigné le b-a ba du métier, était celle-ci : toujours se garer à l'ombre. Un conseil d'autant plus important que la journée était chaude.

Roujio fit un créneau, coupa le moteur et s'assura que personne n'avait suivi Peel dans le parking.

Peel descendit de voiture et se dirigea vers le bâtiment, sans montrer qu'il avait aperçu Roujio. L'Anglais lui avait déjà indiqué que l'immeuble était sûr et qu'il était donc inutile qu'il le suive à l'intérieur.

Roujio se trémoussa sur son siège, guettant la présence éventuelle d'un inconnu déjà sur place ou en train de se mettre en position pour guetter le départ de Peel. Au moindre signe jugé menaçant, il devait avertir Peel grâce à son téléphone mobile. Ils conviendraient alors de la conduite à tenir.

Assis dans la voiture sans rien d'autre à faire que le

guet, Roujio se remit à penser à son retour au bercail. Les problèmes de transport avaient été réglés pour l'essentiel, et il n'aurait pas de mal à trouver un moyen de rallier le continent. Le journal de la veille citait encore le cas d'un inconscient qui avait réussi à franchir les grillages et à déjouer la surveillance des vigiles et des caméras pour s'introduire dans le tunnel sous la Manche. Il lui avait fallu la journée pour se rendre d'Angleterre en France, et c'était un miracle qu'il ne se soit pas fait happer par un des innombrables convois filant à cent soixante à l'heure dans ce boyau – l'imbécile n'ayant même pas eu la jugeote d'emprunter le tunnel de service...

Ce genre d'exemple prouvait bien que lorsqu'un homme voulait absolument se rendre quelque part, il trouvait toujours un moyen.

Roujio ne devait rien à Peel, et la somme qu'on lui versait ne signifiait rien, il avait déjà bien assez d'argent. Mais il allait continuer encore quelques jours. Ce n'était pas inintéressant et surtout, Peel avait tout de même réussi à le repérer et à le surprendre. Dans son métier, c'était le genre de détail qui compte. Non, deux ou trois jours encore ne pouvaient pas faire de mal.

30

Mardi 12 avril
Washington, DC

Plus ou moins planqué dans la boutique d'articles de sport, Tyrone surveillait la sandwicherie. Il avait séché les cours pour se rendre à la galerie marchande. Bella était là, assise à une table devant une Tortilla Maria, entourée d'une demi-douzaine de copines et de deux mecs. Les mâles n'appartenaient pas à son harem, pour autant qu'il puisse en juger : ce n'étaient que des planétésimaux en orbite autour de leur étoile éclatante. Dès que Bella riait, tous riaient. Dès qu'elle ouvrait la bouche, ils écoutaient. C'était quelqu'un.

Ses sentiments à son égard étaient partagés. D'un côté, il la détestait franchement pour l'avoir largué. Sans avertissement, paf ! En plein buffet, hasta la vista, l'ami Tyrone ! C'est qu'elle n'avait pas l'habitude d'entendre des mecs lui dire ses quatre vérités ; or, c'était tout juste ce qu'il avait fait. Comme ça, tilt ! et te fatigue pas à remettre une autre pièce dans le bastringue, parce qu'il n'y aura pas d'autre partie.

D'un autre côté, il suffisait de la mater. Elle était si belle, le centre d'attraction dès qu'elle se pointait quelque part, les mecs faisaient la queue rien que pour baiser le sol où elle venait de poser les pieds. Et, miracle ineffable, il s'était trouvé qu'elle l'avait gratifié, lui, Tyrone, de ses faveurs. Qu'elle l'avait embrassé, touché, qu'elle l'avait laissé la toucher, et la simple idée de pouvoir recommencer, de savoir qu'il avait à nouveau captivé son attention, eh bien, c'était quelque chose de magique, pas à tortiller. Il avait un beau jour posé la main sur ce sein parfait, joué de la langue entre ces lèvres parfaites. C'était excitant d'y repenser – encore une veine qu'il soit planqué entre deux rangées de doudounes, ainsi personne ne risquait de constater son état d'excitation...

Elle l'avait quasiment invité à se rendre à la galerie marchande. Il pouvait sortir de la boutique, faire mine de s'approcher d'elle, l'air de rien, et voir de quoi il retournait. Lui sourirait-elle en l'invitant au club, le conviant à s'asseoir à côté d'elle ? Parce qu'au bout du compte, elle le respectait pour avoir osé lui dire la vérité en face ? Ou bien était-ce quelque jeu pervers dans lequel elle allait le battre froid devant sa petite cour, le plonger dans l'embarras et le faire passer pour le dernier des crétins ? Il ne la pensait pas capable de faire une chose pareille... elle en avait eu cent fois l'occasion, alors pourquoi attendre si longtemps ? Mais il n'était pas sûr non plus.

Récemment encore, il serait accouru aussitôt sans se poser la moindre question. Il l'avait aimée. Vraiment. Et cru qu'elle l'aimait aussi. Mais c'était avant. La vie pouvait changer drôlement vite en quelques mois. Sans déc'.

Quand il pensait à Bella, il se faisait encore l'effet d'être une serpillière tordue, essorée et mise à sécher en tas au coin de la baignoire, sans même qu'on prenne la peine de l'étendre. Il était peut-être temps de faire le point, d'être fixé une bonne fois pour toutes.

Seul problème : est-ce qu'il tenait tant que ça à le savoir ? Se faire plaquer une fois, ça craignait déjà un max. En plus de ça, se faire humilier en public, c'était la méga-tasse au cube. Il entendait d'ici Jimmy-Joe et le reste de la bande : « Ouah, le mec, tu t'es fait congeler en beauté par la belle Belladonna (donna-donna-gla-gla-gla) au beau milieu de la galerie ! Remis à zéro, ratiboisé le mec, redémarrage à froid, le plantage intégral. Ça fait quoi, comme effet ? »

Tyrone hocha la tête. Il n'avait aucune envie de jouer ce scénario en RV et encore moins en MR, putain de non merci.

Pas de risque, pas de gain. Mais pas de casse non plus, pas vrai ?

Mais... mais si ça te permettait de récupérer Donna, de te réintroduire chez elle et sur son divan, de ravoir une chance de peloter ce corps superbe, d'avoir ces lèvres sur les tiennes, est-ce que ça n'en vaudrait pas la chandelle ?

Oh, que si !

Il inspira un grand coup, expira lentement. Recommença.

Scénario-catastrophe, il passerait pour un grand couillon. Le scénario idéal ?

En un éclair, il eut l'image fugitive de Bella, nue, les cheveux répandus sur un oreiller. Une image assez réaliste pour qu'il en oublie de respirer. Il avait quatorze ans et c'était le genre d'image à mourir – et tant pis si c'était également le genre à vous expédier en prison, même si elle était plus âgée que lui. Bella. À poil...

Seigneur !

Quand il lui revint l'idée de respirer, il se dirigea vers la porte. Tu fonces ou tu crèves, mec. Pas d'autre choix.

Mardi
Londres

Debout en face de l'entrée du MI-6, John Howard vit son patron traverser la rue et se diriger vers lui. Il lui fit signe, Michaels le remarqua et répondit à son salut.

« Colonel, comment va ?

– Plutôt pas mal, monsieur. Tout bien considéré.

– Du nouveau dans l'enquête sur l'assassin ?

– Oui et non, concéda Howard. Nous savons qu'il a pris un vol au départ de Seattle, mercredi. Nous savons qu'il a débarqué ici. Nous en avons confirmation par un examen de la liste des voyageurs qui ont passé la douane. Fiorella a collationné toutes les arrivées en provenance des États-Unis jeudi, tôt dans la matinée. On a un cliché qui correspond. »

Il lui tendit une copie couleur d'un homme traversant l'aérogare d'un pas décidé. Un réseau de lignes fines avait été superposé à la photo.

« Vous êtes sûrs que c'est lui ?

– Ça lui ressemble, en tout cas. Et l'endroit et l'heure correspondent. L'ordinateur indique que la forme des oreilles et des mains correspond à notre référence. À moins qu'il ait un frère jumeau, c'est lui, sans aucun doute. »

D'un signe de tête, Michaels indiqua le bâtiment. « On rentre ? »

Alors qu'ils passaient devant les gardes et s'engageaient dans le hall, Michaels remarqua : « Cela fait près d'une semaine, il pourrait être n'importe où, à l'heure qu'il est.

– Certes, monsieur, c'est exact. Il aurait pu poursuivre sa route avant que tous les réseaux informatiques de réservation ne soient devenus cinglés. On a pu obtenir du temps de calcul sur le Baby Huey, et avec la coopération des Britanniques, le lieutenant Winthrop se charge, à notre siège, de collationner l'ensemble des données de réservation de billets d'avion, de train, de location de voitures, et jusqu'aux cabines sur tous les bateaux au départ de Londres pour n'importe quelle destination. Même une photo sur un faux passeport devra bien lui ressembler plus ou moins.

– Il pourrait s'être affublé d'une fausse barbe et d'une perruque, nota Michaels.

– On examine de près tous les hommes qui voyagent seuls et dont le signalement – taille, âge, corpulence – approche du sien.

– Il pourrait avoir payé une fille pour l'accompagner.

– Bien sûr, et il pourrait aussi trouver un sorcier capable de le transformer en gorille, monsieur. Il faut bien qu'on parte de quelque chose. »

Michaels sourit de cette remarque.

Ils arrivèrent au bureau où Howard avait laissé Toni Fiorella.

À l'intérieur, Toni et une superbe grande blonde à cheveux courts examinaient la projection holographique agrandie de douzaines de visages alignés en rangées successives.

« Je viens de recevoir la première série de Jo Winthrop, mon colonel, expliqua Toni. Tous les sujets ont les oreilles qui correspondent au signalement ou bien sont masquées par les cheveux, ce qui nous empêche de les voir clairement. Hé, salut, Alex ! Alors, bonne balade ?

– Ouais, merci. » Michaels semblait mal à l'aise. Il était pâle.

« Oh, mais je manque à tous mes devoirs, rectifia Toni. Colonel John Howard, permettez-moi de vous présenter Angela Cooper. Elle est notre officier de liaison avec le MI-6. Le colonel Howard dirige les équipes d'intervention sur le terrain de la Net Force. »

La blonde tendit la main et sourit à Howard. « Bonjour, colonel. Ravie de faire votre connaissance. »

Il inclina la tête, lui rendit son sourire. Du coin de l'œil, il observa les traits de Michaels. L'homme avait un sourire contraint plaqué sur le visage, mais il sentait bien qu'il était à deux doigts de vomir.

Cooper lâcha la main du colonel et il nota qu'elle jetait un bref coup d'œil à Michaels. Il en suivit la direction et remarqua que Michaels détournait les yeux, refusant de croiser son regard. Ce n'était rien, ça n'avait duré qu'une demi-seconde, ou peut-être était-ce uniquement son imagination. Malgré tout...

Oh, bon Dieu.

Le plus souvent, Howard accompagnait sa femme et son fils les dimanches à l'église mais il ne se prenait pas pour autant pour un prophète capable, mieux que les autres, de déchiffrer l'âme des gens. Cela dit, il avait pas mal bourlingué et il s'estimait assez fin psychologue.

Il y avait quelque chose entre ces deux-là. Quelque chose dans l'œillade que la belle blonde avait lancée à Michaels, quelque chose dans la façon dont ce dernier avait évité son regard.

Oui, il y avait anguille sous roche.

Howard, comme tant d'hommes longtemps éloignés de leur foyer, avait parfois été tenté par l'éventualité de liaisons extra-conjugales. Et plus d'une femme avait manifesté l'envie de le connaître horizontalement, une ou deux s'étaient même révélées suffisamment séduisantes pour que l'idée lui soit venue à l'esprit. Qui pouvait dire ? Quel mal y aurait-il eu ? Comment disait la chanson, déjà ? Faute d'être avec celle qu'on aime, ne pouvait-on aimer celle avec qui on était ?

Ça n'avait rien de mal ou d'infamant, pas vrai ?

Par chance pour lui, depuis le temps qu'il était marié, toutes ces pensées s'étaient dissipées avant même qu'il ait pu envisager de sauter le pas. Il ne se considérait pas comme spécialement vertueux – il en avait fait pas mal quand il était jeune soldat, avant de se marier – mais il avait tiré un trait sur tout cela le jour où il avait dit « oui ». Peut-être était-il plus chanceux que d'autres ; depuis ce jour, il n'avait jamais commis de faux pas. Mais il connaissait plus d'un homme qui avaient choisi de continuer dans la voie du péché. Combien en avait-il vu côtoyer, l'air de rien, des femmes qu'ils faisaient mine de ne pas connaître quand la vérité était tout autre.

Howard n'en aurait peut-être pas mis sa main au feu, mais ce bref échange de regards entre Michaels et Cooper lui révélait une chose qu'il aurait préféré continuer d'ignorer : il y avait quelque chose entre ces deux-là. Et pour couronner le tout, à voir son comportement, Toni Fiorella, elle, en ignorait tout.

Allons bon. Tout d'un coup, Howard s'estima heureux de ne pas être à la place d'Alex Michaels. Très heureux.

Mardi
Londres

Roujio vit le tireur à la seconde où il ouvrit la portière de sa voiture.

Une veine, en fait, qu'il se soit trouvé garé à proximité et qu'il ait tourné les yeux juste au moment où l'autre emboîtait le pas à Peel, une douzaine de mètres en retrait. S'il n'avait pas regardé à cet instant précis, il aurait été sans doute trop tard, mais il avait aperçu le reflet du soleil sur l'inox quand le type avait boutonné son veston pour planquer le flingue glissé sous la ceinture, côté droit. Une demi-seconde plus tard, il l'aurait raté, sans pouvoir être certain que le tueur n'était pas qu'un simple piéton hâtant le pas pour se rendre à un rendez-vous ou faire quelques dernières emplettes avant la fermeture des boutiques.

Le tireur n'était plus qu'à un mètre derrière Roujio qui continuait d'avancer, en obliquant légèrement vers la droite, comme pour faire du lèche-vitrines devant un chapelier. Le tireur, un type plutôt grand, blond filasse, coupe-vent sur un polo beige, pantalon kaki et tennis, le dépassa d'un pas vif, polarisé sur sa cible.

Coup d'œil de Roujio alentour. Il ne vit personne en soutien. Il s'écarta de la vitrine et se lança sur la trace du tireur, pressant le pas à son tour. Sa main se porta vers le téléphone clipé à sa ceinture et son doigt pressa la touche « envoi ».

Le numéro était déjà programmé : c'était l'un des deux que Peel lui avait confiés et le téléphone mobile de ce dernier devait en cet instant vibrer à sa ceinture. Personne d'autre n'avait ce numéro, lui avait dit l'Anglais : si l'appareil vibrait, cela voudrait donc dire que Roujio avait repéré une menace mortelle trop proche pour lui laisser le temps d'utiliser l'autre numéro et s'en expliquer de vive voix.

Peel bifurqua aussitôt sur la droite pour s'engouffrer dans la boutique la plus proche. Une librairie.

Le tireur à son tour bifurqua.

Roujio accéléra, de sorte qu'il atteignit la porte cinquante centimètres derrière le tireur. Il n'aurait pas été difficile de lui tirer dessus et de le descendre une bonne fois pour toutes, mais ils voulaient le garder en vie assez longtemps pour découvrir qui l'avait envoyé. Cela risquait d'être un tantinet coton en pleine rue, mais à l'intérieur du magasin, le nombre réduit de témoins devrait leur faciliter la tâche.

Peel était au courant et il s'empressa de guider le supposé assassin vers une allée déserte bordée de hautes étagères remplies de livres poussiéreux. Avant que le tireur ait pu sortir son arme, Roujio le coinça. Il lui enfonça le petit Beretta entre les vertèbres et souffla : « Un pas de plus et t'es mort. »

L'autre était un pro. Il se figea.

« C'est bon », annonça Roujio.

Peel se retourna, la main glissée sous son blazer, à la hauteur de la hanche droite. Il souriait. « Henry ? Je croyais que t'avais pris ta retraite ? »

Le blond filasse répondit : « Visiblement, j'aurais mieux fait.

– Un peu tard, à présent. Si on allait quelque part causer entre quatre-z-yeux ?

– Ça ne servira à rien, Terry, tu le sais.

– Tu ne peux pas gagner, Henry. Mon gars, ici, est un ex-Spetsnatz. Il peut te rendre paraplégique et ça ne nous empêchera toujours pas de te forcer à parler. Alors, pourquoi ne pas régler ça entre gens civilisés ? On pourrait même parvenir à un arrangement qui éviterait à quiconque de bouffer les pissenlits par la racine.

– Franchement, Terry, je pensais que tu me tenais en meilleure estime... »

Sur ces mots, Henry fit un brusque écart sur le côté, un mouvement assez inattendu pour que le coup de feu de Roujio rate la mœlle épinière et fasse un petit trou au-dessus de la hanche gauche du type. La détonation retentit bruyamment, à travers les livres et les rayonnages, qui la répercutèrent vers les trois hommes. Ils n'avaient plus que quelques secondes, maxi, pour régler leur affaire.

« Vivant ! » s'écria Peel en dégainant à son tour.

Roujio surveillait la main droite d'Henry, sachant que c'était la plus proche du pistolet caché. S'il tirait, ce serait vers cette main, et s'il ratait sa cible, une balle de 22 dans le ventre ne serait pas immédiatement fatale...

Peut-être l'autre se rendit-il compte qu'il n'aurait pas le temps de dégainer assez vite pour les doubler.

Il ne chercha même pas à le faire : au lieu de cela, il porta le poignet gauche à sa bouche et mordit dans son bracelet-montre. Roujio comprit le sens du geste, et Peel également, car il s'exclama : « Bordel de merde ! »

Roujio remit le pistolet à sa ceinture, fit demi-tour et regagna la sortie du magasin à grands pas. Peel était sur ses talons. Des gens, même des rats de bibliothèque, pouvaient toujours venir voir, attirés par le bruit.

Quel qu'ait été le poison ingéré par Henry, il était sans aucun doute foudroyant, et il n'y avait aucun moyen d'extorquer des informations à un homme qui préférait se suicider plutôt que de les révéler. Un pro, sans aucun doute. Henry serait probablement mort avant que quiconque puisse lui porter secours, et de toute manière, plus personne ne pouvait rien pour lui. Roujio respectait un homme qui savait mourir. Si vous saviez que votre heure était venue, mieux valait s'en aller de la façon qu'on avait choisie. Vous aviez perdu la guerre, mais si vous parveniez malgré tout à priver l'ennemi de ce qu'il désirait, il vous restait au moins cette infime satisfaction à emporter avec vous dans la tombe.

Dans la rue, revenu sur le trottoir, marchant d'un bon pas mais sans précipitation, Peel dépassa Roujio pour se diriger vers sa voiture. Au passage, il nota : « J'aimais bien ce vieil Henry. Dommage. »

Tout en lui emboîtant le pas, Roujio songeait déjà au meilleur moyen de se débarrasser du Beretta. Il allait devoir le faire au plus vite. Un homme était mort dans une librairie, le décès était dû au poison, mais même une balle à pointe creuse laissait suffisamment de fragments pour qu'on puisse retrouver par expertise balistique l'arme qui l'avait tirée. Et un pistolet qu'on pouvait relier à un cadavre, c'était toujours un talisman encombrant.

31

Mardi 12 avril
Washington, DC

Jay apporta un verre d'eau à Saji, hocha la tête et remarqua : « Tu prends vraiment ton pied avec ça, n'est-ce pas ? »

Elle sourit, installée au fond du large fauteuil aux capitons épais et concéda : « Plus que de raison, oui. »

Il alla s'asseoir dans le vieux canapé de cuir gris qu'il avait récupéré lors d'un vide-grenier. Une vague odeur de patchouli embaumait l'atmosphère. Son parfum ? Un reste d'encens accroché à ses cheveux. Bon sang, ce qu'elle était belle. « J'aurais dû me méfier, après toutes ces années passées sur le Net, mais je ne m'attendais pas à ça.

– Ça te turlupine à ce point ? »

Il ne réfléchit qu'une seconde. « Non. Pas vraiment. C'est l'esprit qui compte. Pas le corps.

– Voilà qui est tout à ton honneur, Jay. Tu y crois vraiment. Si je l'avais su quand on s'est rencontrés, je n'aurais pas pris la peine de me déguiser.

– Dans ce cas, satisfais ma curiosité... pourquoi, alors ? »

Elle fit danser les glaçons dans son verre. « Tu veux le résumé ou le cours complet ?

– Oh, va pour le cours complet. Les condensés sont en général indigestes. »

Elle sourit. « Très bien. Le bouddhisme ressemble à bien des religions traditionnelles, en cela que de tout temps presque tous ses adeptes de haut rang ont été des hommes. Oh, certes, il y a toujours eu des nonnes et des sœurs laies qui suivaient la Voie aussi bien que les hommes, mais pour une majorité de gens, encore aujourd'hui, la religion demeure une affaire d'homme. Et dans la plupart des livres saints traditionnels – Bible, Coran, Upanishads, comme dans l'essentiel de la littérature bouddhiste –, quand on fait allusion aux femmes, c'est toujours sur un ton paternaliste et condescendant, même lorsqu'on prétend chanter leurs louanges : les femmes sont les gardiennes de la vie, porteuses des enfants, le sexe faible qu'il convient de protéger des rudesses du monde, et patati et patata. La majorité des religions classiques voient en la femme plus une propriété qu'un individu autonome. Un homme a une ferme, des chèvres, du bétail, et une femme. Dans ces pays-là, les femmes ont le droit de vote depuis moins de cent ans. Tu me suis toujours ?

– Vas-y, je suis là.

– Parfait. Donc, les philosophies aiment bien voir les nanas rester pieds nus et enceintes, à s'occuper du foyer familial tandis que les mecs vaquent aux affaires sérieuses. À de rares exceptions près – quelques cultes de divinités féminines et autres –, jusqu'à tout récemment, les femmes n'intervenaient pas de manière déterminante lorsqu'il s'agissait de doctrine ou de pratique, même dans les religions les plus “neutres”. La preuve, il n'y a toujours pas de femmes prêtres catholiques. Dans certains pays musulmans, les femmes n'ont toujours pas le droit de dévoiler leur visage en public. Ce n'est pas aussi marqué dans le bouddhisme, et de gros progrès ont été accomplis ces derniers siècles, mais chez certains, il reste toujours cette croyance informulée que les femmes ne sont pas tout à fait équivalentes aux hommes. Physique mis à part, les nanas ne pensent pas de la même façon que les mecs. Les joueuses d'échecs de haut niveau ne battent pas les champions de sexe masculin. La plupart des hommes surpassent les femmes dans les tests d'aptitude spatiale, dans tout ce qui fait fonctionner exclusivement le cerveau gauche. Les hommes – et certaines femmes – en tirent prétexte pour juger que c'est à eux que doivent échoir les responsabilités. Non, l'égalité a encore du chemin à faire, et dans bien des endroits, elle n'existe toujours pas. »

Jay acquiesça. Il savait tout cela. Et il voyait bien où elle voulait en venir mais il répondit néanmoins : « Je suis toujours là.

– Dans de nombreux cercles, dès qu'on te voit comme un vieillard, tu es bien plus respecté que si l'on pense que tu es une jeune femme. La vérité est la vérité, mais beaucoup de gens prêtent plus attention à celui qui l'énonce avant de l'accepter. Tu connais cette vieille blague qui court à Hollywood ? Sur le producteur et l'écrivain ? L'écrivain envoie au producteur un scénario qu'il lui réclamait avec insistance. Les semaines passent, le producteur ne rappelle pas. À la longue, l'écrivain le rappelle, lui demande s'il a lu son script. “Oui”, répond le producteur. “Alors, qu'est-ce que vous en pensez ?” Et l'autre de répondre : “Je ne sais pas trop. À part moi, personne d'autre ne l'a lu.” »

Elle hocha la tête. « C'est parfois ainsi que ça se

passe avec la religion. Si tu as le choix entre un vieillard de soixante-dix ans et une gamine d'une vingtaine d'années pour t'offrir des pépites de sagesse, au bout du compte, tu vas choisir le vieux chnoque. On préfère toujours les vieux sages aux jeunes cons.

– C'est idiot, observa Jay. Si tu connais la chanson aussi bien qu'un vieux, quelle importance ? C'est ce qui est dit qui importe, pas celui qui l'énonce. »

Elle le gratifia d'un large sourire. « Je t'aime. Épouse-moi. »

Il plissa les yeux. « Hein ? »

Elle rit, un rire profond et mélodieux. « On reviendra plus tard sur cette partie du Dharma. Comment se passe la chasse au monstre ? »

Soupir de Jay. « Ça va pas tarder à devenir terrifiant.

– C'est bien pour ça que je suis ici. J'ai pensé que je ferais bien de t'accompagner. »

Mercredi
Londres

Conduisant la Bentley à un train de sénateur, Stephens se dirigeait vers l'usine informatique. Goswell était avachi à l'arrière, baigné par l'odeur agréable et familière de l'huile de vison avec laquelle les cuirs avaient été frottés à la main.

La circulation était, comme toujours, chaotique, mais Stephens avait toujours su se tirer des embarras londoniens. Bien carré dans sa banquette, Goswell goûtait le plaisir du trajet.

Bientôt, Stephens annonça : « Monseigneur. Il y a un appel téléphonique pour vous. Sir Harold.

– Bien, je vais le prendre. »

Stephens lui passa le portable. « Allô, Harry ?

– Allô, Gossie. Alors, en vadrouille, à ce que je vois ?

– Dans ma voiture, oui. Je suis sorti faire une petite tournée d'inspection d'une des usines. C'est qu'il ne faut pas trop leur laisser la bride sur le cou, n'est-ce pas ?

– Certes non. Euh... dites voir, Gossie... c'est-à-dire, *harrumph*...

– Un problème, Harry ?

– Ma foi, oui. Vous avez eu une conversation avec un certain... euh, Pond-Sands, dernièrement ? Au sujet d'une affaire... délicate que nous avions évoquée au club ?

– Je m'en souviens fort bien, effectivement.

– Euh, eh bien... il semblerait que M. Pound-Sands... soit décédé.

– Oh, doux Jésus.

– Oui. Une disparition inattendue.

– Une maladie soudaine ?

– Très soudaine, j'en ai peur. J'ai cru comprendre que la chose s'est produite alors même qu'il se chargeait justement de cette affaire fort délicate. Et que... eh bien, ce serait plus ou moins une conséquence directe de ladite affaire.

– Comme c'est fâcheux.

– Je ne vous le fais pas dire.

– Enfin, ce sont des choses qui arrivent.

– Oui. Désirez-vous que je passe un petit coup de fil aux associés de ce M. Pound-Sands ? Voir si l'un d'eux serait intéressé par la reprise de l'affaire ? »

Goswell y réfléchit une seconde. « C'est fort aimable à vous, Harry, mais peut-être devrions-nous attendre quelque peu...

– Comme il vous plaira, Gossie. Croyez que j'en suis terriblement désolé.

– Ta-ta-ta, vous n'y êtes absolument pour rien, Harry. Il est évident que j'ai moi-même sous-estimé la difficulté du problème. N'y pensez plus. »

Mais alors qu'il rendait au chauffeur le téléphone mobile, Goswell ne put s'empêcher d'y penser. Ainsi donc, M. Pound-Sands bouffait les pissenlits par la racine. Ce qui voulait dire que Peel était soit chanceux, soit bon, soit les deux. D'un côté, cela lui procurait un certain sentiment de fierté de constater que l'homme était assez expert pour avoir empêché un assassinat en engageant un autre tueur professionnel. Mais de l'autre, cela voulait dire aussi que Peel allait être désormais plus que jamais sur ses gardes. S'il n'avait pas été évident d'essayer de l'éliminer, ce serait dorénavant deux fois plus difficile. Hmm. Voilà qui donnait sans aucun doute matière à réflexion.

« Nous sommes presque arrivés, monseigneur.

– Quoi ? Oh, oui. Tout à fait. »

Enfin. Chaque chose en son temps. D'abord, s'assurer que Bascomb-Coombs était hors du coup. Ensuite, trouver un moyen de régler son affaire à ce traître de Peel.

Mercredi
Siège du MI-6, Londres

« On a quelque chose, mon colonel », annonça Fernandez.

Howard quitta des yeux la pile de rapports qu'il était en train de lire. Ils se trouvaient dans le bureau provisoirement attribué à Michaels, et le commandant et son second étaient au bout du couloir, en grande discussion avec un des gradés du MI-6.

« Comment cela ?

– Mlle Cooper vient de nous dénicher ça. » Il lui transmit une photo tridimensionnelle imprimée par graveur laser.

Howard examina l'image 3D. « Roujio !

– Affirmatif. » Longue pause.

« Parfait, sergent, dites-moi tout. Où et quand ?

– À vos ordres, mon colonel. » Il souriait. « Hier, la police de Londres a été appelée pour un incident survenu dans une petite librairie près de Piccadilly Circus. Les flics ont trouvé un cadavre, tué par balle. La victime était un dénommé Henry Wyndham, ancien agent du MI-5 qui dirigeait un "service de sécurité". Cooper dit que les autorités locales suspectaient l'individu de s'être reconverti comme tueur à gages discret et fort coté pour de richissimes clients, mais personne n'a jamais réussi à le pincer. Il se trouve que ce n'est pas la balle qui l'a tué : il s'est apparemment suicidé avec un poison foudroyant. Cette photo a été récupérée à partir de la caméra de surveillance planquée au-dessus de la porte de la boutique. C'est celle d'un des hommes qui sont sortis à peu près au moment où les clients ont entendu la détonation. Et là, voici notre autre client. »

Fernandez lui présenta un autre cliché.

« Connu ?

– Pas de nous. Cooper est en train d'essayer de l'identifier. »

Howard opina. « Donc, il est toujours à Londres. Et il vient de tuer quelqu'un. Je me demande pourquoi.

– Pourquoi il est ici ? Ou pourquoi il a descendu quelqu'un ?

– Les deux.

– Eh bien, ce pourrait être une coïncidence. Il était en train de chercher un roman sympa d'Agatha Christie pour passer le temps quand quelqu'un s'est fait rectifier dans l'allée voisine.

– C'est ça. Est-ce qu'on peut remonter la trace du cadavre ?

– Cooper bosse dessus également, mon colonel. »

Howard opina derechef. « Bien. Est-ce que ça vaut le coup qu'on file interroger les employés de la librairie ?

– Cooper nous envoie les rapports de police, elle précise qu'on pourra y accéder sur le réseau informatique d'ici deux minutes. Mais elle ajoute que personne n'a vu les deux types entrer ou sortir.

– Je parie que feu M. Wyndham les aura vus entrer.

– Mais pas repartir. Les flics n'ont encore jamais rien vu de tel. Le cadavre était armé. On suppose que son agresseur lui a enfoncé l'arme dans les reins, qu'il a essayé de s'échapper. Il a pris un projectile de petit calibre à bout touchant, sans doute une balle de 22, qui n'aurait pas été fatale, estime le légiste. Mais il a dû juger qu'il était fichu et s'est lui-même rayé de la partie. Le poison est une de ces nouvelles capsules explosives de neurotoxines. Il s'est écoulé quatre-vingt-dix secondes, pas plus, entre le moment où il a croqué dedans et celui où il a claqué.

– Intéressant.

– Ouais, n'est-ce pas ?

– Bon, ben, ne reste pas planté là, va voir si Mlle Cooper peut te trouver quelque chose à faire. Notre gars est tout près, Julio. On va l'avoir. Je le sens.

– Ouais. »

Mercredi
Washington, DC

Un grand soleil, pas de vent, le temps idéal pour s'entraîner au boomerang, et Tyrone se rendit au stade de foot, tout imbu de sa personne. Bella lui avait rendu son sourire, elle avait envie de le revoir, de l'avoir près de lui, elle l'avait même invité chez elle, pour ce soir ! La vie était non seulement belle, elle était formidable.

Quand il arriva sur le terrain, Nadine était déjà là. CPI !

Mais quand il parvint à sa hauteur, elle était déjà en train de remballer.

« Hé, Nadine !

– Hé, Tyrone !

– Où vas-tu ?

– J'ai un peu mal au bras. Je ne veux pas me surentraîner.

– J'ai de l'Ibuprofène en gel.

– Merci, ça ira. J'en ai aussi à la maison. À plus. »

Il y avait quelque chose qui clochait, il le sentait bien, mais il ne voyait pas quoi. « Tu vas bien ? »

Elle le fixa droit dans les yeux. « Je t'ai dit que j'avais mal au bras. T'as oublié d'allumer ton implant, ou quoi ? » Pas de doute, il y avait de la colère dans sa voix.

« Hé-ho, on se calme, je t'ai pas traitée de vieux Pentium, je posais juste une question, point-barre. »

Elle se remit à bourrer son sac à dos. « Qu'est-ce que ça peut te foutre ? T'as pas besoin de traîner avec des nanas dans mon genre. T'as Belladonna.

– Je vois pas le rapport. »

Elle boucla son sac, le souleva, se le passa à l'épaule. « Ça va, Tyrone, tu vois très bien ce que je veux dire. Tu traînes avec les entraîneurs, tu partages pas le podium avec les joueurs. Tu prends ton p'tit déj avec les cuistots, tu plastronnes pas à table avec le gratin.

– Mais enfin, qu'est-ce que tu racontes ?

– Tu veux vraiment que j'te fasse un dessin ? Tu tournes autour des canons, tu tournes pas autour des cageots.

– C'est qui le cageot ? »

Elle lui adressa un sourire triste, tout petit. « Tu voudrais me faire croire que je joue dans la même catégorie que Bella, Ty ? Que t'aimerais mieux sortir avec moi qu'avec elle ? »

Il était abasourdi, il n'arrivait plus à reconnecter ses neurones. Pourquoi Nadine lui sortait-elle ce numéro ? Évidemment que Bella était plus jolie. Elle était plus jolie que n'importe qui au bahut. Et après ?

Il essayait encore de piger ce que Nadine voulait

dire, et ce qu'il pourrait bien lui répondre, quand elle hocha la tête, désabusée. « Ouais, ben j'ai entendu la tonalité. On se reconnecte un peu plus tard, salut, Ty ! »

Et, glissant l'autre bras sous la courroie du sac, elle s'éloigna.

Il la regarda partir, et quoiqu'il ne vît toujours pas ce qu'il avait fait de mal, il se sentait coupable. Quelque part, il venait comme qui dirait d'échouer à un examen... sans même savoir lequel.

Merde. Chierie. Il aurait bien voulu avoir son père à la maison. Son vieux en connaissait un rayon de ce côté. Il fallait absolument qu'il lui parle.

32

Mercredi 13 avril
Siège du MI-6, Londres

Quelque chose ne tournait pas rond, Toni le sentait. Les petites failles écaillant la façade d'Alex avaient été colmatées et replâtrées, ne laissant apparaître qu'un mur lisse masquant ses émotions. C'était moins ce qu'il avait pu dire ou faire qu'un changement d'attitude, invisible mais pourtant détectable. Au bout de plusieurs années d'entraînement aux arts martiaux, elle avait tendance à évaluer les choses en termes d'engagement physique. L'impression qu'elle avait c'était que, tout d'un coup, Alex s'était mis sur la défensive. Quand ils s'étaient retrouvés, sa garde était levée, mais il s'était détendu un peu au bout d'un moment, la laissant approcher à nouveau. Or à présent, il était de nouveau replié dans sa coquille, et battait en retraite, en se protégeant le visage.

Assise dans ce drôle de bureau de l'autre côté de l'océan, bien loin de ses repères habituels, Toni s'interrogeait, inquiète. Qu'est-ce qui s'était passé ? D'accord, il avait des tas de soucis en tête, la menace de la bataille juridique pour la garde de sa fille, le pirate fou, et les récents heurts dans leur relation de couple, mais enfin, tout ceci ne suffisait pas à justifier la distance soudaine qu'elle sentait naître entre eux...

« Mademoiselle Fiorella ? »

Elle leva les yeux. Cooper. « Oui ?

– Votre colonel Howard a des informations sur son assassin. Il aimerait avoir votre opinion. Il est dans la petite salle de conférences.

– D'accord. J'arrive tout de suite. »

Cooper ressortit et Toni mit de côté ses inquiétudes concernant Alex. Elle avait un boulot à faire, et même si Alex était un facteur de complication, elle ne pouvait pas non plus passer sa journée à se morfondre sur ses problèmes de vie amoureuse. Elle récupéra son écran-plat et se dirigea vers la salle de conférences pour retrouver John Howard.

Howard quitta des yeux l'holoprojecteur quand Toni Fiorella entra dans la pièce. Julio était là, mais Angela Cooper et Alex Michaels étaient en réunion avec un des pontes du MI-6 et ne devaient les rejoindre que d'ici quelques minutes.

« John. Qu'est-ce qui se passe ?

– Toni ! Le commandant sera là dans un petit moment, Mlle Cooper est allée le chercher, mais je tenais à vous mettre tout de suite au courant pour l'affaire Roujio.

– Bien sûr. Allez-y. »

Il lui exposa les faits, illustrant son exposé avec les images holographiques. Il commença par un bref résumé de la situation, puis vint rapidement à ce qu'il y avait de nouveau.

L'image de l'holoproj afficha la vue prise par la caméra de surveillance de la librairie. « Cet homme a quitté la boutique après l'incident, à peu près au même moment que Roujio. D'après ce qu'ont découvert Mlle Cooper et les gens de son service, il s'agit de Terrance Arthur Peel, commandant en retraite de l'armée britannique. Julio, veux-tu poursuivre ?

– Bien, mon colonel... madame... Peel a effectué une carrière exemplaire jusqu'à son affectation en Irlande du Nord, il y a deux ans, au sein des forces britanniques permanentes dans le cadre du traité de paix. L'équilibre là-bas demeure fragile, il y a toujours des petits groupes d'agitateurs incontrôlés, et d'après les éléments que nous avons pu recueillir, Peel aurait été responsable d'un incident qui aurait pu compromettre la paix. Il aurait interpellé des gars qui n'avaient rien à faire là où ils se trouvaient, et leur aurait extorqué de force des confessions. Apparemment, lui et ses hommes se sont rendus coupables... d'excès de zèle. Plusieurs prisonniers ont été sérieusement malmenés, le résultat est que certains en sont morts. »

Toni hocha la tête. « Hmm, je vois. »

Fernandez poursuivit. « L'armée britannique reste relativement discrète sur ce regrettable épisode, mais il semble que Peel se soit vu laisser le choix de se trancher la gorge ou de se faire virer, il a donc pris sa retraite et l'on a tiré un trait sur l'incident. Quand il réapparaît, il est gorille au service d'un ponte local, Lord Geoffrey Goswell. Son nouveau patron est non seulement noble, il est également plus riche que Crésus. Un vieux milliardaire encroûté qui possède une demi-douzaine d'entreprises qui fabriquent un peu de tout, des ordinateurs aux condiments en sauce. »

Toni réfléchit quelques secondes. Elle avait une vague idée de ce qui se tramait, mais préférait l'entendre énoncer par Howard. Son regard quitta

Fernandez pour se porter vers le colonel. « Je vois. Et cela vous porte à croire... ? »

Howard haussa les épaules. « Nous n'avons pas encore vraiment assez d'informations pour conclure. Mais ça paraît une coïncidence incroyable qu'on retrouve dans une librairie le cadavre d'un ancien agent de renseignements transpercé d'une balle et mort empoisonné, et que quelques secondes plus tard, un tueur notoirement connu, suivi d'un ex-officier supérieur chassé de l'armée pour avoir liquidé des prisonniers, jaillisse de cette même boutique. Si j'étais d'un naturel joueur, je serais enclin à parier que ces deux types ont quelque chose à voir avec cette mort suspecte. Ainsi que l'un avec l'autre.

– Vous pensez que Roujio travaille pour Peel ? Qu'il a été engagé pour capturer ou tuer le gars de la librairie ?

– Comme je viens de le dire, il est encore trop tôt pour sauter le pas, mais il me semble incontestable qu'on devrait avoir une petite discussion avec ce Peel. Même s'il est blanc comme neige, il était à tout le moins sur place au moment de l'incident, il ne peut pas ne pas avoir vu Roujio sortir... si ce dernier avait tardé une seconde à quitter les lieux, Peel lui aurait marché sur les pieds. »

Toni acquiesça de nouveau. « D'accord. Et comment procède-t-on ?

– Cooper va nous arranger ça. On peut l'accompagner au titre d'observateurs. Inutile de prendre des armes. Apparemment, Lord machin-truc est un homme qui a des relations et qui est au-dessus de tout soupçon.

– D'accord, intervint Fernandez. On va se pointer à sa porte, on accepte une tasse de thé, puis on lui demande poliment : “Dites donc, vieille branche, auriez-vous descendu quelqu’un dans une librairie, tout récemment ?” Et lui, il nous répond : “Il se trouve que c’est effectivement le cas, mon brave. Y a-t-il un problème ?” C’est que tout le monde est très civilisé, ici, genre prout-prout ma chère, n’est-il pas ? »

Toni éclata de rire.

Vu son air enjoué, Howard en déduisit qu’elle n’avait pas encore eu l’occasion de discuter d’Angela Cooper avec le commandant. Enfin, bon. Ce n’était certainement pas ses affaires et ce n’est pas lui qui allait...

Son virgil pépia. La tonalité indiquait un appel personnel. Il fronça les sourcils. Il n’était pas vraiment en opération, aussi n’avait-il pas filtré les communications autres que tactiques ; malgré tout, il était inhabituel que son épouse l’appelle ainsi.

« Si vous voulez bien m’excuser un instant », dit-il aux autres avant de s’éloigner de la table pour décrocher l’appareil de sa ceinture. Par mesure de précaution, il laissa la liaison vidéo coupée.

« Allô ?

– Hé, p’pa !

– Tyrone ! Tout va bien ? Ta mère... ?

– M’man va très bien, tout baigne cinq sur cinq, ici, p’pa. »

Howard se relaxa. Personne n’avait eu d’accident de voiture ou quoi que ce soit. « Qu’est-ce qui se passe, fiston ?

– Je voudrais pas t’embêter si t’es occupé.

– Je ne suis pas occupé à ce point. Accouche. »

Il y eut un silence. Qui s’éternisa.

« Hé, fils, on n’est pas en tarif local, là...

– Oups, désolé. Eh bien, il y a cette fille, au bahut... »

Howard écouta son fils lui débiter son problème, et il ne put s'empêcher de sourire. Chaque fois qu'on lui demandait s'il ne voudrait pas remonter le temps et revivre son existence, il répondait immanquablement : ça ne risque pas. Il n'avait pas commis tant d'erreurs qu'il éprouve le besoin urgent de revivre sa puberté pour rattraper le coup. Non, monsieur, pas question.

Fiorella et Fernandez l'ignoraient, plongés qu'ils étaient dans l'examen des images de l'ordinateur, et au bout d'un moment, Michaels et Cooper les rejoignirent.

Finalement, son fils parvint au bout de son exposé. « Alors, qu'est-ce t'en penses, p'pa ?

– Ma foi, je pourrais me tromper, mais je pense que ta championne de boomerang a un faible pour toi. Et il se pourrait bien qu'elle soit jalouse de Bella.

– Ah ouais ?

– Ouais. Et elle pourrait bien avoir ses raisons. Pourquoi est-ce que t'aimes bien traîner avec Nadine ?

– C'est une super-lanceuse, p'pa. Elle est intelligente, drôle, et elle a un bras qui vaut de l'or.

– Mais c'est pas une fille canon...

– Non, pas vraiment.

– Et Bella ?

– Merde, p'pa, elle, elle est méga-top !

– Et si ma mémoire est bonne, elle a également un caractère de cochon. Tu te souviens de m'avoir déjà parlé d'elle quand elle t'a plaqué comme une vieille chaussette ?

– Ouaip.

– Donc, elle t'a déjà fait le coup. T'as pas dans l'idée qu'elle pourrait recommencer, si ça lui chante ?

– Euh... non. Et puis, p't-être qu'elle s'est rendu compte qu'elle a fait une erreur.

– Peut-être surtout que tu es devenu plus désirable depuis qu'une autre a jeté son dévolu sur toi.

– Nadine ? C'est pas pour être méchant avec Nadine, mais je vois vraiment pas en quoi elle pourrait inquiéter Bella. D'accord, elle est marrante et tout, mais c'est pas le genre de nana sur laquelle on se retourne dans la rue.

– Si Nadine est athlétique, intelligente et drôle, certaines pourraient trouver ces qualités intimidantes, surtout si elles en sont dépourvues.

– Quoi ? Tu veux dire que *Bella* pourrait être *jalouse* de *Nadine* ? »

Howard se mit à rire. Son fils avait le même ton que s'il venait d'entendre son père lui annoncer qu'il comptait rentrer à la maison par la voie des airs, rien qu'en battant des bras très fort.

« À ton avis, quoi d'autre a changé, fils, depuis qu'elle t'a plaqué ?

– Rien. » Nouveau silence. Puis : « Meeerde...

– C'est chouette d'être désiré, reprit Howard. Mais tu dois te demander qui te désire, et pourquoi. Tu ne peux reprocher à personne la tête ou la silhouette que Dieu lui a donnée, mais ce n'est pas une raison non plus pour en tirer gloire. À moins d'avoir payé un max en chirurgie esthétique.

– Qu'est-ce que t'essaies de me dire, là, p'pa ?

– Si Bella n'était pas belle, si elle était banale, et même moche, est-ce que tu aurais toujours envie de la voir ? Est-ce qu'elle a quelque chose pour elle, mis à part son joli minois ? Est-ce que tu traverserais la rue pour aller lui causer, si elle n'était pas franchement regardable ? »

Ces longs silences commençaient à devenir coûteux.

« Euh...

– Réfléchis-y. Laisse mijoter un peu et vois ce que ça donne.

– Oh, flûte. Je crois qu'il vaut mieux que j'y aille... Euh, et merci encore, p'pa.

– Et dis bonjour à maman de ma part.

– D'accord. Discom !

– Salut, fils. »

Howard raccrocha le virgil à sa ceinture. Il était soldat, et il allait être absent un bout de temps, c'était le lot du métier des armes, mais ça le tracassait de ne pas être là pour aider son fils. Un homme avait sa tâche à remplir, mais il avait aussi des responsabilités vis-à-vis de sa famille. Quoi qu'il puisse arriver par ailleurs, il avait un fils qui avait besoin de son père. Il y avait des valeurs qu'il convenait de transmettre, des leçons à enseigner. Il faudrait qu'il s'en souvienne. C'était important.

33

Mercredi 13 avril
Crétacé supérieur
Dans ce qui deviendra l'Europe occidentale

Des fougères hautes comme des pins s'agitaient dans la touffeur de l'air et des libellules de la taille de faucons voletaient parmi la végétation luxuriante, poursuivant des moustiques qui auraient pu passer pour des moineaux étiques. C'était une ambiance primitive, primordiale, infiniment plus torride, humide et moite que dans la jungle équatoriale.

Le Humvee à empattement rallongé buta dans un monticule d'humus destiné à faire partie d'un gisement de pétrole d'ici trente à quarante millions d'années. La roue avant droite rebondit dans les airs et tourna dans le vide, mais les trois autres pneus à crampons avaient encore suffisamment d'accroche pour extraire le véhicule de la masse en décomposition avant qu'il ne retombe sur ses quatre roues motrices.

Jay se mit à claquer des dents.

Attachée sur le siège du passager, Saji remarqua : « Merde, Jay ! Tu veux que je prenne le volant ? »

Le jeune homme accéléra. Le Humvee fit une embardée. « Parce que tu crois que tu pourrais faire mieux ?

– En tout cas, je ne vois pas comment je pourrais faire pire. Sauf à nous jeter du haut d'une falaise. »

Le sol humide redevint à peu près horizontal et les sculptures des pneus réussirent à y mordre pour propulser le 4×4 un peu plus vite. « C'est pas si facile que ça en a l'air.

– Ma foi, vu comme tu t'y prends, facile n'est certes pas le mot qui vient immédiatement à l'esprit. »

Il essayait de trouver la repartie qui tue quand il avisa les fougères piétinées. Il rétrograda, s'approcha au ralenti des plantes écrasées, puis tira le levier de vitesses pour ramener l'engin au point mort. Coup d'œil à Saji. « Reste dedans pendant que je vais jeter un œil. Tu peux toujours te poster à côté de la mitrailleuse, si tu préfères. »

C'était une Browning calibre 50 chargée par ruban, montée à l'arrière du 4×4. Arrimé à côté, il y avait un lance-roquettes antichar à guidage laser avec une demi-douzaine de missiles. Jay avait envisagé d'emporter fusils et carabines, mais décidé de ne pas s'encombrer. Toute arme de calibre trop réduit serait inefficace. Il aurait certes préféré disposer d'un char d'assaut équipé d'obus perforants à pointe d'uranium appauvri, mais d'un point de vue relatif, le lance-roquettes était l'arme la plus importante autorisée dans ce scénario. Plus gros, ça ne passait pas.

Hélas.

« J'aimerais mieux pas », répondit Saji. Elle était en chemise et short de brousse, chaussée de godillots Nike et de chaussettes montantes qu'elle avait roulées. Elle était splendide dans cette tenue tropicale. Il se demanda comment elle était sans rien sur le dos.

« D'accord. Dans ce cas, change de place et glisse-toi au volant. Laisse le moteur tourner. Il se pourrait qu'on doive filer en vitesse. »

Il descendit et s'approcha des tiges de fougères géantes sectionnées. Le sol spongieux était recouvert d'une sorte de mousse verte.

Il ne risquait pas de manquer l'empreinte de pied : trois doigts et une paume, sans talon. Un peu d'eau s'était accumulée au fond de l'empreinte, si profonde qu'une fois complètement remplie, on aurait pu sans peine s'y intaller et prendre un bain.

Jay avala sa salive. Bon Dieu, incroyable, ce truc ! Il suivit la direction donnée par les doigts. Huit mètres plus loin, il découvrit une autre empreinte. Aucun doute : au-delà, la piste dans la forêt était bien visible, comme si quelqu'un avait traversé la jungle avec un gros semi-remorque diesel, en écrasant tout sur son passage.

Jay contempla ce sillage de désolation. Ce n'était pas un semi. Ben non. C'était Rex Regum, le roi des rois, *Carnosaurus supremus*, le prédateur ultime. Un truc à faire passer le tout-venant des tyrannosaures pour un vulgaire iguane domestiqué. La bête pouvait vous traverser la longueur d'un terrain de foot en une douzaine de pas. Pas loin de quinze mètres de haut, sans la queue.

La suivre à la trace n'allait pas être un problème. Mais comme pour un chien qui poursuit une voiture, restait la question, que faire lorsqu'il l'aurait rattrapée ? Cette mitrailleuse risquait de ne pas être de taille à s'acquitter de la tâche, et s'il s'approchait assez pour pouvoir tirer au lance-roquettes mais qu'il ratait sa cible, il n'aurait pas droit à un second coup.

Il fit demi-tour pour remonter en voiture. « Pousse-toi ! lança-t-il à Saji.

– J'ai pas l'impression que le pistage nous pose problème, observa-t-elle.

– Non, effectivement. » Il se mit au volant, embraya et entreprit de suivre le monstre à la trace.

Depuis que son cerveau s'était plus ou moins remis en route, quoique avec une certaine lenteur, Jay avait tourné et retourné le problème pour essayer de trouver une explication, n'importe laquelle, à l'existence d'une telle brute. Pour savoir ce qui avait pu la créer. Or, avec la technologie qu'il connaissait, il n'avait aucune réponse. Mais comme ils parcouraient la piste virtuelle sur les traces de la bête, il se remémora la vieille maxime de Sherlock Holmes : une fois éliminé l'impossible, il ne restait plus que l'improbable. Rien selon lui ne disposait d'une telle puissance, et pourtant il s'y connaissait en informatique. Mais puisque la chose existait, qui pouvait en être l'auteur ? Que lui fallait-il ? Il n'y avait pas des masses de possibilités, une seule se tenait, et elle n'était que théorique, aucune machine à ce jour n'existant pour la concrétiser.

Et si, par quelque miracle, c'était pourtant le cas ?

« Mieux vaudrait tourner à gauche, indiqua Saji.

– Tu crois ? Je pensais plutôt foncer droit dans ce gros arbre.

– J'essayais juste de me rendre utile. »

Il secoua la tête. « Pardon. J'étais distrait.

– Quelque chose te turlupine ?

– Une théorie.

– Ça te dit de me la faire partager ? »

Jay contempla le sillage de destruction qui transperçait la jungle virtuelle. Il devait certes rattraper le frère monstrueux de Godzilla, mais plus il en saurait sur son compte, mieux cela vaudrait. Tout élément susceptible de lui éclaircir les idées serait le bienvenu. « Bien sûr », fit-il.

Mercredi
Les Ifs, Sussex, Angleterre

Monseigneur était parti à son club, sous bonne escorte, et Peel était dans la chapelle, au téléphone, attendant toujours son correspondant. Dehors, en plus de son personnel habituel, il y avait le Tchétchène qui attendait dans une voiture de location, guettant des ennemis potentiels. Il estima qu'il devrait être relativement en sécurité, mais il n'y aurait pas mis sa tête à couper.

Qu'allait-il faire de ce putain de scientifique ? Devrait-il le liquider tout de suite ?

Naturellement, la première chose qu'il avait essayé de faire dès qu'il avait commencé à nourrir des doutes sur la fidélité de Bascomb-Coombs avait été d'essayer de retirer le million de la banque indonésienne. S'il avait pu transférer les fonds en Angleterre, il se serait senti soulagé, et cela aurait pour une bonne part contribué à apaiser ses craintes. Hélas, toutes les formes de transactions électroniques avaient été interrompues par l'ordinateur infernal de Bascomb-Coombs. Tout ce qu'il avait pu obtenir de sa machine lors de la connexion avait été un message « transfert en cours », bloqué en permanence à l'écran, dans l'attente d'une validation qui n'était jamais venue.

Au vu des pannes informatiques qui affectaient toute la planète, il n'aurait pas dû s'en étonner.

Mais il pouvait être tout aussi possible qu'il se fût agi d'une ruse habile de Bascomb-Coombs, une machination aisément dissimulée dans le chaos qu'il avait lui-même créé. Le temps que la situation se clarifie, il risquait bien d'être mort.

« Ici le vice-président Imandihardjo, annonça une voix masculine. En quoi puis-je vous aider ? »

Peel reporta son attention vers le téléphone. Enfin ! ce satané banquier indonésien. « Très bien, je suis M. Peel. J'aimerais avoir une situation précise de mon compte. »

Il aurait presque pu entendre son interlocuteur froncer les sourcils. Vérifier la situation d'un compte ? Et pour ça, il lui fallait un vice-président ? « Votre nom et votre mot de passe, je vous prie. »

Peel les lui donna.

Il y eut une longue pause. « Ah... monsieur Batterie, oui, je vois. »

Peel hocha la tête. Batterie... accus, piles... d'où le jeu de mots de Bascomb-Coombs. « Pile » pour « Peel »... même prononciation, juste une orthographe différente.

« Alors, vous l'avez, la situation de mon compte ?

– Oui, monsieur, tout à fait. » Le ton du vice-président changea, il avait à présent ces relents obséquieux que donnent parfois les grosses sommes d'argent à ceux qui en sont dépourvus. Excellent.

« J'aimerais transférer une partie de ce compte dans un autre établissement.

– Certainement, certainement. Si vous voulez bien m'indiquer les références bancaires... ? »

Peel lui débita son numéro de compte en Angleterre et son mot de passe. Une fois le transfert effectué, il sentait qu'il pourrait enfin souffler.

Quelques secondes plus tard, le banquier observa : « Ah, monsieur Batterie, il semble qu'on ait un problème avec notre système informatique.

– Vraiment ?

– Oui, monsieur. Je suis sûr que ce n'est pas bien grave mais j'ai peur de ne pas pouvoir vous fournir autre chose que votre position. L'ordinateur ne me laisse pas effectuer de transfert. »

Peel hocha la tête sans mot dire. Tiens donc.

« Hum. Il semble que plusieurs dizaines de comptes aient le même problème que le vôtre. Je suis certain qu'il ne s'agit que d'un dérangement temporaire.

– Vous êtes en train de me dire que je ne peux pas récupérer mon argent tant que la panne ne sera pas réparée ?

– Ma foi, j'en ai bien peur, en effet.

– Je vois. » Il n'avait pas besoin d'en entendre plus. Ses entrailles se nouèrent, il sentit un grand froid l'envahir. Il eut le brusque soupçon qu'au terme d'un examen un peu plus attentif, la banque indonésienne ne tarderait pas à découvrir qu'elle détenait des dollars virtuels qui scintillaient quand on les regardait du coin de l'œil mais s'évanouissaient en fumée sitôt qu'on s'avisait de poser la main dessus. Il s'était fait rouler par cette petite crapule de Bascomb-Coombs.

« Je suis sûr que tout ceci va être réglé dans les plus brefs délais. Si vous voulez bien me donner un numéro auquel je puis vous toucher, je vous rappelle sitôt que nous aurons résolu le problème. »

Ben voyons.

Peel lui donna le numéro, mais il n'avait pas l'intention de poireauter jusqu'à ce que son argent soit à nouveau disponible. Il s'était fait arnaquer et il connaissait l'auteur du coup.

Il était plus que temps d'avoir une petite discussion avec M. Bascomb-Coombs. Entre quatre-z-yeux.

Mais presque au même instant, son téléphone sonna. La ligne privée.

« Oui ?

– Allô, Terrance. » Tiens donc. Quand on parle du loup...

« Allô.

– J'ai peur que nous ayons comme un problème. Il semble que monseigneur ait donné ordre de bloquer mon accès à mon... euh... joujou. Il a fait couper toutes les lignes extérieures visibles et posté un garde pour m'empêcher physiquement d'accéder au bâtiment.

– Vraiment ? Et pourquoi cela ?

– Je soupçonne le vieux de ne plus me faire confiance. »

Et il a de sacrées bonnes raisons, songea Peel. Puis une autre idée lui vint : « Les lignes extérieures *visibles*, avez-vous dit ? »

Bascomb-Coombs avait coupé la vidéo, mais Peel pouvait presque le voir sourire. « Très bien vu, Terrance. Naturellement, j'avais pris soin de planquer plusieurs liaisons bidirectionnelles numériques par micro-ondes. Plus une liaison terrestre multiplexée sur la ligne d'alimentation électrique, au cas où quelqu'un s'aviserait de recourir à des brouilleurs... Il faudrait qu'ils démontent le plancher pour couper mes connexions, et comme ils en ignorent l'existence, ils n'en feront rien. Et s'ils coupaient l'alimentation générale, ils pourraient bien ne plus être capables de remettre en route le système.

– Je vois. Ce qui veut dire, en clair ?

– Je crois que nous allons devoir traiter avec le vieux. En faisant appel cette fois à *votre* domaine de compétence.

– Vous croyez ?

– J'en ai peur, oui. Bon, il faut que je raccroche, mais je vous rappelle dès que possible. Laissez-moi un temps de réflexion, d'accord ? »

Le scientifique coupa la connexion. Peel fixa le mur de son bureau.

Bon Dieu, ce type avait des couilles en béton. En même temps qu'il essayait de faire liquider Peel, il faisait comme si de rien n'était en lui ordonnant d'éliminer leur employeur commun. Il fallait avoir de sacrés nerfs, pas de doute.

Peel se rendit compte qu'il respirerait beaucoup mieux sans ces deux-là sur le dos. Bascomb-Coombs devait disparaître, bien sûr ; on ne pouvait guère s'encombrer d'un homme qui cherchait à vous faire assassiner. Quant à Goswell, tout gâteux qu'il fût, il n'était pas totalement sénile. Tôt ou tard, il finirait bien par s'apercevoir que son chef de la sécurité l'avait vendu au savant fou, et ça, ce serait très mauvais pour lui. Il doutait que le vieux aille chercher sa pétoire pour le descendre, mais il ne faisait aucun doute qu'il veillerait à empêcher Peel de retrouver du travail au Royaume-Uni. Avec un million en banque, cette perspective ne l'avait pas inquiété outre mesure, mais si l'argent n'était qu'une autre ruse de Bascomb-Coombs, Peel allait se retrouver, pour le compte, bel et bien baisé.

Si Bascomb-Coombs disparaissait, et si monseigneur succombait à une attaque ou à un infarctus, Peel aurait enfin le champ libre, sans personne pour lui monter le coup. Il ne serait peut-être pas riche, mais il pourrait toujours se placer sur le marché. Avec ses états de service sans faille auprès de monseigneur, il trouverait bien un autre vieux con bourré de fric pour l'engager.

La victoire valait mieux que la défaite, mais il fallait parfois battre en retraite afin de survivre assez longtemps pour tenter une nouvelle action. Il avait engagé Roujio parce qu'il avait besoin d'un bouc émissaire pour éliminer le vieux, mais à présent, compte tenu du changement de situation, autant que Goswell meure de cause naturelle, ça passerait mieux sur le CV de son chef de la sécurité.

Quant à Bascomb-Coombs, il disparaîtrait simplement de telle façon que personne ne retrouverait jamais sa trace.

Peel sourit. Oui. Tout ceci était bien regrettable, mais nullement irréparable. Le temps de rattraper le coup et de régler la question une bonne fois pour toutes. Tuez-les tous, Dieu reconnaîtra les siens. C'était bien ce qu'avait dit un des premiers papes... *Plutôt eux que moi.*

34

Mercredi 13 avril
Londres

Profitant d'une brève accalmie dans l'activité de plus en plus frénétique du MI-6, Toni trouva le temps de passer un coup de fil à Carl Stewart.

« Allô ?

– Carl ?

– Ah, Toni. Comment vas-tu ?

– Bien. Écoute, je suis dans le boulot jusqu'au cou et je ne vois vraiment pas comment je pourrais me libérer pour venir à ton cours, ce soir. Désolée.

– Pas grave. Tu nous manqueras, mais je comprends.

– Merci. »

Après un bref silence, il ajouta : « Enfin, il faut bien que tu manges, quand même, non ? Peut-être qu'on pourrait se voir à déjeuner ou dîner d'ici la fin de la semaine ? »

Toni sentit comme un coup au creux de l'estomac. C'étaient moins les mots que le ton sur lequel ils étaient prononcés qui la mirent en alerte. Est-ce qu'il n'était pas en train de lui proposer un rendez-vous ? Elle aurait pu lui poser la question tout de go mais elle ne se sentait pas encore tout à fait prête. Devait-elle répondre à l'invite ? Ou bien au contraire la décliner ? Elle pouvait certes toujours dire qu'elle était trop occupée, mais non. Elle avait par trop tergiversé à son goût, ces temps derniers. L'heure était peut-être venue de prendre le taureau par les cornes.

« S'agit-il de deux adeptes du silat qui se retrouvent pour manger un morceau, Carl ? Ou bien d'autre chose ?

– Eh bien... je pensais plutôt à deux personnes qui trouvent leur compagnie mutuellement agréable et qui s'avèrent partager un goût commun pour le pentjak silat... »

Un rendez-vous, donc.

Sa réaction instinctive faillit être de lui dire qu'elle était déjà prise et de décliner poliment. La fenêtre s'ouvrit... et resta ouverte. C'était un homme plein de vie, séduisant, et dont le talent forçait son admiration. S'ils devaient se retrouver sur le *gelanggang*, le tapis de combat, pour une vraie compétition, il la vaincrait, aucun doute là-dessus. Alors qu'elle était sûre que même son propre gourou, aujourd'hui octogénaire, n'était désormais plus à son niveau, qu'elle était à peu près certaine de pouvoir tenir tête en combat singulier à la plupart des maîtres d'arts martiaux de l'un ou l'autre sexe, si prétentieux que cela puisse paraître, elle savait avec certitude qu'elle ne pourrait vaincre Carl. Et c'était, pour une grande part, ce qui le rendait si séduisant. Elle imagina, fugitivement, ce que ça pouvait donner de se retrouver étendue nue sur un lit en compagnie de cet homme plein de force et de séduction, et le fantasme n'avait rien de désagréable. Bien au contraire. En fait...

Elle sentit, brutal, l'aiguillon de la culpabilité. « Je suis très proche d'Alex, Carl, tu sais, et je suis sensible à ton invitation, mais je pense qu'on ferait peut-être mieux d'en rester sur un plan strictement professionnel.

– Ah... eh bien, tant pis. Mais je comprends, bien sûr. J'apprécie ta franchise. Préviens-moi dès que tu pourras reprendre les cours.

– Sans faute. Merci. »

Dès qu'elle eut raccroché, Toni eut le cœur tout chaviré. Pendant un instant, la tentation avait été si forte... Plus qu'elle n'aurait voulu l'admettre. Elle aurait pu suivre cette voie, et ça la tracassait que l'idée même l'eût effleurée. Elle admirait Carl, elle éprouvait même pour lui une certaine attirance sexuelle, mais elle aimait d'amour Alex, et il y avait un monde entre eux deux. L'espace d'une seconde, pourtant, elle s'était interrogée, elle avait eu une hésitation, avait envisagé la chose.

On ne peut pas vous pendre pour vos pensées : ce vieil adage disait vrai parce que personne ne pouvait lire vos pensées, mais on ne pouvait jamais se leurrer longtemps soi-même. Comment une idée pareille avait-elle pu lui traverser l'esprit ? Non, vraiment, c'était moche, très moche.

Mercredi
Les Ifs, Sussex, Angleterre

Roujio rajusta le pistolet 9 mm Firestar dans l'étui de hanche sous son imper, basculant légèrement la crosse vers l'avant pour que la position soit plus confortable. L'arme de poing précédente, celle fournie par Peel, le Beretta de fabrication américaine, était à présent au fond de la Tamise, soigneusement nettoyée et cassée en plusieurs morceaux, le mécanisme et le canon séparés par plus de trois kilomètres. Si, par le plus grand des hasards, quelqu'un parvenait à les récupérer avant qu'ils ne rouillent, à les assembler, puis à effectuer des tests balistiques et en conclure que la balle dans le corps du cadavre de la librairie provenait de cette arme, cela n'aurait guère d'importance, puisque de toute façon il n'aurait rien pour la relier à Roujio. Mais quand on ne laissait rien au hasard, le hasard avait alors d'autant moins de chances de vous retomber sur le paletot.

Il n'appréciait pas trop la nouvelle arme, mais au moins pouvait-il s'en servir. Solide, fabriquée avec soin, c'était un semi-automatique plaqué chrome dont le fonctionnement était assez proche de celui des antiques Colt 45 de l'armée : fiable, peu encombrant, bien qu'un peu lourd. Il était doté d'un chargeur de sept balles chemisées à pointe creuse, plus une engagée dans la chambre. Tous ces projectiles avaient une pointe rayée pour exploser à l'impact dans un corps humain et provoquer le maximum de dégâts. Bref, pas une arme conçue pour faire des trous dans du carton au stand de tir, ou dégommer de vieilles canettes de bière dans les bois : non, elle était destinée à tirer sur de la chair tendre, l'endommager sérieusement, voire la faire passer de vie à trépas.

Roujio sourit. Ces dernières années, surtout aux États-Unis, les fabricants d'armes s'étaient trouvés en butte aux attaques des trusts anti-armement. Leur dernière tactique avait été de poursuivre les manufacturiers pour défaut de dispositifs de sécurité ou de mises en garde. Il avait du mal à imaginer la stupidité d'une pareille attitude. Poussée à l'extrême, elle aurait conduit à l'apposition d'avertissements analogues sur les véhicules, les ustensiles de cuisine, voire les allumettes : « Attention ! Vous pouvez vous faire tuer si vous percutez un gros camion au volant de cette petite voiture ! » « Attention ! Ce couteau est doté d'une lame affûtée – ne pas la plaquer contre votre gorge ! » « Danger ! Les allumettes peuvent déclencher un feu susceptible de vous brûler ! »

Cette idée d'étiquetage des armes à feu lui semblait d'une monumentale sottise pour quiconque avait deux doigts de jugeote. C'était une chose d'exiger un dispositif de verrouillage difficile à actionner pour des enfants, et une autre d'imprimer sur le canon d'une arme à feu : « Attention ! Ne pas pointer sur quelqu'un en pressant la détente ! » De toute façon, celui qui ne comprenait pas à quoi servait un flingue ne serait pas non plus capable de déchiffrer une telle mise en garde. Tout ça lui rappelait la vieille publicité qu'il avait pu lire jadis dans les trolleybus de sa Tchétchénie natale : « Vous êtes illettré ? Si oui, contactez telle adresse... »

Le 9mm se chargerait du boulot, et il avait toujours le parapluie, au cas où. En supplément, il s'était acheté un couteau automatique Benchmark tactique, avec une lame crantée de dix centimètres. Compte tenu des lois en vigueur dans le pays, avec deux armes à feu et un couteau, il était sans doute mieux armé que n'importe qui, y compris la majorité des forces de police. Comme naguère en plein désert du Nevada, Roujio éprouvait le besoin d'être armé. La situation risquait de tourner au vinaigre, il en avait le pressentiment.

Il envisagea la possibilité de filer. Sauter dans un bateau, un train ou un avion pour gagner le continent, puis retourner au pays, en faisant des détours pour éviter d'être pisté. C'était encore possible, Peel s'apercevrait trop tard de sa disparition pour l'en empêcher, quand bien même il l'aurait voulu.

Seulement Roujio était las. Et regarder sans cesse par-dessus son épaule accroissait sa lassitude. Il avait toujours les Américains aux trousses ; ils étaient quelque part aux aguets et ils allaient bien finir par réussir à le repérer. Inutile de se retrouver avec un autre ennemi sur les talons. Non, il allait d'abord terminer cette affaire avec Peel, et quand il tirerait sa révérence, ce serait de sa propre initiative. D'une manière ou d'une autre, il réglerait le problème. Une fois de retour au bercail, eh bien, advienne que pourra, il aviserait le moment venu.

Peel ressortit de la chapelle reconvertie et lui adressa un signe de tête avant de se diriger vers sa voiture personnelle. Roujio répondit en acquiesçant puis démarra à son tour. Ils devaient retourner voir l'informaticien à l'endroit où Roujio avait détecté la fameuse filature qui s'était achevée par un cadavre dans une librairie. Apparemment, le commandant Peel avait des plans qui risquaient de ne pas être du goût de M. Bascomb-Coombs.

Le scientifique était le cadet des soucis de Roujio. Il comptait rester aux côtés de Peel jusqu'à ce qu'une occasion favorable se présente, et à ce moment-là, salut la compagnie ! Et ce serait pour bientôt, estima-t-il en sortant à son tour de la propriété derrière lui. Pour très bientôt.

Mercredi
Washington, DC

Il y avait eu un interminable conseil de discipline au collège, et une fois celui-ci achevé, Tyrone s'était retrouvé dans le préau ; il salua Jimmy-Joe au passage. Essai, le monstre du bahut, s'était bel et bien fait exclure, pour au moins deux semaines, et alors qu'il restait encore quelques spécimens à éviter dans les corridors, ils ne jouaient pas dans la même catégorie que l'autre grand idiot.

Alors qu'il allait prendre la queue du car de ramassage, il avisa Bella, son livre électronique à la main, qui marchait en riant avec trois copines. Elle le remarqua et lui sourit : « Hé, Ty, par ici ! »

Il sentit cette bouffée d'excitation qui le transperça comme une aiguille de glace pour venir se ficher dans son bas-ventre. Il se tourna vers elle, en retenant ses pas pour ne pas donner l'impression d'être pressé. Il essayait de garder l'air dégagé, tranquille, QC – Quasi Congelé – tant il était hyper-cool. Bella voulait le voir ? C'était super-CPI et tout, mais surtout pas de panique, Nick, d'accord ? Cool, Raoul. Peinard. C'était l'image qu'il voulait donner : le mec peinard. Mais il allait peut-être un poil trop vite pour ne pas se trahir. Genre démarche à douze images par seconde qui aurait fait nettement meilleur effet à vingt-quatre.

« Hé, Bella !

– On va faire un tour à la galerie marchande. Tu veux nous accompagner ? »

Il sourit. Et à la seconde précise où il allait lui servir un « Bien sûr, pourquoi pas ? » hyper décontract', il avisa, derrière Bella, Nadine qui traversait le hall.

Nadine le vit elle aussi et détourna les yeux.

Bella remarqua son regard et suivit aussitôt sa direction. Juste un coup d'œil fugitif, avant de faire comme si de rien n'était, mais Tyrone avait deviné son manège : Nadine venait de subir l'inspection, de recevoir le label « éliminée » et d'être oubliée, tout cela en un clin d'œil, au revoir et merci.

Alors tout d'un coup, Tyrone Howard, bientôt quatorze ans, se trouva à la croisée des chemins qui devait marquer le reste de son existence. Devant lui s'ouvraient deux itinéraires partant à angle droit, et il n'avait guère de chances de sauter de l'un à l'autre dès lors qu'il aurait fait son choix.

Tu as le com dans la main, Tyrone. Alors, qui vas-tu appeler ?

Peut-être qu'il pouvait encore jouer sur les deux tableaux. Il répondit : « Si on se retrouvait plutôt au bus ? J'ai un truc à régler d'abord. »

Bella n'était peut-être pas la diode la plus brillante au tableau d'affichage, mais elle n'était quand même pas nulle au point de ne pas saisir aussitôt de quoi il retournait. Elle ne manqua pas de le lui faire savoir : « C'est tout de suite qu'on y va, Ty. » Sous-entendu : c'est maintenant ou jamais, Tyrone. À toi de choisir.

Eh bien... flûte. Ce serait chouette de pouvoir en profiter aussi, mais aucun risque, pas question, il n'était pas zéro-formaté-brouillé à ce point.

La seconde s'éternisa quelques millions d'années. Il

avait l'impression qu'il était sur le point d'exploser. Zut, zut et superzut.

On pouvait se dérober d'un côté, se dérober de l'autre, mais pas des deux côtés à la fois.

Et puis merde. Il prit sa décision. « Nadine ! Hé, Nadine ! Attends une seconde ! »

Nadine se retourna, surprise, c'était manifeste. Il n'osa pas se retourner pour regarder Bella, pourtant il aurait bien voulu voir sa tronche. On venait de lui accorder une seconde chance de monter au paradis et il venait de la balancer aux chiottes et de tirer la chasse. Il avait envie de fuir se cacher dans un trou de souris.

Nadine sourit et son visage n'avait plus du tout l'air aussi quelconque. Quand il fut à sa hauteur, elle remarqua : « Ta petite amie vient de filer sans toi. Elle avait pas vraiment l'air ravie. »

Il haussa les épaules. « Et alors ? » Il se sentait mal mais il se sentait vachement bien en même temps. « Comment va ce bras ? Tu veux quand même t'entraîner un peu ?

– Ça te dit ?

– Ça me dit. »

Le sourire s'élargit. « Mon bras va nettement mieux maintenant. Ouais. Allons nous entraîner. »

Et en marchant à ses côtés, Tyrone sentit lui aussi le sourire le gagner. C'était un truc que lui avait dit son père. Quand on a fait le bon choix, on se sent toujours mieux que dans le cas contraire.

Et un point de plus pour son vieux.

35

Jeudi 14 avril
Crétacé supérieur
Dans ce qui deviendra l'ouest de la France

« On dirait qu'il sait nager », nota Saji.

Jay arrêta le Humvee et coupa le moteur. Les traces du monstre aboutissaient au bord d'un océan pour disparaître dans les eaux. De petites vagues soyeuses couronnées d'une écume immaculée dévidaient mécaniquement leurs rouleaux sur le rivage. « Apparemment.

– Et maintenant ?

– On change de véhicule. Bateau ou hélicoptère. Je pencherais pour l'hélico.

– Je comprends. Mieux vaut dominer la situation de quelques centaines de pieds que de voguer au risque de le voir nous débouler par en dessous, tel Moby Dick. »

Jay hocha la tête. « L'inconvénient, c'est qu'on peut armer le bateau plus fortement que l'hélicoptère. On est limités en capacité d'emport, donc, si on l'aperçoit du haut des airs, l'un de nous devra se pencher à l'extérieur pour pouvoir lui tirer dessus. Pas question d'utiliser le lance-roquettes dans le cockpit d'un hélico. Les gaz d'échappement nous rôtiraient comme si on avait été nous-mêmes touchés par le missile.

– Agréable perspective. Pourquoi ces limites à l'armement ?

– Ma foi... Même en sim*, il faut toujours garder à l'esprit la situation réelle correspondante. Ce truc est plus gros, plus fort et plus rapide que nous, et on ne peut pas se contenter de lui balancer une bombe atomique, tout simplement parce qu'on n'a rien d'équivalent face au matos et au programme contre lequel on se bat. » Il descendit de la Jeep et contempla la plage. Il sortit de son blouson un GPS et le consulta. « Là, j'admets, c'est une tricherie par rapport au scénario. Je devrais consulter une carte papier, puisqu'il n'existait aucun réseau de satellite de positionnement à cette époque. Mais ça encore, on peut laisser passer. En revanche, pas un submersible de classe Seawolf, et ça, c'est vraiment dommage. De toute façon, je ne suis pas certain non plus qu'il ait existé ici une telle masse d'eau. J'avoue que mes connaissances en géologie ne sont pas si pointues. »

Saji descendit à son tour, s'étira, puis remarqua : « Et c'est où, *ici* ?

– Les côtes françaises. Ce qui sera un jour la Grande-Bretagne se trouve par là-bas, derrière l'horizon.

– Donc, dans le MR, c'est là qu'aboutit la piste ?

– Apparemment, ouais.

– Ça te conforte dans ta théorie ? »

Jay opina. « Ouais. Peut-être.

– Tu vas te lancer à ses trousses ?

– Ça oui. Je veux juste sortir momentanément de RV pour vérifier d'abord deux ou trois trucs et appeler le patron. Je pense que ce ne serait pas une mauvaise idée de lui faire part de ma théorie. Au cas où. »

Jeudi
Siège du MI-6, Londres

Dans la salle de conférences du MI-6, Alex Michaels attendait l'apparition de l'image de Jay dans la sphère holographique bleutée qui flottait au-dessus de la table. Autour de lui, il y avait Toni, Howard, Fernandez et Angela Cooper.

Michaels expliqua : « Je voulais que vous entendiez tous ceci, c'est pourquoi j'ai fait transférer ici l'appel de Jay. Nous l'aurons dans une minute. Autre chose, en attendant ? »

Howard prit la parole : « On a un rendez-vous avec ce commandant en retraite, chez son employeur, dans sa résidence... (il baissa les yeux vers son écran-plat) ... du Sussex, cet après-midi.

– Chouette balade, commenta Angela. La région est superbe, même si les routes sont un peu étroites.

– Pas de nouvelles attaques notables contre les grands réseaux ou les systèmes militaires, intervint Toni. On dirait bien que notre pirate a battu en retraite – momentanément, du moins.

– J'apprécie toutes les bonnes nouvelles, d'où qu'elles viennent, commenta Michaels. Bon, assez fait attendre Jay. »

L'holoprojection vacilla et le visage de Gridley se matérialisa soudain dans les airs. « Hé, patron. » Sa voix paraissait presque normale, juste un rien pâteuse. Il récupérait vite.

« Jay, c'est Angela Cooper du MI-6. Sinon, vous connaissez tous les autres. »

Jay murmura un salut.

« Très bien, reprit Michaels. Raconte-nous ce que t'as trouvé. »

Soupir de Jay. « Ben, pas grand-chose. Nous... je suis sur la piste du programme et il semble qu'il mène dans votre direction. Il pourrait être juste de passage, il pourrait vivre là-bas, j'en sais rien. Je me remets en chasse dès qu'on aura discommuté*.

« J'ai réfléchi au problème. Aucun ordinateur existant à notre connaissance ne pourrait, rien que par la force brute, factoriser des nombres premiers comme le fait cette machine, même avec une architecture massivement parallèle, donc c'est qu'il doit s'agir d'autre chose. La première idée qui vient à l'esprit quand on se demande quel genre d'ordinateur pourrait en être capable, c'est bien sûr un ordinateur quantique. On en a déjà discuté. Le problème, c'est que jusqu'ici, aucun prototype n'a dépassé les premiers stades expérimentaux à petite échelle, de sorte qu'aucun n'aurait la puissance nécessaire pour réaliser les dégâts qu'on a constatés.

– Je suis peut-être lourd, intervint Fernandez, mais c'est quoi, un ordinateur quantique ? »

Jay leur fit un bref exposé, expliquant ce qu'étaient les Q-bits et les états quantiques multiples. Michaels était familiarisé avec le concept mais, comme l'avait souligné le jeune homme, personne à ce jour n'avait réussi à fabriquer en vraie grandeur un OQ opérationnel, de sorte qu'ils n'avaient jamais sérieusement envisagé l'hypothèse.

« Oui, mais si quelqu'un en avait un, malgré tout ? insista Jay. Un modèle pleinement opérationnel ? Un truc d'une puissance de cent ou deux cents Q-bits ? Il vous pulvériserait n'importe quel cryptage à base de nombres premiers comme une tornade explose une meule de foin.

– Ça fait un gros "si", observa Toni.

– Ouais, mais j'ai mené ma petite enquête. Aucune des organisations politiques ou militaires qui sont passées au nouveau standard de cryptage à matrice pluridimensionnelle AMPD (Abstract-Multidimensional-Point-Distance) n'a été inquiétée par ces attaques. Ce pourrait être une coïncidence, mais un OQ ne serait pas en mesure de percer ces algorithmes de chiffrement. Peu importe la vitesse de traitement, la méthode AMPD est, par sa conception même, à l'abri de telles attaques. D'un autre côté, bien sûr, seule une poignée de systèmes ont déjà basculé sur cette méthode.

– D'accord, dit Michaels, mais si quelqu'un avait créé une telle machine, est-ce que nous n'en aurions pas eu vent ?

– À la longue, sans doute. On ne peut pas la garder cachée éternellement, mais durant un temps, cela reste possible. La technologie et le matériel nécessaires ne se trouvent pas sous le sabot d'un cheval ou dans le labo d'informatique du premier lycée venu. On parle là d'installations de plusieurs millions de dollars, de matériel fabriqué sur commande, de tout un tas de périphériques coûteux, sans compter le personnel de laboratoire, de maintenance, les programmeurs et tout le bastringue... Tôt ou tard, quelqu'un de l'extérieur va tomber dessus, ce n'est pas une bidouille d'amateur qu'on peut planquer sous un bout de filet de camouflage. Une fois localisé, même s'il est le seul de son espèce, il devrait se voir comme le nez au milieu de la figure.

– Oui, un OQ, ça paraît une hypothèse tentante, admit Toni. On a des informations pour la corroborer ?

– Aucune preuve tangible à mettre sur la table, reconnut Jay. Mais encore une fois, si une telle machine existait, elle correspondrait parfaitement aux paramètres.

– Et selon ton opinion d'expert, c'est le genre de système vers lequel tu pencherais ? » C'était Howard.

« Oui, mon colonel. Aucun autre ne répond mieux aux critères. J'ai fouiné sur le web et recensé toutes les publications sérieuses concernant le domaine. Dans la liste des auteurs, on trouve deux types au Royaume-Uni. Le premier, un certain Peter Bascomb-Coombs, a publié sur le sujet un article théorique brillantissime il y a deux ans. Il est à plusieurs coudées au-dessus du lot, je ne lui arrive sûrement pas à la cheville. Je ne vois même pas qui pourrait. Il résidait à Londres mais il semble avoir disparu de la circulation.

– Est-ce qu'on doit le considérer comme quelqu'un susceptible de nous aider ou bien comme un suspect ? s'enquit Howard.

– Dans l'une ou l'autre hypothèse, je l'interrogerais si j'étais à votre place. Je ne suis pas arrivé à trouver son adresse électronique dans un annuaire public. Ça paraît tout de même bizarre qu'un type de cette carrure se soit volatilisé comme ça. Il était trop jeune pour prendre sa retraite, et s'il avait cané, on l'aurait su par les journaux.

– File-nous tout ce que t'as sur lui et on va vérifier de notre côté, suggéra Michaels.

– C'est déjà transmis », indiqua Jay. Il y eut une brève pause, puis il reprit : « Bon, il faut que je me remette en chasse. Je crois que je vais parvenir à abattre ce monstre, il n'est plus loin.

– Sois prudent, Jay. » C'était Toni. Il était inutile de lui rappeler pourquoi. Si quelqu'un le savait, c'était bien lui.

« Ouais. Merci. Je vous tiens au courant. »

Angela, qui était en train de taper des instructions sur son écran-plat, leva les yeux au moment où Jay coupait la connexion. « J'ai récupéré les infos sur M. Bascomb-Coombs. Je lance une recherche...

– Quoi ? fit Michaels.

– Voilà notre homme. Employé par ComCo Angleterre. C'est une petite boîte d'informatique qui fabrique, entre autres, des cartes-mères pour stations de travail haut de gamme.

– Bref, c'est un informaticien qui bosse pour une boîte d'informatique, observa Fernandez. C'est vraiment une surprise ?

– En soi, non, admit-elle. Mais ComCo Angleterre appartient à Lord Geoffrey Goswell. »

Michaels se demanda où diable il avait déjà entendu ce nom. Et puis ça lui revint.

Howard l'avait devancé : « N'est-ce pas le type dont le chef de la sécurité se trouvait dans la boutique avec notre assassin et le cadavre ?

– Oui, confirma Angela.

– Tiens, tiens, fit Howard. Comme le monde est petit.

– Ça ne veut sans doute pas dire grand-chose, poursuivit Angela. Goswell possède plusieurs entreprises, et il a des milliers d'employés dans tout le pays. Où qu'on aille en Angleterre, en Écosse, au pays de Galles ou en Irlande, on a des chances de tomber sur quelqu'un qui bosse pour lui ou qui connaît quelqu'un dans ce cas. »

Alex hocha la tête. Les coïncidences, ce n'était pas son fort. On avait sans doute déjà vu des trucs plus troublants, mais toute cette histoire sentait quand même brusquement le roussi.

« Vous savez quoi, on va reporter momentanément cet entretien avec Peel. Faites comme si de rien n'était, dites-lui que vous avez résolu votre affaire, que vous le rappellerez plus tard si on a besoin de le voir. Je pense qu'on doit d'abord en savoir un peu plus sur son patron avant d'aller farfouiller dans son antre. »

Howard était d'accord avec lui, tout comme Fernandez et Toni. Angela lui adressa un petit sourire, et il sentit son cœur tressaillir et cogner dans sa poitrine. Il évita de regarder Toni. Il ne voulait pas prendre le risque.

Jeudi
Londres

Peel passa en voiture devant l'usine à gaz qui bordait Old Kent Road, et il était franchement en rogne.

Bascomb-Coombs s'était pris sa journée de la veille, et quand il était allé le retrouver, il l'avait manqué. D'après ses agents, l'informaticien n'était pas chez lui, et il n'avait pas pris sa voiture qui était toujours parquée dans son garage. Il ne répondait pas non plus au téléphone.

Une nouvelle visite à son bureau ne donna pas plus de résultat.

Où diable était-il passé ?

C'était de sa faute, Peel le savait. Il avait demandé à ses hommes de se retirer parce qu'il voulait s'occuper en personne de Bascomb-Coombs. Il n'avait pas envie qu'ils soient dans les parages à ce moment-là ; par conséquent, il ne devait s'en prendre qu'à lui-même si le salaud avait disparu. Où avait-il pu filer, ce connard ? Et pourquoi ?

Son téléphone carillonna.

« Allô ? Peel à l'appareil.

– Commandant Peel ? C'est Angela Cooper. »

La fille du renseignement. Manquait plus que ça ! Ils l'appelaient de temps en temps, après cette histoire en Irlande. Chaque fois qu'un de ces excités de bouffeurs de patates faisait sauter quelque chose, ils appelaient à tous les coups, comme s'il était personnellement responsable des conneries de ces cinglés. « Mademoiselle Cooper. Je n'ai pas oublié notre rendez-vous cet après-midi.

– Il se trouve justement que nous n'aurons pas besoin de nous entretenir avec vous, en définitive. À vrai dire, l'affaire en question s'est résolue d'elle-même. Désolée encore une fois de vous avoir dérangé. »

Dieu merci, c'était toujours ça de gagné. Au moins

n'aurait-il pas à se carrer ces foutus imbéciles. « Vous m'en voyez ravi.

– Bien, je vais raccrocher. Encore une fois merci pour votre coopération. »

Après avoir coupé, Peel jeta un coup d'œil dans son rétro pour s'assurer qu'il n'avait pas perdu de vue Roujio. Non.

Bien, et maintenant, où vas-tu, mon brave vieux Peel ? Notre savant fou semble avoir pris la poudre d'escampette, il n'est pas dans sa piaule ni à aucun de ses points de chute habituels, et tout cela ne fait que confirmer tes soupçons. Il t'a menti, a essayé de t'éliminer, et t'a piqué en prime un million d'euros. T'aurais intérêt à le retrouver et à régler le problème avant qu'il n'empire.

Plus facile à dire qu'à faire, toutefois.

C'était une journée chaude et ensoleillée, et Howard, en civil, déambulait sur les trottoirs à quelques pâtés de maisons du siège du MI-6, profitant du beau temps en touriste. Londres était une vraie cité cosmopolite. Des gens le croisaient, curieusement accoutrés, parlant toutes sortes de langues, et qui pourtant avaient l'air d'être parfaitement chez eux dans la capitale britannique.

À ses côtés, habillé en pékin lui aussi, Julio sourit en croisant deux adolescentes en minijupe et chaussées de semelles compensées épaisses comme un annuaire téléphonique. Les gamines lui rendirent son sourire avant de gratifier Howard d'un long regard appréciatif. Merde, l'un comme l'autre auraient pu être leur père. Et si elles se cassaient la figure avec ces godasses monstrueuses, elles avaient toutes les chances de se péter une cheville, ou pire. Howard regarda le sergent, le sourcil levé.

« Hé, vous savez ce qu'on dit, un beau spectacle suffit à vous embellir la journée.

– Et une mineure reste une mineure, où que tu ailles. Tu ne dois pas être bientôt père de famille ?

– Faut vous décoincer un peu, John. Entre regarder et passer à l'acte, il y a de la marge.

– Tu es resté célibataire un long moment, Julio. Tu es sûr d'être capable d'assumer la transition ?

– Pour être franc, je n'en sais rien. Je pense que oui. Je vais tâcher de faire de mon mieux. Mais vous savez aussi bien que moi qu'aucun plan de bataille ne survit au premier contact avec l'ennemi.

– Parce que vous envisagez le mariage comme une guerre, sergent ?

– Pas exactement une guerre, mais sans aucun doute un territoire inconnu. Je veux dire... j'aime Jo, j'ai envie de m'éveiller tous les matins à ses côtés, et elle va être la mère de mon enfant, mais je ne suis pas non plus une jeune recrue de dix-huit ans, tout juste débarquée de sa ferme et qui découvre la ville pour la première fois.

– Ça, c'est certain. » Il laissa provisoirement cette question de côté, puis enchaîna : « Alors, qu'est-ce que tu penses de toute cette affaire ? »

Fernandez haussa les épaules. « Ce Goswell qui fait partie de la haute, le type inattaquable, j'ai l'impression que c'est un refrain qu'on connaît. Peut-être qu'après tout, il n'a rien à voir avec ça. Mais, que je sache, tous les hommes politiques ou tous les hommes d'affaires riches et célèbres ont toujours eu des squelettes à cacher dans leur placard. Et ça me paraît quand même curieux que notre tueur russe soit comme par hasard en cheville avec ce commandant qui bosse pour notre chevalier sans peur et sans reproche.

– Ouais, c'est aussi mon avis. »

Une superbe nana café-au-lait en robe de soie rouge et noir les croisa avec une démarche langoureuse. Juchée sur ses talons hauts, elle dépassait le mètre quatre-vingts, facile. Un mannequin, peut-être. Elle était suivie d'un sillage subtil de parfum de luxe. Julio se retourna sur son passage et Howard jeta un œil par-dessus son épaule, en essayant de rester discret.

« Pas mal non plus, vue de derrière, commenta Julio. Vous n'êtes pas de mon avis, mon colonel ? »

Il avait noté le regard à la dérobée de son supérieur.

Ce dernier sourit, pris la main dans le sac. « Je dois avouer...

– Vous, un homme marié et tout ça ! »

Howard se contenta de sourire.

« Bon, et maintenant, John ?

– On laisse le renseignement britannique rassembler tout ce qu'il jugera utile de nous fournir, et ensuite on avise. Puis on règle cette affaire et on rentre au bercail. Avec toutes ces filles, je commence à m'ennuyer de ma femme. »

Rire de Fernandez. « Reçu cinq sur cinq. »

36

Jeudi 14 avril
Siège du MI-6, Londres

Quand Toni ressortit des toilettes et regagna la salle de conférences, elle y trouva Alex et Cooper en grande discussion, tout au bout de la table. Ils étaient quasiment tête contre tête, assez près pour s'embrasser.

Toni ressentit un accès de jalousie. Ils levèrent les yeux, l'aperçurent, mais ne bougèrent pas. Bon point. S'ils s'étaient écartés d'un bond en la voyant, c'est qu'il y aurait eu anguille sous roche. Malgré tout, elle n'avait aucune raison de s'inquiéter. Elle connaissait Alex.

« Du nouveau ? demanda-t-elle.

– On a obtenu les renseignements sur Goswell et Peel, dit Alex. Et certains développements intéressants. Le colonel Howard et le sergent Fernandez nous rejoignent. »

Au moment même où il le disait, les deux hommes arrivèrent.

« Angela, si vous voulez bien... ? »

Cooper resta debout tandis que tous les autres s'asseyaient. Elle effleura son écran-plat et une projection apparut au-dessus de la table de conférence.

« La propriété de Lord Geoffrey Goswell, dans le Sussex, commença-t-elle. Elle s'appelle les Ifs. Il y passe le plus clair de son temps. Le domaine occupe plusieurs centaines d'hectares et comprend le corps de logis principal, des bâtiments annexes et plusieurs dépendances. »

De nouvelles images arrivèrent.

« En dehors de son personnel, monseigneur – l'homme est veuf – vit seul. Il a plusieurs pied-à-terre à Londres, Brighton, Manchester, une villa dans le sud de la France ainsi que divers appartements et résidences secondaires au pays de Galles, en Écosse, en Irlande, en Espagne, au Portugal, en Inde et aux États-Unis. Voici la liste des entreprises dont il est propriétaire ou actionnaire. Sa fortune personnelle est estimée à près de deux milliards d'euros.

– Sa vie doit pas être tous les jours facile », laissa tomber Fernandez.

Cooper poursuivit : « Peel, que nous avons déjà eu l'occasion d'évoquer, dirige le service de sécurité personnelle de notre lord. Il a sous ses ordres entre six et dix hommes, tous anciens militaires, tous puissamment armés, qui patrouillent en permanence sur l'ensemble du domaine.

– Je pensais que les armes à feu étaient plus ou moins illégales ici ? observa Fernandez.

– Pour le citoyen lambda, oui, convint l'agent britannique. Pas d'armes de poing, tous les fusils et carabines doivent rester sous clé hormis lors de leur utilisation, et celle-ci reste exclusivement limitée à la chasse ou au tir sur cible. Et en toute hypothèse, aucune arme d'assaut de style militaire n'est autorisée. »

Fernandez nota : « Laissez-moi deviner : quand vous avez deux milliards dans le petit cochon, les règles sont différentes, c'est ça ? »

Sourire crispé de Cooper. « Tout juste.

– Continuez, je vous en prie, intervint Alex. Laissons de côté les remarques journalistiques, voulez-vous ?

– Nous avons placé deux de nos équipes sur les routes menant à la propriété et, il y a moins d'une heure, une voiture de location s'est rendue là-bas. Une vérification auprès des agences indique qu'elle a été louée hier à Southampton par Peter Bascomb-Coombs. Nos hommes ont réussi à avoir une photo floue du chauffeur et il s'avère qu'il s'agit bien de notre informaticien. »

La nouvelle fut accueillie avec satisfaction.

« Le commandant Peel, lui aussi sous surveillance, a quitté Londres et fait route actuellement vers le Sussex. Il devrait arriver à destination d'ici une heure.

– Pas trace de Roujio ? demanda le colonel.

– Non.

– Pourrait-il être déjà sur place ?

– C'est possible, admit Cooper. Nous n'avons aucun satellite-espion en position pour couvrir le secteur avant quatre-vingt-dix minutes. Et quand bien même ce serait le cas et que notre homme se baladerait sur les pelouses, on risque d'avoir du mal à l'identifier sur ce seul élément. Avec la bénédiction de la Sécurité nationale, nous avons mis sur écoute toutes les lignes téléphoniques de la propriété, et nous surveillons également par scanner toute activité radio-électrique.

– Ça doit être sympa de pouvoir organiser aussi aisément une écoute, remarqua Alex.

– Aisément n'est peut-être pas le terme exact, rétorqua Cooper. En tout cas, jusqu'ici, on n'a rien relevé de notable. Voilà, en gros, la situation telle qu'elle se présente à l'heure où je vous parle.

– M'est avis qu'on a fait le plus gros du boulot, commenta Fernandez. On n'a plus qu'à filer faire un saut là-bas pour avoir une petite discussion avec tous ces mecs. »

Cooper contempla l'image holographique, puis son regard s'abaissa vers la table. Elle semblait gênée aux entournures. « Eh bien, oui, logiquement, ça serait la prochaine étape.

– Mais... ? fit Howard.

– C'est un petit peu plus délicat. On ne peut pas se pointer là-bas comme ça.

– Et pourquoi pas ? demanda Toni. On a un suspect dans l'affaire de délinquance informatique qui a ébranlé la moitié de la planète, suspect qu'on a réussi à localiser. J'ai du mal à croire que vous n'ayez pas envie de l'interroger. Lui et le type pour qui il bosse, en prime. »

Toni vit Julio Fernandez et John Howard acquiescer avec vigueur ; quant à Alex, il semblait curieux d'entendre la réponse de Cooper.

« Certes, admit cette dernière. Toutefois, on ne travaille pas comme ça, ici. Imaginez que vous soyez aux États-Unis et que vous deviez soudain interroger un milliardaire qui se trouve être aussi un personnage politique influent. Un sénateur, voire le Président en personne. Vous iriez comme ça frapper à sa porte en exigeant qu'il vous ouvre ? À votre avis ?

– Non, reconnut Alex. Mais si nous avions des raisons suffisantes de le soupçonner d'être impliqué dans une action criminelle qui a eu pour conséquence indirecte d'entraîner la mort de centaines de personnes, on pourrait obtenir d'un juge un mandat d'arrêt ou de perquisition. On a déjà contraint nos présidents à témoigner quand ils ne le voulaient pas. On en a même destitué.

– Après des semaines de palabres avec leurs avocats, observa Cooper. Quant à la destitution, c'était un tour de passe-passe... il n'a jamais été jugé et déclaré coupable, n'est-ce pas ?

– On a tenté le coup, rétorqua Alex. Personne n'est au-dessus des lois.

– Ici non plus, Alex, mais nous sommes un petit pays, et malgré nos efforts pour le faire entrer dans le XXIe siècle, il conserve encore un très fort esprit de caste. Lord Goswell est au summum du pouvoir. Il a fréquenté les mêmes écoles que les plus anciens membres de la Chambre des lords. Il connaît toute la noblesse fortunée, il fréquente les meilleurs avocats et il connaît les juges, les hauts fonctionnaires de la police. Tous les quinze jours, il prend le thé avec le chef du gouvernement conservateur. D'un simple geste de la main, il peut accomplir plus que le Parlement en une semaine de délibérations. Il joue au bridge avec le roi. Obtenir l'autorisation de le mettre sur écoute a été un petit miracle, dû uniquement au fait que Goswell n'était pas au courant. Non, ce n'est pas un homme à la porte de qui on va frapper pour exiger quoi que ce soit. Quand on veut traquer ce genre de lion dans son antre, on doit négocier en douceur, le chapeau à la main. C'est une chose d'appeler son chef de la sécurité pour lui annoncer qu'on va passer l'interroger ; c'en est une autre de faire de même avec l'un des hommes les plus riches et les plus influents de ce pays. »

Nul ne trouva rien à répondre durant quelques secondes.

« De la couille, oui », commenta Julio.

Toni retint un sourire. Elle ne pouvait qu'être d'accord.

« C'est bien possible, sergent, mais je suis venue vous prévenir que le gouvernement de Sa Majesté n'interrogera pas Lord Goswell, sinon par le truchement de ses avocats, et encore, en marchant sur des œufs.

– Même si on le soupçonne d'être impliqué dans les piratages informatiques ? » Toni était outrée.

Cooper se tourna vers elle. « Même si on en avait la certitude et qu'on avait les éléments pour le prouver, mademoiselle Fiorella. Ce qui n'est pas le cas. Nous n'avons aucun indice sérieux, en dehors d'une preuve indirecte et bien légère : Bascomb-Coombs, qui pourrait éventuellement être l'auteur du forfait, travaille pour Lord Goswell et lui rend visite. Point final. Ça ne prouve pas grand-chose, vous ne croyez pas ? »

Toni savait que Cooper avait raison. Mais elle savait aussi en son for intérieur que Bascomb-Coombs trempait dans toute cette histoire, et que Peel et Roujio y étaient liés d'une manière ou d'une autre. Seulement, que pouvaient-ils faire si les autorités locales leur refusaient jusqu'au droit de s'entretenir avec les intéressés ?

« Bref, reprit Alex, on ne peut pas débarquer sur les terres de "monseigneur" sans carton d'invitation. Très bien. Est-ce qu'on peut au moins coincer Peel ?

– Je vous demande pardon ?

– Peut-on demander à vos agents sur le terrain

d'intercepter Peel pour l'empêcher de filer se planquer dans la propriété de Goswell ? »

Cooper le regarda, éberluée. « Pourquoi diable irait-on faire une chose pareille ?

– D'accord, fit Alex, avec patience. Suivez mon raisonnement : supposons que Bascomb-Coombs soit responsable des pannes informatiques.

– Jusqu'ici, je vous suis.

– Si tel est le cas, il a dû recevoir de l'aide. D'après Jay Gridley, ce n'est pas le genre de truc qu'on monte avec trois bouts de ficelle, donc il doit recevoir le soutien financier de quelqu'un.

– Oui. Et après ?

– Le rasoir d'Occam. Il travaille pour Goswell. Il est logé chez Goswell. Combien d'individus ont les moyens de financer un projet de plusieurs millions de dollars et de garder le secret ? Ne faudrait-il pas quelqu'un jouissant d'une énorme influence ? Par exemple, une personne qui détiendrait l'intégralité du capital et du pouvoir de décision d'une boîte d'informatique de pointe ? Cela nous donne Goswell. Et vous ne croyez pas que le chef de la sécurité personnelle de Goswell devrait avoir une petite idée des activités de Bascomb-Coombs ? N'importe quel agent de surveillance digne de ce nom ne manquerait pas d'effectuer une enquête approfondie sur quiconque cherche à se mettre bien avec son patron. Si j'avais la responsabilité de veiller à la bonne santé d'un homme fortuné, je m'arrangerais pour tout savoir sur quiconque s'avise de franchir le seuil de sa demeure. Je mettrais un point d'honneur à savoir ce que ses visiteurs ont mangé au petit déjeuner, l'endroit où ils l'ont pris, et le montant du pourboire qu'ils ont laissé.

– Vous êtes en train de me dire que Bascomb-Coombs est le pirate dément, et que Goswell est au courant, ainsi que Peel ? L'enchaînement logique de vos déductions est un peu faible, à supposer même que le premier maillon soit solide comme l'acier.

– Si on les retrouve tous ensemble à boire le thé, ça se tient, non ? »

Cooper lui adressa un demi-sourire. « Voyons, Alex, ce n'est pas parce qu'on boit le thé ensemble qu'on partage forcément tous ses secrets, n'est-ce pas ? »

Alex rougit. John Howard détourna les yeux et parut soudain prodigieusement fasciné par une tache sur le mur. Le sourire de Cooper s'agrandit et devint radieux. Pris isolément, tous ces éléments ne prouvaient rien, mais ainsi réunis... Toni sentit d'un coup, à un niveau purement instinctif, comme un poignard glacé lui transpercer le cœur :

Mon Dieu, est-ce qu'Alex aurait couché *avec cette salope ?*

Comment ? Quand ?

Et pour l'amour du ciel : *Pourquoi ?*

Alex se racla la gorge avant de poursuivre : « Écoutez, je sais que Peel est lié à Roujio dans la mort d'un individu suspecté d'être un tueur à gages.

– Le décès du type de la librairie était, d'après les premiers éléments de l'enquête, dû au suicide.

– Après que Roujio ou Peel lui eut logé une balle dans la peau ! Peel n'est pas blanc-bleu dans cette histoire. Vous savez que j'ai raison. Interceptons-le et cuisinons-le avant qu'il y ait de nouveaux morts et que des millions de vies soient bouleversées... »

Il y eut un long silence. Toni dévisageait Cooper, tiraillée désormais par ces nouveaux soupçons qui lui taraudaient l'âme. Tout le reste n'avait plus d'importance. Elle se contrefichait de Peel, Goswell ou Roujio. C'était sans intérêt.

Alex l'avait-il trompée ? Non. Impossible. Quoique ?

Elle sentit la nausée l'envahir.

Enfin, Cooper répondit : « D'accord. Il va falloir que je demande une décharge au directeur général Helms, mais j'imagine qu'on peut au moins faire ça dans l'intérêt de la sécurité nationale. »

37

Jeudi 14 avril
Autoroute M23 – au sud de Gatwick

Roujio inspira profondément deux fois de suite avant d'expirer avec lenteur, cherchant à se relaxer. La tension n'avait fait que s'accroître, il était crispé au volant, penché en avant, et c'était très mauvais d'être une boule de nerfs quand il aurait dû au contraire être parfaitement détendu. Un homme crispé ne pouvait pas évoluer convenablement. Mais, même en connaissance de cause, ça arrivait toujours. Il fallait prendre sur soi pour se dominer, malgré les années d'entraînement et d'expérience.

Devant lui, dans la file voisine, la Toyota grise avec les deux hommes qui filaient Peel depuis Londres roulait cinquante mètres derrière la voiture du commandant, noyée dans le flot de la circulation. Ils étaient tellement absorbés par leur filature qu'ils n'avaient pas remarqué la présence de Roujio.

Dès qu'il les avait repérés, Roujio avait pris son mobile et prononcé un seul mot : « De la compagnie. » Cela avait suffi pour alerter Peel.

Qui avait répondu : « Compris. Je vous rappelle. »

Ils avaient dépassé l'aéroport de Gatwick depuis plusieurs kilomètres et continuaient de filer vers le sud sur l'autoroute, comme s'ils se rendaient toujours dans la propriété du Sussex. Le téléphone mobile posé près de lui sur le siège se mit à sonner. Roujio décrocha. « Allez-y.

– Est-ce qu'ils vous ont repéré ?

– Non.

– Bien. On quitte l'autoroute à la prochaine sortie, dans trois kilomètres environ, direction est. Cinq kilomètres plus loin, il y a un grand chêne, à une intersection avec une vicinale sur la droite. Trois kilomètres plus loin sur cette route, côté gauche, vous verrez une grande bergerie. C'est là qu'on doit avoir notre petite discussion avec notre compagnie. Si vous passiez devant pour préparer le terrain ?

– D'accord. »

D'un coup de pouce, Roujio coupa la communication. Il accéléra et dépassa en douceur le véhicule de filature, puis celui de Peel ; il avait huit cents mètres d'avance sur eux quand il quitta l'autoroute à la bretelle de sortie. Les poursuivants ne lui prêtèrent aucune attention.

Le chêne était à l'endroit indiqué – Roujio avait vérifié la distance au compteur – et la grange, devant une prairie où paissaient des moutons, se dressait, isolée et tranquille au milieu de nulle part. L'endroit rêvé pour organiser un tête-à-tête loin de toute oreille indiscrète.

Roujio entra se garer dans la bergerie et referma la porte derrière la voiture. L'endroit était poussiéreux et sentait le foin séché, la laine et quelque chose qui évoquait la cire chaude. Des odeurs de ferme qui firent remonter brièvement en lui le souvenir douloureux des jours passés avec Anna. Il inspecta les issues – il y en avait deux au rez-de-chaussée, en plus de la porte par laquelle il était entré en voiture, et deux autres au niveau supérieur, équipées de treuils et de poulies. Peel était un professionnel ; il allait s'arrêter et sortir de manière à ne pas obstruer la vue sur ses poursuivants depuis l'intérieur de la grange quand ceux-ci descendraient de voiture. Sans doute, estima Roujio, en se garant devant la plus petite des deux portes, celle située du côté sud-est du bâtiment.

Roujio vérifia le chargeur du Firestar, pour s'assurer qu'une balle était bien engagée. Il arma le pistolet puis remit le cran de sûreté. Il n'y aurait peut-être pas de fusillade ; si jamais on devait en venir là, il avait huit coups à tirer, et sept de plus dans un second chargeur, au cas où le premier ne serait pas suffisant. Aucun semi-automatique n'était à l'abri d'un pépin, mais il avait ajusté les chargeurs et poli la rampe d'alimentation, et tous les projectiles étaient suffisamment propres et lisses pour qu'il ne doive pas y avoir de problème. Après avoir tiré quelques balles dès qu'il avait eu l'arme en main, il avait manœuvré à une centaine de reprises le mécanisme sans qu'il s'enraie une seule fois. À la distance où il aurait éventuellement à tirer, quelques balles devaient suffire, et la première était déjà engagée.

Il entendit un bruit de moteur, aisément audible au milieu de ces pâturages tranquilles. Il inspira profondément encore une fois, souffla, étira sa nuque, fit rouler ses épaules. Il était prêt. Prêt à suivre les instructions de Peel.

Peel engagea sa voiture sur l'aire de terre battue devant la bergerie et contourna celle-ci par la gauche pour forcer ses poursuivants à s'interposer entre lui et le bâtiment. Il s'arrêta, dégrafa l'étui de son pistolet et descendit de voiture. Il laissa la portière ouverte pour avoir un minimum de protection. Il n'avait pas aperçu Roujio mais il avait remarqué les marques de pneus fraîches menant à la grange et savait donc que l'homme s'y trouvait. S'il avait été à sa place, Peel se serait placé derrière cette porte, juste en face de sa voiture, et il était prêt à parier que l'ex-tireur d'élite soviétique était déjà là. Il se sentait nettement mieux de savoir qu'un vieux pro surveillait ses arrières.

La Toyota quitta la route et s'arrêta pile à l'endroit prévu, dans un nuage de poussière gris rougeâtre. Quand celle-ci retomba, il vit deux types descendre de voiture. Ils portaient des impers et se déplaçaient comme des gars qui portent une arme, ce qui était sans aucun doute le cas. Mais ils n'avaient pas une dégaine de flics, en tout cas pas de flics en civil. L'un des deux était brun, taille moyenne, l'autre était petit, râblé, courte brosse de cheveux gris souris. Appartenaient-ils à l'armée ? Aux renseignements ? Merde, c'était quoi, ce plan ?

« Bon après-midi, messieurs. Puis-je vous être utile ? »

Gris-souris se présenta : « Commandant Peel, nous aimerions savoir si vous accepteriez de nous accompagner, monsieur. » Ce n'était pas une question.

« Si vous avez l'obligeance de m'expliquer qui vous êtes et ce que vous désirez, nous pourrons peut-être nous entendre.

– Nous ne sommes pas là pour répondre aux questions. Nous enverrons quelqu'un récupérer votre véhicule. Vous allez nous accompagner.

– Je ne pense pas que je vais faire une chose pareille.

– Dans ce cas, nous serons contraints d'insister, intervint le plus grand. Veuillez avancer par ici, monsieur. Et laissez vos mains bien en évidence.

– Insistez tout votre saoul. Je m'occupe de mes affaires, et je ne pense pas que cela vous regarde en quoi que ce soit. »

Les deux autres échangèrent un coup d'œil et, sans un mot, se séparèrent et s'éloignèrent. C'était la procédure habituelle lorsqu'on se trouvait en face d'un individu considéré comme armé et dangereux. Même s'il dégainait rapidement, il allait devoir balayer ses deux adversaires avec son arme, et plus ils seraient éloignés, plus la tâche serait difficile... surtout si l'un et l'autre étaient prêts à riposter. Ils n'avaient toujours pas dégainé leur arme, ce qui était à son avantage.

« Ne compliquez pas la tâche, commandant, dit Gris-souris.

– Messieurs, je vous conseille de rester immobiles et de garder les mains éloignées de vos armes. »

Le plus grand des deux sourit : « Sauf votre respect, commandant, je vous ferai observer que nous sommes l'un et l'autre de dix ans plus jeunes et dix ans plus vifs que vous. Vous ne vous croyez tout de même pas de taille à nous tenir tête ?

– Peut-être, peut-être pas... ce serait certes plus risqué si j'étais seul... »

Gris-souris remarqua : « Il n'y a personne d'autre dans votre voiture, Peel. Vous nous prenez pour des idiots ?

– Passablement idiots, oui, je l'admets. À ton avis, pourquoi penses-tu que je me suis arrêté ici, fiston ? Dans ce coin paumé en rase campagne ? »

Gris-souris s'interrompit dans sa manœuvre de contournement pour jeter un bref coup d'œil à son partenaire.

« Il nous raconte des craques, répondit celui-ci. Il bluffe.

– Vous croyez ? » fit Peel. Il sourit. « Vous me filez avec votre japonaise depuis qu'on a quitté Londres. Vous croyez peut-être que je ne le savais pas ? J'ai eu tout le temps de demander à un collègue de se pointer ici. Vous me semblez des gars sensés. Dites-moi qui vous a envoyés et ce que vous savez et peut-être que vous aurez une chance de vous en tirer sans bobo. Sinon... » Il conclut par un haussement d'épaules théâtral.

« Arrête ton char, mec, dit le plus grand. On n'est pas nés de la dernière pluie ! »

Peel éleva la voix. « Monsieur Roujio ! Êtes-vous là ? »

La porte de la bergerie s'ouvrit à la volée dans un craquement de charnières rouillées, et Roujio apparut sur le seuil, même s'il se garda bien de sortir à découvert. « Je suis là », confirma-t-il. Il tenait à deux mains un pistolet argenté, braqué sur le plus grand.

Les deux types le regardèrent, éberlués.

Des hommes qui avaient déjà connu l'épreuve du feu auraient compris qu'ils n'avaient aucune chance. Vous pouviez être plus rapide que Billy le Kid s'il avait encore le flingue dans son étui, mais sûrement pas assez pour dégainer si son pistolet était déjà braqué sur vous.

Les deux types paniquèrent et cherchèrent à dégainer.

Roujio tenait en joue le plus grand, Gris-souris était

donc pour Peel. Mais avant qu'il ait pu dégainer, Roujio avait déjà fait feu – *pan ! pan ! pan !* Une infime hésitation, puis encore une fois : *pan ! pan ! pan !* Six balles à peut-être cinq mètres de distance, et tirées si vite qu'on aurait cru deux rafales d'arme automatique. Bon sang, c'est qu'il était rapide, le bougre !

Le grand type et Gris-souris s'effondrèrent, fauchés comme des épis.

« Merde ! » s'écria Peel. Il termina de dégainer et se rua vers les hommes à terre. Les deux portaient sous leur imper des gilets pare-balles, comme il put le constater en approchant. Les gilets avaient intercepté deux projectiles chacun, comme c'était prévisible. Mais ils n'avaient rien pu contre le reste de la salve de Roujio : deux balles dans la poitrine et une dans la tête. Les deux types l'avaient reçue entre les yeux et ils étaient déjà morts avant d'avoir touché le sol. Peel n'avait jamais vu ce genre d'exercice effectué avec une telle maestria, même à l'entraînement, et encore moins en situation réelle. Roujio était un tireur d'exception.

« Bigre, et comment suis-je censé apprendre quelque chose si vous ne m'en laissez pas un en vie pour l'interroger ? »

Roujio lui adressa un haussement d'épaules très slave. Il éjecta le chargeur vide, le laissa choir à terre, rechargea l'arme avec le second tiré de sa poche, puis se pencha pour récupérer l'autre sur le sol. Quand il se fut redressé, il porta une main à son oreille pour en ôter le bouchon de cire, puis il fit de même avec l'autre oreille, avant d'enfourner les deux tampons dans sa poche en même temps que le chargeur vide.

Dieu du ciel. Le type était assez décontracté pour avoir pensé à se protéger les tympans avant de descendre tranquillement deux hommes armés, vite fait bien fait, avec une froideur toute mécanique. Ce Roujio devait avoir de l'azote liquide dans les veines.

Enfin, on n'y pouvait plus rien désormais. Mieux valait découvrir qui étaient ces deux-là, s'il le pouvait. Peel fit les poches du grand jusqu'à ce qu'il trouve un portefeuille. Il l'ouvrit, contempla la carte d'identité dans son étui plastifié. « Nom de Dieu ! Ce sont des types du MI-6 ! On vient de descendre deux agents des Services secrets de Sa Majesté ! »

Roujio haussa de nouveau les épaules : il parcourait des yeux la campagne, cherchant des témoins.

En dehors des moutons que les détonations ne semblaient pas avoir affectés, aucun regard indiscret.

Peel hocha la tête. « Venez. Aidez-moi à déplacer les corps. On n'a que quelques minutes avant qu'on s'aperçoive de leur disparition. »

Ils n'étaient pas dans la merde, à présent.

Jeudi
Siège du MI-6, Londres

« On a un problème, dit Cooper à Michaels. On a perdu le contact avec l'équipe qui filait Peel. »

Howard, Fernandez et Toni étaient descendus à la cafétéria manger un morceau en vitesse, et Michaels se retrouvait de nouveau seul avec Cooper dans la salle de conférences. « Perdu le contact avec eux ?

– Il y a plus d'une demi-heure. Leur dernier rapport

indiquait qu'ils avaient quitté la M23 près de Balcombe et qu'ils s'apprêtaient à interpeller Peel. Nous n'avons pas réussi à les toucher depuis.

– Avez-vous un moyen de les localiser ?

– Pas exactement. La balise de leur voiture a cessé d'émettre son signal quelques minutes après leur dernière transmission. Nous savons où ils se trouvaient. Nous avons envoyé sur place un détachement militaire héliporté.

– Ils se sont fait enlever ou tuer, répondit Michaels, sèchement.

– Ça, on n'en sait rien.

– Vous n'auriez pas fait décoller en alerte un commando parachutiste si ça ne vous semblait pas probable. »

Elle soupira. Posa la main sur l'avant-bras d'Alex. Le contact était tiède. « C'est vrai qu'on redoute un drame. »

Il fixa cette main. Au bout de quelques secondes, elle la retira. « Aucune chance pour nous, n'est-ce pas ?

– Je... je ne crois pas que ce serait une bonne idée. Désolé.

– Mais ça vous a plu, pourtant ? Jusqu'ici ?

– Ah... ça oui. Aucun doute. »

Elle sourit, mais d'un sourire sans joie. « Les meilleurs sont toujours pour les autres... Dommage. Votre Mlle Fiorella ne connaît pas son bonheur, vous savez.

– Je crois que c'est moi qui ai de la chance. »

Elle s'écarta, consulta sa montre. « On devrait avoir bientôt des nouvelles du commando.

– Peut-on encore arrêter Peel ? S'il est en route vers la propriété de Goswell ?

– Compte tenu de la situation actuelle, je doute que le directeur Helms ait envie de risquer la vie d'une autre équipe. Il serait moins risqué de le coincer aux Ifs, si telle est bien sa destination, et de l'interroger ensuite. »

Assis dans la dans la cafétéria du MI-6 avec Howard, Fernandez mastiqua laborieusement un morceau de son espèce de vague steak-purée noyé dans un demi-litre de sauce brune, puis remarqua : « Qu'est-ce qui se passe avec le sous-commandant ? Elle a l'air toute chose. »

Fiorella était descendue au snack avec eux, mais elle s'était rapidement excusée avant de s'éclipser, livide.

Howard contempla sa salade au poulet thaïlandaise. Il n'avait rien d'une pipelette mais il connaissait Julio depuis qu'ils étaient adultes ; ils n'avaient guère de secrets l'un pour l'autre. Et à voir la tête de Toni, elle ne se faisait plus d'illusions : elle avait deviné les activités extra-conjugales de Michaels. Howard n'avait pas toutefois besoin d'entrer dans les détails, aussi se contenta-t-il d'observer : « Je pense qu'elle et le commandant pourraient avoir certains... problèmes personnels. »

Julio fit passer un autre morceau avec un grand verre d'eau puis il opina. « Cooper... Le patron l'aurait-il connue... charnellement ? »

Howard haussa un sourcil.

Julio précisa sa pensée : « Elle est belle, intelligente, et elle n'a pas arrêté de l'allumer, poursuivit Julio. Et le patron regarde la pointe de ses chaussures chaque fois que Cooper le serre de trop près. Elle a l'air possessif et lui, il a l'air culpabilisé. Pour moi, ça me semble une affaire entendue. Cela dit, je ne pense pas vous apprendre grand-chose. Vous l'aviez déjà remarqué.

– Oui », opina Howard.

Julio reprit une bouchée de son infâme ragougnasse brune. « Je ne comprends toujours pas pourquoi on fait toutes ces histoires sur les horreurs de la cuisine britannique. Jusqu'ici, je n'ai pas eu à m'en plaindre.

– Je vois que j'ai affaire à un véritable carnivore amateur de patates.

– Oh, ça va, Jeannot Lapin, vous avez le droit de continuer à brouter votre gazon. »

Un jeune homme s'approcha de leur table. « Colonel Howard ? Le commandant Michaels voudrait vous voir dès que possible, mon colonel. »

Julio se dépêcha d'engloutir une autre bouchée, alors que son supérieur, hochant la tête, était déjà debout. Allons bon, quoi encore ?

38

Jeudi 14 avril
Près de Balcombe, Angleterre

Le MI-6 avait réquisitionné un second hélico qui se posa avec Alex, Howard, Fernandez, Cooper et Toni. L'appareil du commando était déjà posé et une douzaine de paras britanniques en tenue camouflée et béret, l'arme à la main, étaient en train d'encercler la vieille bergerie à l'instant où l'équipe de la Net Force émergeait du nuage de poussière soulevé par le rotor.

Toni avait mis ses peines de cœur dans sa poche avec un mouchoir dessus, pour se consacrer entièrement à sa tâche. Malgré tout, elle n'avait pas été capable de regarder Alex dans les yeux durant le bref saut de puce en hélico.

Un capitaine de l'armée britannique s'approcha et s'entretint avec Cooper. Toni arpenta les alentours, se pencha pour examiner le sol en deux endroits, puis se dirigea vers la vieille bâtisse. Une voiture était garée à l'intérieur – pas depuis longtemps, car elle n'avait pas pris la poussière. Le sol, en terre battue, était recouvert d'une fine couche de foin séché. Elle ressortit et fit à nouveau le tour du propriétaire. Le sol crayeux était assez meuble pour permettre des prises d'empreintes, mais les militaires en avaient piétiné beaucoup, leurs bottes de combat laissant des marques bien caractéristiques. Elle songea aux événements qui avaient pu se dérouler ici, compte tenu du peu qu'elle savait et qu'elle avait vu.

« Toni ? » C'était Alex. Il se tenait près de Cooper et du capitaine.

Elle pouvait tenir le choc. Mettre de côté ses sentiments et faire son boulot.

« Je te présente le capitaine Ward. »

Cooper intervint : « Si vous mettiez le sous-commandant Fiorella au fait de vos déductions sur ce qui a pu se produire ici, capitaine ? »

Un sursaut de colère l'enveloppa brièvement. Comme si elle avait besoin qu'on lui fasse un dessin... Elle aurait eu envie de lui voler dans les plumes. Au lieu de ça, Toni fit bonne figure et remarqua : « Cela paraît assez évident, non ? »

Cooper accusa le coup. Aurait-elle décelé une note de défi dans la voix de la jeune femme ? « Oh, vraiment ? Et si vous nous expliquiez votre version, dans ce cas ? » Ouais, elle l'avait décelée.

« Avec plaisir. Peel avait un ange gardien, c'est sa voiture qui est dans la grange. Un véhicule de location, qui ne nous donnera aucune piste, sans doute loué sous une fausse identité en donnant l'adresse d'une société bidon.

« Vos agents n'ont pas dû remarquer l'ange gardien. Il y a de bonnes chances pour qu'il s'agisse de Mikhaïl Roujio, qui doit être lié à Peel d'une manière ou d'une autre. Peut-être se sont-ils rencontrés sur les bancs de l'université ou lors d'une action quelconque quelque part en Afrique ou en Amérique du sud. En tout cas, ils ont un passé en commun. Sinon, la coïncidence est trop belle.

« Toujours est-il que Peel a conduit vos gars ici, droit dans un piège. À ce moment, Roujio leur est tombé discrètement dessus... non, rectification : pas question de se pointer en voiture depuis la route sans être vu, et à pied, c'est trop loin de tout, donc il était sans doute déjà planqué sur place quand Peel est arrivé. Qu'est-ce que vous en dites, jusqu'ici ? » Elle regarda Alex, et le visage de celui-ci était figé dans un demi-sourire. Il devait sentir sa colère, elle le savait. Elle lui adressa un petit signe de tête.

Je sais tout, mon salaud. Et tu sais que je sais.

Cooper ne dit rien, Alex non plus, pas plus que le capitaine, aussi Toni poursuivit-elle : « Il y a deux petites tachcs de sang par terre, encore visibles, bien que quelqu'un ait essayé de les recouvrir de terre avec le pied... là, et encore là... » Elle indiqua l'endroit. « Vos hommes étaient-ils armés ? Portaient-ils des gilets pare-balles ? »

Cooper lui jeta un regard incendiaire et ce fut le capitaine qui précisa : « Ils avaient leur arme de poing et pour les gilets, oui, ils auraient dû en porter. C'est la procédure habituelle pour ce gcnre d'opération.

– Bien. Donc Peel et Roujio les descendent, sans doute d'une balle dans la tête. C'est là qu'ils sont tombés. Puis ils traînent les corps des deux agents dans leur propre véhicule, et repartent avec celui-ci et celui de Peel. J'imagine que si vos hommes n'avaient pas consciencieusement piétiné tout le secteur, vous auriez retrouvé les traces de pneus des deux véhicules... À l'heure qu'il est, je pense qu'ils ont emmené la voiture avec les cadavres dans un endroit où on ne risque pas de la retrouver de sitôt. Deux agents disparus, c'est un problème, mais pas autant que deux agents morts. Si j'étais responsable, je demanderais à la police locale de fouiller toutes les mares, les lacs et les cours d'eau dans un rayon de plusieurs kilomètres. C'est l'endroit idéal pour cacher une bagnole. »

Le capitaine secoua la tête. « Dans l'ensemble, c'est quand même un peu tiré par les cheveux, vous ne trouvez pas ? À part les taches de sang, nous n'avons aucun indice concret. On n'a retrouvé aucune douille.

– Roujio aura récupéré les siennes et je suppose que Peel est assez malin pour avoir fait de même. Le temps qu'on leur remette la main dessus, les armes utilisées auront disparu depuis longtemps. Je ne sais pas trop pour votre commandant Peel, mais Roujio est un vrai professionnel. Il ne laisse jamais beaucoup de traces. »

Ward acquiesça, comme pour confirmer qu'il s'intéressait moins à ses explications qu'au cheminement logique qui l'y avait menée. « Le scénario que vous envisagez n'est pas impossible. Dès qu'il a compris à qui il avait affaire, Peel a su qu'ils avaient une balise dans leur voiture et l'aura neutralisée. On a fait établir des barrages routiers, mais on risque d'avoir pris du retard à l'allumage... »

Du retard à l'allumage, tu l'as dit.

Toni rassembla son courage et gratifia Cooper de son plus aimable sourire. « Vous voulez savoir autre chose, mademoiselle Cooper ?

– Pas pour l'instant, merci, mademoiselle Fiorella. »

Cooper jeta un bref regard vers Alex et Toni crut y lire de l'inquiétude. Voire de la pitié.

Donc, Cooper avait compris, elle aussi, que Toni était au courant. Et la pute britannique en éprouvait de la compassion pour Alex. Formidable. Voilà qu'ils formaient à présent un putain de sordide ménage à trois.

Michaels saisit son virgil pour passer un appel prioritaire à Jay Gridley.

« Ouais, patron, qu'est-ce qui se passe ?

– Si je te donnais une adresse, une adresse physique où pourrait se trouver ce système d'ordinateur quantique, est-ce que ça t'aiderait dans ta recherche ?

– Ça pourrait pas faire de mal. Je pourrais éventuellement repérer une piste si je ne suis pas trop loin, même si ce n'est pas garanti.

– Reste en ligne. Je te la télécharge. On a retrouvé Bascomb-Coombs et l'endroit où il bosse. On ne peut pas encore lui mettre la main au collet pour l'instant, mais peut-être qu'on arrivera à une solution de ton côté.

– Merci, patron.

– Sois prudent, Jay.

– Bien copié, haut et clair. Discom. »

Michaels se dirigea vers Cooper. « Est-ce que ça modifie la donne ? Est-ce qu'on peut filer chez Goswell et capturer Peel ?

– Je peux toujours voir avec le directeur général, mais j'ai peur que ça ne change rien. Nous avons deux agents disparus mais pas grand-chose pour relier leur disparition à monseigneur ou même à Peel. Pour autant que je sache, Peel s'est échappé en voiture avant qu'on ait pu l'interroger ; quant à nos hommes, il se trouve, pure coïncidence, qu'ils ont été agressés par des voleurs de troupeaux.

– Ouais, c'est ça.

– Désolé, Alex, mais c'est ainsi. On a les mains liées. »

Michaels traîna les pieds pour retourner à l'hélicoptère. Il lança : « Attendez voir une seconde, colonel. »

Howard ralentit.

« Cooper dit que le MI-6 a les mains liées. Qu'ils ne peuvent pas s'introduire sur les terres de Lord Goswell sans un carton d'invitation.

– Formidable, ricana Howard, sarcastique.

– Colonel, je ne sais pas comment fonctionne votre téléphone arabe, mais vous êtes bien placé pour une promotion... »

Howard hésita une seconde avant de répondre : « J'avais entendu la rumeur, commandant. Mais merci, je suis sensible au compliment.

– Je mentionne ceci uniquement parce qu'un incident diplomatique international risquerait de gâcher vos chances. Non : les gâcherait sûrement. »

Grand sourire d'Howard. « Si ça me permettait malgré tout de mettre la main sur Roujio et ce pirate fou, je pourrais vivre avec. »

Michaels lui rendit son sourire. « Quelque part, je sentais que vous me diriez ça. Dès qu'on sera de retour au MI-6, j'estime que nos hommes auront besoin de souffler un peu... Aller s'aérer à la campagne, par exemple...

– Oui, monsieur. »

Michaels contempla l'hélicoptère, les yeux plissés pour se protéger de la poussière soulevée par le rotor.

En général, il suivait la ligne tracée. Mais de temps à autre, il devait emprunter des chemins de traverse.

Il y avait une différence entre la justice et la loi, et parfois, la fin justifiait les moyens. En général, dans son boulot, quand on s'aventurait là où on n'aurait pas dû mettre les pieds, on pouvait toujours se trouver de bonnes raisons *a posteriori*. Mais en cas d'échec, on était baisé. Leur boulot était de traquer des terroristes, qui tuaient directement ou par ordinateur interposé. Le pire qui puisse lui arriver en cas de dérapage était de se faire virer sans gloire et foutre en taule pour vingt ou trente ans...

Alors qu'il regardait Toni monter dans l'hélico en prenant bien soin de ne surtout pas le regarder, il comprit qu'il y avait des prix plus lourds à payer en cas de dérapage... ou, dans son cas personnel, quand on avait failli déraper avec quelqu'un...

Peut-être que s'il avait de la chance, il se ferait tuer lors de cette opération clandestine...

Jeudi
Crétacé supérieur
Dans ce qui deviendra Londres

À pied, le lance-roquettes accroché à l'épaule, Jay huma l'air. Les odeurs de jungle habituelles étaient là, mais il y en avait une autre qui les dominait, tenace. Impossible à ignorer, en fait.

Près de lui, Saji fronça les nez et remarqua : « Bon Dieu, c'est quoi, cette puanteur ?

– Sans vouloir insister lourdement, c'est de la merde de monstre. »

Il tendit le doigt.

Devant lui se dressait un autre fourré de jungle préhistorique, représentant des piles de paquets de données codées, un nœud de transit électronique qui, dans le monde réel, correspondait à une société d'informatique londonienne. Sur le chemin menant à la jungle, formant grossièrement un triangle avec deux immenses traces de pas, il y avait un monticule de fiente, un monceau d'excréments bruns et puants, haut comme un tas de fumier et entouré d'un nuage de mouches vrombissantes.

Sur les côtés de la piste, une douzaine de monticules identiques, séchés et durcis, formaient des amorces de coprolithes géants. Bienvenue à Chiottes-ville.

Ils contournèrent le dépôt tout frais. Vu de près, on voyait émerger des bouts d'os non digérés et l'on sentait la chaleur qui en émanait. La puanteur était littéralement à couper au couteau.

« Sans vouloir ramener ma science, je crois pouvoir affirmer qu'il est passé par ici... Et je parierais qu'il est sorti faire ici ses petites affaires parce que c'est là qu'il habite. »

Saji contempla le monticule. Elle hocha la tête. « L'idée de rentrer là-dedans ne m'enchante guère. »

Jay fit glisser le lance-roquettes. « Moi non plus. Mets-toi sur le côté. » Il épaula, visa droit vers la jungle, pressa la détente. Le missile jaillit en chuintant, suivi d'un sillage de flamme, décrivit une parabole vers les bois avant d'exploser avec une détonation sonore qui répandit en tous sens feuilles et fragments de branchages.

« Une ou deux encore devraient suffire à attirer son attention. »

Jeudi
Les Ifs, Sussex, Angleterre

Peel descendit de voiture et claqua la portière avec un peu plus de vigueur que nécessaire. Il domina son irritation, adressa un signe de tête à Huard qui montait la garde à l'arrière du corps de bâtiment principal, puis se retourna pour regarder Roujio descendre de son côté. La voiture avec les cadavres des deux agents et l'arme qui les avait tués gisait au fond d'un trou d'eau de neuf mètres qui servait d'abreuvoir au bétail d'une des fermes de monseigneur, dans l'est du Sussex, pas très loin de l'endroit où ils avaient descendu les deux hommes. Enfin, où Roujio les avait descendus. Les services secrets ou la police locale finiraient tôt ou tard par retrouver la voiture et son macabre chargement, mais sans doute pas dans l'immédiat. Il devrait avoir tout le temps pour régler ses dernières affaires et quitter le pays. Dommage, mais prolonger son séjour risquait de devenir à coup sûr malsain. Et alors qu'il pouvait tirer un trait sur sa fortune fantôme dans la banque indonésienne, Peel n'oubliait pas que Goswell avait un coffre-fort dans sa résidence qui devait être bien garni en billets. Son plan était donc de refroidir le lord, ce salaud de Bascomb-Coombs, et enfin Roujio – ce dernier avec précaution : par-derrière, et au moment où il ne s'y attendrait pas. Ensuite, il disposerait les corps avec soin pour laisser croire que l'ex-agent soviétique avait descendu les deux autres avant de se faire tuer par un de ses hommes – Huard, par exemple, qui devrait disparaître lui aussi – et la voie serait libre. La situation était mauvaise, mais pas désespérée ; il aurait bien sûr préféré que les choses tournent autrement, mais il pouvait y survivre. Il était un soldat entraîné, un officier avec une expérience de commandement sur le terrain, et il y avait toujours du boulot pour des gens de sa trempe quelque part dans le tiers monde. Il pouvait former une armée dans un des pays de la CEI, commander un bataillon en Afrique centrale, assurer la sécurité d'un prince arabe. Les mercenaires avaient encore leur place, même si le monde était devenu plus paisible. On ne savait jamais si votre voisin ne lorgnait pas votre territoire, et il fallait toujours être prêt à le protéger, malgré ses sourires et sa main tendue.

Ce n'avait pas été son choix initial, mais difficile de faire autrement.

« Restez ici et ouvrez l'œil », dit-il à Roujio.

Ce dernier salua avec son parapluie roulé. Il n'allait sans doute pas tarder à en avoir besoin : le ciel devenait menaçant, avec de gros nuages sombres, avant-garde d'un front froid venu de l'Atlantique. Parfait, un orage ne pourrait qu'ajouter une touche de sordide.

Peel s'approcha de Huard. « Dis aux gars de se

disperser sur le périmètre. On pourrait bien recevoir de la visite. Toi, tu gardes la porte de derrière.

– Oui, mon commandant. »

Peel se dirigea vers la maison. Il allait régler tout ça. Ensuite, il attendrait la nuit pour pouvoir s'éclipser à travers champs, au cas où quelqu'un surveillerait le domaine. Il devait supposer que s'ils connaissaient son identité – puisqu'ils lui avaient mis aux trousses une équipe du SIS – c'est qu'ils savaient pour qui il travaillait. Ils n'allaient certainement pas investir les Ifs par la force, mais ils pouvaient essayer de le coincer à la sortie du domaine. S'il s'en éloignait à pied, il pourrait piquer la voiture d'un des voisins, rejoindre la côte sud, et traverser la Manche à bord d'un des bateaux de Goswell. Il n'y avait aucune honte à battre en retraite devant une force supérieure en nombre. On pouvait toujours se regrouper pour revenir ensuite. Avoir perdu une bataille ne signifiait pas obligatoirement avoir perdu la guerre.

Goswell était en train de prendre l'apéritif au salon.

« Bonsoir, commandant.

– Monseigneur. Où est M. Bascomb-Coombs ?

– Au bout du couloir, au bureau, je suppose. En train de jouer avec son ordinateur portable. J'ai fait fermer son accès au système principal, mais il a bien dû trouver un moyen de contourner le barrage, j'en suis sûr. Son portable s'est mis à biper, il est devenu tout agité et s'est excusé pour aller voir de quoi il retournait. Un verre ?

– Excellente idée. » Applewhite se matérialisa aussitôt – dommage qu'il doive mourir lui aussi, il avait de l'affection pour le vieux bougre – et Peel tendit deux doigts, pour indiquer sa dose de scotch. Oh, et puis, au diable l'avarice, il en ajouta un troisième. Il fallait qu'il tienne le coup jusqu'à la nuit, pas vrai ? Et la journée avait été longue et éprouvante. Personne n'irait lui reprocher d'avoir besoin d'un bon remontant.

Une brise soudaine ébranla l'encadrement de la fenêtre et les premières gouttes de pluie s'écrasèrent sur les vitres. Bon, la soirée s'annonçait orageuse, pas de doute, et dans tous les sens du terme.

39

Jeudi 14 avril Londres

L'équipe de la Net Force avait embarqué dans ce que le colonel Howard avait baptisé son PC tactique mobile – en fait, un gros camping-car loué en catastrophe. Julio Fernandez, qui était au volant, pestait sans arrêt : « Pourquoi tous ces maudits crétins conduisent-ils tous du mauvais côté de la route ? »

Le reste du groupe d'intervention s'était déjà entassé dans plusieurs voitures et camions à la base militaire et se dirigeait vers le point de ralliement – en l'occurrence, une caserne de pompiers du Sussex.

Howard avait posé un ordinateur sur une tablette ; Michaels et Toni, assis à côté, regardaient l'écran. Howard fit apparaître une image, une vue aérienne retravaillée d'une grande maison et de plusieurs bâtiments annexes. « Voici la résidence de Goswell.

– Vous l'avez eue par le MI-6 ? s'enquit Michaels.

– Non, monsieur. J'ai demandé au Gros Loucheur de l'enregistrer ce matin.

– Avant même qu'on ait pris la décision d'intervenir ? demanda Toni.

– Oui, m'dame. Ça fait jamais de mal de garder en tête le principe des 6P. »

Michaels opina. Tout le monde ici connaissait la

signification de l'acronyme : Planification Préparée Pour Prévenir Performances Pitoyables. Howard ne faisait que son boulot.

Le colonel poursuivit : « On serait nettement plus à l'aise si on avait deux jours devant nous pour étudier la situation, monter des scénarios tactiques et simuler d'autres plans d'attaque, mais puisque ce n'est pas le cas, on fait dans la simplicité. Ça passe ou ça casse.

« Bon. Voilà comment je vois les choses : on attend la nuit avant d'investir la place. Mes hommes détournent l'attention des gardes du domaine tandis qu'avec le sergent Fernandez et deux autres gars, on saute la clôture et on se dirige vers le bâtiment. On balance quelques flash-bang, des lacrymos et on neutralise les gardes, on entre, on ramasse tout le monde, on récupère ceux qui nous intéressent et on se dépêche de quitter le pays. Roujio, Peel et Bascomb-Coombs : ça devrait faire l'affaire. On pourra toujours transmettre par la suite à nos hôtes un mandat d'arrêt contre Goswell. Qu'ils s'occupent de lui s'il est impliqué dans l'affaire. Avec un peu de veine, le temps que les autochtones aient pigé ce qui s'est passé, on sera déjà dans notre zinc au-dessus de l'Atlantique.

– Avec un détail encore, intervint Michaels. Je vous accompagne. Eh oui, je sais, ce n'est pas ce que dicte la prudence, mais on a déjà eu cette discussion auparavant et puisque j'ai la responsabilité, ce choix me revient. » Il tourna les yeux vers Toni, prêt à lui demander de rester au poste de commandement.

Le regard de la jeune femme était reptilien. Elle savait ce qu'il s'apprêtait à dire. Et il sut aussitôt que s'il le disait, les maigres chances qui leur restaient de recoller les morceaux seraient définitivement réduites à néant. Alors, à la place, il lança : « Et Toni va venir aussi, bien sûr. »

Elle lui adressa un bref signe de tête. « Merci. » Sa voix était sèche, glaciale, mais au moins daignait-elle encore lui adresser la parole. C'était toujours mieux que rien.

Lorsqu'ils arrivèrent à la caserne de pompiers, près d'une petite ville baptisée Cuckfield, le commando de la Net Force était déjà là. Mais quand Toni sortit sous la pluie vespérale, une surprise l'attendait sous l'abri de l'auvent à l'entrée du bâtiment principal : Angela Cooper était là, elle aussi. Elle était en tenue de combat camouflée, maquillée, bottes, treillis et chemise.

« Et merde, murmura Fernandez. On dirait que la partie va être annulée. »

Ils coururent s'abriter sous l'auvent. Alex s'avança mais avant qu'il ait pu placer un mot, Cooper leva la main pour couper court à ses objections. « Si j'avais voulu vous arrêter, Alex, je ne serais pas venue seule.

– Alors, que voulez-vous, au juste ?

– Officiellement, le gouvernement de Sa Majesté ne peut mener aucune action contre Lord Goswell sans des preuves autrement plus tangibles que celles dont nous disposons actuellement. Toutefois, le directeur général et notre ministre sont au courant de ce que nous avons découvert et, à titre officieux, ils croient la même chose que nous, à savoir que Bascomb-Coombs a toutes les chances d'être l'auteur des actions de terrorisme informatique et que le commandant Peel comme Goswell trempent dans sa machination.

– Donc, vous avez décidé de détourner les yeux ?

– Oui. À la condition expresse que nous ayons un observateur officieux pour s'assurer que notre position officieuse... comment dire... continue de le rester. »

Toni intervint : « Bref, on se tape le sale boulot, on vous règle votre problème, et si jamais tout nous pète à la gueule, vous vous en lavez les mains.

– On ne peut rien vous cacher, n'est-ce pas, mademoiselle Fiorella ? Enfin, ce n'est peut-être pas la stricte vérité, qu'est-ce que vous en dites, Alex ? »

Des années de pratique des arts martiaux vous procurent une certaine assurance. Quand on se sait capable de tuer ou blesser grièvement quelqu'un rien qu'avec ses mains, ses coudes, ses genoux ou ses pieds, cela vous pousse à réfléchir avant de faire un geste inconsidéré. On doit être en mesure de réagir presque instinctivement dès que l'action est engagée, mais on doit également savoir quand il convient de le faire. Un jour, à la fac, un copain de dortoir s'était glissé derrière elle et l'avait saisie par la taille, dans le couloir, dans l'intention de la chatouiller. Sa petite blague lui avait valu un tour à l'infirmerie et une bonne contusion. Il avait fallu plusieurs années à Toni pour qu'elle dépasse le stade de la réaction instinctive, pour qu'elle soit à même d'évaluer la situation avant de risquer d'envoyer au tapis quelqu'un à qui elle ne voulait aucun mal.

Seule cette expérience durement apprise retint Toni de se ruer sur Angela Cooper pour la tailler en pièces. Ce n'était pourtant pas l'envie qui lui manquait. Au lieu de cela, elle réussit à sourire. Elle répondit : « Oh, je suis peut-être parfois un peu lente, mais je finis par piger.

– Très bien, coupa Alex. Le colonel Howard va nous récapituler à nouveau les opérations. On a encore deux heures devant nous avant d'y aller. » Il regarda Toni, hocha légèrement la tête, puis écarta les mains, en signe d'excuse impuissante. Il avait le teint pâle, presque gris, et elle espérait bien qu'il se sentait mal à l'aise. Il avait de quoi.

Roujio était appuyé au mur de pierre sous le large surplomb de la toiture. Le vent était presque tombé avec l'arrivée de la pluie et les chéneaux guidaient les eaux vers les chaînes d'écoulement situées aux angles du bâtiment, ce qui lui évitait d'être mouillé malgré l'humidité ambiante. Et puis, il avait toujours son parapluie, bien sûr, et gardait le pressentiment qu'il allait devoir recourir à ses fonctions cachées avant que la nuit ne s'achève. Tous les services de renseignements qu'il connaissait voyaient en général d'un très mauvais œil quiconque descendait un des leurs. Ça faisait désordre. Et en matière de vengeance, le Spetsnatz avait toujours été réputé. Un jour, dans un de ces pays toujours troublés du Moyen-Orient, un de leurs agents avait été capturé et tué par un groupe de fanatiques. Une semaine plus tard, seize d'entre eux avaient été retrouvés alignés avec soin dans un fossé, leur pénis tranché enfoncé dans la bouche, les yeux arrachés.

Tuez un des nôtres et on détruit un de vos villages. Ça donnait à réfléchir aux fanatiques de tout poil.

Les Britanniques étaient plus polis et moins sauvages, mais ils devaient désormais se douter que leurs hommes étaient morts, et ils devaient savoir qui en était responsable. Tout du moins étaient-ils au courant de la présence de Peel, et s'ils en savaient assez pour le retrouver et le filer, ils devaient sans aucun doute savoir aussi pour qui il travaillait et où résidait son employeur. Peel devait s'en être rendu compte, et avoir à l'heure qu'il était mis en place un plan pour éviter de se faire prendre.

Huard, vêtu d'un imper, faisait les cent pas derrière la maison, observant Roujio en silence. Huard ne l'aimait pas, mais Huard était un gamin.

Bon. À la place de Peel, qu'est-ce qu'il ferait ? La fuite était la seule option viable ; même Goswell ne le protégerait pas s'il restait ici. Et le temps jouait contre lui. Peel allait devoir disparaître avant qu'il ne fasse trop chaud pour lui. S'il avait été lui, il aurait déjà pris la tangente. Avant que le petit jour ne facilite la tâche de ses poursuivants. Et il quitterait les lieux sans laisser derrière lui de traces compromettantes. Peel avait envoyé ses hommes le long de la clôture du domaine, ne laissant près du bâtiment que Huard et Roujio. On pouvait les sacrifier, comme le reste des occupants de la maison. Oui, c'est ainsi que Roujio voyait la situation, quand il se mettait dans la peau de l'officier britannique.

Donc, à un moment donné de la soirée, Peel allait l'appeler à l'intérieur. Ou peut-être se servir du com pour dire à Huard de se charger de la tâche. Le tuer ? Non. Il ne lui ferait pas confiance. Et puis, en cas d'échec du garçon, son maître saurait que Roujio ne resterait pas les bras ballants.

Roujio pouvait simplement disparaître à la faveur de l'averse nocturne d'ici quelques minutes. Aucun des hommes de Peel ne le retrouverait ou ne pourrait l'arrêter, même s'ils arrivaient à mettre la main sur lui. Il pouvait fuir à travers champs, se faire prendre en stop ou piquer une bagnole, et dès demain, il serait en

France. La partie était presque terminée, alors à quoi bon traîner pour assister à une fin prévisible ?

Il haussa mentalement les épaules. Non, aucun intérêt, effectivement. Et c'était peut-être là la raison. Il n'avait plus nulle part où aller. Cet endroit en valait bien un autre. Alors, quelle importance quand votre sablier avait presque fini de s'écouler ? Au bout du compte, qu'est-ce qui importait désormais ?

À l'abri près du camion garé, Howard mit son casque et vérifia le fonctionnement du communicateur de son LOSIR.

« Équipe du périmètre, coupez le son, nommez-vous dans l'ordre. »

Les hommes du groupe d'intervention répondirent docilement. Tout était nominal.

« Groupe à l'entrée, son coupé.

– Ici E1, Cooper.

– E2, Michaels.

– E3, Fiorella.

– E4, Fernandez. »

Et il était E5. Cinq, ça devait suffire, si chacun faisait ce qu'il avait à faire. Fernandez et lui sc chargeraient des tirs à l'arme lourde, et même si Michaels et Fiorella n'avaient pas l'entraînement des troupes d'assaut, il les avait vus assez souvent en action pour savoir qu'ils en avaient dans la culotte. Non, la seule inconnue restait Cooper, mais si elle était agent traitant du MI-6, elle devait avoir au moins quelques notions de base. C'était une action improvisée, montée à la va-vite avec des bouts de ficelle, mais il devait faire avec, et c'était bientôt le moment. Tous étaient équipés d'Intellicombis allégées : en gros la tenue pare-balles, les coms et l'ordinateur tactique gérant le casque. Tous étaient dotés d'armes simples et fiables, des pistolets et des mitraillettes H&K 9mm, sauf Howard et son inséparable 357 Magnum. Et d'ailleurs, dès qu'il l'avait dégainé, Julio s'était mis à beugler : « Wouah, mes aïeux, je dois avoir la berlue ! Mes vieux calots doivent me trahir ! C'est quoi, cette horrible bosse qui défigure l'antique talisman du colonel ? Ne serait-ce pas un viseur laser ? Pincez-moi, je rêve !

– Julio...

– Non, je dois être drogué, ou alors je suis devenu fou. Le colonel John Howard que je connais ne s'abaisserait jamais à améliorer son équipement sous le prétexte futile que c'est moderne et utile ! » Il leva les yeux vers le ciel chargé de pluie.

« Vous cherchez quoi, sergent ?

– Ch'sais pas, mon colonel. Un signe, un présage. Une grosse météorite sur le point de nous tomber dessus, une assemblée de chérubins, une pluie de feu, enfin un indice quelconque que notre fin est proche.

– Personne n'a jamais dit que ton supérieur était un parfait rétrograde. » Il sourit.

C'était l'heure à présent. Ils allaient se séparer en deux groupes d'ici trois kilomètres, celui chargé du périmètre atteindrait la grille et escaladerait la clôture. Howard inspira un grand coup et souffla lentement.

« Tout le monde en piste », lança-t-il.

Peel regarda sa montre. Bientôt neuf heures. Il pleuvait toujours, mais pas aussi dru que tout à l'heure, à en juger par le bruit des gouttes sur les ardoises.

Bascomb-Coombs n'était pas ressorti du bureau, il était penché sur son ordinateur, coiffé d'un casque et de gants capteurs, immergé dans un scénario de réalité virtuelle. À la bonne heure. Il pouvait bien crever sans savoir ce qui l'avait frappé... bon débarras.

Goswell s'était rendu d'un pas chancelant vers la salle à manger pour souper, et Peel avait désormais le salon pour lui tout seul. Il terminait son troisième scotch, léger celui-ci. Il ne voulait pas trop boire... il restait le problème Roujio.

Il allait devoir s'y mettre bientôt, mais il traînait la jambe. Il fallait que ce soit fait, bien sûr, mais il avait une certaine réticence à se lancer. Encore une page tournée dans le livre de sa vie, et une page importante. Enfin, bon. Ainsi allaient les choses. On gagne, on perd, mais l'essentiel est de survivre pour se battre un nouveau jour.

Il but une nouvelle gorgée de whisky.

Le monstre, qui évoquait un croisement entre Godzilla et quelque Vélociraptor spielbergien géant, entra d'un pas lourd dans la clairière qui lui servait de toilettes et lâcha un beuglement qui effeuilla les fougères. Il était pourtant encore loin, dans les deux cents mètres. Sans doute était-il capable de couvrir la distance en quatre ou cinq secondes, une fois lancé. Une roquette... peut-être deux.

« Le voilà », annonça Jay, bien inutilement.

Saji leva les yeux. « Pas possible. »

Jay déglutit, la bouche sèche, aligna le réticule du viseur laser sur le torse du monstre. La croix tressauta quelque peu mais finalement l'image holographique se mit à clignoter en rouge, indiquant le verrouillage de la cible. Jay pressa la détente – et eut un instant de panique, redoutant d'avoir appuyé trop fort.

La roquette fila. Percuta le torse du monstre et explosa.

Quand le feu et la fumée se dissipèrent, le monstre gisait abattu.

« Excellent, Jay ! » s'écria Saji.

Leur triomphe fut de courte durée. Devant leurs yeux ébahis, le monstre roula sur lui-même et, avec sa queue en guise de béquille, il se releva. Aussitôt, il chercha alentour l'origine de l'attaque.

Et meeeerde !

Saji était déjà en train d'introduire une autre roquette dans l'espèce de bazooka avant que Jay ait pu dire un mot. Elle lui tapa sur l'épaule. « Chargé ! »

Le lance-roquettes entra de nouveau en action. *Boum !* Une fois encore, le projectile renversa la bête.

Et une fois encore, celle-ci se redressa, avec un rugissement d'une force à réveiller tout ce qui était mort depuis le commencement des temps. Il se pencha vers l'avant, tendit sa grosse queue à l'horizontale et avisa Jay et Saji. On aurait dit un chien de chasse géant en arrêt.

Bigre ! En tout cas, leur attaque avait eu de l'effet. Le problème, c'est qu'ils n'avaient plus qu'une roquette et la partie était terminée. Ils pouvaient toujours décrocher de RV s'il les serrait de trop près, et ils auraient même intérêt à le faire : vu comment le petit tigre lui avait arrangé le cerveau, Jay avait le sentiment que si cette bestiole leur mettait les griffes dessus, image virtuelle ou pas, leur intégrité physique serait réellement en péril. S'ils devaient décrocher, cette chose remporterait la victoire et Jay ne voulait surtout pas de ça. S'il désirait un truc, c'était la vaincre. Et pas seulement la vaincre, mais lui botter le cul, l'expédier au diable Vauvert, la piétiner longuement.

Toutefois, l'affaire s'annonçait mal pour l'équipe invitante.

« Rechargé ! »

Jay inspira un grand coup et se prépara à tirer son ultime projectile.

Pas de problème, Bascomb-Coombs était toujours dans le bureau, agitant les mains et les doigts, commandant quelque invisible sorcellerie informatique. Peel avisa les deux bouts du couloir. Personne. Il se faufila dans la pièce. Retira le petit couteau Culloden de l'étui à sa ceinture. L'arme était courte, pointue comme un stylet, avec une grosse poignée caoutchoutée donnant une bonne prise. Il s'approcha de l'informaticien par-derrière, lui plaqua la main gauche sur le front, puis, de la droite, lui enfonça le couteau à la base de la nuque. Bascomb-Coombs se raidit...

Le monstre ouvrit sa bouche pleine de dents, exhiba des crocs longs comme l'avant-bras, et poussa de nouveau son terrible cri. Puis il se figea dans cette position, bouche bée...

« Qu'est-ce qu'il fout ? »

Jay hocha la tête. « Du diable si je sais. En tout cas, j'ai ma cible. » Il aligna le réticule sur l'œsophage béant de la bête. Retint son souffle et pressa la détente...

Bascomb-Coombs eut plusieurs soubresauts, puis il s'affala, poids mort soudain trop lourd à retenir. Peel se pencha, ôta le couteau de la nuque de sa victime, l'essuya sur la chemise de celle-ci, remit l'arme dans sa gaine.

« Désolé, vieux, mais quand on joue avec le taureau, on se fait parfois encorner... »

Le couteau était l'arme idéale, pas de problème. Il ne voulait pas attirer l'attention. En revanche, une fois qu'il en aurait terminé ici, il utiliserait son pistolet pour liquider Roujio. Celui-là, il n'avait pas envie de le serrer de trop près.

Bon. Récapitulons. Restaient encore à l'intérieur Goswell, la bonne, le cuisinier et le vieil Applewhite, puis Roujio. Huard, il pouvait le réserver pour la fin, le gamin ne se douterait jamais de rien. Ensuite, ouvrir le coffre (dont il avait la combinaison depuis des mois), récupérer le fric et les babioles qu'il pouvait contenir, puis : petite promenade vivifiante dans les prés humides et salut, la compagnie ! Sa longue et dure journée était loin d'être achevée, mais enfin, il n'avait pas le choix, ce qui devait être fait devait être fait, pour Dieu et pour le roi !

Il reprit le couloir en direction de la salle à manger pour dire deux mots à monseigneur.

Cette fois, quand la roquette explosa, elle emporta la tête du monstre. Des fragments d'ersatz de cervelle, d'os et de sang se mirent à pleuvoir en tous sens, certains atteignirent Jay et Saji, mais peu leur importait.

« Tu l'as eu ! Tu l'as eu !

– Tu m'as l'air diablement joyeuse pour une bouddhiste, compte tenu des circonstances... »

Saji le serra dans ses bras. « Attends, pour avoir fermé un programme informatique ? Parce que c'est tout ce que t'as fait, en somme, non ?

– Tout ce que j'ai fait ? Hé, c'était pas un logiciel ordinaire, ma petite ! » Mais il lui rendit son étreinte. Il avait réussi. Il s'était racheté. Et il se sentait plus que vachement bien. Il se sentait comme un dieu.

Jay Gridley était de retour, ouais !

40

Jeudi 14 avril
Les Ifs, Sussex, Angleterre

Le groupe de pénétration arriva jusqu'à quelques centaines de mètres de la maison sans aucune difficulté. Michaels s'était attendu à entendre les vigiles tirer lorsqu'ils seraient parvenus à la grille, mais soit ils étaient trop loin, soit les choses avaient tourné mieux que prévu.

Howard demanda dans son micro-casque : « Tu vois quelque chose, E4 ?

– Négatif, répondit Fernandez. Je... attendez... je viens d'en voir passer un sous la lampe de la porte de service. On dirait qu'il est en patrouille.

– Bien compris. On y va. »

Michaels attendit qu'Howard l'ait dépassé pour se relever de sa position accroupie dans l'herbe humide et se mettre à progresser, le dos baissé.

Rester baissé, avancer lentement.

Howard avait bien insisté là-dessus.

Toni et Cooper le suivirent, et la boule qu'Alex sentait au creux de l'estomac n'était pas due seulement à la crainte de se faire descendre.

Roujio entrevit le mouvement dans le pré à la faveur d'une accalmie de l'averse. Pas grand-chose : juste une ombre dessinée à contre-jour par la lumière au-dessus de la porte d'une ferme voisine, mais cela suffit à attirer son attention.

Quelques secondes plus tard, il crut discerner un autre élément. Un mouton égaré, peut-être. Un agneau qui aurait perdu sa mère. Mais il n'y croyait pas. Des formes sombres traversant un pré sous la pluie ? Non, plutôt un commando britannique. Et arrivé plus vite que Peel et lui ne l'avaient prévu. Puisqu'il n'avait pas entendu de coups de feu, il devait supposer qu'ils avaient dépassé le cordon des gardes. Pas vraiment une surprise. Les hommes de Peel étaient de bons soldats mais la propriété était trop vaste pour qu'ils puissent couvrir le périmètre dans de bonnes conditions.

Roujio s'enfonça un peu plus dans l'ombre du surplomb du toit, fit le tour de la maison et s'éloigna vers le bâtiment annexe qui servait à Peel de bureau. De là, il pourrait embrasser le domaine et voir combien d'hommes étaient là. Ensuite, avec un peu de chance, il pourrait toujours s'esquiver. Les assaillants pouvaient être une douzaine ou une centaine et, faute d'avoir localisé les failles dans leurs rangs, toute tentative de fuite précipitée s'avérait risquée.

Goswell s'essuyait les lèvres au moment où Peel entra dans la salle. Il arborait un petit sourire un rien désabusé. Bien. L'heure était venue.

Il avait envoyé Applewhite à l'étage avec la bonne et le cuisinier, en leur ordonnant de se boucler dans le bureau du premier et d'y rester jusqu'à ce qu'il leur dise personnellement de sortir. La porte du bureau, en acier, était dotée d'un robuste verrou et d'une barre de renfort, installations réalisées dans le cadre du dispositif de sécurité mis en place sous l'égide de Peel. Plutôt ironique...

Il s'agissait à présent de finir de régler cette désagréable affaire. Il remit la serviette sur ses genoux et laissa les mains posées dessus.

« Prenez donc un siège, commandant.

– Je crois que j'aime mieux rester debout, si cela ne vous dérange pas, Geoffrey. »

Geoffrey ? Dieu du ciel, Peel était devenu fou. Quelque peu désarçonné par cet accès de familiarité excessive, Goswell chercha à se ressaisir : « Eh bien, avez-vous vu Bascomb-Coombs ?

– Ah, ça oui. Je viens de le quitter. Il est dans son bureau. Raide mort.

– Mort, dites-vous ?

– Oui. Une brusque attaque cérébrale. Due à ceci. » Et, glissant la main sous son veston, Peel exhiba un méchant petit stylet qu'il brandit dans les airs. La lame en acier brillant étincela sous les ampoules du lustre.

Goswell considéra la chose. « Vous l'avez tué, n'est-ce pas ?

– J'en ai peur, oui.

– Quel dommage. Un homme si brillant.

– Et aussi un psychotique prêt à se plier à vos quatre volontés, qui avait en outre essayé de me faire tuer. » Peel agitait son couteau en tous sens, en fixant l'acier, comme hypnotisé.

« Pas possible ? Eh bien, il semble donc que ses assassins n'aient pas eu plus de succès que les miens. »

Peel fronça les sourcils. « Les vôtres ?

– Mais oui, bien sûr. J'ai bien peur que vous n'ayez commis une erreur et que ce pauvre Bascomb-Coombs n'en ait fait les frais. C'est moi qui avais chargé des gens de vous tuer, mon ami.

– Mais... pourquoi ? » Sa perplexité ne semblait pas feinte.

« Voyons, franchement, Peel. Pour avoir comploté avec ce même Bascomb-Coombs que vous venez d'assassiner dans mon bureau. M'avez-vous cru assez idiot pour croire que j'ignorais qu'il convient toujours de surveiller les surveillants ?

– Ah, c'est donc vous qui m'avez fait suivre. Et ce type dans la librairie...

– J'admets avec tristesse que c'était nécessaire. Votre pauvre père n'aurait pas été fier de vous. Je vous pensais fait d'une autre étoffe, commandant. »

Peel rit de sa remarque. « Ma foi, je vous dois cet aveu, monseigneur, je ne vous aurais jamais imaginé capable d'une telle initiative. Je fais amende honorable. Et ce n'est pas comme si Bascomb-Coombs était un innocent n'ayant pas mérité son destin. Même si, je dois l'admettre, vous êtes d'un calme incroyable pour un homme à qui on s'apprête à trancher la gorge. Gentleman jusqu'au bout des ongles, n'est-ce pas ?

– J'ose l'espérer. Bien que, je le confesse, je doute qu'un tel sort m'attende ce soir. »

Sur ces mots, Goswell saisit la Rigby à double canon qu'il gardait posée sur ses genoux et la pointa droit vers le cœur de Peel.

Le vieux était lent et à moitié aveugle, et si Peel avait réagi assez vite, il aurait pu se dégager de la ligne de mire et poignarder Goswell. Mais telle fut sa surprise de voir apparaître le fusil de chasse qu'il en resta interdit. Le temps qu'il ait retrouvé ses esprits, Goswell l'avait mis en joue. Il n'était peut-être pas fichu d'atteindre un lapin gambadant dans son potager à quinze mètres de lui, mais à trois, il aurait eu du mal à rater une cible de la taille d'un homme. Et à si courte distance, bien ajustée, une volée de chevrotines serait fatale.

« Allez-vous m'abattre ?

– Je préférerais ne pas maculer de sang ma salle à manger, mais si vous battez simplement d'un cil, je le ferai sans aucun doute. Le nettoyage fera pester Applewhite, mais c'est un homme très discret.

– Bon, et maintenant ?

– J'avais dans l'idée qu'on aille dehors, que vous fumiez un ultime cigare, buviez un dernier verre de cognac ou de ce que vous voudrez, et puis qu'on se... sépare. »

C'est qu'il était sérieux. Goswell s'apprêtait à le tuer. Après un dernier cigare et un dernier verre.

Pas tant qu'il avait un couteau dans une main et un pistolet à quelques centimètres de l'autre... le vieux fou pouvait toujours se brosser. Il allait le distraire et compter sur ses réflexes plus affûtés. C'était le seul moyen.

« Bon, très bien. S'il doit en être ainsi. Je pense que je prendrai un de ces cubains et peut-être un ballon de cette fine Napo... »

Laissant sa phrase en suspens, il plongea...

« Je ne vois toujours que lui, indiqua Fernandez. Vous voulez que je lui expédie deux pruneaux, que je prenne sa place et vous donne le signal ? »

Howard envisagea les différentes options. Le garde avait une mitraillette à la hanche, prête à tirer, et il risquait de disjoncter au moindre bruit suspect. Des balles de mitraillette ne perceraient pas le blindage de leur Intellicombi, mais elles feraient certainement assez de boucan pour prévenir les occupants de la maison qu'ils avaient de la compagnie. Idem avec des flash-bang ou des lacrymogènes. Howard s'était préparé à une fusillade, et dans ce genre d'hypothèse, on faisait ce qu'il fallait pour maîtriser la situation, mais jusqu'ici, il n'y avait pas eu de coup de feu, et il semblait possible qu'ils règlent cette histoire sans effusion de sang. Il préférait de loin cette solution, compte tenu de l'aspect délicat des implications politiques. Michaels s'était plus d'une fois mouillé pour couvrir Howard, le moins qu'il puisse faire était donc de lui rendre la politesse.

« Je vais me relever, dit Howard. Pour détourner son attention. Pendant qu'il s'intéresse à moi, tu le dégommes. De manière non létale, si possible.

– Non létale, bien compris, E5. »

Howard s'approcha de la maison en rampant jusqu'à moins de vingt mètres, puis quinze... Le garde avait fait demi-tour et revenait vers lui et il devait attirer son attention assez longtemps pour que Julio puisse lui sauter dessus et le neutraliser.

Il fallait qu'il trouve un bruit pour éveiller la curiosité du garde sans susciter son inquiétude. Un miaulement serait l'idéal. Il fit une imitation passable d'un chaton réclamant sa mère. Même si le garde était une espèce de pervers qui aimait piétiner les petits chats, il faudrait d'abord qu'il le repère. Ça laisserait assez de temps à Julio.

« Miaou. Miou, miou, miou ! »

Pas de doute, le garde s'était détourné dans sa direction.

« Miou ! Miou ! »

L'homme sourit. « Hé minou ! Minou-minou-minou ! Alors comme ça, t'es perdu sous la pluie ? Viens par ici, je vais te sécher. »

Parfait, un amoureux des chats.

Ça devait marcher. Et ça aurait marché... si, à cet instant précis, quelqu'un dans la maison n'avait pas tiré un coup de feu.

Le garde pivota pour se ruer vers la porte, vit Julio lui arriver dessus à toute vitesse, et releva aussitôt son arme.

Et merde, pensa Howard. Puis il fit feu avec sa propre mitraillette, une brève salve de trois balles dans le dos du garde. L'homme ne portait pas d'armure. Il s'effondra.

« Go ! cria Howard dans son micro-casque. Retour au plan A ! »

Peel contempla le trou sanglant au milieu de son ventre, sentit la brûlure des plombs, et il comprit qu'il ne se remettrait pas de cette blessure à l'abdomen. Une épaisse fumée obscurcissait les lampes, l'odeur de poudre brûlée était épouvantable, et, gisant à présent au sol, il n'avait plus qu'un seul désir : entraîner avec lui dans la mort ce salopard de Goswell. Il empoigna la crosse de son pistolet, le dégaina...

Goswell s'approcha et braqua son fusil de chasse vers le visage de Peel.

« Désolé », fit-il.

L'explosion suivante mit fin à la partie pour de bon : plus de son, plus d'image.

Howard franchit la porte de la cuisine par une roulade. Il se redressa aussitôt mais, en dehors de Julio, déjà en position, il était seul. Sans un mot, il indiqua le couloir et Julio acquiesça.

Ils visitèrent les pièces une par une. Quand ils parvinrent au bureau, ils trouvèrent un corps gisant au sol, à côté d'un ordinateur portable. Le cadavre était muni d'un équipement portatif de réalité virtuelle. Ils le firent rouler sur le dos et découvrirent son visage.

« Bascomb-Coombs, commenta Julio. Définitivement refroidi.

– Ouais. »

Dans son casque, Howard entendit quelqu'un à l'extérieur pousser un gros soupir.

Quand ils parvinrent à la salle à manger, ils découvrirent le second corps, masse sanguinolente dont la moitié du visage avait été emportée, et un vieillard assis à la table, un fusil de chasse à canon double posé, cassé, devant lui. Un épais brouillard de fumée blanche planait dans la pièce.

« Vous tirez en chargeant ce truc à la poudre noire ? » s'étonna Julio.

Le vieillard était Lord Goswell. Howard le reconnut d'après ses photos.

« À ma connaissance, vous ne ressemblez à aucun des mes vigiles. Américains, n'est-ce pas ?

– Ouais, on vient de débarquer, répondit Julio. Qu'est-ce qui s'est passé, ici ?

– Le commandant Peel a eu une crise de démence,

j'imagine. Il a tué Bascomb-Coombs puis s'en est pris à moi. J'ai dû l'abattre, je le crains. Lamentable histoire. »

Peel et Bascomb-Coombs, morts tous les deux. Howard hocha la tête. « Bon Dieu. »

Dans son com, il entendit Cooper pousser un juron identique. Ou peut-être Fiorella.

Julio demanda : « Où est Roujio ? »

Le vieux fronça les sourcils. « Qui ça ? Oh, vous parlez du nouveau qu'a engagé Peel, ce Russe ? J'imagine qu'il est quelque part dans les parages. Il était ici tout à l'heure.

– Ne bougez pas, dit Howard. On revient. Tout le monde bascule sur l'affichage tête haute. Roujio est toujours en vadrouille. »

Ils enclenchèrent l'affichage tête haute. Michaels, Fiorella et Cooper couvraient l'arrière et Julio annonça dans son com : « E4 et E5 ressortent par la porte de service, personne ne nous a tiré dessus. »

Lorsqu'ils débouchèrent dans la cour, la pluie avait cessé. L'affichage tête haute du casque d'Howard clignota, indiquant un message sur le canal tactique 2. Il activa le deuxième com. « E5 pour P1. Nous tenons le périmètre.

– Bien reçu, P1. Laissez-y la moitié de votre unité et envoyez-nous une escouade. Nous avons un malfaisant en vadrouille à travers champs, il est armé et c'est le plus dangereux de la bande. Alors, ouvrez l'œil.

– Bien copié, E5, on ouvre l'œil. »

Howard intervint : « On se divise. Commandant, vous restez avec moi. Cooper et Fiorella, accompagnez Fernandez. Faites ce qu'il dit. On va aller le chercher. »

De sa cachette dans l'angle de la dépendance, à cinq ou six mètres de là, Roujio entendit la voix de l'Américain mais sans bien distinguer ses paroles. Ils étaient cinq, plus d'autres dans les champs, qui devaient sans aucun doute converger par ici. Son arme était sans effet contre les armures protectrices qu'ils avaient revêtues, et il était douteux qu'ils relèvent leur visière ou ôtent leur casque, sachant ce qui était arrivé à leurs hommes la dernière fois qu'ils l'avaient fait quand ils avaient voulu le capturer. Il était en infériorité numérique, en infériorité matérielle, et encerclé. Naguère encore, il aurait vu cela comme un défi personnel. Pas ce soir.

Il pouvait tenter un coup de feu sous une visière avec des balles chemisées, mais ses calibre 22 en plomb mou ricochaient mal, même si elles étaient susceptibles d'éclater en frappant une surface rigide. Il pouvait peut-être en aveugler un, mais ça ne l'avancerait guère.

Le seul autre point faible de ses adversaires, c'était les gants, qui étaient en Kevlar fin, pour ne pas trop entraver les mouvements des doigts. Toutefois, une fracture de la main ne risquait guère d'être fatale.

Non, s'il voulait survivre, il avait intérêt à courir sa chance en fuyant à travers champs. Avec du bol, il pourrait franchir leurs lignes et s'échapper.

Il soupira. Il aurait dû fuir depuis longtemps. À l'heure qu'il est, il serait de retour en Tchétchénie. Mais sans Anna, ce n'était plus vraiment le bercail... son bercail avait été là où elle était. Avec sa mort, il avait perdu toute attache, et s'était retrouvé à la dérive, feuille morte chassée par les vents du destin.

Il poussa un nouveau soupir. Assez de jérémiades.

Il déplia la détente de sous la poignée de son parapluie et quitta l'abri du bâtiment pour s'avancer dans le cône de lumière. Les cinq types n'étaient qu'à cinq ou six mètres, le dos tourné.

« Je vais vous faciliter la tâche. »

Ils se retournèrent comme un seul homme, tous l'arme braquée sur lui.

« Lâche ça ! lança l'un d'eux. Lâche ce... ce parapluie ? »

Il les vit se détendre imperceptiblement. Il avait cédé. Ils le tenaient.

Il releva le parapluie et se mit à les aligner à bout portant.

Howard sentit l'impact de la balle et, quand il voulut riposter au pistolet-mitrailleur, il tira un coup, bien trop bas, puis son arme s'enraya. Il la laissa tomber et s'empara de son revolver.

Il entendait hurler les autres, même s'il ne pouvait séparer les diverses voix, proches ou lointaines, dans son LOSIR.

« Merde !

– Bordel !

– Ouch ! »

Le Smith & Wesson jaillit de son étui, le capuchon du viseur, attaché au rabat, libérant l'oculaire. Il brandit le revolver, trop haut, repéra le point rouge lumineux, le rabaissa...

... merde, pourquoi était-il seul à lui tirer dessus... ?

... fit redescendre le point rouge vers la poitrine de l'homme... puis lâcha deux balles – *bang ! bang !*

... le vit s'effondrer, tassé sur lui-même, au ralenti...

... et le fils de pute, en tombant, *avait le sourire* !

Howard se rua vers l'homme gisant à terre. Les deux balles de 357 l'avaient atteint à la poitrine, les deux en plein cœur, il avait eu son compte, même si le SAMU avait été là, il n'aurait rien pu faire pour lui.

Le mourant leva les yeux vers Howard : « Anna », fit-il. Et ce fut tout.

L'affaire était quasiment réglée. Fernandez s'approcha, tenant le parapluie utilisé par Roujio. Il le tenait de façon à révéler à Michaels le mécanisme niché à l'intérieur : « Vous voyez ? un revolver à cinq coups ! Ingénieux, non ? »

Michaels opina. Il nota également le pansement sur la main droite de Fernandez, à l'endroit où la balle de petite calibre l'avait touché. Elle n'avait pas transpercé le gant, mais l'impact avait été assez violent pour l'empêcher de riposter. L'arme automatique de Michaels avait été neutralisée quand une autre balle avait touché le chargeur. Toni, comme Fernandez, souffrait d'une blessure légère à la main droite, et pour Angela, son gant n'avait pas réussi à bloquer le projectile et elle souffrait d'une fracture du pouce. Quant à la mitraillette d'Howard, elle avait pris une balle dans la culasse.

Ce Roujio les avait donc frappés tous les cinq au point de les empêcher de riposter, et seule l'arme de poing d'Howard était en fin de compte parvenue à venir à bout du forcené. Incroyable. Personne ici n'avait vu quelqu'un tirer aussi bien. S'il avait disposé d'une arme capable de perforer les blindages, il aurait pu tous les descendre.

« Pas de pot qu'il n'ait pas été dans notre camp, remarqua Fernandez. Il aurait fait un sacré maître d'armes.

– Tu regrettes sa mort ?

– Non... et, ma foi... oui. Quelque part. »

Michaels le comprenait.

« Très bien. On remballe et on décolle, annonça Howard. La fête est finie. »

Épilogue

Vendredi 15 avril
Londres

Toni avait pris une chambre à part, sans même discuter de la situation avec Alex. En descendant dans le hall de l'hôtel pour la retrouver, il se demandait ce qu'il allait bien pouvoir lui dire. Ils étaient censés rentrer aujourd'hui. Leurs places étaient réservées. Le voyage s'annonçait long si elle refusait de lui adresser la parole.

Il prit l'escalier, il aurait voulu être seul.

L'affaire était close. Les Britanniques avaient nettoyé le bordel chez Goswell. Ils n'avaient aucune charge à relever contre le vieillard. Tous les éventuels témoins à charge étaient morts.

L'ordinateur miracle de Bascomb-Coombs également. Une sorte de code d'autodestruction programmé qui n'avait pas été neutralisé, personne n'étant là pour désarmer le dispositif. Les Britanniques avaient la machine mais ils ne savaient pas ce qu'ils détenaient. Un jour peut-être réussiraient-ils à en décrypter les rouages.

Donc, pas d'incident international. La plupart des méchants étaient morts. Ça aurait pu être pire.

Mais il y avait Toni, debout dans le hall, près de la grande plante en pot. Elle ne lui avait pas parlé de

Cooper, avait refusé d'écouter toute explication de sa part.

Elle le regarda et son visage était si triste qu'il la crut sur le point d'éclater en sanglots. Si triste qu'elle lui donnait lui aussi envie de pleurer. Il fallait qu'il trouve le moyen d'arranger ça, d'une manière ou d'une autre.

« Toni, je suis désolé, je...

– Non, coupa-t-elle. Pas aujourd'hui. Ton avion décolle dans deux heures.

– *Mon* avion ?

– Oui. Je reste ici un moment.

– Mais...

– Non. Je dois réfléchir à pas mal de trucs, Alex. Et toi aussi. » Elle le regarda et il vit les larmes lui monter aux yeux, se mettre à couler.

« Toni, tu ne comprends pas...

– Non. Pas maintenant. Ne parle plus de ça. »

Les larmes ruisselaient maintenant sur son visage.

Elle ne savait pas qu'il n'avait en fait jamais couché avec Cooper. Elle devait être persuadée du contraire. Et s'il voyait les choses en face, cela faisait-il une telle différence ? Il avait désiré Cooper. Il avait bien failli la posséder. Se retrouver nu, allongé sur une table avec une femme, nue elle aussi, quelle importance s'ils n'avaient pas consommé ? Il fallait qu'il lui explique, mais le regard qu'elle lui adressa fit s'étrangler les mots dans sa gorge. La situation en serait-elle meilleure ? Ou pire ?

D'ailleurs, est-ce qu'elle le croirait même ?

« D'accord, pas de problème, prends du recul, autant que tu voudras. On pourra... régler tout ça lorsque tu reprendras le boulot.

– Non, on ne pourra pas. Je ne retourne pas au boulot. C'est trop dur à assumer pour nous, ce mélange entre vie privée et vie professionnelle. Je raccroche, Alex. À dater d'aujourd'hui, de cette minute, je ne travaille plus pour la Net Force.

– Quoi ? Tu ne peux pas !

– Tu ne vas pas me dire à présent ce que je peux ou ne pas faire... tu ne me le diras plus. Adieu, Alex... Tu... tu me manqueras. »

Et sur ces mots, elle s'éloigna.

Alex la regarda partir, incapable de parler, de bouger, de respirer, même.

Oh, bon Dieu, Toni ! Qu'avait-il fait ?

Il resta figé ainsi un long moment, comme en transe, et quand il en sortit enfin, elle était partie.

Partie.

GLOSSAIRE

Note du traducteur : *Le lecteur trouvera ici, panachés, des termes en usage à l'époque de la rédaction de cet ouvrage, ainsi que d'autres apparemment usités à l'époque, un peu plus lointaine, où se déroule le récit...*

Com : Dispositif de communication miniaturisé, analogue au *virgil* (voir ce mot).

CPI : Ça passe impec. Argot des cybersurfers. Équivalent du « ça baigne » usité au XXe siècle.

Discom (DISconnect COMmunication) : Formule de politesse pour mettre un terme à une transmission vocale sur un réseau télématique. Par dérivation : *Discommuter* : couper la communication.

Écran-plat : Comme son nom l'indique, ordinateur portatif se présentant sous la forme d'une simple dalle d'écran tactile faisant en même temps office de clavier, sur lequel on peut directement écrire ou dessiner.

Flash-bang : Terme d'argot militaire qualifiant les grenades à concussion ou détonantes/aveuglantes : il s'agit de grenades offensives incapacitantes comprenant une charge au phosphore ou au magnésium (pour aveugler), complétée d'une poudre détonante (pour assourdir et provoquer un effet de choc). Selon les armes et les services qui les utilisent, elles ont plusieurs noms : « phosphorescentes » (pour les commandos de la marine et pour l'armée en général), « fulgurantes » pour les forces d'intervention civile (SWAT, GIGN, GILO, RAID, FBI, Net Force).

GPS (Global Positioning System) : Système mondial de localisation par satellites.

Holoproj : pour *holoprojection*, projection holographique.

Humvee : Véhicule tout-terrain de l'armée américaine, remplaçant la Jeep.

Infosphère : Dispositif de mémoire statique miniaturisé, de la taille approximative d'une balle de golf. Les derniers modèles sont à peine plus gros qu'une bille.

Intellicombi : Combinaison utilisée par les militaires, formée d'un tissu pare-balles à camouflage actif, procurant une quasi-invisibilité. Elle est dotée en outre de balises de repérage et d'un casque protecteur équipé d'une visière à affichage tête haute permettant une relation permanente et bidirectionnelle entre tous les membres d'un détachement et leur PC arrière.

KT (kick-taser) : Pistolet électrocuteur. Cette arme d'autodéfense lance des fléchettes reliées par fil à un générateur de courant haute tension. Immobilise l'adversaire en provoquant une tétanie musculaire momentanée. L'appareil dérive du *taser* inventé dans les années 1980. Grâce à la transmission par micro-ondes, la dernière version (2010) s'affranchit des fils.

LOSIR (Line-Of-Sight InfraRed Tactical Com Unit) : Appareil de communication tactique à transmission directe par infrarouge.

MR : Monde réel (par opposition à la RV, la réalité virtuelle – voir ce mot).

Nouille : Argot des cybersurfers (par assimilation avec « couille », erreur). Absence de piste révélatrice d'une intrusion de pirate sur un site ou dans un réseau informatique. Dérivé plaisant de penne (voir ce mot).

OQ : Ordinateur quantique.

Pare-feu : Firewall en anglais. Système de protection logicielle, et par extension nom du serveur d'accès d'un réseau informatique chargé de filtrer toute intrusion extérieure pour éviter le piratage informatique ou les actes de malveillance (vol de fichiers, destruction de données, prise en main du système, introduction de virus). Faisant écran entre le réseau local et le reste de l'Internet, ce routeur spécifique contrôle en permanence les accès pour ne laisser passer que les paquets de données autorisés.

PENNE (Piste EN Négatif) : Absence de trace révélatrice laissée par un pirate après une intrusion. L'application de ce concept contre-intuitif a souvent permis de démasquer des pirates particulièrement rusés enclins à trop bien masquer leur passage. Voir également *nouille*.

Plaque-mémoire ou **Puce-mémoire :** Composant de mémoire de masse statique, miniaturisé sous la forme d'une *carte* ou d'un *jeton*.

RV : Réalité virtuelle (par opposition au MR, le monde réel – voir ce mot).

Sim : Abréviation de *simulation.* Programme interactif reproduisant dans un environnement virtuel un univers imaginaire, contemporain ou historique. On dit également *simul.*

Taser : Arme d'autodéfense. Voir *KT*.

TR : Temps réel.

UC (Unité Centrale) : Cœur d'un ordinateur.

UC tactique : Unité centrale miniaturisée dans un boîtier dorsal. Reliée à divers capteurs et afficheurs, elle constitue le central d'équipement et de transitions électroniques du fantassin moderne (voir *Intellicombi*).

Virgil (VIRtual Global Interface Link) : Liaison par interface globale virtuelle. Version améliorée et complétée de l'organiseur électronique : il s'agit d'un micro-ordinateur intégrant scanner, balise GPS, téléphone mobile avec fax-modem et radio-TV.

Virus : Fragment de code informatique qui s'introduit dans un système et qui, à l'instar de son homologue organique, va se répliquer automatiquement pour se propager ou déclencher des actions plus ou moins incongrues... du simple affichage de messages anodins à l'écrasement de fichiers ou à l'effacement complet d'un disque dur.

Voxax (VOICE ACtivated System) : Dispositif à commande vocale.

Nous voudrions remercier ici les personnes suivantes, sans qui ce livre n'aurait pu se faire : Steve Perry, pour son aide à la mise en forme du manuscrit ; Martin H. Greenberg, Larry Segriff, Denise Little et John Helfers, Robert Youdelman, Esq., Richard Heller, Esq. et Tom Mallon, Esq. ; sans oublier Mitchell Rubenstein, chez BIG Entertainment ; la merveilleuse équipe de notre éditeur, The Putnam Berkley Group, en particulier Phyllis Grann, David Shanks et Tom Colgan ; les producteurs de notre mini-série chez ABC, Gil Cates et Dennis Doty ; le brillant scénariste et réalisateur Rob Lieberman et toute l'équipe d'ABC. Comme toujours, nous tenons à remercier Robert Gottlieb, de l'agence William Morris, notre agent littéraire et notre ami, sans qui ce livre n'aurait jamais pu voir le jour, de même que Jerry Katzman, vice-président de l'agence William Morris ainsi que ses collègues de la télévision. Mais d'abord et avant tout, c'est à vous, nos lecteurs, de décider si nos efforts collectifs auront été couronnés de succès.

Tom CLANCY et Steve PIECZENIK.

Net Force en vidéo et sur Internet

Vous pouvez retrouver sur Internet les jeux interactifs basés sur les romans de Tom Clancy à l'adresse de Red Storm Entertainment ***<http://www.redstorm.com/>***

On trouve également sur ce site des présentations, des démos, des actualités, des forums de discussion... Les divers jeux sont accessibles aux pages suivantes :

Politika :
<http://www.redstorm.com/politika>

Dominant Species :
<http://www.redstorm.com/dominant-species>

Rainbow Six et ses variantes :
<http://www.redstorm.com/rainbow-six>

Rainbow Six Eagle Watch :
<http://www.redstorm.com/r6missionpack>

Rainbow Six Rogue Spear :
<http://www.redstorm.com/rogue-spear>

Force 21 :
<http://www.redstorm.com/force21>

Pour tout savoir sur l'actualité concernant Tom Clancy, le site de référence américain se trouve à l'adresse :

<http://www.redstorm.com/corporatehq/updates/clancy.html>

Les sites de référence en français se trouvent désormais à l'adresse :

<http://clancy.anotherlight.com/>

<http://www.multimania.com/sphead/RSE.htm>

La série Net Force a donné lieu à un téléfilm diffusé début 1999 aux États-Unis (disponible sous forme de DVD double face, *Zone 1*, chez Trimark Vidéo). Le film écrit par Lionel Chetwynd a été réalisé par Robert Lieberman.

J. B.

Tom Clancy dans Le Livre de Poche

(extraits)

Le Cardinal du Kremlin n° 7586

L'auteur du best-seller *Octobre rouge* nous entraîne ici dans les arcanes de la recherche militaire, autour d'une arme à laser susceptible de bouleverser l'équilibre des forces mondiales. Jack Ryan a pour mission de percer le secret de cette invention. Et pour complice le colonel Filitov, alias le Cardinal, haut dignitaire russe acquis à la collaboration avec l'Occident. Tom Clancy déploie dans ce roman la parfaite connaissance des enjeux militaires, stratégiques et techniques du monde contemporain, qui a sidéré les experts les plus chevronnés du Pentagone. Et l'art époustouflant d'un maître du suspense.

Code SSN n° 17138

21 février 2003 : la United Fuels Corporation annonce la découverte en mer de Chine d'un gigantesque gisement pétrolier, au large des îles Spratly. 21 février 2003 : coup d'Etat en Chine. Le conservateur marxiste Li Peng s'empare du pouvoir. 26 février 2003 : la Chine envahit les îles Spratly. Un pétrolier américain est arraisonné. 27 février 2003 : l'US Navy est placée en alerte maximum. Les porte-avions *Nimitz* et *Independence* font route vers l'archipel. A bord de l'USS *Cheyenne*, un sous-marin nucléaire de la dernière génération, fleuron de la flotte américaine, le commandant Bartholonew « Mack » Mackley reçoit l'ordre de les rejoindre. Sa vraie mission : empêcher la déflagration mondiale...

Danger immédiat n° 7597

Le directeur du FBI assassiné en Colombie, ainsi que l'ambassadeur américain... Le jour où cette information tombe, plus de doute : la guerre totale est commencée contre les seigneurs de la drogue. Armements de pointe, réseaux clandestins, agents d'élite, rien ne sera négligé pour éradiquer le mal. Mais le fléau a gangrené le monde, les enjeux sont énormes, les ramifications planétaires... Comment faire cette guerre-là sans déclencher le troisième conflit mondial ?

Dette d'honneur, tome 1 n° 17015

Le monde, en cette fin de millénaire, serait-il enfin délivré de ses terreurs, l'apocalypse nucléaire, l'affrontement final entre les super-grands ? On a le droit de le croire... à condition d'oublier que la guerre, devenue économique, n'en est pas moins impitoyable. Et que les vaincus d'hier n'ont pas forcément renoncé à la revanche. Quelque part dans le Pacifique, un homme d'affaires japonais met la dernière main à une offensive destinée à paralyser l'Amérique : l'introduction d'un virus informatique dans les circuits boursiers de Wall Street. Tiré de sa retraite, nommé chef du Conseil national de sécurité, Jack Ryan se retrouve face à cet ennemi aussi dévastateur qu'insaisissable. Et c'est tout un monde complexe, celui des ordinateurs et des mécanismes financiers, qu'il lui faudra maîtriser pour venir en aide à un président nouvellement élu...

Dette d'honneur, tome 2 n° 17016

Au cœur du nouvel ordre mondial, les vaincus d'hier n'ont pas renoncé à se venger. Et la guerre économique n'est pas moins meurtrière que l'autre. Jack Ryan poursuit la lutte contre un adversaire redoutable, d'autant plus dévastateur qu'il est invisible : un virus informatique, infiltré au cœur des systèmes bancaires et boursiers dont dépend l'économie des Etats-Unis. Cependant, les navires d'une marine étrangère croisent à proximité d'îles américaines. Et tout laisse craindre une réaction en chaîne qui pourrait mener à un affrontement non plus seulement économique mais militaire. Scénario de science-fiction ? En un sens, oui. Mais dont les points de départ se situent bel et bien dans les réalités économiques, financières, technologiques d'aujourd'hui, décrites ici avec une précision qui ne nuit en rien au suspense.

Jeux de guerre n° 7575

Tom Clancy abandonne la guerre sous-marine (*Octobre rouge*) pour le terrorisme. Paisible professeur d'histoire navale, le héros de ce livre se trouve à Londres quand un attentat se déroule sous ses yeux. Il s'interpose instinctivement ; blessé, il apprend qu'il a sauvé la vie du prince et de la princesse de Galles et de leur fils, visés par l'IRA. Le voici promu héros national... et cible, à son tour, des terroristes.

Net force n° 37018

Au cœur du dispositif de défense américaine, la Net Force est une antenne du FBI spécialisée dans la protection des réseaux informatiques. L'homme à sa tête vient d'être assassiné. Son successeur s'appelle Alex Michaels. Sa mission : retrouver les commanditaires du meurtre. Assurer la sécurité de l'Etat. Filtrer le Net. Piratages, plantages, pertes de données sc multiplient sur le réseau. Un bug géant se prépare. Le responsable : un commando de terroristes des pays de l'Est, mené par un certain Plekhanov. Leur intérêt : contrôler l'économie mondiale. A Alex Michaels de déjouer une machination qui pourrait être fatale. Avis aux internautes et aux cybersurfers. Mais il faut faire vite. Après *Op-Center*, une nouvelle série-culte signée Tom Clancy. Entre réalité virtuelle et géopolitique, espionnage et technologie de pointe, *Net Force* explore les arcanes du Web.

Net force 2. Programmes fantômes n° 37019

2010. Panique sur le Net : vols de fichiers, blocages de réseaux et détournements de fonds bancaires se multiplient. Ce n'est que le début. Bientôt, des informations confidentielles sont divulguées : formules de fabrication de puissants explosifs chimiques, liste des agents de la CIA opérant à l'étranger... Les unités d'intervention de la Net Force doivent faire face à ce qui pourrait être un fléau. D'autant plus qu'une commission sénatoriale met en doute l'efficacité de l'homme qui est à la tête de ce service : Alex Michaels. L'enjeu est de taille, la sécurité du monde en danger. Pour les agents de la Net Force et autres internautes, le temps presse. L'ennemi est peut-être plus dangereux qu'on ne le pense... Après *Net Force*, la suite de la série-culte signée Tom Clancy. Entre réalité virtuelle et géopolitique, espionnage et technologie de pointe, *Net Force* explore les arcanes du Web.

Octobre rouge n° 7547

Le bâtiment le plus précieux de la flotte soviétique – un nouveau sous-marin balistique commandé par son plus brillant officier – tente de passer en Amérique. Devant cette trahison d'une envergure sans précédent, la flotte soviétique entière a reçu l'ordre de le traquer et de le détruire à tout prix. Si la flotte américaine, alertée par la CIA, parvient à localiser *Octobre rouge* à temps pour l'amener à bon port, ce sera le plus beau coup de tous les temps. Mais le sous-marin a près de deux millions de kilomètres carrés pour se cacher, ainsi qu'un nouveau système de propulsion silencieux, impossible à détecter pour aucun des deux camps. La chasse dure dix-huit jours... A l'approche du but, tous les bâtiments convergent... Un thriller unique en son genre : l'imagination fertile de Tom Clancy, doublée d'une remarquable connaissance des technologies avancées, lui a permis de créer un univers complexe d'aventures, un jeu de cache-cache mortel qui se situe au seuil de la réalité.

Power games – Politika nº 17157

La mort de son président amène la Russie au bord du chaos. Les trois hommes qui assurent l'intérim – un nationaliste, un réformiste, un communiste – se révèlent incapables d'empêcher une famine accrue par de mystérieux attentats contre des silos de grains. Au même moment, le terrorisme frappe en plein New York, faisant des centaines de victimes. Comme si on voulait rendre impossible l'aide que les Etats-Unis s'apprêtent à apporter à Moscou. Businessman à la tête d'une société de haute technologie, Roger Gordian a compris la menace. C'est à son propre réseau, composé de managers et d'experts, mais aussi d'anciens agents des services secrets, qu'il confie la mission d'enrayer cet engrenage. Le prix à payer sera terrible. Le combat haletant. L'auteur d'*Octobre rouge* nous entraîne dans les coulisses du vrai pouvoir mondial.

Rainbow Six, tome 1 nº 17185

Alors que le monde se prépare à suivre les jeux Olympiques, des attentats terroristes endeuillent l'Autriche, la Suisse, l'Espagne. A la tête de l'unité spéciale Rainbow Six, qui comprend des agents de divers pays, John Clark, le héros de *Danger immédiat* et de *La Somme de toutes les peurs*, a pour mission d'y mettre un terme. Bien vite, il va se trouver face à un foisonnement d'énigmes. Quelle relation y a-t-il entre ces attentats et les disparitions de jeunes femmes sur lesquelles enquête le FBI ? Quelles recherches mène donc le trust pharmaceutique du docteur Brightling, nécessitant l'installation d'un laboratoire au fin fond du Kansas ? Le péril que Rainbow Six va devoir affronter dépasse l'imagination. L'enjeu n'est rien moins que l'anéantissement de l'espèce humaine. Jamais l'auteur d'*Octobre rouge* n'était allé aussi loin. Et de façon aussi vraisemblable...

Rainbow Six, tome 2 n° 17186

Rainbow Six : tel est le nom de l'équipe, formée d'agents anti-terroristes de différents pays, dont la direction a été confiée à John Clark, l'ancien des commandos de l'US Navy, héros de *Danger immédiat*. Tandis que le monde se prépare à acclamer les jeux Olympiques, cette unité d'élite, habilitée à intervenir partout sur la planète, va tenter l'impossible pour sauver le monde d'une menace mortelle. Car tel est bien l'incroyable objectif des fanatiques : déchaîner un virus d'une violence sans précédent...

Sans aucun remords n° 7682

John Kelly, l'as des commandos de plongeurs de la guerre du Vietnam, a voulu décrocher, mais la violence le poursuit. Pam, la jeune fille qu'il tentait de soustraire à la drogue, a été sauvagement assassinée par un réseau de dealers. Et presque dans le même temps, le Pentagone lui demande de récupérer des pilotes américains toujours détenus dans un camp nord-vietnamien. Deux affaires moins distinctes que ne le pense Kelly, qui devra apprendre à reconnaître ses ennemis avant d'agir... sans aucun remords. Une aventure hallucinante de réalité, où les séquelles de la guerre, le marché de la drogue et de ses ravages, les rouages les plus secrets du pouvoir sont impitoyablement démontés.

La Somme de toutes les peurs n° 7623

Après l'effondrement du communisme et la fin de la guerre du Golfe, un plan de désarmement mondial est possible, à condition que rien ne vienne enrayer un processus de paix encore fragile. Surtout pas une bombe nucléaire perdue dans la poudrière du Proche-Orient... Tandis que s'ouvre une crise sans précédent, le président des États-Unis perd tout contrôle de la situation. De la paix à l'apocalypse, il n'y a plus qu'un pas. À Jack Ryan de ne pas le franchir...

Sur ordre, tome 1 n° 17066

Un Boeing 747 s'écrase sur le Capitole, entraînant dans la mort le Président, les membres du Sénat et de la Cour suprême. Telle est la déclaration de guerre d'un dictateur islamiste fou de Dieu au « Grand Satan » américain. Plus que jamais Jack Ryan est l'homme de la situation, le seul capable d'enrayer la machine de guerre et d'expansion conçue par un cerveau mégalomane, résolu à unifier l'ensemble du monde musulman et à déclencher la guerre totale contre l'Occident libre.

Sur ordre, tome 2 n° 17067

Dans la guerre totale qu'il a déclarée au « Grand Satan » américain, le dictateur iranien Darayaei ne recule devant aucun des moyens les plus implacables. Après le crash volontaire d'un avion sur le Capitole, tuant le Président et les membres du Congrès, une équipe spécialisée porte sur le territoire des États-Unis l'horreur de l'offensive bactériologique... Face à une crise pouvant à tout instant déboucher sur une conflagration internationale, Jack Ryan dispose de tous les pouvoirs. Encore lui faut-il contrôler le jeu médiatique, éradiquer à l'intérieur les complots de la corruption et affronter la pire épreuve : l'enlèvement de sa fille.

Tempête rouge n° 7559

Tom Clancy était déjà l'auteur de l'éblouissante odysséecavale à l'Ouest d'un sous-marin soviétique (*Octobre rouge*), si documentée qu'elle avait été éditée par l'Académie navale américaine d'Annapolis. Il récidive avec un roman-fleuve à mi-chemin du jeu guerrier, cher aux stratèges et aux surdoués de l'informatique, et du grand roman de guerre. L'invention géniale du livre, c'est la *maskirovka*, savant coup de bluff destiné à égarer les Occidentaux.

Composition réalisée par IGS-CP

IMPRIMÉ EN ESPAGNE PAR LIBERDÚPLEX
Barcelone
Dépôt légal éditeur : 48812-09/2004
Librairie Générale Française – 31, rue de Fleurus – 75006 Paris
ISBN : 2-253-09915-5

30/1918/9